# The Gusty Deep

# The Gusty Deep

Lee Morgan

New Orleans

Published in the United States of America by
Queer Space
A Rebel Satori Imprint
www.rebelsatoripress.com

Cover & initials are Baskerville Caps™ © Three Islands Press (www.3ip.com)

Paperback ISBN: 978-1-60864-221-2
Ebook ISBN: 978-1-60864-222-9

Dedicated to Rebecca Rose, the gifts that exceed common speech, and the fraternity of beings beyond description that we body-forth between us. Without you this story would never have grown these paper wings.

Ye who have yearn'd
With too much passion, will here stay and pity,
For the mere sake of truth; as 'tis a ditty
Not of these days, but long ago 'twas told
By a cavern wind unto a forest old;
And then the forest told it in a dream
To a sleeping lake, whose cool and level gleam
A poet caught as he was journeying
To Phoebus' shrine; and in it he did fling
His weary limbs, bathing an hour's space,
And after, straight in that inspired place
He sang the story up into the air,
Giving it universal freedom. There
Has it been ever sounding for those ears
Whose tips are glowing hot. The legend cheers
Yon sentinel stars; and he who listens to it
Must surely be self-doomed or he will rue it:
For quenchless burnings come upon the heart,
Made fiercer by a fear lest any part
Should be engulphed in the eddying wind.
As much as here is penn'd doth always find
A resting place, thus much comes clear and plain;
Anon the strange voice is upon the wane—
And 'tis but echo'd from departing sound,
That the fair visitant at last unwound
Her gentle limbs, and left the youth asleep.—
Thus the tradition of the gusty deep.

John Keats' Endymion

# CONTENTS

# BOOK 1

BOOK I

# 1

Lux was getting good at managing the bodies. Her mother had allowed her to help wash and dress them since she was young. She used to say that corpses had a quiet story to tell, even though their tongues had gone still in their heads. There had been her dear little brother only nine months before. The boy was her only full sibling, with the others belonging to her father's first marriage. The death of the boy had broken her mother, and that was when cleaning the family's bodies had first become Lux's responsibility.

He had been so little still his body had almost no story. The boy had just whitened away day-by-day, not eating enough, not thriving enough, until one morning near the end of winter he didn't wake from his sleep. Lux had wept bitterly but it had been nothing by comparison to her mother's heart-rung despair. She had clasped the tiny white body in her arms and refused to let go. After that Agnes couldn't face it anymore.

When Lux's sister perished only a fortnight ago, Lux had been called home from the nunnery her mother had sent her to and dissolved her novice-hood. Immediately Lux had known why, and she had dreaded every item she packed to return. It was partly because her mother was no longer coping, and partly because her sister Amelia had been promised to Father's best friend who was now short of his bride.

Unlike her brother's body, Amelia's had a big story to tell. It had been the first time Lux had done the job alone. She had entered the room with a basin of warm water and plenty of washcloths and opened the shutters on the window. This was done first and was crucial, as without it there was some chance the soul could become trapped. Also, a reason Lux had barely dared name for herself, it would throw light on her sister's body and allow it to tell its own story better.

She had expected to feel more when she saw her sister lying there. There was a certain dull relief at first, for Amelia's sake, as she was free of the world's ownership. It wasn't that her gut wasn't churning when she looked more closely, mainly that it had its origin in horror rather than grief.

There are some stories that one doesn't want to hear a body tell. Amelia's body told such a one. Her mother had taught Lux well enough to recognise which bruises were grab marks, and what kind of marks have been done to the body before or after death. She knew the faint bruising of suffocation. Although being a woman grown meant being able to deal with births and deaths Lux had tears in her eyes as she cleaned her sister.

It was difficult to know what to make of the bruising around her sister's vulva, whether it had occurred pre or postmortem. Surely her sister hadn't been dishonoured? Not after Father had policed their virginity so carefully? She had tried to talk to her mother about it. Agnes had shut Lux down as if it were an emergency, as if even mentioning it somehow made it her fault, as if the last of her sanity would crack apart if she had to hear it.

Then it had been her mother's turn, the final disavowal of her responsibility to protect her last living child… As much as she hated her father for allowing the fair to come to town with her mother still laid out on the table, her rage and hurt was for her mother as well. *She knew and she did nothing. Worse than nothing…* Now it was Lux who had to be diplomatic with the priest as he argued about whether he would have her mother's body in hallowed ground. Were faerie women indeed children of God who could be given Christian burial? The priest quoted the well-known folklore attributed to faeries: "'Not from the seed of Adam are we, but the proud angel fallen from heaven', they say of them."

It was take him on or allow her father to threaten him with violence. Angry as he was, De Rue had still allowed the fair to come to town… There were

2

bells and jugglers, minstrels and fools now, in their time of mourning. The occasional splash of animal torture, which seemed to bother none but her (a mark of her strange faerie nature that caused her to turn green at the sight of blood -so she was told), tinkers mending pots and pans, telling fortunes, selling cures, children running and playing. Creatures, sometimes even including humans, shat and pissed about the place in such abundance that you had to lift your skirts and dodge as you moved.

People looked at her but didn't give their commiserations. None of the simple people believed that Agnes was really dead. The body back in the parlour was a faerie stock placed there to trick mankind, whilst Agnes was taken back to her own herd. They whispered that she didn't have to worry about that brute De Rue anymore. Lux wished she could believe it. But the smells of her mother's death were in her nostrils still. Surely faerie stock aren't *that* convincing?

It wouldn't be long before they'd send someone to fetch Lux back and scold her for being out of sight. Her older brother Geoffrey, who was so often tasked with following her around and keeping watch on her, had seemed quite relaxed on mead last she saw him. She had been under tightened watch ever since the betrothal had been swapped from Amelia to herself. It's almost like they know the marriage is against my will, she thought sarcastically.

Lux had been seeing visions of things that no one else could see all her life so she didn't jump when it appeared. Yet it was so strong that her heart leaped up in her chest and it was all she could do not to cry out 'Mother!' at the top of her lungs. Forcing herself to walk at a fast but dignified pace, Lux headed rapidly for where she thought she saw her mother standing in a shaft of sunlight, just within the trees. She had never seen a ghost stand in the sun like that. Somehow the simple folk were right! Her mother had just been taken back by the faeries and wasn't really dead at all!

Agnes retreated into the trees as she approached but Lux followed at a run as soon as she hit the cover of the green.

"Mother!" she cried out softly.

3

Turning slowly from where she was shuffling away through the early autumn fall, Agnes came to face Lux. Lux gasped when she saw her mother's face. She was ghastly pale. A thin slither of blood ran from her nose, she didn't bother to wipe it away. There were many recent tales of revenants rising from the dead. It was known to happen in troubled times like these.

"Lux, my sweet child," she said, her voice as flat and serene as one who had never known weeping. Her pale hair was undone and uncovered, disreputably tousled like an unmarried girl. "You should come with me where I go. This world is cruel and its men are made of cold hard iron. Where I am headed there are men made of starlight and honey dew."

"But, Mother! Look! You're not even really dead! Come home with me. They're going to put you in the ground soon if you don't come home." Lux felt desperate. She loved her poor strange mother, despite her many betrayals, which were all born of fear and the weakness that came of so often being afeared. Without her mother there, Father would be crueler to her still. It had been her, after all, who had prevailed upon Father to send her to the convent when she had been reaching a woman's years.

"Look, baby child," Agnes whispered, her voice full of awe and child-like joy now as she raised her skirt. Lux stared in horror as her mother exposed herself. "It's all coming out now. All of it! All of that human mess." Lux covered her mouth with both hands and tried not to make a sound of disgust as wide-eyed she watched blood, and shit, and possibly parts of organs begin to clot and slither down her mother's legs. "It's for the best, girl," her mother was saying while it happened. "Can't enter Faerie with that rot still inside me. No point being ashamed anymore. Humans and their stupid shame…" She crouched down then as though to better evacuate the toxic humanity in her. She made a grunt of pain like someone in the late stages of childbirth. Something awful slithered out of her and then she became nothing but light.

"Mother," Lux whimpered, falling to her knees. She thought she had reached out to clutch her mother before she disappeared, but all she was holding to her chest was an armful of muddy leaves. She threw them from her in revulsion as if they were the severed hands of faerie children, reaching up from the mold to pull at her hair.

Before she could get to her feet she heard a quiet but distinct sound in one of the trees above her. Lux jumped and swung around. There was a young man sitting on one of the high branches. His relaxed posture suggested he'd been there for some time. Getting hurriedly to her feet Lux tried to brush her clothes down. He had seen too much already. Doubtlessly he'd heard the whole exchange and thought her mad.

"It is nice to meet another with The Sight," the young man on the branch said. He had a strange accent. Not just common, *strange*. Something from deep in the base of her skull told her she was in danger because his voice sounded like that.

"I have no idea what you're talking about," she said stiffly, trying to stop crying and wiping at her face.

He swung his legs down so he was sitting up on the branch and she was able to see that he was wearing greenish brown leathers in a style that reminded her of the tinker boys. When she caught a flash of the arrows in the quiver at his hip she took a few steps back preparing herself to run. She hadn't been old enough to speak yet when the cautionary tales had started. The tales that involved men who looked like he looked, spoke like he spoke, those stories that never ended well for girls like her.

"Be not afraid," he said softly, as though she were an easily frightened bird or startled doe that he wished to win the trust of. "I mean you no harm. I have the Seeing also."

"Who are you?" she demanded. She was conscious of trying to reestablish the sense of herself as the social superior, it was all she had in this situation, after all.

"My name's Robin."

"I'm Lux de Rue."

"Oh, I know who you are, my lady. My condolences for your loss."

"Thank you," she whispered. "Did you... did you see her also?" It was

5

hard to ask because she had been punished too many times for Seeing. Her mother had no longer even been able to speak of it, so deeply did those scars go.

"I saw some light. I'm not sure if that was hers or yours. I heard one of Agnes' daughters survived her, and I immediately knew it was you. You weren't here last time my people came through though."

"I was destined for a nunnery," she replied. "I was in fact a novice nun before my older sister died. I was then hastily brought out to fill his lordship's convenience. One sister is much like another I suppose. Her betrothed, though distraught you understand, was able to simply keep his wedding arrangements unaltered and substitute me. The bride's dress merely needed to be brought in slightly at the hips to conceal the difference. Her name was Amelia, by the way, the disposable girl that died."

"You do not wish for this marriage then?"

Lux realised it was the first time anyone had asked her. She laughed bitterly. "If they had me in shackles I'd try chewing through my arm."

He didn't laugh, though she'd intended it as a joke. It seemed best to try to laugh about as many things as possible. "But you're not in shackles," he observed. With no warning he leaped down from the branch in one motion disturbingly feral in its agility. Without words a sense of his greater animal power conveyed itself to her. A feeling that he was just coasting in his body at this moment, a latent force she couldn't predict.

"This is true. But I'm watched."

"Not too well though." He pretended to do a quick scan of our environment. "We are both outlaws you and I -after a manner of speaking."

"For me you mean this symbolically, but for you…"

"For me I am an outsider because I see straight through all the lies the people in power tell us to keep us quiet," he added. "They say a girl is less than a boy, but they say it only to convince her not to fight while they get what they want of her."

She couldn't breathe because her heart was going so fast. Lux wanted to believe it was possible for a man to see through the lies the rest of his sex seemed to uphold to all their detriment. "Are you trying to charm me?"

"No. I don't even know if I'd want to charm you yet, not until I work out what sort of person you are. I simply see differently to what people tell me to see. I see in you a mind the equal of my own, and they trussed it up in vain baubles and a superfluous number of under skirts."

Lux could feel herself blushing at the mention of her underthings. She couldn't guess him, she wasn't sure if he meant to be suggestive or not. "I think they're a perfectly adequate number."

Instead of answering he came around in front of her and Lux saw his eyes for the first time. She realised that she'd not actually really looked at his face until now. "I…"

"Know me?" he finished for her quietly, his eyes engaging intensely with hers. He was close to her though nothing about his body language seemed sexually threatening or even suggestive. It was just intense. She nodded slowly as she began to place from where.

"Yes. You're the tinker's boy that-" She paused because what she wanted to say was, 'that I wished I was brave enough to kiss' but that memory was buried too deep beneath the layers of the ritual humiliation that had followed later at the hands of her father. It was on that very day that she'd had her first lesson in not being elf-wanton like her mother. He always told her he knew you could turn a faerie slut into a proper wife with use of the strap, because he'd done it to her mother.

"Say it, please," Robin said, his tone showing a confusing vulnerability. "I want to know for sure that you know me."

He had no way of knowing how he was wrenching at her damage. Robin wouldn't have known about what De Rue would do with the strap later, how he used it to make her renounce her connection with Faerie, all because of how she'd touched that little boy… She had promised God she wouldn't be a faerie like her mother. When the words finally got to the surface they tasted and felt bleak in Lux's mouth. "You're the little boy the guards beat that day."

7

She seemed to look right through him. Her voice was toneless because she was seeing the scene again before her. "Your mother tried to stop them..."

"She was my aunt. But she was indeed as a parent to me."

"You say was... Is she... dead?"

He nodded but did not look at Lux. "That same night after what you saw, they slipped into our camp with another man. We were playing music when they forced themselves upon her and killed her when they were done. That night was the end of my childhood."

*Mine too.* She wanted to say. He had been brave enough to speak of his terrible trauma maybe she should meet him there and tell him what had happened to her because she touched Robin's face?

"I'm so sorry," was all she muttered. "There are many brutes among us, though we act the part of better to the Saxon. In truth I wish I were not one of them."

He raised his eyebrows. "Do you truly wish it? Or is that a wish made by rich girls who have never had need to wish for anything serious?"

His question stung like her father's strap stung bare skin.

"Do you mean other than her freedom? Or her dignity? Or perhaps her right to know what it's like not to belong to another human being as though one were cattle? To walk the road alone as you do? Other than those wishes, I suppose a woman of my class has nothing else left to wish for but frivolities."

He looked at her for a moment before smiling ruefully. "You stretch my speed with French and my vocabulary to frayed edges, my lady. But I am picking up new words from you already, and I'm guessing you probably proved me wrong just then?"

She *had* been talking very fast. "This is not your first language... Of *course* Norman French is not your first language..." Her assessment of his intelligence began to take flight and her eyes lit up as she lifted them eagerly to his. "How many languages do you speak?"

"Cymraeg, what they call Welsh, is the tongue of my mother. I learned English second. Norman French is still in a growth phase. I have a little of whatever the lowland Scots speak as well. Or at least think I do; they seem to nod to me."

She laughed and continued to gaze into his eyes, feeling slightly light headed and off balance. "I've never even been out of our village." Hot on the heels of the dizzy feeling she realised her danger, and even more serious, his. "Goodness. How long have I been standing here? I have to go back immediately!"

"Please don't go!" he cried, taking her arm as though it was involuntary and then removing his hand quick as a reflex. He would have been struck for such a liberty in any other circumstance, if he were lucky. "I'm sorry. I'm sorry, my lady."

She flinched at being grabbed by a man because she was used to meeting with force. Afflicted by class rather than gender violence Robin flinched back equally at her flinch, as if he too expected a blow. A voice of cool reason in her head saw things more clearly. *What would happen to him if you screamed and said he touched you? There would be no trial for him when my father's men got here. They'd kill him for sport.*

"I'm sorry," he said again. "My fault, too faerie. Too much like my father."

"What did you say?" she asked, moving toward him.

"That I'm sorry? Oh, and about my father. Now that you know, you will never like me."

"Why would I never like you?" she asked, mystified by the way this breaking of the touch barrier between them had shattered the edges of his mischievous confidence and made all his youthful damage hang out.

"Because I can't lie," he replied. "You will know who I am and as soon as you do you will run away and never come back here again."

She frowned. "Who are you, Robin? You said before that you are faerie?"

"I'm Robin Goodfellow. The one your nursemaid probably warned you about."

"The one whose father was a faerie man just as mine was a faerie woman?"

He nodded. "The same. I'm not nearly half so bad as the Wanted Posters

9

say. A lot of things were taken out of context."

"My people say you deflower virgins."

"Well your people *would* see what they do in others. Barely a third of peasant girls escape the unwanted attentions of your people's men long enough to bleed a woman's first blood."

"They are little better to our own women! They are giving me no say in whom I marry, and shall be raped just as shamefully on my wedding night as ever your women were."

"Will they do it in front of your six-year-old nephew, do you think?"

Lux just stared at him for a very long time before murmuring. "It was wrong of me to compare my troubles to those of your women."

"No, I apologise," he said quietly. Suddenly he dared a light touch on her arm, which carried a heartbreaking need for comfort in it. As though he just needed to make physical contact with someone, dangerous though it may be.

"But after what happened you have every right to feel-"

"Oh, I know," he said with a sudden steely certainty in his voice, a confidence that seemed to come out of nowhere. "I don't need your people's permission to feel. That alone is mine. I only mean that my Aunt Eliza is many years dead and buried. Your fear is current; you have every reason to find it more immediate than my kinswoman's long-ago murder. It is wrong of me to assume that you find her life less important because you are.... what you are... Yet it is hard for me to not... This is why I ask you again if you would like to be following your words about denying your blood with a matching action? Or are they just words? Baubles?"

She was breath taken by his cheekiness. It was as if he truly couldn't help it. Some puckish instinct put this edge of pride in him whether he liked it or not. The head ducking and the flinching was a learned behaviour, possibly even a sham, but the glimmer of challenge in his eyes, that part went to the bone. *Cheeky is a word we use to describe the defiance of children. Why do I describe his pride that way? I've heard them described all my life as the 'little people'. Many years ago I realised they weren't talking about physical height and some part of me let them tell me their lives mattered less than ours. This was not what Christ taught us of our fellow man. And yet even the priests don't seem to think it's wrong.*

"I should go," she whispered. "If they find me with you, they will kill you. You must know that."

It was fascinating to see the intricate work on his leather jerkin up this close, the tiny bones, beads and teeth that had been sewn into it. It was impossible not to wonder what he would smell like if she could get closer. She fancied he'd smell like the forest, as if he were a part of it. Not as ordinary human men smelled of ale and stale sweat.

"You could say the same for nine out of ten things I do," he said softly. "If it's worth doing, you can guarantee someone has thought of a rule against it." He was close enough to her then that she could smell the leather of his clothes and the scent of horses that clung to him. He did indeed smell more like the outdoors than as others smelled.

"Yes," Lux said suddenly.

"Yes what?"

"Yes, I intend to follow through on my words." She pulled him close and stood up on her tiptoes to whisper to him with urgency. "I am being held prisoner against my will at fear of my life. My sister died with restraint bruises and lividity around her womanhood. I am watched almost all the time. I am beaten if I resist, examined, humiliated… If I am given to the man, they mean for me I may end up like Mother."

It felt good to put the truth into words, as if, just by doing it now she could breathe again.

"What sort of interior guards does your father keep and how many are there?" Robin asked with all the appearance of seriousness. She looked at the unusual bow he carried and the knife in his belt and wondered what on earth they could possibly do against men in chainmail with proper swords. It was true that he was not the same as Norman men were. He was not a man of cold iron as her mother's shade had called them.

"You're not really *that* insane," she murmured.

"Are you joking? I'm *barking* mad. Norman men saw to that. Even I don't know what I'll do next. Meet me back here tomorrow same time."

"What if I can't get away?"

"Then I will kill the people who prevent you leaving," he replied. Lux couldn't tell if he was joking and wasn't sure whether she should have been more afraid of him than she actually was.

"Have you ever loved a man, Clarice?" she asked her nurse as the older woman bedded her down for the night. "I mean really loved. Not what they made you do, but what you wanted to do," she whispered the last part, like the words themselves were part of a conspiracy between her and a fellow member of the powerless.

Her old wet-nurse made a quiet sound in the back of her throat. From the sound she knew that old as she was now Clarice knew and remembered, both about what it was to love a man and about The Conspiracy. Clarice dropped her voice accordingly, as people will when stepping into the presence of the holy in a cathedral. She lay down next to Lux.

"Ah… You stretch a woman's memory, sweet Rue. Those memories are old now and dust covered."

The poignant edge to her words told Lux otherwise. Tones of voice like that were a secret language between them that no one ever mentioned but all understood. It was a way of communicating without committing to words that could incriminate either of them should they be dragged out to testify against one another. Until Lux had met Robin as an adult man, she hadn't known that men could speak that language. "And yet you remember him," Lux said cautiously.

"Aye, I do at that. Memories don't keep you warm at night though, my girl. You know what keeps you warm at night? An intact maiden head!"

Lux laughed and sat up in bed, turning to face the other woman. "What, shall my hymen serve as a shelter from the heavens and come to house the poor in time? As its girth grows ever wider until the whole village can shelter beneath its majesty?"

Clarice laughed despite herself. Lux had developed wit for this very reason. Often, she made angry people laugh despite themselves and they would calm down. She had discovered that even powerful people who pay no heed to wet, frightened eyes still love to laugh. She had deflected more blows to both herself and her mother through her sense of humour over the years than she had through begging or weeping. She was quick, but sometimes her wit carried the scent of fear. Some men grew up parrying for their life with a sword edge. She had parried with her tongue, which had been oiled and sharpened with anxiety.

"You know what I mean, Lux. The getting of memories is never so important as the keeping of a maidenhead. All of your future rests on that fine veil. No matter how handsome he may be or how kind he seems. If there was a man, which of course *there isn't.*"

"Of course. What with my mother lying dead below? But to take our minds from all the death around us, at least tell me what his name was?" Lux hit Clarice with one of her most winning smiles. She was lucky to have straight, white teeth. *They are an asset. All purchasers of livestock check the teeth.*

Clarice sighed. "He's not the man I married, sweet rue. But you're old enough to guess that. Some stories are better left untold."

"Those are the only kinds of stories I'm interested in," Lux said, seeing how far her former wet-nurse was willing to go when it came to The Conspiracy. In Lux's mind she heard Robin's voice. *If something is worth doing you can be certain they'll have come up with a rule against it.*

Clarice sighed. Lux sat re-braiding her long mid-blonde hair. *My selling point, that only my husband will be able to appreciate ever again, after my hair is covered by a wimple and veil on the day I become a wife.* Lux worked on her hair in the hope that it would make Clarice feel relaxed and not set upon.

"His name was Edwin. You've bled your first woman's blood a while hence now, so you're not too young to know. There's a summer there when you're young, maybe two if you're lucky, where love seems so real. You believe for a moment that it's worth risking things for. But then they discover you are bleeding a woman's blood, and then it's time to abandon childish things and start learning what we have to do to survive."

Lux frowned. She sensed without needing to see Clarice's face all the unspeakable hardships and subjugations that those tight-lipped words glossed over.

"What if we don't have to," she whispered in the half dark. Such words were not safe to say with all the lights on. There were other words she kept buried even deeper, words that had been with her for many years now words to do with poison. "Have I not tended enough of your welts for you to have learned it's otherwise, my dear girl?" Clarice said, the edge of tenuous pain still there in her voice, echoes of the Summer she glimpsed where she'd felt love touch her face like the sun and the terrible shadow it cast over the things she'd had to do since that day.

"Your lord husband will be no kinder than your father, and can hurt you in ways you don't know about yet, unless you learn to survive. You should count yourself lucky you have a warm bed and a roof over your head. I have not always been so fortunate. When you're caught outside four walls with nothing but hunger and cold… that's when you learn what men truly are. Tell me what good is the fickle promise of your summer-boy then? Pray you never trust a man!"

"Men with power," she muttered, her objection nearly inaudible.

"What's that, my girl?"

"I said, 'men with power'."

"All men have power!" Clarice snapped back in a fierce whisper. "Even the best of them will take your maidenhead without a pause with never a thought for how you will bear the burden of the consequences."

"But think, Clarice, about what some women of my class have had done to men beneath them… I think… Well, it seems to me there is more than one kind of power."

"You think *too much*, that's what you do," Clarice snapped. "You have

14

dangerous thoughts."

"If thoughts are dangerous there must be something very wrong with our world," she muttered to herself more than Clarice.

"You're like a child playing with her father's blade. You're going to slip soon and cut yourself. We'll bury you too before the grass grows on your mother's grave at this rate."

But Lux couldn't let it go. She couldn't. It felt like her life depended on this debate, and perhaps it did. "They're important thoughts," she cried, turning and taking Clarice's weathered hands in hers. "Think about it. We are none of us innocent. We all pass the cruelty along to someone else who is less than us, don't we? Father strikes me and I strike a servant the servant strikes a bondsman and the bondsman beats his wife and children who learn to beat the animals for fun. Look around you, Clarice! That is the world of man for you. What if this is a bad place she came to, my mother?"

Clarice gripped her hand hard and shook her head. She looked furtively around the room as though she feared spies.

"Now don't you start talking like that! That was how your mother talked right before she did what she did. And don't go saying in the town that she did what she did, alright? We all know. But part of being an adult is knowing when to be economic with the truth. Your father is trying to convince the priest it wasn't her who did it, but we all know it was. T'was no accident."

"Economic," Lux whispered, turning the word over in her mind. It was the perfect word to describe the way the human world dealt with both truth and kindness.

Lux knew the truth of her mother's self-murder better than anyone; it was madness inducing to be expected to pretend it was an accident. How does one hang themselves from the willow trees by the river with her own apron by accident? Lux had found the body after all. Nobody else had thought about it but as Lux had pointed out, it wasn't the apron her mother was wearing on the day, which suggested she had not been attacked and hanged by an assailant but had brought the apron with her to the site. How her father had glared at Lux

15

for pointing out this piece of logic! It had seemed so obvious that she'd just assumed the adults had already seen it until they began talking murder. Sometimes it took Lux a time to realize when others dealt in deliberate duplicity.

Lux was fairly sure that if someone asked her outright what she saw that day and what really happened to her mother she would just start laughing hysterically and be unable to stop.

"Who could blame her really?" was all Lux whispered. She didn't mention how she'd watched her mother take the house apart in a frenzy only the day before her death. When Lux tried to calm her and ask her what she was looking for she just kept saying 'my faerie clothes' and 'where did he put it! My faerie clothes! My faerie clothes!' Lux knew what that meant. When she couldn't find the clothes she'd been wearing when she left Faerie, her mother had simply found a different way to put her wings on and fly away.

"Now, Rue, your mother called you 'light' for a reason, she wanted you to conquer the darkness that swallowed h-"

"And yet you call me 'regret'…"

"You're speaking like you have faerie devils in you. You promised your father they were gone."

Lux could tell she was upsetting her nurse so she began to put on her placating tone. "I'm sorry, nanny, really I am. I won't have faerie devils in me anymore. Tell me one more time about how they found my mother and her brother in the wolf-pit? One more time before I must grow up and learn to survive?"

"Oh, very well then," Clarice said, lying back down and playing into the pleasing fiction that Lux was still a child and that all was well, when they both knew full well that it was not.

"The wolf-pits of Suffolk were still catching a lot of wolves in those days, when King Stephen was on the throne. These days the traps only catch a thin drizzle of wolves. The forests are nearly tamed now, but back when your mother first arrived it was still fully wild. Some villages were checking the pits when they found instead the two children. Their skin was green in hue, and

16

they wore strange clothing, not speaking the common tongue nor eating the common food of mankind.

The little boy pined away so for the land of Faerie that he died within weeks, but the little girl... She was a survivor. She started to get well. It took a while but soon she was able to eat human food and her skin began to pinken. Many experts and men of learning came to look her over before and after the change and they all agreed it was miraculous. Now of course, Agnes, as they christened her, she was... different. It was hard for her. For a long time she used to go to the grave where they buried her little brother and talk to the mold there in her strange tongue. Many times she would speak of going back to her land with neither sun nor moon.

"But such was not her fate, as none knew how she had come to be here in the first place. She had just appeared one day in the wolf pits, as though she were one of those wild things they were trying to net and push out of the forests... Made sense that they caught her really. Whatever she was she was as wild as a she-wolf and as wanton, with a little cat in her and some crow besides. Mad as a headful of songbirds that one. But allowances were made up and to a point for her because she was a miracle. A faerie bride such as was spoken of in the time of heroes! Your father was willing to ignore her lack of dowry to win that prestige. To tup himself a rare faerie wench and father a line with faerie blood...

"Of course, the poor man had no idea what he was getting himself into... That he didn't! She was a beauty alright. Perhaps you'd say she still is even down there in her shroud. She looked too good to have a girl of your age, that is for sure. Though of course grief had left a darkness under her eyes at the end. Many men would have wed her for her locks and her eyes alone. But your father was not a man to be taken for a fool... If she'd married a younger man... Or perhaps a weaker one... things may have been different. But there are some men you don't cuckold without carrying the mark of it for life," Clarice said grimly.

Lux didn't need to be told about how her father had held her mother

17

down and cut the word *whore* into her back. She had heard the screaming and been the one to wash the wound.

"One can only wonder what the little boy would have done in the world had he lived? Agnes was bright; brilliant they'd have called her, if she'd been born a boy. But she had no damned common sense. None whatsoever…"

"I'm starting to feel this story is developing an ending containing a moral with a certain directional component?" Lux asked with raised eyebrows.

"Do you think?" Clarice asked sarcastically. She gripped Lux's hands sudden and tightly. "If there is a man, -which there isn't because if there was and I knew I'd have to tell your father immediately. But if there was, whatever he might seem, he would never be worth the risk you'd be taking. And he won't stand by you, Rue. He'll take your virginity like it's light as air to him and then he'll-"

"Is that how your summer ended?"

"Child, winter has been so brutal I can't remember even the taste of summer."

"If you knew I was going to… do something…"

"Then I would have to tell your father! That's why I don't know anything. You go to sleep now, foolish sweet child."

The tinker-man had been watching the house and the people who came and went. He knew the routines of the estate better than those who lived there. At nightfall like this when the shadows lengthened he took note of where the guard's line of sight ended and where light was cast. Robin noticed much, but he himself was not the object of notice. As he moved around the grounds, he learned a lot just from overheard conversation.

Settled folk never really saw things, he knew, even things that were sitting right in front of them. They missed the extraordinary even more often than they missed the commonplace. They missed the small epiphanies that are always happening, the portends and prodigies… and the big ones too. Robin spent most of his time engaged in Noticing. Partly he did so with the patience of a hunter, engrained since childhood, partially because his survival and success depended on it, but also just because the world had not yet become over familiar to him.

Because the settled people lived in one place all the time and became complacent and bored with their environments their minds would just shut down after a while. Believing they had seen everything there was to see and observed all there was to observe about that same old place. After that a sleepy arrogance settled over them. They expected things to remain how they left them. The settled folk reminded him of a rider asleep on the horse's back, going where the horse finds the sweetest grass with the rider having neither say nor awareness.

Settled folk were easy to fool. Lulled by repetition as they were, small things in their environment could change just a little each day. Even with a greatly significant change, a dangerous change for instance, so long as it happened as gradual as heating water over a fire, they would never feel it, or see it, until it was too late. He used this understanding to insinuate himself into environments over time so that people assumed he was meant to be there.

Robin had been picking their pockets while his family kept the crowd busy with music since he was five years old. He had the lightest touch in the business, but there was more to the art than just sensitivity in your fingers and a lot of gall. When you pick pockets, you learn all about how to tell whether someone's mind is asleep or alert. With a little observation it was possible to see, that nearly everyone he met outside of his own people was asleep on their horse nearly all of the time.

You could tell it was true by how many of their purses you owned. *It almost makes you feel bad when it's as easy as it is with them. Like stealing from a baby. With Lux's people all you have to do is nod, duck your head and say yes master and you could rob them blind, so asleep and fat and drunk on power are they.* Was this why the girl had stood out?

As a woman she was not in control of the men's actions. In her foremother blood would be women the North-men claimed as slaves back before they

19

shortened their name to Norman. Mixed with Lux's Viking ancestors would be those of the native Briton also, an internal soup of slave and plunderer. Would the energy of conquest or that of submission be the strongest in her blood? It was easier not to attribute his feelings to when they were children. It felt too raw to admit how desperately he'd needed that tiny shred of compassion she gave him. Was she merely there at the right time?

Every year when his caravan passed this way, he had looked upon her from a distance, watched her grow and wished her well. People said his imagination was susceptible at the best of times. He saw the world backlit by a mysterious light others couldn't see. Some said that it was because of his faerie father who begot him on May Eve. Or because he was pulled loose from the womb of a dead woman through her stomach after her ghost eyes had already glimpsed the infinite?

They said he was touched. But after he'd found out who the girl was it was only reasonable? *How many other young people alive in England at the moment have been the child of a faerie? There is me, and then there is Lux… We live in a bounded world inside, we hear about lands outside this, on the other side of the sea, but common folk never see them. There is only this white isle exploding with evil portents of war and revenants said to walk in many towns.*

Robin both feared that the dead may again walk and thrilled to it at once. For he knew that whilst there were some dead whose memory he feared to look upon, there were also many due a reckoning, if the graves were indeed emptying. *Faeries walk among us and there are strange light bodies seen to cross the sky in these times.*

Or was it less about prophecies of coming doom and more that Lux seemed effervescent among the asleep-on-their-feet dullards she moved among? Was it like spotting a lioness pacing in a sheepfold unaware that she is a lioness? Does the sheep backdrop make her appear more wonderful than other lionesses that move with their own kind? Robin hoped it was just that. He hoped he would just help her to get to freedom and realise quickly that he felt nothing for her but the basic regard for another trapped, desperate human creature.

When he watched Lux de Rue from a distance, he watched her not like a man observing a woman, but like a man observing his own potential death and what features it possessed. Mentally he planned possible escape plans and for the ordeal this premeditated act would involve. There was nothing metaphorical about this risk he planned to take. He had never dared something like this, not with a family as powerful and highborn as Lux's family. This wouldn't just be breaking a young girl out of an arranged marriage, something he'd done before, it would be to thumb his nose at the occupiers.

Lux woke at the first thump, and the groan that followed it chilled her through to her marrow core. It was hard to wake, the sleep remedy her father had given her made it almost impossible some nights. Things would happen in the room, people would enter and leave, sometimes she dreamed she was touched in her sleep and she still couldn't wake to verify it.

Clarice, who lay beside her most nights was still breathing deeply as Lux got quietly out of bed. Beyond the sound that woke her everyone else seemed to be at rest. There was no light under any of the doors as she stole her way down the hall. She wished she could take a candle with her, light it from the coals of the half-out fire, but she didn't want to risk waking anyone.

When Lux heard or saw something she wasn't always inclined to assume that everyone else could see or hear it too. So, woken in the night as she was by strange sounds coming from the room where her mother's corpse lay, she didn't dare get a second opinion about the sound. If they knew she was hearing things again father would have to beat the faerie devils out of her.

The fear of going in there, in the dark, alone, was not worse than the fear of her father. There was only an eerie quiet followed by a rustling of fabric that made the earlier chill in her bones feel balmy and warm. Swallowing hard and steeling herself Lux reached for the door, willing herself to push it open. It was a time of chaos in the land to be sure and there were many tales of prodigious happenings. Often it was told that those who went to the grave with a terrible secret had been known to return.

What could there possibly be to see more terrible than what she had already seen? She asked herself. Having seen her mother hanging there by her own apron, her bloodshot eyes bulging from her head and her purple tongue forced out between her teeth, piss and blood running down her legs, what was there left to see to shock or hurt more than that?

When she swung open the door the faint smell of death hit her in the face. It wasn't strong but knowing where it came from made her gag on it. *That's all the rot inside her mother said had to come out before she could go back to Faerie.* But it was only for a second she thought of this, because in the next instant she perceived the figure bent over the table. For a terrible moment she thought it was her mother somehow, bending over the table she'd formerly been laid out on. When a girl suddenly appears in the bottom of a wolf-pit one day you don't necessarily assume she can't come back to life as well.

But then, as her eyes adjusted further, she perceived her mother's body lying beneath, and in that same instant she saw and understood the movements of the upper figure.

"Father?" she whispered, unable to prevent this whisper or horror.

He stopped thrusting immediately, took two panicky steps back and reached furtively for his breeches.

"Lux! What are you doing out of bed!"

Lux just starred with her mouth open. She looked at the uncovered body of her mother, partially unwrapped from its shroud with its legs pushed apart. Then back at her father doing up his belt. Then something even worse than what she had seen occurred to her. As it did, she tried to run but before she could make it to the door her father had crossed the room and grabbed her by the hair.

Lux cried out with pain and went limp. This had happened before and her body knew not to struggle. Before the sound could fully leave her mouth her father had clapped his hand over her face. His hand smelled faintly of her mother's decay. Again, she knew something else that was coming before it happened. This wasn't the time for going limp. *If I do not get him to let go of me now it is my death I smell as well as hers.* She knew the truth of those words as she'd never known or trusted anything in her life, it was like a voice from an older, wiser part of herself who knew everything that was coming slightly ahead of time. There had been many times when she'd been forced to submit but it was time now to fight.

This knowledge was like a surging wave in her. It rose up her centre as a strength she'd never known. As soon as it reached her head she wrenched her head violently backward and bit into his hand at the same time. Although he let go immediately, she didn't stop biting. It seemed that now she had hold of him and could taste blood between her teeth she would never let go. If she let go she would die.

"Get off me you crazy bitch!" he cried, cuffing her in the side of the face. She fell back and jumped to her feet. He was after her she knew; she was only a few steps ahead of him. Soon his men would come, or he'd catch her in the hall before she could even make it to the front door. *If he catches you you're dead.* The voice in her head gave her a burst of desperate adrenalin. Almost at the door she could hear his step behind her, hear his breath.

Lux tore out through the front door and it slammed behind her. It was too late for stealth. Her father could wake the guards if he wanted to. She was counting on him not calling for them. She was counting on not giving her the opportunity to start raving of what she'd seen him doing to Mother's body. There would be no choice but to tell no matter the consequences.

Within a few steps she knew she was right because her father hadn't paused, he had just pushed on after her. It was then that she knew she wasn't going to make it. There was no way she could outrun him at a distance of this length, not with no shoes on. She was still running as hard as she could, and she could hear her father calling the guards now. It was his word against that of a hysterical girl child, who was going to believe her? So, he had sent the younger, faster men out to catch her.

Even with the big start Lux had on them she knew they would catch her quickly once she reached the forest. She wondered if they would just send the dogs after her. Would father set the dogs on her and claim it was a tragic accident? The dogs frightened her so much she considered turning around and putting her hands up, going down on her knees, begging for forgiveness, enduring whatever she must to avoid that fate. Then she smelled the forest…

It was close enough for the cool, mossy, clean joy shout of the forest's perfume to hit her nose and mouth, cleansing her. If servitude inside the house was linked to the secret decay on her father's hand over her mouth, then freedom smelled like green moss. Tears stung her eyes. She couldn't lose it now that she'd smelt it. It was too late, just as with love sometimes it is too late. Even if it cost her life now she had to run towards freedom at any price.

Her body wasn't strong enough but her faith in what she wanted was. It would have to be because faith was literally all she had left. Throwing back her head as she ran, tears streaming down her face like a child Lux yelled into the darkness with all her might.

"Robin!"

His name shattered the night, birds flew up at its wildness. Animals started in the dark as if were the cry of a witch shrieking for her devil lover. "Robin Goodfellow!" she cried again, her feet only steps from the edge of the forest and the guardsmen only steps away from catching her. "Robin Goodfellow!"

She was just about to plunge into the trees and cry his name again when something whizzed past her face so rapidly she didn't see it, but it was close enough she felt the air displacement. The hissing was followed almost immediately by two hard 'kthunk' sounds. Spinning around to see what had happened, Lux got a brief moment to look back at the two guards lying on their backs with arrows sticking out of their chests. Lux stared for only a moment before turning back to try to see the source from which the arrows were coming. There was nothing except a branch moving in the gloaming-light.

Less than a second after she looked, she heard another arrow loosed that hissed for slightly longer before finding its hard, wet target. The hidden marksman had shot at this distance a man that was only just coming down the front steps. There was a new fear in Lux's heart then. A man doesn't learn to shoot

24

like that from firing at targets, nor come to be in the trees outside her home by accident, long before the agreed on meeting time. But what use that fear when this other was so close behind her?

A strong hand grasped her in the darkness and pulled her further into the trees. "Run!" Robin's voice said from up close.

His Lordship paced up and down in front of where she was seated, the iron of his spurs still clanking on the flagstones and all his weapons still in his belt, including his horrible mace. In truth he only really needed his fists with Clarice, there was something more deeply threatening at work when he came into the house wearing a blade or his morning-star. "So, what you're trying to say to me is you don't think we should look for my daughter? Is that what she asked you to do, Clarice? To try to convince me not to hunt her down?"

Clarice swallowed hard and knitted a little faster. Her stitches were getting almost too tight to move from needle to needle. "No, my lord. It's just I know it to be fruitless. The faeries took her back, they did. Saw it coming a mile off the way she's been of late. Did you not hear her cry out the name? They say if you're in trouble you call on Puck three times aloud-"

"I know what they say, woman. And of course I heard what she cried out, the whole county heard what she cried out!"

"I think the people half expect it, my lord. What with who she is and all."

"Half expect what?" he demanded. Coming to a stop. Clarice wasn't sure if she had just said something to her extreme credit or extreme detriment.

"Her to get taken back by Them. I mean, they somewhat always were looking to see if her folk would come for her… Now they did. The faeries…"

"Do they now?" he asked, seeming thoughtful as though she had managed to present a perspective he hadn't thought of. "So, you don't think they'll just assume she's run off with some boy like her whore mother?"

Clarice crossed herself rapidly in a way that was almost involuntary, even though she was still holding a knitting needle in that hand. "I don't think they will say that," she ventured tentatively. "After everyone heard her call to the

Hob who shouldn't be spoken of, I think they'll say he was a faerie."

"What kind of faerie horse throws an iron shoe?" He demanded to know. When she didn't reply immediately and sweat began to break out across her forehead, he added, "I had my men sweep the area with flaming torches. They lost his tracks pretty quickly, but shortly before they 'disappeared into thin air', as the simpleton I sent to track them tells me, his horse kicked a shoe. Do you suppose faerie men have horses shod with iron, Clarice?"

*Well, I've bought you all the time I could, sweet Rue. And argued as hard as I dared against him chasing you. I hope your man has grown wings by morning and he truly is a faerie. Because De Rue's men will have razed the countryside for miles around by lunchtime tomorrow. You mad girl...* Unbidden a little smile came to the edges of Clarice's mouth as a touch of moisture crept into her eyes. *You go, my girl,* she whispered. *Go fast. Go for all of us.*

fter he pulled her up behind him on a half wild stallion there was only his body and the body of the horse, which seemed like one integral being. That and there was chaos. Or perhaps his body itself was chaos?

"Hold on tight to me and keep your head low," he said at the beginning of the maelstrom of movement and sound. She didn't get time to tell him she'd never ridden astride a horse before and wasn't sure she knew how. The snorting beast had half reared before shooting into a crazy gallop so there was no room for words. Fine branches whipped around them at times, or she was jolted when the horse jumped something. With the light of the near full moon everything seemed to be made of blurry silver and black lines and the pain on her inside thighs, which were not protected under her nightgown.

She could feel the animal's heaving breath and its immense muscles rippling against her calves. For a second, she noticed the smell of the forest, the fresh rush of ozone, and she closed her eyes and let it happen. Whatever was about to happen to her it was life, *real* life outside of captivity. Lux surrendered to the jolting, the whipping with branches, the cold, the chaffing, and the strength and certainty of his body that was also the horse's body. She held him tight not like a woman holds a man, but as one who fights to live holds life no matter how much pain it keeps doling out.

They rode through a river, so that the horse was up to its knee and they were sprayed with freezing cold water. She made a squeal of shock, though most of it must have flicked on Robin whose back she was sheltering behind. They went through water more than once until she felt like she'd been turned around in a circle a few times. The bottom of her skirt was wet and cold against her bare legs. If someone had told her they were descending into Elphame and had travelled through blood up to the knee and that the surrounding greenery had risen up to swallow them she would have believed it.

By the time the horse was beginning to tire Lux couldn't say yes to it anymore. Now the letting of it happen was just teeth gritting and no other choice. She was now in quite some pain and trembling with cold and excess adrenalin. It was uncertain whether she was being kidnapped or rescued or some combination of the two.

When it got to the point where he let the horse walk for a time through some rugged terrain, she considered the possibility of asking him for mercy. Then she thought of the spoilt, soft, little rich girl he would think her and the idea of such an injury to her pride hurt even more than her thighs did. Robin must have intuited something because he paused beside a small pond that reflected the moonlight brightly and dismounted, letting the horse drink. He dismounted by throwing one leg over the horse's head as though he not only had normal use of his legs but was still feeling quite spry. After he jumped down, he handed her down from the saddle.

"It is safe to let the horse rest and drink here," he said quietly. "They would have set the dogs out if they meant to use them before morning."

"Are you sure it will be safe to rest?" she asked, afraid to dismount because she wanted to so much.

"I'm sure. We have lost them many miles back."

Her hands were trembling in his and when he set her feet on the ground her legs immediately went from under her. He caught her and supported her body weight for a moment before gently lowering her to a seated position on the ground.

"I'm not used to it," she explained, hot in the cheeks with shame. "They don't let us… he doesn't let me ride astride the horse."

"Of course he doesn't. That would give you too much power in the saddle. Make it easier for you to get away."

The words 'get away' recalled Lux's ordeal in her mind so vividly she started to shake violently. Only a couple of hours ago she'd been facing the possibility of death at the hands of her own father.

"What happened in there?" he asked, leaning forward slightly so that she felt obliged to make eye contact with him. Although the moonlight was shining directly on his face she barely noticed his features. All she could feel was the pounding of her heart and the churning in her stomach as images of what she had seen that night ploughed through her.

When she didn't answer him, he quietly took out a cloth from his saddlebag and some water from a bottle and cleaned her face. As he wiped the blood away, some of which was her father's and some hers from the blow he'd struck her, he gave her also a gentle pat to the cheek of encouragement. The gesture might have seemed creepy on a Norman man but it carried a strong sense of basic decency in it, the way one might stroke the head of a wounded child.

"Did they hurt you anywhere else?"

She shook her head, biting her lip to try to avoid bursting into tears. It was no good, her disgust and horror had to get out somewhere. She began to sob as well as shake and suddenly it was hard to breathe. Just as when she was on the horse and all control, boundaries and normality had disappeared now it was all happening in delayed time.

"You wouldn't believe me if I told you what I saw!" she managed to say at last.

Even though he was stopping her from falling, totally supporting her in fact, she as yet had no sense of him as person. He could have been a rock or a strong tree.

"I wish that were so," he murmured.

Part of her didn't want to sully someone else's mind with the knowledge of it, but the faerie part of her couldn't keep silent. She felt like she might explode. "I found him raping my mother's corpse! My father! He was... He was... My mother!" She cried some other almost incoherent things and he soothed her. He didn't say whether he was indeed shocked or not.

"What a parody of a man," he said at last. "That he needs to assert his control over her even in death."

"Do you think that's why?"

"I'd say he got off on being able to do whatever he wanted to her without resistance, yes."

"Is that what men really want? Just a body lying there?"

"Broken little boys who abandoned their toys only to play with other people never become men. "

Lux had never heard someone critique her father so matter-of-factly. "If he's broken should I feel pity for him?" she whispered.

"No," Robin replied, his voice firm. "I don't think you need to ever say should again when it comes to what you feel, Lux. Feel as you like. It is your own wild heart. Where it loves let it love, where it hates let it hate. Everyone else will try to control what you do with your body, but nobody can ever force what you do with your heart."

His words felt the way the forest had smelt. She was afraid of the dizzy freedom in them, like it was too much oxygen all at once. Yet she leaned into this letting of the heart like he said to, and there she found her rage.

"Damn him!" she cried, getting to her feet unsteadily. Her legs wobbled but she turned in the direction she believed her father's house to be and pointed her finger on her left hand at it. With her other arm she covered her right eye and let the curse boil inside her.

Quietly and unobtrusively, Robin got to his feet beside her and guided her arm to be pointing true to where they had indeed come from, which was not particularly close to where she had originally been pointing.

"The eye and the blast and the dart upon them! May the host take the eyes out of the heads of the men of the House of De Rue!" she cried the curse out with all her rage behind it. "To the third generation!" she added.

"May their crops wither on the stem and their wells turn to poison. May grass grow between the flagstones in their grand hall and toads nest in their hearths," Robin whispered softly from behind her. "May their cradles rock empty and their graves all be full, let joy be as a stranger in their hall from this moment forth, may bats roost in the eaves of their ancestral seat."

After a while she turned around and laughed. "You really know how to fling a curse!"

He laughed quietly too. "We tinkers don't just mend kettles."

"I need to get back in that saddle don't I?" she asked, trying to ride the feeling of levity that had come for a moment with their laughter.

"I'm afraid so. But look," he said, going for his saddlebag again. "I've some trousers I borrowed from a boy about your size. If you put these on under your skirts, it will protect you some."

She took the item of boy's clothes from him without saying thank you. Lux was too busy thinking about the amount of planning that these trousers represented. Again, anxious questions about what Robin had planned to do with her moved through. He turned around, busying himself with the horse while she pulled on the extra item of clothes. For a wild second it occurred to her that this was an opportunity where she could run. "Do you usually carry around emergency boy's clothes?"

"Only when I'm planning to abduct a rich man's daughter," he replied.

"Is that what this is? Abduction?"

"That is what they will say it is."

Lux only remembered parts of the ride. There was Robin lifting her down off the horse at daybreak, standing around out of sight, in the cold, while he spoke with someone in Saxon English. Then she was being lifted onto a fresh horse. Once, when the wind was coming in from the west she caught the sound of the far-off yell of hounds on the scent. She didn't need to ask him if this was anything to worry about, she could feel his muscles stiffen and the ripple of tension in his body as he kicked the new horse into a hard gallop. The exhaustion was too immense for Lux to feel fear anymore.

They avoided all main roads and cities, making a jagged path across the landscape, darting from copse to woodland and across empty moors. During

31

the few moments where Lux was fully awake she noticed how well Robin knew this land and all of its features, the knowledge made her feel safe in her weary state. Even though logically she knew she was anything but.

It wasn't until the horse slowed to a walk and she could hear seabirds that Lux put her head up. "Where are we?" she asked.

"Near the coast," he replied dismounting. "Here," he said offering her his hand. "Can you walk?"

She wasn't sure. Taking his hand, she half dismounted and was half lifted out of the saddle by him. The trousers under her skirt had protected her only a little. They were wet with fluid from the broken blisters on her inside thighs. Lux's pride bit down on the sound, but she cried out in pain nonetheless as he lifted her.

"I'm sorry, lass," he murmured. There was real sympathy there mixed with a species of resignation. She knew the resignation was in his voice because there was nothing for it but to keep on moving. If they didn't keep moving they were dead. She appreciated this rare humanity in him, nonetheless.

He led her quickly towards a ridgeway that gave to a long downhill path, sloping to the sea. The small sharp cold rocks hurt on her tender bare feet but she bit her lip and didn't complain. For a moment she paused and stared out at the greyish-blue heaving expanse of it. The briny smell and the deep surging power of the ocean pulled a lump up into her throat.

"I've never seen the sea."

He didn't say anything in response; he just took her hand in his and led her quickly down the incline.

When they reached the edge of the water Lux was swallowed by a boundless awe. For a moment there were no hounds on her scent, no violent men on horses scouring the countryside for her, there was only the grey low hanging sky, scattered with birds and the sound of the waves. She could have dissolved into it if she stood there long enough, as though she had found her way home already. Lux went to the edge of the water and let it wet her feet. There was a small rowboat coming towards them out of the churning mist.

"Give me your knife," she said turning to him.

Without hesitation he removed the hunting knife from his belt and handed it to her, hilt first. Standing in the foam, her feet aching with cold, she took a handful of her hair in her hand and cropped it off with the knife right under her ear. Robin didn't say anything as the first handful or two of her blonde hair rained down on the sand around them. As she moved on to the third and fourth cut, he picked up a handful of it, but he never attempted to order her to stop.

"Do you want to keep some of what you cut away? It may be bad luck to leave it like this," he said, offering the long, wet lock of her hair back to her.

She frowned, still cutting at her hair with a manic intensity. "Who says it's bad luck?"

"Well…" he said. "Among my people we believe hair provides a link to you. It is also a symbol of a woman's fertility."

"Then let the ocean have it. I want no baby brought into this world to fight as men fight, or suffer as women do."

Robin went to relinquish the lock he was holding into the sea in accordance with her wishes.

"You can keep some if it bothers you to release it."

She didn't watch him decide and instead set to cutting away the skirt on her night dress so that she was left standing in the trousers and what had now became a long white shirt. Lux had small breasts so it seemed possible that without her hair she could pass off as a boy with a little more work on her stance. There wasn't much time to think it over though as the boat was almost to the shore. She passed him his knife back.

When they reached the ship Robin paid the ferryman extra for his silence and goodwill. There was a strong rush of relief when he saw his brother on the deck. It wasn't that he doubted Blaith would be there as he said he would, it was just the immediate sense of heightened strength he always felt in the presence of his people.

He woke Lux and offered her an apple to eat.

"Where are we?" she murmured, biting into the apple and looking around blinking. It seemed entirely possible she was yet to remember what she'd done. The juicy fresh flavour of the apple would bring her back down into her body.

"We're in good hands with those I trust most in the world, sailing for the port of Whitby," he explained, eating his way quickly through an apple himself.

"This is my brother Blaith," he told Lux and then swapped to speaking Cymraeg for Blaith's benefit. "This is Lux. We've ridden hard all night and she's not used to it, so I might go and make her comfortable below deck."

Blaith did not question or lecture only held out his arms to Robin. Their foreheads came together in greeting. For the first time since the chase had begun Robin felt the tension draining out of him. When they were together it felt like there was nothing they couldn't handle between them. Others might not, but Blaith would understand his decision and his actions.

Without them needing to speak he felt the evident solidity of that allegiance, as had been the case since they were boys.

"It's so good to have you back," Blaith said. He kissed Robin and released him.

"It's good to be back," he said.

"I'll let you settle your girl. But come back to me afterwards, cariad, yes? We need to *talk*."

Just as with Robin she had not had time or emotional energy to properly observe him, all she'd caught of Blaith was his dark, mysterious eyes and the long hair, a style that was unusual among her people. He was beautiful rather than handsome, as sleek dangerous predators are beautiful. But her tired mind only caught a brief impression of it.

As Robin settled her on a pile of sheepskins and tartan rugs below deck, she couldn't resist questioning him. Trying to understand this strange new world she was moving in seemed key to her survival somehow. If she didn't learn to swim here she feared she'd soon drown. "Did you say Blaith is your *brother*?" she asked cautiously.

"Yes," Robin replied. "We had the same mother, different fathers. Now, before I go and get raked over hot coals for my reckless behaviour by said brother, will you let me treat your wounds?"

Lux was confused for a moment by what he meant. The only wounds she was currently, deeply, painfully aware of where those on her upper and inner thighs, and he couldn't possibly mean those!

"Which wounds? You don't mean…"

He looked at her blankly for a few moments, as though this time he really didn't understand what she meant at all. Then it seemed to dawn on him that this was a matter of modesty.

"You needn't feel uncomfortable with me. I'm a faerie doctor, as well as my other… sidelines. When I'm in doctoring mode the man in me is tucked away somewhere."

"I don't understand."

"If you trust me, I can take the pain away. If I put so much as a glance wrong then never trust me again."

Lux swallowed hard on a knot in her throat. She wanted to tell him that trust wasn't even on the table. After all it wasn't yet clear what he meant to do with her. Trust was too painfully delicate. You couldn't simply extend it like that with your only recourse being to remove it in future. Her trust, since early childhood had been too badly violated for that. With a sigh she gave in due to exhaustion more than anything.

"Alright," she whispered. "What do you want me to do?"

"Just roll over on your stomach for the time being," he said.

Confused as how that was going to help with her blisters she did as he told her. Lux could hear him rub his hands together briskly before he touched her. When he did, she almost cried out with the shock of it, although it was impossible to word why. His touch was hot and alive and focused in a way she'd not felt before and it went straight for all the places in her back where she was

35

holding her pain. His strong fingertips worked into the muscles and released their tension, and right when she wasn't expecting it, he compressed her and her spine issued a series of loud cracks.

She gasped and tears of relief rushed to her eyes.

"That will feel better," he said, rolling her over onto her back. Lux was embarrassed when he did so because he noticed the tears spilling out of her eyes. He squeezed her shoulder. "Let it flow." He indicated her trousers. "I will turn around while you take those off. Cover your womanhood with this cloth if you like. I won't look while I patch you up."

She was utterly confused by his decency; it was something new and strange. It left her helpless. Most of her wanted to trust it utterly and to believe that such things existed in the world. Gingerly she undid the boy's trousers and pulled them off, quickly covering herself over with the cloth he'd handed her. "I'm ready," she said timidly.

He turned around and came over to her, carrying a bundle. It wasn't lost on Lux that he indeed did not look at anything of her but the wounds. He was intent, cool and professional as he examined her. When he had to move her legs slightly apart, he said, 'my apologies' and pushed the cloth down further so he couldn't see between them.

"Ah, you poor thing," he said quietly as he examined the mess of weeping sores and inflammation. "You were very brave."

The praise brought more tears to her eyes. It was perhaps even more unexpected than kindness. He got out a small bottle from the bundle and began to lathe a thin fluid onto the insides of her legs. Although Lux knew her herbs and poisons well, she couldn't guess what was in this one. Because whilst it stung like wildfire at first application it soon numbed the area so that she felt little pain. After he had done this and let it dry a little, he covered the wounded area in a soothing thick ointment and bandaged her legs.

"The bandage will give you some padding so it's not rubbing on everything," he said, leaning back on his knees and going through the medicine bundle looking for something else. He took out a powder, put it into a cup and covered it with water from his drinking bottle. "Now drink this, it has milk of the poppy in it. It will ease your pain and allow you to sleep."

"Ah, my old sleep remedy." She recognised the opiate and drank the potion eagerly from his hand as she had missed the stupor it cast her into. All of her fear of Robin seemed to have evaporated, and at the first effects of the medicine he'd soothed her with. While she lay there waiting for it to take full effect he covered her over with blankets.

"Robin," she murmured, already feeling woozy. She reached out for his hand, to catch it before he tried to leave.

"Yes?"

"Thank you!" she hadn't meant for it to come out with so much emotion but after everything that had happened it was impossible to hide. He stroked her forehead briefly before getting up to leave. "You didn't have to... You could have left me there... You didn't need to get yourself into trouble. You could have done anything you wanted to me... But you helped..."

"Think nothing of it," he murmured, a faint sadness in his voice. "I *did do* what I wanted."

"So, no telling-off for what I've done?"

"Is it her?" Blaith asked.

"Is it who?"

"Don't pretend with me."

Robin sighed and nodded. "I think so."

"Then what use would there be in me telling you off? If it's her, if it's actually *her*, you won't listen to me anyway. It's all foretold. An inevitable thing."

"I know," Robin said. "But then I tell myself it doesn't mean anything to me that she is one of them, that I don't see her as one of them-"

"Yet is it true?"

"Sometimes."

"Then perhaps you mean to make her one of us? Then she would no longer be one of them?"

"The thought has crossed my mind. She is the daughter of a faerie woman after all."

"That she is. Remember though this world doesn't see you as a faerie prince. In this world she was born master, and you slave. No doubt she thinks because she was born a woman that she knows all about servitude, yet she's never washed her own under garments, let alone lived on the road. I can tell she's very quick witted. Probably she is one of the few people almost as smart as you. I sense her intentions are sincere, yet in the end she is what she *does*."

# 3

The swaying of the ocean brought Lux gently awake. There was a soft-focus, a gradual edged confusion, which was followed by immediate panic. Between last night's shocks and being drugged with the opium poppy for pain, there was discontinuity about how she came to be below deck in a boat with some half-wild tinkers. Out of habit she double-checked that her clothing was still in order, and that she had not embarrassed herself whilst under the influence.

Light poured in through the cracks between the deck boards above. It was thin, fragile, golden light, spangled with dust and it fell across Robin's face while he slept. Lux found herself staring. It was like seeing him for the first time, and in terms of *really* seeing him, she was. She went through the times they had looked at each other over the past day or so, and she realised that until now she'd had actually never really looked at him at all. She had glanced at him in the forest, scanning his eyes, looking for signs of aggression. He was strong, highly physically capable and quite a bit taller than her. These things were evident from the abduction but they'd involved senses other than eyes. On the beach she'd barely noticed him, the previously unseen ocean had been the face of infinity.

It was easy to look now he was asleep and seemingly defenceless. For the first time she noticed his dark-gold hair, his honey-coloured skin, a shade or two darker than her own, his high, noble seeming cheekbones and the slight imperfection across the bridge of his nose where a break had probably occurred. His brow was strong yet not stern and cast shadows across his long eyelashes. Both a shallow dimple and a combat scar marked out his chin that wore three-day stubble. Beside these manly features his lips were striking for their open sensuality.

Lux's gaze became bolder at this thought; the thought that noticing was a matter of daring and a kind of new privilege she was claiming for herself. She scanned his visible shoulders, biceps and forearms, and in the process took in a little of Blaith's arms which were intertwined with Robin's body. It wasn't for long, because she didn't want to wake them with the weight of her gaze.

She took in that Blaith's body was more wiry and a little less powerful looking than Robin's, but that both of them were tall and long limbed, and were covered in a good many tattoos and scars. There was a bracelet of some kind around Blaith's wrist, something pretty that caught the light, but only the sharp canine teeth of what was probably a wolf and some bone beads adorned Robin's chest.

It was when she was looking at Robin's half naked chest that it occurred to her; she was alone in this room with two adult males and no chaperone. Lux sat up abruptly, using the blanket to cover her breasts that she was concerned may be visible through her shirt. Clarice had told her once that when it came to virgins from noble families like her that in the event they were seized by enemies, or ran away with a boy, the search would scale down after the first twenty-four hours. The reason being that the girl was assumed already defiled after this time.

Lux had been young enough to be horrified that a girl's worth was lost so easily. "So, they don't bother looking for you after that?"

Clarice had shaken her head matter-of-factly, as if she had been merely preparing Lux for the nature of the world they lived in and it couldn't be helped. Instead, she had put the seed of an idea in Lux's head, that if she could just get away and get clear for over twenty-four hours... Like so many things they had been wrong on this score. Unless torn by the astride horse riding she'd done, as far as she knew her hymen was still intact after over a day and night in the wild.

With no chaperone, though, she had no idea how long such a condition would persist. Not only this, but it was unclear under what conditions she might be called upon to yield her maidenhead, whether to the condition of wife or whore, to one man or more? The uncertainty was indeed unnerving. She was used to a particular and familiar threat to her person, one that Lux had cultivated a lot of behaviours around avoiding, placating and enduring. What sort of dangers might exist on the other side of the hedge was entirely unknown.

"Do you not think people will assume me a boy?" Lux asked tentatively.

"Maybe a very young one," Robin replied. It was clear he was unconvinced even after the more detailed haircut. "At least with the dye in anyone looking for someone with blonde hair will be slowed down a bit."

Robin found her a spare belt with weapons in it to finish the look.

Blaith indicated something in their language and Robin found her a smaller belt. When it was done Robin turned Lux to face Blaith. Although he was still reclining on the blankets and had not yet spoken directly to her Blaith said something in Welsh, which Robin translated.

"He says you make a very attractive boy."

Lux stared at Robin unable to think how to say or do anything beyond blushing. She felt something in response to this strange compliment she couldn't quite explain. There wasn't language to talk about that feeling. But if she'd had to put words to it, she'd have said that she liked this type of compliment, and was at the same time certain it was very sinful of her to like it. After all it seemed to suggest that boys may be looked upon in a way that quite levelled the playing field.

"And he's right," Robin added with a wink.

Lux looked away and down. The twinkle in Robin's eyes during this remark was so brazen it made her wonder if now was the moment he would claim what a man usually wanted. Would she have any more choice in that than she had in her hair being dyed?

"Excuse me," she said, turning to go. She couldn't think of anything else to say she just needed to quickly get out of that space for the open air.

The port of Whitby was nothing to her but a rat warren of fish-head-smelling streets, and alleyways awash in hops fumes, the hollers of hawkers and the forlorn cry of the gull. Over the top of other impressions was the sound of Lux's rapid breathing under the hood. She was afraid the whole time they were moving through open streets but she tried not to pull her hood down so far it would have the opposite impact and draw attention to her.

Robin and his kinsfolk seemed to know every path in England, every short cut or long way round, every nasty rutted backstreet or crooked back alley. They seemed to know people when it came to the maritime world. People recognised Robin everywhere they went. Both the crew of the ship, the ferryman and the owner of the rooms they were staying at were to be trusted, he said. Lux had no idea how it could be safe to be with a man with a face so many people knew, but there was nothing to do for it.

When they were finally behind closed doors Lux pulled back her hood and turned to Robin. "I'm not as dull-witted as most people in this world, you know?"

"I wouldn't have taken you with me if you were," Robin replied quietly, his back still to her and his hood still up while he disarmed himself and threw his weapon belt onto the one bed in the room. Blaith was hungry and had gone in search of provisions.

"Yet you think I can't see what's going on? That mark that you and Blaith have on your little finger, the woman who just gave us this room had the same mark on her hand."

"You've got good observation skills for a Settler," was all he said, taking a seat on the bed. "Tell me what's going on then." He sat there looking at her with his arms crossed.

Lux frowned. She could sense the mild challenge in his tone and didn't quite know how to respond to it. "Well…" she hesitated for a moment but his gaze hadn't shifted from her eyes. He was clearly waiting and possibly even assessing her. "It's perfectly clear that you are… some kind of criminal network or…"

"Or?" he prompted, and his eyebrows rose.

"Or you're rebels, people trying to start a revolt to take back control of the country."

"Or?"

"Or witches! Or a little of all of those three."

Robin smiled then. It was a slow mysterious, gradually kindling sort of smile. For a moment it made Lux wonder whether it was time to run. She had taken him for somewhere between nineteen and twenty-three but when he looked like that he seemed far more knowing than he had a right to be.

"A little of each perhaps."

"*Witches* also?" the word was a bit of a hiss, hardly over a whisper. She had been taught always to emphasise the difference between faeries, the folk who worked with them, and witches.

Robin neither confirmed nor denied just continued to look fixedly at Lux, never moving. "You know who I am, Lux. You said the name three times in all. And I came for you, just like the stories say."

"That was just panic. Some superstitious streak in me from early childhood must have risen to the fore. I was terrified and in shock, I wasn't really trying to invoke the d…"

He grinned again, his eyes twinkling with something between dark humour and some fiercer emotion she couldn't name. "Go on, say it. The sooner you get that word out of the way between us the more we're going to like each other."

The challenge in his eyes and tone was clear. She paused for a long time as she looked back at him, meeting his gaze and not letting herself drop her eyes. "Devil."

She wasn't sure if she meant the word as an answer or an accusation. The word felt abrupt in the air and immediately she wished she hadn't said it. But Robin smiled and nodded very faintly, very slowly as though this was what he wanted. "I hear he's very good to his own..."

There was a long silence.

"You're not going to run away?" he added eventually.

Lux sighed and shrugged. "Where would I run to? There's an array of tempting offers: probable death at my father's hands, or perhaps gutter prostitution. I'm going to throw my lot in with the devil I suppose."

He laughed as though he hadn't expected to. "You're funny."

"I'm wittier in French," she replied, her sass trying to hide the thrill she got out of that particular compliment which was so seldom accorded women.

"Then we shall speak French," he said, swapping to French. "But you place me at a disadvantage. I'm wittier in Welsh."

She smiled. It was close to impossible not to like him, devil or not.


"While we are asking each other personal questions, may I ask how you got the scars?"

"I thought you didn't look around while you were doctoring?" She flushed hot with shame in her cheeks.

"I said I only notice *wounds*," he replied. "Scars are wounds. Who hurt you?"

"My father."

"How were they made?"

"He beat me with his weapons belt. He said it was to stop me being a slut. I was only six at the time and didn't know what that even was. I was too ashamed to show anyone because of the location of the welts, up until they became infected. That is why it scarred."

Robin shook his head. While he washed the raw skin and re-applied ointment to it, he mentally added this story to a bank inside his memory of appalling things he'd heard or seen people do to innocents.

"Did he do this to you through clothes?" he asked, as he began to re-bandage her leg. He saw the immediate shame. She shook her head quickly and tears rushed into her eyes. "I was always undressed and exposed for his punishments."

As soon as Robin indicated he was done she rapidly huddled herself into a sitting position, pulled down the tunic over her legs and hugged herself with her arms. He sat down next to her on the bed and invited her confidence with his silence.

"He would make me take off my underwear, then he pulled my skirt up."

"Did he do anything else beyond the beating?"

"He would humiliate me, but only in such ways that I remain pure. He had me examined to make sure I was intact while he stood there and watched, because he didn't trust the women to get it right." She had stopped crying now and her voice had gone flat but for the odd sniffle. "Later on, as I got older I would be exposed and punished with only the two of us in the room. I am intact though, still, in case you wonder."

"So that's how they do it," Robin muttered to himself, as he put his doctoring kit away.

"Do what?" she asked, sitting back again and hugging herself.

"How they kill a woman's sex, break you into just a receptacle for the man's sex and seed."

"What do you mean by kill our sex?"

"To hurt and humiliate you so that your body will still be capable of giving life to his grandsons, but not to yourself."

He could tell that Lux didn't understand what he meant about her sex giving *her* life, but that didn't matter. It felt like enough for now that she was presented with the idea.

# 4

Before dawn the master and his men were out there again, disturbing the geese, and preparing for another day of putting the hounds on the scent, tracking, and torturing accomplices. Their absence meant Clarice could do her work without fear and she did her jobs rapidly. Today was a special day after all. The parish priest had finally been worn down through threats to allow the mistress to be buried on holy ground. The master had given his orders that Clarice prepare her to be moved into her coffin.

It was dark enough that she still had to use a candle to get about in the halls when she went to prepare the mistress. That was one of those odd little details that she remembered quite clearly later. From the moment she entered the room she was struck by the overwhelming smell. Covering her nose and mouth with one hand she held the candle high with the other. Despite the intensity of the odour there had been many odors in her life and her main concern was that this one didn't make sense. Clarice had been in the room only yesterday and there had been only very little corruption, only a mild smell of death as the room was as cold as an icebox.

Then she saw.

For a moment her mind couldn't wrap around the absence of the mistress's body from the bench where she'd lay for so many days. She just stared at the table and the blackish mass of bodily fluids, waste and what appeared to be human organs that lay in a congealed mess where her mistress's body had been. Clarice made a quiet sound of horror and covered her mouth with one hand. The only sound was the clank the candleholder made as it hit the floor and the flame went out.

Clarice began to tremble. She didn't know what it meant. A sweat of pure dread had begun to break out on her skin, especially between her breasts and at the backs of her knees. The crypt-like iciness of the room seemed to move like cold breath against that creeping moisture. Not far behind the nameless horror she was facing came the fear of retribution from the master if she didn't produce a body. The worst part was the way it had ruined her precious time alone. She had been planning on hiding and eating a handful of grapes she'd stashed from the master's leftovers, which, on the rare occasions she managed such treats was the highlight of her month.

Instead, now she was forcing herself forward heading gingerly around the table with its filth and gore and going for the window. If she could only open the shutters and let in the fragile light of the dawn, then she would be able to see what had gone on and clear the air a bit. It wasn't the first time she'd found a body moved around a bit by morning. Surely gases had simply built up and forced the internal organs out of the body, pushing the corpse onto the floor. Somewhere…

On her way to the window, she didn't see any body. Even with the window open and the faint light she couldn't perceive anything else on the floor. She tried not to think about all the horror stories of strange happenings concerning the dead that were currently gripping the land. Clarice told herself it was just the anxiety surrounding the succession, a stress held by the whole country. Everyone had a feeling that the crown would not pass peacefully and that terrible upheaval was afoot.

"Are there soldiers coming?" Lux asked nervously, awkwardly donning her own belt with numb, woolly fingers. Everything she was doing felt too slow, but she couldn't make herself move faster. It was like one of those dreams where you know you need to go quickly but your body is heavy as lead.

"Always."

He seemed so calm and matter-of-fact. As Lux pulled on the pair of boy's boots Robin had acquired for her she blinked away tears from her eyes. She wasn't upset, she was desperately afraid. Lux was afraid that she was going to freeze up out there like she felt close to doing now. Even with the mead in her she felt a whole lot less courageous from feeling the urgency in the air and the sense of battle-readiness about him.

"How do you know?" she asked tentatively.

"Because I have one who walks with me," he replied. "One of my father's kind. He lets me know they're coming. That's why they never catch me."

Blaith tossed her lately acquired backpack to her and that was that. Lux's head was spinning with the speed and efficiency of it. *So little to pack, the ultimate in travelling light...* It wasn't until then that Lux realised she had left all of her possessions behind, every keepsake from childhood, every piece of family heirloom jewellery, even locks of her mother's hair - and it didn't matter. It was as if she had died that day on the edge of the forest when Robin shot those men for her, died at the moment she would have died if it wasn't for him.

She followed them down the crooked stairs and out a back entrance into a courtyard. Once they hit the open air they walked smartly but didn't run. Blaith said something in their tongue that she didn't understand and then slipped away, they kept walking through the tangled back alleys.

"Where is he going?" she whispered to Robin.

"To find horses," he replied.

"How does he just *find* horses?" she asked.

Robin just looked at her with raised eyebrows for a second, long enough to realise he meant theft. They slipped out through the gates of the town long before dawn and shortly afterwards Blaith met them on horseback, leading another. As he leapt down from the horse's back with agile grace Robin smiled at him.

"You were quick," he said to Blaith in English, looking up at the rising sun and gauging its position in the sky. "I was expecting at least another ten minutes." There was an air of carnival about this for them. As though the business of committing felonies punishable by death and running from the sheriff's men was all in a good day's sport.

Blaith grinned and said something in Welsh.

"What did he say?" Lux asked as Robin lifted her onto the horse.

Robin appeared to think about it for a moment. "Roughly: when the grave beckons speed pays."

"The quick and the dead?" she suggested.

"That pun wouldn't work in Welsh," he said, kicking the horse into a gallop. "Are you scared?" he asked her, having to yell a bit to be heard over the movement of air.

"Terrified!"

He laughed as though with some exuberance. "I warrant you feel very alive right now though?"

"I'm feeling something!"

"Always better than feeling nothing."

At one of the cooling down lulls of the riding, Robin felt Lux stir against his back. "Where are we?" she murmured wearily, as though she'd been half asleep.

"North Yorkshire Moors," he replied. It still struck him as surprising that she didn't already know these things. It was so natural for him to assume that he was less educated than her on all matters including geography.

She perked her head up with interest. "Is that anywhere near Stokesley?"

"Very near Stokesley," Robin agreed.

"We need to stop there," Lux asserted. "There is a man that lives there, Old Devil Jack some call him, he was my mother's... very best friend once, so close to her that father forbid him access to our property and retracted her permission to travel."

Robin figured the word for that was love or lover, rather than very best friend, but he didn't say so. He was aware enough of her world to know there was shame around that kind of extra-marital arrangement in their eyes.

"They knew each other since they were children. He taught her to speak human. She used to tell me, over and over again when I was young, she would say: if ever you are in trouble or need you can always go to my friend Jack Daw who some call Devil Jack, up in Stokesley."

"I've never met Devil Jack personally I only know him by reputation. They call him The Warlock of Stokesley, a great horse breeder. Would he remember you, Lux?"

"Most certainly! Everyone knows that mother was the only woman he ever loved. Oh, Robin I absolutely must inform him of her death. We don't have to stay long if you don't trust him."

"What made you think of him just now?" Robin queried. He found it intriguing and potentially significant that she should have this thought pop into her mind when they were so near the edges of the moor that backed onto Stokesley.

"It just popped into my head."

"We must go to him then," Robin said, turning the horse to better speak in Cymraeg with Blaith.

Blaith nodded his agreement. "Stokesley... Wouldn't the old devil be Broomshead Coven stock if he hails from there? We might have some kin ties with him. They'd be thin ones but all the Broomshead folk join with us nine ancestors back. They'll remember."

"They're known for being territorial," Robin pointed out, wondering what the necromancer would make of them.

"I don't think we have much to worry about," Blaith replied. "It's just that most of the ones left now are old and grumpy. They're a dying breed the old settled families."

Robin nodded. He knew this fact to be true and he had a queasy sense that itinerate families weren't doing much better. *We're just like the wolves. Only a few left now... Them they trap and hunt and catch in pits, us they are killing by locking up the forests up for Norman hunting and filling them with officials to punish us for eating.*

When they arrived outside the necromancer's cottage in the edge of the moor, Lux was fairly sure that she had now seen the most drear outpost of the world. Had it always been so bleak here? Every thorn tree seemed tortured in some foul position suggestive of extreme inclement weather. The exposed rock of the land felt like the skeleton of some slain giant from the old stories. There was something about heading into this northern rebel territory that made her afraid she was the enemy.

Lux was unnerved, in fact, by how often her journey since leaving the house had included echoes and shadows from the old stories that nannies tell children in the nurseries. Like all children and young adolescents, her mind had been a fear-scape of hobgoblins, giants, headless shades, hell hounds, water horses, jenny green teeth's, enchanted fruits, witch's cottages in the woods, untrustworthy wolf men, spells of sleep broken with kisses and a very great number of tales of the doings of the King and Queen of Faerie and Robin Goodfellow, all her remembered life.

For her such folk stories had always seemed brighter and louder in her consciousness than the stories of Jesus, if perhaps only for the fact they occurred in the place she lived, not in faraway Jerusalem. As much as she liked the moral attitudes of Christ they had never really lined up with the behaviour of the people who claimed to follow him, and pray as she had at the convent she found it hard to overlook. On the other hand, it was impossible not to see giants in the land, were-lycans in the men at her side, hell hounds lurking in every dark hollow, and an evil witch of some kind in the cottage ahead.

Stories or no stories, the cottage wasn't exactly inviting looking. Its partly unhinged gate swung in the wind, making an unpleasant sound that vied for creepiness with the creaking of the ancient yew tree that grew outside the tumble down half-ruin. It was a very modest stone structure, the thatch was well rotted and patched in places with pieces of wood or even hide. There was a gnarled broom leaning near the front door and an amulet with knots and hag stones in it was suspended from the low hanging awning.

Robin jumped down from his horse. Lux followed. She was pleased to see that she was no longer so cramped she couldn't walk when she hit the ground, and she certainly didn't need a man to hand her down from the saddle anymore. Faster than she could have imagined her soft body was beginning to harden.

Blaith went first to the door, while Robin was still looking at the hag stone and taking a closer look at the bird of prey feather in it and the iron key.

"Ah, but what if he doesn't speak the tongue, Blaith?" Robin said in English.

Blaith replied in their dialect.

"He speaks English just fine, you know," Robin pointed out to Lux. "He just refuses."

Lux smiled faintly; she was a little charmed by his stubborn resistance. Robin ended up knocking, and very soon you could hear the creaking and shuffling of movement coming from within. A cat meowed in protest as it was moved out of the way and the door was unbolted. Lux stepped forward so that Jack would be able to see her and hopefully recognise her.

For a moment she couldn't see the man under his slightly floppy black hat with the light of the fireplace behind him, his face seemed black as coal though it was only an illusion.

"You came then," he grunted, stepping back to let them in. "Robin Goodfellow, I presume?" Robin was obviously about to confirm his identity and introduce his brother, but it appeared the older cunning man was already aware.

"And you'd be Blaith, Devil of the Twll Du blood-thread? *Bendithion a chroeso, cefnder* Blaith," he muttered, going over to stoke the fire.

Blaith smiled, showing a mouth that had rather too many teeth that sat oddly but not unattractively. He replied in Welsh but Jack held up his hand. "Oh, it was a granny's granny's granny who last had the tongue in full. I just know the important words, like the words for welcome and bless, brother, cousin, sister, words. Don't even know how to put them together right. Come to the fire," he said, ushering them closer to the blaze.

Lux went towards it with some enthusiasm. She'd watched Robin say a prayer over the fires he lit as though he reverenced the flame. She would never have understood that until she'd been this cold in wet clothes. Privation, it seemed, brought out the inner heathen in man.

She felt more comfortable the moment Blaith had smiled at Jack. Lux had noticed that Blaith didn't give full smiles to many people, so when he did you knew he really approved. For some reason though they'd barely communicated she already placed a great store in his opinion. "Blessings for your hospitality."

"Oh, don't bless me at all," the rugged woodsman-looking fellow said, taking off his hat in a gesture of respect. "It's for Lux's mother I take this risk, not for you."

Lux frowned in a pained sort of way. She found it very hard to give people bad news of this sort. Knowing that Jack had loved her mother she found the idea of saying the word dead close to unbearable.

"There's something we need to tell you, about mother…"

"Don't take on so, lass. I already know."

"But… how? Who told you?" Lux asked with a puzzled expression.

He sighed deeply. "Ah you're too young to understand yet. But there are some loves that never leave us. Some things the wind speaks to you of for the rest of your life."

# 5

So, what you are expecting me to believe is that someone came in here and stole my wife's body without you noticing?"

"No, my lord," Clarice murmured, ducking her head.

"Then what?" he bellowed at her suddenly. His voice was so loud and sudden, echoing in the stone chamber that she jumped and had to stifle a cry of fear. For a moment she was afraid she'd lose bladder control, so she pressed her legs together harder.

"I… I don't know, Lord. I think maybe…"

"You *think* do you?" he said sarcastically, taking a threatening step towards her. "I wasn't aware you people were even able to think. What precisely do you think when you think?"

All she could think of was escape but unlike for Lux there were no handsome stranger going to whisk her away to safety. She started to weep. "I think the faeries took her back," she cried.

"Just like how the faeries took Lux?" he asked, backhanding her across the face. She bit down on the involuntary sound of pain.

"I might have been wrong about Lux," she muttered rapidly, through the blood that was coming up in her mouth, trying to swallow it. "But mistress was brought here by the faeries! Why not taken away by the faeries!"

"What use do the faeries have with a half-rotten corpse?" he shouted at her, hitting her again on the other side of the face. This time she fell to the ground, and she immediately went into a defensive posture expecting him to kick her. Clarice was winded. Hitting the ground was getting harder the older she got. He got down on the ground with her and grabbed her face, forcing her to look into his cold blue eyes.

"You're not lying to me this time," he declared, after a few horrifying moments of having to stare into his total lack of human compassion. There was something stark about it, like a desert scene.

"No, my lord," she whimpered.

"You would lie for Lux because you gave her suck and watched her grow, and women are weakened to the intelligence of a sow when they give suck. But you had less love for Agnes, much less. She was cold and aloof, wasn't she?"

Clarice knew this was a trap. "I hold no such opinions of my betters, my lord."

He got up then and began to pace once more. "You're common," he pointed out, somewhat redundantly Clarice felt. "Surely you know of a conjure man or a necromancer, a renown wise woman or cunning man who can give information into the hereafter? There must be at least ten of the vermin in the villages surrounding."

"Doubtlessly."

"If you would avoid suffering for the lies, I know you've told and possibly for the ones I'm not sure about as well, I task you with this: find me a witch or some such devil's spawn. One who is not troubled by superstition regarding Agnes or Robin Goodfellow, one who will not hesitate to uncover their treachery. Can you do as I've asked?"

"Yes, my lord," she whispered.


Robin was glad he'd been asked to be the one to sit with Jack while Blaith attended to the horses. Usually Robin found that job soothing but tonight he wanted to keep a close eye on everything and assess this man they were staying with. From a seat in front of the hearthstone Robin looked up at the raking antlers of a huge red deer that adorned Jack's mantel. "Shoot him yourself?" he asked.

Without his hat it was possible to see his dark, silver-streaked hair. Despite his slightly turned foot Robin judged him to be a strong man yet, perhaps in his forties and definitely a fighter. He was quietly feeling him out and also trying to work out if Jack could tell he was being appraised. The older man crouched down to poke at the fire. "Aye. Shot him up in the Pennines many a year back now."

To someone who didn't know their world this might have seemed innocuous conversation, little more than small talk; but it wasn't. This was a conversation about poaching, though nobody said the word. It was a conversation about a capital crime and implicitly they were recognising each other as rebels. Jack wore his position on current events proudly on his mantelpiece. He also undertook his resistance a long way from anywhere it might have mattered.

"What's he got, about seven tines? He must have been a monster. What sort of bow did you shoot him with?" Robin asked, still taking his time scanning subtly over all visible fetish items and sorcerous objects and most importantly its owner and his rebellious antlers.

Instead of addressing how many tines the stag had, Jack sat down and looked at Robin very directly. "Why did you take her?" he asked bluntly.

Robin frowned for a moment and then laughed. "I like you," he replied.

The other man smiled in a reluctant way. *As if I charmed a mild flicker of mirth out of him against his better judgment. I wonder what story carved this man out of stone in this manner? His home is a boarded up re-occupied ruin that was one of the ones burnt out during the Harrying of the North, so I guess he's rebel stock and carries the scars we all do.*

"Which is all well and good, lad, but not an answer."

He shrugged. "She was in trouble, De Rue was going to kill her. She called out to me in her extremity and I answered. Can't think what else a man could do upon seeing that?"

"Have you claimed her hymen in exchange for this help?"

Robin frowned. "No. Would you ask me that if I wasn't a tinker?"

"I don't give one squirt of piss whether two usurious, tinker lepers bred you on a dung hill, only your actions matter to me. The world is full of pig-shit men of all classes. But you realise I've known Lux since she was this high?"

he said, indicating an improbably small height for any standing human to Robin's way of thinking. "She would have been my daughter, not his, if Fate wasn't a mean old bitch who likes to break pretty things," he muttered the last part bitterly to himself as though half in defiance and half in fear of retribution. "That bastard De Rue has lost the right to call her his daughter, so as far as I'm concerned Agnes' child is my responsibility now."

"Well, she can't stay here with you. They will go to everywhere that Agnes' daughter might hide, and De Rue would no doubt love an excuse to come after you. So, I'm guessing this is a talk about my intentions?

Jack sighed. "Just tell me you're only half as black as you're painted on the wanted posters and I'll sleep better at night for it."

"That's amusing coming from the Devil of Stokesley, the Black Warlock himself."

"Yeah, well the Devil of Stokesley isn't trying to court my woman's child and if he was I'd come after him too."

"Court?" Robin inquired. "Is that what I'm doing?"

"Yes, court, because that's what you're doing if you're doing it at all. You do it her people's way not your people's way."

"Her people's way? Through selling her to an old rich man against her will?"

"No." He sighed as though Robin were being deliberately obtuse when in fact he genuinely didn't understand why there was anything good about the Norman way of treating girls and women. "Just not wild in the hedgerows."

Robin sighed. "So, this *is* a tinker thing."

"I'm just being straight with you. This country is full of people who believe that their one true omnipotent god who created the entire firmament has told them not to touch their naughty bits." He laughed. "These idiots believe that fine girl sleeping in there is worth nothing more than a milking heifer. Vast majority of them would tell you that judge-not-Jesus, who they all make so much of, would have wanted your brother put to death on account of his boy love. An all-seeing peeping tom who cares where boys stick it! Men like

57

you and me? We're freaks in their world. Maybe in any world... If Lux doesn't stay inside their parameters she has no future." Jack passed Robin a hip flask of mead to drink from.

Robin took it, nodding to himself as he swallowed the honey fire of it. "Fuck their parameters. Fuck what they say. Fuck what they think. Fuck what they believe. Fuck everything they stand for. And fuck their authority." Robin said with quiet conviction while he gazed fixedly into the coals of the fire. He figured that should about nail his colours to the mast.

"Fuck their authority indeed," Jack agreed, swigging from the mead as Robin passed it back. "Fuck their usurper tyrant kings, and their forest laws."

"Ready to help us take the land back, friend?" Robin asked, getting to his feet as though to warm himself at the hearth, before turning to face Jack. "My people believe there are certain people who are always reborn right when it's time to reshuffle the cards."

Jack grunted. "Well sure as shit I'm not one of those folks. I'd rather sit tight here and shuffle my balls instead." It was clear he found this a great joke. "Show the bastards my arse from a distance from time to time."

"And yet you just invited some very wanted people into your home... Didn't really think that one through too well did you?"

Jack sighed heavily. "It ain't what I wanted for my later years. But they'll be getting at Agnes' girl over my dead body," he declared. "Don't care if the King of England himself wants her."

Robin clapped him on the back affectionately. "Welcome back to the rebellion, my friend."


When Lux heard someone knocking at the door she tried to pull the somewhat oversized men's tunic she was wearing down over her knees. She was seated on the edge of the pallet near the fire, drying her short dark hair more quickly by brushing it with a comb. "Come in," she said.

She felt a little leap in her chest when she saw that it was Robin. What he was asking her to do pressed outside of all the conventions she'd been brought up with. He himself was down to some hose and a tunic loose at the waist. It was impossible not to smile. It made her happy to see him able to relax like that for a moment, no iron, weapons, or studded leather jerkin. It made him seem more like an older boy suddenly, rather than a man grown.

"Do you mind if I sit?" he asked.

"Not at all."

He crouched down on a mat in a very lithe way that further accentuated the sense of the boy in him. Lux noticed that he was looking at her exposed thigh. But it was with such an unusual expression in his eyes that she found she couldn't interpret the gaze as anything to offend her modesty.

"What are you thinking when you look at me like that?" she asked, her head cocked on one side with curiosity. He glanced up at her quickly and smiled, his mischievous Puckish grin.

"Do you really want to know?" he asked, cheeky humour twinkling in his eyes.

"Yes." She felt challenged now so she couldn't back down.

He came and sat up on the pallet beside her. "Well," he said, picking up her forearms that lay against her thigh and in the action exposing more of her thigh. "I was thinking," he said, pausing again for effect. "That you have very long thigh bones and forearm bones proportionally for your size. Very much a young swordsman's build, a great runner, or perhaps like a faerie bowman."

Lux smiled with a quirk of her eyebrows and then laughed. She wasn't quite sure how to explain why she found this appealing.

"What?" Robin asked after a moment. "Is that not what I'm meant to be thinking when I look at your thigh?"

"I have no idea what you should be thinking when you look at my thigh," Lux denied. "I just find it... I don't know... amusing that you are assessing my combat potential."

Robin shrugged. "I suppose I do think of you as little different to another boy."

"That's just how I would like you to think of me," she blurted out. "I

59

mean… Not as a boy, exactly. I mean… I suppose I just mean I'd like you to think there isn't much difference between us."

Robin nodded as though her explanation was clear. "Of course. It's because only half of you is a girl, the other half is a faerie and would like to be seen. It is the same with me that I am only half a man, the other part does not belong to their world of two-by-two. I can see that faerie who is neither girl nor boy in you. In your thigh and this turn of your arm," he said, getting up and kneeling on the bed behind her. "Where you imagine," he took her elbow in his hands and drew it back in the posture that one might fire a bow. "That it's been designed to draw back and let fly an arrow."

As he said this his body touched hers lightly from behind and she flinched. He let her hand fly as though she were firing the bow. "Yes," he remarked, as he studied the arch of her forearm that he had posed and her extended arm. "There is a distinctive, shared, faerie form I see in us both." He cleared his throat and sat back observing her blush. "We will meet with my cousins on the road in the next day or two. They are women… What I mean is, you will not be only around men for much longer."

Finally, Clarice got up the courage and knocked twice on the oak wood door. Although small, the place had a sturdy stone hearth and walls, you could tell that well enough from the outside, as smoke billowed forth from the of the roof rather than diffused through the thatch. Whilst the place was small it was clear the owner wanted not for new thatching or fuel.

"Come in and sit by the hearth, I'm almost ready," a woman's voice called out in English with a Norman French accent.

Clarice frowned, hesitated and then finally let herself in. She was overcome by the combined smell of animal life, macerated herbs and blood. Her entrance disturbed a bustle of what Clarice originally thought to be cats until she realised that there was a hare with a gamy leg among the menagerie. The lady of the house had her sleeves rolled up and blood up to her elbows, as she leaned over a basin gutting some feathered creature.

She hadn't aged as much as would be expected; there was still a lot of dark hair mixed with the silver that was piled up on top of her head half concealed under a red cap.

"Good morn, Ma'am. I wondered if…"

"Take a seat near the hearth, Clarice," she said abruptly, looking up for the first time and fixing Clarice with her sharp dark eyes. Her high forehead and the dimple in her chin marked her as De Biron stock, but her clothing did not suggest she was highborn.

"You remember me," Clarice muttered, taking a seat by the fire while the animals mobbed her for her attention.

Nanette grunted. "I remember things well enough. But people only remember Nanette in return when they have dark works they want brewed." She looked up from the goose in the basin and wiped back a stray strand of hair from her face with the back of her arm. "What unspeakable thing do you need done? Not another bairn fetched out of you, I'll warrant, not at your age."

She hadn't owned that crime, the conceiving or the undoing of the babe to any those long years. "No, indeed," she said quietly. "And I've thought of you kindly many a year for your skill and discretion."

Nanette laughed. It was an unlovely sound. "I bet you did. Saved you a beating and a half, I'm sure, and probably a turning out onto the street. What do you want now?" At that Nanette placed a large bowl of entrails down on the ground and the cats quickly covered it, devouring it, and hissing at each other in competition.

"It's not on my account I come, mistress," Clarice said, hoping Nanette wouldn't detect the slight lie. "My master needs to track someone down who does not wish to be tracked."

Nanette narrowed her eyes and squinted at Clarice in intense scrutiny. "A simple finding of a lost object? I don't believe you. You could have gone to any old friendly herb peddler and fortuneteller for that. Yet you came here when you are both afraid and embarrassed. You need greater work done than that."

Cleaning the excess blood off her hands with an old rag, Nanette came and sat down opposite Clarice. A small dog with only one eye came up and began licking at her hands to get at the blood. It was strange to her, the compassion this black-hearted woman had for lesser creatures. Clarice sighed. She knew she wouldn't be able to tell a half-truth to Nanette.

"Do you remember Agnes the faerie girl? Whom my master married?"

"Of course," Nanette replied immediately, interest seeming to quicken in her dark, intelligent eyes. "Her name is legend."

"Her daughter Lux has run off with Robin Goodfellow. Master refuses to believe he is a spirit and holds he is a man and can be caught. Only days later my mistress's corpse... disappeared. Master believes there's witchcraft at work, wants me to find-"

"A stronger witch?" Nanette finished for her.

"Yes, mum."

"To do battle with them, too, I take it? Because they have their own sorcerers, don't they, those tinkers? Or at least you suspect they do. It's that caravan family they say has faerie blood? Well, you're smarter than you look, Clarice. Aren't you?" she laughed under her breath quietly, as she pushed her over enthusiastic animals away. "The Biron's are known for liking a fight, it's how we earned our land and carved out our inheritance. My brother and son have their battle mace and their broadswords, I've only got my blasting rod, but I don't mind a good set-to. You knew that already though, that's why you came to me."

Clarice was conflicted. She knew her life could well depend on Nanette's agreement to come and meet her master, yet some secret part of her had hoped that it would be impossible. She knew enough about Nanette de Biron to fear what she could be unleashing on Lux if it went ahead, and upon all of them.

"My lord wants me to tell you that you'd be handsomely financially compensated for your trouble if he gets the results he wants."

"Do you think I work in this little hovel because I want for gold, woman?"

"I have no idea, my lady. I was just sending the message."

"Tell your master I don't care for his gold, I have my own if I need it. But

I would meet with him, and have him prepare objects ready that belonged to both the woman and the girl. The more intimate the item the better."

"Why would you do it for then, if not for pay?"

"Glory," Nanette replied immediately. "Why do men fight each other? You don't know your witch families like I do. I know who Robin Goodfellow is, he who they call Robin Dhu on the other side of the Marchers, everyone does. I know the awe with which the people speak of him and his brother. Witch royalty they would name them. They are feared, but Robin is also loved by the common folk and people link their names with rebellion and insurrection. If I defeat them people will know that it was a Norman woman who bested them.

"The fear they once had for them they will have for me. Never the love, but never mind the love, they can keep that. Love doesn't last, it sours on the vine long before winter. And believe me Clarice's fear is the only kind of power that men understand. If we would get by in their world, we can do so by being beautiful for a time, but beauty fades," she muttered, poking at her fire. "Even the fairest of them, faerie-get or not, she will fade, she'll eat the bitter fruit of grief and time like we all must taste and it will line her pretty face... But *fear*, when men *fear* you, then you can have whatever you want. Now *that* only grows sweeter with time."

Robin was leaving Lux's room when Jack came striding up to him rapidly. "I thought I told you to court her!" he said, when he reached Robin, he shoved him in the chest. "Huh? What were you doing in her bedroom?"

Robin had come to react poorly to being struck and his body responded in certain semi-automatic ways to the energy of male violence. It happened often enough as a child that aggression followed by strikes, and since he'd grown up he didn't tend to put up with it now that he could prevent it.

"We didn't do anything," he said quietly, putting his hand over Jack's arm and trying to diffuse the situation with calmness. He knew this behaviour stemmed after all, through the lens of a very different culture, from Jack's regard for Lux. As he shared this same regard it seemed folly for them to fight. "She was just telling me-" Robin didn't get to finish the situation because Blaith interrupted.

"Get your hands off my brother before I kill you," Blaith said in disconcertingly clear English.

Immediately Jack let go of Robin and with surprising speed threw Blaith into the wall by his throat. "You think to draw on me in my own home, boy!" Jack roared at him, seeming to nearly lift the finer boned man off his feet. What Jack didn't see that Robin did was Blaith's hand close around his side arm.

"Blaith no!" Robin shouted, rushing forward to step behind Jack's ankle and throw one arm across his throat, immediately leveraging the older man to the ground. Jack hit the ground but Robin went down with him, keeping his forearm up under Jack's chin and across his throat firm enough to prevent further struggle. Although he was subduing him in this manner Robin had always very deliberately placed his body between Blaith and Jack to prevent Blaith following through with his intention to draw his blade.

"Stop it!" cried a female voice. Lux was standing in the doorway in only her shirt. The candle behind her showed her shape through her shirt. Her intense distress made Robin immediately feel somehow ashamed of himself, even though all he'd actually done was prevent his brother knifing their host. "Please don't fight... Nothing was happening."

Robin did as he was told and so did Jack. Blaith was still glaring at Jack in a manner that suggested that the job of keeping Blaith's weapon in its sheath might not be over yet. The balefulness of Blaith's sharp black eyes was so intense Robin gestured it to earth with his hand instinctually, *a little of it upon the bare rock, a little on the salty sea, none of it upon our host.* To aid in diffusing the malefic atmosphere Robin took Jack outside to talk.

After he closed the rickety old door Jack turned to Robin. It was left ajar to provide some light. He looked at the wall and the ground and finally made reluctant eye contact. "Sorry for jumping to conclusions and handling you

64

like that. Had a bad experience with a very dear sister and a tinker boy once. Sweet tongue on him, left her with a bairn," he said, holding up his hands. "I'm just looking out for Lux like I wish I did my natural kin."

"I feel like that towards Norman men. I'm sorry about my brother moving to draw on you." It was only a partial truth because he didn't think it was exactly the same somehow, with one group having the whole power of society and the other nothing. Yet he knew from the look of terror on Lux's face that he needed to prevent any further outbreaks of violence.

"He's a hothead," Jack grunted.

"He's had reason to be," Robin replied, his voice firm but patient. "He was all I had growing up. No father to take care of me, our mother dead, and I got myself into a lot of trouble."

"Wouldn't be the only ones," Jack replied bluntly. "Don't you tinkers follow any codes of hospitality?"

"After the way you grabbed Blaith by the throat you are lucky I didn't break both your arms. Consider that my concession to the laws of hospitality our people indeed teach us."

Jack looked him up and down as though appraising him. Eventually he nodded. "Fair enough… I don't know why, but I like you, lad." Jack looked at him almost puzzled then, as if he were searching for something in Robin's face that continued to elude him. "I swear to the gods old and new you remind me of someone I once knew."

# 6

The patchy woods and moorland gave way to real forest about mid-afternoon. Lux became aware that she didn't know where they were headed. Although it disturbed her that they didn't tell her she had a feeling she knew where they were headed without being told. It was as if some ancient part of her had followed these crooked, winding paths before, so many times that her feet would have known them.

"Robin? Where do tinkers come from? You speak Welsh but your people are far from home."

"They say we're the children of Cain."

"Well, they sure know how to put people at their ease." Once again Lux was joking because she was uncomfortable.

"Putting people at their ease is probably not our top survival strategy."

"But seriously, Robin. Was Cain a Welshmen? Because unless a traveller came from the East everything suggests you're not descended from Cain."

Somehow, she sensed rather than saw him smile in response. She could tell he'd thought it too. They were both thinkers after all, the few in a world of the thoughtless. It was what excited them both so much about each other. Lux was fairly sure that Robin's thinking mind had seen the thinking mind in her and rescued her so as not to waste it. That idea elated her far more than whether or not he thought she was pretty.

"It's complex because our family is made up of three caravans that came together as one with each having their own history. They say we came from a mixed Welsh-Irish settlement and we went on the road because our brand of Christianity wasn't considered Christian anymore after some new law or another passed hundreds of years ago."

Lux considered this information for a while. "But your people consider themselves to be Christians?" In the world she'd been raised in this was among the most important issues of conformity she'd been asked to accept. It was hard to *think* outside the framework of it, just as it had always been hard to *feel* from inside the same framework.

"We worship Our Lady as fervently as anyone in England."

"You're Marian Christians?" she narrowed in as he tried to skip away.

"Yes, we call ourselves Marian."

"But you also refer to yourselves as witch families and use the word devil."

"*They* called us witches. *Theirs* is the word devil. These are English words. We do not call ourselves witches."

"In French then? *Sorciere*?"

"*Sorcierère*," he corrected, giving the more gender-neutral version of the word.

"But how can you be both *sorcierère* and Christian?" Lux asked. As she asked this a parasite from one of the ancient oaks they were being enveloped by wetly caressed the back of her neck. She shivered. It felt like she was going down into the belly of a green beast that was slowly digesting her.

"Some might find our take on Christianity a touch... heretical," Robin admitted.

Lux knew about heretics. Her father had been involved in slaughtering heretics by the hundreds in the crusade. This was something you were brought up believing you should be proud of, the mighty tally of your father's killings. Her father had told the tales about how many he personally butchered around the meal table since she was old enough to remember. "My father used to proudly tell us of slaughtering the children of heretics so they couldn't grow up and breed."

"How Christian of him," Robin replied, his tone cuttingly dry.

"That's what I was thinking when I said it," she admitted. "Alright, well... What about the devil? Explain to me how he's involved in this heretical take on Christianity?"

"Well, my people will tell you that the devil and Jesus Christ are but two faces of the same being, the light-bringer who-"

"Whoa! Whoa, alright… Look, you shouldn't say that out loud, Robin! Goodness! People could hear you! That's just a *touch* heretical?"

He shrugged. "We believe Jesus saves, if that helps? And the limitless divine made everything that is including the potential for magic working."

"But you're witches! You're… you're… witches! And you just admitted you worship the devil!"

"No, I didn't. I didn't say anything about worship. I just told you that my people believe that Jesus is Lucifer. If we worship anyone it is Our Lady Mary."

"Do you know what people out there would do to you for having such… thoughts?"

"No doubts punish me in cruel and unusual ways. Thinking is quite the unpopular hobby. But consider it this way Lux, you used to share a meal table with a man who bludgeoned to death someone's babies, now you're just in the company of a man with peculiar thoughts. I have a feeling you were in more danger in your father's house than you ever will be around my people and I. Out of the way ideas notwithstanding."

Lux wanted to tell him of her gut knots, about how life had taught her that people's ideas got enacted upon the bodies of others. How ideas became actions and how, never having met someone with his kind of ideas, she therefore had no way to predict his actions.

Lux only caught a few snippets like: 'Should we try to outrun them?' and Robin shaking his head adamantly and replying something about the horses carrying two. It took her a bit longer but by the end of their discussion she could hear hoof beats in the distance.

"Blaith?" Robin said in English. "Please get Lux out of sight and range, along with the horses." He said this very coolly, yet under the surface was a battle-readiness that made Lux's stomach churn. You didn't need to understand their language to hear the objection in Blaith's tone of voice. But Robin's quiet determination appeared unmoved by his brother's protestations. "I know, but you hold the Virtue of our blood-thread and we cannot risk you."

Blaith muttered some words under his breath that she was fairly sure were resistant. Robin turned to Lux. "When I've dealt with this, I'll come for you. Follow Blaith's lead in all things until I return." He turned from her then, grim and business-like. "Jack? Will you stay?"

"Wouldn't dream of doing anything else, lad," the older man said gruffly, taking out his bow. "I'm a hunter. I mislike being hunted."

Lux's fingers felt frozen to stiffness on the horse's reins. She wanted to point out to Robin that she'd never ridden astride a horse alone and actually been in control of the animal before. Her tongue was as frozen as her fingers. Deeper inside herself she wanted to protest leaving Robin's side the way Blaith had, but she was so thoroughly trained since childhood to obey men that in this moment of stress she just couldn't find the words to do it.

"Alright, Lux. Let's go," Blaith said in English, taking hold of her reins.

Lux was still looking back at Robin, her mouth so dry she could barely breathe let alone say anything. He noticed. "Expect me in the time it takes for the horses to recoup their breath," Robin reassured her making brief eye contact, before giving her horse such a smart smack on the hindquarters that she was suddenly cantering her way into a gallop.


Jack could feel the vibrations in the ground through his feet now and when the air was suddenly rent by the crazed cry of a hound the hairs went up on the back of his neck.

"Jesus' cock end," he muttered. "They've got dogs with them."

The younger man just nodded as if it was expected. "They wouldn't have found us otherwise," he said.

"What's our plan?" Jack asked. Even in the midst of the emergency, he found himself looking Robin over and trying to place the strange feeling that they'd met before. The boy wasn't old enough to have crossed his path back in the old covenant days, he thought. But it didn't matter. Jack's bones told him he could trust the other man. His experience as a fighter and the brief moment of being restrained by him back at the cabin told Jack that Robin's obvious confidence was probably not over-confidence.

Before he answered Robin took out a torn piece of a woman's gown and threw it down in the clearing before taking a seat on a fallen log. Immediately Jack joined the dots and realised that he was purposely attracting the dogs to them with a decoy carrying Lux's scent. "If you could take cover behind that rocky outcrop with your bow at the ready. There will be a moment, you will know it when you see it, when they are just about to realise I'm not what they think and menace me, at the moment I want you to shoot the one most likely to be a threat."

"Shoot him dead?" Jack enquired with a deep frown on his heavy brow. It had been years since he'd killed a man, and even then, he hadn't really set out to. Whenever he'd killed it had been hand-to-hand in a fair fight. The young man's green eyes flickered up to his with an enquiring expression in them for a moment.

"Well, I don't want it to tickle him, friend. I assume you can shoot a man dead reliably at this close range?"

Jack nodded grimly. "It's not the range or my accuracy that bothers me, but I'm good for it. Sounds like there's a few of them. I'm hearing three horses at least."

Robin nodded his agreement. "I've got the rest covered. Unless it looks like I don't," he grinned.

"And what do I do if you don't?" Jack asked, already assuming his position behind the rocky outcrop.

Robin laughed as though with genuine humour. *The boy is half touched and that's being generous.* Jack's palms were sweating. *Fucking elf-get.*

"Then save me!" Robin replied with a grin, as if these were perfectly ad-equate and detailed instructions. He sat down then and pulled his cloak hood down over his face. Jack frowned in fascination as he watched. Somehow the outward facing wooden edge of Robin's partially visible bow had become an old man's walking stick. Assuming a hunched position Robin suddenly went from having the form of a strapping young male to appearing smaller and more vulnerable under his cloak. His only half visible hand on the bow had a tremor in it, like an ageing man.

The hardest part was waiting. Waiting as the hoof-beats got closer and you could hear the slavering of the dogs. Jack hated dogs. It had been years ago now since he'd been scarred on his leg by one of De Rue's dogs which had left him with a permanent odd gait. In all honesty, he admitted to himself, he was lucky to still have all his fingers and hands after all the poaching he'd done in his life. A bite in the calf from one of the lord's dogs was probably the least he deserved. He was a poacher and a rebel, but he was not a cold-blooded killer.

Sighing to himself he notched an arrow and thought about how delicate Agnes had felt in his arms. He thought of their lovemaking and the lifelong scars he'd found on her body that De Rue had put there. *Love makes killers of us all in the end. I'd end that monster in cold blood, preferably with my bare hands. But what are these? Bounty hunters? Desperate men? Not so different to me? I'm only a few good feeds off having to sell my blade for coin myself; like most of us. I'd sooner kill the master than his dogs.*

The dogs made it into the clearing ahead of the men and went straight for the material Robin had left on the ground. So far, so good, Jack thought to himself. His heart was thundering and his palms were sweating. He just hoped that the dogs wouldn't give the game away before he could get his shot in.

"You seen any horses pass this way, stranger?" one of the mounted men demanding of Robin as he rode into the clearing. The dogs were still gathered around the material whining and worrying at it with their frothing muzzles.

"Ow, I think so yes, sir," said a creaky old voice that somehow emerged from Robin's throat. "These old eyes aren't what they used to be but I heard 'em, my good friend, oh yes I heard 'em and they dropped that in passing." He said indicating the material from Lux's gown. They dismounted then and came over to examine what the dogs had. Jack appraised the three of them and he didn't like what he saw. Dangerous men. You could tell it in the way they moved and even in how they scoped out their environment. They were probably ex-mercenaries turned bounty hunters, or worse yet they were foresters from a nearby warren. Foresters were often some of the best trackers.

"And what were you doing out here just sitting in the woods, old man?" one of the other said, a swagger of aggression in his walk as he headed toward Robin. Jack's heart beat harder still.

"Just collecting sticks for my fire when I came over tired," he said, his voice still so convincingly weak and cracking on certain words that Jack would have judge him to be three score and ten if he was a day.

"You were collecting wood from a crown forest?" the bounty hunter demanded. Jack made a quick assessment of the situation. He had already worked out roughly what weapons each were carrying and only one of them was carrying a bow. But there were throwing knives on them, he was certain of that much.

In a moment the one who he judged to be their best fighter was going to reach out and try to push back Robin's hood. Jack had a feeling that the hand he touched Robin with was never going to touch anything again, but what would happen afterwards was anyone's guess, and that's the part that Jack hated, the uncertainty, the taste of chaos in the air.

"Did you hear me, old man?" he said, roughly attempting to push back Robin's hood. As Jack predicted he never got the chance to finish the motion. What happened was almost too fast for Jack to follow. But he gathered that Robin captured and broke the man's hand or wrist in one motion. The man cried out in pain and then became a human shield who was then shot by one of his own companions. Jack heard the man who fired the arrow swear at his own misstep and realised in the same instant that this man was the one he needed to shoot.

Jack dropped the man with the bow the same way he'd have put down a deer. He was saddened slightly by how little he felt doing it. Given how many years it had been since he'd taken human life, he'd thought his heart had become tenderer.

"You're him!" The still living man cried, reaching franticly for a weapon. "You're Robin Goodfellow!"

Robin laughed, but there was something cold and elfin in it, different to his other laughs. The man dropped to the ground. It was only a couple of seconds afterwards that Jack realised it had been the result of Robin's bow, so fast was the young man's draw. The dead man Robin had been using as a human shield fell limply to the ground.

Slowly Jack got to his feet as he watched Robin brush himself down and push back his hood. "Jack, could you capture their horses please?"

Looking around he realised that the dogs had run off at the sound of arrows flying. "Sure," he agreed.

While he was calming and capturing the horses, he glanced back occasionally to see what Robin was doing. He realised with mild distaste that Robin was rifling the dead for valuables and supplies.

By the time Jack returned with the horses he saw that Robin had the men's chests and rib cage open. He frowned as he passed.

"Would you like to offer the heart of your own kill?" Robin asked him, as casually as if they were talking about a stag they'd just dropped.

"I've only ever done it with deer," Jack muttered. "Didn't know it was in tradition to do it to a man."

Robin shrugged. "The heart is in much the same place. We do it for all things that bleed red. I can do it if you prefer?"

Jack was too mature a man to feel he needed to prove himself in front of the young fellow. He was years past caring about other men's opinion of him and only cared for his own. "Yeah, you do it."

"Tender heart or queasy stomach?" Robin asked, as he opened the man's chest with his hunting knife.

Jack gave a half laugh that was closer to a grunt. "More my heart than my stomach, friend."

Robin nodded to himself. "I like the company of a man with a tender heart," he observed. "It's rare enough in our world."

Jack didn't bother to remark that it was hardly excessive tenderness to balk at the idea of gutting the newly dead and taking their valuables before they were cold. But he didn't bother, he figured the tinker lad had lived a different sort of life than himself; one lived closer to the edge.

"It is a gesture of respect," Robin said, wiping away the blood that he had nearly to his elbows with some water and a rag. "Just like with a deer. Chances are these men deserve my respect less than any deer I've ever shot, but it's not the point. I was taught to honour life."

Jack nodded thoughtfully as they led the new horses. "What makes you so sure they don't deserve it? Me, I could see a few missteps of youth having taken me down the same road they went, selling their blade to the highest bidder…"

Robin looked over at him then, and he had the feeling that now they were on the opposite sides of an ethical judgment. "Really?" he asked, a slight note of surprise and maybe even judgment creeping through in his otherwise neutral tone.

"I've seen enough to know what a desperate man will do," Jack muttered. "And enough on top of that to know I'm just a man."

Robin made a faint exhalation of air through his nose that quietly seemed to suggest disagreement. Jack chuckled after a while. "Well, I guess you aren't just a man are you? Elf-get as you are."

Robin shook his head slowly. "I'm a man as other men are. But I'd never use *just*. The soul of man is a proud thing to possess. I'd die, or starve, or cut my own throat in the fields before I threw dishonour on that soul and the womb that bore me by taking an honourless man's coin to hunt down a woman and child for a bully like De Rue." He spat on the leaves of the forest to fully express his contempt.

Jack smiled to himself enigmatically. He'd seen enough of the world that it had made him cynical, this was not a cynical smile though. There was a wildfire that burned in the boy that made Jack believe his words, wanted those words to convince him to believe again.

"So, you kill them so easy because you judge them bad men?" Jack asked, riding up level with the other man.

"No. I kill them so easily because I want to live," Robin shrugged. "And if I don't they won't let me."

It didn't matter that they had to ride through bandit-haunted woods through the early hours of the night to reach their destination. It didn't matter that Lux was riding into the maw of a wild green beast that had tooth and claws, or that the parasites hung down close and scraped her skin. It didn't matter that death dealing had likely happened on the road behind them. It didn't even matter that some of his family were ahead and that she would soon be plunged headlong into their unfamiliar culture. All that mattered was that Robin was riding unharmed beside her.

In truth it hadn't been until she'd been forced to separate from him that she knew how much she dreaded the idea of him being harmed on account of her. And weren't they now bringing his family into peril also? She wanted to talk to him about it. Her adrenalin had been leading everything until now. But Robin had made it clear no one was to make any extraneous sounds, let alone conversations. It wasn't until Robin whistled into the darkness ahead, mimicking a birdcall and was returned by another such call that Lux saw it was all too late.

What sort of person, especially female persons, was out here at this cross-roads at this time of night waiting in the dark in total silence? Watching? Doing what in a dark wood at night with no lanterns? How many of them were there and were they watching her? By peering ahead Lux was soon able to see three figures on horseback moving forward at a walk to meet them on the path ahead. It was clear Robin and Blaith knew and recognised who they were by the way they increased the speed of their horses and didn't draw weapons.

Finally, they were close enough that Lux was able to brush back a partial wall of parasitic greenery and glance through a patch of moonlight to see them. Lux noticed the woman in the centre first. Her body conveyed a fierce whip-like strength in the whole way she sat her skittish horse. The woman to the right of her had darker hair, cut in a simple bob with a fringe. As they moved into a column of moonlight Lux saw she wore a kind of apron, which Lux knew to be used by physicians, with small pockets for all their herbs, powders, and implements. Lux had never seen such an apron on a woman before.

On the far left was a young man, armed much as Robin was, but slighter in his build. Within an instant the woman in the middle had swung down out of her saddle in which she'd been sitting astride, all in a single agile motion, as if she was born nestled in the curve of a horse's back. It wasn't until Blaith jumped down from his horse too and their bodies met that she identified them as lovers.

Jack made his favourite grunting sound of acknowledgement. "Well, I'll be damned. Oh, no, hang around there... His door swings both ways then. Looks like they follow the hardline way here," Jack commented, more as though it was to himself than to Lux. "No shackles of any kind, not even the marriage one."

Lux frowned. "Do you mean there are no husbands and wives here?"

"If they're hardline then they have what's called hedgerow wives and husbands. It's usually only used when linking an outsider to their clan. It's to indicate who your primary connection is, though from what I understand you remain free to sleep where you choose."

As she didn't know how to process such an idea Lux asked no further questions.

"Come," Robin said, handing Lux down from her horse after noticing her freeze. "Let me introduce everyone. These are my cousins. This is Sariah." He indicated the woman whose hair was worn in braids. "Eilish." The woman doctor. "And Meredith," -the younger warrior. "Cousin, this is Lux, someone I was fated to meet. And Jack, the Black Warlock of Stokesley."

"Welcome strangers dear to the blood-of-my-blood," Sariah said, smiling in her direction and winding her arm around Robin's waist. Although her affectionate behaviour with Robin seemed natural and playful there was a quiet authority to her. "You cannot argue with Fate, so you must come and drink mead from our horn and break bread with us, then we will not be strangers any longer," she declared, showing the way forward along the path with her arm and formally inviting them to be her guests. Lux could tell that this young woman, who she judged no older than twenty-three was somehow high ranking in their world. Was it because she was Blaith's hedge wife?

Sariah slipped back up effortlessly into the saddle and nudged her mount into a walk. She doubled back to ride beside her and Lux immediately felt nervous. It wasn't like with Blaith who had only once or twice deigned to speak to her, this lady spoke English well and clearly intended they do more of it. Her nerves came from the fact Sariah moved so effortlessly in the world that Robin was a part of, in exactly the way that had been punished out of Lux.

Would she herself ever be relaxed enough to joke with him and touch him so freely and unselfconsciously? This woman seemed to break about ten rules imposed on women in her upbringing every minute. The thought made Lux's chest ache in the centre. It was not an ache of jealousy, more one of sadness in the face of the knowledge that whatever was so switched on in Sariah's hips and whole body was switched off in her own.

"Greetings, Lux," the other woman said in very good but slightly artificially rendered English. Sariah even pronounced her name correctly as 'lukes'. "I hope you don't mind if I ride with you back to camp?"

"It's my pleasure," she said shyly. Despite her other feelings a certain surge came up in her stomach at being in the presence of someone other than men finally. All her early life had been a primarily single gender affair, so this past few days had been a grand anomaly in which she was by turns oddly comfortable and at others, especially when the men tried to fight each other, entirely at sea.

"I'm both delighted and curious to see Hob's prophecy girl. But of course, it all makes sense," she said, after examining Lux. "Now that I see how fae you are. Is it true that your mother was as Robin's father, one of Them?"

Lux frowned slightly. She hadn't heard that euphemism before. "It is, or was, yes. She is dead."

Sariah burst out laughing and then prevented herself cutting it off with her hand. "Oh, I am sorry. My apologies and condolences, that was just the most faerie way you could have put it. Even with that indigo in your hair what you are is clear."

They had passed through a column of moonlight that indeed had been bright enough for the colour to be perceived. "Is your hair dyed... green?" Lux asked, thinking the topic of dyes might keep the conversation away from Robin, faeries, or her mother's death. "How do you obtain that hue?"

"It's woad, bluish for a while but on hair my colour it turns greenish, we mix it with other dyes to use it for camouflage. A lot of our kin who have bright coloured blondes or reds in their hair put woad through it to blend with the forest."

Lux didn't know what to say in response. She was suddenly overwhelmed, like a wave hit her, one consisting of the idea of a whole life spent having to worry about things like camouflage. It seemed all too apparent in those moments of mentally crashing through space that this was exactly what she had chosen for herself, and the enormity of her own decision was terrifying.

"You will have to dismount now. It's best to lead the horses down on foot from here."

Lux gazed forward into the ever narrowing, dark, vine-choked path ahead and shivered. Robin appeared on her other side then, dismounting from his horse just as she did from hers. He took her hand in the darkness. Before they began the descent into whatever lay before them Blaith called out something to the trees and forest itself, an imprecation of sorts. When he was done Lux whispered to Robin, feeling as though they were suddenly in a cathedral, "What is he saying?"

"He's alerting the sacred wood and the ghosts in the mist that we're coming. This place is special to us, so he's telling the spirits of darkness to swallow up any who betrays our hospitality or discloses our location."

"Oh," Lux replied, teetering for a moment as she hesitated to lay down her foot on what she knew was their holy ground. *There will be no going back. When you've trespassed into their space with your Norman blood and your hips that don't move when you walk, and your baby-soft hands...* For a moment she felt giddy in space, diminished by shame, as though an abyss was opening up under her. And yet she kept tight to Robin's hand. Letting it go had never been an option so perhaps there was already no going back. Only forward moves were possible on this crooked and treacherous path before her.

hen they had arrived at the caves Lux had felt a strong tremor go through her from her feet to her fingertips. It felt a little like fear. It was also dread of further discomfort, if she was to be honest with herself. Sleeping in caves was associated with a primitive state in her mind, and she imagined an intensely cold and hard experience.

Inside Sariah's nest it was anything but. She had taken possession of a chamber and put up a kind of curtain out of found fabrics and parts of old tapestries sewn together. Once inside the space was warm with a sandy floor covered over in rush matting. Immediately, Sariah had turned attentively to her. "You must be so exhausted. Come. I've prepared you some hot water to wash and some of my clothes to change into."

"Thank you," she whispered, afraid she'd cry if she spoke too loud. Lux stripped off readily. Nudity around other women was a commonplace thing in her culture. Other women seldom showed the amount of undisguised interest in her bare flesh that Sariah did though. Too shy suddenly to look at Sariah she busied herself looking around while she washed.

When it came to colour the tinker sense of decor was certainly on the more-is-more side, as every mismatched colour and shade appeared somewhere, either on the wall hangings, the cushions or Sariah's crowded shrines, covered in saint images caked with the wax of many candles, ribbons, coins and beads. Not wanting to look too curious Lux dried herself hurriedly and donned Sariah's clothing. It was a little too baggy around the bust, shoulders, and hips but immediately she loved the style of their women's clothing. They were basically slightly longer tunics with loose, comfortable pants underneath.

When Lux was dressed Sariah indicated some cushions for Lux to sit on. The tinker woman didn't have anything under her tunic, so with her legs crossed under her in a way that afforded a glance up her skirt, Lux very diligently looked at the bone beads in Sariah's hair instead. Despite this hint of the wild about the woman, she was, like all of Robin's family, meticulously clean and had polished, strong white teeth that Lux knew to be treated in charcoal and then polished with clove and salt grit, something Robin could be observed to do every morning.

"Have you lain with him yet?" she asked.

Lux shook her head. Sariah smiled a little wider. There was something almost lascivious about that smile, as if the older more experienced woman had transformed into a cross between a big cat with gleaming eyes and a coiling serpent showing its glistening forked tongue. "Well…" she murmured, her green eyes glimmering so that Lux felt compelled to continue looking into them. "You realise you are at liberty to do so, should you want to?"

*I am at liberty…* This simply didn't make any sense, so much so that she didn't even know how to ask questions that would make it make sense. What did whether he chose to lay with her have to do with her liberty? It wasn't as if she could just decide something like that herself. It was forbidden for a woman to take the man's part. Involuntarily she found herself thinking of a particular sermon she'd heard in church where the priest spoke out against lewd and depraved women who engaged in terrible perversities of this sort.

"I… I… I wouldn't know… I mean… That's up to him… surely?"

Sariah put her hand on Lux's. "What you've already done is so brave. I can't even imagine being raised in the Norman world. You must be so scared out here."

Lux nearly teared up again at this empathy. She felt a strong desire to cry into Sariah's breasts as they seemed like they might be the warmest and softest place to fall she could imagine. "Not half so scared as I am of my father!"

"Did our Hob kill him when he rescued you?"

Lux couldn't help noticing that she used the term rescued rather than abducted. She also liked learning that Hob was his nickname. Hob was a folk word for a male faerie, yet also a variant for Rob in those named Robin or Robert. Most of all she liked it because it made her feel like she knew him better now somehow for being privy to it.

"No. My father sent others to do his dirty work. Those others are now beneath the turf."

Sariah nodded with approval. It was possible to detect a certain pride in her cousin's abilities. "Such it is for many bullies who meet a man of the Twll Du blood thread."

"Right now what I'm most afraid of is that I've brought danger to your family's door."

She shook her head decisively. "Do away with that. You were at risk of your life, and no one can be expected to do anything in such a moment but run. The responsibility for you being here is not your own. If anyone has brought trouble to our door it is Hob, and trust me, that wouldn't exactly be an isolated incident." She grinned. Clearly, she found this charming despite the dire possibilities. "He solves twice as many troubles as he causes though."

"I'm actually so afraid I'm not brave enough to face the consequences for what I've done."

"Do you know how rare it is for girls of your kind to do what you just did at all?"

She shook her head. Other than the story from Clarice about the twenty-four hour expiration date on an abducted girl's value Lux had certainly heard no direct stories of escape. From the very first days of the conquest the Normans had demanded all the daughters of the Saxon lords be rounded up and brought to Westminster to be handed out to their men as wives, and as far as she knew no one had escaped since.

"I've never even heard of it happening before. Not a girl of your rank. The hate and fear they teach them to feel towards people like us normally wins the day. That is how I know you are uncommonly brave and will overcome.

Because your love is stronger than their hate."

As soon as they entered the humble abode Clarice was overcome by a smell that was partially that of newly butchered meat and in part the odour of early decay. She assumed that Nanette had another of her geese in the basin, bleeding it, but when she followed the master into the room she saw the body of a woman. She gasped and covered her mouth with her hand when she saw that the woman had been cut open from groin to sternum.

Clarice stopped near the door and crossed herself. She stared at Nanette and the younger girl who were sitting on either side of the body as if in the middle of some form of instruction. Nanette looked up, not even bothering to feign surprise that they had been caught with blood up to their elbows. It had the feeling of a staged interruption.

"Greetings, my lord" she said, getting to her feet. "I'd offer you my hand to kiss but as you can see…"

"Don't be silly, my lady," De Rue said, taking her unoffered hand whether she willed it or no and forcibly kissing it. "I don't mind a bit of blood."

Clarice could see that Nanette understood the menace that lurked behind this act of force. Coolly she retracted her hand and made eye contact with Clarice. "Don't be off-put by this," Nanette said, indicating the cadaver, which was half naked and bleeding into two separate basins. "She was one of my patients. The business of fetching out an infant as formed as that one is always dangerous," she said, indicating a bowl with a greyish coloured dead baby. "We warn them of the risks, but they are desperate and haven't options."

"You procure abortions?" De Rue asked.

Lady De Biron raised her dark, arched eyebrows. "Oh, don't be sanctimonious, my lord! How many men have you ended with your broad sword? With your mace and your battle-axe? What is it to a man like you if I end them a little earlier than you do?"

To Clarice's surprise De Rue began to laugh. "I like your way of thinking. Who is this charming girl here, your younger sister? Is she wed or unwed?"

Clarice cringed inwardly for her, being talked about as though she were not in the room. Perhaps the daughter of a warlord like De Biron and a woman such as Nanette had no such squeamishness? She was, after all, slowly and carefully soaking her cap in the blood of the dead woman while her mother spoke with the master.

"Augusta is my daughter. And I suspect you of being gallant in suggesting she is my sister. The maid hasn't yet bled and is thus unwed. We have received a few good offers. Have you got a better one for me?"

De Rue scoffed as if she was joking. "An offer for you? I would speak to your husband about it certainly. I find myself inconvenienced of a wife. Let me look at you, girl," he said. Augusta dutifully turned her head to him and allowed him to manipulate her chin to make her look up at him. She kept her dark, almost black, brown eyes downcast.

"I am a widow," Nanette said coldly. "The girl is mine. I will dispose of her as I see fit."

"Is that so?" De Rue murmured thoughtfully, still examining the unripe maid like she was a young filly he was thinking of buying. "I think you'll find by law that your eldest son now wields that power." He said it almost casually, as if he wasn't even trying to rub salt into an open wound.

"I am his mother," she said through clenched teeth. "A few seasons ago the green boy was still playing with wooden swords."

De Rue smiled at her. Taunting. "All the same. You must obey him now, galling as I'm sure it is."

"He will do as I counsel." She said, her voice about as tight as it could get without snapping.

"Well, that is convenient for me I suppose. I'll have your daughter as soon as she blossoms," he said, finally letting poor Augusta's chin go. "I don't require a splendid dowry. I've tried a faerie woman, now I'd like to try a girl of a famous sorcerer house. I take no interest unless there is some challenge in it."

"I will consider your offer."

"Well consider quickly. I don't like to wait for things. Before I put our business before you, explain to me what you are doing to this corpse?"

"Does it bother you?" Nanette asked, some mysterious, half hidden emotion lurking under the surface.

"Hardly. I've done worse to the odd alive one. This just evokes my curiosity," De Rue said, coming over to the body and lifting the skin flaps back so he could peer inside. "It reminds me of the killing of a tramp woman some years ago."

"I don't tend to keep track of the murders of vagabonds and I must own myself surprised to hear a man of your caliber recalling a thing of such inconsequence."

De Rue smiled to himself with a hint of approval. "I feel you are dodging my question."

"Hardly," Nanette replied. "We are sorceresses. This you know, it is why you came here…"

"We use the body parts for our work," Augusta said. "The eyeballs for instance," she said, her voice very sweet and well pronounced. "Strengthen our inner eye that allows us to see into other people's secrets." With this she delicately placed one of the dead woman's eyeballs in her mouth and with one pointed swallow took it down whilst looking at De Rue. There was an air of challenge in her gesture and in her composure.

"Interesting," he said, not ruffled, not even blinking at it. "And what does all the blood do? Are you bathing in it to keep your youth Nanette?"

Nanette laughed softly, it was a dark sexy sound but it made Clarice uncomfortable. She wondered if any of them would notice if she slipped quietly away and just ran? There was a queasy feeling coming up in her that went beyond the smell of blood. It felt all of a sudden like she had chosen a path she couldn't un-choose.

"Oh, you do flatter, Lord," she said, no warmth making its way into her voice at all despite the words sounding flirtatious. "No, blood is mainly good for creating a flash of raw magical power. Such as the power to do the thing you come here asking of me, for instance. That's what you want isn't it? You want me to deliver you means to the heads of Robin Goodfellow and your recalcitrant daughter? On a platter, as if I were your Salome?"

"That is indeed what I came for. Though I have asked for my daughter to be taken alive. I don't mind if the bounty hunters want to have their fun with her, as she's no doubt been ruined already by those outlaws."

"Doubtlessly," Nanette agreed. "Those tinker boys are a menace. Far too popular with the ladies it seems."

"Not after I cut his cock off," De Rue said. "I do not precisely understand how they have managed to elude us for this long. How can an inferior people with less weapons and provisions disappear from under the noses of this country's best?"

"I couldn't imagine, Lord," Nanette said, her tone very neutral.

"So, what do you need to do this work? You mentioned blood?"

"This blood will do," Augusta commented. "Though fresh is always best."

"Well we have fresh available. Why settle for this old congealing mess?" De Rue asked. As soon as he turned around Clarice felt her legs turn to water. She knew suddenly that she wasn't ever going to leave that room. Her mind commanded her body to run but she didn't, she froze.

"Clarice, come here," he demanded.

When she didn't move the master strode over to her and grabbed her by the hair. It was so casual like that, his brutality. Over the years Clarice had stood by and watched terrible things be done to Agnes and her girls by this man and for the reasons of this same paralysis she had never been able to even try to help them. Now there was no one to help her. Within seconds the sharp, cold edge of a blade was pressed to her throat and Clarice stopped breathing, afraid to so much as move her head.

"Would you like to do it, my lady?" he asked, the challenging ringing clear in his voice as he offered the knife to Nanette.

# 8

The acoustic effect of the underground drums undulated and made the air thick as honey inside Lux's ears. The harp players layered each other's music in improvisations around and inside the percussion. Lost as she was in a tapestry of musical but incomprehensible Welsh speaking, everything became sensory. Instead of thoughts she was left with sensations. For a time, she no longer even had an internal voice in her head. It was a relief, to step outside of words, it was like how the forest had smelt during her escape. Wordless-space was a forest, or the forest was a wordless space.

The drums caused little trails of ancient dust to be dislodged from the roof and enter her nostrils. She fancied she could feel the past getting up inside her. It mingled with an intoxicating incense smoke burning on coals. The music took her back to the fairs of her childhood where she'd first heard them play and sing. Such was their musicality that it was easy to understand why some folk said they were faerie people. Like faeries they were dangerous so she could not play with their pretty golden-haired boy. But their music had been her first hint at life outside the walls.

Robin had been a few years older than her at that time, but that hadn't seemed as large a difference as it did now. *Tinkers grow up fast...* Now, as she looked at him, what she had previously estimated as a difference of three or four years between them when they were children she now guessed as at least five or six. His harp playing was masterful- she noticed this quite fixedly to avoid seeing he'd taken his shirt off- and this alone seemed the mark of greater maturity. Lux certainly as yet possessed no signs of this kind of discipline.

Though in some circles it was considered a bad one, he also had a reputation all over the country.

He was playing almost competitively against Eilish's harp, which was an achievement because she was a magnificent musician. Lux was able to watch him for awhile she found herself fascinated by the very thing that had originally seemed so foreign. It was seeing him like this, shirtless with his tattoos and scars, both ritualistic looking ones and injury ones, and the clear definitions of his musculature in contrast with the delicate skill of his fingertips, that really revealed him to her.

In the presence of this so-called underling, this ditch-born traveller, part of an uncivilised culture, she stood humbled. It was clear to her quite suddenly why she remained unravished. How could her unfinished girlhood be of interest to someone who wore the scars as well as the accomplishments of full manhood in his own culture?

"I can't keep up with you, Eilish," Robin said in English, as he laughed and pushing his harp aside.

"It's probably the swelling around your knuckles where you are developing fighter's hands. I have a good poultice you could-"

Robin leaned over and kissed her on the forehead. "Oh, I do love you, cousin," he declared. "If I ever need a little wee poultice for my handsies, it will be you I come to!"

She made sport of trying to slap him and he ducked. Lux took the opportunity of him leaning forward to inspect the tattoo on the back of his left shoulder. It was a skilful depiction of St. Michael slaying a monstrous dragon. The tattoo felt like a ghost. An ancestral encounter with an anachronism from her own Northman forebears, back when they were still heathen, and wore tattoos and braids.

Lux felt a bit woozy looking at it. There was a sensuality encoded into it somehow, in the posture of the archangel and the almost yielding supine serpent. Robin's movements as he pushed the harp aside to stand caused the muscles to move under the tattoo, bringing the scene to life. As Lux watched she saw the golden-browed hero. Here he was, the saviour everyone is looking for, but what if he's just another bully? The white charger beneath him reared in erotic frenzy trampling in the serpent's blood, the serpent reared back also and threatened to strike.

Together they circle, neither stronger. The dragon bares its teeth almost seductively, threatening and inviting all at once, before the angel of light's shaft splits into her skin, blood flowing from the open wound as she writhes around the solid oak spear and sinks her teeth in turn into the leg of the brave charger. A circle rather than a dominion seethed between them.

"Lux?" Robin's voice broke her out of the vision.

"I'm sorry," she murmured. "I just-"

"You're Seeing?" Robin finished for her. "You had the horizon-gaze. I think tonight might all be a bit much for you. I might take you to the-"

Someone bumped her right into his body. It was just a second of breathless and awkward contact, but it rushed through her body like fire, bringing her back into herself and the moment. The smell of his bare skin up so close sent an immediate rush of heat all over her. His hand slid gently, experimentally around the side of her waist, drawing her closer to him. His hands never applied enough pressure that she couldn't have easily indicated resistance, yet they guided her to where he wanted her all the same. And where he wanted her was closer against his body. Her breath came as fast as the drums, filled with the smoke in the air, mingled with the heat of Robin's body against hers.

"Let's get you somewhere quieter," she heard him say near her ear and then he was leading her away, out into the cooler corridor. "Come," he said, gently taking her arm. "The temple room should be quiet with everybody gathering in the cathedral chamber for sabbat. Would you join me there?"

Lux nodded, knowing as she did she had said yes to something of more significance than just going into a temple. He led her into a dimly lit circular cave with a huge icon of the Madonna with her face painted black, a wooden one that looked like it might have come from a church. The sparseness of the space, and its sandy floor made her feel like they were in one of the original places of Christian worship in the Holy Land. Such a place as Mary Magdalene might have retreated to for contemplation.

"Are you alright?" he asked.

She nodded. "Your tattoo started coming to life. It made me feel... strange."

He smiled, and for a moment she saw a hot-cold lupine glimmer in his eyes. She took a half step back from him. This is what it was, why he seemed so much older than her when he really wasn't, he carried with him something ancient, something tribal, something animal. Lux's head didn't understand it at all, she had been trained not to, but her ancestor-women understood. Her ancestor-women had squirted their wetness for him. They recognised that bit of wolf in him.

In her intoxicated state she wondered if she too had an animal inside her? When people looked at her sometimes when she didn't know anyone was around did they see in her eyes the moon-crazed wild eyes of the hare, just as she saw Robin's lupine shadow?

"What kind of strange?" Robin asked, his eyebrows dancing up slightly.

"Just... strange... I don't know."

"What did they do when they came to life? St Michael and the dragon?"

"Well..." she murmured, her eyes doing a round of the Black Madonna draped in dried flowers and chains made of wheat. "St. Michael moved with lots of vigour. And the dragon almost seemed to dare the angel by offering her throat and underbelly. When St Michael thrust in the spear it was..."

"*Suggestif?*" he supplied.

"Ah... almost, yes." There had been nothing almost about it.

"Did it feel threatening?"

"Sometimes it seemed yes, but then it didn't," Lux murmured, gaining confidence in what she saw as she went along she kept going. "For a moment I thought of two great houses going to battle and then it felt like they were gearing up to mate and one would swallow the other." Suddenly in speaking her vision she began to feel dizzy.

90

"Come. Sit down. The plant magic in the smoke is strong."

"Is that what that smoke is?" she murmured, as he sat her down on a prayer cushion.

"It relaxes most people, but for people like us…" Robin made a gesture with his hand that indicated something a little one way, a little the other way.

"Does it do that to you too?" Lux asked. "Make you see things?"

He laughed. "Oh, gods yes, I am out of my head as we speak! I'm seeing things everywhere. I'm just used to it so I can act almost normal while it's happening. When you first came into the room and I was still playing the harp all I could see out of the corner of my eye was light. And then when I looked up you burst open like a chrysalis and spilled wet light everywhere."

"Wet light?" Lux queried. She blushed at the mention of wetness.

"Don't you find wet light a perfectly natural state of being? I know I do. Does not wet light run from you now?"

Lux looked down at her own skirts in a paranoid fear that her excitement fluids were suddenly somehow incandescent. "I don't think I'm glowing, no."

"Ah, then you are looking with the wrong eyes. I think you have been taught to mistrust your faerie eye, for only one of your two eyes is human. Look again with your faerie-eye. I think you will find both our bodies are making wet light."

Just the way he was speaking alone was causing the growing boldness of her arousal to war with her embarrassment. "I want to see with my other eye, Robin. Will you show me how to see as you see?"

Robin smiled, and there was the wolf-gleam again.

Without warning he lifted her and sat her before the Black Madonna. Lux yelped quietly, partially because he lifted her so easily and unexpectedly, and partly because he had sat her on what she took to be an altar.

"Do you want to take this further?" He picked up a clay flagon and filled a cup. As she reached out her upturned hands to take the cup and drank, he continued to look very intently at her. She had never had her face, her responses and her reactions studied like this before. He was reading her with all his senses, as if what she felt and wanted was important somehow. The feeling of this exotic interest in her inner life rippled through her like the wind in her hair on the back of his horse. She drained the cup.

Sitting on an altar would usually be an act of sacrilege, but she could only assume it was permissible among his people and their customs. There wasn't any time to dwell on it because as she watched the Madonna's face began to morph and move in and out of focus the way Robin's tattoo had. Lux felt herself pulled into some special current unknown to the herd of humanity. It felt like she was being claimed by warm honey, or maybe dark blood. There was a primeval forest sprung up inside her. Or perhaps it had always been there.

"I want to do something for you," he said kneeling down. It occurred to Lux for a dizzy second that he was facing the wrong way in turning his back to the Holy Mother. "Stop me if you don't like it." He parted her knees. Lux had expected to have her knees parted sooner or later. In the world she'd grown up in she would always be expected to pay her way in this manner eventually. But this was something else. Robin's head disappeared into her skirt and within seconds she felt him slide his tongue straight into her. Lux gasped. For a moment or two she was overwhelmed by both the suddenness of the intimacy and the taboo nature of what he was doing.

Lux's foremothers had been working away inside her too efficiently for her to be able to hang onto that inhibition for very long. With the herbal smoke and the sabbat wine, it didn't take very long before he teased away from Lux her shame, her shyness, her self-consciousness, and even her fear someone would see. What was he even doing? Even that thought melted in response to the skill of his tongue.

He slipped her shoes off and took her feet in his hands, arch of her foot to the palm of his hand and pushed her legs back wide and apart while he licked her, hard and deep inside her, and then up to the spot that undid her. Had someone asked her beforehand how she would want it to start she would have said with kissing on the mouth and maybe her breasts being touched, but she had not known about this.

Robin made a sound of deep enjoyment in the back of his throat, indicating such a plain and obvious pleasure in the act that it pushed Lux over the edge. Every punishment, every shaming, every fear of exposure converted itself somehow into a rebellious reason to feel excited, in a cresting crescendo of rising triumph over the things that had been done to her. Even the prospect of someone walking in and seeing her like this, with her social mask torn down… The idea helped to push her into the throes of orgasm. The pleasure trod down the shame like the serpent Mary bruised beneath her heel.

A black substance from behind the Holy Mother reached out and it was into this blackness of outer or inner space Lux subsided. Gradually after she was able to open her eyes, and her daily self began to return, there was a creeping shyness of exposure. As though sensing it Robin stood up and unbuckled his belt and unbuttoned his trousers. Lux left her legs obediently open as she assumed he would now claim her. Instead, he exposed some of his manhood but didn't move any closer to her. "Look," he commanded her. She did as she was told and gazed down at the shimmer of fluid on the tip of his cock. In her altered state it seemed to glow. "Liquid light," he confirmed, before using his finger to capture the fluid. Holding her behind the neck with his other hand to force her to look into his face he very carefully anointed her clitoris with it, and then down into her vagina. Without warning he pushed his finger deep inside her. Her mouth fell open, with a mixture of surrender and surprise, but he withdrew almost immediately. "So that she can get to know me," he explained, before tucking himself away.

Blaith ran his fingertips over the stone skin of the cave's interior. It was only through the pulsing of the drums that the black silence-drone behind them would open up like this, until the walls were spilling all their memories. His connection with this particular Creswell Crags cave was more ancient than his body or those even of his forefather's bodies stretching back into perpetuity. Those same forefathers had been *nadredd,* serpent-wise men, but even they were not the true guardians of the place.

The spirits that dwelled here were older than the ancestors of his body, they were the ghosts of the very oldest people. He had received something of them, long ago, something that was not necessarily allied with mankind. When roused it stirred, hungered, and prowled, this feathered thing. It opened a grave pit in his chest and let the blackness pour in, and light would seem to pour out of him as in stigmatic wounds.

This was what allowed Blaith to open and unseal something primal under his people during sabbat. He need only knock on the old stone floor, worn away by the feet of giant hyenas and two-legged ones who were not yet as humans are. Blaith would knock with his blackthorn walking stick, darkened with elder berries, and the depths would answer him, yielding up secrets of hidden knowledge and power.

Mostly though people weren't really interested in those things. They all paid homage to the idea of taking the forbidden fruit on the Tree of Knowledge and growing their power, yet really what most of them came to him for was ecstasy and freedom. It was his skills in these areas that created the intense loyalty of his band. Rumours abounded that he had once killed a man with magic at a single touch. The truth was more complicated, but he was never one to put pay to a useful tale because healthy fear was always a little spice that didn't do any harm with humans.

One of the youngest wardens, Meredith, appeared beside him. "Do you want me to do a quick sweep outside, make sure everything is okay?" Meredith and his two brothers were orphans and Merrie was the youngest of the cohort with which Blaith had grown up. Though he was now a young man Meredith had been orphaned at a young enough age where Blaith had come to feel an immense protectiveness of him over the years. Not only was the young man charming he was also possibly even wilder than Robin.

"Hello, Merry," he replied, sitting down next to him. "Let's let someone else take this scouting mission."

"Surely it will be my turn soon?"

Meredith hadn't meant the comment to sound macabre yet for a moment he could see a death's head in Meredith's skin. Sometimes the Seeing wracked him. He couldn't look at Meredith and face the image of his bones shining through his skin like a light from behind was making his skin transparent.

"To take on missions alone?" Blaith managed to reply, glossing over the ripples of anxiety he was feeling.

"Aye," Meredith said.

"Very likely, Merrie."

Meredith smiled. He always softened when Blaith used his childhood endearment, which had not so long ago been his nickname from everyone.

"I'm entirely ready you know. I feel like you just don't trust…" Meredith went still quite abruptly.

"What's wrong?" Blaith snapped, almost shaking Meredith in his sudden contagious anxiety.

"I feel the wind blowing over the feet of the graves," Meredith whispered. From the look on his face, it was as if they'd both seen two halves of the same vision.

Blaith sniffed the air. Something uninvited walked there, something that sought to know their weaknesses.

"You have no invitation," he whispered. Blaith sent the words out as a challenge. His eyes rolled back, sniffing at the air, Blaith extended his awareness like a dark web filling the cave system until he caught the unfamiliar presence as in a web. It slipped away from him quickly, but not before he had some sense of it, just as it no doubt went away with some knowledge about them.

"A Norman," he murmured. "A woman."

"Well, there can only be so many of those surely," Meredith replied.

"Indeed."

"Two things I have for you," Nanette said, a mysterious smile spreading over her face. "I know the ones who have captured your daughter, they are the witches who ride with the rogue Robin Goodfellow your daughter called out to. I recognise among them one I have ties to, which will give us their whereabouts."

"Wouldn't wish to be any of them for the world now that Lord de Rue knows what they've done," Augusta threw in, to a tacit look of approval from her mother. Her mother had taught her the importance of flattering a man's pride.

"As to who took your wife's body… Well, that is stranger. I can only say that there is no body, as such. A kind of magic is afoot there belonging to the Good Neighbours."

Was this just a ruse of her mother's? Or was Nanette telling the truth? Surely even faerie women's bodies didn't disappear? Tales about true revenants were popular of late since upheaval had come to the land, but Augusta had always taken them more as the common folk's way of expressing the intensity of their fear of ghosts.

"What? You mean to suggest she is getting around with a pulse again?"

"No. But I'd stake my professional reputation on the fact there's no dead body," Nanette said firmly.

"You'll be staking more than that on it, I assure you," De Rue replied with a quiet, stomach-churning menace just under the surface.

"Tell me more about what you saw. Where was it?"

"They are inside a substantial cave network, and they can't be more than two days ride outside of Stokesley, given that they have my bastard brother with them."

"I will have my men overturn every cave within three days ride of Stokesley, and burn out any settlements near the caves, just to be sure. If I find people around a cave and they aren't someone's peasants I will put them to the sword, be they man, woman, or child. But if one of them isn't Lux…"

# 9

**R**obin moved toward Blaith at the same pace his brother moved toward him with matching urgency, neither of them needing to give a signal to meet. This happened so often between them it was almost unremarkable. When they met Blaith pulled Robin into the Chamber of the He-Goat that was faintly illumined from a lamp on the shrine. His hands immediately found Blaith's shoulders where he administered supportive pressure.

It hadn't occurred to Robin that their bond was more profound than most siblings when he was a child. It was only when others mentioned it later that he'd had cause to become conscious of it. Perhaps it had something to do with their mother's death in childbirth, which Blaith had witnessed? As if some ethereal bond had struck in that moment of birth and death biting each other that kept their nervous systems intertwined? Nowadays Robin knew it was a bond of spirit as much as flesh, for he had known this man before in other times and other skins.

"What happened?"

"There was a foreign sorcerer's shadow upon us tonight, brother," he announced. "It fell across Meredith's face and made it appear a skull. She's good, and I suspect she's working for De Rue. I feel like she saw enough, maybe too much, before I threw her off. I feel like she saw Meredith."

"She?" Robin queried.

Blaith nodded his head. "A Norman woman."

"A De Biron woman," Jack added, walking in and joining them.

"You are just who I was planning to look for next," Robin said. "I figured with your connections if there was a Norman witch family of note you'd know about it."

"Aye. I felt an unwholesome draft of cold myself. And if Blaith says she's good then I warrant I know which De Biron it is."

"Who is she?" Blaith asked. There was an inky fire in his eyes full of deep resentment to this trespass, and that it was a Settler of all people…

Jack sighed. "Well, it isn't good news. It's probably Nanette De Biron. She is very well known as a magical assassin. People say back home that if she opens her evil eye upon you then you may as well stick your head between your legs and kiss your arse goodbye."

"They say some pretty unflattering things about me also," Blaith muttered. "I have killed many a man with magic, many are they who have in turn tried to kill me. What I am more concerned about is how she goes at divining locations and lost objects? Because that's what we really need to worry about right now."

Robin closely observed Jack's facial expression, eyes, posture, and he had his answer from the faint wince around his mouth and frown before the words came. Jack cleared his throat.

"Let me put it this way, if it were up to me I would start packing up the women and children right now and be out of here before morning."

Sariah could smell it on her. It wasn't just sex after all, it was Robin, sex, and magic, which were up there in her list of favourite perfumes. It was only really the officers who knew how to speak English, and she knew she was probably the better choice than Eilish. Love her as she did her cousin was hardly adept at a light social touch. Tasked with keeping Lux out of the way while strategy was discussed didn't mean Sariah couldn't use the time to pursue those intriguing scents.

Wafting past and sniffing Lux Sariah made a sound of appreciation. "You have him all over you."

The girl blushed, all the way up to the tips of her cute little ears. Sariah loved blushing… It all just added to the eroticism. "Is it that obvious?" she whispered.

"Oh, only to my slutty nose!" Sariah laughed. "You'd have to be looking for it."

"And you were looking for it?"

"Of course! What else would I be looking for? It's got everything… Shy upper class girl meets wild tinker fucking in a cave…"

"Oh, we didn't…"

"Didn't fuck?"

She was even more flustered now. Sariah both wanted to soothe the poor little thing, and was taking a gently sadistic pleasure in watching her writhe. It was the polecat her foremothers had bred into her fetch that did it.

"No. I mean… not in the traditional sense."

Sariah's eyebrows jumped up. "Well! Now you have me really curious. Nobody should be fucking in the traditional way anyway. Let me guess, did he use his tongue on you?"

Lux's reaction to the question, with eyes darting down and to the side quickly told Sariah the answer was yes.

"Ah, well that does explain why you're so pink. I bet that didn't half take you by surprise!" Her eyes narrowed in concentration. "He's done more than worship your cunny though. He's tuned you, inserted you into the blood thread."

Lux didn't say anything, but Sariah could see her words sinking down into the clear waters of her mind and finding a place there. It was easy for them to do so because they made perfect sense to her. Lux knew the warm honey feeling of belonging that had overcome her during this act with Robin. That was really the only way to teach as far as Sariah was concerned.

Their conversation was interrupted by the sounds of hasty male boots in the corridor. It was Robin and he was armed. As soon as Sariah took note of this fact she began to put her shoes on. She had learned cues like that growing up with a warrior father as a single parent.

"We need to get ready to go," he said, in the tone of his you always knew to take seriously. "As quickly as you can get packed." With that he was gone, striding off again to move, rally and prepare. Lux gazed after him like the source of everything that still made sense in her life was walking away with no explanation. She would learn over time that emergency-Robin wasn't like other versions of Hob. "What do you think's happened? Do you think we're under attack?"

Sariah had already started to pack and she didn't slow down while she answered Lux's questions. The poor girl was at sea, but she knew she would do her no kindnesses with coddling. "You don't ask those things when Robin says get ready to go. When he says that, you just get ready to go, and you do it as fast as you can."

The shoes for stealth were ingenious. They were very well tailored to protect the foot, padded with rabbit skin to create an almost silent step. At the end your foot was wrapped around in old, soft rags to protect the fur. It seemed to make a lot of sense to Lux that she was making an escape on rabbit feet. Because her heart felt like that of a little rabbit, going way faster than a human heart and seeming to beat in her throat not her chest.

The women and those too young to fight fell into formation with almost military discipline. Sariah went at the front with Blaith. Seemingly it was their collective responsibility to get the civilian population to safety. It was only now that Lux was beginning to discern the sense that certain people held leadership roles in different areas. Blaith's role seemed to make him indispensable, though she knew from a lifetime of growing up around soldiers that Blaith could fight and probably very well. Despite this something singled him out from the other men to be sent on this mission. At the back of the column was a strapping, armed woman she learned was Sorcha, who brushed away their trail as they went.

Eilish, second from the front, had Lux's hand and was guiding her unerringly though forestland too dark for proper visibility. Before they left Sariah had briefly explained to her that they knew this trail very well and could therefore walk it in the dark. Never had Lux felt such a challenge to her bodily awareness. Not even when her skin had been sloughing off from her inside thighs when fleeing bareback from her father's men. Painful as that had been the situation had called on her to do literally nothing except hold on. With Lux's upbringing hanging on passively through pain was not unknown to her and she was braver than most. But never had she been asked to participate in saving herself, to use her own body's intelligence to escape.

The training she'd received in place of an upbringing was insidious. Perhaps the most damaging part of it had not so much been being constantly under threat from men, it had been being under the protection of men. They hurt you themselves but what they did was made out to be nothing by comparison to what the men from the outside would do to you. All unless you had the protection of such-a-one man with a scary reputation for smashing his enemies heads open with one strike of the mace. The very horror the tyrant represented in the home was turned outward upon a hostile-seeming world, where the worse kind of man your protector was the safer you felt from the other men outside.

Now Lux was separated from Robin her vulnerability became excruciating. Terrible things would be done to her if she was caught. She might not even be offered the mercy of death. It hit Lux like a horse barreling into her that she couldn't endure it now, if she ever could have, to be taken by the man of her father's choosing and forced to bear infants. The very thought of that invasive, shackling pregnancy that would be forced upon her made her feel physically ill. Perhaps this awareness she was developing, where it felt like her feet had eyes and she was starting to exist in all of her body at once, made it worse.

She cast around to place her faith somewhere and it alighted on Blaith as the only adult male present. For a moment it wanted to set down on Sariah, yet her past experience made the allocation wobble and not feel safe. After all she had no experience whatsoever in women leading, let alone trusting that such an unprecedented thing could happen and be solid. It was going to take some time to sit with that feeling, but it wasn't going to happen while they moved at a smart pace in mute almost silent formation through the night wood.

Desperately she wanted to ask Eilish things, such as whether they were close to their destination, or whether it was likely they'd got away from the unspoken horror that was bearing down upon them. But the instructions had been clear and sharp. No talking for any reason. Do not break the rhythm of movement. Silence had become death to her mother and sister. Yet somehow in this back-to-front, upside-down world she'd entered, speaking was now death.

Robin headed down to the river to pray. The place he chose was rocky and strong in the sound of running water. The white noise rushing by him, making him feel like he was plowing through space on someone else's fresh stallion. A deep cleanliness of motion seemed to anoint him. It was the way the Queen of Heaven taught them to wash off the calcifying debris of Settler consciousness. Whilst they heard the slurs and the un-Christ-like judgments they received from others they never stayed still long enough for them to get stuck in their fur or hearts. As travellers, to move on was to live on.

The river did its work tonight as always. Robin thought of how these caves had been occupied back into deep time, and how ancient hunters must have come here to drink. It reminded him he was part of a long thread of people living by their wits under stars and around campfires, hunting and scavenging their way along the old crooked paths, the ones that were carved out with the land, rather than a destination in mind. Nobody knew the ground, the water and the trees like travelling folk and so it wasn't going to be easy to hunt them here of all places.

What he needed to happen tonight was not of the world of men and metal. De Rue had a lot of resources and power on his side, whereas most of Robin's weapons were those nature gave him, and ones he got himself through paying attention. One of the most important was from somewhere a little to the side of nature, it had to do with his faerie birth. This would be above everything a magical battle, even before it was a physical one. Whilst in the world of men he was an outlaw in the world of Faerie, he was a prince.

Before he knew Eilion was coming he would always hear the bells. It was eeriest when you saw them and heard them at the same time, because they always rang faster than they moved. The sound stirred something deep in the part of him that was of his father, the ancestral memory of the Other Herd, and ghostly recollections of earlier lives. Now he knew the ringing of bells was the noise reality makes when another awareness pierces it.

There was a flash of illumination among the leaf litter. The starlight spangled the frost on the grass and turned the spider webs to crystal patterns that captured his gaze. Somewhere during this hypnotic state, he was no longer alone. The faerie man who was with him was not his father, the relationship between them did not answer to human terms exactly. Robin gazed into the slightly-too-large blue eyes as the long, thin fingers that reached for his. His cheekbones were high, and pronounced, his eyes wide and long, blinking very infrequently. It was true that he was beautiful in a way that was entirely alienating.

To any full-human seeing Eilion for the first time, his stare might be read as cold, his expressions lacking in emotional texture, difficult to read and therefore unnerving. But Robin was born able to discern a greater range of micro expressions than most people, a trait from his father's side. It was something that aided him whether fighting someone or charming them. He always knew what people were just about to do or feel right before they did.

"Danger comes for you again," Eilion whispered. "I think she likes you. She is like a she-hyena stalking your trail."

"Straight to business then?"

"Your survival is one of my highest priorities."

"Sometimes I find it over-rated," Robin muttered.

"Of course you do," Eilion said. "It is from the death love leads us to, your love of it. I'm not surprised you can smell the nectar but, it is not time for that perfect moment yet. So, for the sake of your myth and that which is artistic, I suggest you listen."

"Well we do know the respect I have for the artistic…"

"Blaith and Jack are right. De Rue has brought in Lady De Biron, which means the collective intellect and magical clout of your enemies has risen considerably."

"Is there a way we could stop her?"

"Not at this point, he has something over her, something I can't see clearly into. I've looked at it every way and Nanette leads to catastrophe, unless we eliminate her and all her seed."

Robin raised his eyebrows. "Kill them all, burn it all to the ground, leave none standing? Like a Harrowing of the North upon the De Birons?"

"Yes, indeed, it appears you understand."

"Even the children?"

"There aren't any. The youngest are fresh women and men."

Robin knew his faerie kin were fate-weavers, that their existence lay somehow closer to the warp and woof of things than that of humans. "Something of magnitude changed in the threads, something that shouldn't have been able to happen. I see your future witch-house tightly wrapped around the fate of the House of De Biron now. But their House is curse-laden. It is a curse they haven't fully put on themselves yet. It's Nanette who conceives it, but it will not be she who births it, for it must be wetted with blood of your blood. Yet the complication is: in the far future, one of them, many, many human moons from now, will come for you when you've forgotten who you are and remind you. You'll meet him at the ford of a river when Avalon is again an island. Blood will be again be shared between the houses."

"Surely killing them all and leaving none left as you suggest would get in the way of this other prediction?"

"If it were up to me the scorched earth policy would be enacted. But it is not up to me and there are no fate threads in existence where you help kill a girl of twelve. I had to try this human vice of futility, for you are a miracle in this world of shabby, lesser men, Robin Goodfellow. I would commit a considerable number of murders to keep you alive. And, when your moment is right, to see you to your best death in the artistry."

Blaith sat with his eyes closed feeling them all. The witches, rebels, and whores that made up his crew were static against the night. He was crouched like a black scavenger bird, an infernal Jesus surrounded by his apostles. Some were blood aunties and female cousins, a few were old people, over half of them were gifted rescues and runaways like Lux. The blood thread of their heretical church was formed by adoption as often as it was shared nativity. All of them, except Lux, had faced nights like this many times and they knew how to keep silent.

The light from the fire was concealed by the placement of the three caravans with canvases stretched between them. Communication was only in signs and when otherwise unavoidable close whispers once inside the caravans. For those who knew the detailed sign language of their people the sign of silence indicated a shift to hand speech. Silent as death in the night one of their wardens patrolled their boundaries on a shift basis. But they were not the only protection.

It was important not to become distracted by the loud emotional currents of those who were afraid, because Blaith was *listening*. It was the hearing version of Seeing. He wasn't just listening with his ears but with his feet, with all of the hairs on his body and those deep senses below the pit of the pore, that belong more to the Underworld than they do to living men. In this state Blaith could never be snuck up on by anyone. It would have taken the country's greatest tracker to know they were there. Nobody ever expected a number of humans gathered together to be there in silence and darkness.

The country's greatest tracker was in their company now. The Black Warlock of Stokesley had quite a reputation. In many ways his name as a tracker preceded that of his name as a magic worker, though it was understood by

105

those in the know that the two trades were no strangers. Blaith never felt good about not staying to fight when the ranks closed around the vulnerable, the young and the precious. Some of the people most precious to him personally were out there, and it was in his blood to fight at their side, he had the same training as the other boys after all.

Their reputation for abductions and rescues was ideological as well as practical for Blaith. He refused to accept that anyone could be stolen *with* their own consent. It was only a crime if one admitted Lux was not a person and hadn't the space to make decisions about her own movements. With these thoughts in mind Blaith squeezed Sariah and Eilish's hands that he held in his.

He indicated to them with his thumbs on their palms alone his intention to leave and return soon. Both women tapped back to say they had understood him. He got up so quietly the only sound was the darkness rearranging itself where he had once been. Gently he brushed Lux's shoulder with his fingertips. She jumped as if struck by a punch, her face as white as a dead woman's. He beckoned to her to follow him into the caravan. Modelling the slowness he wanted her to move with for the sake of stealth he took her to the door and showed her inside.

A lantern was kept burning inside to avoid having to move flame around and attract attention but no one had yet turned in. As soon as Blaith shut the door behind them Lux turned around and started talking like pressure had been building up inside of her. "Have you heard-" Immediately Blaith gave her the hush gesture and she fell silent. He led her to the lowest rung bed and sat her down.

"Only in the barest whisper," he said in her ear.

"Even in here? Surely no one would hear," she whispered back.

"If I let thirteen people all talk inside them without whisper? How much noise?"

Lux appeared to concede the point. "Are you their leader? Is that why you are here with the women?"

"It is hard to say in your words just what I am. In one way I am what you call leader, in another Sariah is leader, in one way Robin is, in another the elder of most seniority…" He shrugged. "It is different to your world." For now this would have to do. Blaith had already exposed a vulnerable place in him by allowing her to hear him as a second language speaker who was not masterful in that tongue.

"You and Sariah are considered too precious to lose though, Robin is not?"

"Robin is leader of the Warden Company who are a war band. Do not worry, he is ridiculous, almost crazy good at it." Her fear felt like trying to save a drowning victim, complete with the concern you'd be pulled under by them. Open as his sensorium was, he felt the power of a river in her, of still lakes and ponds with river-weed and of pounding waterfalls, a power potentially full of grace and by turns deadly. Robin had said that during her escape from De Rue, she had bitten into her father's hand and clamped down, determined not to stop until her teeth met. He admired fighting spirit like that. This is why we do it, he thought as he took note of her potential. *What would we be without these regular infusions of roadside talent?*

# 1 0

The yew wood bending made a quiet creak and he breathed out slowly, entirely emptying his lungs. After the first shot it would start and from then on there wouldn't be a moment of slowness again for some time. With his lungs Robin's mind fell empty. There was a glorious quiet inside him and things began to slow down. Growing up he'd been taught that the divine existed in all things, inside a split piece of wood, in the frolics of a new lamb, and also in the brutal artistry of archery visited upon human flesh.

When his body suddenly accounted for air currents and the motion of the target Robin would hear the perfection of the shot the way a great musician can hear a perfectly tuned note. Unleashing this meant Robin let himself go. He wouldn't even be slightly trying to hide how good he was so as not to overshadow other boys, he would be unselfconscious, so it was easier for his wings to unfurl. This was why he was the Twll Du band's sharp-shooter. Just like Jack's tracking was a form of witchcraft, Robin experienced archery like a mystical discipline.

Most of his shots would be ones of extreme difficulty aimed at the exposed eyes, or the join of the chainmail at the throat. Nobody but the victim would really see what he'd done and he would be alone while he was shooting. It felt intimate. Robin's spirit-eye seemed to travel with the arrow along the line of his long-sighted daily eyes, travelling to the place where the arrow would penetrate. Only the stock of him was left with its hands on the bow.

Meredith's scouting skills said mercenaries had made camp two hours ride south. He had been able to count a company of two-dozen souls based on the tracks. They were a comfortable distance from the caravans that were placed northwest of there. Their scouts had sighted no other likely hostiles near the caravans. Meredith had even managed to draw close enough to hear their conversation and heard De Rue's name. This confirmation was the gold of the scouting world, as well as hideously dangerous and something he would have words with Meredith about later.

About five minutes earlier he'd heard a scout's whistle announce the approach of someone hostile and he'd climbed the tree to assume his position for the ambush. There was no hurry as they had different whistles to indicate different degrees of proximity. Robin would find his position and attempt to mow down as many of them with his bow as possible during the phase where much could be made of his accuracy. When they were within range of the other archers who were defending the cave they would enter phase two.

With even lighter poundage, faster firing, and more accurate bows, they would start to hem the survivors in with rapid arrow fire. It was hoped it would never come to hand-to-hand fighting, but if it did Robin would shoot the combatants in the back. This was undesirable as with the poorer light and his more powerful bow the risk of hitting his own people with friendly fire would exist regardless of skill level. His heavier Welsh bow was designed to hit hard and punch through chainmail, and if the target wasn't wearing chainmail it was a killing rather than a wounding weapon.

His ears told him it was about to start. In a moment, he'd have his first clear view of them and he'd see a few options. There he was as soon as thinking. Robin was able to discern the typical costuming of a mercenary. The act was also done as soon as thinking. As the man was thrown backwards from his horse, then there was the standard human delay that always gave Robin such an advantage. Four men were dead, one after the other, a smooth rain of arrows, each just a little whistling fate-note from the sky, death from above without explanation. It took till the fourth for the other men to process it. Soon the panic responses would start and they would scatter making them harder to shoot.

A fifth man had died. His horse galloped away with his dead body flopping in the stirrups, before the well-trained were visually separated from the untrained. The untrained tried to run, whether on horseback or on foot, they all met the same fate. The ones with a bit more experience went to ground and tried to take shelter under shields or behind a rock or tree. Now it would get interesting. It was significantly harder to shoot men that knew you were shooting at them, so you had to fight dirty.

"Forgive me noble beast," Robin muttered grimly, as he shot one man's horse in the throat. When the horse stumbled it half unseated its rider who lowered his shield for just long enough to meet one of Robin's arrows. Robin gritted his teeth and narrowed his eyes. He watched them as a remorseless predator watches something approaching with the intent of consuming their young.

Phase two kicked in with the first rain of arrow fire from inside the cave mouth. All of the shots were accurate and delivered mortal wounds via the back. They had been stepping backwards under the cover of their shields when they stepped into range. The death dealing was rapid. Robin began to tally the deaths he'd seen occur. It didn't seem like as many as Meredith had said, and yet after a while the plain of green and red stood still and the first raven cawed.

*They have not shown us the respect they should have today. But if we live to be the tellers of this and so do they, they will not make that same mistake twice. If we prevail today and some of them yet live they will tell tales of our better bows to explain their defeat. We will need to make sure none live and then we move far and move fast, because next time they will give no quarter in our extermination.* With this in mind, Robin jumped down from his hiding place and went in search of Meredith's missing men.

Near evening Blaith beckoned to her to join him a little way off from the fire. As they had seen the victory smoke from the wardens but not yet made contact with them they were on silence half-measures where quiet whispers were allowed. Blaith pulled her very close to him in order to speak to her.

Because his words were whispered directly into her ear they seemed somehow magically charged.

"There is ritual to confirm you as us. We offer to you if you want to it?"

Lux took a deep breath. There was a good chance they worshipped the devil and that she was about to be asked to sell her soul. *They may yet be wicked, though the evidence stacks up in their favour. They are the ones who have put food in my mouth and blankets over my flesh. They have cared for me at turns both tenderly and fiercely. Shown me far more respect than the apparently godly people inside the walls.*

"Yes."

"Without even knowing what the ritual is?" he asked.

Lux couldn't help noticing a twinkle of some type of humour in his eyes.

"Without even knowing," she replied. It felt courageous, like a huge leap of faith, for a moment, then she quavered, wondering if she was equal to her own boldness.

"Undo your dress so you pull down off shoulders," he said this in such a business-like way all hint of humour gone. Suddenly she had gone from being in the presence of a highly sexual man who flirted constantly with both sexes, to being with a strange dark priest. She obeyed but paused before her breasts. "Here let me do mine too," he said, pulling his tunic off over his head. Shyly she glanced down at his hard torso and got an impression of highly visible stomach muscles and bones with dark chest hair and an assortment of tattoos, and then looked away. It seemed he felt taking off his shirt was equal to her removing hers.

Feeling very intensely aware of what she was doing, stepping to meet him in some way, Lux revealed her breasts. She did so because she wanted to live in a world where two people of different sexes removing their shirt was roughly equal. Though the action felt erotic to her, Blaith the Priest didn't bat an eyelid.

"Now kneel for me, rest your forehead on my knee and flip your hair over to reveal your spirit door."

Lux felt one of Blaith's hands slide under her shin and the other over her head. He muttered in Welsh and she could feel a heat building in his hands against her skin and hair. Again she felt the hot, pulsing red snake she'd known with Robin, the one that was made of warm blood. She was becoming part of something, something that bleeds.

"Do you come to me at the crossroads of your own free will, Lux? Forsaking all previous allegiances to God, Father, Creed, and People, made either by you or on your behalf?"

"I do."

"To show me that you are free place your foot upon the cross." He let her kneel up before drawing a cross in the dirt. She placed her foot upon the cross. Next, she felt a sharp burn across the back of her left shoulder. Lux gasped. The cut was deeply sensual somehow and it didn't hurt in the normal way, even after she could feel blood running down. Blaith licked the blood off her back and then bit her shoulder over the wound.

He helped her to her feet. Although Lux's dress was still undone to the waist and her breasts were showing she no longer thought about it. For the first time she was able to hold eye contact with him. Looking down finally she realised her foot was still on the cross and she stared at it like it was a foreign thing she couldn't account for. Nor could she account for the horror with which the gesture should have filled her, but didn't.

He stepped towards her and stood so close they were touching. Lifting her chin, he took a few deep breaths of air. "Empty your lungs," he said.

She did so and he covered her mouth with his, filling her lungs with air. Lux felt a serpent of wind fill her, filling her up down to every nook and cranny.

"Now that you are of my house know that you do no misdeed standing on the cross," he said. "As your feet are holy for it is they that remembered your way to the crossroads." He knelt then. "Among the priests in the walled church the congregation kneels before the man who speaks for God, among our people we kneel to the newly made one, for you are the future." He kissed her feet. "Your feet are as holy as the cross they rest on." He kissed her on the top of the pubic bone through the fabric of her skirt. "Your sex is as holy as the wafer and the wine." He kissed her open-mouthed upon each nipple she felt a hot flush go up into her cheeks as the kiss had a little suck in it.

"Your heart and all its many loves are as holy as the burning heart of Our Lady, before whom no act of love is impure." He stood then and kissed her on the spot between her eyes. "Your Fire is of the Holy Spirit and *the Kingdom of Heaven is Within You*." Leaning even closer he whispered in her ear the final part. "You have been lied to. The apple and the woman who took it were *good!*"

His last words seemed to hit her like a slap they had such impact... She knew this urgent whisper had been passed from mouth to ear many times and that finally, finally, she was beginning to meet others who were part of The Conspiracy. Blaith pressed a sixpence into her hand while she was still reeling. He murmured to her as he did: "When you need to buy your way out of the worst moment of your life use this six pence. Throw it over your left shoulder and cry out his name three times. I think you already know how to do that, Lux?"

# 11

eredith could see the four men who'd gone for cover. Robin had told him to announce a victory and then Bran told him to return to this position. It was lucky he had, otherwise the nervous whinny and the threat to the horses would never have been seen. "It will be what it will be," Meredith murmured to himself as he slipped out of his hiding spot and into another closer one.

Yes, the men had heard the sound. From here the small company of mercenaries were a clear target, easily in range... Could he shoot all of them accurately before they could retaliate? Perhaps it was better to rely on his strengths, Meredith thought. He crouched down and obtained a few rocks, before putting them in his pocket and shimmying up the nearest likely oak.

He knew the branches and the connections points where it would be possible to get away to the confusion of the less agile. From the branch he threw a stone that hit one of the men in the back of his helmet. Meredith couldn't help giggling at the 'doink' sound it made. "Hey, you sell-sword, pig-shit!" He didn't know many phrases in English but this was one Blaith had taught him.

This time Meredith didn't engage in any bravado. He took the shot carefully, taking his time. When the arrow whizzed through space it cut open the jugular vein of the man closest. Meredith was soon firing at the second closest man who he hit in the shoulder, throwing him from his horse. The animal careened in panic away from them and towards Meredith. He thought to swing down and jump onto its back to ride away. But there was still two able men, and a wounded one alive and sure to follow.

Meredith had fought a good few times, killed a good few people, yet he'd never been alone like this, forced to make his own decisions. He decided to try and take one more shot. It missed and lodged in the tree behind one of the men. The man's horse reared but he was not unseated. Leaping from his position to run across a branch that would let him down to a place he could quickly usurp the horse and run home yelling: Robin Goodfellow! Robin Goodfellow! Robin Goodfellow!

What it felt like to Meredith was as if something wrapped around his ankle, like a glance of The Eye had tripped his step. By the time the pain signal from his ankle reached him and told him a projectile had hit him there was the hard impact with the ground. Despite years of training, Meredith did not break fall as his instructors had not prepared him for a fall from quite that height.

There was leaf loam to cushion him, and he may have woken up quite quickly if they hadn't started to beat him. There were strange painful moments where he felt a blow and then time where the whole reality was the throbbing in his head that seemed to drown out the sun. The overwhelming quantity of pain around his ribs and the constriction in breathing from being winded by stomach kicks dominated. Having for one moment won his breath and voice Meredith did the one thing with it he believed could bring him help, and he emptied his soul into the cry so it reverberated around the forest. "*Robin!*"

The pain of being lifted brought him conscious. Meredith could feel Robin's sobbing breath and tried to reach out a hand to him.

"I had to try to do something, they were too near the horses."

"Fuck the horses, Merrie!"

"Is that an order?" he tried to laugh but it hurt too much and led to a bout of coughing. "Because I think… I'm too weak for it."

Robin rested his weight gently between himself and a strong oak to keep Meredith steady while the choking wracked him and Robin laughed and cried at the same time. "We'd have stolen new ones!"

He nodded painfully. "We could not leave… those men alive, Hob. None must… live… who come for us… it was part of… what we agree."

Lux held back the flap to the healing tent they'd set up while Robin carried the wounded boy inside. The two parties had been slow to meet up because Meredith had been missing. From the facial bruising and the way Meredith was bracing against the pain of being lifted Lux guessed he'd taken a savage beating and may have cracked ribs. She had helped to treat her mother after The Worst Time, her mother had taught her how as they went.

From the wet, clean trails through the dried blood on Robin's face and the glazed look in his eyes Lux could tell this young man Meredith meant a great deal to him. Blaith came unstuck in a mixture of frenetic Welsh speaking. Meredith was trying to calm Blaith down by making a pretence he was nothing more than mildly winded. Lux could tell all this through the language barrier, and also see straight through it to the strain in Meredith's eyes and the pallor where shock had blanched his lips.

Eilish immediately covered Meredith over with two blankets and began gently wrapping and enfolding him in it like he was a baby. Inside the cocoon was placed warmed rocks that were at just the right temperature to give comfort. Blaith shouted something angrily in response to other words that involved Bran's name. Eilish began to shoo them all out of the room then, including Blaith. Repeating her message loud and strong so as to cut through the male voices, saying it in both Welsh and then English.

"Please everyone out now. I need to treat Meredith, and for just a spell that means you too, Blaith."

Lux didn't know how Eilish managed to stand her ground against the fire in Blaith's eyes and the immense wall of fierce emotion that came from his body in wave after black, crushing, wave. It felt like if he'd wanted to he could have ended her life magically just by striking her with his fingertips. But Eilish, coming up to his chin as she did, did not back down or move a muscle.

When Blaith hesitated she added in English, as though she meant the statement to be heard by the outsiders as well as him. "This is *my* healing tent, Blaith." Her calm-seeming blue eyes were as implacable as a stone wall.

Blaith gave ground to her. In all her life Lux had never seen anything like that happen before. *That a woman might stand against a man and not be knocked down...*

He left the heads hanging by their hair. Robin had already cut two of them off during the rescue. One man, unfortunately for him, had been delivered to Blaith alive. That man would now be telling stories in the Underworld about what happens to people who touch a member of the Twll Du blood thread. In each of their ears Blaith whispered to them what he saw for them on the pale shores by the waters of blood and sorrow.

Blaith could feel Jack looking at him and it was hard not to interpret the older man's gaze as critical, or at least appraising, though there was no outward sign of it. "What?" Blaith demanded.

Jack shrugged. "Head sculptures aren't going to put Meredith back together."

Blaith hated these kinds of redundancies more than he hated the majority of other twaddle people said. Of course he knew that taking heads wasn't going to undo the outrage, it was just going to make him temporarily feel better. "I come from a warrior people. We don't know how to breathe when we're not fighting."

"I've noticed," Jack snorted, making dry reference to the time Blaith drew a knife on him.

"We've not had a whole lot of choice. The justice of revenge is the only sort our kind can expect to know."

"If you go against everything they stand for all at once, you will probably end up limiting your choices."

"That," Blaith said, pointed viciously in the direction of where a young man of sixteen lay beaten so badly he might not recover. "Is an example of what they stand for. Attacking in unfair numbers, and hurting women, and children. They stand for land theft, they stand for salted earth and burnt crops. They might not talk about it in front of the ladies, but the men do when they're alone, if you let them live, they'll be back in their castles bragging of their atrocities, because *that* is what they stand for. So yes, I go against everything they stand for, all at once, each chance I get."

Jack didn't deny any of it. He had the weight and heft of time behind him so he didn't need to argue. Jack had this sense about him that he'd let time prove you wrong instead. "That boy's got more guts than I'll ever have anyway. He spat in their faces when they caught him."

Blaith closed his eyes again and tears ran out down his face. He just nodded. Jack's words left a bittersweet ache in his chest. It was a form of comfort that only those who've led the harshest of lives could possibly understand. The comfort taken by a boy that hears his father died well. The cold comfort of remembering your mother's valiant last words, 'save my baby', as she fought for your brother's life right up to the end of her own… *He's right, the old bastard. Taking heads won't make me feel better. Instead it will be my people's bravery, the unending revelation of our collective courage.*

"My heart aches with pride," Blaith replied.

By the time Lux sensed his gaze layered thick upon her skin she wondered how long Robin had been watching her. It was uneasy suddenly. As if he had upon him a buzz of mars and death that came in with him from the battle, even after his bath. Physically his face was a bit scratched up but there were no real signs of the slaughter he'd perpetrated. Robin's eyes had that same lupine hunger in them now as when he'd pinned her thighs apart in the temple. The memory made her feel naked again, even in an apron and dress.

That Norman runaway who blushed and unraveled for him wasn't the same one who stood before him now, for this young person had taken an irrevocable step without consulting him. If he'd asked her about the initiation she couldn't have put words to her decision either, it was the result of trusting her stomach intelligence. His people had already shown her that a woman might either choose to stand or kneel before their powers that be, and the devil was better to a girl than god.

That knave Robin Goodfellow stood in the doorway of the main tent and looked at her, neither coming nor leaving. She wanted to throw her arms around him and tell him how she could barely breathe while he was out there, yet it felt awkward now after the terrible thing that had happened. Was he regretting ever bringing her here? So, she made herself say the thing she feared to say. "How is Meredith? What does Eilish say of his condition?"

The pain in Robin's eyes was back again at the mention. "It's hard to say until the swelling goes down how dangerous the injuries are, whether they are cracks or breaks, whether there is organ damage... But he's taken about as much milk of the poppy as you can without choosing the path home."

"You must be exhausted," she said instead, trying to show her love through fussing. She meant emotionally as well as physically, but Robin chose to ignore the first part.

"It wasn't arduous work," he replied, his voice somewhere between toneless and dry. "I just sat in a tree and shot a lot of people dead." The flat way he delivered it disturbed her in an altogether different way than the when her father used to talk about killing. "And then I shot and beheaded three more men."

"But what you're feeling about it..." She hoped it wasn't foolish to say it. He was just this man-sized shadow there with her, someone who had lived through experiences so different to any of hers. "The emotional impact of that."

"Oh, we aren't going to look too closely at that for now. I haven't got time for feelings until we make good our escape."

"We're getting straight back on the road with Meredith so gravely wounded?"

"There's nothing else for it," he murmured. This time those feelings he said would have to wait cracked into his voice. "We can't be anywhere around here when the Sheriff's men arrive. They'll bring dogs next time. We were lucky this once. They thought too little of us inbred tinker scum, imagined we'd be easy to kill. Now they know how wrong they were we're in real trouble."

Lux put her hand on his chest and stepped close to him. It was as if her gentle touch brought him back into his body, for he took a deep breath that had a shudder to it. "I had to kill a horse. There was no other way in. Couldn't afford to be sentimental. Mercenaries are human refuse, but I've never met a horse I didn't like…"

Sariah's words took residence in Lux's mind. Lux pressed Robin gently backward until he yielded to the suggestion and leaned on the tree. Her heart was hammering in her chest as she knelt down in the leaf loam before him. *Your love is bigger than their hate.* She opened her mouth and took his fingers, showing him a thorough tactile impression of her open mouth.

"I want you to put it in my mouth, Robin." It scared her to hear her own voice saying these bold words. She didn't experience it for long because Robin proved very efficient at unbuckling and unbuttoning his trousers. Closing her eyes she opened her mouth wider and stuck her tongue out a little. He groaned as he pushed his cock over her tongue and into her open mouth. Lux knew she was no longer in control of this act as he took her face in his hands and thrust deeply into her throat. An ecstasy of willing surrender burst over her like an array of falling stars and her throat gave way to him.

Her body became as water. Nothing could hurt her. She breathed when his pleasure decided. Finally, he was claiming some pleasure from her for the pains he'd taken. Lux loved that he wasn't shy about it either. It made her feel more confident in not being shy with him. When the peak came he was half way down her throat already so there was no need to swallow. At that moment she thought of her foot trampling upon the cross, and how she was consuming rather than bearing his young, which was forbidden.

Such thoughts were replaced only with ones about him. For she felt that violent shimmer around him, dangerous and attractive, but not belonging inside the campsite, come undone from his muscles and leave him along the river of her surrender. Robin slid slowly down the tree and they sat in the darkness together. After a while he reached out his hand and took hers.

# BOOK 2

# 1

It was said of his people they were born in the saddle. It was a way of expressing they had been travelling for as long as anyone could remember. Despite this homily even Robin had saddle sores today. He'd switched to his winter diet that, during a forced march such as this, consisted mainly of chewing hawthorn berries, claiming to have already eaten when delivering the kill to the women and children, and extending to everyone helpings of almost belligerently good humour.

He was amongst the most resilient members of his clan when it came to deprivation (with the other contender being a stick fighting aunty called Eldri, now in her early seventies who also hadn't been sick a day in her life). This meant he could and would ride longer, rest less, and save the food for those who most needed it. He could take it for the time being, and make it up later. Not all of them could. His family had always taught him: *to each their need, from each their capacity.* All strong capacities were, therefore, both a gift and curse. From him a very great deal would always be expected.

As Robin scouted the road ahead his mind was on his job and nothing else. He had no regrets about his decision to abduct the daughter of a wealthy and vengeful Norman nobleman. Always under the surface of Robin's chaos was an agenda. What he had done made sense inside it. Lux's liberation was an act of resistance. One his family regularly committed. It was a provocation, but it was not the mindless type. His actions were part of a tapestry of threads that reached way back into the events of what would come to be known as The Dark Ages.

At some point someone was going to have to strike back against the force

125

grinding forest and hedge-side dwellers out of existence, in some way, at some point, it would have to happen. At the moment this small act of defiance, removing their unwilling captives, was all he had in his arsenal. Meredith's dire condition even couldn't change the fact Robin knew in his balls his people couldn't just run like this forever, from one patch of contested forest space to another as the surveillance increased and the possible penalties with them...

There was a difference between travelling and running, and his people hadn't been travelling people for some time now. They had been fleeing people, and not all of them had all their fingers any longer. Never since before William the Bastard locked up the forests as his personal hunting playground had they really stopped being ready to run at a moment's notice. Their women increasingly went out of their way not to get pregnant.

Through the less than marvellous weather conditions, he got visual on what appeared to be a scout they send before large parties to tell them to yield the road. Quickly Robin stashed his bow in the hiding place all their horse's saddles had to hide their weapon when meeting with strangers. It was illegal, after all, for someone like him to bear the kind of arms he did. It was illegal to do nearly everything he was obliged to do to keep his family alive, and it was certainly illegal to do most of the things he enjoyed doing.

The scout hailed him and as the man dismounted Robin dismounted also. Despite the appearance of casualness, every fibre of Robin was alert in this situation. It always had to be when meeting a stranger on the road. Whilst still looking friendly and affable he was evaluating everything about the other man, starting with whether or not he was a fighter, what weapons he had on him and whether or not he could smell the man's fear.

"Hail," said the scout in the Scots tongue. "King David's army is on the march; your caravans will need to cede the way at the next away in the road."

"Hail, we shall do so. Why does the King march?" Robin's easy command of the tongues of the realm made it his job to collect useful gossip.

"Have you not heard before now, stranger? King Henry is dead!"

Robin frowned. The tapestry was now reforming in his mind. Armies were on the march as a response to a sudden power vacuum. This meant the English succession was to be contended, which most likely meant war. But heading into winter as they were this movement of armies was likely to be uncontested seizing of territory for now.

Real hostilities wouldn't be expected until at least spring. Then, if someone didn't make a decisive move on Westminster beforehand, the crows would get a feed. Robin sighed. He was only young in human years, though his forefathers within him were old and battle-tired from centuries of conflict. Part of him just wished they could all embrace as equals, *Welsh, Scots, Saxon, Norman, whatever! Let us just share what is here together and now and never count that once it was mine, but do not think within that generosity to make yourself master of where I shall walk, what I shall hunt, not upon the land that bodied my people forth from nothing.*

"Where is the army bound, friend?" Robin always corrected the word stranger with friend where he could, it seemed to help build up familiarity and made people less likely to try to fight with him. In small ways every day he tried to encourage others to think friend instead of stranger.

"Carlisle and then Newcastle."

"As low as Newcastle?"

"The King is claiming his own."

Robin nodded in a non-committal way, the attitude he kept for all the machinations of power between powerful men. For in his mind none of it belonged to anyone, or if it did it was to everyone for we all belonged to it. *What else will the crows feast on but for our insanity?*

"What about Wales? Will he cross the Dee?"

The scout shrugged. "I'm not his advisor, I'm just the scout."

"Peace be with you," Robin said, as he stood back to watch over his people as they pulled into the away.

The scout snorted with skepticism. "I very much doubt peace will tarry here with any of us."

Robin felt a quick jump of enthusiasm, much like the leap of a salmon in his chest, when he realised the warden joining him on night duty was Jack, when he'd thought it was Bran. The two men were roughly the same height and stocky build and moved through the trees in a similar way, like trackers move. Gazing deep into the coals of the fire as he had been, it was an easy mistake, and a happy one.

"Well met," muttered the other man, as he sat beside Robin and gave him a pat on the back. The language of Jack's gestures always spoke his truth more thoroughly than his words. Robin refused to allow what he regarded as the other man's emotional inhibitions, to get in the way of his own natural effusiveness.

"By the cunny of the Almighty! Am I glad to see you!" He leaned over and inflicted a warm hug upon the burly woodsman. It had been a long time since he'd met a man outside the immediate blood thread he felt so comfortable with. His affection seemed to partially amuse Jack based on visual signals, but Robin's fetch could sense the older man returned the sentiment.

"Why?" he asked, gruffly. He passed a wineskin of something alcoholic to Robin. "You thought I was Bran didn't you?" He laughed quietly with a certain wicked enjoyment at having caught Robin in a mean thought.

"I did indeed, my friend," Robin admitted with a grin. "I will own it."

"Don't know whether to be most delighted with the fact I've caught you not liking someone, or that I got one over on your creepy faerie senses?"

"Indeed, there are many men I dislike, you have seen me kill them. You move just like Brain. And that's a compliment as Bran's like a ghost."

Jack grunted. "Most trackers are. You pay that much attention to the ground you become a dirt artist. Having a turned foot means I've always have to pay attention to the Grandmother so she doesn't pull me down there to say hello."

Robin smiled with enjoyment. Jack was beginning to come on a little eloquent and more talkative it meant the wineskin had already been in solid use. "I like the term dirt artist. I aspire to know every wrinkle of the Grandmother's face and hands one day, the way you do." Robin nodded to himself while he considered life from the perspective of the slower warden art.

"Well, I'd say I aspire to scramble up and down trees like a monkey one day like you do, but it ain't gunna happen!" Jack laughed and slapped his knee.

"What do you see coming to the Old North now the King's dead?"

Jack sarcastically pretended to read the dregs in his ale cup. "War, strife and bitter weeping."

"So, any old day in the north country then?" It was part of their survival strategy, Robin knew. Dark humour was the life's blood of this place.

Jack laughed and then came over serious. "Your people adapt differently than mine did."

"In what way?"

"My family tried to stay away from the place where it happened. Your people fashion the skullcaps of the dead into drinking bowls and camp right over the scene of the horror."

"So, we are forever drinking in the spirit of rebellion and bravery that's gone into the stone here, my friend. This is more than just a massacre ground it's a place where a whole people said no to an unstoppable force and held their ground until they couldn't."

Blaith had been called to deathbeds since he was a boy. Under cover of darkness people would come to talk to him in superstitious whispers about how it was time to gently stop the breath. Adults didn't talk about it aloud -the fact they regularly hastened the deaths of their suffering loved ones by taking around the little boy with the death touch. But he of all people knew how common it truly was for people to want it to end before it ended.

So far he'd sat through each night with Meredith and he wasn't sure if it was despite or because of his nature that it had to be him. Some had started to say he was sleeping a lot or that he had become indolent. People under hardship and grief say such things. Things they don't mean. Of late he himself had said a few things born of pain that he didn't mean. Namely threatening to physically harm Bran for ordering Meredith to go back out after Robin had told him to come in. It was his pain speaking, and so he in turn held those who spoke unkindly of him during this hard time in no contempt.

His was a fitful rest, full of dark, moist shapes of dread. No hour until Meredith's pain had passed would contain true respite. His focus was maniacal and unbending. Until something changed in one direction or the other there was no such thing as light for him, and little of nourishment. He appreciated Sariah's hand on his back, rubbing him around the kidneys like she was trying to keep life moving in his vital organs, yet in his flesh he could hardly feel it.

The numbing effect on Blaith, of sitting staring at Meredith's bruised and battered face and holding his slowly cooling hand, went far beyond the scope of the emotions he felt for the other man. He had known Meredith all of the young man's life, of course. Yet even through the grief, guilt and fear of losing an aspect of that connection Blaith knew this coldness was more than human grief.

Death had loomed behind Blaith all his life. Meredith had seemed fearless of it. Most people talked a big talk in relation to Death's icy touch, all until they understood the true brutal, visceral, lastness of the struggle that precedes it. The strangled silencing and suffocation of the process of getting dead... But not Meredith, he thumbed his nose at it, cracked jokes to the very face of Death…. And it was this very thing Blaith had so loved in him that had probably got the boy killed.

Now Blaith wasn't allowed to just sit there and soothe him till eventually that bone fragment fully punctured the lung. Confused with lack of sleep and grief fatigue, Blaith was becoming Death. Death looked out at the world through his black eyes, non-verbally telling each person who met his gaze directly that they had a future appointment with Him. Some would look away quickly. All could feel this extra presence winding up in him, slightly behind him, to help someone cross over. Only a few still came up and touched him despite it. He didn't blame the ones who didn't. "Are people blaming Lux?" Sariah murmured. While she spoke she laid her warm stomach against his back. He appreciated the care behind the gesture even though he couldn't feel warmth at this point.

"You mean am *I* blaming Lux?"

"Both or either." Some people would have taken his tone as contentious or even picking a fight, but Sariah didn't tend to react to him like that. She had always known how to whisper the black serpentine force that lived in his spine into warm elasticity. For that reason he was careful not to take advantage of her patience with him by snapping at her.

"I'm not." He lifted Meredith's bruised hand and checked the pulse again while he spoke. "Lux is part of a destiny of Robin's, and of this caravan's. Robin will be Magister after me, as I will never see a live son born."

"Oh, my lover… I hope not. You know it would be Robin's worst nightmare to outlive you, even by a few heartbeats."

"And yet it will be so."

"Do you feel whether Merrie-"

"If Bran hadn't-"

"Cariad," she whispered, wrapping her arms around him. Her tender tone and the kiss on his neck that followed dissuaded him from minding that she'd interrupted him. "It will do no good to lift blame from Lux to give to someone else. What is done cannot be undone and Meredith too has a fate."

He shook his head mildly irritably, but he wouldn't have thought to pull away from her on account of it. Sariah had within her such a potent red life force that he never feared he'd blight her and in a wrestle between the red serpent in her and the black one in him they were well matched. "I'm not. I'm just saying, there were fates there where we could have taken Lux and still saved Meredith.

"And blaming a frightened young girl not much passed her first blood, who is fleeing a corpse-raping madman is less than I am. It may not be less than what Bran is, but it's less than I am! Even if…" Blaith cast his eyes over Meredith's sleeping eyelids. He knew the pattern of the veins in each of them individually and could have drawn their blue-green tracery from memory.

"Even if… The worst should happen. I shall not have it come back upon the girl. It is easy to blame the outsider," he muttered under his breath. "Always easy to make a scapegoat of one who is different, even better to most if it be someone helpless also… They prefer Lux over Robin for this reason as she is both. But the Magister isn't here to make things easy."

"You are very strong, Blaith."

Without words he acknowledged her with the gesture of respect, which began with touching the brow.

"Know that whatever happens your maidens are with you."

He squeezed her hand with a profound demonstrativeness and deep sincerity. His deepest bonds were always with the people he believed understood the language of his body best, with whom he needn't utter too many words. They were also the people whose bodies he had been given license with and leisure enough to know every nuance of in return.

"And thank the saints for it," he whispered.

"Well! You've Eilish and I to thank for it, in truth!" she declared. "The saints had less to do with it."

He eyed her for a few moments before answering. "I am contrary on this. My lovers are how Divinity reveals their hands, eyes, and lips to me. So, as I said…" He inclined his head to her solemnly, and in the gesture much was spoken.

When Meredith stirred, Robin considered running to get his grandmother and Blaith. He didn't though. Young as he was, Robin had watched a number of people die a slow death from injuries and he knew the signs when time was running out. As much as he wanted his people to be with the boy he also didn't want to risk leaving Meredith alone for so much as a minute in case it happened. He turned his head in Robin's direction. It was clear from small signs around his mouth and eyes that he was in profound pain. The instinct was to dose him with more milk of the poppy, but at this point such a thing might finish him.

132

"I'm here. It's Robin." It seemed like a good idea to be clear, as judging from Meredith's eyes he was seeing with the horizon-gaze.

"Hob? I'm seeing a lot of people that aren't with us anymore"

"Aye. It's me, Merrie." Robin squeezed his hand.

"It must be… your hand's so hot it almost burns… Nobody… except you feels that warm at this time of year."

Robin wiped at his eyes with his fingertips, trying to stop tears before they could begin. He didn't know exactly what it would be like to die, but he had a good idea that he didn't want anyone weeping for him while he was still in the room. "Who're you seeing out there beyond the curtain of falling snow?"

Meredith closed his eyes again. "Aunty Eliza and Uncle Gaelyn."

"Do they wear their wounds?" Robin whispered, clammy sweat formed on his palms.

"Yes. The omens of rising war, ice, and hunger in the North."

"Ha! A standard day in Norman-occupied Britain then?"

Meredith tried to laugh and ended up coughing. Robin pulled out a rag for him to cough into. When the painful spasm ceased a small amount of blood was evident on Meredith's lips and on the cloth. Coughing up blood was part of the endgame, as he understood it. "Speaking of Norman occupation… how is Lux holding up?"

"She's holding up as well as can be expected, given that she's never really been cold, hungry, or hunted." Robin's empathy extended over her too, even in that most foreign of experiences of transitioning from the domestic to the wild state.

"Don't let them blame her… when I'm gone."

"Don't say that. You are still going to-"

Meredith shook his head, impatient. "I'd have run away if I were her too and not stopped running. Escape or die… Bite through his fucking bully hand…" Something was shifting fast in Meredith's eyes. Robin got up quickly and ran to the door of the healing tent. "Somebody get Blaith!" he yelled out, before rushing back to Meredith's side.

"Don't let the bastards… break you…" he was muttering now. The drop from the lucidity of a few moments ago was fast and staggering in its brutality. "Take a few of them with you…run… fight to the end…die wild." Towards the end of his sentence the fits and starts of words faded.

"That I promise you. It will be in your name, Meredith."

# 2

Lux was starting to pick up on a small vocabulary in their tongue -which was in fact a language, not a dialect. What she'd pieced together was that there was pressure on Blaith because it was up to the maidens to say when the caravans moved on. Yet Sariah was the leader of the maidens, and she and Blaith were lovers, so she was thought unlikely to contradict his wishes. Especially not when it came to something as important to them all as Meredith.

"The problem is," Robin muttered to Lux around the campfire, while Blaith was sitting stock-still beside Meredith's bed, waiting to see if he'd speak again. "If we don't move soon, we are putting the survival of our whole family at grave risk. It is my job not to allow that." Robin was still wearing all his weapons, which included his very heavy belt with sword and knives.

"Is it all up to you, Robin?"

He shook his head, but you could still tell he didn't feel the answer to be no in his bones. "It is up to the maidens when we move the caravans, but even then it's complex because the First Warden can override that decision in an emergency when issues of survival are immediately at stake."

"So, it pretty much ends up being up to you?"

He nodded. "Blaith wants to stay put for Meredith, if a different decision has to be made then only the First Warden will make it, and only in a situation of imminent mortal threat."

Among her own people it was frequent enough to see a young man of Robin's age assume his father's title after the older man's untimely death, so in some ways she understood what he had to carry and why. "And you are the

135

First Warden?"

"There are many wardens. I am what's called First Warden, it is my job to lead our warrior company, and in an emergency the band as a whole."

"Why do you have such a job when you are so much younger than many of them? Surely, it's difficult being in charge of one's elders?"

Robin sighed. "It's sometimes hard. It's complicated. The Magister chooses his wardens and they swear to him in a certain order, and the one picked first is usually the man he most trusts. So, partly I'm here because Blaith chose me. Partly because of my mother's blood line. But we also have this more savage custom of challenge by single combat."

"So, you were made to fight and defeat all your elders before you could assume the position?"

"Not defeat with injury or bloodshed, just subdue."

"It sounds like a lot to carry."

Robin shrugged eloquently, his shoulders going up high and being held there for a long time before releasing fully. "It is all I know. We were trained for our roles since boyhood, Blaith and I. So, I do not know what it would feel like to carry something lighter."

"So, there is a matter of order of birth and who one's parents were in the mix too when it comes to who holds office?"

"Aye. A whole tapestry of bloodlines, traditions, and prophecies, my friend. But yes, Blaith and I were groomed as Magister and First Warden from birth."

"What if you'd wanted to be something else?" she asked quietly, before finally looking up to make eye contact with him. Part of her mind was trying to work out what the flaws were in their system and where the oppression was hiding. "Just like how I was born to be an enslaved baby maker, but I wanted to be a person instead."

"And what does being a person entail for you?"

"I...I... suppose I wanted freedom."

"What does freedom mean?"

"To make my own decisions about what happens to me."

"Hmm. Well life has seldom just *allowed* me what you call freedom. I've had to fight for it and steal it. But being Blaith's First Warden, serving my First Maiden, making sure our way of life survives and grows. These don't feel like impositions upon my freedom, if that's what you're trying to tease out. They feel like purpose." He shrugged again. "If not for this purpose what else am I for?"

The question took Lux aback. She certainly didn't know how to answer it for Robin and she had a feeling it was rhetorical. Also, Lux couldn't help applying it to herself. *If not a Norman wife then what else am I for?* If she was honest with herself Lux had not been so bold to imagine anything else beyond that Robin would claim her for the same purposes. The question of purpose sat with her the rest of the night, the way Blaith did with Meredith, still and deep, studying her.

The next morning the still air was rent by the first of the wails that signified a passing. Lux would remember it ever after as if a great black bird came down and covered the sky, darkening out the sun before a collective and terrible primal screaming began. It started off with just the keening of those who knew Meredith best but was soon joined by wild lamentations and sobs.

Terrified, Lux gripped the side of the caravan. For a long moment her body was convinced she was to be killed immediately in retribution. Outbursts of intense emotion had, back at her father's home, been followed by violence. Never had she been amongst such a powerful swell of collective emotion that didn't seek a rage outlet of some kind. It took a moment or two before she saw through the people surging forward, Blaith, his face almost concealed by the hood of his black cloak, carrying Meredith's body. The image burned into her mind and memory as one with the grief-grandeur as to befit the old sagas.

Only moments afterwards, Blaith's walking careened unevenly and he fell to his knees, taking Meredith down to the earth with him. Their people moved in around them. Lux just stood there with one hand over her mouth. Her body wanted to run but her legs had no power in them. Unlike the power they'd seemed to have on the night she'd run for her life she couldn't have moved to defend herself had someone chosen to strike her down.

Unlike usually where Robin would be behind Blaith steadying him, placing his cloak around his Magister's shoulders, this time Robin was on his knees beside Blaith and hitting himself in the chest with the most intense distress. To see it broke Lux's heart but terrified her also. It was only when the mourners blocked her view that Lux realised she was also on her knees. She didn't remember falling, but perhaps her body had followed Blaith's in the action, just as Sariah and Eilish had done.

For a moment they were all part of some dread sabbat where they were kneeling before a two-headed man that was Lord of Death, and because all things were now in reverse, instead of letting down their hair to him in sensuous bliss, they were tearing at their hair like wild animals. The frenzy of Blaith's grief seemed to carry the weight of group hypnotism.

The lamentation rose to a great intensity until the mob of arms holding each other they had formed around Meredith, rocked back and forth collectively like they were trying to soothe an infant. Meredith was clasped in the arms of The Master, at the centre of the sabbat and instead of waking him up, we were rocking him to sleep. Just to confirm that they had passed to the infernal plain and that all things had reversed, instead of throwing her out of the group hands were pulling her deeper into the heart of it.

Under normal circumstances she'd never have dared to force her affection on a virulently grieving man in this manner, but they were thrusting her toward Robin. To her surprise he eagerly accepted this offer of comfort and immediately clasped her to him. She became one with the throbbing of his heart and his hurting, heaving lungs. He held her tightly, so that she was only just able to breathe.

Sariah swapped to holding Robin, and Blaith pulled softly upon her arm and with his body language invited her into his embrace. The gesture shocked her, as much for how gentle and unassuming it was as for the fact he'd want anything to do with her under the circumstances. She accepted even though it meant closer proximity to Meredith's semi-shrouded form.

"Ah do not fear him, lass," Blaith whispered, a kind of desolate yet poignant tone that came in between his weeping. "For he is only as we all will be one day." There was a great profound darkness in him, yet also an unstinting generosity of spirit she'd seen in few people.

Lux had never been so drunk in her life as she was when they carried Meredith. Nobody explained the rite beyond saying they would bear up the body of their loved one and walk it up and down till dawn. When her turn came to help shoulder the bier of birch saplings that held the wrapped and shrouded remains of Meredith, nobody could have prepared her for seeing them walking through desert places of the heart together, burnt out parts of the Old North…

Her feet walked through the harsh terrain of the Underworld wastes. Around her in this lunar-scape giant jackals followed with red eyes. Tears rolled down Lux's face. *You shall not have him*, their collective presence said to the scavengers who take the weak upon the road. *For he who is loved in life need not walk a step in the empty spaces between death and life but is robed in fire, cocooned in love, defended on all sides by unending brotherhood and the shield of friendship. He will not falter once for when he does we will hold him.*

People would spontaneously begin to toast Meredith's courage and tell a memory of him and then all would have to drink that memory, something that was taken quite literally. Everybody was weeping freely. There seemed no way to stop the trickle roads of salt that opened at the eye.

Robin watched Blaith's every move, ready to sweep in with his cloak and his arms with support that he needed to give every bit as much as Blaith needed to receive. Now she'd been absorbed into the collective salted and blooded river running to sea, the seething warm red serpent that, even in its pain-writhing, remained warm with motion and the open sharing of pain.

Nobody who shared this rite was an outsider by the end.

Meredith's grandmother, Henwen, his closest, living blood elder, wrapped in a bear skin, sang a haunting, primal lament. A fresh run of tears came out from being in the presence of a type of exquisite rawness Lux had never heard before. It made her feel like the song was coming from the caves and rocks of the land itself. As though the grandmother woman had somehow given the land a mouth to express pain that mellowed into a welcoming song as she called him back to her bosom like an infant.

Lux leaned her back against the caravan trying to catch her breath and watched Robin and Blaith carrying Meredith. The bier was laden with greenery and whatever flowers could be found that you could hardly see him. Lux jumped when she realised what she'd thought another human was someone from outside the clan. Normally her reaction would have been one of alarm but tonight she was transfixed.

The androgynous-looking young man was suspiciously still amid a seething sea of human feeling that he seemed entirely detached from. To see him was like the comet observing the fixed star. Lux surrendered entirely to the maelstrom of collective humanity she was enmeshed in, yet there was a not so small part of her that envied the stranger his aloof non-involvement with the mess of humanity. Immediately Lux knew from this what he was, as faerie is want to know faerie.

As soon as she knew what he was the faerie man was gone, and Lux found that alcohol had decided to sit her down against the caravan. Lux was struggling not to be sick when she felt someone staring at her and looked up. This time it was one of the red world watching. Meredith's grandmother was coming towards her. It was clear from the way she fixed her eyes on Lux that she intended to communicate with her. Rooted to the spot in fear, Lux had no idea what to do. How do you convey your sympathies when you can't speak the language?

The grandmother woman was shorter than Lux yet her body felt whiplash fierce and strong. As she took Lux between her hands at shoulder height she was sure she couldn't have pulled free if she dared try. Reluctantly she met the other woman's eyes. They were red rimmed with crying and her face bore puffiness not only from tears but from having struck herself in the face during the keening.

Looking at her visage, weathered with character and hardship like the land around them, facially tattooed, dark eyes like a bear looking out through those of a woman, Lux felt humbled and so much less-than in her unfinished girl-hood. This woman who stood before her with her wolf and bear teeth about her neck and tokens of her many grandchildren worn at her belt, represented a power that Lux had never dared dream women might possess without op-position.

The grandmother woman took Lux's face in her hands and looked closely into her eyes. Lux saw a warm, kindly look in them that seemed to mingle naturally with the sadness into poignancy. The older woman embraced her tightly. Not just a brief hug which one might give in passing but a long, deep hold as if Lux were a child, her child at that. Lux hadn't known how much she'd wanted such a hug until then. This woman's body seemed to say, in absence of a common language, there is no shortage, no giving or taking, trusting or not trusting, there is just this truth: here we stand, or here we fall -as one.

"It's too cold against the earth for you to stay down there," Robin whis-pered softly as he lowered his warden cloak over Blaith's body. They had cov-ered Meredith in greenery, soil and stone and now Blaith was lying on the covered grave. It wasn't unusual to grave-lie and seek vision, but now was both a cold and a dangerous time.

"I don't care."

Blaith's face looked blanched against the black soil and Robin felt afraid it would somehow open and claim his brother also. There had always been something about Blaith's body as well as his soul that seemed to have an inti-mate communion with the world of death, the make-up of a true necromancer.

"Well, I do." Robin's heart and entrails were spasmed with tenderness. Wind was blowing through him now, like a worn old rock that had been whipped by the North Country winds for too many millenniums. "I'm afraid now is that moment. I would give you whole seasons were it in my hands." It wasn't humane to drag him from the grave when the sod had barely settled in around their family member, but Robin knew this land and this sky and what it promised to bring down upon them very shortly. If they didn't make it through the serpent road of the Peak District before the snows set in Meredith would not be the last roadside burial of the season.

"I know," Blaith muttered grimly, nodding to himself, but still not opening his eyes or moving. His brother's grace even in the face of his own heartbreak didn't make it easier. "Ah gods that it should be so though, Hob!" These simple sounding words tore through Robin until his own throat thickened with tears. You didn't hear many such complaints against Fate from Blaith.

"I know."

"I'll try to get up. I don't know if my legs will work."

"If they don't, I'll lift you."

After they got him on his horse Blaith rode like a statue carved in alabaster, staring forward, acknowledging no one but the task he must face. Sariah had been on her feet all day and he could see she looked pale. She and Robin made anxious eye contact with each other regarding Blaith. Robin rode to where Sariah was in the line and without speaking held his mead skin to her lips so she could drink. Sometimes when there was nothing to be said such small comforts meant the world.

She drank hungrily from it. "Blessings upon you, Hob. How is it warm?"

His brand of heat had always been the thing he'd been able to bring to the officers. "It's been against my skin."

"You're not natural."

"It has been said."

Their banter had no spirit in it that grey day but they tried it out anyway.

"It just doesn't seem right," she murmured brokenly, giving up on their usual semi-flirtatious play fighting. "Packing up caravan like this."

He swallowed down hard and didn't reach out to comfort her. He knew it was best to let the tears flow and do nothing to try to stop them up, as hard as he found it to see. Tears made his maiden look like she had when she was little and it tugged at his heart to see her pink and wet like that.

"I know." He fell in to ride beside her. "I just tell myself he's out there in the trees somewhere. He always did so much prefer the spring and summer to the winter." He reached over to squeeze her hand and left rode off, for he had no choice. Robin moved his horse to a different position in the caravan where he could see everyone better.

He hated this mountain pass because some of it was quite overgrown and haunted with bandits. With the sound of the wind they would have to rely entirely on instinct at times to know if someone was coming. The weather was unpredictable here and it wasn't the kind of country Robin preferred to take his people through, but this was another manifestation of their freedom he had little choice in, if they were to cross the pass before the serious snow arrived.

# 3

Lux had the job of watching over the children while the rest of the adults made camp. The weather was frosty but clear and windless, so tents were being pitched. People planned to spread out and enjoy the brief reprieve from caravan life. With no experience of the smooth and efficient camp-making procedure the clan followed, so Lux didn't know how else to make herself useful.

The boy was called Zorien, he was Meredith's half-brother from the Gyre Carlin caravan. His jerkin had a strip of leather down the front to which were affixed saint medallions from different locations, holy stones and coloured bones. There was a threadbare tartan around his neck, a bearskin hat on his head and a strip across his eyes had been blackened with soot. It made Lux think of how Clarice had described someone as: dark and sooty as the devil.

The children habitually went around like this, but the adults would sometimes black their whole face out when they moved around at night in fairs or markets. Apparently, it was meant to make them harder to recognise, but Robin admitted it was as much a matter of custom and cultural dress as one of expediency. Lux couldn't quite help wondering if it wouldn't help them somewhat to be less obvious?

The little girl was Bran's daughter. Lux couldn't remember her name, which was frustrating because she was the oldest of the child cohort, and if Lux needed to call them back it was the lead girl's name she'd need. When the picturesque little waif beckoned her to follow the children down the other side of the mound and into what appeared to be a ruin of some kind, she followed without question.

There was a stark quality to the land here, with large patches of dead vegetation and fields where nothing grew and only dirt and stones were to be seen. Ravens outnumbered man and they looked at you like they were making dark plans for you. But she was gradually starting to interpret the landscape as less threatening even so. It was as if Robin's stories were beginning to give the land faces and identities and not every one of them appeared to be grimacing at her.

Lux's newfound confidence wavered when the children standing around were obviously trying to repress giggles. She hadn't had many friends during her growing up years and she still felt awkward around children, even though she was technically a woman now. They would have been flogged for their insolence if she were back at home... The lead girl pointed at the crunchy ground at their feet. In response Lux looked down to see what was of interest. It felt like she was moving around on broken pottery shards. Picking her feet up and down a few times Lux frowned as she examined the strange rocks the children were trying to show her.

"Cymry!" Bran's daughter uttered fiercely, indicating the white gravel beneath their feet and then pounding her little chest firmly with her fist. Lux knew the word was thought of as Welsh for being Welsh, but really it just meant 'one of us' or 'our people'. When Lux didn't catch on the girl made the universal gesture of throat slitting to indicate killing. At the same moment she saw the human jaw with teeth. Immediately Lux's gaze darting around the interior of the floor of the ruin spotting a blackened cranial casing here, a human vertebra there...

"Normans!" The girl said, immediately after the kill gesture. This time she swung her accusing finger in Lux's direction as if she personally were to stand for all Normans. Lux suppressed a scream by throwing her hand over her mouth but still made a yelping sound. She frantically tried to pick somewhere to stand that wasn't on top of human remains and nearly tripped in the effort.

The children's laughter followed her as she fled back up the hill. She hadn't yet reached the top of the mound before she almost collided with one of the wardens. He was only about the same age as her, but the fox's tail in his belt marked him out as a scout. It was humiliating to be standing before this almost complete stranger sobbing, having been rattled by small children. The young man took her about the shoulders gently in his hands. He was quite a bit taller than Lux but his limbs still had a youthful awkwardness about them that prevented all sense of threat.

"I'm sorry," she murmured.

Seeing her flustered and hearing the children he spoke firmly to them. They answered him and appeared chastised. After he'd ascertained what he wanted to know he merely pointed and uttered one emphatic word that she imagined meant 'go!' and the children dispersed.

"Rory," the young man said, touching his own chest. "Meredith *brawd*," he said pointing back to camp. "Zorien *brawd*," he pointed in the direction the children had gone. Lux began to nod inferring their word for brother.

"You're Meredith's younger brother!" She dabbed at her face with her handkerchief. Rory patted her on the back in a comforting fashion, as warmly as if they'd been friends for years and it were perfectly normal for boys and girls to touch one another in this mate-like fashion. Rory made a gesture in the direction the children had run that seemed to say, 'never mind them'. "Hob," he said, giving her the gesture of 'stay put', and then ran off to get Robin.

Lux felt awkward standing there while everyone else bustled around and worked, especially as Rory was interrupting Robin's warden duties to deal with the fact she was crying. Rather than engaging with the embarrassment of looking at them she cast her eyes back down into what had appeared a pleasant glen with the picturesque ruins but now had been exposed as a killing field, or at the very least a mass grave.

*Why in Heaven's name would they choose to camp so close to so recent a killing ground?* The longer she looked around the charred or half mossed over bones the more she noticed. She had an uncomfortable feeling the mound she was standing on itself wasn't Nature's handiwork. What sort of a slaughter resulted in exposed dead with no one left to give them proper burial rites?

When she turned Robin was moving rapidly towards her in his grey warden cloak. They looked threadbare like something a beggar might wear on the outside, having seen a great deal of inclement weather, but underneath they were lined with wolf's pelt like something a lord might display on the outside. Only Norman noblemen were allowed to sanction the killing of wolves and wearing their pelts openly would be an act of provocation.

"Are you alright, Lux?" he asked her in Norman French.

"I'm so sorry you were interrupted-"

"Please don't apologise. Rory explained to me what happened. I meant to tell you the story of the place we were coming to beforehand but my work swept me up."

Lux stared at him for some time trying to fathom how on earth he existed…"Your work is *only* the safety of the entire clan after all, how remiss of you not to be running around preventing a foolish girl's tears!"

He caught her new sarcasm and looked up from under his brows with an enigmatic sort of expression that bordered on amusement. "We are not reared to suggest what we do is more important than what women do. Besides, I'm off duty now. Will you walk with me back down there?"

"You want to… go back where they are?" She glanced nervously in the direction of the bones, like a skittish horse shying from the scent of death. "Won't we walk on them?"

Robin reached out and took her hand. He sighed. "I'm afraid we already walk upon them. Ever since we've been in the Old North we've walked upon their bones on and off. Rode our horses over them… Eaten berries which grew from their rot… There is nothing here in the soil but rock, sadness, and the bones of rebels."

Lux shuddered. "Why ever do we camp here then?"

"Because we too have not had much left to us beyond rock, sadness, and rebellion. What is deemed cursed land by all else is a safe haven for people such as us."

She paused and involuntarily resisted walking on.

"Come," he encouraged gently with his hand, but his voice held more firmness. "It is a token of your willingness to acknowledge reality, Lux. Do knowingly what you've been doing all along -walking over land riddled with the bones of those who resisted. When you have done so, I will tell you their stories and we will drench their ghosts together."

If asked to declare it before others Lux would have claimed her lowest moment came with Meredith's death. The truth she was less proud of was that it came on the forced march somewhere through the Old North and into the borderlands of Scotland. At first, while they were still meeting people on the road, Lux had the luxury of being hidden in the caravan. As conditions got steadily worse people more vulnerable than herself needed the space.

Any they did meet were heading south rapidly, either for matters of climate or war. They were still heading through a comfortless waste with burnt out huts that gave Lux a new perception of the extent of the ethnic cleansing The Conqueror had inflicted on this land. While she was outside during travel Lux mostly rode a horse, which in itself was a large part of the hardship. Eilish had applied some wonderful ointment and bandaging, but there was only so much it could do.

She opted to try walking. Stoic in the face of the driving sleet and sometimes even more miserable rain, Lux claimed to want to give up her horse for someone older or younger than herself. The reality was that she feared she would scream if she tried to ride anymore.

The extra exercise of the forced march made her hungry. That was when the true misery began. There was the bitter cold, the hard exercise, and scarce food which she'd not been bred to withstand, coupled with the smarting sores. The bleak Northern skies seemed to taunt her with circling ravens she was convinced had spotted her as walking carrion. She was frozen to the bone and it was mainly pride that kept her going.

It was only when Robin would ride up and down the line that hope and a memory of why she was enduring this would flare back up inside her. He seemed like the sun in human form riding along towards her, laughing and engaging in light or dark humour with people who needed a smile here, and helping lift someone down from the saddle there... He was so invulnerable-seeming she could only assume he must secretly scorn her weakness, her softness born of coddling and privilege.

As she trudged on, she was beginning to feel every little unevenness in the path, every loose stone as a major hardship on her ankle joints, requiring as it did some tiny gradation in extra effort to traverse it. For the first time she found herself thinking of her life back at the castle with a kind of nostalgia. She remembered the bed-warmer that Clarice had used to take the chill off her sheets, and the feather mattress. She recalled what it felt like to be full...

It was when they got to the rutted hill where every stone seemed shaped for her personal torment that her vision started to swim. The next thing she recalled she was on the ground, partly being held, looking up at the sky.

"That's it, take it slow," she heard Robin's voice whisper as she blinked in confusion. "You checked out on us for a little while there." When she looked up into his face there was still reassuring warmth in his smile. "I'm surprised you didn't drop before now. Come. I'm taking you inside."

Lux woke up later on a nest of sheepskins by the fireplace. She looked down to see she was wrapped in Robin's warden cloak, which had seemed to act on her as some kind of sleep spell. It smelt like him.

"How are you feeling now?"

Rather than speak and wake the caravan she got up and tiptoed quietly closer to him before answering. He was taking off his wet boots and had obviously just finished his shift on watch.

"I'm... But, Robin, how are *you*?"

He was wet through and cold to the touch, rubbing his hands together vigorously in front of the fire and shivering convulsively. This was terrifying to witness as she had never known Robin to respond much to the cold. If he was shivering, he must be near to death from exposure.

"Oh fine, fine. It's all looking fine out there... We just need to get some hunting in tomorrow and it will be fine we've got some oat biscuits left....

Before the weather really turns-"

"But how are *you*?"

"Who?" He seemed only semi-facetious. Or perhaps the mad gleam in his eye was not humour at all but a genuine moment of confusion, the look of one who has for too long stood in a snowstorm and watched the swirling death flakes dance out the pattern of oblivion before his eyes. "Ah... I have forgotten him quite, too many other people I'm worried about. Things walk out there tonight, Lux."

"What sort of *things*?"

"Things that stalk the living," he muttered. "Powers that can't be fought and can only be appeased." He sounded in that moment like a weathered veteran of three score years who has seen his life's load of horrors already. "I've seen *them*. Just beyond the curtain of snow. The shape of what has been sent to dog our tail till it brings us to earth."

"You need to take that wet shirt off." Her tone came out with a motherly authority and he responded by obeying her immediately and without question. Not waiting for his permission Lux began to undress him. "Even you have limits on how much cold you can take."

"Wash your mouth out, lass! I know not these limit things you speak of," he joked. But it was still in between the kind of breathing you'd expect from someone near hyperthermia. She passed him the drying cloth and began to spoon some bone broth from the jar that was kept warming by the fire for the wardens when they came in. It made her feel stronger to do something for someone else, she realised. While she did this something occurred to her: *He's this cold because he left me wrapped up in his cloak...*

Tears of intense tenderness filled her eyes. It was an act she couldn't have understood before, because until now she'd never known what it was to only have one of something. Sharing had always come easily to her, she was the sort of child to share her toys with others and any treats she was given, but never before had she only had one of something and had to decide to give it to the other.

150

Her body promised his body that no matter what it must endure to stand beside him it would not let his body down. *I will never harm you, I will never shame you, I will never let you down.*

"I'm sorry," she whispered into his hair. "I didn't know."

"Know what, sweet girl?"

"That you felt cold like normal people."

He laughed softly, it had a touch of sadness in it, but did not reply.


The preparations for the horse sacrifice were undertaken with such solemnity that the atmosphere seemed more primed for a human sacrifice. Whilst she understood these people loved their horses, and even drank the milk of the mares, she was taken aback to learn the death would take place out of public view. The horse's sacrificial death was considered too graphic for the children and more sensitive folk to witness. When told Lux had turned to gaze in mute confusion at the half-decomposed Norman heads hanging from the back of their caravan.

"He was Meredith's horse," Sariah explained as they watched Blaith lead the animal away from camp. Only one of the older men from Arva caravan who was known as a great horse-whisperer went with him. Everyone else gathered around in anxious silence and shivered while the wind howled and the snow fell intermittently.

"Is that why he was chosen to be killed?" Lux asked. "Must he go to meet his rider in the Otherworld?"

"He went lame and we need the meat." Sariah laughed then at the surprise her practicality elicited from Lux. "No, it is also that he went lame in his back left foot, which as an omen is interpreted that Meredith is indeed trying to catch up his old horse from the Otherworld. If we don't appease the dead with blood, and the living with meat in their bellies, then Margen will come among us again."

"Is Margen death?"

Sariah nodded. "The *mari lwyd*, the old white mare, they call her. Tonight's rites are conducted in her honour."

Lux continued to watch the place where Blaith had disappeared over the ditch with the horse even though she couldn't see anything. "Why does Blaith have to do it? Surely with it being Meredith's horse this must be hard for him?"

"Oh, it is hard for him," Sariah confirmed quietly.

"But couldn't someone else-"

"He's Magister." She shrugged. "Such killings are always the first death. It is right he should be the one."

It was soon a moot point anyway as Blaith reappeared holding a white object that was quickly soaking through in blood. It took her a moment or two to realize it was the animal's head, delicately wrapped in white cloth -unlike their enemy's heads which were carried around openly by the hair. Nobody spoke in response but instead walked towards the killing site.

Lux followed through the whirling snow, running to catch up with Sariah. When she got there, she found the wardens had already begun to hang and bleed the animal and the rest of the people got to work on building a fire. The site where the actual slaughter had happened was hemmed off from the cooking space by a circle of stones.

"That space is the blood acre, where the Others feast," Sariah said. "Do not ever step inside that circle or they will think it is you who is offered."

And why would she? For it seemed the snow fell slower there and yet it was colder. Their circle had a fire and cooking meat. Once the fire was roaring and had a good coal bank Blaith ceremonially unwrapped the horse's head and placed it among the flames. While this was done a great drumming started that sounded like a horse in gallop. The little children got up and pretended to gallop around the fire, raising a great dervish of movement. It was not until all the flesh was cooked away from the blackened skull that a hook was used to fetch it out of the fire.

Robin appeared before her with a clamshell of freshly cooked meat. The flesh was emergency cooked, unlike their more considered dishes, which were some of the tastiest things she'd eaten. It was a bit charred on the outside and almost raw on the inside, but she didn't care.

"Thank you!" she began to eat immediately.

Robin regarded her in an approving manner, as if he found the animalistic way she was attacking the meat to be attractive. How he could think any such thing when he didn't appear to have yet eaten, and she was hardly at her most well-groomed, was beyond her. "I'm glad you are able to eat with appetite. I was worried you'd be put off by the ritual and the fact it was Meredith's horse."

"Are you serious?" she asked with her mouth full. "I wouldn't care if it was my own childhood pony. I'm starving!"

Robin laughed with real humour. "Ah you are new to hunger, I forget this more than I should, mainly because you hold yourself with such dignity it is easy to forget."

"Thank you." She blushed, her ravenous hunger punctuated by this praise.

"It's quite an experience isn't it? Living this near the edge?"

Lux understood exactly what 'the edge' was without asking because she was experiencing it.

"It grows you fast. Turns fifteen into twenty-five and some tough old horse meat into the best thing you've ever had in your mouth."

"Well," she muttered, in between sucking meat grease off her fingers. "*One* of the best things I've-" It took a moment before her mind caught up with her sudden vitalism leant to her by the meat and reminded her how brazen her comment was.

"Are you flirting, Lux?" he asked, his eyebrows twitched faintly and his eyes glowed with a mixture of warmth and patient-wolf.

"Well…" she tried to deflect with humour. "You *did* just feed me and I was very hungry."

Robin didn't seem to think it was funny though, he just nodded matter-of-factly, as if the connection between the two things made perfect sense. "I understand. It feels arousing to me too. Bringing you food… That is why I haven't eaten yet. I wanted to feed you first and to feel the sacrifice of it for a little while."

She didn't know what to say so she fell back on practical, demonstrative loving. "I will enjoy it far more if you eat with me," she said, taking some of the meat between her fingers and motioning to feed it to him. He accepted it from her without question and ate it. The sensation was with her again, of having hand fed a wolf, a creature capable of deep loyalty and discipline yet, from the eyes you knew was wild to its core.

"He was a good horse," Robin commented as he chewed. "A perfect example of Welsh mountain pony courage and tenacity."

Lux cracked up laughing and had to cover her mouth with her hand to avoid choking out said horse's remains. "Robin! Don't mention that *now*, not while we're... *you know....*"

"Why?" he asked, puzzled. "I am Singing him. May his courage remain in our people's blood. May his hardiness take root in us all. May he never die whilst we are living. And may our cousin Meredith never want for a mount in the Otherlands."

When the Mari Lwyd came clanking the large bells at her waist all the children went running for the caravans, and the adults were not far behind. The now white-washed horse's skull was mounted on a high stick which was held aloft by a man under it, so that Death appeared to tower over them all. Unlike the God of the Dead, the sooty-faced Gwynn ap Nudd whose wild hunt chased the souls to Annwn, the personification of death was utterly white.

"Devil take the hindmost," she whispered to herself, seeing the significance.

Robin grinned. "Good luck to him."

She didn't fully realise what he meant by that until she saw that Robin would not enter until he saw the last person secure of all three caravans. Thus, he himself who would be the hindmost. Unwilling to enter without him Lux lingered on the steps of the caravan, watching the Mari Lwyd's threatening approach. Finally, when the last door closed on caravan Arva and Gyre Carlin Robin came they secured caravan Ama against the onslaught.

The small band beat pots and pans and knocked against the caravans creating a very chaotic feeling. Finally, the mari lwyd team settled on caravan Ama to visit. There was a menacing knocking at the door. The people were encouraged to all hold hands and be touching.

"I thought they would pick us," Robin said, as if this ritual were not terrifying. "It would be insensitive to go to Meredith's caravan, and Arva has an infant in it."

One of the elders rose to answer the summons. As soon as the door was opened the mari lwyd began to speak in verse in Welsh.

"What does she say, Robin?" Lux asked. "Something about singing and asking permission?"

"She says roughly: 'well here we come, innocent friends, to ask leave, to ask leave to ask leave to sing.' But singing also means to make something become or to weave or create it. Now Uncle says: 'You may not, Margen, for I am chief bard and where I sing the thread of life Death shall have no dominion.'"

"It's very poetic."

"Ours is the language of poets," Robin replied. "Now Margen demands Uncle enter into a battle of poetic wits with him or elect a champion." He sighed then. "And he's electing me... You know, between you and I, I really do resent this a bit right now."

She was left smiling to herself and almost blushing at how good it felt that he had chosen to make a secret complaint to her in a language no one else understood. The repartee between the death Margen and Robin was clearly in metre but was far too fast for her to follow. Though she could tell from the laughter and gasps of the audience that they were on Robin's side and voting down the mari lwyd's contributions. She watched Robin's extraversion, laughter, and rapid verbal dexterity in his own tongue and it fascinated her to know that secretly he resented being asked to do this job tonight.

Eventually it appeared that Robin was obliged to throw one round, the *mari lwyd* was invited in and given lots of alcohol to drink, with the intention of getting her drunk and unable to reap any souls. In fact, from where Lux was bundled up on one of the bunks it looked like it was compulsory that Death drink whatever she was served. She was given the best place at the fireside and a great quantity of food and drink.

"What happens now?" Lux asked Robin when he came back to sit down.

"The Margen rides with us and we feast her thus for nine nights. On the ninth night we burn the horse's skull. Then it is done, the ones who watch after a death are appeased and whatever has been sent upon us will be sent back to its owner."

# 4

Lux watched Robin hand over his ward for the night to Emrys, before sitting down to remove his wet boots. Robin stripped off his wet shirt and hung it up on the beams to dry. He also went through the routine of cleaning his hands and feet with the rosemary and sage scented vinegar, even though he must have just been cold and exhausted. It was as if these simple routines had the spiritual air of prayer against the forces of disease and dissolution.

"Come, Lux," he said to her. "Share Blaith and my sleep space."

She watched him take one of the hot rocks from under the oven over to the bunk and climb in next to Blaith, applying the stone to the other man's lower back. He turned and patted the space beside him to indicate Lux should get in. He pressed the warm stone into different locations on his back. Blaith sighed deeply.

"Do you want to come in closer? I'm warm…" he held out one arm offering for her to snuggle against his body.

She was indeed cold but the idea of doing so with Blaith in the bed also made her feel awkward. "Won't you find it difficult to sleep…"

"Do you mean does my cock get hard? Because it's hard already just because it heard us talking about it… You just get kind of get used to it."

Blaith rolled over onto his back and said something in Welsh.

"What does he say?" Lux asked.

"You know what… maybe never mind for now?" Robin replied.

"I say…" Blaith began in broken English when he perceived that Robin was not repeating his words. "I'll fix it for him if it gets in the way."

Lux gasped. Blaith laughed with real enjoyment at her discomfiture. It was the first time she'd heard him laugh like that since Meredith's death. She was glad to see him indulge a moment of levity, even if it was at her expense, but his willingness to push some of the deepest taboos alarmed her like the smell of smoke alarms those who live in houses of thatch and wood.

Again, she felt the animal in them as if she'd found herself snuggled up in a wolf pack to whom the laws of man were unknown gibberish. Whatever was different between them and herself was getting smaller. Now they were no longer wolves tracking her scent in the woods, she had gone where Grandma ended up, into the belly of the wild things.

Lux helped spread the seaweeds and herbs they'd collected on their foraging mission out to dry. They had journeyed there with a small guard, even though Sariah told her that once upon a time the women were able to travel alone to the seaside looking for winter food, but the world was changing and these days it was too dangerous.

Eilish was pouring hot fat into small earthenware jars that would then become ointments when they cooled. Lux picked up after her and began to clean the utensils she'd used in the making, and the mortar and pestle she'd just used to grind the elderberry.

"It feels really good," she said, now she felt safe to do so. "To have contributed to something from the beginning through to the end of a job like this."

"Good," Eilish muttered. "Shows you can be saved."

"Eilish!" Sariah chided gently. "That's a little blunt isn't it?"

"I hope she's right," Lux said, trying to gently defend Eilish. "I don't think there's anything wrong with saying so. After all, most people who've lived off other people's work all their life as I have probably can't be saved." Lux noticed the two other women look at each other, sharing a significant glance that seemed to convey something she couldn't interpret. "What?" she whispered tremulously, a little afraid they were mocking her.

"Oh, we just see why Hob chose you, that's all. It is nothing bad at all, dear girl, quite the opposite. You've a deal of character. One would have trouble finding one girl in a million girls raised as you were who would so quickly understand and take on such new ways."

Lux blushed and looked down. She had wanted their positive regard but now Sariah had generously heaped it upon her she felt ashamed for having looked for it. "Thank you," she whispered. Keen to change the subject Lux picked up some of the rue herb. "Eilish... I wonder is there a herbal preparation I might take to prevent pregnancy?" She had some ideas of how to undo a pregnancy, something her mother had taught her, but she was not aware of how to stop it happening in the first place.

Neither woman reacted strongly to what among her former people would have been tantamount to high treason against husband, church, and race. Such a request, such an action would have nullified her entire value as an individual.

"Yes, very sensible idea. In our clan we all practice pregnancy avoidance strategies and at your age it is extra wise," Eilish replied with a shrug. It was that simple. That was all the reaction her outrageous request got from the tinker doctor, whose true thoughts Lux still felt she could only guess at. "I'll fix something for you to start taking immediately. I thought you were about to ask me for something else."

"What did you think I might ask you?" Lux asked curiously.

"I thought you might want me to knick your hymen a little so you and Hob won't need to worry whether he'll fit without tearing it."

"I've been thinking the same thing," Sariah nodded, like it was just good common sense.

Lux looked at her in in complete incomprehension and then looked back to Eilish in the same manner. She had no idea it was possible for it to fit without tearing. "*Knick it?*"

"Yes. With something very sharp so you barely feel it, rather than risk it tearing during intercourse and bleeding."

"But why?" she asked, entirely confused. Her whole life this little membrane of skin had been made out to be her most important possession, just as important as her ability to breed, a possession that would ensure her a roof over her head when she surrendered it. It was almost incomprehensible after the build up that it meant so little to them. "Does it have no meaning among your people?" she murmured.

Eilish seemed to recognise Lux's struggle and took up position on a crude driftwood stool across from Lux. "What is the point of it though? Are you worried he won't believe you? You believe him when he tells you about his level of sexual experience no doubt? And he has no magic seal on him."

"Oh, I know he would believe me…But… what would be the point in stopping it from tearing and bleeding?"

Sariah frowned in incomprehension and pity as she examined Lux's face, seemingly trying to understand just as hard as Lux was trying. She wanted to cry both from the shock of this discovery and the fact that she felt them trying so hard for her. Nobody had ever reached out for Lux's hand like this or been so patient with her.

"So that it won't hurt you so much, lass. Of course…"

Lux was still frowning and shaking her head in confusion. "But… But why? Would Robin prefer it if it doesn't hurt?"

Eilish made a choking sound as if Lux had said the strangest most inexplicable thing she could imagine. "Of course Robin would prefer it didn't hurt! But-"

"That's hardly the point, is it?" Sariah finished smoothly for her cousin as though they shared one hive-soul of which she was the more tactful part. "The point is why should you suffer it, lass? What wrong have you done, you little lamb of a thing, I ask of you? Wee thing as you are and my cousin Hob… well… he's a nicely put together lad… Why not make it easy on yourself?"

"I don't know," Lux whispered helplessly. "Maybe we are punished for Eve's sin? I don't make the rules, nor did I create the skin seal upon a virgin girl… Why would God, especially if as Robin says it is so, God is a woman, why would she make it if not for it to bleed and tear?"

Eilish looked at her like she had suddenly revealed a partially developed co-joined twin under one of her arms. After a few moments her expression changed to one of distaste at Lux's revelation. "Those aren't men. My cousin is a man and he has no need of making girls bleed to prove it. I think that Robin, who still has nightmares after witnessing his aunt's violent rape killing, would definitely prefer you didn't bleed during sex."

"Well, we should take it off right now then," Lux agreed with great conviction, even beginning to hike up her skirt in preparation, as if she'd expected Eilish to pull out her oyster-shucking knife and just slice it off right now.

Sariah smoothed her skirt back down gently and gave her an unexpected embrace. Once again Lux thought she would cry but managed to hold most of it back. Despite seeing that even the men wept freely here it was hard to get over a childhood of being punished for crying.

"Oh love… Put your poor little self away. We're not going to just have at you here in the drying shed like barbarians with a half blunt knife! We'll prepare you properly so it doesn't hurt and we'll drink mead together and talk about fucking, and laugh and it will be over before you'll know it happened."

Again, Robin found himself seeing Lux framed by the sky and sea. Her hair was like a pageboy's now. He liked the androgyny of it, the way it sat under her little elfin ears as his own had done as a boy. Those little reminders of sameness between them was always endearing to Robin. When he drew level with her he saw her worried frown. He was learning to tell the difference between Lux's concentration frown and her consternation one.

"Something worries you," he observed.

"What happens when the spring comes?"

"We rejoice?"

"I shall not miss the winter. But its exit also means my father will recommence hunting me, sending spies, and otherwise trying to capture you. It is hard to rejoice knowing he's out there."

"Trouble not your heart on that score for some time yet, cariad. With fighting set to break out between Stephen's people and Matilda's, your father is a sworn man who must rise to someone's banner in order to hold his land, yes?"

Lux made a cynical sound. "Well, he *was* someone's man. He was Henry's man, but King Henry's gone now. De Rue will wait as long as he can to pledge his sword to Stephen just in case Robert of Gloucester's forces prevail in Matilda's name. You speak about him as if he has honour… He'll lean towards Stephen to a large degree because he wouldn't well tolerate a woman in charge, but at the end of the day he is self-seeking. He will go with whoever looks like they're winning."

It thrilled Robin that he could talk about politics with Lux and he thought highly of her astute judgment on these matters. She had taught him a great deal already about the doings and structure of the Norman ruling class, including quite a who-is-who of the peerage, details he added to his mental arsenal of resistance tools for future notice. "So, if someone like De Rue isn't motivated by honour, for what does he try to punish me? Is my crime not seen by such as him as essentially an honour crime that he must avenge?"

"Not out of honour," she murmured softly. "Out of *rage*." There was something in her face at such times, when she spoke about her father that reminded him of the look he'd seen in the eyes of others like himself who had also witnessed atrocities. There was a strange calmness, a matter-of-factness when describing the crimes, in it, and in her when she would tell of the monster he was. It was a matter-of-factness that those who had not had similar experiences could mistake for callousness or even that she had not been much affected by her experiences. "Rage that one such as yourself should outsmart him, that one such as I should dare to disobey. He wants to see us both on our knees. Not for loss of honour but loss of property."

"Among my people such a one is still a boy child if he must push others down to hold himself up." Robin sniffed with contempt yet there he stopped himself. Robin tried not to appear to preach to Lux. It was hard though, as he found everything she told him about her birth family so deeply repugnant.

"Are there not slaves owned in Wales? I have heard as much." Slowly Lux was beginning to make little challenges like this in their conversations, and he was glad of it.

"When I say my people, I do not mean the whole land others call Wales. I mean my people, my blood, my family, our thread, our church. We have been separate from the others since our ancestors vowed to strike off the collars of slaves wherever we can. What I did with you… it is in our job description."

"It's remarkable your people have survived as long as you have, moving through a world where slavery is one of the supporting pillars of the structure."

Robin sighed. "Not often do we have the chance to strike off a true neck collar anymore. But to my eyes women are kept as slaves in the Norman world, they trade you for a bride price and most of the time no choice is given. Serfs are not free either. They cannot be traded from one to another location like a slave, yet they are bonded to the land, cannot leave it, do not get paid for their labour and are forced to work for their lord. I have freed a good number of such people, and no, it has not made us very popular. Doing the right thing seldom does."

"Do you view me as a liberated slave? Is that why we haven't…"

He could see the tips of her ears had turned pink, which he had learned was a signal she was either embarrassed or a topic touched her closely, somewhere in her private self he was still trying to fathom. Robin smiled and couldn't resist tweaking her blushing ear gently. "Ah, lass…" he murmured. "But you haven't asked me yet."

Lux did a double take in his direction; her first with the look of someone about to slap you and her second quizzical, as of someone considering if you may indeed be serious. "Are you serious?"

"Not entirely no, nor am I fully joking. When you come by a woman via abduction it behooves a man to be open to hearing her wishes."

"Was not what happened between us after the battle a sign of enthusiasm?" She didn't look at him when she asked, but her ear deepened to mauve. He took pity on the poor, pink and bothering organ and wished there was a way he could simply take away all the trauma layers that were between her and being able to directly reference having lovingly sucked his cock.

"Well, I have to say it made me pretty hopeful, Lux." A playful smile lingered around his mouth. "But people do crazy things in crisis situations."

Lux refused to be drawn into his attempt to lighten the heaviness. "I think we should do it soon, all of it. Before spring comes."

Robin sighed. He wanted to argue that there was no rush and try to assure her that they weren't about to die or be captured. But he didn't know that for sure, so he agreed quietly, with his body. As he took her into an embrace by degrees he tried to surround her with his warmth so that she too could partake of the lack of personal fear that he himself generally enjoyed.

# 5

The armed soldiers intercepted Augusta on her way to her mother's cottage. When she saw them she considered running, but couldn't. It was partially that she knew what her mother would say: *De Biron women don't run.* But it was also that Augusta wasn't sure if she *could* run, her legs had turned to stone like they do in bad dreams.

"What are you doing!" she cried when they grabbed her and began to forcibly march her away from her mother's home. Even while it was happening, she was vaguely horrified that she hadn't managed to catch her breath to scream and that they were able to sweep her up so easily without anyone noticing or putting up much of a fight. She had always imagined it would be different if someone physically menaced her, Augusta had seen herself fighting fiercely.

"My lord is unhappy with your mother," was all the explanation they gave her. It was all she could do to get air when they finally pulled her down and pushed her through the open door of a carriage. After they slammed and bolted the door behind her she sat on the floor while the horses started moving and the wood below started creaking, barely even cognisant of who else was there.

"I warned your mother how I deal with those who won't do what they're told," De Rue's voice said from the other end of the carriage. "And as I still haven't been able to punish my daughter, and your mother is too old for my tastes…" Augusta could hear him taking off his sword belt but she refused to look. "You will have to do."

It was clear to her what was about to happen. She had been prepared for this for some time and her mother had coached her rigorously in the survival of male violence. Nanette had never allowed Augusta to live with any illusion that their rank would protect them from it.

"In what way does my mother displease?" she asked cautiously.

"She said she would tell me when you bled, but she did not," he said, getting to his feet while he lowered the heavy belt to the ground. "I don't have a mind to be tricked by some devil bitches." As she looked up at him from her position at his feet her heart accelerated wildly. That was alright, she told herself. Fear was alright, she could use that to achieve their ends. *He will want to see that you're frightened*, her mother's voice said in her head. *Most of them can't invigorate their jaded manhood without the spice of it.* Well, she wasn't going to need to act much... "The spy that I had placed among your laundry staff informed me."

Augusta pressed her lips together firmly. "It was my maidenly modesty that forbade me mention it, my lord," she murmured, looking away in a manner she hoped was demure rather than desperate.

De Rue laughed, a quiet, insidious sort of laugh that hung just under his breath. That laugh seemed to do invasive things to her. "Maidenly modesty, huh? Well, I'm afraid I plan to outrage your maidenly modesty, Augusta."

Lux stood hesitantly on the edge of the partly frozen winter-bourne stream and looked up at the ice formation above her. Blaith jumped down onto a rock in the middle of the stream and turned around and it became fully apparent what they wanted her to do. She was already nervous and stiff enough about the crown full of lit candles she was wearing on her head! They immediately lifted her into the air.

Even though she knew it was going to happen Lux still cried out in shock at how quickly the boys lifted her up onto their shoulders. It was clear they had done this before and were very sure of not dropping her. When they adjusted their hands to lift her higher so that the candles on her head would begin the melt of the overhanging ice shelf, she was relieved it was them as the act required some fairly intimate hand placement, especially in Blaith's case.

A cacophony of bells, pipe music and tambourines began and a cheer went up. The burst of sound subsided then as if in expectation. Shortly afterwards Lux yelped with surprise and jumped when the first ice-cold droplet of water dripped down onto the back of her neck and ran down her dress. With an effort of discipline, she forced herself to straighten her back to try to keep her head even and not dislodge the candles. There was an appreciative sound from the crowd, a kind of friendly form of sadism, in response to the spectacle of the candles and the ice and her wriggles of discomfort, mixed with her will to remain dignified.

It occurred to Lux as the water really began to drip steadily and she tried to sit still, that she fully understood ritual for the first time. This was what it was, she knew, as she shivered. This physical spectacle, the held breath of the crowd, the heady mixture of identification, sadism, and lust. Yes, there was lust involved in this ritual too, that much was clear. If there wasn't, why did the boys lifting her need to have their shirts off in this cold weather? And why did they cheer louder when the freezing cold water soaked down over her breasts and she squealed in shock at the rush?

Her body sprung awake with her rigid nipples and like the land when spring would eventually come. It was impossible to think much when you were wearing nothing but a white shift sticking wet to your skin, live flame on your head, and liquid ice was running down your cleavage to pool between your legs. When Blaith readjusted his hands and his thumb almost penetrated her through her clothes, Lux jumped again, this time enough to put out the last candle.

Bran stepped forward then and helped to lift her out of the steadily dripping frozen waterfall, Blaith removed the crown. Robin had leapt over onto the bank and Bran and Blaith were lifting her into his arms. She was passed down off their shoulders into his arms awkwardly, so that her wet limbs made an inordinate amount of contact with his naked upper body. It felt like they might have done it on purpose. One of her exposed knees was against Robin's chest and the other around his waist as he struggled to properly take hold of her slippery wet body. Instinctually, not wishing to fall she took hold of his waist with her knees, just as she would have done to avoid coming off a horse. A few people made a sound she couldn't quite describe even whilst she knew what it meant.

"Like catching hold of a landed salmon," he laughed as he caught her up, so he was now supporting her under her upper thighs in a very suggestive manner. Her arms went rapidly around his neck to steady herself and then she blushed because people were looking. Lux was now flushing furiously. Robin didn't put her down immediately. He let her body settle there on his hips as if he could hold her like that all day. It was a casual display of core strength and there was no sign of shyness in him. He allowed her to drop down just low enough that she felt the rub of his belt buckle between her legs.

"Is this why you took pains in teaching me to ride a horse astride?"

"Capturing your horse wouldn't have been sporting otherwise," Robin shot back. His horse snorted and pawed the ground in a tetchy way. She stopped circling him as she could sense it was agitating his mount.

"Where does the custom come from?"

"It is said the women started it. It's how we prove we're fast and bat-shit crazy enough to bed a Twll Du woman and keep up with her on the road."

"What's this about bat-shit crazy?" Sariah asked as she rode up. "You aren't giving away our tactics to the enemy are you, Lux?" she asked with a wink.

Lux laughed. "No. Robin was just informing me about the origins of the bride capture."

"Did he tell you how often we have to slow down to let them catch us?" Eilish asked as she rode up next to Sariah. "Blaith could never capture Sariah's horse, lucky he doesn't mind being ridden astride himself!"

"See what I mean, Lux?" Robin grinned, indicating Sariah's entire person-age as he did. "You can see how it got started right here, no?"

Men of Lux's people would have taken Sariah's and Eilish's words as a full on challenge to their manhood and would never have allowed a fair competition. Not every Norman insisted on women riding sidesaddle like her father. Those who did insist put women at an immediate disadvantage, and then would use the evidence as signs of the inferiority of female horsemanship. Here, in this strange new world, Robin responded to Sariah like her banter was fun. It almost seemed like their competitiveness had a certain sexual charge to it. Here most of the chemistry between people looked sexually charged, even Robin's with Blaith.

Sariah beckoned for the other two women to bring their horses up close. "Okay, so what I'm thinking is we ride Lux out like a guard of honour at a hard gallop, in formation with Lux at the front and centre. Then we come back around and do a ride by, kick some dirt up and get our tits out."

"Hard-ons will make it more awkward for them to ride," Eilish agreed. "Let's flash our breasts at them during the first ride-by where we present her."

"You don't have to do the flashing part, Lux."

"Good!" Lux replied with a nervous laugh.

"Let's see how good he is, shall we?" Sariah said.

Robin's smile was slow to form, and came up from somewhere around his heart. *How could any man worth his salt prefer the tamed and broken creatures they turn their women into over that... that force of nature... that eruption?* He thought, as he watched the women's horses go pounding past, riding so hard and close that you felt it in your chest, the proximity to the powerful animal's galloping. The danger of it *was* the sex.

Sariah's locks flew out behind her and Eilish's hair jingled, as it was full of tiny bells. Lux was but a streak of light in her white dress and her hair now flaxen again with the dye faded out by the sun. All three of them were moving so fast you barely saw them. When he'd tried to explain bride capture to Lux in words it was lacking a great deal. You had to understand it in your red blood through sensory knowing. They were drawing close to the holy wild forces of life and death, with it the dizzy sex, risk, and possible death in the air.

Robin laughed exuberantly when Sariah and Eilish stood up in their stirrups and bared their breasts. How he loved them! Both of them had taught him so much growing up and he adored their aliveness, revelled in their boldness, took pride in it as though he sourced his own strength from it. He didn't know how to explain to outsiders that a man couldn't remain strong unless he sourced his own freedom and happiness from the equal freedom and happiness of his people. If any one among them was hurt or oppressed then that happened to him too, their bodies were part of his body and his theirs. There was no *us*, and no *them*, only *we*.

Blaith whistled in loud appreciation of their breasts and there was a stirring cheer. For Robin the display made him feel emotional more than aroused. It made his throat choke up and his chest burn with pride to see that he and his fellows were still man enough to ride beside women like these, when so few were any longer. Out of his blood kin Robin had seen the most of what it was like inside the hedge, where the women lived in fear of their own men.

"Those are some pretty breasts," Jack acknowledged. "But it will take more than that to throw you off, I'll warrant."

"Do you have ice water in your veins, man?" Blaith murmured. "I've forgotten my own first name."

It was good to hear Blaith with a little banter in him. Jack snorted and shook his head with a smile and some mild contempt. "That's young men for you. Hard cock all the time and a brain only half the time till you're thirty. That's the truth of it."

"Let's go, then!" he said, kicking his horse into an almost immediate gallop.

Blaith made a high-pitched ululation of a hunting cry in his throat, letting the girls know they were coming. Jack sent out a very realistic wolf howl, which echoed out across the valley. Huge and ancient animal powers stalked that valley suddenly, hunting, gliding, locking horns, preparing to rut... One half of Robin was part of that red swirling blood magic. His hips, which he

170

believed belonged more to his mother's side, did most of the horse riding for him.

She wanted the clan to be impressed, to think she rode more bravely than they had imagined she would. It didn't matter anymore that tears were streaming down her face. It didn't matter that who she really was was showing. Finally, she was showing the daring girl she really was.

As Robin drew alongside her. He tried to pull in front of her but his horse balked and reared, then cavorted on its back legs as she wheeled to the right. There was a collective gasp from the whole Twll Du clan as they rushed forward to see if Robin would come unseated. When Lux tried to circle her horse around it resisted her, pawed the ground and finally reared also. She held on tight with her legs and arms. *If you fall now, they will forever think you the one not fit to ride beside him.* Almost as soon as that was over the animal was pig rooting violently under her, vastly unnerved by the behaviour of Robin's horse.

Lux thought she would be thrown but her horse settled. She sat there still in the saddle, panting furiously, her breast heaving much as her mount's was. Robin was standing in front of her horse, whispering to the mare. The sense of stark danger fell away. She went to him and put her nose in his hands and he gently took her bridle. All of Robin's people made a collective 'awww' sound, as if this magic were sweet rather than terrifying.

Robin blew in the horse's nose, made eye contact with her, finally their foreheads touched, and he slowly went down to his knees taking the mare down with him. The hair on the backs of Lux's arms was standing on end. The audience clapped at his skill and whistled as he handed Lux out of the saddle, a bare moment before her horse simply lay down at his feet.

"I lay my weapons at your feet Lux De Rue, as your horse has lain down for me."

# 6

"re you alright?" Blaith asked, as soon as Robin entered his tent.

"I have some nerves, I'll own it."

Blaith embraced him. Robin was a lot of things to a lot of people, some of them seemingly contradictory: wanted man, no rules fighting champion, holy healer with the faerie touch… One thing he was to very few people was a lover. "You know what you're doing with a woman's body better than most men married forty years. Sariah and I have taught you well."

"I'm not nervous about that, it's how she was raised…"

"Your instinct is probably to treat her with kid gloves because she was ill treated by her father. You probably think to be very different to the men of her people and give her all the power in the act. As if she will be safer that way. But that would be a misstep, as she is so far from being ready she can't even see the shape of her own desire yet. You will need to tease, and coax it out, yes, but also to demand it out, to use the demon of perversity against itself.

"She has been raised to respond to men's demands, to believe she will belong to her husband. Hell, you might say she's been *bred* that way. She will believe that is how being fucked is going to be for her because all her foremothers have been sold and fucked in this manner for generations. They are all in Lux, those other women and their bodies, and the men who perpetrated the abuses are there also, and you can't ignore that either.

"But you will know how to make the poison into medicine because you will demand she free her sex from their control. And, as the ancestors tell it: what you set free sets you free. For what you do with her must be like a game she can stop at any time. Just as sparring is not real violence for one may tap out. All the while as she is opening herself to her own pleasure, and it will feel blameless, like it truly is, because she will be doing it to obey you and your needs."

Robin was silent for a while after he finished. It was rare for Blaith to speak so much in one go, but when he did he always had solid gold to deliver. Robin was usually so quick, as a thinker and learner, when something slowed him down for some deep consideration you knew something had really hit deeply.

"You are a genius whisperer of the human animal, old friend." Robin inclined his head to his brother and touched his forehead in respect.

Blaith smiled. "And you, cariad, are a natural lover. Fear nothing, show her how she might do the same."

When Robin entered the hut Lux covered her breasts with her shawl. It was a knee-jerk response to the sheer night slip the women had dressed her in after the ritual ablutions, and bad associations with men entering the bedchamber without knocking. The last thing she wanted him to think was that she was afraid of him, yet she was afraid of him. It was too soon yet to associate male virility and strength with anything other than fear.

Lux was standing in what appeared to her little more than a wood shed or outbuilding at best, the sort of place her father might have left a bound captive he meant to deal with later, gave the scene an intimidating visage. Granted someone had tied together some hay bales and covered them in furs to resemble a bed. She appreciated the flowers and the fresh herbs strewn around, but it didn't change the fact she was about to be deflowered over straw bale. It was much like how she'd been told an abduction by wild men would play out.

When she made eye contact with him his eyes were burning like they were glass revealing a fierce inner fire. His chest was bare under the wolf's skin around his shoulders. He paused at the door to remove both his boots and his weapons. Lux understood that by the standards of his own culture he was a well-mannered wolf, but he was a wolf, nonetheless. The lupine glint of wildness was there in his eye, seen better in the half-light than in the day.

He took a couple of steps towards her. Underneath all the matters of class and race that sat between them there was more. Into this chamber she carried the weight of shame, and he did not. That was what made his flame so bright.

"Show me," he said, his eyes trailing down over her wet hair that stuck to her throat and lingering where the cloth clung to her breasts. She didn't dare do otherwise than he said. Her hands were trembling, so instead of lowering the material, she lost hold of it altogether. It fell to the floor in a gesture far more provocative than she had intended. Taking another step towards her he pulled down her shift to reveal her breasts.

She gasped. Though she had ridden harder than ever in her life before during the capture she passionately hoped he liked what he saw. "Do I please you?"

He didn't answer immediately, instead he pulled the clothing down till it fell off. Robin spent some time observing every inch of her with exquisite attention to detail that she squirmed.

"You please me, Lux." His tone had something mysterious simmering under the surface of it, perhaps mild amusement at her question. "Turn around."

As soon as she did she could feel his breath against her, though he didn't touch her immediately. Finally, he moved her hair and kissed the back of her neck, twisting it in his grasp. She jumped when his hands took possession of her breasts. He made an immediate low sound in the bottom of his throat, coupled with him pressing his hard-on against her lower back.

Being the fingers of an archer and a harpist, his touch was not exactly soft in texture yet it was *awake* and buzzing with awareness. He lived in his hands in a way that Lux had only really learned to live in her head, and it was as if his hands were calling to her to join him.

When he turned her around to kiss her mouth she kept her eyes closed so she could see who he was better. While they kissed, Lux fought with a rising emotion that threatened to overwhelm her. Somehow without him having said a word she knew, just from his kiss, that Robin *saw* her too. Not just as a woman, as the sex that mankind had made goods and chattel of, but the way she saw him, as a complex many-layered being, immortal in nature.

"What do you want me to do?" she whispered.

"I'll tell you when I want you to do something."

Her stomach quavered in a strange half-weak flutter. She didn't understand her response to his tone of quiet command. She was embarrassed by it. Wasn't she meant to be a rebel, a refuser of men's commands? He moved her backwards two steps and sat her down on the hay bales.

Obediently her body laid backwards on the bed in the expectation of being mounted. Instead, he went down on his knees and began to lick her with animalistic enjoyment. The pleasure was intense, but thick layers of disgust at her own wetness, lay between her and fully surrendering to it. As if he sensed this he stopped and undid his belt. Lux looked away when his cock appeared in his hand and then looked shyly back.

He smiled at her as he pulled her by her hips to the very edge of the bed. "I don't think I can wait any longer."

She found herself thinking of all the hardships his body had endured over winter to protect them, put food in their bellies and fight against the cold with firewood. How he had saved her life. The feeling of service cleaved her open as surely as his member. Finally, this moment… There was no pain when he entered. The ecstasy of the surrender was more than she was prepared for. Here she was, on her back with her legs spread wide with a tinker man's cock inside her.

After a while he withdrew. She nervously put her legs back together. This deviated from the script she was familiar with. In that story the man would claim her and the finalisation of that act was the filling of her with his seed. That was what made the act sanctioned in the eyes of God -not that Lux worded it to herself like this."Did I displease?" she all but whimpered. The shame she would feel in displeasing him in this intimate way would be so much fiercer than anything her father had ever managed to make her feel.

175

"Bend over," he instructed her, without any reassurance beyond the warm tone in his voice. Robin ran his hand up her back applying a slow but steady pressure as his hand climbed her spine, until she had to put her hands on the bed to steady herself. "That's it," he said, his enjoyment clear in his voice.

Lux had another rush of the thrill she felt whenever she realised she was serving him. He frustrated her inbuilt attempt to bend over in the most modest way possible, by using his foot to push her legs further apart and lifting her hips higher with his hands.

He ran his thumb and forefinger firmly up and down her spine before settling his hands on her bottom. The sound he made while he did it reminding her a little of one of the secret sounds he made to skittish horses, but it was followed by something between a groan and a grunt of intense appreciation. As he ran his hands down, his thumbs opened and parted her womanhood. Now that the maidens had widened her hymen it didn't sting or burn.

Robin seemed to be examining and appreciating her for no other reason than that he liked looking at her secret parts, and that he could. Lux was blushing hot by the time he was done.

"Mmm," he murmured, running his fingers inside her. "Good girl." His tone was approving and almost impressed sounding, as if she had done something wonderful. She was utterly overcome. Lux trembled with the joy of his praise. This celebration of her body and its responses thrilled her like solar warmth thrills a plant long denied the sun. He moved his forefinger and middle finger out along the circumference of her vagina until he had her labia spread wide as it could go, before relaxing the pressure and resting for a few moments on the spot where her pleasure seemed to centre.

"Do you want to be fucked now?" he asked, as his fingers languidly tormented her in tiny flickers of movement.

Lux made a quiet, quavering sound that came from the bottom of her throat. It seemed to ripple through the river water that lived in her flesh like an asrai had issued a wet cry of protest against the merciless gaze of his light.

"But I... but I... I don't..." How could she word that she didn't know how to say that, or even how to feel that? "I want you to do whatever you want," she whispered shyly. In saying that she felt twice as exposed as before.

"Is that so?" he murmured, almost under his breath but with a deep smoky quality in his voice. "Put your knees on the bed then," he said, pushing the backs of her legs with his knees to demonstrate. She crawled up onto the bed and he ran his hand hard up her spine again. "That's it, head down." He didn't stop pressing her shoulders until her face was in the furs. Her legs quivered when she felt his belt against her bottom.

She received the head of his cock -nudged inside her hard but not pressed all the way home. At once it seemed he conquered her utterly. In another sense it was not he who mastered her, but the water inside her, the rising and gushing out at all the cracks. She was water and water cannot be hurt.... Pierce it, break it, enter it slow or fast and it reforms just the same. Lux only pulled up short when he parted her bottom and his thumb slid into it touching her in a place she had not expected to be touched. "What are you doing?" she gasped.

"Whatever I want. Is that still what you want?" As he asked this, one of his fingers that were already wet with her fluids went a little deeper. She cried out softly. He made another of his sounds of enjoyment. Lux was embarrassed by the excitement she felt in taking whatever he chose to do to her.

"I asked you a question, Lux."

"Yes, Sir!" she managed to gasp. "Yes."

Robin laughed quietly. "I have many names," he whispered. "But I'm nobody's sir."

"I'm sorry!" She panted.

Without warning he gave her a lightly stinging smack on the bottom with his other hand.

"Don't ever say sorry when my cock's inside you."

"S... Yes, Robin."

"That's a command, alright?" She bit down on her lip. "Do you understand?"

"Yes!"

He slowly removed his hand and leaned down over her to fuck her more deeply. As he did, he gave the back of her neck a soft bite. For some reason it rushed through her mind right then that she hadn't yet experienced the most exposing part of the defloration. In the morning she would have to step out among people and be seen, while she tried not to walk funny. Whether she managed to walk like her hips weren't looser or not, everyone would know what had been done to her the night before, and probably even have some ability to guess the details.

"I love you so hard, Lux," he whispered from just behind her ear. It wasn't too many thrusts after that where she began to melt into the sensation of serving his body with hers, of being taken, of being his, of being willing to walk out there before all the world with her proudly ravaged holes.

Lux came rushing up to the door of a climax full of liquid legs and sobbing sounds where she couldn't seem to get enough air in for the wind serpent to chase the raging fire of it up her spine. Whatever that rising power that burst into her head was it trampled her to the ground and ruined her, like Mary and the serpent.

"Good girl," she kept hearing him whisper, even while she came so violently that her teeth locked down and her back bucked in his grip like a wild horse pig rooting. It felt like some secret door in the back of her head yawned open and power entered her like a needle in the brain. "That's it. Give me everything." He said holding her firmly by the back of her neck as he fucked her giddy and limp. "*This* is what most pleases me. I want to see all that is hidden of you. Yes… oh that's right… My good girl…"

There were storms inside Robin the night he and Lux lay together, great surging subterranean ones that caught him off guard. They were the type with winds you hear driving over the moors for minutes before they arrive. Blaith had been cunning in his suggestion for healing Lux's bruised sex, the advice had brought him here to receive a witnessing of himself as weather event. He hadn't consciously known how much he'd enjoy being firm like that with her.

178

The more it aroused her the more he inhabited the role her desire assigned him.

His drive was strong one, so he knew how, and where, and at what pace, he wanted to fuck. Lux on the other hand wanted to take it like he decided to give it. He understood her need to take something toxic she had beaten into her and reclaim it for her own pleasure. For her the crooked-turning of this demon of the flesh was about gender. But for Robin it was a class upending, the overturning of the social order, with the outlaw able to take the daughter of a noble house. Never in his life had he looked at a Norman woman and thought about bending her over. Yet now that he was doing it he was intoxicated.

He occupied the fantasy that he had abducted her, and here he was taking her virgin cunny in a woodshed, while she was discovering she was not above him but equal as are all animals in the savage kingdom outside the walls. When he stepped into the role he felt an immediate response from her body. There was some part of her that could tell what fairytale they inhabited together. The sense of this non-verbal communication was deeply intimate.

For the first time he didn't suspect these feelings in himself. Even his inner boy who had made very strict rules for his future man after *It* happened wasn't angry with him. Because what he was doing had taken her outside of herself, or outside of the self her people had falsely erected over her half-faerie soul. In his culture Robin had been taught that pleasure was a sign of the goodness of something. He cherished the trust involved in being allowed to hear the shy flesh-voice of hers and telling him things vaguely like: *more* and *harder*.

He wanted to fuck her hips open, to stretch out her whole pelvic cradle so that while she was she might also have her centre of life move down again into the place they had made taboo. There was enormous pleasure to be felt in pounding her like this, and of gently coaxing her to the place where her body would let him do it. Robin felt it as if he were carving her out for herself, giving her more room where she'd been tied up too tight. So that she would welcome her own wild woman, the kind of woman who could ride beside him through the halls of hell where he was headed. He was carving her out for them both.

Finally, when he had filled her and covered her with his seed, he pulled her by her arms until she was sitting up looking at him. For the first time he looked at and acknowledged the small dark mark on her outer left hand finger that distinguished her as one of the devil's company. He'd left it up to her to mention it because generally speaking initiation could be a private matter between the neophyte and the initiator. Blaith had of course told him it had happened but until now he and Lux had not discussed it. He moved in close and gave her swollen, pink nipples two long sucks.

"Is this how the devil did it when you met him at the crossroads?" he asked.

For a moment she could see her hesitation, how she feared briefly that he was jealous or angry with her. But she read the warmth in his flirtation correctly, seeing that he was instead turned on by it.

"Yes," she replied. "You and your brother have a few similar techniques."

"You're watching me sleep," Sariah murmured sleepily, as she rolled in Blaith's direction and opened her eyes slightly. Her tone was somewhere between accusative and affectionate. "I can feel you boring your way through me, how is anyone meant to sleep during that?"

"Easily enough from what I can tell. You sleep through it night after night. I watch you for hours."

Usually after someone had lain with Blaith they felt soporific enough to sleep through floods and earth tremors. Sariah had always had a special gift for nourishing people sexually though. After Blaith made love to someone he always felt like staying awake half the night, so watching his loved ones sleep was a regular activity for him.

"Well, you do always give me a bit of exercise when I share your bed," she observed.

"It is true. I enjoy being ridden by you."

She reached out for him, so he moved closer to allow her to rest her head against his bare chest. He loved the mixture of woad and myrrh ointment that always clung to her locks and the way her skin smelt when tinged with wood smoke. Ever since he'd been capable of a reliable erection the smell of her had been enough to give him one. It was also pleasant how she didn't seem to see his needs as any different to any other man's, as if his intimacy with the death current were no different to any other inclination or sexual practice.

When she looked at him Blaith knew she saw his out-of-the-way tastes to be just another charming diversity of nature among a colourful tapestry of humans being sexual and needing love. For all his knowledge and power, especially regarding the realm of the dead, he was still awed by her natural wisdom about life. It had been she, although she was his junior by a tiny margin, who had taught him most about love, life, women's bodies, men's bodies, and his own erotic potential. In his people's reckoning those things counted for a lot more than they did inside the walls. Those were the kind of things that keep you going on the long winter nights without much food and comfort, as the wild men of the hedgerows live.

He kissed the top of her head rather thoughtfully and slowly, though didn't explain to her why he did it just then, or what he was thinking while he did so. Such feelings weren't really wordable for Blaith. Usually when he did speak about his own inner workings he would say something tangential to the main point that nonetheless stood in for it. "Yet you do not tire of me."

"How could I? You give me so much heart-centre nourishment, Blaith."

"It's kind of you to say so."

She was a prodigy in the art of love in the way Robin was with the bow, and if she couldn't make him feel better no one could.

"It's not kindness," she said, rolling away and propping herself up on her elbow. "It's truth."

"From my heart centre?" he asked, his eyebrows jumped skeptically. "Would that be next to or in front of the great sucking void that also lives there?"

She just smiled lovingly at him, her eyes filled with a glimmering warmth that he imagined was designed by the gods to tell whatever man she looked upon that he was not only adequate, but perfect, beautiful, whole, and just as nature intended him…

"Next to, besides, dancing together, perhaps -the void and the warm, rich human heart in you." She leaned in and kissed him. Even her pecks on the face carried erotic, lingering warmth that just inherently made you feel good. "Perhaps they're making love even," she suggested, drawing back to look at him. "Yes, I think that's how it works. The black void in your chest makes love with your red heart. They circle each other, and cross over each other, pulsating and breathing together in unison, love and destruction, making that thick, hot music in your flesh."

"I do believe that the eagles accidentally dropped some of their poetic honey under your tongue, in between when they were busy hiding it in your cunny," he observed with some seriousness.

She laughed and poked her tongue out at him. "Oh yes, I am the very *awenydd* of fucking!" He began to laugh. "The poet of the fucking-world, or the fucking-poet of the world? Will you remember me thus at my last rites, Magister? Poet of fucking, cock hound, and curer of the malady of chastity?"

"I would certainly remember you thus, Sariah," he replied quite seriously. "But I will never out live you." The certainty with which he delivered this took away a little something from her smile. *Like I always do, wilting the edges of the flower.* It was clear she didn't want to consider this fact, so she took the conversation down the path of pleasure instead.

"What do you think Hob is doing to Lux right now and how much do you think she likes it?"

Blaith smiled despite himself. His brother's happiness always spilled over easily into his. "I'd say he's filling her out good and proper, from behind, I'm guessing."

"Oh, she will get a surprise! Don't their people only do it with the man on top and the woman on her back?"

Blaith nodded, this he knew was indeed part of the torturously basic sex-

182

ual life of the settler. "She'll be getting some surprises alright. But you may be assured she likes them."

"How could you not?" she murmured, straddling him, as if the visualisation she now had of Robin and Lux fucking made it imperative she ground off against him. Blaith undid his trousers. If she was going to do that she may as well do it on his cock. He released his arms at his sides, as if in crucifixion-pose. The first moment of sliding up inside Sariah in this position was always one of pure joy unmixed with suffering. When her hips above him his hips became a whirlwind of red snakes, these were the moments for knowing god.

"Make me come alive again," he whispered to her, as together they carried out this act, this moment of levity. "Fuck me to life."

# 7

Augusta could never remember afterwards whether she screamed when she saw because everything went silent. There had been the sound of her sobbing breath, as she'd run down the stairs when she heard her brother's men. She could remember the shouting and the drawing of swords. Silence had fallen at the point where she rounded the edge of the doorway to see the last motion of her brother cutting down De Rue's son.

The look on Rowan De Biron's face was almost as shocked as hers. Outraged, as her brother was, you could tell he hadn't expected to win. Geoff De Rue was almost as feared as a fighter and vicious of reputation as his father. His had been one of the leering faces. Nobody had ever suggested that Rowan was anything more than a green boy just filling out his dead father's sword-belt. Augusta kept moving forward even afterwards, her own torn clothing and bruising no longer noticed, to try to see if the young man lived.

De Rue fell to his knees beside his son and heir, wrenching his head up off the flagstones while he choked up his own life in a dark rush of blood. It was impossible to say what De Rue was saying other than 'no, no, no', as his son bled out in front of him. Augusta didn't care about that. Geoff wasn't the first person she'd watched die. The reason the sound had gone was Rowan. Augusta was waiting for his death. Her brother had killed De Rue's boy, and now he was going to die.

She had never really noticed that she loved her brother until this moment where he had appeared to place his body between herself and her tormentor. Suddenly in response her body was hurtling through space to try to get between him and De Rue's sword. But the assault on Rowan never came. The intensity of the moment passed and gradually Augusta could hear De Rue's voice again.

"I just can't believe it," he muttered, still holding his son's head. "The only thing of any worth I've ever created… The one living son among all those useless and expensive daughters…Taken down like a guileless peasant bitch with a wooden sword by a boy…"

In truth De Rue sounded more exhausted and defeated than he did grief stricken or angry. His son's death seemed like an opportunity to rail against God's injustices towards him personally. He wasn't even going to kill Rowan…

"Rowan!" she cried, bursting into tears as she ran into her brother's arms. "Oh God I'm so glad you're here. Take me home!" She wept against his shoulder. At first, she was just too relieved that he was here to notice how gingerly he handled her. But it crept through into her awareness gradually.

She stepped back from him and gazed into his face. It was like a punch in the stomach, the realisation that it was distaste she was seeing in his eyes, not compassion, not fraternal identification. As if *she* were the monster rather than the man who did it to her. He shook his head ruefully. "If only I'd been able to get here in time before you dishonoured our family," he said, sounding to Augusta as though he'd arrived to find her already killed.

"But… but… I'm not dead, Rowan. Just…"

"-Dishonoured," He completed for her, patting her arm with that same gingerly touch. "Has he married you?"

"Don't say that, Ro," she said softly, wheedling, hoping to obtain mercy through supplication.

"I'm sorry," he said, throwing his hands up in a helpless kind of way. "There's nothing I can do if he did."

"I've wed her," De Rue said. "She's a girl of good blood and I bedded her, so I've wedded her."

"You ravished her," Rowan muttered, his tone sounding petulant rather than deeply upset. *He was ready to kill or die for me only minutes ago!* Now she

185

was just an embarrassment to cover up however was convenient, no longer his sister, no longer a person…

"We could argue that all day," De Rue said, his attempt at an affable smile on his face as he walked towards his son's killer like he was about to do a business deal. "It doesn't really change anything. Your sister finds herself embarrassed of a hymen and I have made an honest woman of her."

"Your son…"

De Rue threw his hands up. "It could not be called other than a fair fight. And if Geoff could be cut down by a lad of your age, well! What are you, lad? A bare seventeen if you're lucky?"

"I'm sixteen."

The whole time they were speaking Augusta's breathing was just getting faster and louder and she couldn't seem to control it. All she could hear was her frantic breath and the thumping in the vein in her temple. All she could smell was the blood in the air and their small talk was starting to sound like bees buzzing, and the buzzing was becoming shards of glass trying to get in behind her eyeballs.

"Well, I'd be happy to think of you as my son till your sister makes me a new one."

It was probably because the gesture looked so casual that Rowan didn't react at all when she drew his hip dagger out of his belt. But in truth he hardly had time to half-heartedly reach for her arm and smile before she'd buried the blade in his chest. Her mother always told her to remember that it takes a damn lot of force to drive a knife through a man's chest cavity. More than you would think. As he gazed at her with wide stupid dying eyes, she pulled the knife back out with a full-throated cry of effort and will.

As Rowan went down on his knees Augusta stepped behind his body, placing it between her and De Rue. She made eye contact with De Rue while she grabbed a handful of Rowan's dark curly hair (so like her own) and opened his throat onto the flagstone floor. All she could think from the moment she'd rent his heart in two was: *now we're even.*

186

De Rue just starred at what she had done as if he had no context within which to place this experience of female violence. Her hand trembled with rage as she raised her fresh-blooded dagger in De Rue's direction. It wasn't even her that cried the words but the combined voice of the terrible furies of the Underworld, and hundreds of wronged women. Upon him that voice seemed to call a blood sea of eyeless horrors.

"You're next!"

"Eilion?"

"Yes."

"That's not your face, yet I see you. I could pick you out among a hundred who looked just like you."

The young man's face that he was wearing smiled softly, poignantly. Robin found it strangely familiar and frowned as he tried to remember who the boy reminded him of? Was this the face he'd been trying to remember, or forget? Had it happened yet or was it still to happen?

"I am not to be got like that, I'm afraid," Eilion replied. "Though I know it is storied that my sisters must be picked out in such a manner among one hundred who look just like them, but that is the wrong fairytale for me unfortunately."

"What is yours?"

"You are Pwyll to my Rhiannon."

"What? Then I only need to stop spurring my horse? I only need to ask instead? Then I ask!"

"Do you? Can you? Most human men spend a lifetime just learning how to ask. I don't think you even dare believe it's possible enough to ask for it."

"I want to believe it," he whispered.

Suddenly Eilion was behind him, up very close. Robin didn't need to turn around to know that. "Then just believe in the possibility of me. Give me the holy risk of that."

"I'm afraid to."

"Then you must conquer it."

"It's not that easy!"

"I didn't say it was easy!" It was the first time Eilion had ever raised his voice to him. "I'm saying you're strong enough for it. *You can become Him.*"

Slowly but decisively, Robin turned to face Eilion. He was standing face to face with a young man of about his own age. The boy was attractive, but more cute and interesting looking than beautiful, and yet… Robin frowned. "Why is this human skin you've stolen so familiar to me?"

"The wind has started blowing backwards."

"What does that mean?"

"It's means you're seeing things that haven't happened yet."

"Who is he? Who is the Puck? My family say I'm an emanation of his but I'm not him all of the time."

"Yet."

"What do you mean?"

"You're not him all the time *yet.*"

"If you mean…" Robin paused for a moment as he felt the pieces in a puzzle coming together in his mind.

"Keep going," Eilion prompted.

"If the wind is blowing backwards through me as well as through the wood…"

Eilion smiled with a subtle satisfaction in it. "And here in this moment it becomes clear to me that the human brain can indeed be modified to comprehend its own potential godhood."

Part of Robin felt like Eilion was still talking in riddles, but another half had leapt well ahead already. "He's who I become, isn't he? That's what an emanation is, isn't it? An echo coming at us backward through time. The god is our full realisation point. We are them in process, mirrored back from this world of incompletion, allowing completion to be truly whole through union with the incomplete, the innately broken…"

The thought seemed to harrow up his soul for a moment. But the practical, warrior heart of him won out quickly. "There must be a key that I can trick, or steal, to make me capable of what you ask."

"You have more bravery already than you realise," the young man whispered. "All you need to do is be calm in my presence and ask for what you want from The Weaver. Although she seems cruel and vicious from where you're standing, it is she who can set us both free." The boy whispered this like it was a secret that must be kept from the night itself. "Though great hardships will be asked of us if we are to obtain this, it can be done with Lux's help, if you will give me your serenity and your most dreadful risk."

"The only way I could imagine being able to be calm in your presence would be if somehow I could be made to forget how I feel when we're together."

The words felt naked in the air. Robin wondered if this was what it felt like for Lux when he brought her body fully open and exposed her desire?

"I am quite the glamour-lord you realise, Robin? I probably could make you forget anything you wanted to."

"If it would help I'd let you do it. Even though my people say never to taste from the Well of Oblivion."

"One day it might be necessary, if we are to ever break this cruel spell we are all under. And on that day I will drink it with you. But for now you must remember everything as clearly as possible." Eilion moved closer still then. Robin could feel the cold fizz of Eilion's power up and down his own body from head to toe. "Because you must get ready to fight for your life now, and those of your loved ones," he whispered, very softly near Robin's skin.

"What should I do? Having learned what De Rue has done to another innocent girl I see I have two clear options before me and only two. Fight or flight?"

"Fight," Eilion replied immediately. "If flight were an option I'd urge you to it, but he will run your family to ground pursuing Lux. He is out of all children save her now, and he has just lost the boy bartered for his own life against a curse that seeks somewhere to roost. There are less and less roads open to you with the war in England as it is. As it stands in the weave there is one way through this for you, and only one. You need to get De Rue to agree to meet you in single combat."

Robin smiled and he felt his wolf bare its teeth more so than a smile denoting happiness. "I can't imagine anything I'd prefer to do with De Rue than meet him in single combat but he would never agree to it. He would see it as beneath him to face a man such as myself. It's what they always say when they're afraid they'll lose."

"Then you must twist him around to it with your word-cunning, for elsewise why have we invested so heavily in that skill with you? You must word-weave it so there is more shame in the refusal than the acquiescence. He is only human, after all. They are very forceful like iron and very cruel, and not always so exceptionally dim-witted either, but the moment you make them angry or dint their ego somehow they lose all ability to reason and will do anything to regain face. That is your key. Let Puck put it in the lock. It's time to upset the social order, dearly beloved. It's the beginning of your long moment. The one you were born for."

Robin stopped beside the wolf pit and gazed down. Something hurt in an ache that went all the way from his guts down to his balls, and yet he was partially numb when it came to watching the end of the world as he knew it. The forest laws had been the beginning of the end for anyone trying to live off hunting. Slowly those laws were turning his people into thieves as much as hunters. A pit had never appeared so close to the wild lands before...

"Maybe they... *we*...humans... are just bad," he murmured to himself aloud. But as he gazed down at the partly decomposed body of his forebear of fur and fang his eyes narrowed. A quiet but steady determination began to take form within him. He couldn't name his determination and he knew it was about as far from rational as any impulse could get. *No.* That was all there was, just one word. It carried far-reaching consequences. Within it was the seed of a resistance he knew neither word nor deed for, only that it came from the core of who he was and he would die standing for it.

Taking out the piece of parchment in his pocket he stood there and fingered the message without opening it. He thought about the folklore that had built up around him. The idea that you only needed to call out 'Robin Goodfellow' three times and he'd come for you, for better or worse. Robin wondered how many desperate young people had tried it across the country only for nothing to happen.

*How can I make it true? There must be a way. It's happened a few times where I think I really did know. I knew the night I found Sorcha. I was alone in the forest and it was quiet and something on the wind tasted like someone needed help... But to do it I have to do more of what I did with Lux, not less. And there are some among our number who in fear wish to shut tight that radical door of freedom we have stood for. What are we if not breakers of chains who melt them down to fix things?*

Finally, he opened the scroll of parchment and perused the message he'd written. It was a commitment to being Him, that's what it was. Even if being Him meant the death of this body. Robin knew this was part of a thread leading to what Eilion called his long moment. If he did this he was making another move he'd never be able to retract. He was taking a step towards living on a scale that most people only fantasise about with a mixture of dread and excitement. It was a thumbing of his nose at a force that had the potential to roll right over him without even noticing his resistance.

Nonetheless, for all the people out there crying out 'Robin Goodfellow!' into the darkness because nobody else came to help when they needed it. He would make his great act of defiance for them, that way he could hold their pride for them until they had the chance to take it back. For all the frightened people who had too much to lose and had to say 'yes, my lord' he would say: *No.* He'd learnt since childhood that his people had no right to that word. His people had not had their opinion asked any more than the axe asks for the wishes of the tree, yet this time that wall of steel and stone with greedy humans hiding behind it would be forced to hear their voice in his voice. They would hear his voice not because he had learned to wield steel, but because he'd learned to wield language.

*From Robin Dhu to Geoffrey De Rue*

*I was more than a little disappointed with the quality of your henchmen last autumn, as I have often had cause to be with Norman manhood. My interactions with your race suggest you are only fond of killing women and children, being too cowardly to fight anyone who might potentially be able to fight back. For this reason, I strongly doubt you possess the courage of your convictions enough to come face-to-face with me across a blade, but nonetheless I throw this challenge to you. If you truly believe yourself my better, come and show me.*

*Sadly, I can see you penning (or perhaps getting someone else to pen for you as I doubt you trouble yourself with literacy) your refusal. Men like you are only brave against the babies of the Saracen and make yourselves feel powerful by beating and raping. You'd sooner let your hired thugs wield your weapons for you and try to conceal your inadequate manhood within the iron shirts that ill-gotten gold buys.*

*If you should decide you wish to inhabit your manhood I have included details on the over side as to where to come, when and under what circumstances. If you try to do something differently to how we have laid down the terms of engagement, rest assured that our people will slit your people's throats in the forest before you hear or see us.*

*I am distributing copies of this letter to a few town criers in surrounding villages so knowledge of your cowardice can better travel far and wide should you fail to attend. If it is indeed you and your kind who are leaders of this land then you should be more than capable of dealing with an upstart tinker lad like myself. After all I have only learned to fight in the streets and forests.*

*In the meantime you will no doubt be pleased to hear that your daughter is doing well and in good health. I'm not sure whether I've got her with child yet but I have been trying awfully hard. It really is a beautiful thing to have such a willing bed partner -perhaps you should try it? When the happy day comes and our bloodlines fuse would you like us to*

*I'll see you on the day I kill you, Geoffrey. I can call you that can't I? Actually, I don't really care whether I may or not, because in reality I can do whatever you don't stop me from doing.*

Bearing Truth in the face of a whole world that wants you to tell lies felt like an explosion of light and colour against a grey backdrop of conformity. It was a thing of terrible, raw beauty in which Robin saw the face of god.

"Who in Hell does he think he is to even dare to address me directly!" he raged in the hall. "I will teach him how to talk to his betters! Since when can tinkers write letters? You won't believe what that upstart gutter-bred whoreson has done, Augusta!"

"What has he done?" she murmured, trying to stop her voice from shaking while she waited to find out if she would be the one to pay for it.

"You read don't you?" he demanded, throwing down a parchment on her embroidery table. Nodding she picked up the letter. At first, she had thought her wifely duties were the worst thing she'd ever experienced, until she'd endured her first serious beating from him. Now she truly knew what fear was.

The further she read into the missive the more she had to work hard to control herself. Part of Augusta thought she might faint from fear, the other part was desperate not to laugh for joy at the sheer audacity! Because wasn't this exactly what she'd always wished she had the courage to say to De Rue herself? That he wasn't really a man at all just a sad, inadequate bully who picked on children and girls and generally even preferred petite women over any possibility of a physical challenge from a stronger one?

"Can you believe it?" he demanded, tearing the parchment out of her hands before she'd finished. She had the feeling that no one had ever spoken to him like this in his life.

"I'm speechless, my lord," she murmured. "Such insolence is… beyond belief."

He wasn't really listening to her anyway. That was never what she was present for. Augusta had learned that what De Rue called a wife was in fact just something to toss things into, whether that be semen, rage, or his thoughts. "How dare he think I would meet him in combat like an equal? As if he had the right! What do you know of these people, Lu… Augusta?"

It always made Augusta feel physically sick when he'd regularly mix up her name with his daughter's. "Well," Augusta said tentatively, realising that providing useful information would probably mitigate her own suffering. "Robin Goodfellow… let me see…" Everyone knew Robin's story, everyone connected with sorcery at least, but she didn't want De Rue to know that. "Well, I can tell you that in West Riding they call him Robin in the Hood. Opinions about him vary. Some say he's a demon in human form, others that he's some kind of people's hero-"

"Well, he's going to be a very dead people's hero soon!" De Rue exploded.

"From what I hear he's a good fighter…"

"What's that? Have you got a wet spot for the tinker?" he demanded.

She closed her eyes hard and tried to think what to say, but it was hard because the fear made her mind go blank.

"Hardly, my lord," she managed to get out. "He is less than a peasant, baseborn…. Not fit to touch the hem of my gown. There is one thing," she cried, a sudden desperate thought coming to her. "One thing I know about him… Gossip I heard, anyway…"

The whole time he gazed at her in contempt, as if her terror he had worked so hard to engender were a sign of her poor character, rather than something to do with the fact she was a foot shorter than him and under half his body weight.

"What?" he demanded.

"I've heard that his father is the Faerie King Obreon-"

"Everyone knows that. You better have something more than that." It seemed the furious edge was gone off him suddenly.

"His mother died giving birth to him and he was raised by his aunt!" she

194

cried rapidly, stammering over some of the words and then rushing on. "Rumour has it his aunt was murdered in a killing so terrible that even though she was only a tinker, people really wanted to catch the killer for a week or so."

"Is that so? How old do they say the boy was, at the time of the murder?"

"About… five… maybe older maybe seven. I don't know… But a wee little lad they say. He couldn't speak afterwards, for many years."

"What do you mean, couldn't speak? Like had his tongue cut out or something?"

"I don't think so. I think it was meant to be from the shock. It was used to illustrate how awful the murder was."

"Ah…" he murmured. "So he's the boy we left alive then." But then his face seemed to darken. "This is why he's done this to me… If he's the brat of that tinker that's why he's stolen Lux from me! Even though I was the one who put her out of her misery. You'd do the same for a dog by the road if you saw it in that state. I knew we should have killed the boy too. My cousin said not to worry about it. He always likes to leave the young ones alive to carry on the message to any others who would rebel. It was a tactic our fathers used when we harrowed the north. He always told us, leave one of the little ones to run and tell what we did to those who resisted. Unless they're pretty girl children… Then you break them in first. That's how come we had no more rebellions up North."

Augusta tried to focus on her breathing. For the first time she started to relate to the dispossessed, the rebels, and to think on all the suffering of innocent children perpetrated to tame the place to Norman rule. "Well…" she said tentatively. "If you did decide to meet him in combat the people would get to see the truth. That one like him can't stand against the Norman cavalry. And now that you know what happened to him…" Augusta felt a bit sickly about the words in her mouth, something about them felt very dirty, but she knew it was needful for her own safety to remind De Rue that she had helped him. "You will not only be able to humble him in combat, but show the people how weak he is with your words. If your father's tactic worked he may be broken easily just by a reminder of what he saw."

"Do you think so?" he asked, surprising Augusta by asking her opinion. It was unpleasant how much she liked that feeling.

"Oh definitely. Mother taught me a lot about how to manipulate an enemy."

"I don't need any help defeating him," De Rue laughed at her, and the ray of approval she'd basked in for a moment was snatched away. "But it's good to know how to hurt him. I might fight him after all."

# 8

I forget you've not yet seen him fight. If you had you'd be less nervous for him. Robin is the best man in the land. He's been in a lot of fights and he's won all of them."

"I know. But my father's been to war, real battles, and he's won all of them, too."

"This is different though, Lux. Robin is pretty much unstoppable, an old school warrior like the heroes from the sagas. You'll be an orphan in the first three minutes of the fight, I promise you."

"A lot can happen in three minutes," Lux murmured. With trust in Sariah's judgment Lux started counting out the full one hundred and eighty seconds of three minutes in her head. It really was an appallingly long amount of time to imagine two men desperately trying to murder each other with a variety of weapons.

Lux paused in the kneading the bread she was working on. Though they had gone without themselves a good deal over winter Sariah had been instructed to make bread for the poor, so that when all the people showed up to see Robin fight De Rue, they would remember which side it was who looked out for their provision.

Most of the grain had been bought with money from the younger children's pickpocketing skills. Purses stolen from rich men feeding poor men, cut with a decent quantity of acorn flour to make it go further. Sariah said Lux was to put love into it as she kneaded it, because the crowd was their secret weapon and the only thing they had up their sleeve if De Rue decided to try and break the agreed upon rules and conventions.

197

During the ride, Augusta began to regret her decision to accompany De Rue. It was likely he'd simply have forced her to come had she not acquiesced. Now that he'd got the notion into his head that she was secretly championing the outlaw -all because she'd once pointed out that Robin wasn't said to be a small man. She knew De Rue expected her to watch him mentally torture, defeat, humiliate and disfigure the upstart tinker lad, just to make sure she understood.

*The eyes in every oak and the faerie beings that dwell in the rivers and mounds, all of them watch and lurk, they work for that tinker devil, not for me or my kind. This is why no matter how much blood magic we practice we will never be as powerful as he is on his own land.* The further Northwest they went, the deeper they went into wild land where the rules didn't work quite like they did at home. When they'd made camp in the evening the uncanny howls of timber wolves echoed through the night.

"I thought they were almost all gone?" she said nervously, moving closer to her lady in waiting. It had been years since she'd heard them, and when she had she'd been safely behind walls, not outside in their territory. They sounded like the lost souls of the wandering dead whining and keening at their disenfranchisement. She was sure she could hear in their wails the little children De Rue's father had broken against rocks.

"Oh, not out this far, my lady," Prudence answered. "Things are still half savage out this way. We're heading just north of The Marcher's, wild rebellious land up that way, it is. This is territory loyal to Hereward the Wake's old cause. Most of it has been wasteland since the harrying, so the wolves thrive here, on two legs as well as four."

Augusta had shivered and wrapped her fur-lined cloak more closely around her. For the first time since De Rue had abducted her she had felt safer to be behind the wall of cold iron that Norman soldiers could become in battle. She began to think about her Uncle Jack and the fragile blossom of hope opened. So what if he was there? It wasn't like some hedge-born tinker could really defeat a trained Norman knight, veteran of the crusade...

There was no hope for her at all. There was probably no hope for Lux either. Perhaps it was time to take her own life? Death by her own hand would surely be kinder than meeting her end at the hands of wolves or outlaws if she tried to run. Augusta didn't have any tears to weep at the prospect, she just stared into the distance and let her horse take her deeper into a land full of myth and terror, a place where the country itself seemed to her to cry out for the blood of her kind.

"You must be frightened, lass," Jack said, putting a comforting hand on her shoulder.

"I'm trying not to be," Lux replied. "I'm trying to believe in miracles."

"Do you really think it would be that miraculous? For Hob to rip the old bastard a new one?" When Lux didn't reply he continued. "I've seen what he can do. De Rue knows how to fight well as a Norman knight, but Robin has fought Normans all his life, he's fought in the ring, in the street, in the forests and war-bands, on horseback and off…"

She nodded hurriedly, hoping he'd get the message. It didn't matter what anyone said, this sick fear in the pit of her stomach had tendrils reaching all the way back to childhood abuse and intimidation. "What are they doing?" Lux asked. Even after her total immersion in the language and culture of the Twll Du blood thread she still occasionally turned to Jack as the other semi-outsider when she didn't understand something.

Jack grunted. "The Broomshead folk haven't kept up this rite since my grand papa's day, so I only know the basics from the old stories… But they are dressing and painting him for war, so key parts of his body remember the doings and the words of the legends."

These men, she had learned, came out of a just such a legend only found in a story book buried so deep, burned in every nation, a series of fairytales so revolutionary and untamed that only the wind could get away with repeating it. Stories so old they had rattled their way into Britain in the poetic throats of those who crossed the ice-scape were being sung into Robin's flesh. His body was all their bodies. When Sariah poured a cauldron of icy river water over him, other than closing his eyes as the water hit his warm upper body, he gave no other signal of discomfort. This met with signs of approval from his family.

"You of the wolfs-kin and angel-seed awaken!" Sariah declared, striking him on the back with a handful of birch. "Proud son of Beli Mawr, first father of men. Direct descendent of the Goddess Ana who rode the lion. Man of the haunt of eagles, flint-boned, fire hearted, honey tongued, son of Eryri come forth!" She struck him again, a little harder.

Still Robin didn't flinch.

"Dragon man! Griffin rider, storm hunter! Come forth roaring with the strength of a lion, the long sight of an eagle and the cunning of the warg!" She struck him a third time firmly and higher on his back.

All the while she'd been speaking the depth and speed of Robin's breathing had been increasing, as had been the tension across his abdominal muscles.

"Robin Goodfellow! Robin Goodfellow! Robin Goodfellow! Puck. Hob. Robin Hode. Robin Dhu, Master Puck, key-keeper, crossroads haunter! Blood-letter for the thirsting soil! He who was promised to us! He whose coming was known to the fathers of our fathers!" By the time she reached this part Sariah was screaming the words into the wind like a fury. All of her foremothers cried it out with her and the hairs on the backs of Lux's arms stood to attention. "He whose love can save us! Come forth and be terrible with our enemies!"

One of the oldest women, Eldri of Caravan Arva, came forward and armed him with two knives. As she did she whispered something to him about those weapons, words that were only for him.

"I've heard that they are not even formed like men," Prudence whispered to her. "Some are part beast, others quite deformed from all the inbreeding."

Augusta rolled her eyes in contempt as inbreeding hadn't been absent among the De Biron history. "That is merely the chatter of superstitious villagers. I'm sure they are men formed as other men are formed."

"Perhaps, my lady. But no mere men could be guilty of the crimes they say

200

these tinkers do, surely to God."

Augusta's dark eyebrows twitched ironically. *No of course not. They couldn't look just like De Rue.* "And what sort of iniquities are these men guilty of, pray tell?" "Well," Prudence began, clearly warming to the tale. "I have heard such filthiness of them as could not truly be spoken in front of a lady of your high degree."

"I think I can handle it," Augusta replied coolly.

Prudence leaned in closer so that others wouldn't hear. "I hear that their men lie openly with other men among their tribes and the women with the women."

"Never!" she exclaimed.

"Oh yes, my lady! Such filthy creatures are they that the women also take the man's part in bed and all manner of incest, buggery, and perversion follows forth from them because of the women's lack of modesty that attracts the devil."

Augusta found it hard to imagine how taking the man's part was physically possible. Sex as she had experienced it had been so much based on physical force that she found herself trying to imagine women wrestling men to the ground in an arm lock before violently forcing their organs over theirs.

"I *even* heard..." Prudence continued. "That they lie together even during the high holy days when it is forbidden by Holy Mother Church, they make especially careful to do so in the broad daylight like beasts in the field!"

"Do any of their crimes actually occur outside the bedroll?" she asked sarcastically.

Prudence sniffed in distaste. "Oh goodness yes they do! It is said that if you manage to kill one of them the others make this keening, screaming sound as if Hell has opened its doors on you. They will then burn their dead in the manner of the heathen. But if they manage to kill *you*... they slash open your chest and pull back your rib cage like birds wings!"

Augusta had to admit she was far less offended by this description of their old school pagan violence than she of their sexual habits. Something deep and

201

low hit Augusta in the stomach and her horse felt it too. It took her a moment to realise it was drums. It came with music through the early morning mist, before she ever heard their horses or saw them riding out of the low fog like the men of the sagas, a strange, crooked pipe tune wailing amongst the low tones. Graves were opening and expelling their fallen warriors, it seemed Britain's fallen heroes had been vomited from the turf to walk among them.

As the Twll Du people rode by there were strangely coloured faces, eyes surrounded in bands of soot, and wolf pelts, painted symbols and shirtless men who were very nicely built. Augusta raised her eyebrows and nodded faintly to herself as she examined the fine physiques of the men. She glanced over at Prudence. "Well they don't look too deformed to me…"

Lux was glad she'd chosen to come in full traditional war costume otherwise people might have recognised her. The braids in her hair and paint on her face made her feel stronger. As if the essence of the Twll Du blood-thread would make her brave. When Robin had kissed her before riding away, she hadn't thought she'd be able to let him go, but the ancestors who lived inside the traditions behind her costume did it for her.

"Is that really all he's going out there with?" Lux's voice was a bare murmur, but Sariah heard her. She brought her horse over closer until their legs brushed each other. There was some comfort in the other woman's proximity.

"He means to take De Rue's weapons from him," Sariah explained, her eyes never leaving Robin. "Or else it signals that he plans to kill him with his bare hands. These things are kind of like a violent language of flowers between men," Sariah said.

Lux glanced briefly away from Robin, as though Sariah had somehow magicked a little slither of life into this situation. "You know about the language of flowers?"

"Of course! Do you imagine we tinker girls all just skipped the kissing stage and just plonked ourselves down on some man's cock one day? We send boys flowers in our culture as often as they send them to us."

If Lux hadn't have been anxiously watching Robin she would probably have admitted that, yes, she had assumed that Twll Du girls initiated sexual relations by plonking themselves down on a man's member.

"But why then no shoes?" Lux whispered, more to herself than Sariah.

"That part I myself am wondering," Sariah admitted. "But whatever it is you can guarantee it is no accident. Hob always has a plan, or if not a plan exactly then a vision, or perhaps a plan that forms a little later than most people's plans."

Lux wished that she could fully share the other woman's faith. To Sariah it seemed as if the ritual she had performed virtually guaranteed Robin's success. The women and all non-wardens had been placed back so far, surrounded by their warriors and furthest from what was happening, that Lux didn't even hear the brief concession to rules and regulations before someone winded a horn. Then, like the chaos of the Wild Hunt, it began with the furious galloping of horses.

Something sharp iced through her when she saw De Rue. It was a sick feeling that would have made her legs shake if she were standing and her bottom quavered. She saw the truth of how close she stood to her own death, with only Robin between her and it. She watched her father couch his lance and charge, and she remembered all the stories about what happened to the poor Saxons when they tried to stand against Norman cavalry. It felt like every breath she was taking was getting shallower and shallower.

The audience cheered thunderously. There was everything from women's cries of 'Robin Goodfellow come and save *me*!' with a flirty edge to them, to some truly vile racial insults against Tinkers, the Welsh, and travelers in general. During this cacophony a series of seemingly impossible things happened.

Robin's stallion had been galloping toward De Rue and Robin appeared to be only holding a knife in his hand. Then, all in one smooth motion, he stood up in his saddle and balanced precariously. The audience gasped for one brief second to see this feat of horsemanship, where at the end he had his hands entirely off the reins. Lux's hand went over her mouth and she didn't even blink.

Her whole universe seemed to wobble, tilt and threaten to fall over.

It was a fleeting moment because Robin was only standing on the horse's back mid gallop for one terrifying second before he alighted on De Rue's lance and used it as midair stepping stone to leap onto De Rue's horse behind him. It was all so fast because De Rue couldn't prevent himself hurtling forward on his horse and thus covering most of the distance for Robin. For a breathless second Lux thought it might all be over, as Robin came up behind De Rue about to slit his throat.

De Rue foiled this attempt by removing his own feet from the stirrups and lurching sideways. It was a bold move travelling at the pace they were, throwing them both from the horse's back in a way that for untrained folk would likely have ended in death. De Rue had probably imagined Robin would catch the worst of that fall, unprotected by armour and a helmet as he was.

Robin half flipped backwards as he fell and landed on his feet, while De Rue truly fell before beginning to roll to on impact. A huge cheer went up from the audience, even a grudging one in some quarters. They were obviously vastly entertained regardless of whom they'd put their money on.

"I'd start counting about three minutes from here," Sariah advised, her tone cool as if the theatrics were only for the plebs, her eyes set fixedly on the details of the fight that was just beginning. "I know a dangerous man when I see one, Lux, and you have not exaggerated what you've said of De Rue. By the look of this Settler thug he will work Robin hard and die just as bitterly. One fall won't stop him, I'm afraid, horse stunt or no horse stunt. But Robin's given the first and most important blow in this fight, the one that lets his opponent know he has no idea what he's up against. A man who becomes afraid of another immediately begins to lose to him. Now as he grapples for his weapon, winded on the ground when he's used to being on top… after *that* impossible thing just happened to him and *that* just dropped on him… I'd say he's a wee little bit afraid of this lowly tinker man now."

Robin understood what this man on the other horse had done wrong, but in the moment he didn't feel too much about it. Not really, not the things that Robin usually felt towards child abusers and rapists. Instead his whole being had become merely the instrument of a few key actions, the lightning strike that falls after the judgment of the heavens has been cast. He was splitting at the seams with starlight pouring out through the stitched joins.

This happened at times at the height of his passions. It was no harder to make room for violence than for love, perhaps that's what had always truly been so terrifying about Puck? All you needed for almost impossibly good judgment of timing and distance was to be so entirely relaxed. To be calm in a way that it wasn't natural under life and death conditions. He needed to judge leaping from the back of your moving horse, over someone's couched lance handle, just the way you would when reaching for your cup and drinking from it.

What madness careened and screeched, keening with bright insanity through him…When he made first physical contact with the man he had come there to kill he possessed all of Robin's tactile sensitivity, but it didn't bother Puck at all. Puck was ready to feel all the things if he had to. Few people could cope with what he brought to bear when it came to love and joy, let alone when it came to war… The wolf-cloaked, goat-horned old one chuckled to himself as he brought De Rue off his horse. Oh yes… he did so enjoy it when the world turned upside down!

Before De Rue could recover from the winding he'd taken in the fall Puck was on him. De Rue would have liked to have responded to Puck's laughter with violence, that was easy enough to tell, but he was somewhat thwarted by the fact that Puck's knees had been carefully placed and clamped firmly over De Rue's weapon belt. All the frightened human had in his hand was the sad and pathetic crushed lance handle. It almost seemed too easy to kill him that it wouldn't be sporting. Puck was up on his haunches over De Rue, knife in his hand and an I'm-going-to-gut-you smile full of dark fire rippling through his eyes.

De Rue tried to strike him with the lance handle but Puck deflected the blow like it was boring and stuck the point of his knife very keenly into the skin above his jugular vein. You could feel the man's pain, desperation, and total outrage. The surges of it entered Puck's hips in a way that was borderline erotic. The proud man's outrage only made Puck stronger. The more hate you tried to throw at him the stronger you made him, he would just feed on the poison of the oppressors and make it into nutriment and laugh and laugh while he opened their veins to find out if the leaders of the land really bleed the same colour as other men.

"You've grown into a fine fighter. Aren't you the brat of that tinker my cousin and I raped some ten summers back?" He was only halfway through the sentence when De Rue's familiar voice unravelled him. Robin felt himself closing in the middle, and then falling through space. For a few seconds he tried to catch his breath in panicky clutches and his breath got stuck. His fingers were back in the cold black blood on the floor of the tent as he tried to slide towards her. It was a bit like being punched in the stomach by a blizzard, and after it hit him he was so, so very mortal...

Augusta tried to remind herself to close her mouth. Her face wasn't obeying her mind though. The Biron men were known for their bloodthirsty and fearsome intensity in battle, so she had grown up around violence and cavalry charges and seen men die in the lists for sport, she'd seen a number of heads on pikes. But she'd never seen anything like what the tinker did from horseback that day.

Three things went through her mind in quick succession during the crowd's collective gasp that followed when he stood in the saddle. She wondered whether it was true what they said about the tinkers witching horses, because how else was such a feat possible? And thirdly... thirdly and most terrifying of all: what if the mythic elf boy actually won?

"What just happened? I don't understand what I just saw," Prudence murmured. "How did he do that? Without a hauberk or... or... a lance... How did he unseat my lord?"

206

Augusta wanted to feel superior to the other woman's lack of comprehension, she wished she could, but she had to admit it all made as little sense to her as it did to Prudence. It had happened too quickly and it went against everything she'd been taught to believe about how the world operated. At some level it wasn't only unthinkable, it was *unseeable*. So the mind convinced itself it saw something else. Deeply held truths that had been inculcated since childhood were being jostled around in her. The people of the forest were foolish like children, weak-minded from inbreeding, no heads for money, no work ethic, shiftless wanderers with heads full of dreams and fairy-dust...

The uproar in the crowd testified to this as a shared reaction to what had happened. There was utter incomprehension but under that there was also something else. Something Augusta hadn't heard or smelt the presence of before, but she still knew it the way the young of most animals recognise a predator they've never seen before. For an upper-class girl this was one of the most dangerous predators she could smell: rebellion.

"I don't know," she murmured.

The tinker was on top of De Rue for a moment but then paused right when he had the clear advantage. She watched the tinker's midsection and saw the rapid change in his whole way of holding himself, right before De Rue hit him in the side of the head with his lance handle. She knew with sickly certainty that the change in the tinker boy was in response to De Rue using the information that Augusta had given him.

If she herself hadn't suffered great trauma she'd not have known what she was seeing. But the wounded, frightened creature in her saw the wounded, frightened creature in Robin. The shame she felt at having been the instrument of his downfall threatened to choke off her breath. She didn't know why but it was more than what she'd felt in killing Rowan. If she had killed this young tinker man she had killed something good.

She glanced over at Prudence and at how close her guard's horses were. Could it be? She wondered. Was there a little touch of insurrection in her as well? She knew she could gallop away before any of them could grab her reins.

She could reach the men fighting at the centre of the heath before any of them could stop her. And then she would… What? Fall upon De Rue with her tiny boot dagger to put right the wrong she'd done?

To her immense relief the tinker… Robin, she reminded herself, was still moving. Despite the fast and panicked breathing she could see happening under his abdominal muscles he backwards rolled up into a crouched position, blood was pouring out of his face. It was then that she heard someone call her name.

"Guss!" Very few people called Augusta her Christian name, but only one person called her Guss. Augusta couldn't breathe but she still moved, all at once her mare was dancing in half circles as she spun the animal's head around to see further into the crowd.

*Uncle Jack.*

Her knees prepared themselves and her heart thudding so hard in her ears she couldn't hear the crowd roar. Her whole body was a battleground between fear and hope. She readjusted in the saddle to be ready at just the right moment, as Augusta prepared herself for insurrection.

"Why is he stopping?" Lux whispered, her tongue numb.

Sariah didn't answer, she was watching too intently.

She sensed the ripple of battle readiness go through Blaith's body and her own body answered it. Lux knew they would ride forward to protect him together if they must.

"He's having an attack," Blaith murmured. He turned his horse around so he was looking at Sariah over Lux's head. "Sariah, I'm sorry." He didn't need to say what he was sorry for because Sariah had obviously seen what he was apologising for a few seconds earlier when she'd signalled to the wardens to restrain him.

"Let me go!" Blaith screamed at them. "I cannot lose him! Don't you understand! You're not saving me. If he dies, I die first! If he dies we're all lost!"

Robin was on his feet but he wasn't moving. He was breathing rapidly as

De Rue came towards him his sword drawn. There was blood on her father's throat, but it only looked like the amount you'd expect from a knick. Many times Lux could remember him shrugging off far worse in the middle of one of his rages. When De Rue took a vicious swing at Robin he dodged and repositioned himself but did not retaliate.

Blaith was right, this behaviour of Robin's held the signs of the seeds of defeat. She knew Robin's body too. Very soon his legs would go from under him. Blaith's horse reared up crazily, still encircled firmly by the wardens.

"He can do it, Blaith!" Sariah shouted at him. "I believe in him! Believe in him with me!"

Lux's eyes went back to Robin and saw him dodge another near lethal blow but still not fight back. That was it. She didn't care what the rules were; all she knew is that she couldn't just watch. Lux laid her heels into her horse's sides hard. They were holding Blaith back like restraining a rabid animal with what amounted to brute force now, but nobody was holding her. It was likely nobody thought she'd be so crazy.

"I liked you better with that rag stuck in your mouth, remember that?" De Rue asked, as he circled Robin. He could see the other man's eyes looking for the *in*, the opportunity, the gap in his guard that would allow De Rue to cut him in two.

Robin didn't just remember the rag, he felt it there still, stuck against his fear-dry tongue and clagging his arid throat, blocking his scream for help. Every panicked breath would draw the rag further down his throat till he risked choking, and struggled with his bonds until blood ran into his hands. Other than De Rue's voice there was only his own breathing and if he listening to that for too long it started to become Eliza's stress breathing in the darkness…

Robin wanted to make a long, inhuman wailing sound of torment. He had no words to give vent to the pain that waited for him in that semi dark, blood-soaked tent… Only a crazed howl that went on and on against a scorched landscape of ash and smoking ruin. It was the cannibal tent, where you met with the devourers and faceless forms of suffering without names.

"Do you know what I've always wondered?" De Rue asked him, almost conversationally after Robin had ducked an attempt to decapitate him. "How long exactly did it go on?"

Robin didn't hear the rest because he heaved and nearly vomited. He had never gone close to being able to answer that question. Not that anyone had ever been so cruel as to ask it of him before. Now, wide open as he was after the Puck possession, the entirety of the horror seemed to glance in jagged shrieks of memory across his mind like dry nails. He made a sound of deep suffering. It didn't matter if De Rue heard. For one timeless moment of horror Robin gazed straight into the twisted reality at the centre of his nightmares and his mind blanched starkly from it.

Then everything went still and silent. It took Robin a couple of moments to realise it just a part of his panic but something else. *How do we know exactly when things are real? We know because others experience them too.* People cheering or booing were frozen in their actions, their mouths shaped strangely as if their words were cut short. De Rue had stopped moving. His brother's rearing horse had stopped still in the action. Lux's horse that had been pummelling the ground towards them was interrupted mid gallop, with one of the sods it threw up caught in the air and an expression of wild determination in her face.

His gaze went to the only thing in the scene that moved, the figure of a blonde-haired woman wearing a tattered, feathered cloak around her shoulders. Though she wasn't moving quickly it was possible to tell she was not frozen like the rest of reality. One of her hands was up and out flat, palm forward in the universal gesture that meant only one thing: stop.

"Greetings, Robin Goodfellow."

"Who...are... you?" Almost as soon as he had gasped the question out in between his too rapid breaths Robin knew the answer. This was a faerie woman, but her face was too similar to Lux's for her to be any one but a particular faerie woman.

"I am Agnes, Lux's mother," she replied, with neither tone nor expression.

She didn't seem to be looking directly into Robin's eyes but gazing off somewhere past or behind him. "Don't worry. I have taken you into what I think of as a time pocket while you recover. Cry, vomit, empty your bladder, do whatever you require. There is plenty of time. In fact," she said, with the faintest of smiles. "There is no time." She threw a silver coin up into the air and caused it to remain hovering, mid-air, neither rising nor falling.

Almost immediately upon being given permission Robin began to vomit convulsively. The evil miasma of the cannibal tent needed to be strip mined from his gut. Agnes stood there patiently while it happened, showing neither sympathy nor any kind of disgust or distaste. It was as though all human things, the muck and filth of it as well as the cruelty of it were nothing to her any longer.

When he had finished and now was only trembling she took a step closer and gazed down at De Rue's frozen form. "You did not expect today to meet one of the men that killed your aunt. Please do not hold the sire against the daughter, nor let one whit of this come back upon my girl. It was not by my will he put the girl inside me to begin with, nor by hers. It is such with us that this man must die today. For your aunt, for me, for Amelia, for Lux, for you, and if there is to be a future."

Robin nodded. His breathing was beginning to settle now as he processed this, as he tried to swallow down the hate that burned its way up through his gorge as it threatened to rise again. He took the time that Agnes offered him, the time he needed to get back to the bone whiteness of his earlier state. He took a deep breath. "Alright. I'm ready."

As Lux's mount thundered across the green she heard the cries of protest from the crowd. They melted away just like fear had when she'd let Robin abduct her. Except today she was wearing braids with paint on her skin, and she was one flame of conviction. Never had she felt herself the centre of such agency!

Of course there was the sound of her own people giving chase as well but she knew they would understand what she'd done. Most of all she knew Blaith understood. She wasn't just doing this for herself, or for Robin, she was doing what her Magister had wanted to do but couldn't because he was who he was, and his life was so precious. In their devil's name she was going to ride De Rue down with her horse at full gallop, and then turn around to ride back over him twice.

Whatever had to happen to buy Robin time to recover from his attack, she would have placed her own body in the firing line to shield his. Not only this, she believed she would also win. When she was almost there a strange flash of light that made everything seem to wobble, as if a vibration went through the fabric of reality. She thought for some reason of her mother when she'd seen her in the woods the day Robin came for her.

Right when she felt it something changed in the fight. De Rue took a swing at Robin which he dodged. Words; maybe taunts were being exchanged, although Robin did not appear to be speaking back. Both men glanced over to see who was riding towards them. When he recognised her De Rue laughed when he recognised her.

Robin made no indication of his response to seeing her galloping to his aid, instead with no change in demeanour he grabbed De Rue's wrist and stopped him laughing. Her father had thought he was playing with his food and then the food had done something outside the script. De Rue tried to pull his hand away but Robin was clearly stronger than him. He took a step half behind De Rue, protecting himself from the blade with De Rue's own body and spun his arm around into a brutal elbow lock. The type of chainmail De Rue was wearing only covered him to the bicep, leaving both wrist and elbow joints vulnerable.

Lux pulled her horse's headlong gallop up to avoid collecting Robin along with her father. By the time the horse could wheel around she caught a flash of Robin forcing De Rue onto his knees still holding the arm he'd captured, leaving him awkwardly trying to poke backwards at Robin with his sword. As Lux rode back towards them Robin took De Rue's mace from where it had fallen and shattered the man's sword hand with it. While De Rue screamed in pain, a sound she could not have previously imagined him making, Robin used his foot to move the sword slowly and very deliberately out of his reach.

"What is the other man's name? And does he yet live?"

A jolt went through the crowd when De Rue hit his knees. It was as if in seeing the impossible, having seen the boss man brought to the ground by his inferior, some special scent signal was released into the air that could be smelt by the underclasses. The timbre of the cheering changed and something feral began rising, as though up out of the land itself. Those who had put money on De Rue screamed for his blood.

"We should get the women out of here," one guard said to another. "Rebellion is in the air. Sweet Jesu only knows what they'd do to our women if they captured them."

She glanced back at Uncle Jack, and then at Prudence.

"The men are right, my lady. It appears your lord husband is all but slain and we must withdraw hastily. Are not any among you man enough to defend your lord?" she cried out, making an attempt to shame them into action. The guardsmen were quick to avoid meeting her superior's eyes. Robin smashed De Rue's hand, and a great, almost ecstatic cry went up, as if they were no longer divided by who had puts bets on whom.

Welsh and Saxon alike bayed for the blood of the oppressor, and Augusta knew in their eyes *she was* that oppressor. She swallowed hard and looked back at Jack. There wasn't much time, she must decide what side she was on. If Robin Goodfellow wins should Augusta ride towards him, or away from him in fear? Fleeing, as all things of Norman blood would seem wise to flee when the true feelings of the occupied people?

"Guss! Now!" Jack cried out.

She didn't hesitate, she lifted her black mourning weeds found her seat and kicked her mount into a gallop. People were flooding into the space, wanting to get closer to the fight but she kept her eyes fixed on Jack. Augusta could see him riding towards her, and then sweeping to the right with his quarterstaff out. It wasn't until he'd knocked one to the side of her that she realised the guardsmen were trying to stop her. As soon as she'd urged her mare into a run she'd only been able to see Jack, reality narrowed to a desperate tunnel vision.

Her horse reared skittishly at the chaos and nearly unseated her, but she hung on with her knees and hands. All pretence at keeping a stiff upper lip and not showing fear in front of those beneath her was eroded by suffering. Augusta was far beyond terrified. The entire trauma she'd known over her time in De Rue's stronghold was upon her in one big crush of adrenalin.

She felt Jack ride up beside her and take hold of her reins, when she felt his hand take her horse's head she began to cry so freely it was impossible to see straight and her nose ran like a child's. It was another in a long line of public humiliations, yet this time she didn't care.

"I've got you now, lass," she heard his deep, brusque voice say.

Robin knew the hand was one of the most sensitive targets on a person's body. De Rue was likely to be in excruciating pain. It would never be enough for a proper revenge, that much Robin knew. What seemed most important in this moment was ridding the world of these men.

"He's still alive," De Rue grunted.

"Name?"

Robin tightened his grip until De Rue made a sound of pain that he tried to grit out with his teeth. Steeling himself Robin took the other man right up to the threshold of his tolerance, but it appeared pain just made this man angrier. "Fuck you, piece of gutter born to a ditch-drab. Your mother and aunt were whores."

Robin broke his wrist. De Rue fought to not scream but failed. There was no satisfaction in it. "It gets more painful after the shock wears off." Robin could hear how cold his voice sounded and he knew it should have scared De Rue, and himself, more than Puck had. De Rue could never be as afraid as Eliza and Robin had been that night though. He was a man who stood be-

214

neath the sky with only rage in his heart.

"You're going to need to do better than that!" De Rue made an attempt to spit on him. "My men are coming, I can hear their horses," he panted, the pain beginning to sap his strength.

"I'm not your men!" Lux said, as she rode her horse closer and looked down at him. "It's me. And I was never yours."

Robin's pride in her was so strong as to be overwhelming. There she was, seated astride her horse with her war paint on unmoved by facing her former persecutor, ready to strike him down if she had to. Here was the girl who had been running and crying now with her eyes full of nothing but pure fight.

"Your men are all deserting you. I came here to help bring you down because you're a bully and a coward. I'm here for Mother, because she can't be here to appreciate seeing you bettered by a tinker's son," she told him.

"Fucking devil whore! When they get here, I'm going to have all my men fuck you first before we kill you and I'm going to-"

Robin placed the weight of his knee down firmly on De Rue's broken wrist, more because he didn't want Lux or himself to hear the rest. "Tell me his name," Robin repeated, pressing his knife into the side of De Rue's eye. He found he wanted this over with quickly and being able to see the weapon close up had seemed to break most people in all the atrocities he'd witnessed in life.

"You wouldn't…" De Rue spluttered on his own blood. "You wouldn't torture me… Make you… just as bad as us… that did your aunt."

"You don't understand," he murmured, pushing the tip into the side of his eye. "You broke my heart that might have taken pity. I will pop your eye out like a cherry pip without blinking." De Rue blinked. "I will know if you lie."

"De Bracy! Richard de Bracy from over Nottingham way."

Robin nodded once to himself. It was strange to know a name to put to that old hate and pain… Now it was time to take out the grandmother knife. He buried his knife deep in De Rue's windpipe and jugular in one motion and pushed it south under the mail until he felt the organs give. You could feel the air rushing out but not so fast that consciousness was a lost immediately.

Robin kept eye contact with Geoffrey De Rue as the other man's eyes widened and then settled into something like horror, as if he saw a terrible thing on the edge of death, just when the blood began to really come out.

As De Rue died Robin told him: "I am all bondsman you've beaten, every child you've killed, or caused to be starved. I am every woman you've raped. I am the land you claim dominion over. I am the spirits your people have banished. And we find you our inferior."

He pulled his blade out, cleaned it on his leg and re-sheathed it. Robin removed a battle-axe from the dying man's belt. With three savage blows to the man's chest he managed to sever the links in the chainmail enough to get at De Rue's organs. There had been chaos all around him before, but there was stunned and horrified silence now while Robin gutted his kill to remove the heart.

It was strange how the heart looked so normal, as he cut loose all the dark blooded arteries and stubborn veins that clung so when you try to remove a heart. With the man's chronic incapacity to love Robin would have imagined it to be shrivelled and desiccated in the chest. When he had it out, he took the warm quivering thing over to the side of Lux's horse.

"For your mother," he said quietly, his voice low and flat. "I couldn't have done it without her." She accepted it from him hesitantly, her hands flinching at the texture.

He turned back to De Rue's body. Eldri the Arva grandmother that held the crow knife kept it nice and sharp as a duty, as beheading a human being with a knife is inevitably messy and brutal. It was worth it to have done it in the old way with a knife that had taken the heads of many evil men and slave owners. Only when he was standing beside De Rue's body with its chest cavity open to the sky, holding his head by its hair and his bare feet felt the thick, bloody mud squelching up between his toes, that Robin could again feel himself trembling.

Almost as if his people were summoned by that sensation in his blood and bones they began to form up around him. Lux dismounted from her horse and came towards him. Blaith came riding up and dismounted by jumping down while his horse was still cantering, smacking into Robin's chest at such a speed that it was more of an attack than an embrace. Robin felt only numbness. He fumbled with deciding whether to wrap his arms around Blaith with the dead man's head or to put it down and Blaith laughed with a mixture of relief and dark humour at his dilemma.

"Oh, thank the gods! Thank all the gods," Blaith whispered with great intensity, kissing Robin several times on the face. Lux was touching his arm. Sariah and Eilish were close, kissing him and holding onto him. Eilish was checking his wounds while he could catch only snippets as they all talked at once.

"I *knew* you could," Sariah murmured, near the back of his neck. Her faith in him would normally have felt so warm and good but it was as though it were muffled. He closed his eyes and let himself come uncoiled a little in the arms of his people. The warmth of Sariah's body, the intensity of Blaith's protective love, the tenderness of his fierce, brave hedge wife, Eilish's practical care… People laughing, people weeping with relief, and everywhere their hands and arms… Robin let his breath out and felt a rush of tears coming with it, choking their way up past his Adam's apple and thickening in his throat.

He was afraid to love them. He was afraid with all of the power of the cannibal tent De Rue had made him go back to. Every one of them carried that same fragility that Eliza had, all of them were mortal, all of them could be made to bleed and cry and scream… Theoretically it was possible that he wouldn't be able to stop it, that if he lived on further, he could have to go back to that pit filled with Eliza's stress breathing and exhausted weeping… How could he? Knowing that? Having seen that? How could he let it in still? But when it was as strong as it was, this wall of love they became, how then could he keep it out?

"Alright…" he whispered to the air, his head tilted back and his body surrendered to the love of his people with a tremor of relief that felt both ecstatic and suicidal. "*Yes.* Oh gods. But, yes."

# BOOK 3

# 1

Nanette De Biron paused in the doorway and watched the young man duck and weave through the small crowd. Her dark eyes narrowed. He wore a grey, faded cloak with his hood up. If he'd been shorter or hunched his shoulders more he might almost have been inconspicuous. But that's what was so infuriating about the Twll Du blood-thread, Nanette mused. They insisted on carrying themselves more like the princes of the realm than like the hedge-born scum they really were.

Immediately the young man sensed her gaze and glanced up, catching her eyes through the crowd. He'd made some attempt to disguise his good looks with overgrown stubble and unkempt hair but it did little to take away from it. Only a fool would have taken him for your average vagabond. Nanette made an impression of a woman's shyness when caught staring at a man. She saw the immediate softening around his mouth, the faint smile. He was used to being looked at by women and he carried a soft spot for her sex. Nanette smiled back at him.

*This is how I will kill you.*

His hood pulled down over his eyes as he dropped his head and slipped away through the market crowd. Her eyes followed him. After she found out the clan's movements it still hadn't been easy for Nanette to even get into Gwynedd with the foment of anti-Norman rebellion in the mountain country as it was. Robin's people had nestled deeply into the rebellious northern territory, protecting themselves from the Norman authorities in the process. Killing De Rue had made him a hero here and as Welsh language speakers they were almost invisible, as Nanette was not.

Ever since Princess Gwenllian's death at Norman hands insurrection had gripped the North like a fever. She hadn't been surprised when her spies discovered this was where they'd taken Augusta. Robin Goodfellow was known to be rebellion manifest in the form of a man, if somewhere there was chaos, and order being overturned Nanette had no doubt she'd find him right in the thick of it, stealing pretty Norman girls.

So keen was she to be off the streets before being caught not being mute that she ran headlong into someone. She was about to tell them to watch where they were going when she bit her tongue, reminding herself not to speak French.

"Brother, you startled me. Have you been watching me watching him?"

Gilbert smiled. His dark eyes were the same colour as hers yet they sparkled with mirth. One would be a fool to think him entirely nice on account of it. He alone could fully understand the importance of getting Augusta back.

"No, I was watching the tinker boy too. He's far prettier than you."

Nanette cocked her eyebrow at him and he immediately held up both hands in submission. "Seriously though," he said at last. "I followed him from where he parted from another man."

"Was it Blaith?" Nanette clarified.

"I didn't get a good look at him. They are wary creatures. I didn't dare tail Robin for too long, I started to feel like he was aware of me."

"Did you observe anything of note?" she asked, taking his arm and walking with him in the direction of the inn. They were both careful to keep their voices low and hushed so as not to cut through the background sounds of people talking Welsh.

"Only what we already know -that we will have our work cut out for us."

Robin slid into the crowded tavern. It was overwhelming, the noise inside after the night air outside, the smell of ale and male settler sweat, the boiling-point noise of them... But mostly it was the feelings, the swamp of fetch pumped up on emotion that these congregated, domestic humans gave off… Mainly it was lust and barely repressed violence that swum in the air. What did they expect to happen when they crammed themselves all in together like this and added alcohol to their discontent and poured it neat into the wounds of their dispossession?

Robin had long ago realised that they did indeed do it on purpose, because they came here to fight. At first he hadn't been able to understand why so many fights always broke out but over time he'd learned to relate to their frustration. He understood these emotions deep in his belly-wolf. Robin also knew how to use those feelings and the men who had them. It reminded him of horse whispering an aggressive stallion, because first you had to learn how to do it on yourself.

It wasn't until Robin pushed back his signature hood that he was recognised and greeted by several men at once. He favoured them with his smile.

"Well met, Robin," the publican said as he approached the bar. "Can I pour you something on the house?"

He smiled. "Do you have any *uisge beatha*, Liam? It's cold in the mountains tonight and beer smells like Saxons."

Liam the publican laughed, beaming at the fact Robin had remembered his name and that he preferred to be called 'Liam' rather than his full name William. Robin instinctually swapped to someone's familiar nickname quite soon after knowing them. If he'd had to consider why he did this he would probably have admitted it gave people a sense of being on intimate terms with him whether they were or not.

"Only for you, Robin," Liam said, reaching under the bar. "Most of these locals have never tasted more than ale and poor mead and don't know what it is to ask for it."

"Travel broadens one's taste," Robin remarked with a touch of irony. He took a seat before the bar, sitting with his back to the only part of the room where no one was standing so he was only half facing Liam. He knew that Liam had travelled into the lowlands of Scotland when he was a young man and was inordinately proud of the fact. Before Robin even got the chance to take his first sip of the potent but rough smelling fire water in his tankard Liam had leaned in for gossip.

"Is it true what they say that you took down a Norman lord in full chain-mail from a cavalry charge with just a hunting knife? They say you stood up in the saddle at a full gallop and just jumped on him and dropped him."

"That depends, is it English authorities asking?"

The publican laughed. The man's blatant admiration for him bored Robin, he wanted to make use of it and get back out into the night. It was stressful being in here. You were meant to leave your weapons at the door but nobody smart ever did anything except put their bow down. That meant there were about twenty other blades in boots and belts scattered around the room and part of Robin's mind was busy knowing where all of them were. It was hard mental work keeping up a conversation at the same time, especially as he liked to do it looking casual and without letting on how wary he was.

"You're one mad bastard, Robin. Everyone's talking about it that saw you do it. It gives simple folk like us new hope of defeating them. If they can be unhorsed like that…"

"Tell me something," Robin said leaning in closer. "Someone told me that there's some strangers in town, people no one knows…"

Liam's eyes lit up. You could see that he was delighted to be able to offer Robin something on this topic or any topic. "Yes! My daughter has a theory they're Norman spies for the King."

"Normans? What makes Siwan think so, has someone heard them speak French?" The second rule after the nickname was to learn the names of the person›s spouse and children.

"Well my wife's cousin's husband had to re-shoe the man's horse and although he let his servant speak for him the quality of the horse was such as no one has seen around these parts."

"What do you mean quality, exactly? What was special about the horse?" Robin swallowed a deep draft of the uisge, he wasn't planning to be here long now so it was time to drink up.

"My wife says he said that it was almost as heavier than our horses but frisky and that the face had a bit of a dish about it. Sleek, black and perfect and a stallion at that! He hasn't seen one like it. Do you think they're spies?"

"I think they're silly," Robin muttered under his breath.

"Pardon?"

"Oh nothing." Robin smiled. "Your wife's, cousin's husband didn't happen to say where they were staying did he?"

"No, but if you head up to the smithy in the morning you can ask him yourself. Gareth will be happy to tell you if he knows. Any good Welshmen would," he added.

Robin smiled but it felt tight around the prickle of aggression in his teeth as his wolf stirred. "Thank you for the drink, Liam. A little gift for the information." He tipped the publican and left.

It takes the patience of a faerie to stand looking at the inert body of another sorcerer for hours as Eilion stood beside Gilbert's body. A human might have made a move to wake him, but a human would have called it wrong. For what is scarier than being watched while you sleep is surely to know that you were watched while you slept for a very long time, Eilion thought. The shapeshifter's body began to stir.

He jumped the bed in one motion when he saw Eilion. "How did you get in here?" he demanded in a quiet hiss.

"Through the walls and floor," Eilion replied in Norman French.

"You're a faerie aren't you? You shouldn't be able to get in here, this place is filled with iron."

"I am indeed a faerie."

"Well… why are you here?" Gilbert asked, feeling around behind him for his sword belt. It always fascinated Eilion how humans acted like their weapons could protect them from the malice of his kind.

"I'm working out how I'm going to kill you."

225

"Is that so?"

"Yes. And it's going to be easy."

Gilbert's eyebrows jumped up higher still. "Really? And why is that?"

"Because power is about knowledge first and foremost, and you don't even know why you're here doing what you do. You are Nanette's mere puppet. It seems unsporting to harm you actually." Eilion cleared the bed in a movement that was too fast for a human to follow, it made it appear that he'd just disappeared and reappeared in front of Gilbert. The other man jumped back. "That's what I was thinking while I was standing there watching you sleep."

"Get away from me!"

"Laughter." It was easier to say it than try to mimic the way it sounded when humans laughed. "Why don't you change your face into something to upset me? That is your whole skillset, no?"

"What do you mean when you say I don't know why I'm here? I know why I'm here. I'm here because those tinker scum have kidnapped my niece!"

Eilion leaned into the tension of holding all the cards, waiting for just the right moment to reveal his hand. "There's no point telling you. You know what Nanette is. If you serve her as you do you must like being her creature. I'm a puppet-master, Norman, and I don't fight with other sorcerer's pets. I go straight to the owner."

"I am no one's *pet*," he replied between clenched teeth.

"You are Nanette's pet as long as you are doing just what she wants even though she's lied to you. Ask her of the rumours about Augusta, Gilbert. Tell her you heard that Augusta ran away with the tinkers on purpose."

"She would never-" Gilbert cut himself off there. Eilion could see the man's quick mind working under the surface, he was smart for a human.

"I'll leave you to discuss it with your master," Eilion replied, withdrawing.

"I have no master!" he snapped.

Eilion mimicked the smiling expression but without the feeling. "I will believe you are not a pet when I see you doing non-pet things." Without warning Eilion appeared right up in Gilbert's face. "And if you hurt my fetch mate,

I will de-sex you."

Gilbert got his weapon belt and his bag. He paid the innkeeper and stepped out into the night air with a strong sense of satisfaction. Yes, this was how it was going to be from now on. Gilbert was going to do what Gilbert felt like and Nanette could go to the devil. He would just need to wake up one of the stable boys to saddle his horse for him and he'd be on his way. He took a few steps out into the night, closed his eyes and savoured the cool, clean air in his nostrils.

Gilbert began to calm down and comprehend what he was about to do. It all sounded very well in theory, walking out on Nanette. This exercise of his male power was out of proportion with her crimes against him, he knew. Tempting as it was when he imagined the look on her face when she found his horse gone… But what if something serious happened to her without his protection? What with the Wild North all up in arms and insurrection in every alehouse… How would he live with himself if someone realised she was Norman?

He was about to go back inside and think of some more worthy way to wreak revenge upon his sister, something that would leave him feeling less shabby, when he felt the sharp cold intrusion pressed into the divot between the vertebrae that connected his head with his neck. Gilbert froze. Even with his survival instincts stampeding into overdrive his mind was still calculating. Any skill he had as a fighter was for this very reason, as he was of quite average physique.

He took in the precision of the placement of the weapon against his neck. Assuming the man who had accosted him was both skilled and had a decent knife he could end Gilbert's life with one clean incision to that spot, and Gilbert would never get the chance to make a sound. It wasn't until after the cold sweat washed over him that Gilbert noticed the way the man smelt. Whatever it was it was hard to describe but it had a visceral impact on him.

"Undo your buckle and let your sword belt fall slowly to the floor," the man said from behind him. He had the very faintest accent on his French but he spoke it as fluently as if he was born in Normandy.

"You speak French," Gilbert whispered. "Who in god's name are you?"

By way of response the blade bit into the skin between his upper vertebrae. Gilbert froze. He felt a little trickle of blood run down his back.

"Unbuckle and let your weapon belt slide down to the ground." The man repeated. The coolness in his voice itself seemed to carry menace. No one should have a regular heart rate when they are threatening another man's life, if they do it means you are in serious trouble. With trembling fingers, that felt like they were covered in wool, Gilbert managed to get his belt undone. "That's the way, gentle and slow like you'd handle a woman," the voice murmured.

The masterfulness of his tone mingled with the husky richness of the man's French was seductive to Gilbert. Between his voice and the way he smelt, even amidst his outright terror, Gilbert was in possession of an embarrassing erection. The moment his sword belt touched the ground a bag was put over his head. "Apologies, my lord," he heard the man say as he was taken hold of. "But you and I need to talk."

"About what?"

The other man shoved him. Gilbert fell and went into a defensive posture on the ground, trying to get away blindly. But then he saw he hadn't been harmed and that he'd only knocked Gilbert over so he could bind his legs together.

"Keep quiet," the man muttered as he threw Gil over onto his stomach in the leaf loam, to bind his hands behind his back. "I've no love for your kind."

# 2

hen the bag was pulled off his head Gilbert saw the other man's face for the first time and confirmed his identity, he had indeed been abducted by Robin Goodfellow. He had straddled Gilbert and was looking down at him with the curiosity of a top predator that has caught something strange and singular and is trying to identify it.

"Why would they send *you* after me?" Robin mused. "You don't seem anything particularly special..."

"Well thank you very much!" Gilbert blurted out sarcastically, before biting his tongue. His wit was a like an instinct at times, it wouldn't even be silent when his life depended on it. "I assure you this is not my best angle."

"You were very easy to capture..."

"Well, I didn't know you were even there!" Gilbert protested.

"That is usually at least half the problem."

Sarcasm, it seemed, was a language they were both fluent in.

"Are you going to kill me?" Gilbert asked, his voice quavering and whatever spirit he'd felt a moment ago disappearing.

"Don't rush me I only just met you," Robin replied, with that same subtle irony in his tone. "How am I meant to know whether I want to kill you or not yet?"

"Oh wonderful, will you be taking me to dinner first? And is the mood lighting helping you decide?" He was getting his courage up again now, seeing that Robin clearly appreciated humour.

Robin laughed. But Gilbert had an ill feeling that laughter and killing him weren't necessarily things that couldn't happen together with this man. Gilbert checked the weapons in Robin's sword belt and wondered how far he'd get if he tried to grab one. Probably not very far, he thought.

"I wouldn't if I were you," Robin said quietly. "If you try that we'll have to skip dinner."

"And that would be such an awful shame. We can't have that! Now if you aren't going to kill me immediately, I wonder if you wouldn't mind loosening my hands? As happy as I normally am to be lying under a handsome man in the forest at night, this is a tad uncomfortable."

"Who are you and why are you following us?" Robin demanded.

He sighed. It would have all been easier when he still felt outraged, when he was certain they had abducted his niece. Now the whole thing just felt foolish and the meaninglessness of it all enraged him.

"I'm Gilbert de Biron, Baron of Rochdale," he admitted quietly.

If Robin was surprised, he didn't show it. That wasn't a good sign, Gilbert decided. A tinker man ought to be surprised if not terrified to discover he was not only touching but straddling a peer of the realm. Social intimidation was about all he had going for him in this situation and it didn't seem to be working

"I see. So you and your kinsman are pursuing us because of Augusta de Biron? Who is what to you, your niece?"

Gilbert was about to correct him and say 'kinswoman' when he realised it would be better for Robin not to know Nanette was with him if he didn't already. He merely nodded in response.

"Augusta has no wish to come home I'm afraid," Robin said reasonably, as if in his eyes this should put an end to the matter.

"I don't care what Augusta wants!" he exploded. It wasn't true of course, he cared deeply about what Augusta wanted, that was why it mattered to him so much that Nanette had lied to him.

"Then perhaps you are not the kind of man I need to have dinner with." There was a faint twitch of a smile at the side of his mouth but Gilbert caught the implication of violence it carried and began to back-track hurriedly.

"No, no, no! I mean- What I mean to say is…" He sighed deeply, mentally cursing Nanette again. He had all these cunning things he wanted to say, ways he could imagine trying to play a man like Robin. Instead, he just closed his eyes and let the truth come out, as he knew deep in his gut that it was the best path to survival. "I came here because I was under the impression my niece had been dragged away and ravished." He sighed again. It was bad enough how foolish he felt without having to admit the details of it to Robin. "I came to rescue her and take revenge upon her attackers, as any decent man would do."

"Would they?" Robin asked abruptly.

The question was so abrupt that for a moment he wondered if he'd mis-calculated. "What do you mean?"

"Is that what decent Norman men do? You'll have to educate me; I haven't met one." There was so much ice around the edges of Robin's voice that Gilbert swallowed down hard on a shaky feeling in his throat. He felt a shifting in the air as though a million tiny strands were vibrating and deciding how they were going to arrange themselves. It was hard to breathe when he realised he could feel his own fate being determined.

"So this is why you came looking for her, because you wanted to rescue her? Not to restore honour to your family name or because you're worried about whether people think you're a big man or not?"

"I'm here to rescue her," Gilbert asserted.

"Where were you when she was abducted and raped by Geoffrey de Rue?" he asked softly. The question was asked so quietly it was almost a whisper, yet Gilbert knew instinctually that at this moment he was under more threat than he had been in the entire conversation so far.

"We weren't happy about it I assure you. When Nanette came to me and told me what had happened, I definitely thought about getting my sword and going around there. But I wasn't her father, I had no legal right, especially after he married her I…"

"Yet her brother did go around there and try to stop it. A boy of sixteen…"

Gilbert closed his eyes. "He was a hothead," he muttered. "He did it without consulting me. If he had, I would have told him to wait."

"Wait for what? The first child to be born?" Robin's voice was still quiet, enigmatic in tone but it wasn't as soft as it had been.

"No," Gilbert said firmly. "The moment when De Rue would let his guard down and be no longer expecting a reprisal. Besides," he added. "The man had a curse sat upon him. Nanette thinks she threw it but I warrant your brother did a number on him with that death curse -"

"I hate flatterers," Robin muttered. "You're clever though. Too clever. I can't let an enemy of your calibre live."

"But what about a friend of my calibre?" Gilbert asked quickly.

"Friend is a strong word. Let's not be too hasty," Robin said. He took out his knife then and Gilbert prayed that he meant to use it to free the bonds that were cutting off his circulation. "But for now, you may continue living if you are helpful to me. You will avoid lying, if you do lie, then I will *take your face*, and I will add it to my face collection. And I don't mean with magic. Do we understand each other?"

Gilbert swallowed down hard and nodded.

"Owain is straightforward enough, but say the prince's other son's name again slowly for me?"

Robin sighed and looked over at Gilbert. "Cad-wal-ad-er," he said distinctly and with as little accent as possible. "But you won't need to speak to them anyway. In fact, given the current mood here it is probably best if you draw as little attention to your Norman-speaking self as possible."

"So… If these two young chaps are the sons of a local prince… I mean, I don't wish to be rude here…"

"For the love of god, get to the point, man." Robin shielded his eyes from the glare coming through the clouds and scanned his environment. He always liked to be at any meet up earlier than anyone else and find a vantage point from which he could watch their approach and scope out the lay of the land. Even though he continued to speak with Gilbert Robin's attention was partly elsewhere.

"Well, you're an outlaw -of sorts…at least by the laws of my country. To be fair you're also somewhat of a people's hero here in Wales but-"

Robin held up his hand to silence Gilbert. He was already starting to regret his decision to keep the talkative nobleman alive. Deep down he knew that considering killing a man for talking too much wasn't an example of his finest self. "Our country doesn't acknowledge English law," Robin said at last, and in saying so he knew he'd made a commitment to trying to grow and stretch this man. Not necessarily to become his friend, mind you, but to show him another way so he could choose.

"So my outlaw status on land which was ceded to the Saxons is irrelevant to our people who see me as a figure of resistance to Norman rule. The princes of this land are powerful men and like most powerful men they want more power. I have something they want. They have something I want."

"But what could someone like you possibly have that they would want?" Gilbert asked in obvious mystification. Robin smiled faintly at how the other man didn't even know he was being rude. He could have mentioned that the prince's sons wanted him involved in their rebellion because of that 'people's hero' business Gilbert had mentioned earlier, and the morale that it would lend. But letting on that he meant to fight for the prince in exchange for a safe passage agreement for his family would be giving far more away to this man whom he had no reason to trust. When Owain and Cadwaladr arrived, they would be discussing the deal he hoped to make in Cymraeg, so there was no harm in Gilbert hearing.

"So these young men really intend to go through with pitting themselves against the crown?" Gilbert murmured after awhile when Robin didn't answer his last question. "I've heard they're little older than you are…"

"Always old enough for Lady Death, my friend. I would guess that, yes, they intend to resist foreign occupation of their homeland."

He shook his head. "It's just… They're going to get *crushed*…" His face revealed horror at the devastation that Gilbert foresaw for the Welsh people if they tried to stand against the Norman cavalry juggernaut.

"Perhaps," Robin agreed, with a sigh that came out sounding philosophical that was really something much grimmer. "But wouldn't you fight not to live as a slave upon the very land that holds your fore-parent's bones?"

Gilbert made brief eye contact with him and quickly looked away at the grey, mountainous horizon. It had a harsh beauty this land, Robin felt, but he could tell that it didn't fill Gilbert with the same sensation.

Eventually Gilbert shrugged. "I wouldn't know," he muttered. "I've never been to the land that holds most of my people's bones."

Robin winced slightly as he thought about Gilbert's statement. It was hard for him to imagine being born into such dizzying alienation. "I feel sorry for you," Robin said quite sincerely.

"You? You feel sorry for me?" Gilbert asked incredulously.

Robin nodded. "There is more than one way to be born rich. And more than one kind of poverty."

Before Gilbert could reply Robin saw the riders. They had come alone as they said they would, he observed. He mentally made note of this and it got them a little respect from Robin. They may be the sons of a rich man, but they were royalty the way the Welsh do it, they could still go riding on their own in the mountains with just their own weapons to assert their authority and no retinue of hired thugs.

He turned away from the two riders and looked at Gilbert. "I want you to learn two quick words in Welsh. Say after me: *Am Gwenllian.*"

"Am Gwenllian," he said, messing up the double L, but other than that succeeding.

"That will do for now."

"What does it mean?"

Robin sighed. It wasn't an irritated sigh but a heavy one of sadness underpinned with deep emotion. "It means 'for Gwenllian.' Princess Gwenllian was their sister."

"What happened to her?"

"She was murdered by your people, trying to hold her land against invasion."

Gilbert frowned. It was clear that this surprised him and that he even doubted its veracity. "A noblewoman killed when a castle was taken? Are you certain?"

*Am I certain about affairs in my own country…?*

"She wasn't killed when her castle was taken, she was killed while she led her men in battle," Robin felt emotion prickle the backs of his eyes with potential tears at the mention of the story. "Her husband was fighting elsewhere and couldn't get back to her in time. She would not surrender… She led her men on the battlefield because her pride made her strong, because here in Wales our girls grow up to be women. And her grown sons died fighting before her, trying to protect their mother, because that's how a Welshman dies."

Gilbert shook his head. He was clearly shocked and moved and disconcerted all at once. He didn't know how to answer Robin's fierce pride and so he looked away again. "I didn't even hear about it…"

Robin shrugged. It was an eloquent shrug that stood in for a whole lecture about the nature of privilege and injustice under a system of oppression that controls information as well as bodies. "So yes, Owain and Cadwaldr will never surrender to Norman rule, because their sister Gwenllian did not surrender. In her name they will fight." Robin knew this to be a fact because she wasn't even his sister but he would probably have fought 'for Gwenllian', even if he didn't have to for his family. "If you're ever in trouble here in Wales," he added as the prince's sons approached. "All you need is those two words."


Owain and Cadwaldr both dismounted and approached Robin to shake his hand. He accepted and shook the young prince's hands warmly, but he wasn't fooled by the egalitarian gesture. He looked them over carefully trying to discern their potential as fighters and as men.

"Well met, Robin Dhu. I'm Owain ap Gruffydd and this is my brother Cadwaldr."

"Pleased to meet you," Robin replied.

If they'd been expecting a 'my lord' or any other kind of fawning they didn't show it. They were relatively handsome, fair-to-ruddy and well-made. Cadwaldr was almost as tall as Robin was but his youth was evident in his playful smile.

"I thought you'd have dark hair," he remarked. "With the people calling you Robin Dhu."

His brother Owain smiled. "I always heard them tell it that he is called Black Robin from flying at night with the devil, and the other such nonsense the people talk."

Robin laughed, but not for the reason they thought. "Actually, it comes from the black in Twll Du where our stories say my people come from. This is my travelling companion Gil," Robin added, indicating the darkly clad man whose clothing alone suggested his Norman birth. Usually only rich people could afford the black dye that went into creating clothing that dark. Robin knew this because most of the black things his family owned had been stolen from Normans.

"*Am Gwenllian*," Gilbert threw into the conversation randomly while Owain and Cadwaldr briefly looked him over. He noted how they were built and moved and came to the conclusion that they were seasoned fighting men, despite their age that Gilbert had considered so tender for military leaders.

"*Am Gwenllian*," Cadwaldr replied. But from the tightening around his eyes and the set of his mouth it was clear that these were far from random words of solidarity for him. As Robin suspected their sister's death was not merely a matter of dynastic vengeance for them but a deep personal loss. Clearing his voice as though to push aside his emotion, Cadwaldr gave Robin a slap on the back.

"I hear tell your family traces back a shared ancestor with us going back to

Maredudd ap Bleddyn?"

"Let's not divert from business, brother," Owain chided gently, fixing a very serious gaze on Robin. He guessed that blood meant a lot to these men, and it made Owain uncomfortable to consider his connection with a man whose family's safety he was essentially holding to ransom. "Is it safe to talk in front of your 'traveling companion'?"

Robin could tell from the dark irony around the other man's mouth that Owain didn't buy for a moment that Gilbert was anything other than a prisoner but was too polite to say so. He had seen the young prince take note of the fact that Gilbert had no weapons in his belt, and there was only one reason that a man would walk around like that with The Anarchy going on in England and resistance afoot in Wales.

It seemed best to take the approach of charm here, so Robin favoured the other man with a cheeky grin. "Considering the poor thing doesn't speak Welsh beyond '*am Gwenllian*' I think we will be safe."

"He looks like a nobleman," Cadwaldr commented.

"Hush, that is Robin's business," his older brother corrected. "We saw nothing." At that he smiled back at Robin. "So, do we have a deal, my friend? Will you fight with us... for Gwenllian?"

Robin would have liked to agree just out of principle but he couldn't afford honour because he had a family. "I would love to fight for Gwenllian, but alas I must fight for my family, instead. I am forced to trade my sword for their safe conduct through the North. We need Gwynedd as a sanctuary this winter as we have outstayed our welcome on the English side of the border and have no wish to be caught up in their civil war."

Owain looked away for a moment. Robin took note of it. He could tell the idea of bribing Robin like this didn't sit well with the man. "You have the word of the honour of the House of Gwynedd, Robin Dhu," Owain agreed, extending his hand to shake again. "Not only will we give you the road, we will bring down the full force of our family's wrath upon any wayfarer who troubles your caravans."

Robin nodded thoughtfully looking back and forth between them.

"You can trust us, Robin," Cadwaldr said. "We aren't Norman baby-killers. We make our wars against other men with swords."

"Well, it looks like you've got yourselves a deal then, fellow countrymen," Robin replied, shaking Owain's hand after an extended hesitation. "I will fight in your rebellion, as long as my family is safe, and your honour remains of the caliber your brother speaks of it. If I once see women and children troubled in your war I will kill him I see doing it and walk away from the battle."

Owain stared at Robin with his mouth slightly open. Clearly people had prepared him for Robin's egalitarian manner, and up until now he'd coped admirably, but it was likely no one such as Robin had ever spoken to him like that before. Cadwaldr cleared his throat again and laughed to break the tension.

"Understood," Owain replied, his tone low and lacking warmth. Robin held eye contact with him unflinchingly for some time. Eventually the other man snorted with mild amusement. "Well, you've got a set, tinker. I'll give you that. Go to your family, set your affairs in order and return to us. I will spread the word that you are joining us."

"It's a good thing you're doing, Robin," Cadwaldr said. "We need the people's morale boosted. They believe in you like you're magic, and if you are here they will believe that-"

"-We aren't about to commit suicide?" Robin suggested.

"Quite," Owain agreed grimly.

"These bastards killed our sister," Cadwaldr blurted out with a sudden heat of emotion in his voice. "They did not ransom her back to us as they would a Norman woman of rank. They put her on her knees and struck her head from her body before everyone. They will die for it, or we will die seeking vengeance for her. There is no third option."

Robin nodded. "I understand."

# 3

it down and have something to eat," Robin said, indicating the delicious steaming food in what looked like a cauldron made from leather. "I want to tell you a story." Passing him some kind of flat cake he'd cooked on the hot stone he indicated the spoon for Gilbert to help himself. He just didn't explain exactly what was in there. Gilbert was hungry enough not to ask.

While he tasted what he believed to be mushrooms cooked in animal fat and wild herbs he looked the other man over briefly. It disturbed him for some reason to note that Robin had clearly woken before him by enough time to have found water, washed his hair and possibly even bathed -judging by his damp hair and shirtless state. Gilbert took in a sweeping look at Robin's scars and tattoos before quickly looking away. He had become adept at glancing at other men's bodies too quickly to be caught.

Gilbert's covertness seemed unnecessary though. As with some half-savage instinct Robin seemed entirely unselfconscious in his half naked state and didn't seem to notice either Gilbert's curiosity or admiration. How strange and foreign this tinker was… Gilbert judged him to be of an age with himself or younger, yet his body betrayed a whole road map of life and battle experience. *Perhaps they make them men sooner out here. Perhaps his twenty-one is our thirty-one.*

"When I was a boy," Robin began his story, something he also did unselfconsciously, as if story telling was entirely normal over breakfast. "I was excessively soft-hearted. Excessively for the age in which we live, a thinking person might say. But suffice it that I struggled with the immense amount of

239

suffering in the world around me, from the bee stuck in a puddle of water, to the impaled wolf in the pit, all the way to the most grotesque public torture of humans. For the little bees I would become distressed if I wasn't allowed to stop and rescue them. But with the public hangings and other public punishments of people…"

His voice dropped away for a few moments and he looked down, shaking his head as though remembering it all clearly. "I was more than distressed. People said I was touched. I used to sit in the corner of the yard rocking back and forth making a wailing sound and knocking my head again and again into the wall."

"I can see how they came to their conclusion," Gilbert said, and then added. "No offence meant."

"Perhaps so. But should we not all react so to the unbearable suffering of our fellow man? Was my child's heart the deformed thing to respond to horror as if it's horrible, to respond to the terror of my fellow man with terror? Or is the problem not with the hearts of those who swung upon the victim's legs or threw rotten fruit?"

There was a stark brutality of the truth in this that struck Gilbert like a slap. It wasn't just the truth, he was used to ignoring that, it was the strange species of innocence that lay behind Robin's words. "Doubtlessly there is far more wrong with us leg-swinging types," Gilbert conceded flatly, trying but not managing to pull off a wry joke.

"So, to continue my story, my dear brother who cared for me and endured my oddity, who was not himself a leg-swinger, but neither was he a corner-rocker, used to try to do little things to help me… He would find some way I could take out my rescue needs on someone. And sometimes I could save it up… He'd tell me to just hang on and I would; I wouldn't panic, I'd get through it. It was lucky he made me strong like that otherwise I wouldn't have survived what happened next. He taught me a lot about the ethics of survival in those early rescue projects he came up with to placate me.

"Sometimes we would rescue wolves from the pits and there were ways you could rehabilitate them if the wound wasn't too deep. Blaith always said to wait and see if the wolf had any fight in it before you decided whether you had to put it down or not. If it just let you help it, if it didn't try to fight you then it couldn't be saved. You had to learn to pick your battles. Maybe everyone deserves your help equally yet not everyone has what it takes to really *use* your help…"

"Why do I feel like this story is driving at something?" Gilbert said, licking the remains of his food off his fingers and wiping his hands.

Robin laughed and got to his feet. "Because you're smart?"

Feeling nervous because Robin got up, Gilbert got to his own feet also. There was a strange feeling in the air suddenly, as if something unpredictable was about to happen. Gilbert didn't like the feeling at all. "Oh I'm not feeling so smart right now… I'm not even sure where I fit into this story."

Without warning Robin tossed Gilbert his heavy weapon belt with his broadsword in it. It partially hit him in the chest, and he partly caught it having to take a step back to steady himself. "You're the wolf, Gilbert."

All at once it dawned on him that he had his sword back.

Gilbert smoothly slid the blade out of its scabbard. He didn't even know why he did it when he thought about it afterwards, beyond that when you're a predator who gets your teeth and claws back you bare them. Robin continued to look at Gilbert's eyes and didn't move from his arms-folded position. That was when Gilbert noticed Robin wasn't carrying.

Gilbert frowned and hesitated. "You're not armed…"

Robin shrugged. "I've never seen that bother a Norman lord before. That's how your people like the odds, isn't it?"

When Gilbert took a swing at him it should have appeared to come from a clear blue sky. Robin moved out of the way in a manner that made it clear he totally expected to be attacked.

"What is this, some kind of game to you?" Gilbert shouted at him, striding closer so he was almost in range to cut him. "Are you trying to prove I'm inherently violent? Or are you trying to see if I've got fight in me? Which one's the right answer?"

Robin laughed merrily at him, as though the dilemma were the ripest form of comedy. Gilbert immediately swung at him again, this time many times with an unrelenting savagery that Robin had to move much faster and use the environment around him to defend against.

"If I told you that, it wouldn't be a very good test would it?"

"I fucking hate you!" Gilbert screamed at him. "You're meant to be my inferior! Draw your fucking weapon!" Gilbert demanded. Somewhere in the back of his mind he realised he was entirely out of control, in a way that he hadn't been since childhood. Entirely, sublimely, out of control… It felt good and terrifying at the same time. "I will not fight a man not holding a proper weapon! Draw your fucking weapon!"

"But I have no wish to do harm to you, Gil," he said, as calmly as though they were discussing what to cook for dinner. "I've become oddly fond of you. You're the one waving all the blades around."

Gilbert made a sound of inarticulate rage through his teeth, but his mind was always working, even amid his fury. The stupidity of the situation was clear. He took a very deep breath and tried to rein in his wrath. "Well… This is just stupid then, because I don't want to hurt you either." The whole thing was just so humiliating, all that softness in him that Nanette accused him of, and had shamed him for since childhood, it all seemed exposed before this man. But despite this it was hard to pretend he had any desire to do Robin harm.

Robin smiled. "What if I said the only way I'd set you loose would be if you force me to let you?"

"Then I would have to stay here, because I'm not doing that unless your weapon is drawn," Gilbert said immediately. "It's just not who I am. I would, I would have to stay. You think I'm weak now, don't you? I'm one of the wolves with no fight in it, aren't I?"

Robin was smiling faintly. "Quite the contrary."

"What in God's name do you want from me then?"

"I'd like you to teach me to fight like a Norman."

"Yet it seems you handled De Rue just fine without knowing..."

Robin shrugged. "Such a trick as knocking the rider from the horse will not work in a battle."

Being an intelligent fellow, it didn't take Gilbert long to nod in understanding as to why Robin wanted that particular favour. He also took in what teaching Robin those things would mean in relation to racial loyalty. If he did that he really was '*am Gwenllian*'. "I can do that... But... We would need things... Chainmail, swords, lances."

Robin attempted to repress a grin. "I could probably... find some of those things."

Gilbert held up his hands. "I don't want to know how, alright?"

"They will just appear at our camp one day."

Charmed by the man despite his better judgment Gilbert forced himself to sigh with fake disapproval. "Fine. What else then?"

"Well as I said before, you're a powerful sorcerer. I'd much rather have you on my side than on their side."

"Am I understanding you right that you're asking me to help you magically take out my own si-"

"So, Nannette is the one who was driving the hunt for Augusta forward then, not you?"

Gilbert just nodded, but he still refrained from mentioning that Nannette was doubtlessly still this side of the Welsh border.

"Where is she located at the moment?"

He sighed. "I don't know. Really, I don't. She was at the inn when you abducted me but she'd be miles away by now."

"And you wouldn't tell me even if you did know," Robin added.

"Correct."

"So you feel normal sibling loyalty to her then? Despite the fact you've been brought up to believe she's inferior to you because she's a woman?"

"Nannette is another of those things that is *meant* to be inferior to me,"

243

Gilbert muttered. "But like you, she isn't."

"How did you come to determine that she was your equal?"

Gilbert glanced over into his probing, interested green eyes. "Oh, I never determined she was my equal, friend." Gilbert snorted with dark amusement. "No. I've never been good enough for that."

"Perhaps not. I have heard big things about your sister's sorcerous power. It takes strength for a man of your people to admit when he's bested by a woman. Maybe that is a strength of character that you have which she lacks, do you think?"

Gilbert appreciated the compliment. He felt like Robin was trying to get him to talk about this sister's character strengths and weaknesses, which was exactly what he himself would do if Nannette were his enemy.

"You won't tell me anything else because you believe I mean to harm her?"

"Sometimes I think I hate her more than anyone living. Yet she's my sister. It's complicated," he muttered.

"Kinship feelings always are."

"Speaking of which, if you take me back to camp with you how are your people going to react?"

"Mixed I'd say," Robin admitted.

# 4

f course I'm not sure I trust the Princes, Blaith. But it's this or expose the people I love to the possibility of another touch-and-go winter. When it comes to my principles verses love there is no competition. Love is amoral in that way." Robin shrugged.

"Love is the only thing that *is* moral," Blaith murmured, in gentle contradiction.

Robin reached over and briefly squeezed his hand. Between them it was enough alone to say he understood. "The thing is I caused so much of this, I need to uncause it."

"None of it was your fault."

"Be that as it may many see it as my fault."

."It's still not your fault-"

"Will you stop saying that?"

"No, probably not. Not until you give in properly."

Robin grinned. "I give in. Better now? Sometimes we have choices but no good choices available to us. Whether it was my fault or not the situation remains and I must right it. Fate has forced her way through us all of late with long teeth and nails and almost broke us on her way out. I just want to buy us a soft autumn and winter. You know I will survive a battle. From those to whom much is given, much is expected."

Blaith felt humbled for a moment in the presence of his brother's eloquence and inborn wisdom. There was no way to argue with it. "If anyone has managed to keep the clarity of the white eyes of fire when coming forth into flesh it is you, brother."

He could see Robin grin out of the corner of his eye. "Just try to keep that thought right at the front of your brain when I tell you I've brought home another Norman."

It took Blaith a couple of moments to process what these words meant. For some reason he was convinced he hadn't heard them right. He frowned and looked over at Robin almost in a double take. "You did *what?*"

"My Lord Uncle!" she cried, immediately answering in Norman French and dropping the weight of the cumbersome English she was not very good at. "You came for me." They stood staring at each other for a few moments. In a belated reaction of shame she futilely tried to cover her hair with her hands.

"Do relax, my dear. I've seen female hair before." He waved her discomfort away as if he could banish it with his hand gesture.

She looked him over. It felt unnatural after being among these touchy-feely people that she and her kinsman weren't going to touch at all. Among her people it was perfectly normal for men to kiss each other briefly on the mouth or face, or women to do the same in greeting. Yet unmarried, opposite sex people, even when family, would not be permitted that liberty. Everything was hard to manoeuvre now because technically she was married, and then widowed. What was the correct way to act now?

"How did you find us?" she asked, bristling suddenly at the thought he might want to harm her new friends. Augusta would defend them with her dying breath if she must. Her Uncle was obviously here on friendly terms as he had been allowed to keep his broadsword in his belt and he appeared unharmed.

"Robin found me. Your mother gave me the impression you'd been abducted against your will and ravished by these people, though I see that was clearly false."

Augusta pushed her courage to the fore and dropped a belated, slow, and well-executed curtsy. It was still hard to talk about what happened to her but in the name of justice it must be done. "I was only ever ravished by Geoffrey De Rue, Lord Uncle," she replied, before lifting her demurely dropped eyes to meet his in challenge. "And I am not free of my rapist because of a man of the House of de Biron, but instead by the hand of a warrior of the Twll Du blood thread, so if you're coming to harm them…"

Uncle Gilbert held up his hands in a way that appeared a mixture of the submission gesture and a call for silence. "To be honest, Augusta. I am quite enjoying their company."

Lux rolled over on the skins and looked at Robin in the half-light. She was still naked, as she had been since the second time they made love. He was shirtless. That was about as naked as he got these days. His weapon belt was always either on, though his blades had been left at the door in accordance with custom, or it was just within reach. Although the campfire was a little way off and her skin was exposed to the air Lux's skin was still hot, alive and tingling.

"What are you thinking about when we fuck?" she asked, still seeing the blind-man look to his eyes, like someone gazing into the face of the infinite.

He turned his head to look at her. "Sometimes I feel the edges of my death touch me."

So clear it was that she had to look away. Behind his eyes she would see something, just the slither of an image, him bleeding out into the forest loam, his gaze lost in the limitless expanse of blue sky, full of ecstatic surrender. She shivered as if the wind from their graves was blowing backwards into the tent.

"You're not planning on staying long, are you?"

Robin pressed his lips together and she could feel a ripple of pain pass through his being. "I wish I could."

"What's happening?" she asked. Lux tried to keep her voice matter-of-fact, as she sat up and pulled a tartan blanket around herself.

He turned his head away to look up at the roof of the tent with one hand behind his head. "War," he replied, low and quiet. That single word, that intense reality that irrevocably separated his experience of the world from hers most utterly.

"Our Lady be merciful, so it is then," she whispered, closing her eyes. The axis of her world went off kilter and she found herself clutching her bedding to try to stay steady, as if she would scramble off the edge of a cliff. Lux felt Robin's hand reach for hers. She didn't resist it when he sat up and pulled her back into his arms. That night this feeling of his strength and physical power only made her more afraid and aware of how small and comparatively helpless she was. It was why she couldn't follow him where he was going.

"I'm so sorry," he whispered into her hair. "If I didn't have to I wouldn't." Even more quietly like telling a secret he continued. "I care nothing even for whether they take my homeland by comparison to how I want to stay here and be with you." That didn't help at all. The notion that he was being forced to go to war against his will wasn't even a vague comfort. It occurred to her that very little possibly could be. The moment he left to face something like this without her there would be no comfort in anything until she next saw his horse on the horizon.

"Are you scared?" she asked.

"Somewhat," he said. "Certainly more than I was of De Rue. Then sometimes I'm not, and that worries me a whole lot more."

Blinking back the tears in her eyes Lux squeezed his hands hard in hers. "Tell me something I don't know about you," she whispered thickly, tears in her voice.

Silent for a couple of moments Robin lifted her hands to his mouth and kissed them both. "I taught myself to read during the years where I was mute. I had a lot of time on my hands that other people spend communicating, so that's what I did with it."

Lux nodded. She hadn't succeeded in stopping the tears, which were running freely down her cheeks. "You do well at communicating, for someone who missed four years practice."

He sat back up slowly and reached out to wipe her tears away. After he'd done so he, somewhat eccentrically to her mind, licked her tears off his fingers. "Well, when you're not talking you do a lot of listening and a lot of observing, which probably helps more than constantly running your mouth like most children. Being mute teaches you how to communicate with body language and subtlety. Tell me something I don't know about you?"

Lux swallowed down on a lump of emotion in her throat and smiled. "When I was only about nine, I went into some kind of faerie fit in church and spoke in tongues. Open eyed visions, the whole business. The village was divided on whether I was a saint or a faerie devil. People started bringing me things, leaving them outside the door as offerings, because they thought it meant I was lucky or uncanny." She laughed at the memory.

Robin looked at her with an expression of intense fascination. "How are you only just telling me this now, you mysterious little creature?"

She shrugged.

"Let's do another one. You can ask me anything you want and I have to answer it without evasion, and then I can do the same."

"Alright..." She thought about what she wanted to know. There were about three main areas of his life that stood out as feeling closed to her in some way, but only one did she feel it was likely he could answer for her. It was something she had wanted to ask since the day she'd first met Blaith. "When you and Blaith are away together, do you touch each other? I mean, more than other normal brothers?"

"How do normal brothers touch each other?" he asked immediately

"I think you know what I mean."

"Let me put it this way," he said quietly. "Blaith and I have a magical bond that means we can give each other an orgasm through moving power during forehead contact alone. I'm not sure how to compare that to the way people inside the walls go about being normal. My turn. Did you ever have any crushes or feelings for anyone before you met me?"

"Do you mean before I met you when we were children or as adults?"

He smiled sadly. "Children?"

She shook her head. "No. I used to watch you even before that day when the guard struck you. I think I could sense you were like me, that you were not from around here."

"I remember you looking down from the window. I could feel you watching me. You waved to me once, the sunlight hit your hair for a moment and then you ran away. I thought you were the sweetest little creature I'd seen in the world. I saw god in you, a spirit carrying redemption in her smile. I still do."

# 5

I'm coming home, Lux. I promise you."

"I know," she whispered, screwing her eyes shut as she hid her face against his chest for that last few desperate moments. She savoured the smell of him and the sound of his heartbeat, so much more powerful than hers and set eternally to a slower, deeper rhythm. His heartbeat was almost always like this except during sex or hard exercise, giving the message there was nothing to fear because he was still calm. She fought her tears back.

"I want you to *really* know," Robin said, gently drawing her back from him to look into her face. She could feel the others standing around. She didn't need to look at Blaith to know how pale he was, if they made eye contact she knew she'd cry. "I'm a survivor. I'm damn hard to kill."

"Enough people have tried," Jack grunted in agreement.

"And besides," Gilbert said to her in French, pausing where he had been just about to mount his newly acquired warhorse. "I will watch his back, Lux."

She didn't doubt Gilbert's sincerity and watching him mount easily in his chainmail and the smooth way he negotiated the presence of the broadsword in his belt during the motion, gave her confidence. These were cues of a man's power that were deeply imbedded in her since childhood. As much as she had become aware of, challenged and overcome much of that early programming, there was still some that held. The presence of this Norman lord made her feel Robin was safer than if he'd been trying to move alone in their world of iron and blood.

Before she could say anything, Robin pulled her into a final breathless kiss, it was fast, madly passionate and cut off abruptly at the end with an air of firm self control. "I have your girlhood hair tucked away inside my hauberk," he whispered. "There is much power of protection in the girlhood hair of a woman who loves you."

"Shoot straight, *fy nghariad,*" she whispered, losing her battle to keep the tears in still pools inside her eyes just at the moment he turned from her to mount his horse. They ran all at once down her face. Her heart was beating wildly as if her very own life were in danger, but she loved him too much to make this harder for him by calling him back.

She could tell Blaith was holding through the skin of his teeth, onto a similar resolution. Gilbert paused, drawing his horse up in front of Blaith. He took out an embroidered handkerchief and gave it to Blaith and then immediately rode away. Robin went with him.

"May the battle queen spare him, may the angel prince of all just causes defend him," Sariah whispered.

Lux didn't feel she'd reach parity with Sariah's faith in Robin, instead she had learned to have faith in the power of the other woman's belief.

"Why did he just give me a pretty piece of fabric?" Blaith asked Lux, looking somewhere between touched and confused, as he looked back and forth between the object and Gilbert and Robin as they rode away.

Lux smiled sadly, wiping away her tears decisively. "It's called a handkerchief. In Norman culture it's often referred to as a token. Knights usually give them to the maiden they favour, someone they're attracted to."

Blaith grinned with amusement and looked down at his leather-clad and weapon adorned form as though double-checking whether he'd turned into a woman. "Well I'm no maiden."

Lux turned away so she wouldn't witness the moment they disappeared from view. "I'm sure he's noticed. Among Normans this means that the knight intends to fight in your name. I think he's telling you he plans to fight for your people's freedom. It also means he likes you."

Augusta looked up with a jolt. It felt like she'd been jabbed in the back of the head with something cold. She saw Blaith beckoning to her from across the campfire, she got the feeling he'd been staring intently at her for a while. His eyes were so dark they looked all black in the partial shadows. She shivered. This was a conversation she had been waiting for but not looking forward to. With a sigh she got up from her place on the other side of the fire and came around to sit down next to him.

For a little while he didn't speak, he sat there worrying at the coals with a stick, as if she were the one who had initiated the conversation. He went about it for so long that she almost broke first and spoke.

"Do you want to tell me about why it happened?"

Immediately Augusta felt hunted. She wasn't sure which it Blaith was referring to but from the way he was looking at her she felt there was likely no way to escape his snare.

"Which it?"

"Are there a few to consider?"

The darkness in him allowed him to see into your darkness, that was what she perceived while he gazed into her. Before she'd even decided it would be so she was speaking her truth to him. "I didn't have a lot of choice. It was Mother who killed Lux's old nurse. I was just... there."

"I know."

Silence again. Silence with a lot of subtexts, Augusta felt she knew what at least a couple of them were.

"I was almost as afraid as the woman herself."

"I know."

She couldn't imagine how he knew because she had never said that to herself until now, let alone anyone else.

"Because," Blaith added, placing down the stick and turning to make very intense eye contact with her. "If I didn't know you were afraid I would begin to suspect we'd welcomed a stone-cold killer into our camp. There are such people, you know? Who feel neither pity nor affection even for those of their own blood? There is only one true sin in our culture, the lack of love."

Augusta sat still and wide eyed like a hypnotised animal gazing into the eyes of a snake. She couldn't move to nod or respond to him but she wanted to. Her rising fear that he could somehow see the worse thing she'd done that none of them knew about was beginning to peak into a pure panic.

"I suppose what I want to know," he said very, very slowly. "Is are you someone capable of hurting the things you love?"

"Isn't everyone?" she snapped back suddenly, her mouth moving without her volition. It was like in the faerie stories where a truth curse is put upon the tongue. "Doesn't everybody hurt the ones they love?"

Blaith didn't contradict her but his eyes narrowed slightly. She began to tremble and break out in a sweat; she crossed her arms to try to conceal it.

"Do they? You tell me."

Augusta felt confused. She couldn't remember why she'd said it in the first place. It wasn't what she wanted to be true. Yet it fitted her experience of reality like a glove. "Love is just a method to control and own people. And when it's not it's nothing but weakness! " She could hear her voice saying this but it felt like some inner perversity in her was just spewing this stuff out to try to wilfully cause animosity, or even bring about her own downfall. All the while she could feel how this wasn't doing her or anyone else any good but the perverse spirit of the thing fed upon itself. The more she let it speak the more it wanted to say.

"Is that so?" he asked, a faint smile at the edge of his mouth. She hated the patience he was exhibiting, she wanted to make him angry and it wasn't working. Her mind rushed with nastier, lower ways she knew she could bring a rise out of him.

"Let me ask you something: You grew up believing in Christ, I assume?"

Augusta nodded impatiently. This seemed inanely obvious.

"And I assume you loved your Saviour back when you were a little girl? Before you realised he wasn't coming to save you from De Rue?"

Her rage nearly overcame her fear of Blaith and she fought a strong urge to slap him across the face like she would have done to a cheeky servant. That's all he was after all, someone so low he wouldn't even have been allowed in service to her family. "Yes," she answered through clenched teeth. "When I was a little girl, before I realised he wasn't going to save me, I loved my saviour," she parroted back sarcastically.

"And if he'd come to you with the wounds of his passion in his hands and offered them to you, how would you have received his holy blood? With what expression of grace?"

"I can see what you're trying to say!" Augusta raised her voice and as she did she noticed conversations falling off and many eyes suddenly on her. They weren't angry eyes, not yet, nor had the wardens reacted, they were just looking and waiting. People did not often yell at Blaith.

"Can you?" he replied, his voice sharp. "Because I see evidence you do not treat those who have saved you with grace. I see evidence you are capable of lying outright to them."

Her bottom lip started to tremble. The human girl in her was devastated with fear of losing his approval, but there was something else inside her, some terrible thing that raged. If he sensed it Blaith apparently only wished to provoke it further, because he leaned in close to her and spoke with menacing quiet. "Jesus didn't come to save you from De Rue, my brother did. Lux did. We all did. You might want to think about who has been answering your prayers."

Before Augusta could suppress it a power of sickening intensity whiplashed through her body and she head-butted Blaith in the face. Her forehead connected with his mouth as her body jerked up as if on puppet strings. For a moment as she covered her face with horror she felt her mother, she felt De Rue, she felt some ancient evil inside her and she wanted to be sick. She wanted to vomit and purge so hard that she'd puke them all out of her, in a great tangle of black matted hair, needles, kin-murder, thorns and strangled newborns...

Everything happened quickly then. Blaith recoiled back onto his knees. Her arms were grabbed by two of the wardens before she even realised she

255

was fighting them, arching back with a deep, crazy sound coming out of her throat. Before they restrained her, in horror she saw that the force of her blow had hit Blaith's lip against his sharp teeth and his mouth was gushing blood.

To her shock and cold fear he threw his head back and laughed. She saw blood on his sharp, uneven teeth in the moonlight... Blood gushing out down over his chest... A scream and a yelp or two from the women and children not used to witnessing violence inside their camp... She had a sinking feeling as his blood splattered onto the soil before her that she'd somehow despoiled Paradise and they would all be gone in the morning like a faerie camp that packs up silently and disappears before the dawn.

"Alright," he laughed, his voice gurgling with blood and his black hypnotic eyes descended on her from above. "That's how you want to do this, is it?"

She didn't decide to but she began to fight them with everything in her body. Trying to bite the wardens and to kick Blaith. A bucking, scratching, foaming madness ripped through her.

"Fuck you!" she screamed at them all. "Fuck you, ditch-born filth! I'll fucking end *you*!"

She growled and contorted in response to it and tried to fight. Augusta didn't know why she was fighting or what she was fighting, all she knew was the raw struggle. The terrible thing was coming, the thing she'd try to hide from all of them and it was tumbling out in front of everyone and they were all seeing it.

# 6

As the road to Cardiganshire snaked down and out of the mountain country and into a landscape of patchy woodland and rolling hills, Gilbert saw that they would no longer have the roads to themselves. Every ten minutes or so a man on horseback carrying a pike with a little piece of his family tartan or plaid tied around his arm would take the road. Or they would pass a small hamlet or cabin in the woods to be joined by men dressed in forest green tunics and natural suede leggings with longbows slung across their back. Some of them shouldered packs as well, some had a little Welsh pony to do the work for them.

Gilbert glanced over at Robin to see if the scene along the road ahead of him made him sentimental. "Your people are rising," he commented.

"Indeed."

Seeing as Robin's reply didn't give much away Gilbert continued to prompt. "They're very brave these simple men. Given that I can see that Prince Owain has not rounded them up. They come of their own free will."

"Of course they do," Robin replied. Gilbert waited, examining Robin's profile off and on in between looking where he was going. Finally Robin's good nature won out over whatever complex emotions the scene filled him with, and he turned to Gil with a brief smile. "They would rather die free men of the Cymry than as slaves of the invader. But they are not my people. Those 'simple' men leaving their homes in the hills to fight took a different path from me and mine many hundreds of years ago, my friend."

"Is that how your people ended up on the road?"

"My people lived just the same as every other of the Cymric folk until the days of Teyrnon Twryf Lliant the first shackle breaker."

"Tell me more about these shackles, you mention."

"Well shackles are rather at the forefront of the minds of all Cymric folk on this road at the moment, I'd say," Robin replied with mild sarcasm. "Teyrnon was a horse-lord of many years hence. Probably while the Romans were still here for there were many slaves in shackles in those times, our people knew subjugation and learned it at the hands of their captors. Those who were made slaves learned how to make slaves of others. There's a demon in it, that's for sure," he seemed to muse on this sadly.

"What's a horse-lord?" Gil asked, unsure of the meaning of a few of the things Robin had said.

"Oh. We use the word you use to denote ownership of land and people to designate skill, as in 'glamour lord', or 'song lord'. Teyrnon was a great breeder of and whisperer of horses, was said that he bred them from a faerie mare. It was he who stood up to those in power and cut Rhiannon's shackles. The story says that he was the best man in the world and he took the men that refused to do what was wrong, even upon pain of death, and he formed the first company of wardens from them.

"They went through the land breaking shackles and where they found the women and the gentle boys who were Otherwise and unable to help themselves, they helped them. They found the changelings, the men who turned into wolves as they slept, they found the dispossessed, the sodomites, the whores, the ones who everyone else had turned from their doors to follow a way that was never Christ's way at all. Christ said judge not, and he helped the poor when all his followers do is cast judgment followed by stones."

While Robin had been talking the hairs on the back of Gil's arms had stood erect. It was somewhere in that rant about the wardens coming to rescue those who were Otherwise... It awakened in him memories of his early days he thought he had long ago suppressed. "So... in the days of slaves-"

"We are still in the days of slaves."

"Well… You know what I mean. Today we have serfs which is a different sort of arrangement."

Robin looked at him incredulously. "Slavery is current right now in this land you stand on. And, Gilbert, you *own* peasants."

"Well, I own the land the peasants…"

"-Are tied to forever and not allowed to leave. You might not put iron on their ankles or a collar on their necks, yet you own them just the same."

Gil felt such a swelling of sadness in his chest that his throat thickened with it. He watched the other men marching steadfastly towards what he imagined was likely-to-certain death. "If I don't die in this fight I'm going home and cutting all my bondsman loose."

"And what would they do then? Where would they go? How would food come to your household?"

Tears of frustration stung Gil's eyes at the inescapable logic of these facts. "Then why are you telling me this! If there's nothing I can do?"

"Because it's the truth. The truth doesn't need to have any other value in it other than the fact it's the truth. Wouldn't you rather have knowledge than ignorance?"

"Yes," he said, after a few moments of contemplation. "I would rather have knowledge than ignorance."

"Good!" Robin declared, suddenly buoyant seeming, in a way that mystified Gil considering the vent of the conversation. "Because the secret is, knowledge and truth? They get us all in the end anyway. It's only an illusion of choice on this one. Ignorance is only ever a delay to Fate having her way with you." He grinned, as though this notion of Fate having her way with you didn't evoke horrific images of being mauled by bears.

"When we have either rescued someone or given them a clean death, we take the chains and melt them down. From them we mend vessels that have cracked and when we heat and pour and hammer. We put our fire into the metal so that it goes out there among the housewives and the servants, those who cook. We melt their hard, cold iron in our fire, turn it, reshape it and send it out to be cooked and eaten of by the common folk, full of our spells. This is how we fight.

"Our arrows are all tipped with their metal, and our warden's cloaks all lined with the pelt of the wolves they've murdered; these two facts are no accidents. We are the shades of the dead top predator coming for those who killed them, our arrows made with melted chains… These people here on the road?" Robin said, indicating the men who rode or walked ahead in the direction of resistance. "They are starting to listen maybe. It's in their blood, part of them remembers they are sons of Beli Mawr and Ana, but part of them has forgotten. They are not yet my people until they have supped at the Well of Memory."

"And what would I find there, if I went to the Well of Memory and drank? What would I have to remember? I'm a great, great grandson of Viking warlords, not horse-lords. Warlords who were themselves sons of plunderers, and my people clapped on the shackles that your forebears put asunder."

Robin looked over at him and smiled. He appeared to be gently appraising Gil in an odd sort of way. "I believe if you drink down far enough you'll find you and I shared some ancestor not so very far away, some man who hunted for giant deer upon plains where forests now stand."

Gil laughed affectionately at the idea of giant deer. "You Cymric folk and your fanciful imaginations! I can see why as someone who lives by hunting why giant animals would be your fantasy. And this mythical common ancestor of ours couldn't just hunt normal old deer, now could he?"

Robin laughed too. "Ah but I've seen them, Gil! I've seen their giant antler span in my dreams! In my dreams I thrust a spear into its throat at close quarters to win the respect of the Old People, and it was so tall its jugular gush went right over the top of my head!" He announced exuberantly. "I think now we should gallop. I feel him, that old one… That old one we both share, wanting the rush of furious motion."

Gil was about to object that they should save the animal's strength for the journey when Robin hit his mount on the rump so hard it went off at a darting run. For a moment he scrabbled to get the situation under control and then he just went with it, an irrepressible grin spread across his face as he did.

What Blaith pulled off Augusta felt like it had mass, had weight, had its own identity in some way. At first, he thought it was a demon, and what he was performing an exorcism. As he got deeper the word curse seemed more appropriate. *A curse with its own rudimentary intelligence...* Having it out of her into a jar while she slept sedated on milk of the poppy, Blaith now sat staring down at the capped vessel as if he would bore through its secrets with his eyes.

"What do you think it is?" Sariah asked.

He sighed. "It's not like anything else I've ever pulled out of someone," he admitted. "If I had to guess I'd say it started as a curse. It wasn't meant for Augusta but perhaps some of it touched near her when Nanette threw the eye in De Rue's direction. Something has been done to feed it though, something vile. A true crime against nature."

"Do you think she killed her brother?" Eilish asked. Abrupt as the question was it was no doubt what they were all thinking. He passionately wished that Eilish didn't have to be anywhere near this while she was pregnant. As much as they had not planned this pregnancy the further it got along the more protective he felt of her and the unformed life.

"Honestly? Yes, I do."

"What are we going to do with her then? That's one murder of an innocent that she stood by and watched, preceding to not tell Lux of the woman's fate. If she's guilty also of the murder of a kinsman..." Sariah left the words hanging heavily in the air. He knew they would not be able to keep her with them long term if their suspicions proved correct. The killing of an innocent and spilling the blood of one's kin were both grievous crimes among their people.

"Well, we have to find out if she did it first. Our suspicions are not enough. I think Jack is best placed to talk to her when she recovers. She is

261

terribly young, murderess or not, she must be surrendered over into Gilbert's hands or Jack's after Robin returns from the fight. I am not sure the girl even yet bleeds with the moon."

Sariah nodded her acquiescence. "I feel sorry for her too, Blaith. I also feel nervous about how many De Birons are here and how that might open us up to further attack from Nanette. She has more than a few links here to work with. And mother to daughter sorcerous links are one of the most potent." He noticed her glance briefly at Eilish's expanding stomach line. Sariah herself had made a powerful oath to not conceive children, but it didn't mean she lacked a mothering instinct. The bond between the two women as cousins was as strong as if they'd been born sisters and Blaith knew all three of them were invested in this baby. Somehow, even with all the impracticality that came with it, it still managed to represent hope for their blood-thread.

"I know. I don't like it either. I want you to keep well away from Augusta, Eilish. Don't let her touch you above the babe or hand you aught of food or drink or lay a shawl or any garment over your person."

Eilish nodded. "But you successfully pulled the demon off her did you not?"

"Aye. This is no ordinary spirit riding a human, it is more curse than demon. The moment I do anything to let it free it will sniff looking for somewhere to roost."

"What do you intend to do with it then?"

"It needs to be returned to sender. Then I suppose we see what Robin thinks and if the people of the caravans are open to her remaining with us."

"There is a lot of gossip," Sariah said. "Everyone who saw her head butt you was furious and many leapt straight to the conclusion that it was her who killed her brother. I think we will have trouble containing the story now, even if it turns out to be false. She is not trusted, and Gil even less so."

When thunder struck Gil renewed his feelings of gratitude to be in a cave, as the wrath of god marked itself upon the turbulent heavens. Everyone said it meant god was angry but Robin didn't seem at all perturbed by it. Gilbert had thought it quite normal to be afraid of storms. This fact heightened somehow the church's claim that storms were signs of god's anger because nobody seemed to have a better explanation for why the sky was crying and shouting.

"Ah," Robin murmured, his voice rumbling deeply in his chest as though in sympathy with the thunder. "Gwrach, Old Woman is sleep walking... She's strong tonight. Guts of the earth strong..." He placed his ear to the stone so as better to appreciate the reverberations of lightning striking the earth and the guttural voice of thunder. "Gyre Carlin they call her further North of here, and Cailleach. Old Grandmother with long teeth and claws stalking the ice... I hear you... A once adopted son of the Old Folk remembers... Wordless he remembers the voices in the marrow holes from when the ice was giant-sized..." As Robin spoke he moved strangely, crouched and throwing a bigger shadow up on the cave wall behind him.

"You're creepy sometimes, you know that?"

His head darted around in Gilbert's direction with almost faerie swiftness. His green eyes were glimmering with a wicked fire, which was easily as disquieting as it was attractive. As he smiled he immediately started shaking his head slowly. "Oh no, no, no... Not Robin." He left a pregnant pause before cocking his head slightly off to one side. "Puck!" He said it like one would say 'boo!' and it had the same effect on Gilbert, who scrambled back out of his way, to Puck's hilarity. From the other side of the cave Gilbert took stock of the mad god his friend had suddenly become.

"Oh come now, don't run away," he cried, leaping up onto a tree stump that should have been too high even for Robin's considerable agility. Gilbert felt the hairs on the back of his neck stand to attention in a long wave of chills. "Come and be my friend, come, come!" he said, jumping down from the tree stump and squatting by the fire, furiously patting the ground beside him. "I'll only catch you if you run." Gilbert edged closer to the fire. "When will you start being Robin again?"

"I am Robin," he said, moving right up close to Gilbert in a way that was more intense than could possibly be comfortable even with a lover. "I am just Robin without edges," he said, making an eccentric sort of hand gesture to indicate his extravagant edgelessness.

"To what do I owe the honour, Master of Witches?" For this was the god's honest truth of the matter, after all.

"Ha! Puck is nobody's Master… Puck *despises* Masters!"

"But they call you that… Master Puck…"

"Master of me, Master of me," he muttered, hitting himself hard in the chest with his fist. "Master of Puck! Nobody is master of me, but me. Every man a master of himself and what Paradise there is upon the earth then! This is the truth the liars and the oppressors have kept from everyone."

"Then why do they flip their hair over and show you the backs of their necks in the Sabbat if you're not their Master?"

"To let me inside the cauldron of their skull, through the bloody door to the old knowledge slithering up in there. To let me come inside them! They offer themselves to their Mastery, Gil. Puck is but a mirror. Puck is a hollow bone. Wind makes music on his rib cage he is so hollow. Hollow bone man…"

His voice muttered out into the storm and his eyes lost focus in staring into the flame. "I'm a memory of the first bone singer. The people want me to sing in their bones and I want the people singing inside mine…" He leaped up very quickly and took Gilbert's face in his hand to bring his face so close that there was no focusing and he appeared to have four eyes and two mouths. "I suckled the long dead on my bone marrow to clear the passage for my song. I called up the stones. I hollowed all the bones."

"You still didn't tell me to what I owe your visit."

"Blood-of-my-blood, surely you know? It was told to you in what you deemed fanciful words back there upon the road. I am your forebear, sorcerer-brood, witch-spawn, hod's-kin that you are… Whether De Biron or Twll Du blood thread, all, all, my children of Cain."

"You who are old enough to have slain giant deer in some mythical land allow yourself to be called Cain?"

"I am the first horseman, who gentled the horse of the plain with my whispers and became as one with her. I am a man of art who made the gods leap forth from the cave wall in the clay hands reaching! I am first child of fire forged in flesh to land upon the ancestral lands, first vessel of the old magic and the new brought together. Branded for shame upon the forehead by my people for fraternising with the Others... If the myth fits, Cain fits so I can wear him. I am the angel-beast that will carry any name blessed or accursed you give me. Call me your language's strongest swear word and I shall answer to it."

"Are you faerie?"

"I loved a faerie thing... Once when the world was fresh and gazed on the open eyes of the dreaming one... The terrible beauty! That's why I'm mad as cut snakes!" Puck appeared to become distracted but waved the thought away with another odd hand gesture. "Because of love! Let's listen to the Old Woman keening for the blood that must be spilt upon the morrow," He said, leaning back against the cave wall suddenly and closing his eyes. "Sad or hungry? Sad or hungry? Both! Both and always..."

Tentatively Gilbert sat next to him and leaned his head back in the same manner, closing his eyes. "What's she saying?" Gilbert whispered.

"She doesn't speak in words," Puck whispered back. "She has all the little ache-voices in your balls, and the shriller ones with the mouths of the dead sitting in rows in your guts, to talk through. Old Woman's got the first people's sinew-speak to work with, she doesn't need your words! She speaks to your bones. Only you know what she's saying to your redness. That's all you have to Master to be the singing bone man. Know your voices and let what's chattering through you do its chattering. All you have to do to make sure no one is ever your Master, is own all the voices you are and never let anyone make you less than everything.

"Move away from one who would threaten your expansiveness and try and make you small. Feel how sovereign you are truly, Gilbert! How edge-less..." At this Puck took up his hand for a couple of moments and squeezed it

265

with great intensity, shaking it up and down emphatically. "Go with strength to the future your voices remember, blood-of-my-blood."

"Have you learned about Norman fighting from your close study of me?" Gil asked him while they rested to recover from sparring.

Robin smiled and sat down on a tree stump to sip water from his skin. "Yes, I think so," he said, wiping his mouth.

"May I ask what you've learned?"

He grinned wider still. There was a little uptight streak in Gil that Robin found adorable; it made him want to do gently sadistic things like tickle him until he squirmed helplessly with laughter. It was an entirely affectionate urge. "Well, they have no idea from what distance our bows can punch through chainmail that's for sure."

"I'd say you're probably right there."

"And I've learned also," he said, watching Gil carefully to see if he'd take offence. "That my enemy is very complacent. It's a side effect of early-learned arrogance, the assumption of superiority that underestimates those society places beneath. They do not even consider a Welsh victory possible."

"How has training with me taught you that? If anything, I have always assumed you would beat me whenever we train at whatever style."

Robin didn't answer. He just reached inside his jerkin sleeve and pulled out Gil's boot dagger, which he'd taken without its owner's knowledge during their practice. Gilbert checked his boot instinctually when he recognised his dagger. Robin passed his weapon back. "If it was a real fight I'd have severed your Achilles heel when I drew it from your boot. I've also learned what boxes they can't readily think outside of without someone showing them what lies outside the walls. All of that could come in handy during combat."

Gil frowned. Obviously, he couldn't see how. "Robin, you do know that it's up to the Princes to command the battle? You won't need to understand anything… You just follow orders…"

"Oh and legs! Normans don't pay enough attention to legs, either their own or yours. I have killed so many Normans by wounding their legs. It's like their body is an upright for carrying around fists, swords and maces and foot placement is mainly about getting your bludgeoning weapon to a certain position. They don't fight with their whole body to the extent we do."

"That is highly unlikely to become relevant during a Norman cavalry charge."

"That's what Geoffrey De Rue thought when he got dressed for his last day on earth." Robin laughed. "Another dead man who forgot he had legs! I got him on his back pretty much the same way I just did to you, except I didn't have a sword when I did it to him."

Gil sighed. "I don't think you understand how large scale battle works."

"True. That's why I need you. But I don't think large scale battle understands how *I work* either."

# 7

hy is he doing that?" Gil asked, shielding his face from the sun with his mail-gloved fist so he could better see the movements of the other army. All of the men on horses up there on the higher ground looked like his people looked. They bore the same armour as him, they cut their hair the same, and they rode somewhat taller destriers. Among them he saw the family crests of various other noble houses that he knew. "Bringing his army outside the walls? We are not prepared for siege, he could break this army with less than two weeks of bad weather on his side. The fire of resistance gets damp quickly in the rain."

"Because he's complacent," Robin muttered. His eyes had become sharp and lupine, they scanned everything that was happening with the enemy army. He appeared to be making constant decisions based on that about where he and Gilbert would be positioned.

"I'd probably call it confident," Gil said, his tone almost equally grim. It seemed most likely that most of them were going to die, but there was no point dwelling on that. The Underworld always possessed a strange seductive call for Gil anyway; sometimes bravery in such situations could really be about fascination with one's own death. "They have the higher ground."

"Yet the numbers are even, almost exactly," Robin replied, his tone faintly distracted as of one who was actually making calculations rather than estimating. "Their destriers will pick up an unstoppable impact coming down that hill which our cavalry would struggle to meet head on, Norman destriers are higher strung. Welsh horses are stoic and hardy, takes a lot to rattle them, and they turn faster and move and readjust for the unexpected."

"Certainly. If we can survive for long enough to get the chance to use those advantages," Gil admitted. "In the case of a rout you will accompany me in fleeing the battlefield? I won't be stuck here trying to drag you away by the bridle like some battle-crazed Briton of former times?"

Robin grinned at him. "So that's how it is then? You're not leaving me no matter what crazy thing I do? And we haven't even declared blood brotherhood yet!"

Gil felt teased and frowned at Robin. "You know very well I wouldn't leave you, you mad bastard. We're probably about to die here, can you take something seriously?" he grumbled almost under his breath.

"Death is the last thing I plan to take seriously. But seriously, we should cut ourselves right now and share blood before the battle. We may as well if you plan to drag me off this battlefield by my bridle."

"So you're saying it will come to that?" Gil asked, taking out his dagger, removing his glove and nicking his thumb. He was practical about it, he didn't pick a spot that was going to interfere with his ability to use his sword. "Welsh freedom or death and all that?"

Robin cut himself in a place that was also quite practical before smearing it onto his open palms. He held out his open palm to Gil between their horses. For a long moment Gil gazed at the blood on Robin's open palm before he stuck the bleeding side of his thumb into it.

"Oh gods no, we will totally get out of here if it goes south and plan the guerrilla attack on them the moment they try to next leave the castle walls. I didn't live this long by being a stickler for staying in the kitchen when it gets too hot."

Gil could feel that weird stinging sensation that always came of a foreign blood entering yours. He felt strange and hot all over of a sudden. "Are we meant to say something?" he asked.

Robin shrugged. "Not really," he said, capturing Gil's thumb in his bloody hand for a second and squeezing. "You know what a brother is, right? Your fights are mine and mine are yours?"

He nodded, though he didn't know how he knew. Robin removed his hand and licked the blood off it. "I figure you don't need much solemnity when you're about to go to war together. Do you really think we're about to die?"

Gil sighed. "Not necessarily. I don't like to be a quitter. He's confident though, that's why he's brought his army outside the walls. And he has reason to be, only months ago Norman forces refused to be besieged at Kidwelly Castle and drove off the Welsh force in exactly this manner. They are repeating that move."

Robin snorted. "Usually a mistake to repeat the same move in another situation. Fate manoeuvres differently every time, so should we. You never want your enemy to be able to predict you. I doubt he'll find it so easy this time. You should hear them," he said, indicating the Welsh soldiers and footmen who massed around them yelling at the top of their lungs. Some of them seemed to be screaming more than chanting. There were people blowing on cow horns and shaking chains so that it sounded like the Wild Hunt was gathering to fight the Normans. Brought all together it was a rising cacophony that you didn't need to speak Welsh to know was the sound of boiling point fury.

"What are they chanting? Other than 'revenge for Gwenllian?" Even though he didn't understand one other word beyond Gwenllian he didn't need to. Robin had been right, if he greeted every Welshman with 'am Gwenllian' it seemed perfectly sufficient.

"'Not one more step!' Is one of the things they're shouting. It's the rallying cry for the Cymric resistance, the hardliners, the ones who won't negotiate, those who will not be satisfied until all Norman military presence is driven off to the Saesneg side of the river and every Marcher castle sent up in flames."

"Well that's a thing that's never going to happen, I'm afraid. Did you not hear about the Harrying of the North? Did these people not hear about it? What they do when someone opposes them?" Gilbert was only conscious afterwards that he had referred to the Normans as 'them'.

"My grandparents lived through the days where The Conqueror broke the north. It isn't just history to us."

He nodded. Gilbert knew what his ancestors were doing during The Harrowing of the North and consequently he preferred it to be thought of as history.

"My people took in refugees, children who were starving to death in the roads after watching their parents killed and their crops burned by the Conqueror's men. Many of the bloodlines in my clan only go back that far, to some starving child who ran when his Mother told him to go and did not stop running."

"I've heard about it," Gilbert murmured, he didn't want to admit that something in the way Robin told it brought a fierce kind of tears to his eyes. It was as if he could feel the pounding heart of the child as they ran, hear the desperate cries of the Mother yelling 'run, never stop running!' and the last fighting breaths of the father who tried to buy them time... He shook himself to rid himself of the rollicking wave of empathy.

Robin didn't seem to feel Gil had heard about it enough though. "Even by the time Blaith and I were boys there were still empty, desolate former manors where we'd pitch our tents inside the ruins. Blaith was born not so far from such a massacre site. His father said they'd done it on purpose, conceiving him upon the ashes of the harrowed north, to raise a soul from the ruins made of pure vengeance."

"Poor Blaith."

"Sometimes. Other days," Robin shrugged. "He *is* pure vengeance. There is still charnel land so littered with mossy bones that only the witches would camp there. We children would dare each other to run into the charred killing site and back out again. When you went in there you'd think it was gravel crunching under your shoes and realise it was human teeth and bone... The land was sodden with death. Some say it was close to *one hundred thousand souls* put to the sword or starved."

Gil nodded hurriedly hoping Robin would see the conversation wasn't agreeing with him and crossed himself involuntarily. "That is how my family acquired their Rochdale possessions, on the backs of that kind of warfare. You are taught it when you're learning tactics in preparation for knighthood, that it is more efficient to burn crops and villages than it is fight other armed men."

"*Efficient*..." Robin murmured to himself. "That we as a species have come to this... That we talk about efficiency when it comes to ending innocent lives."

"If that shocks you, perhaps you're less ready for the campaign the Normans will wage in Wales than you think," Gilbert had to all but yell to be heard over the gathering storm of the Welsh army preparing to throw their entire spirit behind resisting Norman occupation.

*Not one more step.* Gilbert considered those words and the total commitment he heard rising around him. He doubted there was going to be anywhere to run to even if they wished it. Gilbert knew already that stubborn force coming up behind and all around them would pack them in. There wasn't going to be anywhere to run.

Somewhere in the maelstrom a harsh, broken sound of a pipe began to cut its way through the air. Half like the sound of heartbreak and half like the sound of utter, heels-stuck-in, harsh refusal. A deep-throated drum began to pound. Gilbert felt it in his guts, he felt it in his hips. His fetch roared in the darkness in answer to the call of the war drum.

"Hold my horse for me while I shoot," he said, sliding out of the saddle and passing his reins to Gilbert. The idea of getting off the horse during the Norman cavalry charge and trying to shoot at that wall of steel and muscle coming down on you didn't appeal to Gilbert at all. He pushed his way further to the edge to allow Robin to get back to his horse.

"Shoot straight," he said, grasping Robin's hand for a second as he passed over the reins. "Show them what your Welsh bow can do."

The world suddenly disappeared and went inside, the sun was swallowed up and she was in St Martin's Land where her mother said she came from, a land where it was normal to have greenish skin and see no moonlight. When she closed her eyes she could feel Robin's wolf, smell it, hear its panting breath with her long sensitive ears. Suddenly she was a hare racing along the battle-field. She was running in the direction of the Welsh army, darting diagonally across the field.

There was the noise and panic of pre-battle fervour and crows circling close making a black whirlwind of Underworld force in the sky above, ready to swallow the lives of hundreds of young men, many not so young ones too, and a plethora of horse flesh. Her hare just couldn't follow where his wolf was going, deep into the rage haze of the battlefield. She could smell Robin's skin and sweat. Even with her ability to clear a hedge in one flying leap she couldn't go where he was going, her back broke in two. She made the terrible sound of the broken rabbit, the baby-like shriek of terror.

Where her spine broke two enormous wings, powerful like those of the swan burst through her fur and took her high. They were heavy, powerful wings inside this invisible swan garment of hers. Finally, she understood what her mother's garment was for, the one locked away in a chest, the one that she could never be allowed to get her hands on again. A faerie's swan garment was her ability to see at a distance, to be in two places at once, to sweep the moon roads in the sky and go where she chose without the permission of a man.

She could go up higher than the circles the ravens were making in the sky above where her hedgerow husband was about to fight. But she didn't want to, she wanted to come down above him. Everything of her swan skin seemed to peel from her as if reaching out each fibre to him, to cover him, to shield him with her own hair and body, to protect him, to lay her faerie veil over him like the shield-maidens of old. *Not this one.* Her body seemed to be saying to the crows. *He's mine. He wears my token of favour.*

By the time she opened her eyes in her body Eilish and Blaith were there with her. Blaith was behind, steadying her as if he meant to catch her should she fall back, and Eilish was stroking her forehead soothingly with spring wa-ter on a white feather. "It's alright, cariad," she whispered. "You just went really deep. Take your time."

Lux blinked in confusion at the faces of her loved ones.

"Are you alright?" Sariah asked.

Lux nodded.

"Did you see something that should give me reason to be afraid for him more than I am already?" Blaith murmured near her ear. She didn't need him to elaborate that he meant for Robin. In her hyper-open state the feeling of his heart pounding far faster than normal against her back was enough to trigger feelings of deep identification. She didn't know the answer, but she didn't want Blaith to feel a moment more fear than he needed to.

"No. But his enemies should tremble." That was the sort of thing you were meant to say, she had seen Sariah model it when he fought last. She just hoped her own body wasn't speaking to Blaith louder than her words were, because all Lux had tasted about the situation her beloved was in, was chaos.


Robin took out the lock of Lux's girlhood hair and kissed it. His lips lingered on it for a few heartbeats where he allowed the cacophony and rising whirlpool of thick, heady madness around him to become like the storm around his still eye. There was silence inside him when he focused on what he was doing this for. The emotions and fears of his countrymen overwhelmed his senses in a way he'd never known before, bred as he was for the sounds of the forests or mountains. So intense was the sensory overstimulation that it brought him passed overwhelm, and into an altered state that had a strange peace beyond it.

Calmly, the way he tended to get really calm when things were at their worst, he tucked her pale, delicate hair back inside his hauberk. *By sun down tomorrow I will be in Lux's arms or Eilion's.* A wistful smile played over his mouth for a moment. The process of getting to Eilion's arms could be unpredictable and various shades of undesirable, yet at the end of the day could only last for so long. He took his position. It was just about time to be Him.

Robin breathed the air and tasted the fear of his countrymen, soupy and

274

thick. He stayed in place like all the other archers. It wasn't in his nature to stand up and put himself above and before others, that just made you a target more easily shot at. The early voice training he'd had for his singing had left Robin capable of strong voice projection, so he didn't need to get up to be noticed. He knew what pitch and volume he would need to cut through the racket.

"I am Robin Dhu a son of Eryri! Do not fear the invader or his high horses, my fellow countrymen! There is further to fall from a higher horse! They will be in range sooner than they know! Shoot fast, shoot straight, shoot as if your very freedom depends on it, because it does! The rich boys with their new lances can't win this for us! We will have to win it for them!"

A huge rollicking cheer went through the archers and stamping of feet from the infantry behind. He felt the emotional lift his presence and words brought the farmers and the hill folk. *In this I have kept my promise to you, Owain. I have whispered the common folk for you and I don't think you yet realise how important they are going to be to you. Perhaps even you don't fully appreciate the kind of archers these people are.*

The Norman cavalry charge began then. You could feel it in the earth like thunder and the wave of anxiety that the archers around him felt was almost as tangible to Robin as the pounding of hooves. He breathed all the way out, letting his lungs empty entirely and his muscles relax. If he breathed slow, just like that, he could judge their distance in breaths.

Everyone around him had all been trained to shoot since seven or even younger. All they needed to do was hold their nerve with countless tons of horse, iron and man-flesh bearing down on them at terrifying speed. Robin sent out a burst of hot power sending it through the earth so it lit a fire under the men at his side, all the way along the line, setting sparks through their group-fetch.

"We're going to feed your corpses to our dogs!" One man yelled out at the enemy. More cusses and threats followed. Robin grinned with sudden inspiration and began to translate their cries into Norman French.

"We're going to cut off your heads and take a piss in your skulls!" He shouted up the hill at them in French.

Whenever a colourful curse would rise above the general wall of sound Robin would translate it and shout it out. The thing he'd learned about language was that someone not being able to speak to you in yours is the first step in allowing a space for them to dehumanise you. This power of translation seemed to rouse the men around him to greater boldness. The Norman soldiers laughed even during the charge, as if crushing the Welsh were a casual business where they could afford to guffaw. Robin didn't smell fear on his people anymore, he smelt blood lust fuelled by outrage at the Norman self-certainty.

*Three, two, one...* For a brief moment he struggled to let go the way he would need to under the pressure, and then it came in a sudden rush of looseness and clarity. The first arrow stuck the throat of one horse, the second, the rider on the horse beside, and the third caught another horse in the throat. The other archers came with him, seeing what he meant to do, a rain of arrows hit the horses and the riders, punching right through the chainmail. The laughing stopped. You could feel the ripple passing through the enemy, as they realised they were still outside of range. And they couldn't stop the momentum of the charge, taking them down towards the furious shower of death.

When Robin saw the horse of one of the leaders go down, tripping the horse next to it, he picked his next rain of targets carefully to increase the pile up. Horses fell and tripped other horses who then caught all of those behind them in a turning pile, dead men on out-of-control horses careened across the battlefield shrieking, at times the legs of the horses broke audibly. Robin felt the mad surge of hope that bolstered the archers when they took in the domino effect their arrows were producing.

He threw his head back and gave vent to a wild, discordant wolf howl. "Fast boys, fast now!" he yelled just after. "Take as many as you can before they are upon us!" Robin thudded a quick succession of arrows into four new targets. One man in his chainmail was being dragged by a foot caught in the

276

stirrup as his horse panicked and rode across their own line trying to get away from the remorseless rain of arrows. Some of the men were trying to pull their horses up, but on the downhill gallop it did little beyond cause the beasts to rear and collide with those coming down behind them, creating greater mayhem still.

Robin could hear Puck laughing hysterically with his throat, as he put down two or three more carefully chosen targets. It wasn't that Puck didn't care about the human and animal agony it was more that he liked to see the world turned upside down, and the bully men fall. He'd reached that place where it started to feel like an elegant, well-timed dance with a rhythm. There was the whirl of the bowstring and thud of the impact forming the beat, and the melody was made up of cries of pain and terror.

You could feel the Welsh cavalry getting antsy. It was almost time to get out of the way to let the men on horseback take advantage of the broken line. Robin could feel it, *three, two, one…* An extra arrow went in at each count and then he leapt up, running to the end of the line and found Gilbert and his horse. He stashed his bow in the saddle compartment for hidden projectiles before mounting.

The archers were scrambling to get out of the way before the smaller bows of the Normans could be deployed, but most of them didn't have a horse like Robin did. The Welsh army had broken the Norman line, now they would need the men with broadswords if they were to consolidate their advantage. Adrenalin owned Robin's whole body so that he wasn't aware of the resistance as he leapt up into the saddle like he weighed nothing.

He was conscious of Gil at his side but no one else in an individual sense. From the brief glance at each other they got time for Robin could see the shock on his friend's face. Things clearly weren't happening the way Gil had pictured it. Robin drew his sword and pressed forward with the others. There was so much surging readiness in the Welsh cavalry that it felt like the horses behind them were going to push you into the fray if you didn't move forward.

"Hold! Hold!" Prince Owain's voice cut through the screams of terrified

Norman horses and men, and the thunder of galloping horses just as Robin's had. It was a voice you took notice of. The cries of 'revenge for Gwenllian' had become a *roar*, an immense wall of sound. These were the men, after all, for whom Gwenllian was more than just a name, a national hero and martyr for Welsh freedom, she was sister, kinswoman, wife, in-law, person... "Now!" Owain screamed through the crowd, a primal sound that unleashed the pent-up fetch-force in the group in a great eruption.

But their eruption didn't look like a Norman cavalry charge. They came out galloping forward just the same and they used their shields to block arrows, but their smaller, nimbler horses darted into the fray to allow their riders to stab or hack to death the riders of injured horses. They were finding all the spots where the line was broken and then wheeling out to safety before the uninjured destriers could readjust their headlong plunge. Crazy, blood-hungry cries came up from the Welshmen, both among the foot soldiers and the cavalry that served as incantations to evoke the raven queen battle goddesses of yore.

Robin and Gilbert moved easily together, plunging as one into any spot that opened up in the line. One would take the right side of a man on a panicked horse, the other the left side and they would duck and parry while the other man cut their enemy down. Blood gushed over Robin's head and back as he ducked at the moment Gil decapitated another man while their horses were crammed up against each other. The clang of steel and the smell of blood covered over the very sky.

All Robin could feel was the fear and pain of the enemy, the utter shock, the total disbelief that they were really going to die today on this Welsh backwater field. There were tears streaming down his face with the sheer eye-watering intensity of this overload. As he met a Norman broadsword head-on for the first time he was crying and laughing at the same time.

He took the weight of the wild swing on the flat of his own blade and the power of the blow jarred him all through his arm to the shoulder. In the brief moment where their swords were locked Robin saw the Norman's wide frightened eyes as he plunged his side dagger into the artery in his upper thigh. The man screamed, remembering his legs too late and his guard went down in time for Robin's sword to pass through his chest at the same moment that Gil cut him almost in half with a downward thrust of terrible intensity. Robin and he were both wearing so much Norman blood it was hard to recognise each other.

"More! *Now!* More!" Owain was screaming at them through the chaos. "Take them down, sons of Cymry! Take them! We have them! We have them!" In response to his cries the cavalry surged down and in on the enemy, penning them in.

Robin was carried with it despite himself. There was something in the change of vibration, the sense of a killing pen forming that made him feel uneasy. There was nothing to do but go forward because the desperate men who slashing at you with sharp, bloodied weapons, were the best of the enemy forces, you knew this because they were still alive, and they were dangerous in their desperation.

Unable to move or turn, Robin felt the moment when his horse was killed under him as if someone had stabbed him in part of his own body. There wasn't time to focus on it though because he saw and felt the horrid death of the Welsh man on his right side, whose head was destroyed with a mace, in three massive blows, his helmet only half off in the process. He was still screaming until his teeth were destroyed. Brain fluid and some of the man's broken teeth splattered on Robin from above as his own horse's courageous little life went out of it and the hardy beast slowly went to his knees. Robin leapt to his feet, precariously standing on his horse's saddle as it went down, and looking around him for options.

"Robin!" he heard Gilbert cry out to him. The other man pushed deeper into the fray, coming up from below to cut off the arm of the man swinging the mace bearing down on Robin. "Robin!" He was trying to get to him to pull him up onto his own horse, but it wasn't necessary.

Robin quickly leapt onto the back of the horse next to him, holding the saddle of the dead man for traction while the horse reared. He pushed the man with the caved in head to the ground and got control of the horse, just as Gilbert killed the man with a wild shout of total effort. They were close enough that their legs brushed in the stirrups, he could hear Gil panting like a terrified animal with effort and adrenalin. The panting was interspersed with grunts of determination.

The fighting was desperate and brutal. Horses were hacked and screaming, one with the tip of its nose hanging off and the bone showing seemed to dangle before Robin's eyes for longer than it really did. Tears streamed down his face, washing blood-free trails. It wasn't about Wales, what was happening, it wasn't even about three generations of Norman oppression, it wasn't about not letting them have that one more step, it wasn't for Gwenllian, it wasn't about land or ideals, it was now all about survival. It was all about watching the back of the man that just bought you time to get back on a horse. In battle the focus of the world narrows to the width of a blade edge.

He pushed their horses in close. A very angry Norman lord was pressing Gil hard. It was only when Robin came down on him also and Robin saw the man's eyes that he knew what he was seeing. This was the moment... The one Gilbert had told him about where you felt the battle give. The Normans were starting to separate off into those who were running and the few that decided to stand their ground and refuse to yield.

This man they were grinding down, the sound of colliding shields clattering dying out till all you heard was your breath, your brothers and your victim's, he was a veteran of many wars, this man. You almost didn't want to cut him down like this, just for his bravery and his stubbornness. Robin had the feeling he was just about to cut the head off a man of distinction, though he did it nonetheless. He was afraid if he didn't that the man's mace would get past Gil's guard and end him the awful way the man off to his right had gone. Respect for skill didn't matter, mercy didn't matter, fair play didn't matter, there was nothing else except the next gasping breath and your muscles screaming at you and destroying the enemy however you could so that you and your friend would live and the cacophony of horrors would stop.

You could tell by how the veteran died he wasn't one of those bought mercenaries that were mainly the ones galloping for the bridge back into England. He was clearly a Norman lord with a name to uphold. He intended to stand there and die for that name, standing in the gore of his countrymen with his horse dead at his side...

As he killed him, Robin felt nothing except relief he'd managed it. Because in this melee the fact that he trained harder than most people didn't matter, even his faster reflexes barely mattered, there was something terrifyingly levelling about the mess of battle. As if decided by the queen of battle herself when the Norman's iron-bound head fell to the ground and his blood pumped up into the air, that seemed to be the moment when the rout really began.

"I need to get to the river!" Lux cried. Although the vision had began to clear it had left something in its retreating wake, a message in the beach foam.

"The river? Why?" Sariah said.

Eilish was saying something too, but Lux didn't catch it.

"Will the lake do?" Blaith asked.

His words got through because they carried understanding of her predicament that went beyond the common place, and she couldn't really explain right now. Anyone who was with her was with her, the rest would have to run to keep up. She nodded hurriedly, focusing all her attention on Blaith now because she sensed that at a spiritual level the two of them were now standing alone on the heath. "The lake will do. I need you to come there with me!" She was shaking too much to force herself to make sense. It felt like she was already in deep water over her head, someone was holding her down and she couldn't reach the air. Time was gushing in a cross current.

Blaith took her arm and pulled her hard and without warning into a sprint. There was no explanation for this frenetic burst of energy that leapt from his body into hers. She had to bring out her hare to keep up with him, with his longer legs and his wild-born agility running with him was like nothing her body had had to do before, except maybe riding with Robin. When he reached a fallen branch or jutting stone, she was forced to jump it with the same ease that he moved, otherwise she would have fallen.

Every part of her fetch adored Blaith for his urgency, for knowing that she needed to run, for trusting her body and her vision. For the way you could speak to him with your body and he spoke its blood and bone language and needed no words. Only running made sense and so he was going to run with her until it revealed the heart of the problem. When she could hear her breath ragged and burning in her lungs only then did the twitchy sensation begin to abate.

Blaith didn't come to a stop until they were at the side of the lake. Immediately he dropped to his knees and put his hands in murmuring prayers to the spirit of the place. Lux did the same. The moment her hands dipped below the freezing snow-melt eyes flicked open in her palms, like the ones Robin had tattooed on him. There was a frenzy building in her loins that she couldn't explain and it came with a cooling sensation that went through her whole body. She'd stopped shivering because she was part of the cold things.

"Lux! Lux, what are you doing?"

For the first time Blaith seemed discomforted by her strange actions. She could hear Blaith's alarm in his voice but it was nothing but back ground noise from her heart's perspective. Her people were calling and she could hear the strange underwater distortion of their war cry. They were chanting at her from the depths through blue lips. She went down fast. Like stone falling through water. There was no shock when her flesh slid beneath the iron grip of the chill blackness, for her skin had already become cool like the underbelly of a salmon.

Suspended in the water, her hair fanning out around her, Lux opened her eyes as her body sunk deeper into the water. It was important to stop breathing, or to at least slow right down her need for air. The creatures that belonged to this element found the taking of breath to be foreign and they would suffocate anything foreign. Were they war-pipes that she could hear distorted through the water? She felt the vibration of something pumping and deep like drums. All at once it took her. The great eruption, the rivers of the heavens plunging out from between the thighs of Ana like amniotic fluid after a ruptured membrane. There was one word coming from the frenzied water-asrai as they massed, one sound, one musical note held by all of them. It wasn't really a word at all but if it had been it would have been their soul song: drown!

Lux's head was spinning, as the oxygen got thinner. She felt the hands around her ankles and wrists as she went limp, carrying her with them on the wild current of death. Nothing mattered but the collective howl and surge. 'Drown! Drown! Drown! Drown! Drown!' She would do it with them, they would all go down together holding the feet of the enemies of life.

The vision felt so potent it was mainly just annoying when the scene rippled away like someone threw a pebble into water. The water wasn't disturbed by a pebble but by another body diving deeply into it. The reverberation of the disturbance felt like a bruise on their collective mind. Some of the asrai spirits fled with angry flicks of their tails, others just continued to chant 'drown!', so great was the collective lust to swallow and consume.

It took a moment before she realised that the pair of dark eyes looking into her own were not those of an asrai but of a human she knew from the world above. Rather than grabbing her and dragging her to the surface as she'd imagined he might, Blaith took her hands and began to slowly exhale the last of the oxygen in his lungs, until he was sinking along with her. The time they spent there, still, sinking down through the freezing depths together, while he exhaled the last of his air, couldn't have been more than thirty seconds yet it seemed to last forever. Blaith and Lux were as cold and pale as any of the other denizens of the lake, their hair and clothes suspended around them in eerie weightlessness.

For a second Lux's forehead was against Blaith and darkness seemed to pour through her into the water, as if they'd made forehead-love in the way Robin had described to her. The fruit of their union filled the lake, which in turn filled the river, the river that filled the next lake with the death progeny, which fed the river that forked off to the south and was currently reddened

283

by the blood of battle... "Drown!" Blaith declared aloud with her, their voices joined and garbled by the water in their ears and on their brains.

Then as if he'd felt something peak or give that she had not, Blaith was suddenly kicking for the surface and pulling her with him. When she felt the life-kick in him, the oxygen desperation began to come on in her own body and she kicked with him. It was like both their bodies chose life and struggled for it, out of the amniotic sack of the Underworld.

Blaith was less far-gone than her though, and it was he that did the last few kicks and used his strength on her as everything faded to stars against blackness behind her eyes. When Blaith dragged her onto the bank he struck her on the back and she gasped like a landed fish, before choking out stream after stream of water. Blaith gave her a couple more particularly firm smacks. She began to vomit water then, gushes and gushes of it. It felt like he wasn't so much pushing the water out of her as he was redirecting the river out through her throat.

Although he continued to hit her back until the water stopped, he didn't say anything to her. He didn't ask her why she'd done what she'd done or seem to need any explanation. Blaith worked off a different school of logic than the rest of humanity, and it was clear that her behaviour made total sense within his magical worldview. After choking up what looked like a thin slither of river-weed Lux began to shiver violently. He tried to rub her and hold her close to warm her but he was as cold as she was.

"There's enemy blood in the river today," she murmured, gazing down at the strand of river-weed as if it held a great and terrible secret only she could see. Part of her was still down there in the water with them, with her hair turned green and it wrapping and coiling around their struggling ankles.

When the Welsh gave chase to the fleeing Norman army, Gil and Robin got caught up in the comet tail of their stampeding horses. Neither of them resisted it, everyone's nerves needed the release of the hard gallop after what they'd just been through. He glanced at Robin as they rode to see if he meant to purposely hunt down and kill any of the ones who were running. To his relief he saw that Robin seemed more intent on herding and frightening them to run faster with wild cries and smacks on the bottom with the flat of his sword as he flew past. Gil was on board for that.

He might have been on board for killing the ones who were running, were they part of some small rival tribe where there would be advantage in destroying all the adult males. He was usually pragmatic like that with cruelty; you only did it with a clear purpose. Unless of course that person had hurt someone you love… If more would simply come to replace them, as they would, he saw no reason for needless cruelty. The other army had already lost their dignity, may as well allow them to escape with their lives.

Gil saw infantry men on their knees, begging for their lives, have their head cut straight off in one slice of a Welsh cavalryman's blade, as he galloped past the man, standing in his stirrups as he performed the skillful manoeuvre. Archers shot others down, but most of them were forcing themselves four or five abreast, onto the bridge, when the bridge was only wide enough for three abreast. Without taking his eyes off the scene Gilbert brought his horse in beside Robin, who had almost come to a stop now, as he seemed to feel his work in causing utter panic and humiliation among the retreating Normans was done.

"They are going to crush each other on that bridge," Gil remarked, frowning as he watched the melee.

"Indeed, yes," Robin observed pointing. "Look. A man just went down then and they are stepping on him. They are trampling their own people." He reported it much like one might make an observation about the mating behaviour of pheasants, had you spotted the curiosity in the bushes nearby.

Not altogether in a hurry they walked their horses closer to the scene. It was more to observe history making itself than sadism at this point. The Norman defeat was so total and catastrophic that it was like there was little you could add to it. Gilbert felt a lump in his throat when he thought about what had just occurred. Somehow this unexpected triumph, this strange small miracle…it had rekindled all his hope for miracles. This one event had some-how changed everything. Because if this could happen…What other crazy dreams these people had in their hearts and upon their gilded tongues could also come to pass? The world seemed weightless to Gilbert on the afternoon where the Welsh army took the Battle of Crug Mawr… Dragons lived and gods walked among men.

That was even before it happened.

You felt it in the water first, a cool, coiling presence coming from up-stream. It made Gil shiver. He noticed it before Robin because it was of his world, it was a thing of darkness coming along the waterway looking to take heads and drink hot blood. But Robin noticed the practical manifestation of what was happening just before Gil because he grabbed his arm hard.

"Sweet Merciful Lady… The bridge is going to go down under their weight."

Afterwards it always felt to Gil as if Robin had done something uncanny in pronouncing those words. Because he'd not noticed the strain in the up-rights or the creaking sound over the racket of the killing and fleeing. Gil had been too busy paying attention to the insidious, serpentine coil of Underworld power that had come rushing down river. So when it started to give, it fol-lowed almost immediately upon Robin's words, which seemed to invoke the chaos.

It happened bit-by-bit and then all at once. Men and horses screamed and struggled as wood cracked and groaned, but there was nowhere to go as the bridge went down into the turbulent river. Dressed in iron as they were, from head to toe, the water spirits took no pity on them and immediately packed up their mouths and their nostrils with icy plugs of water and coils of river grass. Horses were swimming to freedom after unseating their heavy rider to drown alone, and kicking other human victims in the face with their hooves as they panicked.

"Look!" Robin said, pointing down river. "She runs with blood this day," he said more quietly. He was right, the water down river was slowly turning red with human and horse blood mingled. But none of it was Welsh.

"Dear God, they can't swim in their chainmail," Gil remarked as they moved closer to try to see what was happening. "Should we... should we... help them?" The words sounded weak and shameful in his mouth. He was both embarrassed to say them and ashamed that he was standing there asking someone else and entirely unsure himself.

"What your conscience asks you to do is up to you, Gil. No man should ever ask you to ignore that holy thing. But for me I cannot rob the river spirits. There are certain rivers that no sane man takes a life from."

Gil shivered. He didn't like the idea of finding out what happened to the less than sane men. He decided it was better just to cross himself and look the other way while the weighed down soldiers cried out for help from Mother Mary and Jesus. He wasn't either of those people after all.

"What if it were an innocent down there?" Gilbert murmured, trying to take his mind off the pitiful cries. "Would you not pluck them from the river spirits?"

"Yes," Robin replied immediately, not taking his eyes off the struggling men for a moment. He seemed to be almost intently watching them die without any sign of either enjoyment or distress. "I'd have to offer the life of some other innocent thing to the river afterward though, or it might come shopping among my own people. If you think you spot an innocent down there in the water I will go pluck him out." Robin looked at him as though for an answer. Grimly Gil shook his head and immediately looked away again. He had to admit he saw no such man there.

"There's none down there I'd sacrifice the life of a Welsh squirrel for," Robin muttered, turning his horse's head away from the scene. "Come, I believe our work here is done. Unless you want to join my countrymen in whacking off to the sounds of Norman soldiers drowning? I'm happy to leave."

Robin cursed quietly in Welsh and closed his eyes for a couple of breaths. From the very first scream for help Robin felt dread drop into his lower stomach like a stone. Opening his eyes, he scanned around to see if Gil was back from answering nature's call, couldn't see him returning, and began to move in the direction of the sound. Robin's instincts told him he was in danger. He sniffed the air and tried to place the feeling, but his hesitation was shredded straight through by the girl's frightened voice.

"Help! Please! No, no, please don't! Please, Sir! I'm still a maid... Please..." She was saying in Welsh. Robin had a feeling it was futile, as her captor didn't speak either the language of Welsh or that of mercy. He knew exactly what he was hearing and a cold sweat in response had begun to make the dried blood from the battle run down the middle of his stomach.

He didn't know why or how but part of him believed he should somehow have conquered this problem by now, he felt annoyed with himself. It was a fruitless emotion, his body was in full panic mode and would not be told otherwise. No part of him was any longer focusing on his own safety. He paid caution just enough respect to slide down from his horse and go quietly into the woods. Robin approached more slowly than he wanted to. It was horrific to hear this girl enduring what she was and move slowly, but he wanted to be sure of his shot when he killed the man responsible. Finally the awful suspense of waiting to see it was over and the scene came into view. He winced.

His teeth ground together and a hot, bright flash of light temporarily obscured the vision in his left eye. Closing that eye and opening his still normal right one Robin swapped hands, drew back his bow and shot the attacker in the back of the neck, killing him instantly. Killing him felt better to Robin than a man perhaps has right to feel outside the bedroll, as if for a second he'd killed the very crime itself.

The girl screamed at being suddenly covered in a dead man gushing blood and for a second she struggled to get out from underneath him, weeping convulsively as she did. Robin went straight towards her. His intention was to pull the man off her, and cover her exposed body in his cloak. To tell her she was safe now. The tenderness he felt for her was all-consuming. He had no problem imagining into her experience, despite his different genitalia. Grown

288

men had tried to rape him as a child too.

As he removed the man's body she scuttled to get away from him trying to pull her torn dress down between her legs to conceal herself.

"I'm sorry, lass," he murmured. "You're safe now."

"Thank you!" she whispered in Welsh her teeth chattering already and her lips pale with shock.

He almost couldn't make sense of it when he was shot. The impact of the blow from a Welsh bow at close range was so hard it knocked him half to the ground. He stared with a degree of incomprehension at the shaft of wood and feathers sticking out of his right shoulder. And then his wolf kicked in. Everything of the life force and surging instinct in his body went into overdrive and he dove behind a tree, pressing his back against it.

He knew, as part of him might have known all along, that he'd just walked into a trap. Someone who knew a lot about him set it specifically for him. Looking down at the position of the wound he made calculations of how long he had before it would interfere with movement. While he was doing so the shock started to wear off and he began to feel the pain of the wound. His wolf snarled in response and all his fight instincts came closely on the heels of his flight ones.

Without further hesitation he began to climb up onto the branches of the tree he was hiding behind, even though using his right shoulder made him feel like he might pass out, so he could get the drop on his enemy. Fuelling the fire-in-the-head that was necessary to push on up the tree with fury, Robin seethed on the creative ways he was going to kill the person who had dared set such a trap for him. Somehow the idea that this young girl had been raped for this in a calculating manner was even worse to him than the standard crime. He could still hear her crying and breathing fast with fear.

When he found a good vantage spot in the tree Robin's eyes narrowed and scanned the greenery below. It wasn't long before he saw what he was looking for.

"Where did he go?" he heard the moving target mutter in Norman French.

"Follow the blood trail, he can't have gone far," a female voice replied. *Nanette*. It wasn't like Robin had been far from guessing he just hadn't expected her to actually be there. With a wave of disgust at the thought he remembered Blaith's accusation that his chivalry would prevent him from killing Nanette. He knew how foolish it was, yet for all he knew it in his head the idea of using hands or blade to do violence to a woman repelled him at such a core level the emotion took his breath away.

With slow silence Robin drew back the string of his bow and shot the male speaker in the middle of the chest. It wasn't instant death like the neck shot had been, but it was the best he could do from above with the searing pain it took to hold the bow. Equally slowly and carefully he began to climb down. If he was going to pass out it was better if it happened on the ground. That was about as far ahead as he felt he had the luxury to think.

Robin felt blood trickling freely down both his chest and back where the arrow had gone out the other side. There was enough of it that it was making its way past his weapons belt and into his trousers. He felt relief when his feet hit the ground and stood holding the tree for a moment to get his bearings. The stiffening and swelling around the wound was happening faster by the minute and he was beginning to fear he would soon no longer have use of his bow arm.

"Drop your weapons and come out with your hands up or I'll empty her innards out onto the woodland floor!" Nanette's voice yelled out to him in Norman French. Again, he shut his eyes for the space of a breath, both because he found this image all too easy to visualise, and because he knew what he was about to do and it wasn't going to go well for him.

Knowing how close he was to Gil finding he was gone Robin hesitated for a couple of seconds. The inner battle whether to cry out for help and risk Nanette following through on her promise or whether to remain silent and hope for the perpetrator's good will was not a new decision for him. Being in its presence again made his palms sweat and his stomach churn. Should he pick the opposite to last time and cry out?

"Alright then, if that's how you're going to be. Shall we start from down here then?"

The girl's cry of pain and terror was too much for him. His body knew that stepping out there would most likely result in his death yet he could do nothing else. With a sigh he stepped into view and let his bow drop from his hand. "Fine. Please, just let her go Nanette, she's an innocent..."

"Ha!" she said, tossing the half-naked and bloodied girl from her with an emotion much like contempt but maintained a handful of her hair, so when she tried to run she was tugged brutally back until she fell to her knees. "Not any more she's not! Now the sword and the concealed daggers too...I wasn't born yesterday, you wretched tinker! Turn out your pockets and take off your shoes! I want to see inside your sleeves as well." The very tone of voice she used with him, as if he were twelve years old ground his teeth. As if sensing his defiance and his quiet rage she continued. "And if you try to run, I will go back to cutting that new hole I started in her, remember that, boy. Now walk!"

Robin did as she ordered but the whole time he watched for when the opportunity would come to grab the girl from Nanette before the cutting could continue.

They hadn't gone far before his vision started to swim. "Nanette, if I had mind to harm you, I wouldn't need my weapons to do it. Whatever you're planning to do here I doubt it works out well for you."

She didn't reply. The only sound was his heart beating harder than it should sound in his ears and the girl's gentle sobs as she was dragged along in a forced march. If there was any doubts how far into danger he was willing to go for this girl whose name he never got to know, they were resolved the one moment where her terrified gaze made contact with his as Nanette dragged her around a corner in the path. Her eyes seemed to silently beg him to make this whole reality she was living go away, and her pale lips bore testimony to the shock of having been gathering water only to suddenly start living a nightmare. It was a nightmare that wouldn't have happened to her but for him, so without even really meaning to, his eyes wordlessly promised her that he would indeed make it go away.

Blaith had changed into dry clothes and was warming himself by the fire. He knew without asking Lux that they had shared flesh-knowing of the battle's culmination. Every part of his body felt the conflict turn in the Cymric direction. In his mind as the oxygen had become thin in his blood he'd seen a great red dragon engulf and put to flight a white one and then he'd seen the water maidens, their sharp teeth red with gore, tear the creature apart between them. That had to be good for Robin didn't it? Blaith trusted the voices that lived in the corridors of his guts and the hallways of his bones, he knew the language of muscle tremors.

It was rare to catch sight of a corpse candle so bright you could see it before twilight really set in, and this would have scared him if it wasn't bluish white in colour. If something had happened to his brother on the battlefield, the candle would be tinged with red blood. There wasn't much longer than the time it took to think about the colour before the light took on the shape and form of Eilion.

"Blaith, I need your help."

"You have it," Blaith said immediately. "Tell me this isn't about Robin?"

Eilion looked confused by this figure of speech. "I can't, that would be a lie."

Blaith felt his stomach drop away like he was falling. It was the same sensation he used to feel when he'd wake from nightmares as a child where he was plummeting from the heavens with his angel wings on fire. That was where he felt it when Robin was in danger, in the stomach and in his invisible wings. "Tell me what I need to do."

"You will need to follow my lead and do no more or no less than I say at every turn." Eilion suddenly came up very close to Blaith in a way that was somewhere between intense and threatening. "I don't care about your emotions. I care about saving him. So *do not* improvise because of your feelings."

Blaith nodded hurriedly. He was too afraid to even feel offended at the fact the the faerie was yelling at him. In fact, amid this white-hot outburst that burned him with its cold, or perhaps chilled him with its heat, he felt he really understood this creature for the first time. In that moment he couldn't have been more grateful for the threat of frostbite that Eilion's presence offered to the fires of hell that were burning the pitch inside his heart. "Lead. I will follow."

"I assume Eilish and Lux can ride well?"

"Better than any Norman man alive, the pair of them."

"Good. Get the three best horses you have and arm yourself. Get Eilish and her doctoring kit and give Lux a bow that suits her body size and tell her she won't need to know how to shoot it, because I do. Do this fast. Meet me back here with only the three of you and the horses, then, follow my light."


Gil felt so much better for drinking a lot of fresh water and washing off the blood and gore of battle. Whilst he usually enjoyed the smell of fresh blood there was something about the moment it was starting to congeal that particularly revolted him. It couldn't be a perfect wash as yet, not the kind he was visualising, he could only get rid of any bits and pieces of other men's body parts that were still clinging through his hair. Somehow it wasn't until after he'd relieved himself and thrown up twice that he realised how shaken his body was.

When he got up onto the road, he saw Robin's horse grazing on the grass over near the woods. Picking up his pace he wondered if Robin was hunting. Often, he would just wander off a bit, seemingly only to answer a call of nature and come back with a dead rabbit or pheasant hung over his shoulder. From observing the surprising amount of food acquired with Robin's bow and seeing what the Welsh version of the weapon had done to the Norman army, Gil was determined to start learning how to fire one.

He didn't want to disturb Robin if he was stalking something to eat, or if he needed privacy, yet he felt an immediate sense of unease when he entered the tree line. Sniffing the air, Gil scanned the trees and bushes around him constantly. He was fairly sure he was alone. Unless the person was as good at blending with their environment as his tinker friend… Far more alone than he should have felt if Robin was stalking an unlucky rabbit… Turning in circles a couple of times looking all around him he frowned.

"Robin!" Gil shouted his friend's name at the top of his lungs, it resounded in the trees and valley in echoes. He didn't care if his concern turned out to be foolish, it was far better to lose a little dignity than to lose his friend.

When no sound came back to him, no whistle or playfully mocking laugh from a nearby bush, Gil swallowed hard. He slid down off his horse and began to lead it by the bridle. Quickly he went forward into the clearing like a dog following its nose.

There was something about this clearing… He didn't like how it felt. *Sharp tears were shed here.* Gil could taste them like brine in the air. Something bad had happened there, but why did it smell so delicious when pain smells sharp? He stopped beside a splash of blood in the leaf loam. Crouching down he stuck his fingers in it. It was still ever so slightly warm. He put his finger in his mouth and tasted the blood. *Robin.* His heart was beating wildly with a fresh rush of stress now. It was like he was at risk of losing his birth brother.

Robin stood and blinked before sharpening his focus on the wagon that had come to a stop by the side of the road. Drawing on deep reserves from muscle and bone he drew his breath in tightly and prepared for the kind of fight that comes out when a man feels his options start to seriously narrow. "You're going to have a hell of a job getting me in that wagon there," Robin observed. He wanted Nanette to feel the uncertainty of what he might do hanging in the air between them. "I'm notoriously difficult to take alive. Surely, you've heard." He glanced back and forth between the wagon and Nanette, his eyes racing between the knife in her hand and the armed man getting out of the wagon.

"You'll get in or I will cut her open from cunny to neck."

In desperation his eyes attempted to find evidence of some soft spot in her that he could play, some hint that she was bluffing and not capable of such an atrocity. None of the gifts nature had given him meant anything to Nanette. He couldn't charm her or plead with her. Worst of all the gifts he'd given himself, his decency and honour, were only liabilities.

"Not for very long you wouldn't," he whispered, his voice getting quieter and quieter with menace. "I can move very quickly."

"Normally, I'd believe that," she said, her voice casual. "But you're close to unconscious."

"Have you ever tried to push a wounded wild animal into a box while it's half mad with pain and rage?" He held her gaze for long enough to let his message find its mark.

He could see her body register the threat, his eyes darted back to the knife in her hand. The only thing he forced himself not to look at was the girl's terrified eyes. The girl whose name he never knew… "Or you could let her go and I will quietly let you tie me up." He held up both his hands, wrists exposed and together in binding position to indicate what she must do. As he became weaker and more desperate the chances he would indeed hurt her increased.

"Tie him up," she said to the soldier in Norman French.

"Let her go first," Robin said.

"You aren't in a very good bargaining position."

"You'll have to take my word for it. Let him tie your hands up and I will let her go."

Nanette was right, he couldn't afford to waste the strength on arguing the point. He held out his hands, the soldier took them roughly and wrenched his body forward, causing the arrow to move inside him and his vision to black out from the pain and shock. When he got a sense of what was happening again he was on his knees with his hands bound behind his back.

Nanette tossed the girl onto the ground beside him. "I'm so sorry!" she whispered to him in Welsh. "Thank you for helping me! I'm sorry I got you into this."

"Run!" he yelled at her in Welsh before she could finish, as the soldier began to drag him into the wagon.

"How can I help you?!" she screamed after him, tears streaming down her face and trying to run after the wagon on bare feet, holding together her torn clothing as the wheels started turning and the wagon began moving away from her.

"Tell the man who comes looking for me which way the wagon went!" he managed to say to her before the door closed and darkness muffled out the noise and drama of the fight for survival.

It was a weary fight…A relentless noise over the backdrop of reality, which was really just endless oceans of light, and that light was Love, and Love was god. He saw god in the eyes of the girl whose name he never knew as she screamed and ran after the wagon, fearless for herself in her fellow feeling for another suffering creature, heedless of the blood running down her legs as she ran… It was so raw and beautiful it caused a lump to thicken his throat.

Tears were in his eyes as he lost consciousness briefly, and a poignant smile lingering on his lips. There was a whole world of divine things springing into appearance in any form at any moment, the whole world was teeming with sacred eruptions and god running towards you, holding Her hands out to you, in the form of a crying girl. The unbearable sanctity of life hadn't seemed quite this rich and overwhelming since he was a half-touched child of five.

As though not quite inside himself Robin realised he was laughing and weeping at the same time and muttering long tracts of Cymric poetry, as if it were not quite him doing it. Then he was saying things in an older tongue. If they were going to shut him in a cage and try to box him in when his body was too weak to fly against their hard edges with his fists, then he'd still sing in his cage. He would sing and curse, weep, howl, and cry his internal wilderness at the moon that he couldn't see in her little box full of iron.

"You're insane," Nanette said.

"Oh…" he murmured, flopping his head over to one side. "You have no idea." Just when he looked like he was going to pass out Robin moved very quickly, swinging his legs out and hooking one around her legs, knocking her straight to the floor on her back. Almost unconscious as he was, he struggled with her, past all awareness of her being a woman, or any rules his inner boy made for himself. "You've underestimated how much I love life."

Nanette snorted in skepticism as the man pinned him down. "If that were so you wouldn't have given yours up over some random peasant girl." Her disdain was palpable but he could only laugh at her blindness, because so much light was infusing everything the closer he got to this weird edge.

"I didn't mean…just my life…what…even…is that?"


"F'arglwydd!" she called out to him. He knew the word because it was what the Welsh called their battle-leaders, he assumed it was Welsh for 'my lord'. "Os gwelwch yn dda…"

"I'm sorry I don't speak…Oh you poor little thing," he murmured, pressing his lips together in distaste as he looked down at her clothing and blood and inferred what had happened. "Here." He unfastened his cloak and wrapped it around the girl.

She cringed back from him when she heard him speak Norman French and took in the mixed message of the cloak around the shoulders with some confusion. Gil felt shame on behalf of his people. The girl appeared to take courage from his kind gesture and the expression of pity and disgust on his face, and she came forward to take his arm. Pulling him in the direction she had come she pointed frenziedly along the trail of blood.

"Robin!" she said. "Robin!" she said his name again pointing to the edge of the wood and the road beyond.

"Yes! Show me! God, that we only spoke the same language…So they said his name then, they knew who he was …" Then a few disparate parts of this picture suddenly came together for Gil with a crash. The ravished girl… Robin gone… The trail of blood… The girl's fear of his Norman French… "They used you as a trap," he whispered.

"Brysio!" she kept saying.

He hurried after her pulling his horse by the reins. When they reached the road she pointed once into the distance and again down at the ground. Following her finger Gil discerned the tracks of wagon wheels in the mud and then she gestured along the northern road.

"In a wagon?" Gil made a pantomime of turning wheels until the girl nodded.

"Cerbyd," she appeared to correct him.

"Cerbyd," he repeated, hopefully saying the correct word for wagon. He sniffed the air and turned a few circles upon the spot where some kind of struggle had occurred. It looked to Gil like someone had been pushed down hard on their knees. "But why would she be taking him North?" he muttered to himself out loud. Pointing due North Gil looked at the girl. "North?"

"Gwynedd?" she replied.

He shook his head, no. He knew that word. Pointing to the four cardinal points one at a time he said: "North, East, South, West."

She nodded immediately, the young lass was bright as well as brave, you could see it from her quick brown eyes, as lively and smart as a woodland creature's. "Gogleth!" she said pointing north and then proceeded to point to the directions. "Ddwyrain! Dde! Orllewin!"

"Thank you!" he cried out to her before mounting his horse. If he had to ask directions at any point he didn't want to run into that problem twice. "Diolch y chi!" he added in Welsh. "And I'm sorry for my countrymen," which he could only say in French. He turned his horse's head north and kicked him into a hard gallop.

With twilight coming on it became more and more dizzy and strange, as if they were chasing Eilion's skittering light down a black tunnel into the Underworld. Tears of effort ran down her cheeks. The way they were riding… Like creatures that were in fact part horse themselves who knew the land like the pattern of their own hand veins… Lux kept reminding herself that Eilish did this whilst pregnant and she seemed to have lost none of her fierce horsemanship for it.

She trusted the group mind that she was part of as they followed Eilion's every twist and turn and sudden leap. There was no mistrusting Eilion's desire to protect Robin. He set a grueling routine for them. The kind that put Lux in mind of the stories where faeries would seize control of the limbs of some unlucky soul and make them dance until they bled, and further still until they eventually died. It was that kind of brutal whip-lash of an experience, like where the Corrigan faeries of Cornwall will throw you up into the air and let you fall in a macabre game that ends in your death.

As she rode, giving herself to the single horse they seemed to be galloping hard on, she started to see through Eilion's eyes. It was like lines and lines of something in a code at first. Yet sometimes she would understand snippets. She could feel his mind calculating, if I have them veer to the left I will save a fraction of a second, which the horses will lose because of inertia when approaching at that incline... It wasn't clear if it was more like mathematics or music, but she could feel the code behind creation and she knew that being half faerie she could read it with her fingertips like a tactile language.

Every now and again she realised that the reason it felt like they were diving down a never-ending hole was because they were chasing the figure of a peregrine falcon in full stoop, just as she had become a swan. To go where he was going they were going to have to fly as the same beast. That wasn't going to be hard because the Magister's power enfolded both of them in his enormous wings, it felt like they would merely be pulled into the comet tail of Blaith's plunge from the Heavens, as he chased Eilion's receding light.

She knew where a fall like this was want to terminate. They were going down into the very depths of Hell to find her beloved. *That's where they say the bird robin got his breast burned, down against the hell fires while he was trying to bring water of mercy to the tormented souls in hell. He got that red burn trying to be kind.* As the half-light got lower and the darkness became increasingly literal, her horse began to hesitate before it jumped a log or stone.

"How the Hell?" Eilish eventually cried out, her breath panting as franticly as Lux's. "Nobody can ride like that! It's not possible!" she yelled after his corpse candle. "The horses can't do it! It isn't possible, Eilion!"

"It has to be!" Blaith growled under his breath. He sat forward further in the saddle and took both her bridle and Eilish's as well as his own. He whispered in the ears of the animals before taking full control of all three horses. She would never have credited the idea that the horses would allow their heads to be drawn together as if they were one monstrous beast in such a way, yet Blaith made it happen. The horses began to relax and let it happen.

Her knees relaxed, her thighs too, and she gave herself over to the horse that moved like flowing silk in the Magister's hands. She was part of the horse, the horse was part of her, and the horse was of one mind with Blaith. It would have run over the edge of a cliff into darkness for him at the merest reassuring touch of his hand, and so would she…As relaxed as a toddler into the arms of its parent.

She was chasing the vanishing light that wouldn't stop moving, it moved fast like it was the fingers of the most gifted of musicians, moving on the strings… Feathers from angel wings were raining down, charred in the air all around her.Despite the black wave of power, Lux could still hear Blaith's labouring humanity via his lungs that were working as hard as her own.

Robin found himself thinking of Lux and Blaith and all the other people who loved him and how they would suffer if he didn't come home. There was never any such thing as just fighting for your own life, as he'd tried to explain to Nanette. There was only fighting for *life*, and if you didn't understand the difference and why it was important then nobody could explain it to you.

He didn't need to look down to see what Nanette was doing because he knew from the force with which the very much-needed blood was sucked out of his wound. He was faintly disgusted by the unwanted intimacy of the act. "Normally, I really enjoy this," he murmured weakly. "But you really need to work on your foreplay."

She drew back from him and wiped his blood off her face. He noticed how she acted like the soldier's question was totally irrelevant as if he were no more than a pet in the room with them.

"You joke still? But how does it feel, for a strong man like you? Being helpless?"

"If you wanted to take the power from a man there are more powerful ones."

"No, I disagree," she said. "I have never had a man of your power under my control before." She licked off the remainder of smeared blood from his upper arm and onto his chest in one long savouring lick. "The witch blood of an old house runs in your veins. I want to swallow your death spasms," she murmured, reaching a hand up to compress his throat so it became difficult to breathe. "I'm your death..."

"Maybe..." he said weakly. "But I have a feeling you're just my nightmare... I always look dead when they pull me out... When the wardens of the Underworld arrive to carry me... home... through blood up to the knee..."

Darkness had fallen before the weak light of the lantern on the front of the wagon came into view ahead. On the relatively flat and clear path Gil had been able to maintain a gallop even after the sunset and the new horse was relatively fresh. As much as his respect for the Welsh mountain pony had gone through the roof over the past twenty-four hours, he was glad he'd stolen himself a new destrier as it would help him to impersonate The Baron of Rochdale.

As he gained on the slower vehicle he assessed what kind of protection she was travelling with. There was an armed man on horseback riding with them, and the driver was wearing chainmail also. He could just tell from the way the lantern light glinted off the metal. There was a high chance that Nanette had at least one other inside with her. Gil sighed. If only he was an archer he could have picked both of them off before they knew he was even there.

As he came up closer to them, he whistled and hailed them. The man on horseback swung around immediately and partly drew his sword. The wagon came to a gradual stop. The other man stayed very close to the fragile light of the lantern as if he didn't want to move out of what he imagined to be its protective glow. "Whose there?" he cried out into the darkness. Gil knew that being close to the candle flame would blind the other man so that Gilbert would be seeing him far more clearly than he was seen. He counted on only the height of his destrier being visible at first.

"Sheath your weapon, knight. I'm Lord Gilbert de Biron, Baron of Rochdale and I'm looking for my sister."

"Are you joking? We've got the daughter of the late Earl of Leicester here. What's this the day for nobles travelling alone?"

"Well, we did just take the worst of a rather unfortunate battle," he said dryly, walking his horse slowly into the light. He gazed down his nose at the man and sat his horse in the way he'd watched other lords do since he was a boy. He'd always loathed them even whilst he was forced to try to copy their stances. "Death seems to have embarrassed me of my entourage. But my ancestral broadsword should prove my identity to any educated man who knows what he's looking at. Would you like a closer look at it?" Gil asked, with a tone of voice that said that if he said yes he might end up seeing it a whole lot closer than he bargained for.

"No, no, of course not, my lord," the man muttered warily.

"Have the wagon opened and announce me to my sister immediately," he ordered.

The bluntness of the order sat in the air heavily. The man obviously didn't want to disobey him but had been told not to by Nanette. Hesitantly he knocked on the side of the wagon.

"What?" Nanette asked testily, from within.

"We have your brother Gilbert, Baron of Rochdale here at your service, my lady," he said, clearly trying to sound like he spent most of his time announcing high society and less hacking poor men's hands off at the behest of people like Nanette.

"That's impossible," she said, as the wagon door came open. "My brother is deceased." She said the last words just at the moment where their eyes made contact. Gilbert's attention went straight to her blood covered dress and hands, and then to try to see behind her. Seeming to relish the tension, she slowly moved her hand around in something behind her and lifted two blood-ied fingers to her mouth, before sucking the blood from them. "Kill him."

Gil's hand went immediately to his broadsword and he wheeled his horse around to be facing the other man on horseback. "I wouldn't if I were you," he said, holding the other man's gaze. "Which of us looks like the real noble-man in this scenario, chaps?" he asked, still taking a few backward steps on his horse to keep both the man on foot and the man on horseback in his view. "Me," he said, displaying his sword in the action of half-drawing it. "Or that blood-sucking witch?"

"Yes, men," Nanette said. "Which of us was highborn from the cradle? I, who has just caught one of England's most wanted men? Or this sad little excuse for a man you see before you? What would the real Baron of Rochdale want with this pretty tinker boy? Although we've all heard the rumours about him. I'm sure such a renowned and tragic boy-buggerer can't be too hard for real men to kill?"

*Well, I suppose I did ask them to consider which of us most resembles a real Norman noble, I can't dispute their choice.*

"He's actually quite a good swordsman, isn't he? Who would have thought it?" Nanette snorted. Maybe he was a proper De Biron after all? Surprised and uncomfortable she squinted to see him fighting in the moonlight. It looked like one of her men was lying dead on the ground and Gil was drawing the other two closer to the tree line. She stepped down from the carriage to see more clearly.

Just as she took her second step something hit her in the leg and she pitched hard into the turf. She screamed; it felt like her thigh was on fire. The intensity of the impact didn't make any sense until she looked down and saw the arrow, fretted with pure white swan-feathers, sticking out of her leg. An androgynous young woman dressed in boy's trousers and carrying a bow was coming towards her with a purposeful stride. "Don't move or the next one goes in your eye socket," she said, her voice little louder than a whisper.

Nanette glanced up into two eyes so mercilessly steely and cold that she immediately thought of De Rue. Nanette was certain she was being gazed on by a being with no human soul who would kill her as soon as look at her. She froze and the girl pinned her shoulder to the ground with her boot, and held the arrow still, aimed at her face, never speaking. She had never seen someone's arrow from that angle before, or seen anyone hold the string at such a tension for so long, until their fingers trembled with the effort and sweat broke out on their brow. Any sudden movement, any slip and the arrow would go flying into Nanette's brain.

Barely daring to breathe, Nanette held the other woman's knife-like gaze. After a while, as the fingers continued to tremble on the string, Nanette began to almost wish for the tension to break, for the arrow to fly home and kill her just so the waiting and wondering when the other woman would move would be over. It was a drawn out form of psychological torture that she would never have guessed could be so terrifying until she found herself there, with the blonde girl's boot on her chest, staring up into that pair of unforgiving eyes.

Gil managed to hack to death one of the men and temporarily use his corpse as a human shield while he fought his way to the tree line. Gilbert was a better swordsman than both these men left alive and his night vision was far better, but after the day he'd had he was tiring fast. In the way that ten mangy dogs may kill a lion, many small injuries he'd sustained that day and earlier in life, were beginning to tell.

As he caught a hard blow on the flat of his blade the jarring pain in his shoulder was becoming painful enough to cause flashes of light behind his eyes. The man who lay dead on the grass behind him had managed to open a small cut in Gil's forearm. One of his legs was badly bruised and stiffening from being trapped between his horse and that of another man. With a last desperate effort Gil forced one of the men onto a backward step with a sustained and rapid attack, before swinging at the other assailant seemingly randomly amongst the onslaught.

Something dark moved smoothly and noiselessly in the branches above the man he was fighting. It looked like a shadow. But then his assailant's throat appeared to explode with blood. Only a second afterwards did Gil see the moon catch the glint of a knife blade, as it sawed off the rest of the man's head. For a second the assailant held onto the dead man's hair from the branch above, as if he was hanging up a pig to bleed, but then the last sinews he'd left, keeping body and head together, severed with the weight, and the body slumped to the ground, leaving the head hovering.

Chilling laughter filled the shrill silence as the man's main artery gulped out his life and his eyes still spun wildly in the column of moonlight while life left the rest of the suspended face. The other man Gil had been fighting stood for one moment gawping in pure speechless horror, before turning and fleeing for his life. Gil had begun backing away the moment he saw the silent shadow above, and he was still doing so, with his sword out, when Blaith jumped down from the tree.

Gilbert recognised him mainly by how he moved and let his breath out in a long exhale of utmost relief. He felt dizzy with the utter levity of seeing the Twll Du Magister walking towards him carrying a severed head in one hand and a knife in the other. Blaith came up close and pulled him closer still. For a brief moment he pressed Gil hard against his chest and put one bloody hand on the side of his face. With it he seemed to compel Gil to lean his head forward so their foreheads briefly touched and black fire danced between them with strong vertigo.

Eilish's hips twinged whenever the shock of impact of running went through her legs, there was occasionally a feeling of weakness around the pelvic floor. Yet she knew her body could do it, just like their women would climb up to Twll Du while in the early stages of labour. Most of all she knew that her cousin was in that carriage.

It was the pressure of being the only one who knew how to save Robin

305

that was making her breath come in panicky gasps.

As she climbed up into the wagon she found the light poor, being lit by only one lantern with a low-burning flame. Trying to get to Robin she slid in his blood and fell onto the slippery floor. Down on her hands and knees she wretched when she saw what she'd slipped in. Other scenes of her relatives in such conditions tried to dominate each other for prime space inside her mind until she had to close her eyes for a moment.

"Dear gods," she whispered in horror. "What has she done?" She was afraid to reach for his pulse in case it wasn't there. Swallowing down tears she pulled her doctoring kit off her back. Her hands felt numb and her fingers woolly and clumsy. Reaching a hand up to Robin's face she steeled herself to feel for his pulse. It was weak and it took her a moment or two of sinking horror to locate it. When she found it she started to sob with relief. "Hang in there, cariad," she whispered.

Eilish rapidly prepared the bulrush paste that would solidify and coagulate inside the wounds. "None of us are going to make it without you."

Blaith and Gil's forms blocked out the moonlight as they appeared in the door. Even without his face visible or saying a word Eilish could sense the terrifying wave of suffering that boomed out from Blaith's body when he saw. "See? Look, sweetheart," she whispered to Robin while she worked. "The men of the Underworld have come to carry you back to the world of the living. That means you're going to make it. You know how the story goes…"


Eilion could feel blood starting to form on the fingers he was using to hold the bow string taut, those fingers that half felt like his and half like Lux's. It wasn't like she was going to be the one to give in first though, not before Eilion did. Not when it was a matter of hating this woman and loving this man as much as they both did. Lux would never have come up with the intensity of this drawn out stand off or gesture of concentrated hatred, but nor was she going to be found unequal to it.

"Just let me go or kill me!" Nanette cried at last. "What is *wrong with you?*"

Eilion, in the end, had better understood what Nanette feared. "For the love of God say something!" Nanette's voice cracked, broke and finally subsided into tears. For the first time Eilion readjusted the focus of his eyes and watched the tears roll down her cheeks. The faintest twitch of a smile of satisfaction formed at the side of his mouth, but it was soon gone. The only movement was where the muscles in Lux's arm trembled with stress as the bow creaked uncertainly. "What do you want from me!" Nanette cried hysterically. It was the nose running type of weeping where an adult is wetly dissolved into child form in only a few breaths. "I'm sorry I hurt him! Alright? Is that what you want? Is that it?"

The silence endured until it seemed to seer the air between them, even though Lux's breath was coming fast and furious with the strain of holding the bow taut. Very, very slowly and faintly Eilion's head moved side to side in a gesture of 'no'.

"I just wanted my daughter to come back to me! Alright? I just... I just... I just don't want to be alone... And he... he took her from me!" She paused breathlessly, searching Eilion's eyes for some signal, for anything, for any indicator of whether or not he was satisfied. "And I just wanted..." she wept messily, nearly choking on her distress. "I just wanted... whatever was so beautiful in Robin that I was clearly lacking because nobody ever chooses me!" Still Eilion didn't move, even though his fingers were screaming.

"Are you happy now!" she screamed at him hysterically, the whites of her eyes showing. "You've got my pride now, don't you? That's what you wanted, wasn't it? That's why you just look at me like that with those... eyes... My pride means more to me than life itself so you may as well just do it! Do it!" she screamed. Without warning Eilion let the string fly. Nanette screamed as the shaft hit the ground and dug in right above her left ear, grazing her temple above the eye. She lost bladder control and covered her eyes like a child that believes the monsters won't see her. Eilion continued to observe the spreading of the urine-stain of wetness through her skirts the same way he had observed her sweat and tears.

When he went to move in the response to the blinding new pain Robin heard familiar voices speaking Welsh. As soon as he heard the lilt and burr of his own people's tongue tears of relief rushed into his eyes and the fight went out of him. Now this terrible new pain of getting treated was feeling like something different, it meant help, which made it less terrible.

It was Blaith and Gil who moved to hold him down, and Eilish that was pushing metal tongs into his wound to remove part of the broken arrow shaft. Still even with them holding him firmly, Blaith whispering comforting things he couldn't make out, Robin's body bucked up off the ground when she got purchase. It hurt far worse coming out than it had going in. Robin screwed his eyes shut tight.

"I'm going to go and get you someone," Blaith murmured.

"I can't give you milk of the poppy because your heartbeat's too weak still," Eilish was saying. "I'm so, so sorry, cariad… Gil, you might need to help me hold him down."

"Gil, Eilish asked you to hold me down," Robin murmured in Norman French, passing the message on more than a little reluctantly.

"I've got you," he said. "It will be over soon, I promise."

A figure carrying a second lantern came crawling into the wagon then. Robin recognised his wife's body but he knew immediately it was not entirely her he was looking at. A strange ethereal light seemed to pervade her skin and hair. Robin knew then who he was looking at for it was one of the strongest possessions he had ever seen. "Eilion?"

The faerie creature smiled at him. "Yes, beloved," he said, stepping over Robin with one leg and then crouching down, straddling him in an elfish way that didn't cause them to even touch at all. "I'm here."

His breath caught in his throat when Eilion's fingers found his and coiled slowly and sensuously through them. The pain of what was happening to his body began to seem like a faint ache next to the shimmering inferno of that feeling.

"Well," Blaith said, standing above Nanette, who was making a futile attempt to get away via crawling on one leg. He put his boot on the hem of her dress until it pulled taught and she stopped trying to tug it free. She rolled over onto her back to look at him. "We finally meet in the flesh, Lady Nanette de Biron." Usually, he wouldn't have acknowledged her stolen title, but he was well aware that these were probably the only words he'd say that she understood. That was acceptable, he reasoned, *if you're someone like Nanette your death ought to be confusing and incomprehensible. Everyone gets the devil they deserve, at least they do while I'm around.*

As he pronounced her title he took a quick visual sweep of her urine soaked appearance before coming back up to her face. He wasn't sure how Eilion had done so much to unravel her, but he tendered respect to it. Blaith slowly and thoughtfully drew his out of its sheath. So worried had he been for his brother that he'd not even taken the time to clean it after cutting her guard's head off in the wood. Using his undershirt to accomplish it, Blaith took some time to remedy that now. All the while Nanette's frightened eyes followed the in and out of the silver item in his shirt.

When the knife was nice and clean, Blaith crouched down next to her and looked closely into her eyes. He saw the demon who had a curse for a wife stirring in the darkness behind her eyes, lured by the presence of what he was. His mouth salivated and his teeth ached to devour it. "My brother is in a lot of pain," he said. "Which you know, because you went out of your way to cause it. He won't scream though, even after the way you removed that arrow from him and left the arrow tip," Blaith said through teeth clenched so hard it was difficult to hear him. "But I think you will scream quite easily, won't you?"

She gibbered something at him in the tongue of the oppressor and Blaith backhanded her across the face. "Ah that's better," he said, when she looked back up, shaking with more blood running down her face. "Let it not be said that I conversed with one who nearly killed my brother and did not draw blood from them." Slowly, he raised his blade to her face and, as delicately as shaving, he lifted the trail of blood from her face onto his knife. While she watched in horror, he took out the jar in which he'd placed the curse he'd lifted out of Augusta, opened the vessel and fed Nanette's blood into it.

"Blood taken above the breath," he said. "I have taken your power and send your curse home to roost."

Nanette gasped when his knife approached her face again and held her breath. But instead of cutting her he trimmed a lock of her hair and dropped it into the jar. "See," he said to her, pleased she that she didn't understand. "I know what you did. The will you wrote for yourself. If you were to die over here that you left provision to have my family exterminated," he said. "Instead, your body will destroy itself."

In one long, cold drawing suck he closed over her nose and mouth and emptied the air from her lungs. In one short, sharp expulsion of power he breathed Nanette's spirit into the jar. When the transfer had been done he leaned over her again and came up close.

"*Mourir*," he whispered in her ear.

'Die' was the only single word sentence he'd ever bothered to master in Norman French.

When he forced the liquid from the vessel into her mouth she tried to spit it out and struggled, very calmly he held her nose shut until she swallowed, like a child taking medicine. "That's it…" he murmured. "You should have just about enough time left to make it back to England if you don't dawdle." He leaned back as though to let her leave but before she could his hand covered Lux's arrow that was still sticking out of her leg. "To help with that," he said, before in one shocking wrench he ripped it clean out of her muscle. She screamed with total full-throated abandon and Blaith smiled to himself. *Ah, there it is…* "As was the mercy you showed my brother."

To the tune of further screaming he shoved a sticky glob of bulrush, yarrow, and sage paste into the hole to stop the bleeding and slow down the march of proud flesh. "And that's so you don't die too quickly."

# BOOK 4

# 1

ou prefer not to come in here, don't you?" Sariah observed as Lux crouched down next to the fire in the bleeding tent.

"Sorry… Is it that obvious?" Lux felt a crushing sense of cultural failure. Sariah didn't seem to find it as dire as she.

"Don't apologise. It's pretty obvious, yes. I was always confused why you came in if you didn't like it."

Sariah was using a small dish with hot water in it to wash blood off her inside thighs while they spoke. She tried not to look at the blood. It was among the last obscenity she struggled with. Whilst she would now look upon Sariah or Eilish's cunny as naturally as their elbow or knee, the sight of the menses was still a challenge. It forced her to confront not only a lifetime of being told it was a curse and made you dirty, but also the fact she didn't at all like it when it was happening to her.

"I don't have to?"

"Of course not! Those who come in here do so to have time off from duties and pamper each other and rest."

"We were forced to stay in our room while we bled back inside the walls."

Sariah nodded as though this was something she was only partly aware of nor was she particularly interested to hear of it. "Strange."

It fascinated her that Sariah had bothered to apply coal make up around her eyes and was wearing an amber necklace whilst half naked and in the steamy, herb and blood scented environs of the bleeding tent. This world where beauty wasn't only for the eyes of men was still a revelation.

"How would you bleed if you were free to do anything?"

313

Lux was caught off balance by the question and therefore answered it entirely candidly. "If it were up to me I wouldn't bleed at all!"

Sariah looked surprised, as though menstruation were something desirable that Lux was unusual in not enjoying. Then after a while she nodded her understanding. "There are people among our culture, Lux, people who are neither really girls or boys but feel themselves to be something other, a third thing blessed by the faeries. It is a holy thing, a mark of power. Does that sound like something that makes sense to you?"

Immediately Lux started nodding and tears rushed into her eyes at the same time. They were tears of relief that Sariah had somehow plucked out of the amorphous realm of floating traditions and customs she seemed to move through some words that made sense of everything. "It makes total sense." She glanced up shyly at the other woman, warming to the confidence. "I think Robin sees it, too. Sometimes he makes reference to my inner boy and implies in other ways that I'm not entirely a woman, or that I'm a woman and also something else, something faerie. The other thing is…"

"Yes?" Sariah's open interest prompted and encouraged her.

"Ever since Eilion possessed me during the rescue the feeling has become stronger. As though the edges of what I thought was my own mind has been expanded."

She nodded. "This is a good thing. A sign of a powerful hedge-partnering. So…" her eyes narrowed as though she were her big cat self again and on the trail of something. "Why is it you speak of it with such trepidation and anxiety in disclosing it?"

"The thing is I think I want to be a maiden." Lux had not yet verbalised this to herself or anyone else and even she was still partly shocked by it when it became words. "And if I'm not a proper woman, if I don't like bleeding then I'm afraid I won't be able to do that."

"Being a maiden isn't about being a woman or bleeding. Being a maiden is about being an expert at unraveling people. You don't even need a cunt for it. It happens in the immaculate heart of Our Lady. And I know you have her inside you. I saw her when you rode your horse straight at your own oppressor to protect Robin. I saw her when we treated your bruised and bloodied fingers after the rescue. When you nearly drowned yourself to complete the magic in the lake…"

"So I could do… other things at the times when you and Eilish use your cunny?" Lux thoughts about the spring festivals in particular where she had witnessed Sariah take man after man. It had transfixed her and been hard to look away. The state was one of intense arousal and fear at the same time, as though she were witnessing a sacred glimpse behind people's human-masks.

Sariah's eyes lit up suddenly. "Has Robin tried arse play on you yet?"

Lux blushed and looked away. She felt a hot stab of annoyance with herself. How was Sariah meant to take her interest in the path seriously when she was still so shy about discussing the sex acts that most deviated from the norm?

"Yes. He does things to me… with his fingers sometimes, usually while he's fucking me or licking me." Lux was enormously impressed with herself and won back some esteem in her own eyes for getting this sentence out.

"And? Do you like it?"

Again she looked away. "I'm pretty embarrassed by how much I like it," she admitted.

"Don't be! Not only do so many men love it, but it's a great way to be sure you won't end up pregnant. Blaith would be such an excellent guide for you, with both the spiritual side of your androgyny and with breaking in your arse."

Lux made a choking sound of shock, partly because of Sariah's frank way and partly because she was aroused in a sudden sort of way that she wasn't sure was particularly feminine.

"What?" Sariah demanded. "I'm just saying. He's very skilled in that area, and besides, his cock is a little more slender than Robin's." She laughed and Lux couldn't help laughing too. "But you know what I think? After your excursion with Robin you should come to my tent one night and we can start you off. Whatever you are the best place for any budding maiden to start is with girl tongue."

"What did you notice about them?" Robin asked as he crouched beside Lux at their campfire and warmed his hands. It was still freezing outdoors but this had to be done now. What she was receiving was training, but it was also a welcome excuse to take her with him on the road. Lux wondered sometimes if Sariah had told him anything of her revelations to her in the bleeding tent?

He had her observing some Welsh folk in a hillside settlement. Most of the time he'd given her no indication of what it was she was meant to be watching beyond that they needed to know as much as they could about these people. At first they had appeared perfectly ordinary yeomen going about their lives, unaware they were being spied on a by a feral outlaw in camouflage paint and a runaway Norman noblewoman.

"I'm not sure where to start."

"Begin with who lives at the settlement."

"Well, there's the ageing parents -but the older fellow still wields a bow like nobody's business," she added, beginning to warm to the activity now she realised that without thinking about it she'd taken note of which ones were most dangerous. "Then there are their grown up sons, two of them. Both decent shots but not as good as their father. The two boys go hunting together in the hills sometimes I think, someone was curing venison... So, I'm guessing all the men can hunt, track and probably fight."

"All the people," Robin corrected her softly. "This is a Cymric mountain holding so you can be assured that whilst the men do it more often, all the people inside can hunt, track, and all of them will fight you, down to the small children armed with sharp pointy sticks. There are no king's men or sheriffs here to keep the law, the four men, four women, and ten children within protect this outpost. As do his four kennelled dogs that whine for the chase from further off on the property."

Lux frowned. "Hang on... If there's only one other man here that isn't the brother of the younger women... How are there so many children of such close ages if only one of the women has a husband?"

Robin's eyebrows twitched up with a flicker of wicked glee. "I don't know,

Lux, what could these folk be getting up to out here in the hills?"

"Multiple births?" she ventured.

Robin laughed outright. "No. I mean that out here in the mountains some of us like our brothers and sisters quite a lot. Many even make marriages that are outside the consanguinity laws of the church."

"That's what you think is happening?"

"It would explain the things we observed."

"Seems a large leap though. Wouldn't everyone in the homestead know and surely deem it a sin?"

He only shrugged and poked at the fire thoughtfully with his stick. "There are worse sins in the eyes of the folk out here. Such as ones that hurt someone."

"But would it not be to inflict deformity on their children?"

"We have been observing them all day, did you see any odd ones?"

Lux couldn't help giggling. "Odd! How would you know what odd looks like? You're the oddest thing that ever was."

He winked. "Well you might need to spot them for me."

She sighed. "No, none of their children look deformed or simple. But I have to say, Robin, if sister-marrying is allowed out here in the mountains maybe they're leaving the odd ones out on the hillside?"

"Oh yes, child murder follows I suppose… Let's get back to work. Do the men keep a watch? Did you notice when they packed down for the evening whether all retired? Where is the guard dog now?"

"The older man removed one of the dogs to the house before the lights went down."

"Indeed. Did you notice any anomalies about any of the younger men?"

"Yes! One of them seemed to be nursing a leg injury and a facial scar."

Robin nodded. "And what might we conjecture from that?"

"Maybe he was in the war?"

"Highly likely. Which means you know their political sympathies are strongly with Gwenllian, because a small, close-knit settlement like this does not lightly give up even one of its men at risk of not returning. Think about

317

what you have seen here today. From where do they draw their subsistence?"

"From herding and milking and there's a kitchen garden and some chickens. But hunting also provides some of their meat."

"Yes, which the men mainly do. So this place is highly vulnerable to resource stress as well as outlaw attacks, if they lose so much as one man it could mean the difference between survival or death."

"Outlaws? Do the Welsh mountains have outlaws? Why haven't I seen any?"

"Lux… I don't know how to tell you this. But I myself am an outlaw… It's awkward that we're only now having this conversation, but there is a significant amount of money on my head and I think-"

She grinned. "Damn. I've really thrown my lot in rather recklessly here, haven't I?"

Making a point of returning to seriousness he cleared his throat. "In answer to your question they don't come near enough for you to see them because you're with me. But trust me, they watch us sometimes from a distance, just beyond arrow range to let me know they mean no harm, but I always know they're there."

Lux shivered at the thought of them watching when she hadn't known they were about. "How do you know?"

He shrugged. "I have the Irish Sea in my hips. A lot of things whisper to me from down there at ball level."

"I thought there were wild horses in your hips? That's what your Spirit Song says…"

He smiled. "Aye! Yes. The wild horses come running out of the ocean spray, their legs are covered in blood and tears from my birth home."

She looked away from him for a few moments. Even now his otherness was still an imaginative gap to be crossed between them that would at times seem to loom uncrossable and vast. "How do you hold so much?" she muttered, her voice suddenly tight and pained.

"Oh I don't!" he laughed. "It spills out all over the place. I'm an awen-sticky mess."

"Robin?" she knew it would seem a strange divergence from topic but she couldn't help it suddenly. The need to confide in him was strong. It was something about him saying he was a mess. "I think I might not be a girl, well, not entirely."

Robin just nodded his affirmation. "I wondered when you'd talk about it. I never really thought you were."

"You are such a strange man..."

"It's been said a time or two," he said, flopping back onto his bedroll.

"Why did you pick me if you thought I wasn't quite a girl?"

"Maybe your in-between-ness is precisely what I found attractive? Come; let's get some sleep. You will have a big day of socialising down there at the settlement tomorrow so you will need your rest."

She lay down and then sat half back up again. "Socialising? What do you mean *socialising?*"

He only chuckled while he pulled his hood down over his face and pretended to be already asleep.


Robin reached down to help the woman with the towel.

"Oh," she remarked. "So you're one of *those* type of men."

He grinned quizzically and set his head upon one side. "What kind?"

"The type who can't let a woman do something for him."

Robin sat there trying not to physically squirm with discomfort as she dried off his feet with the towel. It did indeed require an act of conscious will for him to let this custom happen. When he replied to her it was with an unguardedness that was hard to avoid after this forced intimacy.

"It's probably fair to say I'm more the type of man who finds it hard to let *anybody* do anything for him." He knew it was the custom in the north to bring out hot water and leave the guest sit with their feet in it for a time. Often someone would come out and play the harp while you sat there and no one spoke to each other until their fetch had fully arrived in the foyer to the dwelling. If you put your feet in it meant you intended to stay for the night, if you didn't you would just be offered food.

"Do your people not follow the old ways of hospitality?" she asked, for the first time she looked up at him and met his eyes. She was doing the same kind of work he was trying to teach Lux, fathoming the kind of man she had in her home to keep her household safe. Lux had already been invited in because they were not afraid of her. He was going to be examined a bit more first.

"I'm tinker-born," he said, maintaining eye contact with her. To her credit he saw her neither flinch nor pull back her hands from touching him.

"Ah, well that explains the strange tattoos," she said, taking up his hand she looked first at the eyes in his hands and then turned his hand over to look at his knuckles. Few people noticed the small tattooed marks on his knuckles and some of his fingers. Since Nanette's attack on him everyone noticed his scars though. "What do they mean? Are you a sorcerer or something?"

He just smiled in response. It was his puckish smile that often got him out of answering difficult questions when directed at anyone with the mildest interest in his sex. It seemed to work on this lady. "You don't need to answer that." She put down his hand quite suddenly, but he reached out and gently took up hers instead.

"I don't even know your name…"

With a smile that seemed to melt her a little her hand relaxed in his. "I'm Creirwy."

"You are named for the daughter of Ceridwen. A beautiful name!"

"And yours?"

"People call me Hob."

"Like the hobgoblin? The puck faerie?"

"A bit like that, yes."

"Well, you are beautifully clean," she said patting him on the leg as she got to her feet. "Tinker mothers must teach their children very well. Your hands look like they've already seen water this very morning, and your hair has seen soap within two if I'm not much mistaken." She said rubbing some of it between her fingers like he was a child she was checking for lice. "Have you got something else in you? Your skin is dark for a Cymric tinker."

Robin spent a couple of moments breathing through a racially defensive response that made him want to demand why she would sound so surprised that he'd washed, before replying. "Cleanliness and grace are bred into all of us... I think perhaps I see more sun than most se... non-travelling folk..."

"Well, my mother always taught me it's not a man's skin that matters but what's inside his heart."

He got to his feet with her. It was hard to explain exactly what about this comment got under his skin. "It was good of your Mumma to tolerate us so," he muttered in his fake subservient tone. He usually found if he used it dryly enough he could deliver sentences like that without settlers even noticing he was being sarcastic. Creirwy immediately turned, blocking off his access to the rest of her home with her body while she did. The gesture held clear authority. He smiled. The boldness of Welsh women always gave him a hard-on.

"I'm not talking about tolerance, tinker, I'm talking about hospitality. My people do things in the way of the Old Cymry."

"Did your brothers fight?"

"Damn right they did!" she snapped back immediately, fire rushing into her eyes as if he himself had suddenly become a Norman. "And my father. My sisters and mother would have gone too if someone didn't need to stay here to keep this place running and the animals fed!" Her chin tilted up with pride and fierce tears rushed into her eyes as though daring him to say she couldn't carry the armour.

"Gwenllian would have been proud." He smiled at her.

"Did you fight?" she demanded.

He nodded. Even just the mention of it brought back the clamour of bodies, horses and weapons crashing together and the thick smell of blood and exposed viscera. It was all together in one welter of trauma that seemed to feed without boundaries into Nanette's attack on him and that upon the girl whose name he never knew. "Of course," he murmured.

321

She nodded to herself thoughtfully. "Some say your kind will just wander off to other lands, that you don't attach to any one place so you're not truly dedicated to Cymry."

"I'd die for this land!" he half snapped at her, letting her see a little of the defensive response he'd hidden earlier. He had a feeling she'd need to see the truth of it and little of his edge before she'd trust him.

Creirwy smiled and placed her hands to her brow in salute. "A proud daughter of Ana beholds the sovereignty in you."

He returned the gesture, just from the forehead without the heart part used for one's intimates. "A proud son of Beli Mawr beholds the sovereignty in you."

Robin watched Lux laughing with Creirwy's brother over by the fire. The young man was clearly charming, and his warm behavior didn't seem unwelcome to her. She was likely far more inebriated on their guest's mead than he was, so he checked her body language often.

"Is she yours?" Creirwy asked, looking over too.

"In the hedgerow sense, yes. There are no shackles on her though."

Creirwy snorted with amusement as if Robin had meant to imply the girl was headstrong, when he in fact had just meant what he'd said. "Her accent certainly is not Cymric…" Robin didn't respond for so long that Creirwy tentatively began again. "We keep to the old way of hospitality here."

"I'm guessing you mean the kind of old ways the priests might not altogether approve of?" He asked with raised eyebrows.

Creirwy sighed. "The Cymric way of non-jealousy over one-night encounters was never understood by the priests."

"Tinker folk like us live by a way of non-jealousy also. We do not believe a human can own another human."

He watched Creirwy suckle her one-year-old daughter. Young mothers always made him feel protective and moved at some profound gut level, there were shades of arousal in the feeling too. It made him think about impregnation, an act his body found appealing but his psyche did not. A green jolt of spring tide passed through his entire body to his finger-ends, in response to the thought of emptying his ancestors out into Lux's womb one day. But the feeling made him desirous and anxious at the same time.

"She is inexperienced. I trust your brother is a gentleman and won't press?"

"Oh no, Brynmor would never press her! He's the most considerate of lovers. Well, I mean to say…"

"Is he your baby's father?"

She jumped and the babe detached from her nipple, whimpering up at him as if Robin were the clear cause of all evils in the world. "I beg your pardon?"

"Your baby looks just like him."

"She looks just like me! Brynmor and I just look alike."

Robin grinned and leaned in closer to her with the feeling of bestowing a confidence. "My brother and I love each other more than most brothers, and I'm yet to see it do anyone any harm."

She was still staring at him dumbfounded by his bluntness and shamelessness. "I don't know what you're talking about… You don't think…" she ventured. "I mean, you're not disgusted?"

Robin shrugged. "*Honi soit qui mal y pense.*"

"Pardon?"

"It means: the 'shame be to he who thinks evil of it'." He translated for her.

"Ah… Robin Goodfellow… You really are *everything* they hate aren't you?"

"I don't recall giving you that name…" He smiled slowly. There was a thin layer of playfulness, which made it a little softer than a bearing of the teeth, but he could tell she sensed the rising of his predator.

"Oh come on! You're a tinker, you look like *that*, you were in the war, you speak French and travel with a Norman girl…"

"Did you know all along?"

"What? Did I know I was letting a known fugitive and wolfshead into my home from the first moment I lay eyes on you? Of course! Your wariness gives you away, as do your tattoos and the whole alien feeling of you! But we invited you in because we're rebels too. The people of these hills are yours to a man, woman and child, Robin."

Robin frowned. He understood the term at a military level, but he wasn't in the military so it sat strangely. The other wardens were never 'his' even though it was his job to lead and train them. "Mine? If you are all mine what am I to *do* with you?"

One of her eyebrows twitched up. "Whatever you want..." He didn't miss the sexual invitation wrapped up in this political discussion, but she wasn't heavy handed about it, she moved over it with the skill of a woman who had regularly negotiated sexual encounters with strangers. "I have other offers also. What we really hope," she murmured, leaning into his space and stroking his thigh. "Is that it's true what they say you're planning."

"What do they say I'm planning?"

"There's whispers on the wind, perhaps the forest and the mountains tell them and it starts with nothing but hopes and dreams, but some choose to believe. They say that you're gathering an army of our best guerrilla fighters, men who've lived in the mountains and forests in hiding for centuries and are only now ready to come down. They say that you'll bring together all the war bands of the hills to take the fight to the enemy before they come back at us. They say you won't stop till you've smashed the Norman state and cleansed England with the blood of the tyrants."

Robin blinked a few times but beyond this showed nothing of what he felt. He didn't stop her from caressing his thigh, yet neither did he actively encourage it.

"How far spread is this rumour do you think?" he asked.

"Quite far, I believe. They are telling it from Bangor to Cardiganshire and the sheep herders take the stories as far into England as Ynys Witrin."

"Ynys Witrin isn't in England," he muttered.

She smiled widely, running her hand up from his leg to his hard-on. Clearly she liked the taste of rebellion on a man. "Ah yes, the ancient land of the Brython, stolen from us by the Saxons before the Normans stole it from them.

324

Let us make that true again with our longbows! And every Cymric man shall drink again from enemy skulls!" His ability to focus on her vision of war was greatly diminished by her running her hand up to touch his cock. Gently he removed her hand and kissed it with gratitude for the sentiment. "Don't you like it?" she asked. She didn't sound offended so much as curious and gentle.

"Of course!" he half laughed at the strange question. "But the realities of war and sexual play do not sit well together for me. Do you believe there are many people who want this, who believe we can drive the Normans out?"

"Most of the north would rise for you if you asked."

Robin looked at her pained and confused. "But I'm just a tinker! People don't rise for tinkers, they push us down." He shrugged with an air of helplessness. "People have been *making sure* I understood that all my life. Why would so many people want to follow a ditch-born vagrant?"

"Because they say you're the son of the King of Y Tylweth Teg? And all stories with great heroes in them get started with a child of mythic birth."

Robin didn't mention that for him the first story that came to mind involving boys with faerie fathers was one that called for the sacrificial blood of such a boy, to quiet the fighting of the red and white dragon. *Apt.*

"Is that what heroes do? Start wars?" he asked wearily. A great longing to be back with his people came over him. They saw the saviour in Robin. Blaith, Lux and Sariah and his closest crew did, but they always seemed willing to share the burden of carrying that word. Blaith would look at Robin and shrug: 'what if *we* really are?' But Blaith was a mystic, and mystics always hear prophecies with a subtler ear. He never looked at him like Robin might personally and individually solve all the political and social problems of twelfth century Christendom...

"They already started this war when they set foot off their side of the river! And it will end either with their destruction or in our conquest! We need to round up and kill all the fighting age males and ship the women and children back to France where they belong! Otherwise they will destroy our way of life in time."

He sighed. "Maybe I'm too inclined to live in the moment. But it seems to me that if they started it, we finished it." Again, the sounds and smells of combat rose around him and his voice became quieter and grimmer. The face of the horse with its soft velvet nose sliced away and hanging rose before him again, the whites of its eyes in terrible display. It had become an image for him of the innocent victims of conflicts. No horse knew it was invading anywhere.

"It finished in a few gurgles of water in the lungs of some frightened boys who were drowned after trying to run away from us, shamed into fighting in the first place by their fathers and pleading for The Virgin to save them." After a while of her not speaking he glanced up and made eye contact with her. "Surely with our blood and theirs we've bought our children some time to grow up on the green hills? Surely the Normans will at least need a generation to overcome their humiliation before they come for us again? Especially to Gwynedd..."

"But you admit they will come back? What do you suggest we do then? Leave it to our children to deal with?"

He could sense her irritation that he insisted on bringing up the realities of war. Robin could feel her passion for her freedom though and he understood that well enough.

"I don't know! I don't have all the answers. And that is how it should be. Never trust a man too keen to lead others, or whose mind rests too comfortably upon simple and brutal solutions... My teacher taught me that and it's never set me wrong."

"What would you have us do then, discourage the people who believe in you? That's the last thing Cymry needs! How would you do it then, if not with war?"

Robin sighed. Part of him didn't want to answer her. The moment that he opened his mouth to give her any kind of vision or solution he was agreeing to be who they said he was. Whenever he made a conscious decision to let the myth of himself move through him there was always this moment of vertigo right beforehand. "Do you really want me to tell you?" he whispered, coming

326

closer to her ear. Now it was his hand that ran up her thigh, but the voice that he spoke with was no longer fully his own.

"Yes," she whispered tremulously, her thighs came apart with the yieldingness of butter.

He came even closer so his lips were brushing her ear. "Then tell the women that want to live free, only tell the women for now," he whispered, drawing her hand up the inside of her thigh with his hand covering it.

"Yes?" she gasped again, as he placed her fingers onto her cunny.

"-and such men as will enjoy thinking about me while they touch themselves." Her child awoke at the breast with the sudden motion and began to suckle again. She looked up at Puck for a moment with a weird knowing, as though the foremothers behind her eyes had suddenly flashed forth to say they too heard his message and the girl child would drink it in at her mother's breast, that she would pass the message down until one day there was an uprising led by women. "Tell them to give themselves pleasure in my name and affirm in their self-love their worthiness to be free of tyrants. Tell them…" His words strung out a little as they landed. "To proudly open themselves wide to me and invite me over their threshold. And when they are coming, they must cry my name out three times, to let me know which homes I can enter."

A visible quiver went through her whole body and the babe was nearly displaced from her breast. Milk erupted faster than the child could drink and trickled down her stomach. He reached out a fingertip and took a drop of the milk upon it before putting it on his tongue. "Then I will know which houses are mine and I will come to you each and teach you my remedies and my poisons. Do what I have said, feel for the presence of the other women and men moaning my name, and await further instructions."

"Yes, Robin," she all but whimpered. "I'll tell them."


"What did you learn of our yeoman friend Brynmor?" Robin asked as they rode back to the Twll Du camp.

Lux had a mild hangover and was shielding her eyes from the sun with one hand. There had been many educational parts to being on the road with Robin, many of them were things she'd learned about herself though and none of those yielded too well to words. "Probably not as much as he learned from me, I'm afraid. What he ultimately wants is far more than to defend the border against further Norman aggression, that's for sure. His intent is revolutionary, there is an essential humanity about him though. He worked out I was Norman and he said meeting me changed how he felt about purging Normans."

"That's something. His sister is probably the more militant of the two then. I was able to gentle her a little with flirtation. Brynmor is indeed the father of her child, and this secret is closely guarded from outsiders. She's offered to allow our people hunting access to some of their land and a safe campsite."

"And what does she want out of you in return?" Lux was keenly aware that the last time a Welshman had offered Robin something he'd had to fight in a war to earn it.

"She wants us to hold carnival on their land and under the guise of the fun to talk to the people about insurrection."

"Do you mean local insurrection? As in throwing out the Norman presence on this side of the border?"

Robin sighed. "I think her ambitions are far bigger and bloodier than that."

Once Lux might have thought the light of insurrection was what Robin's soul was powered by, but he seemed older since the war and the attack. It seemed like he'd seen his fill of carnage and cruelty. She sensed he was ensconced in some kind of dark introspection about what rebellion meant to him, and how to take it forward. Just as she had not been able to follow him into the war, she couldn't quite get to his thoughts on it either.

"Do you want to do it?"

"I will wait and talk it over with my family, I think. We've already got enough tensions brewing at the moment without me making any lone wolf decisions."

"Do you like her? Creirwy?"

"Yes and no. Her leaking breasts made my ancestors hunger within me to ejaculate in your womb. Nothing in me would want the result to be a child, but one must own up to such feelings or they will take control of one's reason in time and lead us to rash decisions."

Lux was surprised by this frank admission. As a child of a woman who'd died in childbirth Robin had usually seemed about as anti-reproduction as a man could be.

"I admire her fire and courage," he continued. "I doubt she's personally seen women and children massacred, though. If she had seen the fear in the eyes of a five-year-old child fleeing from an armed man on horseback, she might feel differently. The problem for me is I know all too well it doesn't matter what race they are, angry men will do things like that when they're given the chance, Welsh men included. Or at least some among their number will. And when it comes to seeing a child die by violence, some is enough."

# 2

The last lingering wardens cleared the space around the watch fire for Robin and Blaith at a head gesture. When they were alone, he got up and they embraced. For a moment as they pressed their chests flat to each other the problems they faced were gone. They stood again for a moment on a spectral wood-speckled tundra full of game, almost empty of men, in the golden age of wild living. Afterwards, as they let go and both took a seat on a tree stump they came back to the present in the embattled world they weathered together.

"What did you learn out there?" Robin asked. It was a common question for them to get started with as they reintegrated into the world inside the camp. It was Blaith's perception that the world was made of circles inside circles. They spoke of the Settlers as living inside the walls, or inside the hedge, and themselves outside the hedge. But there was another kind of inside within that outside, and sometimes when you were even outside *that* as well it was highly likely you would learn an important story to bring back to camp, sometimes stories were as important as meat. Blaith prepared to share what he'd collected, heavy as it was to carry and off-load.

"I have it upon the word of one I trust that Nottingham has been sacked. It was at the order of a lord loyal to Matilda. They weren't able to take the castle, but hundreds of townsfolk were massacred. The bodies were found even inside St. Peters where they sought sanctuary. Both sexes. All ages."

Robin winced. Despite conveying the details bluntly, the facts alone were horrific enough to Blaith's ears, and compounded again in having to tell his brother who he knew would feel it even deeper still.

"The fighting has become so vicious they kill innocents even inside a church?" Robin looked so deeply disappointed, as if he were continually learning the depths of the depravity of man. Blaith nodded confirmation. They had seen a lot of killing in their young lives, he had to admit though this was a new increment in violence, a certain level of en masse savagery towards civilians perhaps not seen since The Harrying of the North in their grandparent's time. It did not bode well for moving about the country of the Brython as they understood the paths still. Most advice was not to travel at all unless absolutely necessary.

Information had changed its form now. It moved around in the shape of he-said, she-said whispers. The lurid fragments you received took on a looming, ominous character of something that was in part history unfolding, in part mythic horror fragment. It made what was far away seem more frightening than where one was, causing a kind of regional conservatism that only a traveller might notice taking form. Blaith acknowledged that this prejudice was common to everywhere, regardless of whether that place was a major frontier for violence or quite peaceful.

"Any news of whether Gil is caught up in the fighting?" Robin asked.

His brother wasn't alone in having allowed the Norman lord into his heart a little. There had been some flirtation between Gil and himself, only faintly hampered by Gil's inability to speak Welsh. "No. Only that the Scots were put down after making it as far south as Yorkshire at the price of a terrible slaughter. My man described rows and endless rows of mass burial 'Scot pits', full of the reek and ruin of man and horse alike. In some towns now law and order is entirely broken asunder."

"Did you hear any tell of Nanette?"

"We can guess she lives, or at least *lived* for time enough to cross into England. My drover friend gets all the most salacious gossip when he drives sheep across counties to be sold and gossips with many. He believes something like a Norman noblewoman dying at the hands of Welsh rebels would be on every tongue if it happened."

He wanted to believe his own words as he said them, yet well Blaith knew the truth was as quick to mutate in this new climate as a falsehood. Within only six months from a happening, it was possible to hear tales about his own brother that had greatly changed shape, some that were utterly false and appeared to be deliberate smears, or even with his deeds ascribed to another person. Sometimes it was the other way around, where one of Meredith's most crazy japes from the past had ended up as part of the growing folklore around Robin.

Blaith had begun to understand history in this manner: a grand narrative interrupted regularly by outbreaks of violence and war where people were too busy fleeing or dying to keep the chain of the story intact. Facts and people fell into the abyss opened by that violence, rending the social thread, and with it some truths that would never to be retrieved.

"I have felt nothing of her magically since you drew her blood above the breath. She is either magically de-natured, or dead. Nanette is that sort of person, if she was alive and able, she'd still be fighting us. I just hope Gil is as good as his word when it comes to protecting Augusta. I still think she left too soon, before we could really be sure she was free of the curse and before things could be properly smoothed over between her and Lux."

Blaith nodded. Well he knew it. He resented Bran and Gladys and their adult son Ethan and all the other whisperers who had made the pressure build up for Gil to take Augusta away. Once they had known about Augusta participating in Clarice's murder and keeping it to herself there had been no re-establishing trust. If they knew what Blaith also suspected about her, he doubted they would ever have her at camp again.

He could recognise the stains that the darkness leaves inside a person after certain acts. Blaith was sure it was Augusta who had killed her brother. There were few crimes his people would not forgive someone for, but the murder of a sibling, quite outside the parameters of self-defense… That one would be a hard sell. Yet Blaith had put a lot of work into trying to salvage her, and given extreme youth it was morally complex. By their standards she'd not even been a woman yet at the time.

"If Nanette has not yet died in her convent she will soon. The death mole I send after the guts of a one I want dead does not go away until he's buried his snout to the ears."

"I doubt it not."

"Gil's word has proven reliable so far. I don't think we can get across to the De Biron stronghold to reunite like we planned yet though. Things are too hot to try for Rochdale right now. What did you learn from the homesteaders?"

Robin grinned and his eyebrow twitched faintly. "I learned they are fucking each other, for starters; the brother and the sister who run the place."

"Is that so? How old school. I like them more already."

Robin smiled. Blaith spent a lot of his time in a preverbal intensity of the senses in which only people he shared a subtle understanding with could enter his experience. Between Robin and himself much could be conveyed whilst little was said.

"I learned also that we should stay right here in Gwynedd. Because it has always been the stronghold of the north, and likely the last thing they'll take from us."

"Gods... Tell me it is not so that you see it so bleakly? Do you think even Gwynedd is in danger?" Blaith felt sick to hear Robin speak of 'the last thing they'll take from us'. Gwynedd was their original home, Robin was born here and their mother's bones were in the rocks. Gwynedd had been the stubborn last part of Wales to fall to the Romans, ever harder to hold than it had been to conquer, ever the hardest place to pacify... If Gwynedd was lost, all hope was lost.

"Everything is in danger," Robin said simply with a bleak little shrug. "Looked at purely militaristically it's likely to fall eventually. The Normans will move to consolidate their gains along the border when they stop fighting each other. They already have us hemmed in tightly. We've got dangerous Marcher territory up far too close where every lord is his own god king now answerable to no one in how he dispenses his justice. There is plenty of game

333

here in the meantime, also many other rebel bands of some clout, outlaws and fighting men hunkering in the woods nearly as ready to be at each other's throats as at the Norman's…"

Blaith nodded. So much of their endurance had come from circulating through enemy territory, where they were usually the only skilled guerrilla warriors. They were at once free to make money through plying their trade as they were to cut purses. When you found yourself upon the land of wealthy benefactors a few luxuries began to disappear from their way of living as their reliance upon theft decreased. Blaith sensed that this lack of luxuries, lack of alcohol, lack of milk of the poppy, lack of hashish, lack of flour and honey were as much part of the group's tensions as the now defunct presence of Gil and Augusta. "It feels like we're being slowly surrounded closer and closer until someone's going to push us into a corral we can't escape from and try to throw a saddle on us," Blaith muttered.

There was a long pause during which Blaith intuited this was exactly what Robin feared too. "As ever we are of one mind, brother. Creirwy and Brynmor are feisty Welsh rebels with a decent parcel of land and loyalties at their disposal. They have offered for our caravans to summer there."

"But you feel what they'd really like is for us to stay on forever as a kind of standing rebel army, but this situation might actually be the corral we are being herded to?"

"Aye. And I don't herd well."

"May a thousand ferrets run up the dick hole of every feuding Norman who places us in this position!" Blaith cussed with feeling. He did so because he saw exactly the fate playing out before them and how little they could do about it ultimately. If even Robin thought the eventual conquest of the stronghold of Gwynedd was nigh on inevitable with time, so then was the end of their way of life.

"Dick ferrets aside, we are honour-bound to tell our people of this offer, and I fear it will come at the moment of their greatest weakness. I fear that…" Robin's voice trailed away before he named it. Blaith felt it for a moment as if it were a physical reality, the two of them standing together on the edge of one of those violence-abysses of history which form history's quiet spots. All he had to be glad about was that it was this man's hand holding his while they teetered in the breathless black and not some other.

"-That Bran, Gladys and their click will ride their lingering malcontent over Augusta and Gil all the way into settling?"

Robin nodded. "The worst part is, as their First Warden, I couldn't advise them honestly that they would be safer to follow us to anywhere outside of Gwynedd at this time."

"A pox upon dying a tame death corralled like that!" Blaith spat on the ground. "First it will be we wander only in Gwynedd now, and then it will be one *cantref* only, and finally we'll have a nice little cottage with a gods cursed kitchen garden!"

"It's those kitchen gardens that always do it." Robin grinned in an attempt to suppress his humour at Blaith's strong response to kitchen gardens.

"My soul would skin itself to get away, Robin!"

"As you know would mine. Besides I'm out of choices. I made a solemn promise to Meredith right before he left that I would die wild on the road."

"I made an equally dire oath to Aunt Eliza's ghost we would avenge her death and seek the identity of her killers remorselessly. To know the name of the other man and that he bides in Nottingham and breathes yet while we converse…"

"I know it!" Robin replied. That his brother fully shared the torment Blaith felt in holding back their vengeance could never be doubted. "What are we even if we were to settle? When the caravans have moved for hundreds of years? Since the days of the Old North and the open highways with the South West Brythonaid when you could still count Ynys Witrin as part of our country… A wheel has been replaced here and there until perhaps all were replaced, a piece of flooring here, a beam there, but we've lived like this for so long the time before it has moved into legend. Our great-great-great-great grandparents slept as we sleep…

335

"What are we if we know the name of the man who did what he did and we do nothing to stop this monster breathing? Surely not proud sons of the Twll Du blood-thread, we may as well stop and build one of those kitchen gardens you like so much if we leave his head on his shoulders! For there is neither justice nor deterrent in the land for the murder of our kind except for the swift blades of our sons and daughters."

Blaith nodded emphatically. Never had he heard such a cogent explanation for the role revenge played in their lives and in his thinking. It was a direct shadow of his love for his people who he had to value twice as hard because the world didn't give a damn. Were they to lose not only the freedom of the road but the old school warrior values they were reared on? You took at least a head for something like what De Bracy took from their family! If possible, you took absolutely *everything*, starting at the balls.

This was the only way people learned they could not perpetrate evil without fear of extreme retribution. What else stood between their tiny part of the world and innocent civilians murdered while they clung to the pews and altar in the church they were told would protect them? There were no laws for the prosecution of those soldiers who worked for the two teams of top bullies; Blaith had learned that long ago. The only law left in place when all else was rigged against them was the law of his dagger end in their eyeball. Revenge was a savage justice, yet it was also the same power that had lent Gwenllian's brothers the determination to see through their supposedly impossible victory on the field of Crug Mawr.

Eilish knew she had to be there. It was essentially a council of war, this meeting. After Henwen, grandmother to Meredith, Rory, and Zorien and head elder of the Gyre caravan had quietly passed away in her sleep almost as soon as she was back on the land of Cymry, Eilish was needed more than ever. To avoid their culture becoming one of either youth or age, and preferably sharing in the vigour of both, whilst softening the impact of the flaws of both also, there was a careful balance to the dance of decisions. These people had all

336

paid in deeply to this enterprise they called freedom, and therefore had won the right to speak.

Only the most senior wardens, the elders of each caravan, office holders and former officeholders were present, which covered all sexes, ages, and those with the most knowledge about keeping everyone alive. As a healer and maiden Eilish's presence was crucial yet being pregnant made it harder. Even the work she had to do to save Robin had been harder than treating his previous war wounds, or any other wounds she'd worked on. It wasn't because she was physically debilitated, her pregnancy progressed normally for a first child. It was because she felt more tenderhearted towards the pain she'd had to inflict to save his life.

Many times before, Eilish had run with her healing kit into dangerous situations, focused only on saving someone, never on her own safety. Hers was a warrior art in its own way and in the past fear had only ever come afterwards upon reflection. Now her body wasn't her own anymore, there was another helpless life, one that represented the future and depended on her to protect it. When she saw the fierce pride that glimmered behind Robin and Blaith's eyes she felt a different response to it than normal. Something told her that young, male, and uncompromising responses were at a distance from her right now.

"It cannot be denied," Robin was saying, in a way that indicated the observation was against his own heart. "Creirwy's offer represents a very good chance for ongoing survival, avoiding both the conflict and resource stress."

"Starving," Gladys added. "I think what you mean by resource stress is starving."

"Sure," Robin shrugged. "Starving is a possibility, being killed by the roadside, or in our tents, or rounded up, arrested, shot, these are all possibilities of being on the road, as they always have been."

"They are possibilities in any life," Blaith added. "They were possibilities for three hundred innocent bystanders in Nottingham."

"More so than ever with Scotland fighting England and England fighting itself," Bran said. "They haven't the time to bother with this part of the world.

337

I think the most important part is to keep the caravans moving, even if it is within a smaller space than usual. In that way we can endure until better times come and we will return to the old Brythonaic path."

"What if better times aren't coming?" Robin asked. "Everything Creirwy and Brynmor informed me of suggests Gwynedd will fall to the Normans again, as it has before, almost inevitably, unless we push back now while they are on the back foot, rather than waiting to be exterminated in a smaller and smaller yard."

"Are you thinking seriously about their offer of safe haven, Robin?" Sariah asked, modelling the maiden's talent for the non-confrontational question.

Robin sighed and frowned as he thought about it. Eilish could see in him again her young cousin, not the one who had gone to war and not come back the same, but the one that was before. "I don't know, Sariah. To be honest with you it's quite a big decision. Blaith's informants speak of atrocities done between the two sides and England descending into violent savagery leaving average people afraid. But when have the Normans presented any other face to our kind but violent savagery?

"Aunt Eliza was killed during their idea of peacetime. Even in their peacetime we are mutilated in the hand or eye if caught hunting, we are killed without trial by the roadside, our children mowed down by men on horses for sport and worse. People report panic now because it happens to *them* as well as us. That is what I feel about it, that our lot is unchanged. As to whether to join a rebel army… There is still pink in my last scars, so I'm not in a hurry."

"Understandably," Sariah nodded. Her compassion was tangible. One of Eilish's hands rested protectively on her belly. There were the feelings the ancestor-women were making in her via the child, she told herself, and then there was her spirit, the lucid consciousness she had always been beforehand. *It's just like who Robin was before the war, the woman I was before I was pregnant still lives in me though she may not come out the same. I cannot let her down, she'll be back in a month or two, changed yet the same, and she will hold me to account if I'm a coward during this time. Many pregnant women have defied oppressors, ridden or run for freedom, even fought. I will not be the lesser of my foremothers.*

Eilish knew exactly what pre-pregnancy Eilish would have done in this situation. Her Magister was going somewhere, Robin was going the same place, Sariah's heart and therefore her feet upon the trail were with them. Lux and Jack would be with them, two friendships that increasingly meant something quite solid to Eilish. As would the most loyal wardens… Where they were going would have fighting in it, and these most dear people in her life would need their best doctor.

Tears came to her eyes from a deep swell of emotion. It was her skills after all that had saved Robin after Nanette had ravaged his flesh so horrifically. People said no one else could have done it. If that was true it was what she learned at Aunt Eliza's side before the murder, when she was still a girl that had carried the day. Thus their aunty lived on via Hob's protected life.

"May I make a suggestion?" Eilish said, gathering her most maidenly bearing. People looked at her differently now, somewhat softer now she was pregnant. What the people needed to hear from her now was a pulling in of tradition, an encouragement of continuity, and her belly gave her extra bearing with the malcontents who were focused on blood family, even more so because she was carrying the Magister's child. "What if we take them up on their offer until after my child is born? Then he may take his first breath upon Twll Du as is the custom, if I can make the climb as the mothers of old have always done? Then the Magister can seek omens at the Castle of the Winds as his father did before him. If we will not place ourselves in the hands of the voices that emerge from the gusty deep, what then is our life?"

As First Maiden of the Thread, Sariah had been passed the care of three earthenware jars. The clay they were made of looked very old. They smelled like the caves at Creswell. There was one spirit house for each of the primary female bloodlines that had forged and held the Fire of the Twll Du lineage. It was her duty and her pride to feed the foremothers drops of her own menstrual blood. The blood was mixed with that of the other Maidens after being bled onto a stone and when it dried it was mixed with certain herbal ingredients.

As she sent the ghost food down into the dark mouths of the past, she started to hear The Mothers singing, whispering, humming, laughing, weeping. Often she would put her ear to the hollow to listen better and they would predict the comings of love, war or famine. The dead were very tiny now in the place they lived within the insides of reality. You had to learn to contort your thinking to be able to see them properly or hear their voices as fragile as cobwebs or booming like thunder.

The vessels were needed soon as she was preparing a new maiden, and the mothers would want input into Lux's training. The girl's pupils were dilated in the faint light of Sariah's tent. Certainly, she could feel the potency the spirit houses carried because when Sariah offered her one to hold the hairs stood up visibly on the backs of her arms as she took it gingerly into her hands.

"Even we don't know how old they are," Sariah told her. "Some say they were old even when we found them in the caves and that the spirits were already in them. They're too old even for the genealogies, these mothers. As maidens we are the ones who feed them and keep the clan's soul-force strong. We carry the memory. The stories tell of the first people, that we call the Old People being made from Raven spitting his saliva and spraying the blood of the animals together on some shell-grit, chalk and pitch-black soil of this land and raising from it the first of the Old People, long before the coming of the Children of Ama."

"Which pot is for the Children of Ama?" Lux asked, gazing down into the mouth of the Ama pot. Her curiosity was naturally engaged with that vessel because she travelled in the Ama caravan and was closest to that river of the blood thread.

"This one," Sariah said, pointing to the one that she had instinctually thought to hand Lux. "The People of Ama walked into this land following the rivers as the first mother rode upon a lioness."

"And is that how yours and Robin's ancestors arrived here?"

"Some of them, yes. Though we are each born of all the caravans when you look at the genealogies. The Arva caravan says they have been here since the land was formed. Eldri, the elder of Arva, carries the distaff blood thread of the Old People."

"No one carries it after her?" Lux enquired tentatively.

Sariah just shook her head. The sadness was too much to speak of.

"Which do I belong to? Am I of Ama because Robin is? Is it that simple?"

"The intelligence of the flesh is anything but simple, cariad," she said, gently taking the vessel from Lux and placing it back down with the others. "When you start to trust the foremothers who live inside you, you'll see that this matter was decided long before you met Robin or I ever put the vessels before you. Sometimes we just need to take the long way round to arrive somewhere we were already."

"Do you think that because Ama's people walked into Britain that maybe they followed rivers from France? Could she truly be my blood foremother also?"

Sariah could hear the nostalgic note of hope in her voice. Although it was hard to imagine into being her, Sariah sympathised with the poor creature, orphaned of Place as she was. Yet at the same time this *hiraeth* for something never known that the girl felt was based on illusion. For Lux was home, in a way that meant just as much as being born to a Twll Du mother. Sariah knew this more clearly than many others, as her own mother had not been of the blood. This was something most would never have guessed about her.

Unlike Blaith and Robin she had no mother who came from a mother who came from a mother going back to the ancient three who were alive before time was measured. Instead, Sariah had a father who came from a mother who came from a mother, and she had always been rich enough in that, blessed to have had that good man to raise her up all the way to womanhood and office-holding. Before she had lost him she'd had the chance to see the pride in his eyes when he looked at her in her full power. These memories had kept her warm ever after.

Sariah patted Lux's leg. "Never mind that. It doesn't matter one way or the other. Your adoption is not a mere idea and your blood as a solid reality. Hob's blood in you is a solid reality too, as is Blaith's breath in you from initiation. What do you think babies are made out of but the pattern of the blood that is passed through fucking? This is why our maidens in privacy call ourselves Magdalenes. Mothers make new blood kin for us with their womb and their cunny but so do maidens, only we and Blaith and some of the strongest of wardens know the rites that make new kin out of fully formed adults…"

"So I already have the blood? Robin wasn't joking about him being my sovereignty bride?" The girl grinned.

Sariah shook her head. It wasn't clear to her what was funny about this yet she accepted that it was seen this way. Sometimes she had to ask Robin to explain some of the Settler mentality to her so she could better teach the newer members of the family. "Not at all. Hob is as expert as I am at using his Grandmother-given charms to bring new people over to us."

"Are there men here you brought over?"

"Aye and women too."

"Whom did you bring in? And why didn't Bran and his cohort have a problem with them like he did with me, Augusta and Gil?"

"They were all Cymric folk from this side of the river, see. I only speak Welsh and basic English, so until recently only Hob has had the skill to break the Norman language barrier. Now that we have you who can… well… imagine what we can achieve."

Lux frowned. "Are you… are you suggesting we should try to rescue more Normans? Wouldn't that provoke Bran and his crew all the more?"

Sariah grinned mysteriously. "Never mind Bran. I'll handle him. Gladys will be the harder one, as she is a maiden of the past Magister. But a true maiden is always working to diffuse and redirect conflict inside the group."

"Are there plans I can know about yet?"

"Oh, you'll find out about them soon enough! Just trust me that he will be sweetened towards you shortly, and from there I am hopeful for a new direction. Why not use your language skills? Even Hob said that if we don't fight back all will fall in time. The maiden's way of fighting back is a bit different." Sariah leaned forward and touched Lux's thigh. The gesture was platonic enough at first but while she spoke she moved it a little higher up her leg. "Hob's told me that you used to fantasise about starting an uprising among the Norman women and creating a language of women, maybe we need people like you who can talk to those among the Oppressors who might side with us?"

"Could I... could I still... bring someone over without having to risk pregnancy?"

"Blaith can teach you so much about that. He works with no cunny at all and yet can still perform a maiden's magic."

Lux smiled crookedly, there was shyness and roguishness vying for dominance in her at times now, almost as though both a boy and a girl lived within her and one seemed far more experienced than the other. It was as though some slutty water asrai struggled within her with a shining court boy. "You really don't mind sharing him, do you? You would tell me if you did?"

"Of course! Why would I mind?" Sariah asked with puzzlement. It was more than sharing. It was a whole other kind of thrill again to experience Blaith via and through others. She felt as though she didn't just know what it was to fuck him as herself, but as Eilish, as Meredith, and maybe now Lux as well. "His soul is vast as the night sky is vast. There is enough of him."

To her pleasant surprise Lux put her hand on her knee reciprocally. "I think I've only just truly perceived your innocence for the first time. I always saw that you were strong and confident. It's only now that I see that you're also... also just very sweet and lovely and lacking all the awful bitterness and competitiveness Norman women display towards each other."

Sariah clasped one hand to her chest and the other onto Lux's upper thigh. "Oh, thank you, cariad, you're so sweet also! I'm not sure I fully understand about the innocence part, but if you'd like to learn the finer points of fucking a woman I'd love to be the one to show you."

Lux didn't look away. "I would like that."

343

It was attractive to Sariah, this new confidence Lux was carrying after she'd been on the road with Robin. It was true in regards to her innocence, Sariah had to own. She didn't know much of anything first hand about how Settlers lived. The boys had always gone to great effort to shield her from the kinds of responses a woman like her would get within that world. Sariah knew this was the case, but the full details of what it was they were protecting her from was only hazily known in flashes of horror put together from traumatic things which happened to their women when they interacted with Settlers. What drove that barbarity was knowledge she still sought and hoped Lux could help her understand and learn to heal in others.

Slowly she moved her hand up over Lux's outer hip, along her waist until she found her breast and made her gasp by giving her nipple a little pinch. "Robin and Blaith are like the boy parts of me, much like you have your boy side. If you've been with one of them, I've already had you. Their desire for you spills into me, as naturally as tidal motion passes creates a holy stone."

"Did you ever think about being with a girl when you were younger?"

Sariah's question unsteadied Lux even though this very act was what she'd come here to do. The exposing of this truth hit a nerve tenderised by punishment. The quantity of mead she'd had to drink made the barrier between thinking and talking very thin.

"Before I'd even bled I had this dream once- it was only once, among many dreams about young men and attraction to boys- yet it was so vivid almost luminous… I dreamed I met this girl down near the river. She seemed about my age yet she had a strangeness to her. Looking back, I'd say her strangeness derived from the fact she was not in fact my age but only appeared so. I was filled with the most intoxicating desire to kiss her."

"Did you kiss her?" Sariah asked.

"I can never remember whether I did or whether I actually fantasied it in the dream, like a dream within a dream. I feel perhaps we were kissing as I woke up. For the first time I woke feeling wet between my legs. As I'd never heard about anything of the sort I asked my sister Amelia about it. Rather than behaving as a good confidante she told my father, perhaps to score some kind of points with him. Or so she might have thought. The truth was he despised a snitch…"

"What did he do?" she asked, urging her past her hesitation.

"He punished me. It was after that he had the physician supply me with a sleep remedy, to prevent me having any more perverted dreams…"

"Kissing is perverted among Normans?"

Again, her face appeared to Lux in this moment as a being of perfect and unspoiled innocence. "Kissing of the fondling, passionate sort between two girls is considered perverted by most church-goers, Sariah. My father was not to be taken as an example of a good Christian by any stretch of the imagination. When I look back on it I think he feared that if I was dreaming about another girl I might have within me the capacity to take the man's part. That's what they were all so afraid of, a woman making her own first moves for pleasure."

"And do you have that capacity in you? To take the man's part, as they call it?"

"Maybe… I can with Robin. I don't have much idea what I'm doing with another woman yet though."

Sariah smiled, her big cat smile where both her teeth and eyes seemed to gleam in the candlelight. "Never mind. I have *every* idea what I'm doing. Every cunny and tits are different from each other, and I have known them all!"

With that she pulled down the loose bodice on Lux's outworn nightgown. It was the half-cut-away one she'd been wearing on the night of her liberation, and after the trials it saw it was easy for Sariah to reveal her breasts. She did so in one bold sort of tug that seemed to imply she was leaning in to the idea of taking the man's part. Lux gasped when Sariah gave her what she could only describe as a semi-rough feel up. Sariah hadn't been wrong when she said she had every idea what she was doing, because she handled Lux as if she already knew all the things that most made her wet. With playful firmness she pushed

345

Lux down on her back on the furs.

"Close your eyes and spread your legs."

She did as she was told. Within moments she felt Sariah's tongue and Lux sucked her breath in hard. How had she known that Lux would want her to go straight in like this? Or that this very act was what she'd thought about Sariah's first reference to introducing her to girl tongue? The deep taboo of doing this with a woman turned her on so much it almost didn't seem real that it was happening. Was there something in the body knowledge of someone who also owned a cunny that gave her this arcane skill?

Sariah could make you wait, tenderise you, and then tantalise you again, keeping you right where she wanted you until she bestowed Our Lady's own orgasm upon you. It was at the rising point during this dance that Lux had a visceral, non-mental knowing come upon her that this was an art, and Sariah a great artist. Just as they said Robin was the best shot in the land, that no evil eye surpassed that of Blaith, and that no other doctor could have saved some of the people Eilish had, Sariah was gifted in the art of human unraveling.

And it was only now as she surrendered to a shattering orgasm that she knew it wasn't a joke when they said such things of Sariah, it was a fearsome power too strong for the fake men Lux'd grown up with. Lux also knew she had met in Sariah the first woman she'd ever wanted to be like, and that she only ever wanted the kind of men who weren't afraid to share the road with a woman like that.

# 3

obin scrambled up onto the outcrop in the gushing bright moon spill. He was deep into the area known as outlaw country, but the hairs on the back of his neck told him they didn't yet know he was there. He jumped up onto the highest stone and threw back his head and opened up his throat to the moon. The sound came out with all the stark aloneness of the wolf's voice, that haunting sob of lost souls taken by the wind for so long their voices no longer remember human... But still with the signature touch of human melancholy at the dying tone.

He waited for the echoes to fade away as his voice bounced off the surrounding valleys and the emptiness toyed with it. Then he jumped down and slipped back into the shadows to wait. Robin found himself a vantage point where his back was covered, he had more than one exit available to him and yet was in the shadow. After settling into that spot, he closed his eyes and put his hands palm-flat on the ground beside him. As he knew the others weren't close by closing his eyes would allow him to hear them sooner.

Small changes in the air began to sting his nose with intense sensation and the flavour of the loam in the night wood made his mouth water, there was a certain change in taste when the loam was disturbed nearby or recently before his arrival. With his hands it was harder to explain how he used them to see the men coming. It was more like using the Seeing to tap into the woodland's existing network of sentience. As soon as a human foot crunched down above the below soil fungal threads of alertness would go through the web and it would seem like a thousand eyes just came open in the dark beneath.

In this listening, feeling, smelling state Robin was entirely still for a long time. He heard-felt their feral motions as they moved through the undergrowth coming to meet him. It didn't escape Robin that the intelligence of the forest barely recognised these men as human and closed their network of eyes again. Suddenly the silence was broken by an answering howl. Instinctually Robin knew it came from their lead male, yet it wasn't a challenge. It sounded wary, but with cautious welcome. His inner wolf sniffed the air again. He wasn't sure about the idea of packs with no females, his belly wolf suspected- as Robin did about such unnatural environments in human communities too- that it would likely bring out the worst in the species.

Yet if he was going to try moving his family's caravan through these mountain passes at some point, and hunt nearby, he needed to know where he stood with these men who moved like ghosts. There was a fairly good chance Blaith would have had an apoplexy if he knew Robin's precise method for finding out if they were friendly or not. It was alright though, he just needed to make sure Blaith never found out.

He knew the history of these outlaws as well as he did the history of the tinker folk. They had begun with the old war bands where the young men were sent into the hills for initiation into the warrior-hunter craft. Just like for their own wardens the totem of the war bands had been the wolf. The Princes had been trying to rein the practice until their recent realisation that these dangerous men from the hills were good for the country when they came down to kill Normans.

This had of course been their original purpose, to kill Normans in their original form. They were the reason Wales wasn't overrun by Vikings, the Northmen now called Normans. All the young men of the country were armed and ready to fight at any time in case of invasion by Vikings at sea, or Mercian Saxons on land. They didn't marry for years so there was no squabbling between brothers jostling for the father's land. They dedicated themselves only to two gods, the mountains and the goddess of death. In the past they went up the mountain a boy and came down a man. These days, their ranks were packed with miscreants and most of the gentler families didn't want their sons associated anymore.

If Robin answered the cry this time, he'd give away his exact location to men like these who lived on the land by their wits. He knew just from how little noise they made creeping up that they were dangerous. *If there's a man alive today in Britain who can track and kill me it would be a forest man such as these.* It wasn't boasting or pride for Robin acknowledging he was hard to kill, so much as a statement of experience. Robin had killed so many of the men who were sent to kill him now, assassins, bounty hunters, lords, and sheriff's men included, that he now judged some of their efforts insulting. Some of his hunters had passed so close to him and never known how close their quarry, or how lucky they were to still possess throats.

But these men... the Cymric men outside the law with their hardy little bands of guerrilla fighters, each in contact with the next group over, knowing not nor caring for the borders of country or county... They were living wild with no children or elderly to slow them down, nobody they would shield with their own body if push came to shove, no one they would throw down for ... Robin swallowed uncomfortably. Realistically he had many more weaknesses than they did. If he was to protect his family these men must become, in the language Creirwy had used, *his*.

Making a decision in that moment, thinking of his people's vulnerability, Robin threw his head back and howled again, this one was full-lunged and savage, full of the raw proclamation of physical power. Getting up from his hiding spot he shimmied back up onto the rock and silhouetted himself against the sky in the moonlight. He was the perfect arrow target, and yet he made a full circle, slow, turn with his hands out at his sides and his own bow still slung across his body. He embodied calm self-assurance. It was just like confronting a vicious guard dog when you needed to break into somewhere. *Only if I show fear will they attack. But they'll smell it if you're bluffing, so you just have to feel no fear.*

The leader answered his call again and there was excitement in the sound, it set off a volley of answering cries. Even though Robin's hood was half down over his face he still had enough peripheral vision to make out their wraith-like forms as they slipped into the moonlight like the ghosts of our Stone Age selves. But Robin didn't shiver because he was as blanched cold white in the brain by the icy rivers of the moon as they were. Standing in the wolf-mind was like standing under a freezing waterfall of sharp lunar light. The crystal-line clarity of the gaze was terrible. You could cut flesh with it like the gouge from a shard of broken glass.

They didn't bother with human words but came up around him cau-tiously as animals would. Robin paid close attention to their dynamic and to what extent they moved with one mind, and to what extent they deferred to the leader. But most importantly it was to that man in particular that Robin paid attention. Because if he was going to have to fight someone tonight it was likely to be this man, the one who was their best. Being leader in all-male bands like this was different to in a mixed sex pack. You only needed to master one skill, and that was fighting. Generally speaking, they ended up really good at it.

Like his own the other man's body was both strong and agile, the kind of body few Settlers had. He came right up close to Robin. So close that in civilised circles the gesture could only be read as a sexual come-on or threat. Robin knew not to give any ground. He could smell literal wolf on these men and in the moonlight see that their clothes were made from the skins.

"Were you initiated among the war-bands?" the man half-growled at him under his breath as though remembering to speak human was an effort.

"The spirit of the wolf was fed me in blood and my manhood was burned and cut in among the bands."

"As was mine," he grunted, taking a half step back. You could feel the spike of pungent expectation in the air. It smelled of testosterone and violence. "So all that remains is to know one thing."

"And what is that?" Robin asked.

"If you're as good as they say you are."

It was clear to Robin moments before the other man's attack that this question wasn't going to be solved via verbal inquiry. But only *just* before. His opponent was very good like that, he didn't telegraph his intention to strike you until the very last moment when some subtle energy flashed in his eyes. It was enough time for Robin to half block and redirect the blow yet the impact half connected nonetheless. From that Robin could tell that the full strength of the other man's punch was something to avoid.

Cries of excitement and blood lust went up from the other men. Enveloping what Robin had managed to grab of the sweaty wrist or forearm of the other man he pushed it across his opponent's body and went for the man's legs while holding him unstable. Robin's body had not been given to understand a kind of fight that wasn't a fight for one's life. Nonetheless he didn't try to break the man's kneecap with his boot, which would be a death sentence out there.

He managed to get a hand free before Robin could fully put him down on the uneven rock surface and punched him in the mouth. It was a strong punch and blood gushed from Robin's nose and mouth down over his chest. If it wasn't for his time in the ring the intensity of the feeling might have slowed him down more. The pack howled and cheered. At least they did for a few moments. Robin licked the blood off his chin and bottom lip, during which time his opponent might have tried for finishing blows but did not.

"Lucky," Robin murmured, smiling and showing the man his bloodied fangs in the cold, sharp moonlight. "If you got me above the breath, I would have had to kill you."

Robin hit him in the face so quickly then there was no opportunity to dodge. Immediately he hit the man again, beating him with his fist till he hit the ground hard. Although the air went out of his opponent audibly a lifetime of fighting for survival allowed him to roll to one side, his face spewing blood like Robin's, and half on his feet before Robin kicked him back to the ground again.

He knelt down on the other man's throat, not hard, a fully intended pressure to the windpipe that was just enough to tell the opponent's body it was out of control of a vital function. The man tapped out, signaling his submission, and Robin immediately released the pressure. "It's mighty fine to meet you, Robin Dhu," he choked out while he panted. "Whom the Welsh call Black but the English call Good... You're everything they say you are as a fighter."

Robin snorted. Since De Rue his boredom with flattery had become difficult to conceal. He was getting this a lot lately, people knowing him before he introduced himself. It was dangerous this type of notoriety and he felt it accordingly as a cold prickle of impending doom. Getting up off the other man Robin handed the outlaw back up to his feet.

"More vicious than I expected. I'm Hereward."

"A fine rebel's name, friend. Seeing as Lady Luna is full above, we're both blooded already and the night is young, how about we steal a lamb from somewhere and call it a party?"

There was a chorus of answering howls.

The priory was a beautiful, peaceful place full of bird song and gentle wind in the fruit trees. It seemed particularly wrong that her mother should be on her deathbed in such a place. Augusta felt bad for sneaking away from Rochdale under Uncle Gil's nose. Although he was now the legal owner of most of what should have been hers, he was a benevolent and gracious owner, treating her like she had a right to come to decisions with him about the running of 'their' estates. Nonetheless, the time she'd spent riding with the Twll Du tinkers had left its mark of independence on her.

The seriousness of Nanette's situation was underlined when the Abbess met her along with a monk skilled in physic. "My Lady," The Abbess dropped her curtsey and the monk bowed to her. She had to admit she had missed that when she was on the road. Every day this battle raged inside her, between the part that was bitterly disappointed to have to leave the tinker camp, and the part of her that had missed her comforts and privileges. "Please follow me. I'm sorry we can't greet you with better news. When your lady mother first arrived here, we tried to stop proud flesh forming with an application of leeches. This seemed to work but then the rot started up again. We resorted to cauterising the wound, which as you'll understand is bitterly painful. For some time it seemed this too had done its work but return it did, spreading to other parts of the leg. There is a poison in there that would not be still. In the end we've had to take the leg."

"Take the leg? As in… as in… cut it off?" The child inside Augusta quavered. She had been alright with staying away from Nanette for her own safety, but the idea her mother had weathered this terror alone weakened her with guilt.

"Amputated," the physic corrected, as though the medical term somehow made the situation less horrible.

"She survived the operation and the blood loss. Once again, we thought we'd stopped it… But two days ago the redness began to appear around the hip and pelvis, shortly afterwards the fever began. It is as if something were eating her from the inside… She has fought a very long battle, longer than I've ever seen before with a wound so determined to march slowly towards gangrene. Now all her native hardihood has been exhausted. It is my hope that seeing her daughter will allow her to let go and die at last."

Augusta didn't reply. She felt bitter rancour towards the Abbess for trying to make her feel bad about not being there sooner. They opened the doors to the sick room and a vile odour came with it, as of something between stale sweat and the rot of death. Augusta gagged and took out her handkerchief to cover her nose and mouth before venturing in.

"We do our best with flowers to cover it," the Abbess said quietly. "But she rots while she still lives."

"Leave us," Augusta ordered, and the holy people did so with shallow bows.

Her mother's face was perhaps more shocking even than the smell. Once proud features were wan and drawn through shock and trauma into some sort of doll of a human skeleton. Grey as it was Augusta could still see the face of the woman she had most loved all her childhood. She picked up one cold, dry hand.

"Hello, Mother." It felt strange to use that word again after so long. It brought with it a long tug of melancholy and unwelcome feeling.

"Rowan?" Nanette whispered distracted.

With one word it was gone. All the old reminders of hearing her say she wouldn't sacrifice her boy child for her girl child came back, and for the first time since she'd felt her hands sticky with her own De Biron blood she felt something almost like a surge of triumph in knowing she'd robbed Nanette of her son. Her mouth set in a different way.

"No. I'm afraid it's only Augusta."

Nanette's eyes flew open and she turned her head. What she saw there in her mother's eyes was not the same woman she'd once been at all, she was reduced, piteous. "Augusta?" she tightened her grip on her hand like a skeleton with a strength she shouldn't have possessed. "You have come back to me?"

Augusta involuntarily pulled her hand away. Weak as she was there was an insidious power that seemed to weave around her and tightened far more inextricable than her grip had been. In an instant Augusta remembered everything Uncle Gil had said to warn her off this encounter. Though she hated it she feared he'd been entirely right. She had not felt that since Blaith had pulled the tendrils of the curse of demonic presence out of her.

"I was told you were dying." The whole time she'd stood there Augusta had tried not to look down at the absence that would be under the covers where her mother's other leg used to be.

"I'm getting there... but we're... tough stock," she whispered. Reaching around for Augusta's hand she eventually found it. Whilst she winced Augusta could not bring herself to rip it away a second time. "I'm glad you're here."

"Well, I know I'm not Rowan. But I'm something, surely?" she blurted out.

Nanette ignored her bitterness and ploughed on with her own agenda as she always had. "I need to tell you... warn you. I cast such a curse over De

Rue and those tinkers both." She closed her eyes again. It was as if she needed a moment to savour the sweetness of her height of power. A sly smile drifted across her mouth. "But something happened… on that day that Rowan killed De Rue's son and then you killed Rowan-"

Augusta gasped. This time she did pull her hand away. Her mouth couldn't even form the lie, the denial would have been in the teeth of her mother's immense confidence. Furtively she looked around to make sure no one was listening in nearby.

"Let's not play games. I know it was you. It's the only way the curse could have metastasised like this. It was fed on kin-murder. That is the only way it could have jumped from them to you-"

"De Rue married me and by law I was Augusta De Rue at the time you cursed his family."

The little smile again. "You were never… a De Rue… you will always… be a De Biron."

This was about as close to a love sentiment as she was likely to get, Augusta realised.

"Kin-murder is an ancient and primeval curse. It doubles it, triples it… Trust me, I've had that one on my tail before… Cain's own sin… The act fed it. Attracted it to you. But it's worse now… so much worse…"

"In what way?"

"That tinker devil… the one with the black eyes. He took everything I'd sent after his family and De Rue's line both and turned it inwards on me. It's been eating me slow, digesting me ever since."

"What happens when you die?"

Her mother opened her eyes again and this time her gaze was as sharp as it ever was. "You must be nowhere near here when I die! Put running water between us, put the sky and the mountains between us. Let a little of it fall upon the heath plants… a little of it…" Her voice disintegrated into a clear death rattle. "The tinker devil who threw it must die. This will take the edge off. I've made provision for it in my last will testament. If it is done, you might

355

yet outrun it... outlive it...."

Augusta shook her head. "That tinker devil worked all night to try and pull this out of me and off me. In truth, mere vagabond as he is, he showed me more kindness than you ever did."

"Don't come over sentimental with me now, Augusta. His power signature is immense and alien. Like nothing I've ever seen before. What he's done to me... what he sent winging home to me, it isn't escapable for long. It will dog your heels all your life, waiting for a moment of weakness or carnage to ascend your back. Then it will do the same to your children afterwards. It contains everything I wanted for De Rue, after what he did to you."

"Love turned into spite, the only way you know how to express it."

"I said don't get sentimental. There isn't time. You need to go now, before it happens. Put every talisman around you and go far from me. Come nowhere near my body or my grave, ever. I designed this curse to jump from father to son down the line but after what the tinker did with it, I fear that with Rowan gone it will be upon you."

As she tiptoed out into the sun and onto the mossy rocks by the river's edge, he watched her feet more than he did her hands or face. It was always through watching people's feet that he could tell when they were starting to fade out in bleeding edges in the land while they moved across her. Robin spoke of Blaith's body genius to describe his way of practicing deep noticing.

It gave Blaith a hard-on and a heart-swell to feel so *seen* by him, yet until Robin had told him Blaith hadn't realised his intense sensory immersion was rare or special. If he had to explain it he'd say even his curses, the thing he was most famous for, didn't come so much from his appetite for retribution, but from his deep noticing. There was a reason so many euphemisms were called things to do with watching, the eye, overlooking, the owl's blink...

"Afon Conwy," she said, naming the river lady correctly in Cymric as they'd taught her.

He nodded once. Like everything else he did with her he had brought her to this very spot, at this very hour, with *purpose.* Her feet were fading out nicely, as though translucent for moments, with rock, water, or moss showing through. It seemed to him that she felt down into her feet as she moved like one native to place. For a moment he thought he saw moss growing on her. She had become part of the land as well as of their blood.

Wading into the ice-cold edges of the river Blaith stood beside her. Her dress was drawn up to the knee and she gave no indication of feeling the scorching intensity of the cold. Her eyes were fixed on the white water rapids at the centre of the river upstream and their powerful tumult. *She feels in looking upon this as I feel watching ravens circle the battlefield or the bloodied sheepfold that the wolf has been among. She sees her soul mirrored back to her and is in awe at the extent of herself.*. Bringing a new maiden through, one that he'd not grown up beside, seemed to emphasise the truth of everything they believed in. Striking off shackles was still possible. If you could free one, inside her rested the possibility of all freedom.

"When you were initiated did you have to fuck?"

He was used to the students asking him things about their own experiences, not about his. She was precocious in showing reciprocal interest in him and his experiences. Blaith appreciated this about her in the deep, silent way that was his. "I met with the ancient hag of the mountain quite close to here."

"And did you fuck?" Lux asked, with one of her eyebrows darting up. For a moment, and for a reason Blaith couldn't place, she suddenly reminded him of Eilion.

"Of course," he replied with a faint frown, as if he'd entirely missed her sarcasm. "It's only polite."

Lux burst out laughing at his words and the musical sound of her giggle seemed to dance in the air and join the sound of the water. He gave no greater elaboration, but instead stooped to scoop up the water of the holy river in his hands to wash his face in.

"Blaith?"

"Yes, sweet one?" He got to his feet, the water coursing down from his wet hair.

She smiled. "You look like a dark Jesus with your hair like that, standing in the river during the baptism with John."

"Aye. I will soon be your anti-christ."

"First I'd like to hear your Song." She stepped a little closer to him and nearly slipping on a rock. He reached out his hands to steady her. "As Sariah performed Robin's song before the fight?"

It didn't seem necessary to him to ask why she wanted to hear it. He nodded with a certain solemnity and closed his eyes, retaining her hands in his. The numbness from the cold in his feet was coursing up his legs, turning his blood reptilian. Yet he felt the sun on his face and bare shoulders, and the snow melt in the water gushing around him held the memory of the light on high. It all combined to make and churn the Awen he would need to reimagine and rearrange himself in words. They leaked up in him like a water stain creeping across parchment.

When he began to speak the words bubbled up from below ground without effort, starting as a mere whisper but gaining force and power. He almost wanted to call it back when it was too late, the terrible self-revelation of it...

""I am the ache sorrow of every dead or dying people." He spoke from the place Guidgen the first Magister had carved out in him, right from the beginning, sharp with the knowledge of his own lastness, or more properly second-lastness. Before it had even begun for him Blaith had known he would witness the demise of their life way. It was why one such as him was Magister. He was to sit with their tradition at the death bed, the way he'd sat with Meredith. Somewhere inside him a lonely wolf wailed at the sky, the last of his kind, crying out into the night.

"I am the keening of the women on the battlefield, and the long ache of nostalgia years later when a certain flower blooms that flowered that first spring when love was first known." As he spoke, he was those fragile, dew-laden parts of life. "I am Retribution," he said more strongly, feeling black pitchy liquid fire run out of his eyes and down his cheeks. "Under my gowns are the shroud washers and the stile wailers. They make dry bone rubbing sounds when I move. I'm the shell-grit and bone marrow shards of massacres crunching under foot. I lay down as a bridge for my people. I am wolf mother, serpent charmer, trickster man, eyes in the back of my head, one devil's foot cloven." As he spoke the many-headed, androgynous, queer, monstrous, beautiful thing he was seemed to congeal into manifestation as the words naming his aspects were spoken into form.

"As I walk I make the wet sound of the sodden winding sheet dragging on the crooked path," he murmured. Shivering slightly with a cold rush of having evoked a fear and dread of himself. "I am a murder of ravens blackening the sky, an unkindness of Memory and Lore. It was I who blinded the left eye of the Gwrach when I was raven king rising from the long dark to throw around the boulders of the land. My heart is as bottomless and unfathomable as the great lakes, and sharp-edged all around with jagged flint. I am Insurrection. I am the long-awaited sweetness of vengeance served cold. I have been upon this land since the fall of light following the hyenas of a people's dreams, and all that time I have suffered the endless hiraeth of being..."

He was breathless for a long moment as though the abyss that lived in his chest were suddenly so wide there was no room for lungs. The great black wings with white eyes that lived in his back stretched out across the sky like a crucifixion victim. "For I have within a hunger that will never cease. I am a travelling man, whose heart belongs to the freedom of the endless horizon."

Lux entered Blaith's tent, the light was low but she could see well enough to know he was already naked. His form was half in shadow; his black hair was wet and wrung into a strand over his angular shoulder. Blaith put his towel down at the sight of her and stood very naturally and comfortably before her. Her bodice was fastened under her breasts that not only revealed them but pushed them up and out, accentuating them. "You were taken through the camp like this then, up to the door of my tent, in the traditional way?"

She nodded. "Sariah let Bran put these flowers here for you."

"Hmm. Very clever of her. Softened and hardened him all at once, I'd warrant. How did it feel, having him touch you like that?" As he spoke, he reached out and took the flower from her cleavage.

"Uncomfortable and exciting at the same time."

"I hope tonight we will find you have saved me some of your blushes. Now you realise, Lux, whatever of you is left that is Norman, or of their church, will die here in this tent tonight? Yes? You are about to be claimed as a maid of the one they call the devil? Do you do so with full understanding?"

"I come here of my own free will." Sensing the right moment she went down on her knees before him undoing her plait. Leaning right forward she swept her hair over his feet, her hair that she had grown with this moment in mind, exposing the back of her neck to him. "And let down my hair for you."

As she came up onto her knees, he held his hard-on in his hand directing it. She opened her mouth and took it in eagerly. It was with the same feeling of spiritual reverence she'd once compared to receiving the eucharist, except now she didn't even think of the comparison, as she had got so much less pleasure out the eucharist than this. He held her head in his hands and thrust deep into her throat over and over until her throat relaxed. When she gagged he withdrew.

He turned around and bent over the prayer stool. She was guided partly by understanding of what he wanted, and partly by a queer urge to be as another man towards him. "Put your tongue in the devil's arse."

Hesitant at first she gently filled the pink part between his black hairs with her tongue. He was clean and freshly soaped and she wondered quite suddenly at the reason for the great taboo? When he moaned her enthusiasm redoubled. How could anything he was enjoying so much not be exciting? She licked him very slowly and sensuously at first, pushing him with her tongue, teasing. She loved the sounds he made that were not altogether like a man's sounds of pleasure, more of an intermingling of masculine and feminine. She experienced the strong intuition that this was his cunt. Of course, the great obscenity of their devil was that he was neither man nor woman, but complete unto himself.

"You are very good at that…" he said breathily. "We will need to move on or I will empty my balls right now." He got up and faced her again. "Now we will transform poisons and pain into powers and pleasures. Now you must bend over the prayer stool."

Lux did so. Blaith came up behind her and pulled down her pants, but only to the point where they were still loose around her legs just above the ankle. The first strike of the belt to her bottom was much harder than anything Robin had ever done to her in their play, and she cried out in shock as well as pain. It was far closer to the strength of the blows De Rue had struck her with, and it was followed by another couple of stinging additions. She tried not to cry out but she could feel her bottom cringing, flinching waiting to see if he would do it again.

With a sort of rude abruptness, he spread her labia apart and opened everything, having a good detailed look at her. She could feel his examining eye like its path gave off black heat. When he shoved his finger inside her she was given away for he found how wet she was. He laughed softly. It was not a laugh of mockery though, but an aroused one that seemed to carry surprised approval. "Ah, I think you will be good at this lesson." He gave her a more controlled, lighter smack across her cunny with the belt. She shivered with a strange chill of delight.

"Look at this," he showed her his glistening fingers. "What a good little whore you are going to be with some training. Stand up now."

Extremely flustered and red in the face she turned to look at him. Noticing her pinkness with a smile he took her chin between his damp fingers and made her maintain eye contact with him. "How are you going? Are you alright?" There was this brief, companionable, relaxed warmth in his eyes while he checked-in with her. His fetch was reminding her body it was safe with him and that this was play.

She nodded. "I'm ready for your next lesson."

He smiled, acknowledging her playing along with him. "Then we must sit with trust -perfect trust." He took out a small bottle of the sort that Eilish would keep medicine in. "You understand that milk of the poppy is one of ingredients in this wine?"

Blaith took a deep swig from it, pulled her close and covered her mouth with his, spraying the liquid deep into her throat while kissing her so that she was forced to swallow or choke. She took it in and sought his tongue with hers. As she kissed him her kiss said yes to trusting him. Without words he was telling her he knew what happened. He called that child out from where she was hiding after the violations, and when he touched her she grew to adulthood in one instant. Without words he called on her to drown out the echoes of the past with life. "Oh, I am really going to enjoy this," he said huskily, pushing her back from him.

He put her back on her knees again, but this time with her back to him. Coming up behind her he gave her bound breasts a fondle ending in a hard pinch on her nipples. She made a little high-pitched sound, and almost as though in punishment for it he pushed her neck down to the ground. Vast sexual experience and confidence emanated from Blaith's every touch and it gave her a last minute jitter. Before she could regain any composure, he was spreading her arse cheeks and she felt his ointment-covered finger go up into her.

When she heard him unbuckling, she thrilled with excitement mingled with fear. There was no further warning before she felt his cock pressing up inside her. "It was nice of Hob to leave me your arse to break in." He took her around the hips and began thrusting in deeper and out again. It didn't take very long before something roused in Lux, a profound sensation of rightness about it came over her and flushed its way into her cheeks. She could feel the opiate seeping through her, making her go limper, making her muscles relax.

Blaith gripped different parts of her and used them for traction to ravage her in her unresistant hole, he grabbed her tits, her ponytail, or her arms behind her back. The sounds he made were of abandon, and the vigour with which he took her seemed to speak of deep erotic focus. "Ah that's it, Lux…

362

Let the poppy take over your senses and relax you. Give it up to me.... I bet you never thought you'd find yourself on your knees in a roadside tent with a tinker's cock in your arse, did you?"

He asked each bit with a hard thrust as though punctuating, until on the last words a strange new orgasm gripped her anally, intestinally, stomach-to-throat until it came out her mouth in a low moan. She felt herself open up like her body was preparing for childbirth and her fetch begin to unravel for flight. "Oh yes, that's it, little witch…" Blaith murmured. "Come out, come out, wherever you are…"

For a moment or two she felt lifted into the air and seemed to levitate above the scene. Able to look down upon her own body being fucked by him opened out another plane of enjoyment. When she had finished convulsing in his grip, her body lay still but Blaith continued to hold her head down against the furs. "The light is set so that the wardens outside have watched all of our unholy marriage in shadow play upon the tent wall," he informed her from close to her ear.

The words meant nothing at one level and some darkly, exciting freedom at another. Some expansive comet-like part of her wanted them to see it. She felt as if she were made of darkness that crackled and fizzed with life, shame was just another mask over the honey-smooth beast of the flesh. Something to be flushed out like her mother's ghost had once voided her human shame. You could take it off at will if you learned how.


Lux ran her fingers both tentatively and tenderly over the swelling under Robin's eyes. "Will you let me put something on it?" She had observed the bruising on his upper body as he disrobed for the night but he had not said much about how he got them.

"Only if it's your cunny." He seemed to be only half joking.

With a smile carrying a hint of promise she let him know they would come around to all that. "You say it went well, yet you seem to have a lot of bruising…"

"I would have a lot more if it hadn't gone well." Obviously, her desire to know was not subtle because he looked at her before continuing. "Those kind of outlaw bands they don't have any women in them see, it's unbalanced. They work off some pretty basic approaches to dominance."

"So, you had to fight them to win their respect?" she ventured. Although he had refused ointment she was itching to do something for his swollen lip and the spot under his eye where the skin had split and colourful bruising was coming out.

"Oh, go on then, put some of your comfrey ointment on it or something," he grinned.

Given permission she quickly and gladly rummaged through her growing emergency doctoring kit until she found some things she felt would make it more comfortable. He put his head back and accepted the fuss with resigned grace.

"Just their best man. I had to fight their leader."

"And you beat him?"

He nodded. "Not sure if it's about respect or whether they just love to fight. I don't know if I went too hard on him actually. In my experience every fight is potentially to the death. In the ring when I was younger it was that sort of dirty illegal no-rules fighting where sometimes people died. The boys and young men were usually homeless or wretched folk who nobody would miss."

"Did you want to do it? The fighting? Or did you have to do it for the money?"

"The money didn't go astray. But Gaelyn, Sariah's father, bless his memory, mentioned to me once that if he was young again, and he wanted to make himself unbeatable he'd go into the ring. With multiple serious fights a night you got so much more experience than in sparring. I got ten colours of productive shit kicked out of me."

She shook her head in wonderment.

"Gaelyn would come and watch and bet on me after I found my feet. I was smaller than the people I fought most of the time, so only he knew my

speed and agility would count for more than they reckoned for, and he'd make a fortune off me.""When you fought this outlaw did you feel unbeatable like Gaelyn said you would be?"

"That would be expecting something, a sure way to lose."

"So you fought him, you beat him, I assume he looks worse than you do. And then you all just sit around and chat and are best mates afterwards?"

Robin laughed. "Pretty much. Such is the absurdity of the human man cut away from the human woman. But they told me a lot of useful things. They are in contact with the next band over, who in turn knows the next band over, as far afield as Rochdale. I am going to use their networks to get a message to Gil."

Lux nodded. She knew Gil meant a lot to Robin. And having helped save Robin's life as he had, it gave the Norman lord a place in Blaith's and her heart, too. "What are you going to tell him?"

"I want him to know precisely where we're summering if he needs to get out of the kitchen if it gets too hot in his area. I hope for news in return of Nanette and whether she lives."

"That would be good information to have to be sure. We all owe Gil a debt of gratitude beyond any of our repaying." Lux murmured, tenderly stroking his forearm and sitting with the deep gratitude she felt every time he rode away and came back again.

Gil felt sick as he stood there staring at the empty place Augusta's horse should have been. "Damn, Nanette," he muttered, one of many such ill-wishings he'd directed at his sister over a lifetime. Something beyond reckoning was wrong with her. He'd lied to himself his whole life that it wasn't really that bad, but what she'd done to Robin, and the girl who was used as bait and raped.

He was about to have his own mount saddled and go looking for her when he was partly relieved and partly alarmed by the sound of horses approaching at a gallop. His hand already on his sword hilt Gil ran outside to see who

was coming. Shielding his eyes from the sun he saw Augusta riding full-tilt towards him astride her horse, with the escort she'd taken with her left far behind in the dust. Catching the sense of urgency, he began to run towards her. When they met she swung down from the saddle without his assistance in the manner of the athletic Twll Du women.

"What's wrong, Guss?"

"It's mother. It's mother who's wrong! She's about to die and she told me I need to get clear of her by some distance to avoid inheriting the curse Blaith turned back on her."

"Let's get you inside then. We'll put you inside a circle and-"

"That is the least of our troubles, Uncle," she said, taking him by the arm and leading him to walk with her as if she were the man and he the woman. She gestured for the stable boy to attend to her horse. It all came so naturally to her, he observed, all this ordering others around. Coming back from the egalitarian world he'd known with Robin it had been hard for Gil to fully reestablish his lordly behaviour, but Augusta was not so hampered.

She stopped and rounded on him only when she felt certain they were far enough away to be out of any potential ear-shot. "Mother told me in her ravings that her will contains a hit on Blaith, or possibly even the family as a whole. She has put by money to pay the assassins to have him killed upon her death." She was sweating with stress. It pleased him to know she would come to him with something like this breathless, that her loyalties indeed had not swung back towards her mother. What didn't please him were the implications. "I know they are good, and have put pay to so many hired thugs over time but-"

"You are worried because you know Nanette is a cunning bitch. And you should be."

Augusta nodded. "I doubt she'll have failed to notice all the unsuccessful hits that have been put out on them before. With the price on Robin's head alone most people could settle down for life if they brought him in. The fact few people choose to try these days is not a just a matter of him being such a

366

good fellow."

Gil nodded grimly. "Indeed. In making her Last Will and Spitefulness I doubt Nanette will fail to outdo herself in either respect. We need to get a warning to them. God damn it all to hell!" he cried, suddenly needing to take his frustration out by kicking a fence paling. "I should be at their side!"

"If you were there at their side, you wouldn't be here to receive this information, would you?" Augusta replied with startling practicality. "I feel the workings of Fate in all this, Gil. I'm not giving in easily to this curse. And I'm not giving up on our friends easily either. We need a solid plan."

# 4

obin clenched Sariah's hand hard before he let it go. This part of the carnival was as necessary as it was inevitably stressful. He didn't need to say anything else to her, the hand squeeze and the eye contact were enough to reassure her. It let her know he wasn't just physically there, every part of him was engaged in her safety, in this dance of sex and potential violence that played out when she would perform in public. Creirwy and Brynmor had passed the news far and wide about the event, so they had visitors as far-flung as the Marcher lands. This meant there was a stew of cultural difference there that night. There were Gwynedd folk, and then there were Norman-ized Welsh and even English speakers.

His feelings about exposing her to this were complicated, yet the mechanics of what would happen in their respective roles was not. She was going to go out there and work her magic and he was going to make sure she had the space to do it, if anyone tried to disrespect her work he was going to hurt them or scare them until they wet in their boots, at the very least. His whole body felt her free-fall of trust in this situation, as if she was going to fall through space and it was his job to catch her. The responsibility felt heavy at the start, but that was just the fear that he always felt around the safety of his family. After a few moments he'd remember down to his bones that he was doing what he was made to do, just as she was. He was good at it, and so was she.

He made eye contact across the crowd with Jack who was placed inconspicuously close to her. Their friendship had been deepening of late, and Jack had visited Sariah in her maiden tent on and off. This meant that although he wasn't trained in the manner their wardens, he was one of the most trusted

sources of back-up when it came to her defense. Next, he visually checked in with Emrys, who was Eilish's lover and a good fighter. Finally, on the other side of the crowd Robin glanced over at Sorcha, who was a regular visitor to Sariah's maiden tent and was also deeply motivated. It was important to remember he wasn't alone in his role.

As he watched her beginning to unwind to the music, turning inward, spiraling into her womanhood and her abandon the beauty of it ached in his chest. They had done this so many times the two of them, this dynamic, and not just in this lifetime. He knew it although he couldn't remember the specific details of how he'd guarded her in the past. This was just what they did. Blaith fucked her but he held her space and watched her unravel and spin the Lady's Bower into manifestation on this earth. He enjoyed that in a way that couldn't be fully worded. He understood what they were doing in presenting this to the public. At a mundane level it was about distraction, as the young thieves of the blood thread had often used the opportunity to pick pockets of any more wealthy or obnoxious viewers.

Sariah's dance, always the peak of the carnival's entertainments in the evening, was about more than that. It was about Our Lady riding her, it was about beauty and surrender and letting a little bit of the nectar of Paradise spill out into the shabby, damaged world of man. It softened them up later to hear new ideas. It challenged Robin down to his core, this dance that part of him had to do with her, because he didn't know if he felt most of these men even deserved to look at her. As he relentlessly scanned the crowd looking for signs someone would overstep their mark, he ground his teeth on a regular basis. He knew he wasn't meant to step in over mere words, no matter how disrespectful. Sariah had given him that order. He would only touch them if they tried to touch her, or if they put a finger over the line. But it wasn't easy sometimes.

"Hey beautiful! Over here! Show your tits if you want the coin," one man was yelling out, dangling money to her and coming perilously close to putting his hand over the line. Robin began to move closer to him, his eyes fixed on that hand. He was glad they spoke in bastardized Norman French and Sariah

couldn't understand them much. *Why can't they just enjoy watching her? They don't know what they're dealing with. She'd eat them all for breakfast and they wouldn't even touch the sides of the insatiable power she holds.*

The shouts and banter were becoming increasingly crude, it was the fault of the Marcher folk who'd come out for the evening he decided. Sariah appeared almost entirely oblivious to them or their words, as if she were dancing alone in a forest clearing with only the moon looking on. Her eyes looked glassy with trance, and she was so within herself that they couldn't touch her. She was something to behold. Robin felt chills all over his body that made his hairs stand on end just as strongly or more so than heat to the groin. As if the goddess that wound in and out of her could sense him and his thoughts and feelings, Sariah turned in his direction. Her movements reminded him of a snake and when her gaze fixed on his it had the same hypnotic quality. He almost expected her to lick her full lips with a serpent's cleft tongue.

He smiled faintly. She held his gaze for a long time, as if she were dancing exclusively for him and the other men present had ceased to exist. He didn't look away, even though his peripheral vision was still taking in everything the audience was doing. She was slowly revealing her breasts during this sinuous movement that undulated through her body, but Robin couldn't stop looking into her eyes long enough to glance at them. In her eyes she was revealing something far more intimate, terrible, and beautiful.

"Over here!" someone shouted again. Obviously frustrated by the fact her back was almost to them while she was looking at Robin and revealing herself. With a teeth grind of intense irritation, Robin began to move his position again. It was always like that for him during this act. It wasn't just Sariah who was in an intense mystical state, he was fully open when he held her security too. The whole crowd had to be held within his empathic sense. He had to accept full knowledge of the ugliness around him and hold onto it somehow, preferably without killing anyone just for feeling things. He knew exactly when they were going to do something stupid.

He caught the man's hand just as it passed the line and resisted the urge

to break it. Pulling the stranger back firmly but gently Robin put a subtle lock on the man's wrist at his side so no one would notice.

"I wouldn't do that if I were you," he murmured in the man's ear from behind. "I don't want to have to hurt you."

That was a lie, Robin acknowledged to himself. He did want to hurt him. But it would have been scapegoating. He would have been breaking that man's hand for so many other men, and it would have been too easy.

"Oh, come on, mate. She dances for money then she's a whore! I just want to see her-"

Robin tightened the lock till the man started to whimper. He felt into that flesh space with the eyes in his hands, even though it hurt him too, taking the other man right up to the threshold of a bone break, and holding him hovering just over it. Robin was steely calm through it with a discipline born of long practice. Being a warrior with a pronounced sympathy for all living things hurt like hell. It was a deal of sorts with Fate though, because it's what made him the best. He understood the body of his opponent in the way only the very best of lovers usually understands the flesh of another person.

"She's my cousin."

"Alright! I'm sorry!" he gasped, clearly barely able to think with pain.

"And if you touch her, I will kill you. Slowly. Intimately." He began to release the pressure on the man's hand as he spoke. When he let go, the man collapsed to his knees and the other men around him began to enquire what was wrong, as people had been too busy watching Sariah to have observed their exchange. Later some of the most unpleasant ones would also notice some of their purses were missing.

When Lux had first seen Blaith in his little black tent, with his black polished obsidian stone in front of him, and the sign where Robin had painted: 'When will you die?' in three different languages, Lux had laughed at the idea people would pay for such a service. Yet by mid-afternoon there was a queue there. It was like the more he looked morose and unenthusiastic about talking

371

to them, the more they wanted him. It didn't even seem to matter that old maids and rich young women alike often went away with a handerchief or rag to their face trying to hide their tears. If anything this seemed to enflame punters with a dark zeal to experience the same ordeal.

By nightfall most of the women – who made up the backbone of Blaith's clientele- had gone home and the night was mainly full of men. Lux understood that it had been at this time of night when De Rue and his cousin De Bracy had slipped into their camp all those moons ago. This fact wasn't lost on any of the Twll Du people and the place was visibly crawling with alert looking wardens. Lux herself had several concealed weapons on her, beyond her more obvious boot knife. The fact she was wearing trousers and a boy's style tunic caused her to get the odd double take, as people tried to work out what gender to categorise her as. She felt resilient to their stares though. The self-defence lessons she'd been getting from Sorcha probably helped with that. Lux carried a bow scaled to her size quite openly, and she didn't feel silly with it anymore because she knew how to use it.

She came to a halt at Blaith's tent. "Broken the spirit of a lot of housewives tonight?" she asked with a playful smile.

He grinned, one of her favourite type of his smiles where he let you see a bit of his teeth. "Enough," he indicated, showing her the coin he'd collected. "I can't count this high. But a good few dozen are out there reevaluating what they're going to do with the time they have left above ground."

She took a seat where the customer would sit and he waved her away with a loose-wrist dismissive gesture. "Ach. I know yours already. You will die the same day as Robin and I."

Lux could sense the gentle tug of melancholy in his words and she smiled sadly. "I wouldn't want it any other way." It was true, she knew, as she looked down into his black stone of prophecy. She had given herself up for dead the moment her jaw had decided to chomp down into De Rue's hand and not let go till she'd taken his thumb so he'd never hold a sword again. When she'd run she'd not expected to survive for this long, so everything beyond was an

unfolding bonus. Nonetheless she couldn't resist adding. "Do you see us having long?"

"It depends on some moves we make. That is the thing about being a sorcerer, Lux. Most of my predictions come true on normal people. They have access to a smaller number of moves on the board." He sighed deeply as he packed away his kit. "It is a great feeling, and this work is a stark reminder of it, to know you still have so many possible hands left to play. Some of these poor people have almost none, or only one." He got to his feet and put his black cloak on, though to her judgment of temperature the evening air was warm. "Usurpers have taken all their hands, both figuratively and in some cases literally. Come," he said, inviting for her to walk with him. "Let's go and find him. I heard Robin had to threaten idiots tonight over Sariah."

"Was anyone hurt?" Lux wasn't allowed to be there when Sariah danced, neither was Blaith. It gave Robin too many people to worry about.

"Probably not as much as I would like. The wardens are all aware of it though and they're heading down to the Creirwy's hall to make sure the crowd is the right sort."

"What sort of crowd is the right sort for this?"

Blaith snorted with dark amusement. "The kind that might be willing to fight Normans, but not to fight us? It's a fine line category as thin as a hair bridge."

"May I retain this copy?" she asked, as her eyes devoured the words, looking for the salient part. Of course, Mother had willed her possessions to Augusta and not to Uncle Gil, including a parcel of land she owned in her own right that she'd not mentioned to her daughter until now. At this point that was hardly of consequence to Augusta. "Excuse me." Without waiting for an answer Augusta took the will and went to look for Uncle Gil. "Could you show them out?" she said to one of the servants, as she swept past. "Where is my lord uncle?" She asked the next to pass her in the hall.

"In his study, my lady." The upstairs maid dipped her a curtsey but Au-

gusta was already gone. Within little time at all she was knocking on his door.

"Come."

"Gil, you have to see this," she said, bursting in. "I just got her will!"

He cleared a place on his desk for her to spread it out. "Is it as she said it would be?"

"Worse. This is the bit here, she writes: 'I leave 200 marks to Lord Malcolm de Bracy for the execution of my wishes in regards to bringing to justice the wolf's head, Robin Goodfellow, and his brother Blaith, who did abduct my daughter. This in accordance with previous instructions and verbal agreements between De Bracy and myself.'"

You could see the colour leave Gil's face. Which one of them was he in love with, she wondered? Or was it both of them?

"Just when I thought I had accepted the true depth of her depravity... She has gone to the man who killed Robin and Blaith's aunt..."

"Would she have known though? Do you think perhaps she went to him because she thought him motivated in hatred towards Robin who has slain his cousin?"

Gil sighed deeply and sat back in his chair. It was clear he needed a moment or two to process the question. "I suppose we will never know for sure. De Rue could have told her himself. Rumour could have told her. Spying could have told her."

"Regardless, from what I know of the crime he and De Rue committed he is a man without pity and greatly to be feared."

He nodded rapidly, leaning forward and grabbing up parchment and quill. "I will write to De Bracy telling him I wish to take care of this act of vengeance by my own hand with my own men, and that the money is his nonetheless."

"It's worth a try, but given that the revenge is personal for him with Hob having killed De Rue I wouldn't count on it working. We need to act immediately as well as write."

"What would you suggest we do, given we don't know their precise location?"

374

"Well, we need to find out the location. I will start to prepare. To get to Gwynedd fast we will need at least three changes of a fresh horse. What did Robin tell you to do if you needed to make contact in an emergency?"

"He gave me a coded message to tell the inn-keeper at Capel Curig where he checks in weekly. Ideally, we'd get to him faster than that though. Who knows how fast De Bracy will be if he had foreknowledge?"

"What if we send the carriage and a messenger to the inn at Capel Curig and tell the driver to wait there for further instructions? You write the letter, I'll organise transport."

Augusta was just about to sweep away as purposefully as she come when Gil grabbed her hand. "Augusta?"

"Yes?"

"I just want you to know... You're ten times what Rowan ever was. You'd be better at being me than I am, and it's god's own pity you weren't born a man. What a De Biron warlord you would have made..."

They all sat around on the floor in Creirwy's family's hall on cushions. Lux wasn't sure if this was because Robin was unwilling to seat himself above other people or whether it had something to do with custom. She was fascinated to understand that utterings of awenyddion, or prophetic poets as a mainstream custom in Wales even outside of the Twll Du caravans. Most of the people there, including a lot of women who had chosen to come indoors after nightfall and share mead with the family so they could wait to hear Robin talk, understood the practice.

Lux had assumed that when Brynmor and Creirwy had asked Robin to talk to the people that he was expected to give some kind of politically rousing speech. Instead, he had set himself up to speak as an inspired one. From what she'd learned she knew awenyddion were expected to speak in riddles and not give straight answers. Sometimes they gave no answers at all and the audience would accept this. In this way it was probably the best way for Robin to honour his agreement to speak to the people. Lux's upbringing had led her

to expect such practices to be heathen things Robin's family alone did, rather than something the whole of Wales did.

"Amazing," she murmured, as she watched people finding their seats. "These country folk out here make for interesting Christians," she observed to Jack who was seated beside her. Robin had his closest people sitting around him, Blaith in particular sat back to back with him.

"Aye. I think out here if you call something poetry you get to save it from being witchcraft? Inspiration is the true god of this place."

Lux sat with this insightful comment of Uncle Jack's for some time. It was a way of looking at the Cymric identity that pulled together a lot of disparate threads. Some harps began to play in the four corners of the hall where Creirwy and her sisters and mother handled the music. It set an atmosphere, sort of forced people to start relaxing. The amount of mead most people had to drink didn't hurt either. While they were doing this Blaith was rocking back and forth rhythmically with Robin. There was a pewter dish with rocks in it that burned upon coals the same herbal concoction that had so affected her the night she'd seen Robin's tattoo come to life. Sariah was wafting it into his face with a switch made of eagle feathers.

After a time of this Robin's body jerked backwards in a way that might have been violent if Blaith wasn't supporting him. He made a strange, strangled cry as if a creature of some kind of was trying to emerge out of his throat. Immediately upon the cue of the sound the harps stopped and others began to rock back in forth in time with Robin.

"Have you come to lead us, Robin?" someone called out. Despite the grace of the music and the intense love of inspiration these people shared the awenydd was communicated with abruptly on familiar terms.

In his entranced state Robin seemed to not feel the pressure of the room staring at him, many of them expecting him to be some kind of hedgerow Jesus with a bow. When he began to speak his words didn't answer directly. Yet once he began to talk no one yelled out any new questions.

"My story is a terrible one. The lightning storm that ejaculated out my

infant spirit into the death-wrestle for life within my Mumma's body dragon-beget me, my caul-ridden light a disaster of shadow cast on stone three times larger than life and thick with death. I've swallowed the nectar of the awenydd and the goblin poison of the hob men was converted in my body into red-capped mushrooms who spring up in the splatters of my blood because I'm the hedge-dweller the light in the dark sleight of hand man and all the glamour tricks of the Edge Men -walking… The mighty heart of the mountain that haunts the eagles beats fierce in my belly, wolf-turned till my poet's so strong he devours the lover and fighter in me into one sharp edged blade forged in hell. I am he who they say is coming through the cracks in things once in a century. *I'm still coming.* Say my name three times. Tell the innocent to taste hope and let the guilty tremble."

In the silence that fell upon the room when he stopped speaking one person called out: "Robin Goodfellow!"

The room joined in following the first woman. It was clear the people gathered took Robin's trance-delivered words entirely in the spirit of affirmation of their question. Lux felt the hairs on the back of her arms rise up. There was a power in the zinging air, but she wasn't sure if it was the upsurge of new hope in an oppressed people, or the hypnotic thrill of rising death. "Robin Goodfellow! Robin Goodfellow!"

It was disconcerting to know he'd been watched without his awareness. Gil was heading to the woods for some time alone when he saw. The enormous man who stepped forward out from the edge of the green, shouldn't have been as silent as he was. Gil drew his breath in and his hand hovered around his sword hilt. The giant wore bits and pieces of patched together hide of numerous animals, crudely worked, and bore upon his back an enormous quarterstaff. Its position sheathed upon the back seemed to indicate no threat was being offered.

Gil held both his hands up to indicate he would not go for his weapon either, and the outlaw, for such Gil sensed he was, gave a slight nod of the head.

As if he were king of the woods, he stood in rather than standing before their owner the giant waited for Gil to approach him, which he did.

"Do you be Gilbert de Biron?" he asked in a broad Yorkshire dialect of English.

Gil was able to follow along well enough and he was certainly able to recognise his name. "Yes, I'm Gilbert de Biron. Do you have a message for me from him?"

"My name is John from up Hathersage way, best man of the woods about these parts. I had it from the band over, that they had it from the band beside them, that Robin bides in the homestead of the Owens' with Creirwy and Brynmor in the vale above Tryfan. If you cannot find it ask at Capel Curig, you know the place, with the password: legs. He says it will mean something only to you."

Gil pressed his lips together with immediate nostalgia when he remembered them teaching each other new fighting styles, and Robin telling him that Normans never watched their legs after stealing Gil's boot dagger.

"Thank you, John of Hathersage." Gil was touched that this man whose head probably carried its own bounty had bared himself before a lord such as himself. "Thank you for taking the risk to deliver this message so honourably. It's important information to me."

John grinned. In so doing he revealed some colourful teeth in need of maintenance that you didn't tend to see so much among the Welsh. "Oh, I didn't take so much of a risk. I have seven arrows on you."

His eyes did a quick anxious scan of the tree line. "Well, be assured I mean you no evil." Fearing John would melt back into the greenery as stealthily as he had arrived Gil quickly kept talking. "I didn't even know you were here." It was embarrassing because it had been exactly like this when Robin had taken him captive. Gil had flattered himself that his time spent on the road had increased these senses in him, but it appeared being back inside a castle had awakened his dog senses and put his wolf one's back to sleep. The mourning inside him was sudden and deep. Like a hiraeth for a state of being he almost

378

tasted. "Well, you obviously don't eat much. Perhaps I could send you on with a small gift for your troubles?" Gil asked, rummaging in his purse for some coins.

The man's eyes did not seem to convey enjoyment for Gil's half-humorous approach to giving him permission to poach, or the offer of coin, that much he could still read a lot better than he once did. Unwittingly he had hit up against a wall of pride in this man. It was different to the Welsh way of doing pride, more unyielding than fiery. "There is, and can be, nothing between men like you and men like me," he said, before going away as he had come. Presumably, as the best man of Hathersage and surrounds left, the arrows trained on Gil also withdrew, but the barb of the final statement lodged in him and lingered far longer than his forest's resident outlaws.

# 5

There are Norman soldiers… on the road coming here!" Rory cried, coming back to camp at a run.

"How many, and do they wear the crest of any house?"

Rory shook his head, bent over leaning his hands on his knees while he caught his breath. "Their surcoats did not show a crest but they are cavalry soldiers not ordinary mercenaries and they carry crossbows. I think there are about two-dozen of them. Behind them at a rapid pace, appearing to gain on them is a carriage pulled by four expensive looking horses. It is black, the horses are black, and it appears to bear the crest of a noble house, yet still the distance is too great to see which crest."

"Could it be the De Biron colours?"

"Could be. Hope so. The black on black gives me hope."

"How great is the distance, Rory? How much time do we have?"

"Three, maybe four miles away?"

Robin nodded rapidly and gestured for Rory to follow him back to the camp. It didn't take much for his people to be on high alert. They had seen running and already everyone had stopped what they were doing, put down their breakfast, their kettle mending or cleaning up the site and replaced it with a bow. "Bring the caravans up into defensive position. Put up the canvases between caravans to limit visibility. I want everyone who can use a bow to arm themselves with our best archers at the arrow slits in each caravan. Sariah and Eilish, I want you to gather the children and nursing mothers into the centre of the caravans."

"Not inside?" Eilish queried.

"Not at this stage. Clear the caravans for defensive action."

"What's cooking, Hob?" Sorcha asked. "Who's trying to shit on us now?"

"Rory's spotted two dozen Norman cavalry about three miles out carrying crossbows. They have behind them a single carriage with four in harness."

"It's surely Gil come back then," Blaith said, sheathing his side arm in a determined manner that suggested he would not be deterred from joining battle should the need arise. "I feel like Gil is here," he said again, more confidently

"I certainly hope so," Robin muttered. It was encouraging anyway, as the Magister's intuition was one of the things he most trusted. And then, projecting his voice again, Robin added: "Bring the horses in as tight as you can, preferably inside the defenses. I want them there in case we need to get the vulnerable out."

In some ways this was no different to a training exercise. They had prepared in this way a number of times only for the situation to come to nothing but a false alarm. He passionately hoped this was one of those occasions. The gentle mist and songbirds of the morning was too lovely to sully with bloodshed. It still hurt to draw his bow on one side from his last injury. Eilish had done near magic with the way she'd removed the arrowhead and cleaned up the mess of the impact wound. Still, nothing in his body seemed to feel like it did before he was attacked, not his right hand, not this pulling feeling in his shoulder.

"Alright everyone. Let's hope it doesn't come to this, but if shooting starts you need to remember the crossbow can shoot further, so we will be in range earlier than we're used to. They aren't going to be anywhere near as accurate as the standard English bow, and they will only be able to fire off one each in the time our archers can send off ten. Stay a bit back from the walls of the caravan as these bitches hit hard and save your arrows until you're sure you've got a shot."

"This doesn't sound good," Bran said. "Should we really let them get a chance to surround us?"

Robin nodded grimly; he had been thinking the same thing. "It's not a place I like to be, but I'd rather be surrounded with a defendable caravan formation than be chased down on the roadside in a disorganised route. As you often remind me, we have children to think of and we will cover their retreat with our own bodies if it comes to that. We also have our bows and they will have a lot of trouble crossing that distance from the tree line to here without many casualties. There are no Cymric bounties on my head, nor are we guilty of anything this side of the border. If the men of the hills and homesteads of this place spot them this far from the Marcher they are as good as dead. For now, we just need to do what Gwynedd men and women do best - stand our ground."

"The men at arms must have ceded the road to the carriage," Sorcha observed from her peephole around the canvas barricade. This triangular way of parking was designed to give their potential enemy as little visual information about how many of them there were or what weapons they wielded.

"How do you know?" Lux replied. She could barely see that the carriage was at the lead at all as Sorcha's distance sight was stronger than hers.

"Rory said the carriage was at the back but now it's at the front. Which means one of two things, either they are one party travelling together and have changed formation, or the carriage belongs to someone of a superior rank, forcing the others to cede the road."

Lux had learned a lot about ceding the road since she'd been travelling with tinkers. The rule of thumb was to cede the road to everyone, thus cutting down the chance, through immediate submission, of being searched or threatened. She also knew how deeply Blaith despised doing so. "Do you think it could be Gil?"

"I damn well hope so," Sorcha muttered. "If it isn't him then meeting the bully the other bullies pull over for isn't on my agenda."

Other than at Nanette this was the first time Lux had her arrow pointed at other people, but she wasn't afraid. Her gut told her the seemingly unlikely

story that these forces were friendly.

"They are flying De Biron colours!" Robin confirmed from his position. Unsurprisingly it was his eyes of all the far-sighted Twll Du folk who saw the furthest into the distance and spotted the crest. "It must be Gil."

"Or Nanette," Sorcha added more pessimistically. From what Lux knew of the Saxon woman's pre-liberation history, one that had ended with her tied to a tree and left for wolves or men to devour, it wasn't surprising she was cautious.

"Nanette is dead," Blaith said, from behind them with his eyes shielded against the sun. "My death mole has returned home to me; he has burrowed true."

"Because that isn't sinister at all…" Sorcha muttered as if to herself.

Lux grinned and suppressed it. She too always wondered about his death mole, somehow just never quite enough to venture asking.

"Well, I hope you're right. I'd much rather be entertaining Gil than an insane Norman noblewoman who tried to drink our Hob."

Lux shuddered at the evocative comment that placed her right back there in the blood-slippery wagon where Nanette had tortured him. She focused instead on watching the carriage approach and taking note of her gut feeling and its veracity. Finally, she too was able to see that the guards who flanked the carriage were indeed wearing the De Biron livery with the 'Trust Biron' motto. The Latin gave Lux a wry smile. It applied quite nicely to their dealings with Gil, but not so much to Nanette, and perhaps somewhat obliquely when it came to Augusta.

Nanette was dead. Lux didn't consider that to be an 'if' or a 'maybe'. Blaith was confident and she had no reason to mistrust his Seeing or his maleficium. So, with her death what did it mean that Gil had made such an attention seeking gesture as to bring his carriage with its visible crest and all these men at arms wearing the colours of a Norman house into enemy territory? Lux had come to know Gil, and this wouldn't simply be an act of miscalculation or pointless bravado on his behalf.

When the carriage drew close Gil, dressed in a dark scarlet jerkin with a black cloak got out. Robin went quickly to him. "Well met, brother!" he cried, pulling Gil close and wrapping him in his arms. Gil's affection was equal, warm and intense. "It's damn good to see you!"

"And you!" he said in Norman French.

"You received my message then?"

While they spoke this in a language foreign to all except a couple of listeners the wardens eyed the men at arms who milled around on their horses. It was hard for them not to get twitchy around mounted Norman soldiers.

"Thankfully. My sister's Will contained money for a hit on Blaith and yourself. This, it appears, was the retribution she threatened would come to your family in the event of her death. We have got to you first, thanks be to Our Lady, and to Augusta's quick thinking."

Lux couldn't help appraising Gil, despite her gratitude for his saving Robin's life. She took note of the fact he rightly accredited Augusta with the value of her own actions, rather than trying to claim her ideas as his own as so many Norman men would have done. Augusta appeared then from behind him, and Lux saw her in her full Norman noblewoman, rather than the tattered noblewoman mask she'd tried to piece together by wearing dirty clothing every day in the past.

This face was polished, and just like Gil's whole appearance it was an act of theatre. The space between them felt like miles and years. Once Lux would have felt less-than in her simple homespun and suede boy's clothes, but such ways of seeing things had melted away a little more every year in the thaw after the winters she'd now weathered. Changing, she had learned, was an alchemy as much accomplished upon you by the elements upon the body as it was a matter of cultural immersion. The winters honed a new person that grew under the ice, only to plump up each summer and become stronger every year. The old person just wore away like the leather on a much-used pair of boots. You started to think in those terms. These were Lux's third pair of leather-soled shoes since she had run.

Yet still Lux entirely understood what Augusta was doing, and how she had to stand partly inside the heart of the corruption to do so. As someone who had also managed to jump free of the belly of the beast and still carried its marks upon her, Lux saw and sympathised with Augusta. She had come out of her sufferings as a woman with a lot more control over her life than how she'd gone in as a girl. The fact she was here risking everything caused a tenderness to arise in Lux's heart that hadn't been there for Augusta since before she'd found out about Clarice's murder.

"We have a plan," Augusta said, not moving to hug anyone, but all urgent determination and business. "Will you trust me, Robin? Or should I perhaps say, for he has done more to earn it, will you trust Gil?"

"*Crede Byron*," he replied. "It says so upon your coat of arms."

Whatever happened between men in battle Lux knew it must be a strong and fast glue. Her beloved really loved this man he had become as a brother. Her Uncle Jack said that when men go to battle together a whole universe passes between them. They have already saved each other's lives over and over again, risked their own to do so, and seen the other's heart and courage, all in one frenzied bloodletting ritual.

"Tell me your plan."

"When they arrive we pretend to have just captured Blaith and yourself with our own forces. We claim the bounty on your head, but we tell De Bracy's men they may keep Na-"

"De Bracy?"

"Sorry, Robin," Gil said, looking at Augusta as though she'd been mildly insensitive. "Thus is the unexpected evil in all this that I would have thought beneath even my sister. She left the execution of her wishes in De Bracy's hands as an incentive to him to seek revenge for his cousin's death. I don't know if she knew of De Bracy's part in your aunt's murder or not, but it is shabby and it shames me."

"I see," Robin said very quietly. "But the shame lies not upon you."

Augusta didn't apologise, she pressed on. "Yes, Mother was an evil bitch.

Gil is always shocked. But if Gil pulls rank De Bracy will have no leg to stand on should my uncle refuse to hand over his prisoners. With me here as Nanette's daughter we should be able to carry the day without bloodshed."

"I prefer to win without bloodshed where I can," Robin agreed. "Worst-case scenario they don't go for it and decide to fight us, which is what would happen anyway without your plan. Just don't try to make Blaith kneel or anything, it will be more trouble to you than it's worth. If you need to make an example of someone to subjugate with your lordly authority, I suggest myself."

"Understood. But for the record I liked it better when you were kidnapping me."

Robin laughed. "Good times. Alright, come to our fire side, I need to explain all of this in Cymric before my people explode with the not-knowings."

Hob repeated everything very faithfully and honestly to his people in Welsh.

"How is Blaith reacting to the plan?" Gil asked during the translation.

Lux smiled a slightly curbed sort of grin. "Well, I can tell you one thing. He said that if you are going to take him prisoner, he demands anal violation. So, I'm reading that as a yes."

Gil made a snorting, partly choking sound, which was also related to a burst of laughter. "Good gods!" he murmured under his breath.

"Indeed!" she agreed and winked at him.


There was laughter, music, and the sounds of making love in the air, just as Gil remembered it. The caravans had pulled back further, closer to the homestead of the Owens family, deep into the Twll Du family's support base where there were numerous men at arms who could reinforce them. This meant it was safe now for them to play music again. There were few things about being with the Twll Du clan Gil loved as much as when they sung and danced and laughed... Everyone among them felt free to access this exuberance, even the elderly. There were no servants looking on in want whilst others enjoyed pleasures and privileges, all were allowed to reach for their own joy. Gil hadn't

known he'd disliked privilege until he'd experienced its absence.

People served each other in all different ways in their culture, yet everyone's service was judged equal in dignity, and none were shamed for their post, even the greatest warriors among them didn't think it beneath their dignity to wash out their own food bowl. He had so missed the full-souled quality of this life-way and his own vitality thrilled to the beat of this return. There was only one thing left to deal with before he would feel he had come home fully.

He waylaid Robin who smiled and came to him flinging his arm around his shoulders as easy and unselfconsciously as if they were young boys, friends since birth. "There you are, brother! You appear to not have a full mead cup for what reason?"

The De Birons had brought with them a few kegs of mead for the clan, along with some other luxuries the Twll Du people had apparently been scarce on. This again had been Augusta's idea, as Gil could only focus on getting there quickly to make sure Robin and Blaith were safe. Like Nanette, the girl was smarter than him, something he was seeing proved over and over. The relief from deprivation of mead, milk of the poppy, and hashish had made their arrival suddenly a lot more popular than it might otherwise have been.

"It's only that I'm feeling a bit Norman in this get-up. I wonder if you've got a tunic I could borrow?"

"Ah…" Robin murmured looking Gil up and down. "I don't know, I think you look handsome in this deep scarlet colour. It is good with the dark, brooding De Biron thing, no? But if you want to change I think your height is closer to Blaith's than mine. You should go to his tent." Robin made a slight, almost imperceptible gesture with one of his eyebrows that Gil couldn't help reading something suggestive in. Perhaps it was Lux's translation of Blaith's frank request for bound arse violation that put these ideas into his head that he couldn't seem to silence?

"Ah… Well…I'd love to go to his tent. It's just with us not speaking the same language how would I ask him?"

"For clothes?" Robin's eyebrow cocked up again. There was something

in its surface that concealing a subtle directness that Gil recognised as part of male-on-male flirtation. It was if this potential sex act with Robin's brother somehow erotically involved him also. "I think if you just go in there and start taking these ones off, he'll work it out."

Gil hesitated again almost tripping over himself in his desire to say something witty or dignified, something that might save him from appearing like an absolute virgin. Robin came quickly to his rescue – or something like that. "Oh for god's sake, Gil. Just fuck my brother!"

Gil made a light choking sound that was converted into a cough, something he found himself doing around these people a lot. They talked about the unspoken and coupled it by doing the unspeakable, as if every sin and the collective view of society felt as light as air to him. "Do you think… you then… I mean… that he… likes me?"

"It's fair to say the courtship is well established. You gave him your face rag, which is Norman for flirting; he reciprocated by presenting you with your enemy's head, which is Twll Du for flirting. Now I think comes the bit where you put your cocks in each other's mouths?"

Again, Gil was left with his mouth slightly open, as though in preparation for the very act described. Normally trying to determine interest and organise an encounter with another man had been fraught in stress and broad hints, followed by a sweaty palmed fear he'd read the signals wrong. "Gods I wish I could stay here…" The words were out before sanctioned, but they were safe with Hob, he felt.

Robin rubbed his back, a warm, supportive rub that combined understanding and sympathy with firmness also. "Come on. I'll get you a tunic. If you want to wash your Norman off there's some hot water over the central cauldron. You can use the soap and basin in my tent. Wait -do you most like to fuck a man, or be fucked by him?"

"Dear gods, Robin, you remember I am new to even talking about the things I do?" Gil cleared his throat and gathered himself. "Both, I suppose. I like both. Equally enough."

"Good. He is the same. Off you go then, go take your Baron of Rochdale face off. And Gil?"

"Yes?" he asked, turning around.

"I see the risk Augusta and yourself took in coming here for us. It will not be soon forgotten."

Blaith rolled over and gazed blearily at the new figure. A few people had been in and out of his tent that night, but this wasn't any of his regular lovers. Always interested in adding novelty to his taste for intense long-term devotions his ears and other parts pricked with interest. It took a moment or two before he recognised his visitor, changed as his appearance was since arrival. Blaith smiled as he lolled there, one arm behind his head, sizing Gil up as much as welcoming him. He was just in the mood for a man. "Ah… It's you," he said. He spoke in his own language even though Gil wouldn't understand. It was a pointed decision. If the Normans were going to be in their land, and in his bedroll, then they would do so under a shower of Cymric words.

Gil took his shoes and weapons off at the door like a good Twll Du lad and said some incomprehensible things back to him in Norman French. Blaith signed at him to be quiet and beckoned him down onto his bed. The pile of skins and cushions brought together for the convenience of various sexual positions also allowed Blaith to be half sitting up. When Gil kneeled down next to him Blaith saw that he had bathed and changed out of his dark red and black. Blaith was mildly disappointed, as he had been strangely turned on by the taboo violation of wanting a man dressed as a Norman lord.

"You have taken a wash," Blaith said, running his fingers through Gil's faintly wet hair. "Yet I have been cum on by a lot of people since the wash I had a few hours ago. In the spirit of fair warning… You can't understand a word I'm saying."

They both laughed together, as though intuiting a mutual difficulty with remembering the other couldn't speak Welsh or French respectively. Gil responded by saying something that had a charming sound to it but was utter

389

nonsense to Blaith's ear. Robin could always remember languages absurdly quickly. Blaith instead had been blessed by both a lack of aptitude, and an even stronger lack of interest. Languages and lands were one for Blaith. The world was deeply drenched in Cymric so that the only other language he'd ever really been an expert in was body language.

"I think you should just take your cock out," he said, gesturing with his same beckoning finger gesture to the front of Gil's trousers. Seeming to understand but be weirdly awkward about it Gil undid his belt and buttons before presenting Blaith with what he wanted to see. Why did he act so nervous in presenting it? It was a fine enough cock. Blaith made a sound of appreciation that probably crossed the language barrier and took it in his hand. He delighted in how rock hard it was, his own being just above half-mast after a strong earlier workout.

What was perhaps more compelling was the reaction his touch generated in its receiver. Gil's response to having his cock touched was, Blaith judged, that of someone who had not been stroked so in a good while. Such signs of neglect always brought out tenderness in Blaith. To be without sex and touch was as dire to him as being without food or shelter. This lord indeed had lived poor. *Found stumbling in the wilderness with a chronically under-cared-for cock.*

"Don't worry, I work around my teeth well," he said, before taking Gil in his mouth. The half-gagged sound Gil made when Blaith's lips closed around him confirmed it had been some time since someone had performed this act for him. It seemed he might ejaculate almost immediately until Blaith used his hands to flatten Gil out, sort of forcing him to release his shoulders by pinning them. This involuntary proneness of his stomach muscles prevented immediate climax. One of the primary qualities in a candidate for Magister was a blend of the skills of a warden and a maiden. He was an expert in the sexual arts of unraveling that the maidens specialised in, whilst also being one of their most skillful guérilla warriors.

Feeling the needs in the muscles Blaith brought his hands up under Gil's hips, fingers seeking to enter him and deepen the base level of his sexual re-

sponse to include his arse. Reaching over to his bedside Blaith took out an ointment often used to aid in the witch's spirit flight, but in smaller amounts for visionary sexual encounters. Blaith was of the go hard, or don't bother going there at all, school of thinking. He had no understanding of the term 'just physical', as there was no divide between the body and the sacred for him. He showed the ointment to Gil who sniffed it and nodded though it was unclear if he knew what herbs he was consenting to.

Gil's entire hip cauldron surrendered to Blaith as he worked the flying ointment up inside him with his fingers. It took so little effort it was barely a warm up, but it was clear he was already bringing Gil to his peak. Did men where he came from not use their fingers? Blaith felt a little sad that such was Gil's current holding capacity for joy. *Well, stay with us a little while, my handsome Norman, and we will stretch you out a bit.*

Sex wasn't all this rich man was starved off. Blaith found that offering him skin-to-skin contact, holding him chest to chest was craved almost as much as the release Gil had already once experienced. Turning Gil over onto his stomach Blaith lay atop him like the presser, the nightmare that weighs more than the last hour before dawn. As he knew he would Gil sighed deeply and relaxed into that pressure. Very soon afterwards he was getting his arse fucked by Blaith and they were both feeling the effects of the ointment. Blaith was well practiced in how to vision whilst fucking without skipping a beat, and he rode over another of Gil's orgasms, a deep shuddering one this time, it felt as if Gil were the broom he was riding.

Contagiously relaxed Blaith sensed the collision between their houses in a calm sort of way. Only for a second did he see St Michael and the dragon bite each other. The blood threads in an ouroboros swelled between them, a billowing connection between their chests where their respective creatures of darkness had their dens and emerged from whence to prowl. Their ancestries were dancing together on their skin where not only Blaith's fluids were mingling with Gil's but now traces of Sariah's, and of Eilish's had been pushed inside Gil too. Eilish was about to birth Blaith's baby any day now and had

wanted him to fuck her into labour, which he had had a very good go at. To share the Virtue of that coupling represented a particularly magically charged intimacy.

He couldn't tell Gil all this, of course, but Blaith knew the Norman sorcerer and himself both spoke the old witching tongue, so one could rely on communication via under-earth water caverns and channels invisible to the naked eye. Even if daytime Gil didn't know, the creature he was becoming as the ointment stripped him down to his witch knew.

"May I come in?" Augusta asked at the tent opening. Her hair was uncovered and a bit disheveled, a privilege of the wild she had bestowed upon herself, yet she was still dressed the same. Their initial greeting had been a little stiff. This was altered now because Augusta had consumed a generous number of mead cups.

Lux's initial instinct about admitting her to the The Bower was one of hesitation because Jack was still Uncle Jack to Augusta, and he was inside the tent with Sariah having a robust encounter. Would Augusta even be ready to comfortably view him as a sexual being? The close living conditions they all shared made inhibitions of this sort impractical, and so Lux had begun to unlearn them like everyone else. Often Robin wanted to make love in situations where their closest loved ones were nearby.

As Jack travelled in the Ama caravan, she had to stop thinking of him the same way, and he her. Yet her memory of her inside-the-hedge-self and her inhibitions was still strong and clear. This meant sometimes it was easier for her to understand forms of repression that Sariah didn't. Often, they would have to brainstorm about some of the newer members to get a fully idea of how to nourish them. "Welcome, Augusta. There is a basket for you to leave your shoes and weapons."

"A fair enough call really, I probably look like someone who might be concealing a dagger."

"Well, I would say 'concealing a hidden dagger' is your entire noblewom-

an aesthetic in a nutshell." Whereas before it had felt like a drop away from her progress to go back to speaking Norman French now Lux was confident in her Cymric it felt a little fun, in the way nostalgia can be.

"I want to say it's a look I adopt for self-defense, but in reality I've never once felt safe enough since I went back *in* to not have a hidden weapon on me somewhere. The Norman world is a nest of vipers and quite frankly there are some privileges a woman can be given that she will never willingly be able to give up again afterwards."

Lux reached out and squeezed her hand. She didn't say anything though because she couldn't. The truth was Lux would have destroyed herself to avoid falling back into the belly of the beast and whilst she sympathised with Augusta she couldn't exactly altogether empathise.

"I just saw Eilish. She looks like she's about to burst down the middle, poor thing." Augusta shuddered theatrically.

"Yes. I hope the baby comes soon." Lux didn't need to mention the fear. It was an unspoken fact among girls that every woman who had to make the crossing at the birthing wall might not come back down again. Just as violence was the leading cause of death for the men in their life, childbirth would be one of the most perilous moments for them as women. "The birth is somewhat overdue."

"I am glad to see you haven't yet been so encumbered."

"No, thank the gods." Lux didn't mention that they took a lot of measures to make sure they didn't conceive. "There is the question of just how much faerie blood one really wants one's child to have and-" She paused considering whether the next thing she'd been going to say could be read as insensitive, but Augusta seemed to guess what it was and nodded.

"And what if it turned out like De Rue? What if you and I are the delightfully sweet anomalies in a line of evil bastards, but our children start pulling the legs off puppies?"

"You plan to avoid it too?"

Augusta sighed. "As sole heir to my parent's fortune, and as your father's

widow, I now own what should have been yours, as well as what was to be my brother's. I am officially Gil's ward because, though old enough to be married against my will, I am not old enough to manage money… Normally he would manage my estates for me, but he allows me the graceful illusion of independence. So, I am in a good position. I would be insane to ruin it."

Lux nodded. As a widow Augusta could have some semblance of sovereignty over her life.

"One of the perks of being a widow is not being in possession of an intact maidenhead. No one has any way of tracking my sexual activities."

"As long as you don't get pregnant."

Augusta looked at her with raised eyebrows. "Now, who said I was planning on using my freedom with men?"

"It is time I do more for your inner boy," Robin said. "The witch flight finds its way into our dreams best through the arse where the seat of the darkness bides." While he spoke he lined her up with where he wanted her to stand.

"Would you still want me if I was physical a boy?" Lux asked.

"I don't understand. You are a physically a boy… And physically a girl. It is in your nature."

His fingers in her arse agitating the flying ointment, activating the dark magic of the herbs. After being to Blaith's tent she really relaxed into what he was doing more deeply. She let the waves of the ointment take her as surely as he was. He made her wait for it. In waves of vision she had cock, cunt, arse, tits, every sexual part that is human. Lux became the ultimate abomination the people inside the hedges feared, she was the boundary-crosser, the fleet-footed hedge leaper, a key made for no earthly lock.

Then the alarm horn was sounded. Realities folded over each other, tripping, overlapping and inverting leaving her trying to pull her pants back up from around her ankles.

"Fuck!" Robin cried, immediately he was on his feet and doing his trousers up, putting his weapon belt on before Lux had been able to connect with

her current first name. If that meant she had to start moving it was going to be hard whilst she could still taste sound. After he pulled his boots on he crouched down and took her firmly between his hands. "Everything will be alright. Just get to Jack, alright? I have to go!"

With that, he was gone, and Lux could only listen for a time while she tried to reground herself in her body the world had told her belonged to a girl. She caught snippets of words through the distortion of reality that had entered her rear end and was tunnelling deep into her hidden parts, moving backward against the current like a toad bone, telling a story that declared a being-hood for Lux that was more than the world had granted.

A few of the family looked uncertain about seeing their Magister and First Warden in bonds, but the boys seemed to be taking it jovially enough. To Lux's altered vision, the two brothers appeared like a couple of shirtless cheeky satyrs playing a prank. Indeed, Lux had been around long enough to know Hob and Blaith could have those ropes off in seconds if they chose, as escape from capture was literally child's play in their clan.

The voice of the messenger came through the hailing cone with great projection. "We have reason to believe you are harbouring the known outlaw Robin Goodfellow known to be guilty of abduction, murder, and horse theft!"

"That's actually pretty insulting. I am guilty of so many more things than that," Robin stage whispered. A few people giggled at his gallows humour.

"Hand them over and you will not be harmed, otherwise my lord will be entitled to use force."

At this she heard a horse ride forward and people jostled for position to see what was going on. Lux saw Augusta sitting Gil's huge black stallion like the proudest noblewoman that ever gave command. As she rode out into the field, probably closer than was safe, she reminded Lux of a dark warrior queen from times of old, as if she should have ravens on each shoulder.

"She is within range!" someone protested.

"Yet *she* will not be fired upon," Blaith muttered darkly.

Augusta didn't seem to need a voice projector; her voice was neither high nor particularly deep yet it thundered out into the night carried on the wings of her self-assurance. "My name is Augusta De Biron, daughter of Nanette De Biron, sole daughter of the Earl of Leicester, and widow of Lord Geoffrey De Rue! My Uncle, Lord Gilbert De Biron, Baron of Rochdale is here with me and has captured these felons ahead of you. He claims their heads by right of rank. The money paid De Bracy is his as a gift of goodwill of our house to yours, and this is for your troubles!" Her horse pawed the earth as she sent him forward, flaming torch in one hand and a large purse of coins in the other.

Lux started to look around for Jack. Instead, she sighted Gil, still trying to drag his clothes on, his pupils giving away to Lux that she wasn't the only one to have received rectal flying ointment. He was good though. His veteran status gave him a kind of self-ordering faculty in an emergency that excelled her own. Within moments he was mounting, but it was upon Augusta's mare rather than his own destrier, which amused Lux faintly in a way difficult to describe.

"I am Gilbert De Biron!" he declared, following his niece onto the field, his family broadsword catching the light at his hip. Somehow, he just swung back into his role, every move they both made performed a perfect theatre of status and voice projection. "And I have here with me the miscreants Robin and Blaith who have done so much harm to my family and our name."

On what looked like a prearranged signal, Robin stumbled with his hands tied behind his back, his back to Gil, who kicked him down onto the ground with very realistic force. The fact Lux had had Robin's shirt off when they were making love and he hadn't put it back on yet just added some extra spice of degradation to the pantomime of male bondage they were acting out.

Lux made a little involuntary sound at seeing Robin fall, before reminding herself of the tough warrior rapport of men who had fought together on a real battlefield. Gil would know how to kick him so as not to do serious harm, and Robin would know how to fall to make it look worse. "I demand that De Bracy release his claim! As we have seized these men with the understanding

396

that no harm is to come to their family and our word is our family's honour."

There was a long, drawn out tension where Lux held her breath. Then to her amazement the messenger withdrew in the face of their rank-pulling, saying he would inform his lord. As the buzz of danger in the air began to subside Lux found herself looking down at her unlaced boots, and then back up at the rotating stars that had began to appear like a silvery revolving palace. Finally, she looked around her at the other people, and her eyes went to them first. Gil, then Blaith, Sariah, then Jack, and Robin. Somehow, they were the only ones standing there for a while, as if the spirits of the plants in the ointment had carried them to a different ground, a flat dancing ground up high in the witching mountains of the north.

# 6

Sariah was relieved Eldri was with them on the path leading up to the Twll Du birthing wall. The elder was unique among their blood thread in having lived to be seventy-four, old enough to remember the Harrowing of the North. It was her tales they had grown up on, stories of coming outside one day to see what appeared to be a whole line of children and women with babes in arms running towards them framed against a flame ravaged sky. That is what is looks like, she used to say, when the Normans have been through somewhere. Eldri had only been a child herself, but she would never forget their blanched pale faces and their eyes that told wordless tales of horror.

Aunt Eldri still fought with stick and could easily make the scramble up to Twll Du. She was almost as fit still as Sariah was herself. After a whole life lived on the road, she got up everyday at dawn and proved she wasn't too old to shoulder a pack that weighed the same as those of the younger women. She insisted upon it, even when the younger men would attempt to offer her chivalry. Sariah remembered how this elder maiden of caravan Arva passed her the old adage that on the road you were soon for the crows the day you realised you could no longer shoulder your own pack.

Eldri had caught hundreds of infants, both for their women and those of strangers and had seen every complication. Everyone said that if she couldn't deliver safely no one could. That is why people would say Robin's mother had indeed been unsaveable. She had officiated the day Sifanwy died bringing him forth, and she said of it that never had she seen an infant so stuck and un-turnable as Robin was unsuited to his mother's birth canal. Eldri was the last

mother-to-daughter descendent who claimed a direct distaff line back to Arva, and she never had a daughter. The silent tragedy of this lineage death seemed to walk with the older woman, giving strength to her legs on the track. For when she could no longer shoulder her pack then Arva was no more.

Sariah also had dozens of live birth babies to her name and had faith in her own ability to deliver a normal birth. But this child was different. If it was a boy he represented the only male child to be born of Blaith, who was himself the only son born to the Magister, who was born of a Magister, whose father was also Magister going all the way back to the time of the *nadredd* men. If the child was a girl she was daughter of Eilish who herself was daughter of the last mother-to-daughter descendent of Ama. In either case the baby was a lineage carrier, and if those strings snapped, a lineage death. And such reddened and whitened story threads, weaving through their blood thread carried great imaginative impact for their people, if that happened Sariah feared the beginning of a hope-death among them. A person and a whole clan could die of a hope-death.

It mattered terribly to many of them both that Blaith was Garet's son, but also that an appropriate person for the job kept being born as sons to those men. If the lineage fell out of step – such as if one such only son were born simple or otherwise unable to serve- then they would know the Virtue had slipped out elsewhere to the side. So far this had not happened, except for a daughter serving as Magister after her brother had been so and her father before her, with her brother's son stepping into the role upon her death. The lineage stories continued to produce the right souls drawn out of the baby soul lake. These two lineages hovered over Eilish as well as Sariah's lives, carving out a deep personal commitment.

"It's alright, lass. Just breathe. Breathe and rest. Every woman I've ever seen do this had to rest. Even Caer Eileen."

Sariah could tell this encouragement from Eldri carried great weight with Eilish, who immediately burst into tears of release and leaned against the rock to have a strong wave of rising birth rush over her. It was upon this bearing

inward that her waters rushed from her almost in a hissing release of pressure. They filled her boots first and then covered the rock at her feet whilst a primal sound came from the depths of her that made the hairs on the backs of Sariah's arms stand up.

Sariah rubbed the small of her back while it was happening. It was a good thing they were almost up to the cave as things would speed up considerably after a big water release like that, you could tell by the change in the sound she was making. Eilish felt the urgency too, and as soon as the contraction passed, she began to steadfastly climb on, as if she hadn't just been in enormous extremity. Even whilst following her and walking behind her to spot her and protect her from falling, Sariah's heart swelled with pride in Eilish. She was always in awe at the courage of the women she'd seen take on this sacred discipline, as giving birth was enough of an undertaking in many cases. She knew them as proud warriors, just like their men, and she witnessed their quiet heroism.

As harsh as the custom seemed to outside eyes it made sense for those living as they did. Eldri could still make the climb because she was still capable of living wild, and she was still capable of living wild because she could make the climb. What chance did a pregnant woman or a new mother have on a Worst Day like the people of the North had the day it was harrowed, if she couldn't at least climb to a high spot to save herself and her child? When the wardens say 'run with the children' that doesn't always just mean running, it could mean run, ride, climb, fight...

Sariah shivered. There was an eerie prescience that ran across her skin. Something shimmered before her, a certain knowing of threads and paths where she felt Eilish and herself go down different roads with this choice of motherhood or no motherhood. One day Eilish would run with the children in a circumstance where Sariah could not.

Parenthood contained its own kind of sacrificial dignity in their world, as they had all been raised on hero parent stories. Of mothers like Robin's who had chosen to die for their baby. Of mothers who had run while pregnant as if

possessed by the spirit of Macha and somehow made it to safety before dropping to their knees in the undergrowth, their birth brought on by the trauma, to give birth alone with a stick between their teeth. Of the women who had, with their baby in arms somehow found the sheer endurance and pure determination to outrun and outlast their Settler pursuer.

There were stories of the fathers who stood their ground and fought as long as they could to buy that woman the time she needed to save their child. And there were people still alive, precious people, and whole lineages in their clan who only existed now because of such parental courage.

Was it something about the column of unearthly mist that was forced up from the deep below into the sky by the Devil's cook pot that had her thinking of such things? Sniffing the air faintly Sariah narrowed her eyes as she looked back over Ogwen Vale and the blanket of mist they'd climbed up through already. There was something she smelt on that wind; you couldn't put words to it exactly. But in the face of it she suddenly wished Blaith were indeed with them. Fathers, when known, were normally present at a birth, except when the labouring woman was a maiden, in which case usually only other maidens or elder maidens were present.

Her longing for Blaith was more ethereal than practical; it was for his protection from the wraiths that moved in the seeping shadows, threatening to block out the sun. Everyone knew this land had bad as well as good story-threads in it. It was haunted after all, soaked in coagulated fetch, sticky with old memories. The Romans had murdered the people before them in huge numbers all around here, pale ghosts moaned among the rocks. Cancelled stories echoing forth with desirous tongues, slavering for a last chance at meaning.

The smell of burning sweet herb greeted Sariah, mingled with wood smoke from the blessed fire of Saint Bride just like the sacred fires of her childhood. She knew Emrys had climbed ahead of them and had been getting a fire going for Eilish, but he would have left already and would be guarding the way. Sariah suspected he had volunteered for this role because he was Eilish's lover

and whilst he wasn't the father, he loved her very tenderly.

Eilish went inside the rock shelter and immediately was seized by another birthing pain. Sariah let her lean hard on her and squeeze her hands until she couldn't feel them anymore. Afterwards they took her to the spot where she would stand against the birthing wall during the last of her travail.

"She will feel stronger now," Eldri said. "Having her hands in the prints of the foremothers. I remember that relief, after each of the climbs."

There were worn grooves there, probably the product of the elements, but some of them looked like hands. The old stories said that once there were clear handprints, faded but still visible, but they had worn away with time. She could tell from the way Eilish was swaying that Eldri was right, and she was immediately in deep communication with the Mothers.

"I think give her a little space for a time," Edri said, as they built up the fire. "She's still battling to pull the child soul out through the cave wall, I haven't felt the life rush in yet."

Sariah had been present at this, one of the most holy of rituals, since she herself had first bled as a woman, so whilst not herself a mother she had seen a number of women pull a life through. It felt like a sudden hot flush in the faces of all the women present. A few of them she'd even seen do it here in the Holy of Holies. But none of those women had been Eilish, her childhood companion and partner in everything from crime to love, and those few times where both came into play. This birth felt as significant as if it was happening to her, and she knew she couldn't be entirely impartial when it came to sensing good or bad signs.

Eilish moaned quietly and swayed, her hands holding the hands of all the Grandmothers who felt these pangs before her. Sariah guessed that the hairs were standing up on the backs of her arms as they were on hers, as the deep resonance of the cave's unique hum reverberated through her own womb and out into theirs.

"While she journeys, I'll let the spirits use my tongue," Eldri said. The older woman was a much-respected oracle when it came to spirit possession.

402

"Thank you, Aunty," Sariah replied. "I want to hear the voice of every whispering and wailing thing and what it has to say today." She came closer so that Eilish wouldn't hear. "I'm not altogether comfortable with the way the wind feels."

Eldri snorted and nodded. "Indeed, indeed, girl. Our people have got enemies out there walking, talking, spirit walking, talking shit, scheming... coming back in... coming all over again...In blood tides..."

She had already begun to go into the awenyddion state. Sariah knew there was nothing much to be done now but to heed her as though Fate Herself were stirring and murmuring from the abyss below.

It didn't matter that sometimes the wardens would talk while on watch. They always spoke in a certain signature way –interspersed with long silences and sometimes falling quiet mid-sentence to signal turning both of their attention to sniff the breeze and listen- Robin had an easy rhythm of this going with Jack. He would always glance over at the older man and see if his eyes were open. If they were, he wasn't too deep in the listening state, and if he wanted to converse he'd pass Robin his mead flask to sip from. Tonight, Robin received the drink.

"You're worried about Eilish and Sariah being out there, aren't you?"

"I'll own it," Jack said, punctuating with a protracted silence. "I understand it's your people's way. It's just... it's a dangerous place. Emrys is a good fighter, so is Sorcha, it's just... well, it's a dangerous place."

Robin nodded to himself. They had become very close over the years and in fact Robin felt closer to Jack in many ways than he did much of his own blood kin. He sighed. "This life is a dangerous place. *Making* life is even more so. I fear more harm to Eilish from the birth-giving than I do from them making their own way up the Twll Du path."

"It's a hell of a scramble."

"Eilish is one hell of a woman." Robin raised the mead in her honour for a moment before passing it.

"That she is, my friend. That she is." He accepted and sipped from the mead flagon. "I barely got up there with my dignity intact myself, and I'm not working on pushing a person out of my crutch." Jack laughed at himself and his turn-foot limitations.

Robin smiled affectionately. He preferred the company of men a bit older than himself. He liked the way ego wore away in them over time, like a hard rock face exposed to wind, until they could truly laugh at themselves and had nothing to prove anymore. Older men became gradually more carefree about reputation and posturing, and became again their boyhood self, with added patience, less black and white certainties, and a certain wry humour.

"It's a hard one to understand about our people. But you would have about as much luck trying to convince one of our pregnant women not to attempt that climb as you would getting Blaith to stand down on a revenge he owes to slain kinsman. The life we live is hard. Only the strongest babies thrive and end up walking the old crooked ways with us. We choose freedom whilst others choose ease. This is Eilish's hero moment. She does it for the strength of an idea, and at the end of it she brings home life. I just cut up and shoot down a lot of mother's sons." Robin shrugged.

They both listened to the movement of the air in the leaves and to the shriek of a fox. Some bats passed nearby, disturbing the air. Whatever unsettled the darkness the forest animals didn't know of it. There was something there though, something listening, it just wasn't anything human, or at least if it once was it was no longer. "Aye. Yet the warrior deals death so that others might live. His eyeballs eventually feed the battle hungry ravens so little babies like Eilish's don't get their heads dashed out by Norman thugs. Though I would always take a birthing over a killing if it were up to me."

"This is why we're friends," Robin muttered.

There was something so ancient it was macabre about the vision of the old woman framed against the rock face, possessed. Eldri's deep-set eyes were rolled back so far Sariah could see only white. She rocked back and forth in the

coiling fog until foreign voices rose from the depths of her throat. Sariah had attended Eldri during visions since she was a girl, before she was a developed seer herself. So she didn't need to ask who this ancestor spirit was who rode the elder maiden, she knew from voice, from the look of the way Eldri's throat tightened before releasing, from details no outsider could have spotted. It was known and introductions were an unnecessary formality.

"Beware the shade of the one-legged woman," said the strange yet familiar voice through Eldri's slack lips over the top of her strong protruding teeth. She was an old one this one, old as Arva, and she made the mouth she was talking to appear differently, to be shaped like the faces of the most ancient of ancestors and to sound hollow inside like their mouths.

"Is it Nanette?" Sariah queried, but the spirit riding Eldri did not confirm, but continued on as an awenydd utterance usually did.

The spirit reached out one hand that suddenly seemed claw like and grabbed at Sariah for greater emphasis. "Walking as a curse whilst she walks no longer!"

"Are Eilish and the babe safe?" There was a desperate edge to Sariah's voice. The end-knowing in Blaith's body, received during visions on the higher mountain above them, had seeped through to her from so many touches, so many exchanges of fluids, that she sometimes knew things about him he'd never told her. He had never told her, but this feeling that their culture wasn't going to make it had been a bud tight in her throat before this labour, now it was a fully blown flower of sorrow that seemed to throb open like Eilish's womb-mouth.

Eldri's body jerked backwards, Sariah steadied her. "Old blood and new blood mixed together. This is the only way we survive. It was the only way then, only way now…" Her voice trailed away then, as though the spirit were confused or simply inundated by so many rising visions and shapes that no simple words would form for a time. "Just like for Elen…"

"But today, what of today? What of the child and Eilish?" Sariah prompted.

"Choose!" The spirit's voice rumbled in Eldri's throat like a far off storm coming. "Choose with your head, or choose with your heart. No one can do it for you. The heart choice is long... Long winding threads I see them... Spinning out for a long time... consequences... The dance of the heart takes longer but is stronger. You must pilgrimage to the moon-well, scry for a vision of the future there, as the maidens have done before you or else the thread will break. I can't see beyond that."

The sounds Eilish was making changed then, like a thunder that has circled and circled and now begins to zero in on the place you're sheltering, getting ready to pound the caravan around you. Sariah got up and went over to the laboring woman. Eilish had now gone down onto her knees and was panting rapidly. "I think I have it!" she cried out, in between the ever-closer waves of birthing extremities. "I felt it in my hands, a white ghost full of liquid, cold like a fish." The power rose up on her again and she made a sound of intense pain and effort.

"I'll get Eldri."

"I have to push it out right now! I fear I'll burst!" There was fear in Eilish's voice. Sariah had witnessed this moment many times. Right as the woman teetered on the edge, their body about to give way and have new life crash through it, they would shudder and hesitate, almost wanting to back away before the big drop ahead. This was normal, wasn't it?

It seemed the spirit left Eldri in one long shuddering out-breath. Even the dead ancestor woman knew it was time. Sariah took a deep breath. "You have been so brave, Eilish. You've got this, and I've got you."

"Alright, lass, let's do this, it's time for your baby to arrive." Eldri began rolling up her sleeves.

For the first time Eilish stopped staring forward at the birthing wall and made eye contact. When she did something passed between them. It was the result of a bond since girlhood, a jolt of knowledge about things they owed each other, things you couldn't explain to any other. Sariah knew Death. She shared a bedroll many nights with one of his earthly representatives, and she

knew from the piquant sensation of the whole back-story and forward-story of this bond that she was standing in His dread presence.

*This must be what it's like for them*, she thought. The patients Eilish had worked on over the years that had screamed, arched their back and fought the treatment and the stitches even whilst not meaning to. Or the ones like Robin whose eyes glassed over and they mainly just trembled and sweated silently through most of their torment.

They weren't travelling together anymore. She was gripping the spirit women with white knuckles and holding onto them like a child holding its mother's skirts. Sifanwy was there, standing with the other nameless, blood-skirted, unremembered women who gave their lives in childbed. It never occurred to her to break contact with them even when she saw they were the ones who didn't make it. Her hands remained inside the faded prints of Those Who Went Through This Before. There was a buzzing in her ears as of a thousand bees and the invisible threads of things became tangible. She could sense a threat looming power all around her as if even their sacred fire were blotted out to blackness.

When the pain came this time it was white-hot and blanched the space between her eyes. Out of that whiteness the mist came pouring through the gateway in the rock, and she heard them coming... The heathen dead were riding iron-shod horses but they were eyeless. She shivered. There was a rollicking, feral music coming on behind them, like bag-pipes with the crashing of pots and pans and the clinks of chains. The mist smelt like history and old blood when The Company of the Mist arrived. Strange red-eyed hounds whimpered at the heels of their mounts.

She gasped, but she'd no sooner done so as another burst of hot pain struck her like a jolt of electricity and whitened out the image. Eilish cried out and reached for the hands of her people that she knew must be there. Next, she reached for her baby, but her baby slipped through her fingers as the fish would when she was a girl learning to trout tickle from Sariah's father. As soon

as the contraction was ripped away like a wave backing out to sea, leaving the sand eroding under her feet, Eilish could see again.

She could smell blood on tartan, the wet wool of it, the iron and horse sweat. Ever since she was a girl she'd known the story of the gore-smeared tartan of Elen of the Hosts. It wasn't hers it had been made up of the plaids of her slain brothers, but really it belonged collectively to the manhood of Wales slain in resistance to the Roman Invasion. Elen was the ancestrix who had taken the bloodline of Beli Mawr forward into Roman times, but she had carried for life the bloodied tartan of her brothers.

During those dark times the Roman Legion had driven whole families into the sea and forced them to drown or come back up onto the beach and be slain. Official history remembered nothing of the massacres except that they were done. Elen had revealed in vision the images of the bodies of women and children bobbing about with the tide, one day when Eilish had been staring into the water near here. Eilish could feel the hands of the other women lost in childbed but not her living kin. The ancestor woman seemed so much more real than the living did.

Eilish thought she would tear apart now. Some of the power released from her in a low, lingering groan. The sound was so low it must have been pulled up through the stone floor. It came with the rumble of cave lion and bear ghosts that were remembered by the rock. It came with the wail of hyenas following the blood trail of the dying. The wave that was building now was so strong the anticipation made Eilish break out in a sweat. Before the pushing began Eilish felt she heard Elen of the Hosts walking with her, murmuring. "Sometimes the sacrifice asked of us is survival."

Augusta sat up fast and heaved. There it was again, the vomiting of a thousand spiders dream. This time she fought off the furs and rugs that lay on her, pushed her hand hard over her mouth and went for the tent opening. She didn't care if she vomited in her mouth and had to swallow, by whatever powers were holy Augusta swore she would not spill the venom of that dream in-

side the camp. *Dear Gods, but she is in the mead vats I took from her storage room and brought into camp like a Trojan horse. She's the infection. She is the spiders…*

Once she was sick, she would ask them to get Blaith and confess to him. She would throw herself upon his mercy and ask him to exorcise her again. The urge could only be held off for so long, she felt the hot sweat of it take her brow and she vomited between her fingers, just managing to keep it from hitting the ground in her palms until she was outside the glow of the fire. Once it was happening and she was on her knees she let herself acknowledge the full horror of the feeling.

"Are you alright, Guss?"

Jack had been so quiet on his approach that she jumped when he spoke. For a man with a limp he moved with disconcerting stealth.

"Ah… yes… I mean no… too much mead I suppose." The words felt bad in her mouth. Why was she trying to lie to him?

Jack crouched down beside her and offered her what she hoped was a water flask, as she feared she would vomit again at the sick-sweet smell of mead. "I can understand why you'd be scared."

"What do you mean? I'm not scared-"

He snorted. It was the kind of exhalation that alone seemed to refute your entire point, and a few you hadn't even bothered to try yet. "The thing with bullshit is," he said, after a weary sort of sigh that carried the weight of his years. "It's really good with people who you can bullshit to. Problem is, I'm not actually one of those people. This isn't my first passage between bullshits."

"Fine," she snapped, getting to her feet. "Just, spare me, alright? You are right. I am afraid, I'm afraid the curse is come upon me."

"Blaith pulled it off you once he'll do it again."

"What if they were wrong to, Jack?" she cried. "What if they were wrong to trust me?"

"Only you can answer that, lass. I'll tell you one thing though; you show your loyalty best with honesty. Any deception… well it might make people start to wonder if it's got the jump on you. If you try to spin it, bind it, and tie

a ribbon around it, *it means you aren't winning*."

"Well, here I am telling you! Trying to win! This is the third time it's happened. I dream something, then I vomit."

"What do you dream?"

"Tonight, I saw Nanette as this dark mass hovering over Eilish trying to crush her baby. Lying hard upon her like a nightmare upon the chest. In the dream I tried to pull her off, but when I grabbed at her she pushed spiders into my mouth."

"Thank you for trusting me with this, Augusta," Jack said very seriously. "I am going to have to take this information to Blaith and Robin immediately. But I promise you, if you just keep on trusting me, trusting us, if you just keep *telling us*, we'll fight this together, upon my honour you will not be made a scapegoat."

The pain was so complete she was weeping constantly now. "Save my baby!" she would cry and then alternatively: "Help me! Oh gods make it stop!"

Eldri pulled Sariah aside. "I have not felt the baby's breathing-soul enter which usually happens right before a live birth. This stage is taking... has taken... too long. I have done this many times and I would not lie to you to soften the blow. You are First Maiden and you will have to make the final choice. But from what can be told through examination I believe the child will not quicken at delivery."

Sariah nodded once decisively, that was enough for her. She went back over to Eilish. "I'm going to make it stop now, Cariad."

"No!" Eilish wept in anguish. "Let me die instead! You have to, Sariah... Let me die! Save my baby..." There were only a few more words that made it through her pain. "He's Blaith's only... We would not have Robin..."

Tears ran down Sariah's face. In those two short phrases she heard all of Eilish's humanity and her courage reflected like a huge light driving out the shadows on the cave walls... *She is in the most pain she'll ever be in. She's on the bridge between the living and the dying... And these are the two things it comes*

410

*down to for her, the reasons she would give her life for an infant's that might not even still be alive... Because it's Blaith's son... And if Sifanwy hadn't died for Robin then...*

All these two reasons did was to reveal in clarity the sweetness that was in her cousin's soul at its raw centre. Robin always said that you knew someone for who they really were at their moment of greatest extremity. There would never be another Eilish. Not if Sariah chose this unknown foetus over her beloved. "The baby is already gone, sweetheart. Robin was not," she murmured, tenderly wiping back the hair from the other woman's forehead that was wet with perspiration. "And if I don't save your life right now, I will never forgive myself. Blaith will never forgive me. I don't even need to ask. I know his heart."

It wasn't the first time Robin and Blaith had done the Twll Du scramble by night, but it hadn't been since they were boys training in the mountains. Twll Du was only about halfway to the larger Glyder they called Caer Gwynt – the Castle of the Winds. The Magister was expected to go alone to the top of the Gylder Fawr regularly to hear the winds whisper prophecy. Blaith fulfilled this part of his duty regularly, so neither the fitness aspect of this undertaking nor vision in the low light was a problem for him. When alone he would climb and sit among the sharp spines of the dragon's back to listen. Some days he heard nothing except the ancient peace of the great beast whose back he was upon, dreaming.

Other days the wind would talk to him and tell him about things about the future. Upon Caer Gwynt Blaith had been told he was the second last Magister of the Twll Du blood-thread, and that he'd never see a live-born son. For this reason, he hoped Eilish was birthing a daughter. For well he knew that when it came to birth there was nothing he could do in an emergency that that powerhouse of an elder woman, Eldri, could not. Blaith preferred not to appear at births. Things he'd witnessed at his brother's birth, when he was four and lost his mother, were part of it.

Both of them had taken their shirts off and stashed them because they

knew how much they were going to sweat doing this scramble and near run. Neither of them spoke, as even Robin needed all his breath. Nor did they need too. It had often been said that the two of them, whilst filling up two separate flesh vessels, were designed for each other with a synergistic harmony that could only denote a decision of Fate. Sometimes they scrambled side by side, or one at the front, though they never knocked or bumped each other, seeming to know exactly how the other's body would move. Ever since Jack had told them what Augusta saw in vision barely a word had been spoken between them.

Since they entered the sacred precinct, they only used words once, when Blaith's foot slipped and Robin caught him immediately. Briefly he felt both the dizzy rush of space below and the strength of Robin's grip, as though the two forces tussled in the air for a moment. "I've got you." The moon was almost full and as she rose the path became clearer and surer. Below them them the lake was a black chasm, above them Twll Du –the Black Cavern – loomed.

"Please!" Blaith panted. "Go to them. I can see clearly."

"Absolutely not," Robin replied.

It was like that between them. Blaith was in charge all up until he tried to put his own life in danger and then his younger brother suddenly became in charge with utter ease. In the face of it it was easier for Blaith to force himself on, back to a near run, leaping and scrambling, than it would have been to argue with him through panting breath. By the time they crossed the little trickle road that delineated the inner point of the sacred ground his chest was burning and it seemed almost impossible to get enough oxygen without coughing spasms.

Finally, his eyes fell upon them. These girls that he'd run with as a boy... The vast amount of everything to him was standing here with him in this cave. Robin over took him at last and went to Eilish. Though she had been sitting when she saw them she tried to stand. Hob reached her just as her knees were about to let her down and scooped her up into his arms like a child. "It's alright, we're here," he murmured to her, as he took her down to the ground in

his arms by the fire.

Blaith went to Sariah as Sariah went to him. "What happened?" he murmured in icy dread as he embraced Sariah's body that convulsed with sobs. All she could do for a long time was shake her head. In response to this most easily translatable of responses he nodded his own. It was as he feared, he had a son... Looking over her shoulder he was able to see the still, swaddled body of his first-born child. "Was it a boy?" he asked.

Sariah nodded. "I had to choose!" she wept near his ear. "I had to choose the baby or Eilish. I had to use the tongs because she was dying. I'm so sorry, Blaith!"

"Don't you dare be sorry," he murmured brusquely, giving her a hard squeeze that was the gentler cousin of a shake. "Not for saving Eilish! There could be no question. Absolutely no question." He held her tight to his chest. He who had taken more human lives than he had count of, and she whose hands had not until today been asked to do so. Their life experiences were so different in this, yet his compassion for hers was fathomless.

As one they went to Eilish who Robin still had in the pose one might rock a child, her head against his shoulder. What an image of tragedy and triumph it was though... It perhaps would take Blaith's eyes, who could always see the profound and the hidden aspects of things to see it. Here was a woman whose homespun gown was covered in her own blood, having narrowly survived birth, in the arms of a grown son of a Twll Du woman who had given her life for him at that very spot. With them all crowding protectively around her as she wept.

Eldri came gently to them with the child. "Blaith, cariad, do you want to hold him?"

Blaith pursed his lips together to control them from shaking and blinked with tears in his eyes. "Yes I do, Aunty Eldri. Thank you."

They sat there together, the woman snatched from the jaws of death, the Magister with his stillborn son in his arms, the woman who had chosen the path of the heart, and the young man whose mother did. Nobody spoke, yet

413

all knew they sat with the future, and that it had never taken its first breath.

"Down weapons for Lux as acting maiden!" Emrys said loudly.

Immediately all of the wardens stopped what they were doing, moved from where they were into a one-knee position with their weapons out on the ground. They were trained to respond to the presence of one of Our Lady's messengers of mercy the same as to the presence of the Lady herself.

She couldn't help noticing that Bran was a little out of sync with the others and moved a fraction slower to offer his blade. Silence fell on the debate they'd been having. As Lux looked around at the focused self-discipline so well expressed in their perfect stillness and immediate silence the hairs stood up on the backs of her arms. She knew herself to be in the presence of a cult practice full of ancient power and for a moment it was hard to speak, something that had grown strong through many hard centuries and could potentially be as unyielding as the flint in the earth around them.

"What do I say?" Lux said, turning to Emrys because she was unnerved by their utter stillness. "You can… please… stand… you can all stand."

There was a pause before anyone did.

"Oh, I know I *can*, Lux," Bran said, getting to his feet with his aggressive little language lesson. "That is the imperative in Cymric, you should say it: if you see well."

"You need to take some of that aggression down when speaking to a maiden, Bran," Rory said, taking two steps towards him, with body language that didn't seem to aid in diffusing the situation. "Unless you mastered perfect Norman French recently?" Whilst half Bran's age the young scout had a fiery side like all of his brothers. Meredith's closest relatives had held a grudge against Bran ever since the night of the attack.

"That is enough from both of you!" Emrys thundered, losing his temper quite suddenly. His voice reverberated off the rock in a way that cut the air and everyone fell silent. He was a bit of an all or nothing man, Lux was learning.

"Augusta brought their evil into our camp, she head-butted our Magister

414

in the face!" Bran's son Ethan started it off again.

"The *demon* that was on her head-butted him, not the girl." Jack objected, firm but gesturing with his open, palms out hands in a way that was attempting to calm the situation. "If we can stick together around this we can make sure it never takes hold of her again, we can run it to earth, and see that rank curse in the ground in our own lifetime."

"Don't expect that to be the last violence she brings in," Bran added ominously.

"So, is that what we've come to is it, burn the witch?" Jack asked, his arms folded across his chest in a gesture both resolute and refusing to take seriously any threat of violence from the younger men. "That easily, we who are ourselves different, we turn upon the Other?"

"There's witches and there's witches, is all I'm saying," Bran replied.

"If there's violence at the camp this night it won't come from Augusta, it will come from me because Bran can't shut his toxic fucking mouth!" Rory shouted back at him over a cacophony of raised voices. "Is it not enough he's hurled dishonour in the direction of my brother's memory?" Rory pushed Bran in the chest.

"Oh, come on, Rory," Bran replied mockingly. "I'd sooner hit back my nine-year-old daughter in a play fight than I would damage your pretty features."

Three other wardens including Jack grabbed Rory and held him back from attacking Bran while he struggled. Jack and Emrys seemed to understand that much of this blind fury was streaming out from the loss of Meredith and they tried to sooth him. But Bran mocked him by sitting down casually with his arms crossed to indicate his lack of fear. Lux realised that more shouting from Emrys or even reasoning or admonishing wasn't going to restore harmony in this situation.

Quickly she ran between Bran and Rory and held her hands out. Rory stopped struggling as soon as he saw her in the middle. She took stock of the fact that the young man was outraged about his dead brother, but he was also

415

driven by compassion for Augusta and very loyal to what the maidens stood for.

"Sorry, Lux," he muttered between clenched teeth. "It's just that man! He said… before you got here… he said…"

"What did he say?" Lux asked.

"Typical," Bran muttered from behind her.

"What›s typical?"

"Hearing his side first. It's pretty obvious what's going on here," Bran said. "You're one of Blaith's mother coven, and Blaith was with Meredith, now Rory is part of the clique. You all only listen to each other."

"That's rubbish," Emrys said. "Blaith and Robin listen to everyone, as do Sariah andEilish."

Bran snorted with contempt. "Says another of the inner circle. When you get your dick back out of the jar Eilish keeps it in I'll listen to you. Once again, you're here because you're bedding someone from the mother coven… That's the only way to get a say in anything around here."

"How could you?" Lux burst out without her own permission. "How could you speak about Eilish like that while she's up there soaked in the blood of your blood?"

"I agree. Don't talk about Eilish like that," Jack said, stepping up beside her. "She deserves better from all of you. She's stitched the half of you back up a time or two."

"Agreed," Emrys said, triggering an impromptu stepping up of other loyal men that brought tears of emotion to Lux's eyes. "Don't disrespect her."

"I won't hear it."

"Nor I," said Rory.

Unfortunately, the effect of the peer pressure on Bran, the fact that even some of his usual allies thought he was out of line, was to cause him to double down on his error. "She's hurt and she's a brave woman, but it doesn't get Emrys his dick back."

"You sound just like a Norman." Lux hadn't really considered what the

416

impact of what she'd said would be on Bran, it just sort of happened in and out in some faerie, truth-speaking way.

"Take that back!" he growled at her.

Immediately she wished she hadn't said it because Bran was suddenly on his feet and the way he moved towards her with his eyes narrowed made her legs feel like water. He became De Rue for a second. Instinctually and through old habit she cringed and raised her hands defensively preparing for a blow. With the rush of old fear and childhood imprinting she reacted far more strongly than women birthed Twll Du.

Rory reacted instinctually to her fear. Much like Meredith in his agility he moved too fast for Lux to follow as he struck Bran in the face. Bran staggered back two steps from the punch with blood running out of his nose. Lux thought she saw him try to take a swing back right before Rory roundhouse kicked him in the side of the head, taking him straight to the ground.

"It's not the size of the dog in the fight, but the size of the fight in the dog! That's what Meredith used to say." Others came to drag him off. "Did you hear what he said to me?" Rory was shouting as they pulled him off. "Lux! Did you hear him tell me Meredith was to blame for his own death? If Robin were here he'd kick the shit out of him sideways for saying it! You fucking coward!" He spat in Bran's direction as he was pulled back.

Bran's supporters were yelling back at Rory and Emrys was trying desperately to shout over everyone else to regain control, but just not managing to pull it off. A spirit of aggression boiled over. Something shifted in Lux. It was the same unexpected thing that had erupted from her cringing form on the night she'd bitten deep into De Rue's hand and kept on biting determined to feel her own teeth meet.

With a sense of quiet purpose, she climbed up onto the high ledge above the eyrie. It was treacherous up there, slightly damp from where the frost melt dripped down on either side of the jutting rock where the watch fire was set up and stark night looming below. She went up above them in the dark and out onto the slippery rock with the confidence of a cat on a fence. It was a few

moments before she realised they'd all fallen silent. When she turned toward them all the wardens were looking up at her and nothing else at all.

"Lux, come down!" Emrys called up to her. "The rock is slippery. It isn't safe."

"What are you doing, Lux?" Jack called up to her.

She merely came closer to the edge. Rory was first to move to climb after her and get her down but she held up her hand to stop him in a calm but firm no. He hesitated. His warden training told him to get her down, but his instincts recognised her authority.

"Please, Lux, come on down," Bran said, sounding almost contrite. "Robin will never forgive us if we break you while he's gone."

Lux waited for silence to fall again and held her position, teetering on the edge of the darkness. "I am Lux Ferch Agnes," she announced. "Child of Ana of the River of the Heavens, vessel of her liquid starlight and daughter of Shining Ones. I come among you triumphant over demons of hate and fear. I crush them under my heel as Our Lady pressed the serpent, as a strong waterfall may crush a man. But I come before you as one of the Twll Du bloodthread. I will die fighting beside you for this way of life!"

As these words came out they were so true her voice cracked and tears began to flow. She pushed on. "I will fight with my teeth and nails if I have to! To the very edges of the earth, even if there is no hope!" she was sobbing now, but it felt right, it felt like what needed to happen. These were an emotionally rich and vivid people who would not trust fully when they could not see the heart clearly. "I would run with your children in my arms, I would take an arrow for them, and I will never give up!" With that Lux decisively turned her back to the edge and held her arms at her sides.

"Lux no!" Emrys cried out, seeing before the others what she meant to do.

She closed her eyes as she felt it all playing out. Quite suddenly she allowed herself to fall backwards into the air. Her arms flopped out to her sides, her body stayed almost straight in the trusting way that only drunks and toddling children usually fall. There was a collective sound of shock and horror in

the background. Then a weightless rush where this time it was her death that brushed up against her and nuzzled close, before she felt herself caught by the deft and numerous hands of her wardens.

Opening her eyes as she lay there in all of their arms she smiled as she saw Rory and Bran's instinctual cooperation in the act of catching her. They just stared down at her for a couple of moments. Bran shook his head. "You're one crazy bitch, Lux Dhu," he said, wiping the blood and sweat off his face. He laughed and it broke the tension. "And I respect that."

Seeing the softening in him she reached out for his face and touched it. "You caught me because you're my kinsman, Bran," she whispered, not moving from her prone position. "Because you're a good man."

As she got to her feet she made eye contact with Emrys and saw that he was nodding slightly to himself with an odd sort of smile as he looked at her. She had a strong sensation of having passed. No one had come up with it as a test, of course, and yet it was all the same.

# BOOK 5

# 1

obin leaned across the bar a little further in a gesture that clearly encouraged his barman friend Liam to do likewise. He knew he probably smelt of forest smells and horse sweat after his day, but the publican smelt like stale beer, so he figured he hadn't a right to complain. "What is the real talk about the presence of my people's caravans in these parts?"

Liam sighed and looked away for a brief time before looking back. He was known to Robin for his honesty and as far as he knew the man had never passed him false report. It was also clear to Robin's rather astute judge of character that whilst honest, this man was likely no hero. He would give Robin the truth until it became too risky for him. *Few men get grey hair from being a hero.*

"Well, there are some folks who say… just the common sort, you understand? Not the real rebels, the run of the mill people. They worry that the caravans are causing the comings and goings of more Normans."

Robin nodded. If they had caught wind of De Bracy's messenger's incursion into Cymric territory or the De Birons he could see how people would associate them with Norman attention. Though Gil and Augusta had wintered back at Rochdale their exit before the real snows set in had still meant another sighting of their carriage on Welsh roads. "Fair enough I suppose. What else do they say?"

He scratched his unruly white hair while he thought about how to put something. "I've heard tell that someone died exactly in the way a black sorcerer among your people said he would die, after the same time frame, that has some people jittery."

"Alright, sure, that part's true too, but they did pay him to do exactly that… What else do you have?"

Liam shrugged as though there was no accounting for his countrymen and their concerns. "People are saying things about some of the women that travel with you. There is one whose dancing some of the wives object to."

"I bet," Robin grinned. The goodwives of Ogden Vale objecting to Sariah's dance moves only made them sexier to his mind. "And the other woman?"

"She is the Norman who calls herself Marian when she talks in public to disguise her origins. The men, and any great haters of Normans who want Welsh freedom, object to her talking to audiences of women about female insurrection. And it being a Norman girl what said it too."

"I see," Robin replied, rubbing his stubble thoughtfully. "These desirers of Welsh freedom only want it for our men folk? They imagine to be born free from the womb of a slave?"

Immediately Liam held his hands up in submission, drawing his coward's weapon as fast as a warrior might draw a sword. Robin had a feeling he understood how the publican had lived so long. "They are not my words nor my sentiments, my friend. No not at all. Good luck to the women folk, I say. My wife'll have my hide otherwise."

*And you'd say the opposite too if someone applied pressure, including your wife.* "Well, I hope that the people will forgive my caravan's devilish tongues and hips for long enough for us to see out the last of the frosts. We have only tarried so long because my cousin's birth ended in the death of the child and her injury. The Twll Du blood thread does not like to wear out its welcome in any one place, believe me." *Just like how you move on when a camp starts to stink it's the same with the presence of The Ignorant.* He paid the man handsomely for his information. The coin had come out of the purse of a wealthy but inebriated fellow by the door, so Robin could afford to be generous.

"Please don't take it ill, Robin!" Liam called after him.

Robin just waved and left. He would only have been able to take it ill if he had believed in a possibility of fraternity between his people's ways and

424

those of hedge-bound folk. He'd known he was of the people of the outside all his life, part of a bloodline who would be forever turned away to wander like Cain. Ah well, he thought. *The Owens' property has allowed us a soft time when we most needed it. It allowed Eilish to birth at Twll Du and for the child's bones to be returned to Llyn Ogwen. We avoided some English battles. And while we were here, we have dropped some disturbance into the pool of their everyday lives, we have spread some feral seeds and set some minds and trousers racing. What more could you want in return for three years of being someone's pet saviour figure?*

Part of him resented Crierwy and Brynmor for the sedating effect of their hospitality upon his people more than he'd resented Owain and Cadwalladr for sending him to war. Robin exhaled heavily into the frosty night air and watched the vapour evaporate. Greatly did he love Gwynedd, but he had to admit whilst he looked up at the stars and charted his way back to camp by them, he was ready to taste the freedom of the road. Now with Eilish able to ride again, and the villagers beginning to sharpen their pitchforks, spring could be smelt on the breeze, and it was a good time to be on the move again.

Jack found Hob leaning beside the door with his arms folded. It was a common posture for him when waiting. Jack smiled. Robin was brooding as if he had within him one unanswerable question (not an answer) of only one word, but that word would be lightning, setting fire to the old order of things. When he looked up, caught from his reverie, his eyes held a depth that had no right to exist in a man just off his mid-twenty.

The six winters and a bit they'd spent together on the road had brought Robin into the full prime of a glorious manhood, but it had brought Jack closer to fifty than forty. Each one of those winter frosts had left a new ache in his bones, increasing his halting gait. Yet Jack had never yet felt so alive or thrilled to the returning thrum of the spring.

Robin didn't smile as with no explanation he ushered Jack inside. Robin at nearly twenty-five was a sterner, more reserved creature than eighteen-year-old Robin. Today they were not alone. Blaith, Sariah and Lux were seated around

the stove, the two women on the short stools used for spinning and Blaith was reclining on the pallet across from the fire.

"This looks dire," Jack remarked.

"Not dire, just important," Blaith said, his dark eyes appeared to excavate you. The Twll Du Magister never looked *at* but looked *into* you. "It is a meeting of the officers."

Jack looked behind himself. "Last I checked that sure as hell didn't include me..."

Robin took a seat on some sheepskins on the floor so near Blaith that they were almost touching and gestured for Jack to also make himself comfortable. "A First Warden has the privilege to include his second in any councils regarding clan safety."

"But Emrys is usually…"

When Hob shook his head, it was in the decisive way he did sometimes that often worried Jack. It meant the young man was hell bent and there was no point in any council on the topic. "A fighter's second is the man he trusts most to have his back and to carry on his fight should he fall. Emrys is a great fighter and a good man who won't be alive if I fall. I know because he fights after the same style as me, never disagrees with me, he has no different ideas to me, he never challenges me on anything. He has no knowledge base that I do not also possess, nor experience outside of those I also share."

It was a devastating assessment, yet Jack couldn't argue with a word of it.

"My old bones though, Hob… I'd still take most of these young pups at stick, mainly because I can take a thumping. But I'm not going to live through the fight that puts you out..."

"I disagree. I see a man at the full flower of his experience, as well as land and history knowledge. Resourceful and quick witted enough to stay one step ahead of the grave for double my own lifespan. I doubt I'll be around for that long, so I want one close by my side. Besides," he grinned and suddenly when his eyes twinkled, he was as he was when they met, barely out of his boyhood. "You are the warden whose company I most enjoy at the watchfire."

426

Jack was deeply touched, so much so that his eyes misted up a little. That had been happening to him more often as he got older. They were the rich type you shed when you smell the turn to autumn on the breeze or witness the maturation of one you knew since they were a child, tasting with the change the bitter-sweet knowledge that it brings you closer to your last laying down.

"Will Eilish not be with us?" he asked. The subject change was a gentle form of acquiescence. It was also because Eilish was one of his closest friends and confidantes. He felt the loss of her baby and her grief viscerally.

"She isn't ready. She has asked for Lux to attend as acting Second Maiden in her stead," Sariah said. She was wearing the grouse foot and amber broach that had belonged to Robin's mother Sifanwy, and the ancient silver bracelet. Of the symbols of her office only the girdle at her waist was partly unique to her. Jack knew the story of every item of jewelry on Sariah, and every cord and bead in her braids. Such it was to truly become part of a coven.

His gaze jumped across to Lux. The young woman's myth was still ascendant but had taken a great jumpstart that winter. People were talking about her now, this new person. Tonight, she was dressed in a long white tunic over white hose a boy might have worn. Jack perceived the growth of this androgynous, Other, presence in her and it unsettled him in some way he couldn't name, as if it were dangerous.

"It is not just Hob who will be appearing with a new second. Lux will be working with me a lot because Eilish has decided to try for another child," Sariah murmured. It was evident Sariah had complex feelings about the idea of Eilish pregnant again. Lux reached over and rubbed her back briefly. It was low enough on the back that it revealed them to be lovers.

"It is known to me that I will never see a live born son," Blaith said. "But Eilish is a lineage carrier also in her own right along her distaff line, so I can do no other than give my blessing," Blaith said.

"Eldri brought through a foremother prophecy that I'd have to choose between them. I killed the baby to-"

"You didn't kill anything, Sariah," Blaith interjected.

"He's right," Robin added more softly. "I examined the little fellow for traumas, and he was strangled out by his birth cord. What you did to ease Eilish was post-mortem, I promise you."

"Thank you, both of you," Sariah said. She reached out and they squeezed her hands. She had tender eyes for both of them. He knew that Robin and Sariah had a history of light playing, which usually implied performing oral and manual sex. Not only did Jack know all these things about his inner circle he found he actively wanted to share Sariah with Robin.

He knew how good she was at what she did first hand, and he still suspected Robin had wounds, mind wounds, that could do with the attentions of an experienced maiden like Sariah. This form of intimacy with multiple people, in all different forms —such as the desire to share a woman with a man you did not wish to bed yourself- was new.

"I mean that sincerely. With Robin's knowledge of the body and Blaith's of death there can be no doubt that I believe you. But the intent was there, my intent was to kill for Eilish, and so in my heart I did. My hands have taken a life now, and it's opened a new darkness in me. The prophecy Eldri uttered said my heart's choice would lead to a long road, but end in success. Even if there is not a Magister born from our Magister, I believe in her word that there is still a path. I must journey to the Moon Pool and scry there. It is imperative that we take all of the centre with us."

Jack hadn't heard Sariah talk like this before, except when she spoke about her certainty of Robin's victories in battle. There was a quiet, unyielding surety to her, as though she'd undergone an initiation into this darkness she referenced.

"Let us make it a choice," Blaith declared. "The centre will prepare immediately for travel. Those who wish to bide here in the shadow of Tryfan may do so, those who wish to be a part of the work may join us."

"A wise decision," Robin replied. "To cut off before it starts the disagreements about whether we should go or stay. My source says ill-speaking about us is on the rise, the sort of gossip that usually presages the beginning of the

harassment. Most of the talk centres on the people sitting here tonight. So the centre being absent should allay it a bit."

"What do they say?" Lux asked. No doubt Sariah didn't need to ask, and Blaith didn't care to.

"Only that we are too powerful, too insightful, too dangerous, too sexy, and too free for their little village and minds. Much as they always say, and always will, no doubt."

# 2

obin had asked those who wanted to ride with him to meet with their packs and their weapon of choice. He'd done so partly because he thought it good practice when heading into a war zone, but also to make it clear that everyone knew what they were signing up for. It made him thick in the throat to see Sariah and Lux standing there with their bows on their backs and resolute expressions on their faces. It made his eyes mist with fierce pride. He felt it again when he saw Eldri there with her stick on her back. The pride in his eyes met the pride in hers and they nodded at each other, though his was closer to a bow. Respect for this veteran of the road, who stood there with her weapon on her back ready to die wild, moved him to full running tears.

He didn't wipe his face as his eyes scanned along to Eilish who appeared to be dressed in her surgery apron and only holding her doctoring kit. Her face looked pale and her knuckles clutching the handle were a shade whiter again as if she were gripping it for life itself. He went over to her and placed his hand on the side of her shoulder with a reassuring grip. "Is that your weapon, sweetheart?" he murmured quietly to her.

"Yes." She laughed at herself but as she did tears came out. "I thought about it, what we're doing this for. We're trying to be who we are to the end? Well, I've spent most of my life saving lives. If there's fighting going on out there that's what I'll be doing, staunching blood, stitching wounds, giving pain relief… That's what I want to die doing. Just like you want to die on your feet. This is dying on my feet for me. And if there's people out there who won't respect my apron marking me as a non-combatant then… then…"

Robin blinked away fresh tears because her goodness broke his heart and he was sure he would never recover from this moment. "Cariad, where we are going there will be people who will not respect a non-combatant…"

She nodded. "I know," she sniffled. "My doctoring kit has fast acting poison in it with which I could make swift end of myself. And if I must fight in defense of the innocent, my dagger could be laced with it so I needs only manage a scratch against them."

He could tell she was terrified, but he respected her too much to show how it affected him, so he swallowed the rising lump in his throat. "Your medical kit is your weapon, then." It cost him a lot to give her this sovereign right to choose how and in which manner she wanted to face death if necessary.

As he stepped back and looked around, he saw mainly bows and sticks. Blaith was alone in being almost covered in sleek throwing knives. The custom sheaths in his leather trousers built to hold blades were full across both thighs. His boots were loaded with knives, there was another two longer ones inside each of his sleeves which he could draw at once by crossing his arms over. Robin knew that when his brother fought he liked to travel light. Jack, who was the opposite, had his hefty quarterstaff.

The oldest was Eldri at seventy-four, the youngest Zorien at fourteen. The inclusion of both Rory and Zorien meant their party now contained all of the remains of Aunty Henwen's bloodline that Meredith had also been part of. Robin acknowledged and took on board the weight of it. The people who had chosen to be on the road included no children, all of those gathered here could climb, run, and when necessary, fight. Jack was alone in being unable to run, but this fact alone told Robin he'd had to learn to fight well enough that he seldom had occasion to run. The only surprise in any of it was Gladys, there without any of her children or Bran, wielding a stout cudgel. Robin went over to her.

"I'm surprised to see you separate from the family to come with us Aunty Gladys."

"Magic is something we can't afford to compromise on, First Warden

Robin."

He winced. His parent's generation had tended to use the name for their roles such as: Magister Blaith. Times had changed and he tended to associate the use of his office with formality that existed instead of intimacy, or even at times with sarcasm.

"It's saved our lives too many times," she continued. "And besides, there needs to be a representative of your parent's generation of maidens, otherwise it will just be Eldri, Jack, and the rest of you are babies."

Robin attempted the politest smile possible in response, but it was more of a pursing of the lips that seemed to say, 'well then', and stepped away from her. He had a few stories he could have told her about things he'd seen and endured whilst still a baby, things he doubted she had. Regardless of social graces, or lack of them, he respected anyone out of the first flush of youth who after birthing six children picked up a cudgel and headed out onto the road in the name of the old paths.

"Alright everyone, we'll do a last-minute gear check and be on the road. The plan is to travel light and try and snake around above Worcester. Usually, we'd stop there for provisions but I've been hearing tell of fighting between the Earl of Gloucester whose sword is Matilda's, and Lord Waleran in Worcester who stands for Stephen. It's unclear who struck first and who retaliated but we can imagine unpredictable conditions on the roads whichever way we choose. The plan is to get to Gil at Rochdale and rest the horses and ourselves before making a trip to the Moon Well for the scrying."

At this Sariah stepped forward and Robin stepped back to indicate he opened the floor to her. "For at least five hundred years maidens have visited the Moon Pool in times of deep crisis to hear and see guidance. Myself and a few others will make the trip to the sacred place while everyone else remains in the safety of Gil's property."

"Also, understand," Blaith said. "That we will be travelling in highly un-stable country, so Robin is in charge at all times. I don't care if someone else told you to do something else. Do not second-guess him on anyone's account,

including mine. You get a cobbler to make a shoe after all. Otherwise, you'll all end up with Jack stitching your wounds and Eilish fighting with his enormous quarterstaff." Blaith made a faintly suggestive eyebrow gesture at Jack and the company laughed. "Understood?" People nodded their assent. "Well, over to Robin's gear-check now. He's going to pick through your equipment like a monkey preening you. I find it helps if you can convert it into a sexual turn-on."

He caught Blaith's gaze for a second and acknowledged with the faintest of nods his fine work in wrangling the people. The mutual respect they had for each other had a species of eroticism to its intensity, it drew people towards the centre of its magnetism like the central spirit pole of the sabbat.

As soon as the door opened, they were confronted by a sepulchral odour. Gil covered his nose and mouth with his hand. Augusta was steeled by custom. It appeared she'd let the cats out when she left, that was something. Perhaps asking someone to feed them or turning them out to their own plight. But the mummified remains of the hare with the gamy leg lay beside the cold hearth. The songbird she'd kept in a cage also was dead on the floor of its prison. Gil walked over to the cage and stared down at it. "The absolute monster," he murmured, his tone heavy with true horror. "She could have just let them go..."

"When was Mother ever able to let *anything* go?" Augusta exhaled sharply through her nose in a way that conveyed bitter irony.

Her uncle, who never seemed quite able to comprehend Nanette's evil, continued to look with pity and bewilderment at the corpses her life had left in its trail. "But... but... she took these animals in! I assumed it meant she cared for these homeless and injured beings. I assumed it was the only good thing about her..."

"Then you assumed too much," Augusta replied, scanning over the various jars of dried foetus parts and other animal curios. "She liked that their wildness was broken and they would always need her. She liked that she had

control over them. When they were no longer interesting to her, well you see how often she thought of them."

Augusta was honing in on the cabinet and work bench where Nanette kept her most important materials of the art and works in progress.

"Augusta, don't touch any of that! Let me look through it first."

She rolled her eyes as he pulled her protectively behind him. "I can barely walk with the warding talismans and powder satchets upon my person. You forget that I knew her work better than anyone. I've watched her do things in here that would turn you green. I know where she would keep what we're looking for."

"Alright, fine," he said, hands held in capitulation. "You show me but only I'm handling it."

"You are as much De Biron as I am, Gil. Why do you assume yourself so immune and me to be some kind of demon sponge?"

"Because it's her curse. And she didn't care for me," he said quietly. Then he smiled, a half bitter, half sad smile. "She sent someone to kill me and sat and watched me fight him... If it hadn't been for Blaith she'd have succeeded. There wasn't enough emotion in her towards me for her curse to land. You on the other hand, well you were the closest thing to something she loved. Blaith turned her curse back on her, now it can't eat her leg out anymore it's going after what she most valued."

Augusta felt chastened by his response. There was something essentially good in Gil that shamed her by its mere presence. Perhaps it was not Gil who thought she was a demon sponge? "This is where it will be," she said, gingerly pulling open a drawer. "She used to have top shelf magic, and bottom drawer magic. If she kept you on the top shelf it was good for you. If you got put in the bottom drawer it was not so good."

She indicated for Gil to be the one to open it. He did it through gloves. As soon as he opened the bottom drawer a certain new smell was discernible. It was similar to that of mummified hare, but gamey and riper. Inside it was a package of some kind, wrapped in crude muslin and tied with rope including

434

several knots. Gil reached in and picked it up. "Why do I have a feeling I am really going to regret looking in here?" he asked, as he lay the mysterious item down on the bench.

"Should we cut the knots or undo them?" she asked.

"I'm not sure. I don't want to commit to that until I better understanding what we're looking at." Instead he began to carefully unravel the rope so as to remove it in one go without breaking a knot. When he pulled back the muslin the most obvious thing was the badly decomposed, almost dry foetus with its umbilical cords wrapped numerous times about its neck. Gil heaved and stepped back.

"Honestly, dear uncle. You'd think you weren't part of the most feared black magic family in the country."

He frowned and turned to her. "Guss… This *murdered child* is wrapped just as Eilish's baby was… This is probably the curse that strangled him in the womb."

Augusta was nodding to herself. "They were right to want me gone from their camp. I must have conveyed it to Eilish somehow."

"It is not your fault."

"Did I say I thought it was my fault?"

"You don't have to be hard, you know? It's not a pre-requisite of being a De Biron."

"Can we look at what else is with it, please?"

He sighed. "Alright. Well, under the hideous dead baby remains there's this hide that has a runic devise for delivering scorched earth vengeance. I recognise the symbols. This part though," he said taking up a parchment that lay directly under the baby's head. "I've never seen anything like this before."

The parchment had multiple bindrunes for death, this kind of old heathen magic was standard De Biron fare, all of them in circles with an X beside them. They appeared to be laid out over a crude map or confluence of paths all of which were blocked with X's and the names of key members of the clan.

"I have seen Nanette use something like this before," Augusta muttered.

The sight of it brought back a memory almost forgotten from when she was small. There had been some other family who Nanette had wished for the downfall of and she'd written their names like that…

"What was it used for?"

"I… I have forgotten. It sickens me to look upon the symbols. I'd feel better if we just burned it and scattered the ashes."

Gil re-wrapped the bundle and slid the bindings carefully back around it. "I'll neutralise it as best I can, scatter a little of the malignancy upon the rocks and the hillside and a little on the salt sea. Then we'll burn it."

It was obvious he was extra unnerved and Augusta understood why. He was protecting the man he loved. She couldn't resist a poke. "While we get the fire started you can finally give me the details about you and Blaith."

He flinched faintly like she knew he would. "You're not disgusted?"

"By what? Because of the buggery, or because I have to acknowledge that my uncle is a sexual being?"

"Both? Either?"

"I am not easily rattled," she replied in Welsh.

"Nice Welsh. I must be doing alright too because I understood you."

"I copied it from something I heard Robin say."

As they carried the noxious bundle outside Augusta stopped briefly to unhook the latch and swing open the door to the songbird's cage. "Fly free, songhearted one," she murmured softly, looking down at the tiny fragile bones.


As a two-abreast column, travelling with only what their horses could carry they cut corners, left main roads, and rode hard. When they slept, they were less conspicuous without the caravans and they ducked and weaved through both the Cymric and the disputed territories. Sometimes they moved at night and went more slowly. There was not a one of their company who was not an excellent horseman and Robin took advantage of the fact to make good time. He had chosen the path between the garrisoned castles at Shrewsbury and Hereford to make the crossing, because the density of Normans was slightly

less, but he was now questioning the decision.

The air had smelt of human death- something that to the practiced nose smells different to the decomposition of other animals- for the past half-mile. Robin had noticed a few bones in the un-grazed grass, but his archer's eye, accustomed to long-distance targets, spotted what appeared to be a woman sitting by the roadside holding a child in her arms. Immediately he kicked his horse into a gallop and overtook the column to meet up with the scouts who rode ahead.

From the intensification of the odour and the expression on Rory and Zorien's faces, Robin knew before dismounting that the woman was dead. He turned to Zorien. "Can you take Eilish to the back of the column and move everyone past, please? I don't want anyone to see this who doesn't have to." It was enough that Zorien had seen it, in Robin's mind. They would all pass horrors on the road, but he felt wistfully towards tenderness, and wanted it to persist wherever it could.

He crouched down beside the body. The woman had been young, perhaps younger than him. Though bloating disfigured her face along with the preda- tion of carrion birds, he could still tell her age from her hands. She was gone about five days. Animals had gnawed through her clothing in places, beyond that there was no sign of pre-mortum violence. She had been emaciated when she died sitting up and slumped over, perhaps trying to keep her child warm until the end. The deepest horror Robin only saw next. The baby had died more recently, within the past two days or so. He took a deep in breath, having to accept the off-sweetish rancidity of the decomposition.

His pity was mingled with rage. History would record what Lord Wal- deran did in response to Gloucester but it would never tell the story of people like her, the innocent victims with lives as real as his own. What had she done to survive for all this time if Gloucester attacked in November as the rumours claimed? When all the other victims Robin had clocked were moss-gnawed bones? How had she kept her baby and herself alive only to perish without protection on one utterly bleak winter night? Nobody would ever know, yet

while Robin was still able to tell of it people would at least know that she did.

He pulled her hood down and around over her face, so that only her blonde plaits were visible. He used her apron to cover the sight of the child whose want-puckered face was frozen in a terrible expression of suffering. Performing a brief gesture of respect, he got to his feet. "Poor innocent mites."

By the time he turned Blaith had jumped down from his horse and was at his side. "What has done for her?"

"Starvation I'd say, and maybe exposure. The babe, too."

"Ach, it is scarce bearable to think upon!" Blaith exclaimed. "These lands… they were rich in game just last year, so that none of any race should ever needs starve here…"

"Indeed. You can't tell a Cymric woman from a Saxon from a Norman with their face half eaten off," Robin observed.

"Food in a baby's mouth is surely the very least we all owe each other?"

"Surely, brother," Robin muttered, his voice was a different type of low now, for it was a matter of low-simmering rage. "At least this explains why there is no hunting to be had. What does it mean though? What has caused this, so far from Worcester? People starved dead by the road…"

"The lords. The lords have caused this. It means the same thing that happened to the people in Nottingham. When the Earl of Gloucester fights the Earl of Worcester it means Gloucester's army sacked the entire town and maybe the outer villages of Worcester also, and refugees ran for many miles, some of them surviving for months until they'd eaten out the land to empty. Then Lord Walderan sacked Gloucester in retaliation."

"What's our next move?"

Robin glanced at Blaith. His brother looked pale and had dark marks under his eyes. His body had never coped with privation as well as Robin's, for a start he had less to work with when it came to dropping weight. Blaith had been such a sickly child they had held him back from going to the war-bands until Robin's time came so they could go together.

Robin surveyed the bleak skies and smelt the air for rain. "Well, if it was

just you and I, I'd turn north and ride hard until we clear the devastation zone, pass between Shrewsbury and Chester instead. But I fear I've already asked too much of our people and mounts."

"We'd do it for you if you asked it of us," Blaith observed. "Both our people and the horses."

"It's a choice between exhaustion or hunger, for no uneaten animal seems to bide here. I would prefer to choose exhaustion and ride like hell till we can't smell death anymore, and I can again hear living things. The utter silence raises my hackles."

"Indeed. No birds sing here." Blaith agreed. "We should ride through the night until they do."

Lux's life seemed to have become symbiotic with her mount. Their policy was not to name your horse, because it was meant to lead to rapid attachment which would cause heartbreak during a loss. On a long trip like this though, when the mare got a rest, so did she. The relief when they were enveloped by forestland on the other side of the row of Norman castles that perched like the enemy side of a chessboard, hemming in the country of the Cymry, belonged to both herself and the horse.

It was the First Warden's place to ride at the back of the column and the scouts to front their advance. For this reason, Lux always chose a position near the back. When Robin was busy, he wouldn't acknowledge her any more than her position in the clan dictated, yet she could catch his emotions from that distance.

Some time around mid-afternoon, the scouts returned. Emrys and Sorcha had been out and they were returning at a clip. Robin rode up the column leaving Jack to watch the line.

"We crossed paths with someone else's scout," Sorcha announced. "When he realised we'd seen him he headed Nor-west."

"On foot?" Robin clarified.

They nodded. "He was good though, Hob," Emrys said. "He got close

enough to us to raise the hairs on the back of my neck."

"We're entering another outlaws' territory then. Everyone stay close." He swung his horse around as he spoke to make sure everyone was hearing. "Could all the women have their hoods up please and tuck up your hair."

Lux pressed her lips together and did what he requested with a mixture of dread and grim determination. She knew this meant they were riding into a world of fighting men, where suddenly they were all two sexes again. Lux tried not to look at Sariah and Eilish and the women who were also disguising themselves as best they could. If she did she might have seen reflected there her own fear, and on the second day of no sleep, living off dried meat and acorn cakes, she might have lost the edges of her resolve.

They moved without incident for another half-hour until they reached a river. It had white water, which she knew Robin hated staying close to for long because it had the potential to block out background noise. There was no need to guess from which direction a threat was coming though because ahead lay a giant old tree bridge that had been worn flat from the feet and hooves of many travellers, just thick enough to ride a horse of steady temperament over. On the other side of the bridge was a company of strangers in clothing that camouflaged them into their environment so well she couldn't guess exactly how many there were.

Walking out onto the bridge was what amounted to the largest man Lux had ever seen. Following the actions of the archers around her Lux pulled her bow out and notched it but kept it down low, unaimed at anyone.

"John Hathersage, son of Proctor Little," he bellowed out in a voice that rung through the forest. His West Riding accent was so strong it was more of a dialect that made his Saxon English hard to understand. "Best man of the woods in these parts and this is our ground. If you want to cross it your best man is going to have to knock me into that river hard enough that I can't climb back up again."

Lux was close enough to hear Robin sigh and to see him roll his eyes. He seemed more tired and inconvenienced than he did afraid, despite the enor-

mous size of the man.

"Shit," Jack muttered to Hob. "He's enormous."

"Yeah. You know what they say."

"Count in a distended liver," Jack added. "Low heart and lung fitness. Make him move a lot to get at you."

Robin swung down from his horse and Jack tossed him a quarterstaff.

"Greetings, John of Hathersage, son of Proctor Little. I'm Hob, and I'm no one's son and I'd rather not, but I'll fight you if you want to fight. My people just want to pass through here though, we don't intend to put a drain on the hunting."

It was clear that Robin's habit of not drawing first and actively talking his opponent out of the conflict wasn't going to work this time.

"Nah, I want to fight." The man grinned necrotically at Robin with a I'm-going-to-kill-you smile.

"Of course you do," Robin muttered under his breath through the middle of a sigh. "Alright, let's get this over with then." He took off his shoes and his shirt and walked out onto the bridge.

Lux struggled to understand how he could seem so confident against such a mountainous opponent.

Blaith moved his horse around to a different position on the other side of Jack. "So we let this play out?"

"What else do you suggest?" Jack replied.

"That we shoot them all dead where they stand." The quiet, deadly tone of his voice was unmistakable.

"They would have arrows on our people too, Blaith."

"I know. I have seen the leaves move in the places where I would position the cover archers. We shoot them, we shoot the leader and the rest will scatter."

"Let's see what happens first," Jack replied. "I'd just as soon not murder anyone."

Blaith made a quiet snorting sound that suggested this was less of a concern for him.

441

As Robin met the giant close to a quarterstaff's distance apart Lux was able to get a proper assessment of exactly how tall the other outlaw was. She reckoned Robin at about six feet, three pouce. The Twll Du people were all taller than average but Robin was among the clan's tallest men. This man however looked about four pouce again taller than Robin. He looked to be at least twelve years older than Robin, maybe as many as fifteen, which made him old for a fighter. Lux understood from listening to Robin and Jack that this would give him the advantage of experience, and the disadvantage of old injuries to exploit.

"Better watch out," John said, spinning his staff between his fingers to demonstrate his skill. "I can crack a head right open with one square hit."

"I prefer mashing fingers," Robin replied, declining to show off his skill. "Sherwood rules?"

John nodded his assent. There were whoops and yells from the other outlaws in response to the banter, egging John on. This was their first mistake. Lux took note of where each sound came from in case it became time to follow Blaith's plan instead of Jack's. She pressed her teeth together and steeled herself to take them down, one after the other as coldly as she'd held that arrow on Nanette.

"I want to kill him so bad my mouth is watering," Blaith observed, his eyes set on John so intently that she suspected the man may drop where he stood from the ill current of his eye alone.

"Outlaw bands function off reputation. Robin's chosen not to introduce himself fully for now, but if Robin Goodfellow beats John of Hathersage, the rumour of it will spread, and there will be few further challenges in these parts." Jack's persuasion seemed to carry some weight with Blaith for now.

John advanced in high guard and Robin kept his staff in low guard until the very last minute. Robin would seldom strike the first blow in a fight, but once you hit him in any way, shape, or form, it would happen fast. This day was no different, John came in with a few rapid blows that Robin more evaded than blocked. Ducking low and covering a great deal of space in a lunge Robin

managed to touch John's mouth area with a one-handed strike.

This poke-strike looked light and not worth extending over, a mere annoyance. Lux immediately understood this was a magical power move. When John opened his mouth in a grimace of pain there was blood all over his half-rotted teeth and it ran out the side of his mouth.

"First blood is shed," Blaith observed.

The other outlaws had gone quiet. They were obviously used to seeing John beat his opponents senseless immediately. The shedding of first blood also carried considerably psychological impact, which was why Robin always tried to be the one to draw it, all the better if it was above the breath.

"Oh he ain't half mad now," Jack muttered.

Lux wanted to turn her head to look for Sariah, hoping to see her defiant and trusting in Robin's indestructibility, yet she couldn't convince herself to take her eyes off what was happening. From here it happened too fast to follow. John recalibrated himself, repositioned his hands. With the hyper-fixation that came from her pounding heart Lux could see her man's opponent register him as a serious threat. He had taken stock of the fact that Robin was faster than him and far more agile. When John came out now, he came out with everything he had, the products of decades of fighting. He came at Robin over and over again, blows, strikes, combinations of both-end stick work.

Finally, Robin had to take a hard overhand blow on his staff and Lux swore she felt in herself the devastating weight of it as Robin's quarterstaff rang through the forest, over the sound of the pounding river. She felt it in his shoulder where he'd never been quite the same after being shot with a Welsh bow when he was nineteen, even though Robin didn't show the hurt. As she watched she grew a deeper understanding of why Robin tended to hide his pain by virtue of habit. It wasn't some masculine posturing, it was about not showing a weak spot.

"Stop moving around!" John shouted at him, his lungs working moderately hard already. "Stand your ground like a man and fight me!"

"You're the one who wants to fight. So come here to me, old man!" Robin

beckoned him, right before ducking a terrifying headshot.

If John had told the truth about his penchant for cracking heads this meant he was trying for his finishing move. Robin had taught her that in life as much as in combat if your opponent starts using their end game too soon it means they are becoming desperate. That being said, Robin had lied about his favourite shots. Robin had no favourite or habitual moves.

"Keep him moving, Hob," she heard Sariah whisper.

In the motion of the duck Robin made a feint that he was trying for the fingers causing John to readjust his hand, before a sideways one-handed strike to the knee. It elicited a grunt of pain from John but left Robin open for a terrible moment. Thanks to his agility Robin managed to avoid half of the deadly head strike that followed, so that the other man's quarterstaff only caught him a glancing blow across the temple. Lux didn't fully realise the significance of the blow until she heard Sariah's gasp of horror. A glancing blow from this monster was all that it required to whip Robin's head back, and then his whole body seemed to follow, being tossed behind it into the rush of the river. What the rocks made into white water, blood made ruddy.

On the pain scale of being hit with things -in Robin's view- the worst thing you could endure was a quarterstaff strike to the fingers. The second most excruciating was a blow that hit you across the ear. It was up there with a hit in the testicles, yet closer to the fingers in debilitation. As Robin went under the icy rapids the pain was almost blinding and the ringing in his ear was louder than the rush over his head. As he sought purchase in the water a boulder connected with his ribs. He managed to hold on and very rapidly took stock of his situation. The head blow would concuss him later, it would not kick in fully yet.

While he was under the water Jack would have tenuous control over Blaith, who would be about to unleash a massacre in his defense. The longer he stayed under though the further John would be into the process of complacency. Robin had something on his side that dwarfed the injuries he'd sus-

tained; he had a raging, well-honed will to live. He always went into a fight as if it was possible the other person would try to kill him. There were still levels of adrenalin within that though. When true desperation to survive kicked in, which happened only rarely in fights these days, he would enter his Pucked state.

Due to Sherwood Rules, John had to allow Robin enough time to get back up onto the log and have his guard up before he could attack again. Once he emerged from the water Robin ignored his family's relief. He moved quickly back into position. He didn't want to give his opponent too long to catch his breath. The water meant Robin's upper body was sluicing with diluted blood and every second of warming back up would mean stiffening and the onset of mental confusion.

When their gazes met this time Robin's had shifted mode from neutral observer to surrender-or-I'll-kill-you. The joy of victory faded from the other man's hazel eyes. Immediately Robin went in with everything he had. He moved John around, this time also driving him back with blow after blow at his top speed until he felt John's foot lose ground. When he felt that first backward step he committed even more, dizzying volleys of high blows, some coming as one-handed long strikes, others with two handed blows from both sides of the stick, one of them hitting the same knee as last time.

The outlaw bellowed in pain and rage and took another backward step. Robin's full commitment came in waves, dragging out of him raw cries of effort. In truth this man was another outcast like himself, but with the taste of his own blood in his mouth and the whole world ringing as if his head were stuck in a church bell, John became every power that had sought to block the road his whole life. This was no longer John of Hathersage but everyone he'd had to cede the paths to. Dimly he could hear his people yell: 'Take him, Robin!' Sariah's voice called out: 'You've got this!' Hearing her did two things to him: inspired him and made him aware they would have heard her feminine voice.

The actions necessary to destroy the other man were clear to him the way

a good chess player sees multiple moves ahead. He would have to take a couple of blows in the process but Robin knew he could endure it and stay on the tree once in motion against the strike, as long as they weren't to his head or right rib. *My eyes lie to you. You believe me and go a little too low; I come in over the top with a one-handed blow as if I'm going for your throat. I am hit on the shoulder and it is bad. I protect my side and brace, before sending the end of the staff straight up into your nose from slightly below.*

Once he had John in the nose, blood coming out, tears running out of his eyes and visibility low, he took the knee he'd been softening at medium force, not hard enough to tip John into the water just yet. No, that wouldn't be enough of an injury to keep a proud man down. Outlaws like him had a fearsome reputation to protect. Robin would have to make sure he'd not be able to climb out and keep fighting, as every second took him deeper into the blinding onset of his concussion.

The pain in the knee took John back another step and Robin moved into that space assertively getting past his guard with speed to hit him hard in the liver. John grunted heavily and entirely stopped moving for a moment at the shock of toxicity being pushed out into his body. Rapidly changing his hold on the quarterstaff, he finished his work on the left knee. Robin chose a spot that wouldn't shatter the kneecap, which he deemed an unnecessary cruelty. Instead, he knocked his knee out from underneath him with the tip of his staff. It didn't take much. The catastrophic fall would do most of the damage. *It's true what they say.* John's fall into the river was far less controlled than Robin's had been, he hit himself on the bridge on the way down and made an enormous splash.

While this played out Robin continued to stand on the tree in low guard position, panting for some time as if he couldn't convince his adrenal glands the fight was over. He vaguely took in John's companions having to rescue him half insensible from the river. He could no longer hear much of anything beyond the pain-scream in his ear. Suddenly he felt every part of his two days without sleep, and his damage sustained in the fight was getting more and

more shrill.

Usually when well slept, he could have got another half-hour out of his adrenalin. As it was he was fresh out of patience. "My name is Robin Goodfellow! Son of Obreon!" he roared out as he turned on the spot as he spoke and projected so his voice filled the forest. Roused as he was it carried the same punch of testosterone and aggression with which he'd been greeted. It caused the other outlaw band to all turn around and look at him. "And I want to cross your fucking bridge!"

# 3

Excited and urgent as he was in the past old-Gil would have called someone to saddle his horse. These days when he wanted something done quickly it didn't even occur to him to not do it himself. Upon hearing that Robin, Blaith, and a small company of others were at the gate he raced out into the stable and got his horse, didn't bother with a saddle, and rode bareback out to meet them.

When he caught sight of them coming up the road, Gil was surprised to see them all at an exhausted walk. Usually Hob would kick his horse at this point and come rampaging to meet him, they would both jump down and Robin would lift him off the ground in a collision-hug. Today Robin had his hood and head down and Blaith rode so close it appeared he might even have a protective hand on the rein of Robin's mount. Jack rode close on the other side.

Frowning with concern Gil pushed his horse for more speed. When he reached them and reined in, he reverted to Norman French in his anxiety, though he had been meaning to speak his basic Welsh he was working on. "What happened? Is everything alright?"

What he had taken for a slight lad turned out to be Lux bringing her horse up on the other side of Robin and she answered him in Norman French. "Greetings, Gil," she said, taking off her hood. "Robin's had a hard fight and he's hurt. We need to get him somewhere he can lie down."

Gil frowned. "Someone... beat him? As in, fairly?"

"Nah, I got him," Robin replied groggily from under his hood. "But he made me pay for it."

Unable to imagine (through a certain shade of hero worship) who the man could have been to try Robin so, he immediately blurted out: "It wasn't that John of Hathersage monster of an outlaw I spoke to, was it?"

Lux looked at him like he'd been uncanny. "That was precisely the man!"

"Come, you must all be hungry and tired. I will organise food and rest and have your horses seen to. They look like they deserve some hay and rest. Please tell the others I've been working on my Welsh though it's still very clumsy. I'm honoured to have you all here. *Croeso.*"

Lux translated his words to the company. He realised when he heard her fluency in Cymric that he'd moved from thinking of her as a trouble-making loose girl, to admiring what she'd achieved, mentally, physically, and spiritually. *How prejudice misshapes things… how it warps all we see…* Though he still lived like a lord most of the time, he was determined to never un-see what he'd seen. Maybe whilst there wasn't a prospect of immediate freedom for him in the bodily sense there might yet still be a form of mental and emotional liberty that he had won? Something the world could never take away from him?

Thinking of emotions his gaze shifted at last to Blaith. He was pale and drawn. With his colouring and facial features his pallor was picturesque. His body looked purified by the elements after their nights without seeing ceilings or doors. As if wind had lain bare his bone structure and the bleak sky had polished him to this whiteness. Gil wanted to kiss his face yet did not. Blaith's body language made it clear he was too coiled around his concern for his brother to engage in any such expressions of joy in meeting. Instead of kissing, Gil presented Blaith with his best Welsh. "If you see well bring him on slow. I go in front, make things to happen."

His stumbling Welsh wrung out a tender little smile from the fabric of what appeared to be Blaith's last nerve. "Thank you," he said back to Gil in Welsh, giving him the head-heart gesture. "For making things to happen."

Under normal circumstances, Blaith's animal would have been right out of its comfort zone inside a castle, its feathers ruffled and its hair all standing

on end. As much as a fish out of water as he felt right now, he was grateful to be there. Inside a fortified castle with its own garrison was about as safe as his injured brother could be, surely? *Unless there is some hidden place in the world of man, somewhere far from wars for gold and land, the kind of place like which we have never seen, then it must be.*

For the first time in their lives, the hand of a Norman nobleman was extended to them in help, rather than as a mailed fist. Knowing how hard it had been to live his entire three decades pitching his whole body against that unyielding iron, struggling in its grip while they flogged his mute brother for not speaking, struggling in its grip just to eke out a life, he knew a thing or two about the strength of the Norman war machine.

Robin had passed out again when they tried to help him down off his horse. Jack and Gil had half steadied and half carried him up the stairs to a sunny, well-aired room. Blaith reckoned the bed was big enough to sleep Hob, Sariah, Eilish and himself comfortably, though it seemed it was used for a single guest. Towards the top of the stairs Robin fully lost consciousness again, and Emrys joined the other men to carry him up onto the bed. Robin came awake as they lay him down and reached out his arm across bed searching for something. "Blaith," he murmured, without opening his eyes.

Blaith glanced at Lux. She showed no resentment at hers not being the name he called in his disorientation, instead she gently but firmly physically moved Blaith in the direction of the bed. "He calls for you," she murmured. "Go to him."

Thus urged Blaith sat to take off his boots.

"Besides, you can lift him better than I if he needs to drink water or use the chamber pot," she added. "I will go to their apothecary to translate between Gil and Eilish so she can locate extra supplies. Hold him for me." When she squeezed his shoulder in solidarity before leaving, he saw in her eyes a communication of how terrible they had both found it to watch Robin beaten till bloody like that.

Since Lux had joined him in their unholy union non-verbal communica-

tion between them had gone through the roof. For Blaith this meant he could truly talk to her in his native tongue for the first time. He sensed the generosity of her attitude towards his bond with Robin, and he was deeply moved by it.

If you crossed Blaith's family, you'd end up with a knife at your throat in a heartbeat, beyond that he took his shoes off where appropriate, said thank you when given something, and cleaned up nicely if he was planning to fuck. Nonetheless, there was inside him a wild hedgerow boy that took a naughty pleasure in getting the woodlands all over a lord's fine sheets.

"I'm here. I've got you," said near Robin's ear.

Robin had collapsed with a blinding headache quite soon after the fight. When he woke, he had pain in his head strong enough it made his palms sweat and his breath come on too fast. He slept an alarming amount of time, during which he appeared to dream fitfully. When he at length awakened, he'd thrown up twice, said he felt a lot better and wanted to 'just get to Gil's'. On the road though he had nearly fallen from his horse due to dizziness.

Blaith reverted in the face of his brother's physical vulnerability to something more like their childhood and adolescent selves, before the offices of Magister and First Warden had descended upon them. Back when Robin's parentless state led Blaith to fulfil a wide range of roles for him, though Blaith had been only young himself. In his exhaustion he was back in the crude stone hunts, and makeshift camps when they were training with the war-bands, where there'd been little heating beyond each other's body warmth.

Then he was shielding Robin from bullies with his own body when he was still too young to stick an aconite hairpin in them. Alone in the wilderness they had simply been two fallen angels, at other times Blaith was parent, sibling, later Magister, teacher, beloved, and finally himself the watched over, the cherished and protected one whose life Robin was to preserve above all others.

By the time Eilish returned with jars and fresh herbs to treat Robin, Blaith had himself fallen asleep half entwined with Robin. Waking was almost as strange as it must have been for Robin in his concussed state. Not only was Blaith mildly hallucinating from sleeping briefly after a long deprivation, but

how in the names of all things holy and unholy did he find himself inside a god's cursed castle? It took a few moments as well as recognising Eilish and Lux for him to get a hold of himself and sit up.

"I've got some more milk of the poppy for him," Eilish announced. "And some herbs for a poultice. Can you help me get his tunic off, Blaith?"

"Cariad," Blaith said, giving Robin a firm tap on the forearm.

Thankfully Robin stirred this time and looked at him through blurry eyes. Almost immediately he saw stress overcome confusion. "Is everyone alright?" he murmured. "I can't remember how I got here. I've forgotten things... I feel like I can't understand Norman French..."

"Don't worry, your beautiful mind will heal with rest, and everyone is fine, cariad," Lux said from the other side of him. "Sariah is overseeing our people as they eat and rest. Eilish has to treat your ribs."

Robin complied without complaint but flinched visibly when he had to put his arms up in the air to remove the garment. The bruising coming out in his upper body was already colourful. Eilish moved quickly to have him gently down on his back again so she could feel for breaks. Robin endured the examination without complaint. He wasn't fooling Blaith though. "Can I dose him?" he asked Eilish, reaching for the milk of the poppy bottle. She nodded. Blaith measured it out and gave it to him.

"No breaks, thank the gods." Eilish concluded. She followed by covering the area in a comfrey poultice before bandaging him.

"Thank Eilish," he whispered. His voice came out a bit slurred as though under the influence of alcohol. Blaith frowned with concern. This was Robin's third serious concussion in his life, and Jack said that with fighters he'd known it becomes more serious the more times it happens.

"Thank me by resting," she replied brusquely. Eilish packed up her equipment while Lux covered Robin over with sheets and blankets. Before leaving Eilish turned to Blaith and said more quietly. "Wake him every so often, yes?"

He nodded. When they left it seemed he passed out unconscious beside Robin. Yet some instinct- one that Blaith felt went back to habits his young

452

fetch had developed to avoid overlaying Robin as an infant when sharing a sleep space- kept him waking regularly. Throughout the night he calmed Robin from an anguished nightmare, put a cool wet cloth over his forehead, helped him get at water, and woke him gently when Blaith feared he was sleeping too deeply. Despite his exhaustion, Blaith's body did the work of love with barely the need of mind. If their lives had taught him anything it was this: *This work of love that is not work, it is how we keep each other alive.*

He was back in the cannibal tent where they were always consuming his aunt alive. The ghouls that were eating her commanded a primal access to fear, one that Robin imagined must reach back deep into ancient cave origins. It was the power of the first cultural obscenity, humans predating upon humans. Yet, taboo, as the literal act still was, all of society continued to be based upon subtler forms of man consuming man.

"No, no I won't!" Robin cried out. He meant to use his adult-male self-projective voice, like the one he'd used to proclaim his right to cross John Little's bridge. Instead it came out as more of a muffled child's voice. Though he was unable to make himself understood in the dream the tent expanded in size in response to his refusal. Robin had magicked himself back into an adult. Even inside the dream he knew this was a first. Inside this new cannibal tent it was entirely dark, not lit by crazy-making flashes of light, as dancing, the movement of flaming torches, and fire twirlers permeated the tent wall to illume the horror in staccato. There was only the sound, the familiar fast, panicky, breathing.

Robin took a step forward, because, well, *you don't get anywhere if you don't.* As though on the cue of him moving something else moved in the darkness with him. Whatever it was he was also the type to step towards a fight. Though there was no killing taking place before Robin the new tent still smelt like blood and meat. Whatever was approaching him made a *clunk* and shuffle-drag sound as it came on. He was beginning to wonder if tonight the nightmare would make him endure discovering the form of the Other One moving

in the darkness with his hands, having subtracted from him the capacity for sight? Blessedly a kind of light, much like the shifting ones on the night It happened, shone upon the large tent, insisting that the stranger pass through it and for a moment.

The hunched figure using a crutch to compensate for a missing leg, long dark hair matted around her face, revealed itself and then far more horrifically disappeared again in the proximal darkness. "Do you still say yes to life then, Robin?"

"Yes."

"Even when that-" she said the words with a shadowy gesture that appeared to cause a still moment of his aunt's murder to freeze on the tent wall. "Your total terror. Her total pain… When all of this is possible you gaze upon it and you would still say yes?"

Robin wanted to defy her just on principle, but he could not. After all it was Eliza's experience as well as his, so how could he lightly say yes to life, life that does such things? As far as bad goes the experience, when considered for both of them, was terrible enough that its misery matched for intensity the most profound joys of his life. Yet when considered in terms of quantities there had been many more days where the mist lingered in the fields just before dawn and you breathed the perfection of things for breakfast. Many days when no violent men came to consume his family, forcing him also to be a violent man.

Those days and nights of love that rivalled the cannibal tent in intensity of goodness? They had been so many, *many* more in number than the worst night. He knew Eliza had known similar joys, and many more days where she woke safe and happy in the arms of beloveds.

"Yes, I say yes. I don›t deny the horror. I tender up in life's defense only that love exists. And that it is sufficient."

The dream dissolved in response to his words. Robin found himself on his back in what appeared to be Gil's castle, looking upward and seeing Blaith gazing down at him. From the position Blaith was in it appeared he might

454

think himself responsible for waking Robin from the nightmare. *It is sufficient.*

"Hob? Are you alright?"

Robin smiled up at him. He suddenly felt a great joy surge. Some intelligence in his body he believed to stem from his faerie blood had fixed his brain while he dreamed. He felt so lucky to still be here, and that he and Blaith were still together at this moment in time. How precious it seemed suddenly after where he'd just been! "Quite well now. You're a good thing to wake up seeing in the morning."

"It's afternoon, cariad. How are you feeling?"

Blinking in the light he rubbed his eyes. "The headache's gone. Just stiff and disorientated."

"Don't you be sitting up or going anywhere there."

This just made Robin grin wider; he loved it when Blaith scolded him. "I won't be rushing anywhere for a good few days, weeks maybe, I'd warrant. A head injury isn't something I can just walk off."

"Though you tried." Blaith smiled ruefully, as if his affection for Robin were half in spite of himself.

"Well, you don't know what you can do until you do."

"I was afraid for you," Blaith murmured, with a sudden intensification of his presence that seemed to contract to a single point of black heat. He brought his head down in deceptively a gentle forehead-to-forehead touch that energetically packed a healing punch. "I knew you could win. I'd back you against anyone, of any size. I also knew it would cost you. I wanted to kill him because you've already been through enough."

"You would have had to kill all of them if you killed one."

Blaith shrugged. "I am not stinting with my love offerings."

"Of all the many things people might say of you, I don't think that will ever be one of them." He pulled Blaith's head down so he could give him a kiss. "I love you. Even when I appear to be unconscious I gaze upon all you do for me in awe. Even if I'm hovering over my body at the time."

Blaith inclined his head and eloquently touched his head and heart before

offering his hands palm up. He left them offered like that for longer than usual, which translated in Blaith-speak as the difference between 'I respect you' and 'I adore you.'

"I think I just defeated one of my nightmare demons. I made the tent change size and forced it to let me wake up."

He put his hand on the side of Robin's face. "You're so brave, Robin. And not just for the things everyone sees. But for the battles almost nobody sees. Know that somebody sees those that happen in the darkness also."

When Lux first approached the bed that had been made up for her by servants she was tentative. She was afraid that its seductive offer of comfort beyond anything she'd experienced since running from home would somehow undo her in this vulnerable moment. Wanting sleep as she did that might just unravel all of the conditioning and grit she'd developed. Yet despite her concerns she was so tired that it was just happening somehow, she was pulling back the sheets and placing in one tentative leg. Feeling the unimaginable luxury of its softness she couldn't quite hold back from pushing her whole body down in there and pulling those plush covers up to her ears.

It was too good, and she was too tired to further question her motives and whether, despite all she'd done to prove otherwise, she was in fact always going to be a spoilt, soft, little rich girl. For there were only the feathers in that pillow and (oh gods) the mattress itself... Knowing Robin had been treated by Eilish and had Blaith to care for him allowed her to drop the total focus on her fear for him for the first time in days. Only now did she really feel her own exhaustion, so attuned to his pain had she been, she hadn't noticed the myriad of places her own body hurt. Augusta had such plentiful supplies of medicines she'd allocated everyone a tiny dose of milk of the poppy for general three-days-in-the-saddle-with- little-sleep sorts of pain.

Lux took it gratefully. Though she had been riding with Robin for too long to be without a thought of the stockpiling of such things at the castle, and how many were in need of such relief in this time of war. The relief wiped

those thoughts away though and sent her spiraling into thick, dark sleep. It was dreamless, formless, slightly opium enriched sleep. She was aware of nothing until what felt like close to dawn, though in truth her sense of time was all muddled.

At first, she felt hands touching her under the covers. Smiling to herself in her sleep she opened her legs. She loved waking up to Robin's hands taking liberties with her. It was only when she felt a finger enter her that she realised Robin was wounded and in another bed, she jolted back from the touch. When Lux did a terrible weight came down on her. It was like the dead weight of her father's corpse hanging over her, as he had once hung over her mother's.

"Get off me!" she managed to scream. When she woke in a bed inside a castle she continued to struggle, caught in some waking nightmare that her freedom itself had been all a dream, and she was still being held prisoner. She slid rapidly out of the bed as if it had become an object of horror. Lux knew she should never have trusted its appearance of softness. Everything about being upper class was like that, it promised you comfort and wrapped you up in slavery while you were intoxicated by it.

Lux went on bare feet the only direction she remembered: toward where she'd left Robin.

"Lukey, what's happened?" Robin asked sitting up. It was an endearment that he usually only called her when they were alone. She noticed he said it unselfconsciously in front of Blaith. Most importantly he said it sitting up and his eyes managing to focus on things.

"He's feeling much better," Blaith reassured her, perhaps thinking her distress a matter of fear for Robin.

"Oh thank god. Thank god you're alright," she got up onto the bed with them and Blaith pulled back the blankets. "I just dreamed... I dreamed I was back there. The castle had me... My childhood bed had me..." she shuddered. Blaith moved over to insist she climb into the warm space between them. The effect of finding herself in what she discovered was the safest feeling place on earth caused the fear to leech out of her, as if at her back Blaith had drawn it

all out through his chest.

"I just woke from a nightmare too," Robin said.

"Tell me everything that happened, both of you," Blaith replied. "Leave no detail out, this could be important."

"So, to be clear, all of this," with his finger Jack indicated a line from Aberystwyth to Newtown. "The ground contested at the Battle of Crug Mawr of all too recent memory, that is in Matilda's Angevin hands now?"

Gil sighed. He was only in his late twenties but as a veteran of that very war he had earned his expression of world-weariness to Jack's way of thinking. "From what I am told, yes. Hereford as well as Worcester and Gloucester have been sacked. The dead lie uncounted. There are constant skirmishes and raids perpetrated along the border towns."

"The whole Marchers looks like a war zone," Jack muttered. The Harrowing still felt close in the Old North and in his family, the idea he was living to see another generation of atrocities play out did nothing to make him feel any younger.

"Indeed." His brother's tone was just as grim as his own. Having had Nanette for a sibling this fact in its own small way counted towards something a little like redemption. *Damn Robin if he hasn't made me want to live big expansive, expensive, stories with words like redemption in them.* "Here in Rochdale, we're solidly in pro-Stephen country, so naturally at the moment I'm pro-Stephen. If it looks like Stephen isn't winning, I shall lose no time in becoming pro-Matilda." Gil leaned back in his chair. Jack could tell his half-brother was deeply committed to this story they'd both signed up for, not only for the safety of his ancestral seat, for the people he sheltered.

"What are you thinking? Spit it out," Jack prompted.

"If I were Matilda – and this is assuming Robert of Gloucester who is the military strategist behind her is smart- if I'd secured the West Country and South Wales, I'd need more money and levies to move on London. Given that Stephen has the Marchers and everything north and east, and he is not terrible

as a commander there is only one neutral area crushed in the middle now…"

"You're thinking she'll push to take Gwynedd?"

"I would."

"But Gwynedd is known as the heartbreak hill of conquests ever since Roman times. The tales all say you'll lose more men than it will be worth to you trying to take the mountains. After Crug Mawr both armies would know the quality of the fighting men and archers among them. Why would she waste her men?"

"Why waste them to take South Wales?" Gil shrugged. "For the taxation, for the levies, to get some of those northern Welsh archers under her command. Alas, Crug Mawr *taught them* things indeed."

Jack pressed his lips together and nodded faintly while he regarded Gil.

"What?" he asked after noticing.

"Just contemplating how committed you are to all this."

"All what?"

"You know what I mean."

"Yes. Me fighting in an *actual battle* on the Welsh side didn't give that away?" There was a mixture between hurt, ire, and a little of something sardonic all mixed together in Gil's tone. "I spilt my blood for the land of the Cymry, and I meant it."

"You're in love with him aren't you?"

"Blaith?"

"Or Robin?"

"If there is anything my Twll Du blood-brother has taught me it is that there doesn't have to be an 'or'." He looked down then. His gaze rested over the map but no longer seemed to see it. The territory he was traversing mentally had yet to be mapped. Jack felt a willingness to map it with him, in a way that pushed through the class difference based on their legitimate and illegitimate status. "Besides, there are many kinds of love, Jack."

"True enough," he agreed. He too had learned this from loving Robin.

"Many kinds of hate also, some capable of walking beyond the grave… I

459

think we found Nanette's spell. The one she used on Eilish's baby. Or should I say upon Blaith's firstborn son, because I doubt she knew the name of the mother. We neutralised it and burned the remains. Yet I do not feel peaceful upon the matter. It is as though some residue of her is walking yet, clinging to the girl… You must understand," Gil said, leaning forward in his seat urgently. His dark De Biron eyes, so capable of looking malignant were equally able to convey the most heartfelt sincerity. "I love Augusta as if she had been my own. I don't know that she has a choice in being a link…"

"We should dig Old Bitch up and break her last leg to stop her walking and wedge a rock between her teeth to stop her feeding on the living, just to be sure of the thing," Jack grunted. "Stake her through the heart -if she has one."

"I'd join you just for the catharsis at this point."

"Tomorrow the maidens will journey to the well so Sariah can scry. Hopefully if anything of Nanette's invention still haunts our steps it will be made plain then."

"This must be very important to them," Gil observed. "This well… For them to traverse a warzone."

Jack didn't really know how to articulate what he'd learned about the importance of certain features in the land to the Twll Du people. He had to think about it for some time and while he did he stared at that ever-smaller independent Wales Gil had marked out on the map. "The land is part of their body. You take away a well here, a standing stone there, a forest of myth here… it's like you're snipping off their fingers, lopping off whole hands…. Just like the anti-poaching laws do, except in their hearts. You take away this ancestral lake here and their women go infertile for want of new souls. You destroy an ancient Faerie Thorn known to be the grave of a fallen warrior of great prowess; their men will soon be unmanned by it. The loss of the Moon Well would be a loss of vision and connection with the future. Their magic is manifest in these places, and that connection is irreplaceable."

Gil nodded thoughtfully. "I think I understand. It's like how I feel about them. They are magic manifest to me, and those connections are irreplace-

460

able."

Sariah stood with Blaith about ten paces from the well while they waited
for the moonrise to reach the peak position for the work. The other maidens
were spread out a little, doing their mental preparations to support the opening of the well. As a rite, they needed maidens from three different generations, and the man in black who alone knew how to call to the future to step
forward. Blaith didn't seem to need to prepare to become Him, and from long
practice Sariah found the two of them only needed to step forward hand in
hand like this for the work to begin.

"I thought Hob would try and fight me on it when I said he had to stay
home and that other wardens would cover your back tonight. But he didn't…"
Blaith words were a bare whisper, but they fell heavily against the edge of the
night. The Moon Well was looming ominously before them. Sariah was dread
to approach it as if it might pull them directly into the whirlpool of that future
which was stampeding down on them.

"Are you worried about that? Do you think it's a concern?"

"It's unlike him. Eilish says unusual behaviour is something we should be
looking for after a serious head injury. He moves from his bed to the window
where the sun comes into the room, and he reads books, one after the other.
I don't even understand how he does that part; let alone how he does it so
quickly. He's got a read and an unread stack from Gil's library on either side
of his chair. It's almost manic. It makes him tire quickly so then he sleeps for
a very long time. Then he reads again. He insists Gil speaks Norman French
to him, and that Lux speak to him only in Saxon English, whilst I of course
speak Welsh."

Sariah squeezed his hand. "Eilish believes his fetch instinctually has an
extraordinary understanding of how to heal itself. She says it's different to
anyone else she's ever doctored on. His faerie blood in him… it knows how
to exercise his brain, and when to rest it. He is more sedentary than ever in
his life he does this with the same determination he used to get the dexterity

461

back in his hand, and his shoulder strength after the attack. So perhaps, my lover, it is not so very different for our Hob at all? This focused mania, this determination to survive?"

Blaith squeezed her hand, long and slow. It was the kind of squeeze that meant he heard you and what you'd said had given him real comfort. "It's almost time," he said at last. "Let's get the other maidens into position." Blaith walked without hesitation towards the dread well without trepidation it might suck him down. He never seemed to flinch before the abyss, as if he and it were made out of the same thing. As Sariah came forward into her position, with Gladys across from her, Eldri to her left and Lux to her right, she wondered why she had come to feel this place as threatening when she never had before? In a moment there would be no time to think about it or anything anymore because it would be on. The whiteness would have her like a strike across her brain, mediated by the waters of the Underworld, a lightning bolt cutting across time and distance.

Blaith leapt up onto the stone side of the well and whistled sharply down into the darkness. Then he began to walk the leftward way around the darkness that yawned below. With each step his blackthorn stick made a clack sound on the old stone. When he had circled three times he paused and cried out some guttural words in the old witching tongue. He dropped a holy stone down into the water in offering. The darkness seemed to jump up at him then, like a giant black cat, but he darted away having become one with it, before jumping down from his perch. With a bow and flourish of his cloak he stepped back and yielded the floor to Sariah. She leaned forward and drew back her veil that had partly shielded her eyes until the moment where the moon would reflect herself in the water. At that moment the past, the present, and the future would all fold up against each other for a blinding second of revelation.

When she'd first performed as an oracle at this well the elder maidens had told her not feel any pressure, as it wasn't so much a skill as it was something that happens to you. *It is the well that has the skill not the woman. You are just*

*a vessel...* And it was true. As it had happened the first time Sariah's mind was pulled into yoke with the moon and the slow, sluggish motions of the water below. Immediately she reached out with her arms to steady herself as her realities collapsed to a blinding white point. Blaith was there behind her she found, putting his hands around her waist to hold her up in case she slipped in trance, standing in the place Robin would normally have been. If her consciousness had become a star, then his was the black of the night sky that allowed her light to shine.

When she began to speak her voice had gone flat, expressionless. "I see children running through the woods. There are some women too, with babies. Smoke rises from the settlement. There is flint on the ground where they're running. There is blood on the flint. Bones of flint in our men, lion hearts of our women! They came... but we fought!"

Now Sariah's voice began to fall away and a growing horror started creeping up in the pit of her stomach pulling apart the conjunction of place and time in a fracture. It had something to do with hearing her own voice speak in past rather than future tense. It felt like the opening in Blaith's chest reached out through hers like a fanged mouth. An image of Uncle Bran flashed up against her consciousness as if she had collided shields with him in battle. The sensation almost knocked her off her feet if Blaith didn't have her around the waist. "No... no... no...what have I done?" she started to murmur, staring down into the water trying to collect up pieces of the vision with her hands. "I've killed them. I've saved us. I've killed them..."

Blaith was trying to lower her to the ground, but Sariah was struggling with him. She didn't know why her body was doing this. It wasn't clear if she was trying to get back to the well or fight off the curdling knowledge of what she had seen. The worst thing was she was as *certain* of the meaning behind her vision, utterly certain as she had been about the directive to leave Brynmor and Creirwy's settlement. Convulsive sobs wracked through her. Lux gathered to her in support, rubbing her back. Gladys just stood at her feet and watched.

"What does it mean, Sariah?" Blaith asked, his voice low and calm.

"She's moon-touched is what it means," Gladys said. There was a defensive note to her voice, and in Sariah's open state she heard the fear in it. The other woman knew too, though she would deny it as long as she could. After all, he was the father of her children...*Do you not then feel them pass even at a distance?* She had always believed that on the dreaded day when something would happen to Blaith and Robin she would feel it as each of them passed.

Blaith squeezed her hand supportively. "Who have you saved, cariad?"

"The people here with us in Rochdale!"

"So who have you killed then?" Gladys demanded, her voice straining against the runaway horse of fear.

Blaith alone seemed to have enough information already to understand what Sariah had seen. "You didn't kill anyone! You *saved* us. You saved everyone who chose to heed the directive of the Mothers. You were only the messenger," he said flatly, the darkening implications of it sinking gradually into his voice that turned grim. Sariah wrapped her arms around her legs and rocked back and forth.

"What's happening?" Lux murmured, fear thickening her voice.

"She's lying. She is trying to say they're all killed! Those who stayed back at camp!" Gladys cried. Eldri reached out to her but she pushed free of the older woman, fighting reality would get her about as far as Sariah had when struggling with Blaith. "Not all," Sariah whispered, her eyes closed, shaking her head as the visions filled her up like a cup under a waterfall. "The children run and hide yet. Some of the women are with them..."

Gil's hall was a grander one than Lux's father's had been, with far better smoke ventilation and superior hygiene. The walls smelt virgin, like they were yet to know the spray of male piss. Nonetheless, being in a Norman warlord's hall triggered associations of violence, much like their beds did. Lux needed to keep reassuring herself by looking at the man to whom attention most turned. It was not to Gilbert De Biron, Baron of Rochdale, or to the biggest bully, but to a hedgerow-born tinker who Lux suspected might possess one of the finest

minds of his age. He had fought for his gift of late. Lux knew the horror with which she'd have endured the prospect of damage to her mind, and she was awed by his dignity in the face of this silent danger potentially playing out inside his skull.

He sat across the central fire from her wrapped in furs and had another over his lap and appeared unarmed. Blaith's throwing knives were in his thigh-sheaths yet not in his sleeves, which meant he had no one particular in mind to shiv at this time. Jack had a sidepiece; it was just a large hunting knife. Gil had his family broadsword sheathed on one hip. Lux didn't doubt he was relaxed in their company, so it was there either because it looked sexy in his weapon belt –which it did- or for the purposes of conditioning himself to take the weight as normal. Robin was the only male present to not be carrying. In fact, when he moved his hand to reach for his drink Lux saw he was still in sleepwear under the furs.

"We have each in turn attempted to persuade Aunty Gladys to not be hasty about taking the road. So far it's been to no avail and she insists she'll leave for Gwynedd in the morning," Robin's tone sounded a bit tired though calm and steady. "I can't fault her on this," he added. "I might not have even waited till morning were it my nearest love. I would have ridden on Gladys's behalf by now, were I able."

Lux looked over at Sariah's profile to see how she was holding up. Her First Maiden looked a bit pale today. Eilish said that was natural with the Moon Well scrying even without the doom-filled message. In fact, it was considered to be one of the reasons that maidens burned through their blood early, and often did not bleed for as many years as other women.

"But I'm not quite fit enough yet to face Eilish in single combat," Robin added with a faint smile playing over his lips. "If I go trying anything like getting out of my chair too soon."

Eilish laughed quietly, and then had to dab her eyes at the end. He was good at that, Lux thought. Being able to make a joke with a light touch that even in desperate circumstances didn't seem inappropriate.

465

"You'd be fighting me too," Blaith said.

"Oh I know, brother. Believe me… Emrys and Sorcha have volunteered to escort Gladys and Eldri home and are taking an early night on account of it."

"Eldri is going too?" Eilish asked.

Robin nodded. He remained looking down and didn't meet Eilish's eyes when he replied. "She's afraid that if she doesn't… she's afraid she won't die on Gwynedd soil." The quietness of his voice and the flatness of his tone were of a sort she'd heard before, it was how he spoke when he had to give people very bad news. "And I can't blame her either," he sighed. Finally, he looked up and his eyes sought those of each who sat with him around that fire. "Because she's probably right. I don't know if we're ever going to get back from where we're headed. This might be a last chance to bail out."

"Well, I'm not going anywhere. But I need to ask this, though don't take it the wrong way, Sariah," Jack said, holding up his hand in a way to suggest a prior request for quarter. "Has the Moon Well ever given false prophecy?"

"I am certain of what I saw!" Sariah responded, her voice firm though not angry. Lux had heard Gladys accuse her of lying, and then alternatively seen her being shot as the messenger of an almost certain tragedy. She tried to empathise with Gladys and Lux figured she may not be rational either if such a prophecy had just been received about Robin while he was away.

Jack turned to Robin. "Do you mind if I say what I think?"

Robin gestured for him to be his guest. "I asked you to stand as second for me because I wanted to hear when you disagree with me most of all."

"Well, if the Moon Well has never been known to give false report, what Sariah saw is probably what's happened… Terrible as it is to consider. If that is so we will be sending Gladys, Eldri, Emrys, and Sorcha into an unstable situation. Two wardens to escort them isn't going to count for shit if De Bracy has sent men against them in defiance of the Baron of Rochdale's claim on your heads."

"Try telling that to someone when their children and their love are on the other side of that combat zone, potentially in need or danger," Blaith mut-

tered. "All I can say to you is good luck. I would be in the saddle already."

"As would I if it were Robin," Lux said quietly. Robin made eye contact quite intensely across the fire for a couple of moments before he spoke.

"Robin would very much prefer you did not. Robin would like it if in such a situation you turned your horse around and got yourself to safety."

# 4

You know this would have been so much more fun if we did this my way?" Jack remarked, as the grave-warden and another workmen prised away at the coffin lid.

"Why break into the crypt with a stake when you could out her as a vampire who has risen from the dead to harass the living? The clergy have done all the dirty work for us." Gil knew he sounded faintly smug but it was all a front to cover how he really felt about seeing Nanette again under these conditions. One of the workmen who had gone into the De Biron crypt to remove the coffin said the caskets were not sitting as he remembered them and he was spooked by it. This helped to add something to the story.

"I have to admit it was effective," Jack conceded.

"There have been reports of vampire attacks in some of the country, so the hysteria was already brewing, I just fizzed it up a bit by pulling out evidence of some of her more colourful curios from the work shack."

Jack shook his head. "Gods, what is it with this age we are living in? Faerie women walk live and whole out into the world and disappear back into it again. Faerie men siring sons on humans, revenents walking, and now vampires..."

"Either this is what happens to people's minds from the constant stress of seeing so much carnage, this endless killing and fighting and uncertainty... Or else..."

"Or else it's all real," Jack mused, with a philosophical grunt. "Everything you can think of and more."

"Well, Agnes and Robin Goodfellow were certainly real. Maybe these

times of blood sacrifice yield prodigies? Maybe even half of it is a real. If that is so then the world is both more marvellous and more ter…"

The lid came off then. The monk moved forward making the sign of the cross and flicking holy water. As a warrior Gil had extensive experience with the human form mangled in every way and shape, and all the stages of putrefaction. The monk placed his hand over his nose and mouth. "She cannot be vampire for the corpse rots in the casket."

Gil started shaking his head as he stepped closer to examine the body. "No. Look. See? The leg was rotting whilst she still lived! Think of how long she's been in the ground and then behold her bloated and ensanguinate appearance!"

He was not exaggerating about her swollen looking face being late in the piece for bloating. The black blood mingled with sticky yellow brain fluid that leaked from her mouth and eyes was probably normal though had she been in the coffin as long as she had. Maggots still worked away at her leg stump as if never yet content with consuming it where Blaith had blighted her.

"My lord, does it not distress you to see your sister so?"

"Father, this is not my sister. It is merely the foul fiend who has supplanted her. The one who yet walks and who oppresses the sleep of her innocent daughter and drains her of life. Who with her enchantments has been seen walking still in her one-legged state? I will not be able to sleep at night until we have rendered her immobile. I have brought the tools necessary." Gil opened a sack he'd been carrying which contained such things as an iron stake to nail her to her grave, a rock of the size he could shove between her teeth and a mallet and chisel to break her remaining leg bone.

"You certainly came prepared," the monk said with a certain trepidation, which Gil thought might have something to do with him sensing a little too much enthusiasm on the part of her family.

"Had you been tormented by this vampire you too would have brought precautions. Will you do the work of the Lord and send this fiend to hell, set- ﾗg free the soul of my dear sister from its clutches?"

469

There was an uneasy hesitation.

"Here, I'll do it." Jack reached into his sack and grabbed the stone before, in a very matter-of-fact way he put his hands into her mouth, brewing with black slime as it was, and opened it. The sound of the jaw breaking was loud and uncouth in the icy air. He shoved the stone in. "There," he declared. "Stone. Just like your heart. Bite through that before you come looking."

When the deeds were done the coffin was resealed and Jack stood there looking at him while he cleaned his hands on a rag. Anyone would think Gil was the one who had just unleashed this violence upon his sister's corpse in an altogether too casual manner, for how he was being appraised! "You had that all planned, then it came to the execution…"

"Aren't you afraid it will… I don't know… get on you, the rot that's up in her soul? Getting that on your hands…"

Jack gave him a gentle, almost fatherly pat on the back, which despite its benevolence was yet with the same hand he'd just been wiping. "I know my own heart. I wasn't the Black Warlock of Stukley all those years without rotting out all the old dead stuff in me. My heart colours itself dark for camouflage."

As Augusta's carriage passed through the gates of De Bracy's ancestral home she had to wipe the sweat from her palms on her handkerchief. Even the environs of the carriage brought memories of her first rape at the hands of De Rue. Being a De Biron wasn't going to mean for her what her mother had taught her, yet it did mean something. She knew it did because when Gil had exclaimed what a Norman warlord she would have made there was some old-school warrior pride in her she could have sworn belonged to sword-wielding ancestors.

"Lady Augusta De Biron, daughter of Nanette De Biron, here on my Lord Uncle's behalf to see Lord Malcolm De Bracy."

The servant hurried away and Augusta tried to make her wait seem as haughty as possible, as if she were simply arriving fashionably late.

"His lordship will see you now, my lady. Please follow me."

Augusta didn't bother to reply but followed him into a room that contained nothing but a throne-like chair in which his lordship sat redolent. She had to hide a bit of a smirk. The De Bracy family was only recently ennobled, unlike her ancient Norman French family. You could always tell the type, they were bending over backward to behave like a lord. For a brief moment before her curtsy she took stock of him.

He was an average enough looking man around fifty, with a few facial scars. Augusta already knew there was no monstrous appearance to go with the actions of men like De Bracy. De Rue had been guilty of the same atrocity, yet his appearance was unremarkable. He was like many fighters, brutally strong, a bit of damage to his face, but not a gorgon or a troll, not in appearance at least. If anything, the evidence of having once been handsome had existed in De Rue. All that ended though when you got to their eyes. There was a *look*.

"Forgive me, my lord, for my unexpected visit. I come on behalf of my uncle Lord Gilbert."

The man's eyes narrowed. She shivered a little for she found herself imagining how Robin and Blaith's aunt had seen those eyes narrow on her once. "Greetings Lady De Biron. I must say I'm surprised the Baron of Rochdale sends a female in his stead."

Quickly Augusta wracked her brain to come up with an excuse that supported her uncle's honour and appeared suitably subservient all at once. "It is certainly irregular. With my brother and husband both dead I have too oft been burdened with responsibilities that do not befit the frailties of my sex." In between her generally downcast eyes Augusta took little glimpses of him. What she saw she liked even less than she'd expected. There was a stark predatory gleam in his eyes when he looked at her. It looked like the eyes of those who starve for bread on the roadside when Hob was about to distribute food to the refugees.

"Hmm," he seemed to consider the idea and accept it. "What is the matter Gilbert De Biron wants discussed?"

"We encountered your men at the time we arrested the wolfshead, Robin

471

Goodfellow, and his brother and informed them that we had done so."

"You were there for that as well then? Arresting outlaws as well as running errands better suited to your male guardian?"

She threw in another deep curtsy before explaining. "As Nanette's only living heir my Lord Uncle thought it best to have me with him lest his right to seize the outlaw in my mother's name was called into question."

"I see. Well, yes, so far I know this story."

"Please forgive me, my lord. My uncle wants to query the terms of the agreement with you, just in case the messengers failed to convey what was said and in what terms."

"Alright… How do you understand the agreement to have run?"

"My Lord Uncle took the wolfsheads captive before your arrival and offered you a purse representing the money my Lady Mother left for their disposal. He asked that the people sheltering these miscreants be left unmolested."

"Exactly as it was reported to me."

Augusta was unbalanced for a moment. "Thank you for that. It was a chivalry of my uncle's, meant for the innocent women and children who may not have understood their part in aiding and abetting such a man."

At this he smirked. It was possible to know somehow without looking but she glanced to confirm and found it true. "Oh come on, Augusta. De Rue told me it was you who killed Rowan De Biron. Your own brother… Cut his throat like a pig and bled him."

Like a hunted creature she looked franticly around her to check that no one had heard him. There didn't appear to be anyone within earshot.

"Tut, tut, tut," he said, as if to a naughty child. "As far as stories go it kind of gets in the way of your modest young widow act." Seeing that he had thrown her he began to circle at the scent of blood. She swore she could hear him sniffing her like a hyena waiting to see how weakened she was. "He used to tell me what he did to you." He laughed coldly to himself.

Augusta sucked in her breath and held it. *You knew this could happen. You prepared yourself for the possibility he'd talk about it. Do. Not. Flinch.*

"He liked you though. I think it was because of the killing to be honest. He said he'd never watched a bitch tear someone open like that. Charmer, that old bastard… They don't make men like him anymore. It was the Crusade with him. You smash a few Saracen babies and it blurs the edges of things. Once you've been starving enough to eat human flesh, you start realising we're all just the same as that, a butcher's shop on the inside."

"Indeed," Augusta replied quickly. "It was like that when I slit the throat of my brother and felt his blood running out over my hands. I'll never forget the shocked, mindless, dilated expression in his eyes and it was then I knew it excited me." There was a wild freedom in saying the truth of it. For a moment it almost felt like a bond between her and this terrible man.

De Bracy snorted with mild amusement. "You're not looking to remarry, are you? I've taken De Rue's sloppy seconds in the past and I'd do it again."

Augusta dropped another curtsy with her eyes downcast. "Alas, I am still in my uncle's guardianship on account of my age."

He smiled at her then in a way she would never forget. "Just how I prefer it."

"If you will excuse me, my lord. I need to get back before Uncle Gilbert sends people searching." She tried to smile. "He's very protective of me."

"I bet," he said, with a leer and a jump of his eyebrow. "It's like *that* is it? Well, the De Birons do have a bit of a reputation for liking their own blood-line a little too much. Who am I to judge though? In all seriousness, my lady, tell your uncle that I ceded the prisoners to him as a matter of rank, as was his right. I can only trust they suffered before they died. I accepted losing the bounty on Robin's head to Lord Gilbert, too, and continue to pretend I don't know who killed Rowan De Biron, and usurped his birthright. So, I will just kill as many tinkers as I feel like, I think."

Blaith lingered to watch Robin train. He did so with a variety of feelings, including something best described as awe, a marvelling at the physical power of this force of nature his mother's life had been traded for. It was complex to

enjoy the perfect fusion of human and faerie skills that created Robin's combat body. After all, Blaith could tell he was fighting someone in particular in his mind all the more of late. Though he was quite exposed in this state Robin accepted Blaith's gaze with the same unselfconsciousness he always received it with.

So far this morning Robin had repeatedly punched and kicked a sand bag in such a way that suggested he was training to kill someone purely via an unarmed beating. When he was still coming to understand his own strength, speed, and immense adrenal power Robin had killed an opponent with one punch in the ring. Since then, he was more precise about the sort of damage he inflicted. The most telling thing was these foreign broadsword manoeuvres. It didn't surprise Blaith to learn that the person Robin was mind-fighting fought at sword with a lord's weapon. He may have grappled the upper hand over his nightmare demon, yet still their lore taught that neither he nor their community would be free of the trauma until a proper revenge was taken for Aunt Eliza.

This was the unspoken aspect to their presence in Rochdale. Between them it didn't need verbalising or validating. News still did not come of their family and whatever the outcome they would one day have to strike back at their oppressor. Robin certainly looked in full fighting form; in fact Blaith suspected he was stronger than ever he was previously. Perhaps it was the regular food? It was also likely he was only now coming into his full strength, which was believed to arrive somewhere between twenty-five and twenty-seven.

Only someone that knew his every little nuance would have picked up the small behavioural changes. Robin dived straight into what he did best: making things happen. If anything, he was more effective and efficient than ever. Several feelers were put out along the communication chains, both between outlaw bands and via Gilbert's more well to do connections. Nobody knew anything about their people's fate, or had heard anything specific. All they kept being told about was the Marchers were in flames and everywhere hungry refugees, stripping the land bare.

The longer Emrys and Sorcha didn't return or send news the more distressed Eilish became. Their company was pared back now to only those who were fit, not yet elderly, and childless. Blaith had a raven's instinct for weakness and sensing who would falter first, and at this time his greatest worry was for Eilish. Robin didn't seem to be *doing* worry. This was what was at the heart of the changes Blaith noticed since the injury.

Robin's attitude was more like Blaith himself than it was like Robin. *As if I, as Death, have touched him lightly, tenderly, leaving a bruise… a bruise in the shape of an inner stillness that lies behind the ringing in the ear.* When Robin finished, he approached Blaith whilst drying the sweat off his upper body with a bath cloth. He then flopped down on the grass beside him.

"I wouldn't want to be the next person you punch," Blaith observed, reaching over and taking his hand and turning it over in his. He knew it as well as his own, the scar through the palm covered by the matching tattoos of eyes, the calloused fingertips from the bow, the reddened knuckles, and underneath it all still the elegance of a musician's hands. "Do you think you will try again with the harp soon?" He knew it was a tender topic, one that if he could not broach no one could.

Robin sighed. "I should. It is cowardice really, and pride. With music it's harder for me to be bad at it than when I have to get my strength back after other types of injury."

Blaith didn't push into the spot. His heart ached. How he'd wanted to give his younger brother a better world to grow up in! It was as if he personally had been responsible somehow, rather than the Faerie King, for bringing Robin into this incarnation in the first place.

"May I ask you something equally personal?"

"Of course. There is nothing I would keep secret from you." Knowing him as Robin did he would understand what a big call that was for someone like Blaith.

"Do you *know*? Do you sense it? Which of our people have passed?"

It was Blaith's turn to sigh. "I am trying not to…to be brutally honest.

I think you will understand where perhaps no other may. I don't want to *be* Death this time. I don't want people to think of me in conjunction with the loss of our loved ones, as if I were on His side. This time I just want to be Blaith, family member, bereaved..."

"Oh, I understand that one, brother," Robin muttered, his hands behind his head and staring up at the sky. "It's too much to carry all the time, isn't it?" It was only for a moment though, this nebulous understanding floating between them where Robin meant it for both of them and the blue sky was scant clouds with clouds. Blaith felt something emotional rise in his throat. As if he may not see another spring like this one.

Augusta's carriage being let through the gates broke the spell of the moment and caused Robin to sit up.

"Do you notice how she often leaves when Gil does?"

Robin nodded. "It must be maddening to live among us as equals and yet not have one's full freedom of movement. To have another placed as guardian over you..."

"Hmmm." Blaith murmured under his breath. It wasn't that he agreed or disagreed, something about it just stuck in his craw.

"Look what I found," Robin said, carrying a bag of flour into the kitchen where Lux was helping him bake bread and prepare care packages. She had flour in her hair, a piece of which kept escaping from the tie that held her ponytail in an adorable way. He had no particular opinions about how she chose to wear her hair, though there was something about her apron, that she used both for cooking and making medicines that always got him semi hard.

"What I would like to know, my love, is how does someone just 'find' extra flour in a time of famine, burnt crops, and crazy bread prices?"

He grinned at her as he set it down on the bench, with some hope that his smile might allow him to get away with it. "Well... you steal some money from someone who needs is less and spend it on very expensive flour to help feed people who need it more. A form of taxation on the rich for starting the

war in the first place."

She looked at him like it was against her better judgment that she loved him so. "It's that first bit about where you stole the money from someone that I'm worried about. The powers that be tend to prosecute property thefts particularly harshly during times of war."

"Well," Robin said, pulling up a stool and beginning to help allocate things into baskets. "In all fairness they started it when their war stole the people's crops from them. People don't sit there and peacefully starve, they shoot game in the forest, which uses up what we live on. Then, deprived of their sport, the rich call it poaching and steal their fingers and hands."

Robin watched her as she kneaded the bread. He loved the way the tips of her ears would get pink when she did anything vigorous, and her almost translucent eyelids. "You know I share your aversion to walking past and letting people starve. I just don't want to bring trouble to Gil's door. I suppose it's too late for that though." A little mischievous smile crept around her mouth as she looked up at him. "You're already here."

He smiled back at her. It was always best if he could convince them the huge risk he'd taken was charming. Because the truth was, he could do no other, it was more than an aversion he had to seeing people starve. Helping was more of an imperative than optional. Robin was still struggling with trying to un-remember the convulsing, sucking sound of the sobs made by a starving child they'd assisted recently. The mite couldn't have been more than five. Robin had to physically restrain her while she was fed, she fought him the whole time because she wanted all the food at once.

"Robin?"

"Yes?"

"Why have you never asked me about sex with women? Most men... are interested."

Robin shrugged. "I guess I'm different to most men."

"I have indeed picked up on it."

"I don't know how to explain." He sighed. Though he protested this the

truth was he really wanted to. "It's like gender isn't that much of a big thing to me. I don't see it the way most people do, maybe because I'm half faerie?"

Lux nodded to herself. "But you seem to love cunny so much…"

"I love giving pleasure. But I'd suck your cock well too if you had one. Which says more about *whom* I love than it does anything else."

"So you have to be in love?"

Robin lifted the bread tins into the oven while he thought about it. "Yes. That's about it."

She shook her head as if in amazement. "All this time I've been thinking quite the wrong thing."

"What did people tell you about me this time?"

"That you were damaged goods, I suppose. That it was a trust thing that you might not heal from."

He made a cynical exhalation through his nose. "There are plenty of things I might not heal from, that is not one of them. On the topic of gender, do you think you'll talk to the women again when we get the relief rations handed out?"

"It feels a little like proselytising when you do it to hungry people."

"Then we will find some other context. You are so good at it, Lux. Even just the fact you can break down the ideas in everyone's language and you're talking from experience."

She looked a little deflated, as if the last public talk she'd given on Cymric soil had stolen some of her fire for her women's insurrection. "It's hard when the very people arguing back against you for their own oppression are other women."

"What sort of arguments did they put forward?"

"Some of them were pretty base. Like that if they didn't obey their husbands and submit to his wishes who would protect them from all the violence in the land?"

"Wow," Robin muttered.

"Indeed, the ugliness is very clear once you've known better. They quote

478

Ephesians 5.22 at me and say that God's commandments to women were clear. Then you're being forced up against a wall where you have to either identify as a heretic, or yield the floor."

"If I remember that verse clearly, I think it also told the man to love the woman the way Christ loves and tends to his church. So apparently being Christ-like includes marital rapes and beatings of his church."

Lux sighed. "Apparently so. But there are some strenuous in the defense of their own oppression."

"Was there nothing you saw that gave you hope?"

"I admit it there was. There were some tough Cymric women who declared they already co-ruled their home. And there was a youngish woman who stood near the front. The whole time I was talking there were tears streaming down her face."

"There will always be a few smart ones in the mix. I believe there are many more. They are afraid of all this male-led violence. Even when Matilda is queen in name it is Robert of Gloucester bashing people's brains in with his mace. It's like a protection racket; you need us to protect you from what those other men will do to you if I wasn't here. We were raised to respect everyone as equals, that included all women, young, or old, pretty or plain, mother or maid, abled or disabled, rich or poor."

Lux put down the cheeses she was wrapping in cloth, came around the bench, and suddenly wrapped her arms around his waist. Her head still fit easily under his chin, and he felt a rush of delight in her spontaneous affection, and great tenderness for her slight form.

"Thank gods for you," she whispered. "For your insight, your sense of fairness, and your beautiful heart. I have had *a life* because of you and this blood-thread. And believe me when I say I will help you fight for it."

# 5

"re you sure?" Sariah whispered, as though she were afraid the castle walls would hear her.

Eilish nodded. "I've missed two bleeds now, so pretty sure, yes." She could tell that Sariah's feelings about her pregnancy were mixed even though she tried to look excited and happy for her. "You don't have to pretend. I know you too well and you aren't fooling anyone. I'm pretty scared, but it felt crucial. Fateful. Like I don't have a choice in the part I play. Maybe none of us do."

"Ah, my love…" Sariah murmured, squeezing her hands in hers. "We have both made our own sacrifices for this life. Mine was to catch other's babies and to never bear. Yours *was to* bear. After what I saw at Twll Du I applaud your courage for trying again. This time it will be a girl. A continuer for your distaff lineage."

"Indeed," Eilish replied with tight lips. More and more her hand was straying to her stomach, as if Blaith's growing seed there were filling in a carved out absence that had been there since she'd lost her first child. "Do you know what's awful though?"

"What's that?"

"Usually when I get pregnant it would be full holy whore mode for Roodmass, not having to worry who came inside me. But the man I think of when I think about wanting someone other than Blaith to come inside me, is Emrys." A great, thick sadness caught her somewhere between the baby and her heart. "The more time goes by the more I fear…" Eilish prepared herself to say it for the first time. "I fear he's gone, Sariah."

"I know, honey. I know. Not knowing is sometimes worse."

Eilish nodded. "I play out little scenarios in my mind where I wake up in the morning and everyone is smiling at me saying, are you going to tell her, or shall I? And he's arrived to tell us it was all a false alarm. De Bracy hasn't attacked our caravans or burnt out the Owens' settlement." She started to cry. It was harder not to cry now she was pregnant. Intense emotions all too often swept over her so strong they nearly took her off her feet sometimes. "Then when I wake up and it hasn't happened perhaps the disappointment is worse than the hope was good."

Sariah nodded her understanding of this principle. "Does Blaith know about the baby?"

"I just told him this afternoon. I wanted him to know before Roodmass."

"How did he take it?"

She sighed. "There was a muted sort of happiness, also a melancholia more so than the anxiety I feared would be there. He congratulated me, told me I was brave... Which I know is one of the biggest compliments to his mind. But the whole time he looked at me it was more like we were going to a funeral than a birth."

"That is Blaith's deep waters though, Eilish. I wouldn't read too much into it. We have Roodmass to prepare for and I'm sure he can be brought round to a happier state of mind with a little... persuasion."

"I suggest mead," Sariah's voice said from behind her. She turned to see her in her maiden skirt made of leather braids suspended on a girdle, flowers, necklaces, and freshened braids. You could see her breasts, and if she turned certain ways you could see more than that through the leather plaits. She extended the drinking horn to Lux. "You should drink some in honour of your first Roodmass as an officiating maiden. I don't promise that it *only* contains mead, but mead is definitely in there."

Lux drank it without further questions. Even though one might have expected it to do the opposite the continued silence from across the border re-

481

quired a stress-blow-off, it released a thick and heady abandon into the air. A sort of 'drink, fuck and be merry for tomorrow we die' sort of feeling. Sariah's eyes gleamed with it, her body moved with it, understood it, knew how to ride the dragon of it. Lux could feel the pull of it in the sticky fragrance of the hawthorn in blossom mingled with other sweet scents; it called to her to join hers to the wild disjointed pulse of the night.

Sariah smiled, her secretive seductive smile where her eyebrows arched up. Lux was beginning to see the way the feral woman creature they called The Rose Queen came wafting in and out of Sariah on a regular basis, and she understood a little of why so many men were scared of that power and attached cruel names to it. "I would just go to Robin and Blaith if I were you. The foyer is for general touching, kissing, and sensuality so I'd start there."

Lux nodded and took another long swallow of the mead.

"Are you ready for your maiden voyage?" Sariah pulled back the elderberry coloured cloth that covered the door. Giving Sariah a squeeze on the arm meant to convey thanks for her support and so much more, Lux bent down to enter the bower. It was dimly lit inside so it took her a couple of moments to get her bearings.

As her eyes adjusted she saw Robin was engaged with Blaith, who was also equally half naked, and they appeared to be sharing fire between their foreheads and stroking each other. She was just about to withdraw hurriedly when Robin noticed her.

"Lux," he said, patting the furs and tartans they were lying on. Blaith propped his head up on his elbow and beckoned to her. It felt like she'd interrupted something, and yet they were doing this thing, taboo in nearly every culture, where anyone could see… It was strangely unsettling to have this feeling as if only now was she being brought into some private sanctum in their lives.

He didn't sit up; Robin continued to lay sprawled there with his shameless hard-on, offering her a mead flagon to sip from. He watched her as she sipped from it, and when she glanced back and forth between Robin's eyes and

Blaith's their Otherness screamed back into being for her. Robin's eyes had his patient wolf in them again. Blaith's glimmered with black hot fire that you were afraid you'd fall into, and equally afraid you wouldn't. Every line of their supine bodies, the tangible scent of male arousal they carried where their sweat mingled on each other's skin, and the relaxed yet intent gleam of the confident wolf in their eyes told her

"Come and lie down with us," Blaith suggested.

Robin held out his arm to indicate where she should place herself down between them.

"Don't be nervous," Blaith said, holding up the mead so he could actually feed it to her. It was a strange kind of exercise in trust, letting him say how much of it to pour into her mouth and for how long. The whole time he did so he maintained intense eye contact with her. "This is your first May Eve as a maiden. You get to decide what happens."

He forced her to drink a little more than she actually felt she wanted but removed it when she started to make sounds of protest. She was both ruffled and excited by the soft sound of amusement that Blaith's force-feeding drew from Robin. It was impossible not to sense the eroticism that lingered behind this gentle sadism. Suddenly she knew without looking at him that those new edges of Robin she was touching on, and this consensual voyeurism into hidden parts of his nature excited more than it unsettled her.

"I get to decide…" She thought about this for a while, as Robin's hand trailed down over her waist and hips and found her naked outer thigh by pushing up her shift. "But…" she could feel the mead and the smoke in the air starting to go to her head already and she struggled to order her thoughts. "What if it involves other people? What if they don't want to do what I want to do?"

Blaith raised his eyebrows and grinned at her, his immensely sharp and crowded teeth showing for a rare moment. Although they were very unusual Lux had always thought they were more attractive to her than had they been straight. "What kind of twisted stuff are we talking about here? If you can

come up with something I'm not up for, then I'll let you teach me French!"

"He's that confident!" Robin laughed. He was obviously a little drunk. She could tell because being amused by something had to involve touching Blaith in some way to express it.

"Oh, I'm that confident. I'm not learning French for anyone. I don't care what sick stuff she has in mind."

She strongly doubted that she was even imaginative enough to push Blaith's wide comfort zone, let alone come up with anything he'd deem 'sick'.

"Tell me what it is, lover?" Robin murmured, his hand running up over her stomach to lightly pass over her breast. "Remember that it's May Eve so you can do or have pretty much anything you want, there are no rules to-night."

Lux turned slightly so that she was looking up into Blaith's face, who was looking down at her from where he was propped up on his elbow. "Come on, Lux," he murmured. "You can't shock me."

She reached out a curious hand and placed it on his side, just below where his unusual birthmark started. It was a tentative touch but when she touched him lightly with her fingertips he made a quiet sound of enjoyment. She re-alised that when Blaith fucked her she had never taken the initiative like this and touched him back, except when and where he told her to. It disarmed her what a strong, warm sense of his animal being his skin gave off.

There were no walls around him separating the animal of him from the world. He didn't do anything to her, he just seemed to offer his body to be touched by her with a sense of generous intimacy. His comfort made her feel comfortable as if it was infectious. She even lightly ran her fingers through the novel line of dark hair up his midsection that Robin didn't have.

"I guess what I want…" she paused then and removed her hand. These young men, these creatures, were part of some wilderness that she was only just able to enter. They would always be Other though, because they were raised to believe the only sin was the lack of love.

"You are *killing me* with suspense, Lux!" Robin cried, expressively buck-

ling his body up off the ground for a moment to express the sentiment of his frustration with his hips.

"Patience, brother," Blaith chided with amusement flickering through his gaze and his suppressed smile. "This is exquisite. Let it play out."

"You're making fun of me."

"Oh no! Never!" Blaith said, gripping her arm with sudden seriousness. "I would never do that. I'm teasing Robin." He moved closer into her proximity then and she began to see the serpent tattoo around his arm undulate the way she'd once seen the spirit in Robin's St Michael tattoo, rippling under the surface of his skin. "I'll tell you a secret," he whispered. Moving slowly, sinuous like the snake under his skin, he brought his lips right up to her ear.

"I want to hear it too," Robin objected.

"Oh, you'll keep," Blaith said, giving him a light slap just on and below his belt buckle in a spot that must have reverberated through his erection at the very least. "This secret is for Lux. I've got others you can have later." The feeling of Blaith's breath against the side of her neck was intoxicating. "I'm hoping," he whispered very softly. "That if I tease him long enough that explosion he keeps locked up in his hips and chest will burst out and pin me to the ground and…" He lingered on the 'and' with obvious relish before withdrawing and saying aloud. "But that would be telling… You don't want to hear anymore about my *sinful, incestuous* desires, do you?"

It struck her like a slap that he had used the words incestuous and sin together. It was as if he'd plucked it out of her consciousness with his particular brand of gaze penetration. Before she had time to censor herself she said the complete truth. "What I really want is to watch you two kiss."

It was impossible to believe she'd really said it. Robin clearly understood not only her request but the feeling behind it. "Oh sweetheart…" he murmured, pulling her up onto him so she had no choice but to straddle him. "I love you so, so much right now and always… Kiss me first." He kissed her on the mouth, a long, slow kiss with a lot of tongue.

"It moves me so much that you don't condemn it." He said when he

released her, aroused, from the kiss. "I am more than comfortable with that. Blaith?" Robin asked, reaching out for his brother. Blaith sat up then, folding his legs. He seemed to take a couple of seconds to think about it.

"That's something very personal you're asking, Lux. If you'd just asked to watch someone fist me, I wouldn't have batted an eyelid, but this is… something else…. *Yes*. The answer is yes. But first I need to know you better."

She climbed off Robin and sat looking across at Blaith. There was a kind of nudity in the way he looked at her now, as though he was committed to baring something in front of her that would challenge him as well as her. "Would you kiss me?" he asked.

She frowned. It was the wording that threw her off. If he had kissed her as he often did it wouldn't have seemed strange. Carefully, almost shyly she climbed into his lap, straddling him the way she had Robin. He moved his arms to accommodate her legs on either side of him, but other than that he just passively accepted whatever she did. The smell and feel of him was familiar to her, he was her initiator, lover and Magister.

With a surprising gentleness that made Lux think of being with a woman, Blaith slid his hands around her waist. The gesture seemed to indicate consent but he continued to look at her. Not seductive and hypnotic anymore, just waiting. He was simply and frankly offering himself. It was so different to kissing Robin that she almost lost her nerve.

When she leaned down and angled her hips to be able to kiss him on the mouth, Blaith made a soft sound of enjoyment and opened his lips for her tilting his head back. Yet still he remained receptive. She covered his mouth with hers and pressed her tongue into his mouth, grinding her hips against him in unconscious rhythm. He made a long, sensuous sort of moan that had something feminine about it, and pressed up with his hips in a way that was a little more masculine, whilst wholly accepting her tongue. She loved him utterly, every queer, uncanny, dangerous, rule-breaking and strange aspect of him.

She didn't have words for it or know how to describe what kind of love even to herself, but she knew that the bond that existed between this man

and Robin was a large part of it. It seemed impossible to not love what Robin loved. If he liked how Blaith tasted and felt, in his gender-blind approach to love, then she needed to as well. "I love you," she whispered to him. He squeezed her back and drank in her love like it was sunshine.

"Yes," he said finally, as he drew back from their embrace. "You may watch."

Sariah spread her arms wide and lay against the outer wall of the bower like someone embracing a lover. She whispered sweet words to it and sung ancient tunes. Later in the night, after she'd collected the life force of a number of different men and women Blaith would draw it all out of her, and after he'd done that he'd have the power to fuck again when you wouldn't think a man could possible fuck to save his own life. That would happen at some point, many times, as would the collection of life, the gathering of her gift to him... But for now it was about the conjuration of Paradise and she was Her priestess.

"Open your legs red stained, honey sticky, tit-leaking, milk spilling mother of witches! Blood weeper, cunt-drenching, sorrow lady, joy lady, truth barer! Your priestess invokes you! Conjures you with her hips and her tongue... Allow us access to the inside places of your holy skirts. Lift your veil and show us the stars within your cunny," she breathed the words breathily into the woven flowers and the drapes, whispered in a mixture of Cymric and the old witching tongue. "Loosen the Binder's knots that hold limbs tight in bondage, let the red serpent of your passion into the bower this night to go among your people and teach them to writhe to your sweet rhythms... Let Love be the only law our people recognise! Let all oppression be lifted! Let the scales fall from blind eyes! Let all things not of your law be overturned, swept aside, shattered, washed away and obliterated by your eternal revolution of ecstasy!"

Slowly, with her eyes still closed and her lips parted with deep sensual awareness, Sariah withdrew her hands from the walls of the bower. She could feel the movements and the rising pleasure pangs of those within, and she smiled with rich, rising satisfaction. Oh yes, tonight was going to be interest-

ing! *On the edge of the dark it always is. Just where the Lady likes it best. The relief that we still have Eilish, the life inside her, our growing hope and future... The fear for Robin, the cold touch of it like a blade on our skin, the fear of losing him... The knowledge that I can't, and Blaith can't and...*

She knew she needed to hold it all though, how else could she weave the passion of the evening out of it? She had to swallow whole the salt in the grief and the cold in the fear. Sariah knew what her people needed. Some nights you just needed to be brave enough to draw it out of them, she thought to herself. Some nights it would be more terrifying than others. For them terror was always a component of Paradise.

Walking slowly around the circumference of the bower she ran her fingers over it and waited to feel for the right moment to enter. She was just nearing the doorway when she noticed Jack taking his weapons off at the door. Sariah felt Jack's enjoyment of her visible body as his almost roguish gaze travelled up her legs and over her hips. She smiled in response to the spark in it.

"Well, hello, handsome," she murmured, coming up and sliding her arm around Jack's waist. Like most of the warriors Jack could feel a little uptight at first, you had to unravel him. Sariah sensed and knew all her people's wounds the way Robin could feel every ligament and pressure point in the body of his opponent. It was the same body art she and her cousin practiced, she knew, hers was just put towards the work of Venus instead of Mars.

"You're looking particularly irresistible tonight," Jack said, tipping his old black hat to her.

"Great. Because I have plans to suck on your cock in the open air like when you were a drunk lad of eighteen under the stars."

"Ah…" he murmured, both something loving and something nostalgic in his tone. "You make me feel like a drunk lad of eighteen, Sariah. Under the stars and this light rain just starting like the sky's own caress…"

Yes, it was time for the night to really get started now. The big cat that lived in Sariah hips stretched and flexed to prowl. *Let's do this like we've never done it before, and like we may never do it again.*

488

"You understand, Lux, that what is done in the Inner Sanctum of the Bower can't be a game or a pretense of any kind? So we can't just make out for your amusement, doing what you would like to see. This will have to be the way we would touch each other if no one were looking."

Lux nodded in response, letting her gaze wash over Robin. He sat as Blaith did with his legs folded under him and his hands resting loosely on his thighs. His slightly wavy hair was worn half up half down today, the loose bit nearly reaching his shoulders and flecked with dark gold streaks.

His gaze seemed to rest on Blaith's like there was nothing uncomfortable in the world about such a prolonged stare. Yet Lux felt the tension of it like she couldn't stand it for much longer if they continued. The serpent tattooed, crudely yet beautifully, on his flesh matched the patterns and appearance of the one that St Michael was being bitten by and thrusting his spear into on Robin's tattoo. Blaith had a lot more locks in his hair than Robin and someone had plaited one and weaved flowers through it.

Finally, Blaith smiled faintly with a foreign expression of immense softness coming into his eyes, a look that Lux hadn't seen there before, not quite like this anyway. In response to it Robin touched his own forehead, and then his heart before offering his hands to Blaith. Blaith did the gesture too, very slowly and thoughtfully. Lux felt a knot of emotion begin to rise up in her throat. She had expected to be sexually excited by the charge of taboo-violation, she hadn't expected to be *moved* in the way one is when coming into the presence of the sacred.

They left their hands in offering position at the end and in almost perfect unison began to say a prayer.

"Our Lady of Blood and Mercy we pray to you, we of the blood of the Nephilim who are free, loosen the Binder's knots that hold limbs tight in bondage, let the red serpent of your passion into the bower this night to go among your people and teach them to writhe to your sweet rhythms. Let Love be the only law our people recognise. Let all oppression be lifted. Let the scales fall from blind eyes. Let all things not of your law be overturned, swept aside,

489

shattered, washed away and obliterated by your eternal revolution of ecstasy."

They made the gesture of respect again, this time bowing fully over so that their hands were upward in offering and their whole backs and necks were exposed. When they came back up, they moved towards each other at the same time until their knees were touching. Then they each took the others face in their hands and moved in for a first, soft kiss on the mouth. Lux's own lips parted slightly. She hadn't been prepared for the softness and sensuality with which they entered into this. It was clear she was watching two people who each gloried in this intimacy with the other.

Finally, Robin came in stronger, covering Blaith's mouth with his and running his fingers through his hair. They did not try to hide the collision of their tongues as they came up onto their knees to be closer. It was as if she was no longer there, which was just how she had wanted it. Blaith made a soft sound of enjoyment and it seemed to enflame them both. Robin seized him up in his arms. He lifted Blaith around the hips and somehow managed to not only tip him over onto his back in the cushions but contrive in the one action to have his knees separated as well.

When Robin pinned him to the ground as his body came down between Blaith's legs kissing him in this posture. Lux was holding her breath in response to the sudden influx of Marsian aggressive energy that fizzed in the air and mingled in an erotic dance with the Venusian current in the Bower. It felt like those two powers were struggling for dominance over this act of intimacy, engaged in something that was part dance and part wrestle, and that was a big part of the fun.

As she watched Robin lifting Blaith's back up off the ground to gather him up again even more passionately into an even more extended upright kiss, she thought she saw the shadow of black wings emerge from Blaith's back and reach their full and awesome span.

Before Lux arrived, Sariah had come into the bower and taken turns sucking both their cocks. It had been a while since Robin had last felt Sariah's

mouth like that, and he was undone by the erotic charge it held for him. He was certain the Lady herself was sucking him, while Blaith held his hand, touched his own cock and watched. When she did it to Blaith he felt it as though it were still happening to him.

Afterwards she had sat back up, told them to do their trousers back up, and left. Blaith and himself had both groaned in pleasing frustration. Their hands found each other after that, only through clothing, as had been the Lady's priming directive. Robin experienced what amounted to an extra sense in his hands when it came to touch. When someone who loved him touched his body was flooded with wellbeing. It was impossible to express just how much he got off, not only on being able to give pleasure, but to give something they couldn't get elsewhere and were aching for.

Were they as Children of Cain not sprung of the Nephilim, children of The Watchers and the Daughters of Man? Since the first forehead brand did his kind ever walk the earth expecting understanding? Yet now, when he was given it, given permission by Lux's arousal, Robin felt a deep loosening in all his fibres. He could feel her watching them and the exquisite quality of the pleasure she took in what she was seeing. The sense of her acceptance filled his throat with hot, thick emotion and made the tangle of fur and wet wolf teeth and flexing claws that churned around in his guts whimper and howl.

"I love you so fucking much," he whispered fiercely into Blaith's hair, yet he meant the words for both of them.

"*Almost* too much," Blaith agreed, pressing his body upwards against Robin with so much intensity that it took most of Robin's strength to force him back into the posture of total surrender he wanted. Blaith's body was stronger than it looked and had always given him safety to be more brutal in a way he could never do on someone Lux's size. He purposely play-struggled and pressed back against Robin to make him subdue and pin him like an eagle on its prey. "But never quite. Love me as hard as you can."

Robin smiled and closed his eyes. His smile was more of a bearing of teeth than a gentle thing of mere happiness. The feeling was too total to be

nice. It contained ripples and shadows of mythology where his kind dropped out of the sky and battled with creatures like Blaith, tumbling over and over each other in a part battle, part coital encounters, as they plummeted mutually from the Heavens, seeding stars and faerie courts as they fell. They found themselves where shafts of solar radiation were thrust into the side of undulating dragons of the Underworld and where supernovas and black holes try mutually to consume one another.

With the Rose Queen's hand Love had touched those narratives and torn them open, revealing the hungry, ecstatic desire for union at the core. Robin gazed down into Blaith's dark eyes and saw around him the immense black wings that emerged from him like some archangel of Hell, merely sojourning here a time, with numerous backwards facing eyes opening in every feather. He didn't only desire Blaith. No, he knew what it was to *be* Blaith. Robin felt darkness inside himself, howling blackly in his wolf's belly. Blaith, before him, was now shining with a pale, ghostly light, fragile and exquisite as patterns in frost.

Gil was about to come down the front steps when he was met by Robin bounding up them. "Gil! What are you doing so far from where the party is happening?" Even in the uncertain light he felt awkward about the question and didn't immediately answer. "You know I like you in this shade of scarlet," he remarked, stopping in front of Gil, standing a bit too close to him and touching his doublet. Gil could tell he was a little inebriated and exuberant with it. "Though you still having it on this late in the game is a crime."

"Ah, well, I did try to call in on Blaith, but when I came in he had Sariah riding his cock to Valhalla and my niece was straddling his face, so…"

"A fine place to find one's self toward the morn of May," Robin observed.

"For those so inclined."

"Ah! Oh I see, it is not just a lean, you are a man of precise anatomical attractions."

Gil grinned with mild amusement at his way of putting it. "Of course.

Were I able to have sex with women do you not think I'd make my life easier and do so?"

"I see." He could tell that even drunk Robin was deeply considering his predicament. "You know, Sariah has this thing she does where she collects her lover's life force offerings and gifts the energy of it to Blaith at the end of the evening? He often springs back to life afterwards. I'm sure he's thinking to be with you. You two are pretty serious. With all the fine clothes you've been getting made for him he's become quite the kept woman."

He knew Robin was trying to make a joke but it only made Gil feel more anxious. "I hope he doesn't think I'm trying to… you know? To tame him, or something because I love-"

Robin shook his head vigorously as though the question were closed. "No. I know he does not. He knows you love the wild soul in him. Blaith can take care of Blaith. He will let you know quite directly if he feels you've overstepped." Robin shrugged. "He likes clothes. I think he's having a good time."

Gil released the breath he'd been holding. "Thank the gods. He's precious to me."

"He is precious to me also. As is your happiness, Gil." He looked at Gil then in a way he couldn't quite interpret. It came with a smile of the sort one wasn't sure about, as if it contained a multitude of things from soft to hard. It might have appeared at times during Gil's initial abduction. "I've got something for you."

Without further explanation he shoved Gil hard into the wall behind him. When his back impacted with the stone of his ancestral home it knocked the air out of him, even though the push had been casual. His body remembered again the way Robin's strength had thrilled him with this feeling of being utterly out of control, even when he should have been more afraid at their first meeting. Before he could step back, forward, or compose himself Robin's body pinned his, while leaning with one bent arm against the wall behind him. He was about to say something when Robin's mouth covered his. For a moment he was too in shock to feel much, then his attention tuned downward to the

493

feeling of Robin's hard body and his harder, aggressive kiss. A weakened sound of pleasure escaped Gil as he pushed his tongue into Gil's mouth, his body leaning on Gil's so hard it wouldn't allow him to fully fill his lungs.

Just as suddenly it was over. Robin withdrew from him, placed his hand behind Gil's head and lightly bumped their foreheads together. "I've got to go find what I did with my shirt." With that he disappeared. When he was sure Robin would be beyond earshot he let another long exhalation of air out, and with it an incredulous sort of sound. It was a half-laugh, as of someone who had just had a spiritual epiphany, or a miracle bestowed, a miracle like a light moving before the eyes, fast passing out of sight.

# 6

The guards reported the arrival of a lone, elder-nun on a tired horse at the gate. Robin was in an upstairs room when he heard and went to the window. A moment before she rode into sight something twanged inside his belly wolf. As soon as she came into sight he recognised the way she sat her horse. "Eldri," he whispered. Within moments he was racing down the stairs, calling out to his family as he went. "Aunt Eldri is here!"

He ran to meet her and as people either caught what he cried out or just started running too because they saw him running. It didn't occur to Robin to do anything but run at full tilt towards her and news of their people. Only Zorien out of everyone, who was still in the stage between boy and man where they move like lightning, made it to her horse at about the same time as him.

"Aunt!" he cried, reaching his hands out to the woman who had tried to catch him at his birth, and had instead been forced to lift him bloody from his mother's gutted stomach. He was sobbing as soon as she caught his hand in turn. "You're alive." He grabbed her like she was the last salvageable part of their collective past. Zorien was crying too, and gradually the other Twll Du folk arrived who were next in the disorganised running race from the castle to the gate.

"And you are still alive too, you crazy, beautiful, magic boy! Well, I'll be damned…Will you stop getting more and more handsome and hand an old woman down from her horse? I've had a long ride." As he handed her down, he knew just from the skeletal firm grip on his hand and the weight she leaned on him that this was not the same Aunt Eldri he'd parted from. He noticed

that as she was coming down off her mount her eyes were seeking Eilish. Robin turned to see where his cousin was and saw her coming to a stop with pinked cheeks even from this brief exertion, with one hand on her pregnant belly that showed now. Her eyes desperately sought Eldri's, searching them for some sign of which piece of news it was going to be.

Eldri pressed her lips together, pity and sadness was in her expression and it had aged her. Robin knew even before she shook her head slowly and meaningfully that she had no good news to give. "I'm sorry, girl. I'm so sorry."

Robin's eyes continued to search the old woman's face as if more information would come from her expression alone. There was a couple of seconds pause, like the time it takes between a serious injury and the body's ability to process the pain before Eilish's harrowing cry rang out in the harsh air. Robin screwed his eyes shut to bear it, both the knowledge of the loss of Emrys and the shrieking cries of his cousin's heartbreak. Sariah and Blaith were with her, holding her arms while her knees went on her and in the end they had to submit to lowering her down gently on them.

When Eldri looked back at Robin her eyes were overflowing with the tears that had stood still earlier.

"What happened to him, Eldri?"

She nodded and took down her quarterstaff, which appeared to be doing stealthy double-duty as an old lady's walking stick. "I will tell all of it. First, I would like to go inside. This rich man's house can surely spare some proper food and a beverage. Something strong. And maybe one for Eilish."

"Indeed, this rich man's home can provide such things, Aunt Eldri," Gil responded in Cymraeg. "It will be my honour."

She nodded once before beginning to make her way up the path. "Alright then, nephew," she replied, as though Gil had just sprung into existence for the first time now he was speaking to her in the language of poets. "Show me to your hall and I will tell my tale."


"We thought we were doing so well at first. We saw no conflict and hit a

decent seam of hunting. After shooting a deer we had to rest a bit. It was clear we would need to cure some of the meat just in case there were skant miles ahead. The smoke must have been what tipped them off to the fact our camp was there. It sounds sloppy but we were tired and there wasn't enough of us to do watch well without people flagging.

"One of us," Aunt Eldri said, setting down her tankard, and gracefully avoided mentioning who. "Must have fallen asleep at watch very briefly. They were very good, I might add. Proper foresters of the type that know the patch of land they are paid to tyrannise over on the lord's behalf better than any passerby, even us travelling folks. They got the drop on us alright. We all woke to the unsettling sensation of cold steel at our throats. Well, they just started yelling at us in what I suppose was Norman French and of course none of us could understand a word they were saying."

At this Robin made an inarticulate, quiet sound of pain. It would barely have been noticed normally but with the room so still it was the only sound. Lux reached over and squeezed his hand. She knew exactly what that sound was, it was the response to his family member's inexpressible vulnerability in the face of such a situation without their translator.

"Of course, we tried to explain we could only speak Cymraeg and Emrys tried to reason with them…" She sighed deeply. "They took our inability to give a denial as proof of a guilty verdict. By their laws I suppose we were guilty… Or more specifically I was guilty, as it was me that took the shot that dropped the deer, which I tried to tell them. Not that they would have believed me. They would have no doubt thought I lied to protect my grown son and wasn't capable of the shot. I would have taken it for him too if I could have spoken with them…" She held up her two bow fingers significantly and Eilish gasped in horror. "My set are a lot older than his and he would have needed them for longer." Eilish's weeping was now the lone backdrop to the story they had all waited so long to hear.

"As you would all know our folk survive the poaching punishment, even when they take the whole hand, we've gotten some through… Many have

lived on maimed yet unbroken… The problem was in our rush, I suppose in Gladys' rush to have account of her children and Bran we had not packed medical supplies of any kind."

It was Eilish's turn to make a mute sound of horror.

"After they cut him we did our best to treat the wound with what we could find. Gladys stuffed macerated roadside yarrow into the wound. That was all we could do, that and wrap it tight with rags meant for Gladys' blood time."

"Oh dear gods," Eilish whispered. "I should have checked… I should have checked his bag… or been there… oh god my poor boy…"

Eldri gave her some time to cry. After a while she said. "How could you have known, kitten? Wardens generally carry emergency kits but Gladys was in such a hurry to leave... Can you bear for me to continue?"

Eilish nodded wordlessly, swallowing down hard. She was so pale Lux feared her pride was the only thing getting her through the tale.

"He began to falter before we even made it to Gwynedd. There were sweats and trembling. Eventually he began to see things… it's hard to say if it was the blood-loss we failed to entirely staunch or the dirty axe putting demons in his blood. When he was lucid he said to tell people things, which is why I am here and could not bide in my homeland where I very much want to be. He told me tell Eilish that he loves her and that he has no regrets about going, because there was a thing that needed doing for decency's sake. Robin couldn't do it, so it fell to him to give everything to see our family home."

Eilish cried even harder. Robin gave a very slow touch of his head, heart and hands that seemed to offer a heartfelt respect to an unseen presence, while he did it his shoulders trembled with sobs.

"We did reach home. Later we buried his bones on the shores of Llyn Idwal…" Everyone looked at her expectantly and again she shook her head. It was slow and her head drooped at the end, her chin almost touching her chest.

"Oh gods," Blaith whispered. Robin reached over to him and took his hand in his free one.

"There was tragedy there. Triumph also, but a lot of tragedy… Nothing

was even smoking anymore by then. We found the burnt out caravans first. All the relics of the ancestors they contained, gone. Every memory burnt to a crisp…"

Sariah's hand went over her mouth and she made a little high-pitched yelp of a sound.

"We knew as soon as we saw them and Gladys started to run…" Eldri took a long sigh of a breath and had more alcohol. "She would want me to tell you that Bran died a hero, as did her boy Ethan, and all of our brave men and lads save Alun who recovered from his wounds… and from what I understand Creirwy died, fighting on, defending her homestead after her husband fell. The crazy thing about it is nobody knew for sure who sent those men, beyond that they were Normans. Creirwy had forced her sister and her children into the inside of an openable pew and killed as many as she could before she fell. Not a person were they able to take alive…

"The children also gave good account of themselves when they got separated from the women in their panic. Catrin, Bran's girl, being the oldest lead them on such a stealth mission that it took Sorcha three days to track them and bring them in, freezing and scared but alive. Not a one of Gladys' children were lost, or any wee ones for that matter. Our boys did us proud…" she cracked up here. No doubt to her they had all been boys, so recently caught and grown and flown… "They killed most of those assassins, there was only a few left who tried to track the women and children who had run. They never found them though," she nodded emphatically as if to herself. There was pride in this. "That's the strength and cunning in our stock right there. The blood of fallen angels and faerie kings, gods walking around among mere men…" she mused to herself as if having lost the thread of the narrative and wandered into a grander one.

"That's what I want as many of you as possible to do, survive. Don't be ashamed if it doesn't look like the way you were bred. Those caravans are gone now, both in body and in soul. We have to release all that. We are one big family now. Some of you will no doubt die trying to protect others. But those

of you who go on – I don't know where I'm headed either. Maybe into the mountain to take my final journey potion up high on hungry Tryfan where only the eagles will come to pick my bones, or maybe I'll take it easy in a nunnery pretending I give a half damn about their god- who knows." She cackled at the thought. "Either way, it will be upon Cymric soil. Whatever path you have to go down, know this, young people, there is a great dignity in survival. Not at all costs perhaps. It's not to be sneezed at though, there are lessons to be learned the whole way. If some part of what we are… what we were… if some part of our song still rings out somewhere, if some part of us travels on."

Blaith felt suffocated by the environs of Gil's hall, as if the whole thing were some outfit with a tight neckline that he couldn't feel right in his body while wearing. Ever since he'd heard the news about his people and the caravans it had felt like this. With the summer tipping towards autumn there was a chill in the air though, so he had no mind to bear it in a tent outside while his people's loss was still fresh up inside him. Gil had been solicitous and put a blanket around his shoulders and passed him a warm cup of broth he'd fetched from the kitchens with his own hands. Blaith wondered if it was the first time he'd ever been down there?

The biggest relief was neither of these things though; it was in the fact that there was now finally only Robin, Jack, Gil and himself in the room. There would be things to be spoken of which he would wish not to have spoken of before other effected parties. "So what move do you want to make?" he asked, looking at Robin. Protocol seemed looser now, as if the burning of the caravans had turned everything to ash and charcoal dust and it was all floating in the air in its unformed state.

With a broadsword in his belt and the leather jerkin Gil had made for him Robin almost looked like the Brythonic warlord he should have been, in a world that still belonged to them, where people followed the best man rather than the richest. In that world, if such a thing had ever existed, Robin would have been a strong and proud protector of his people, not a vagabond,

a stranger in his own homeland… Today he was lacking some colour, and he had dark marks under his eyes that only served to make them look more fiercely green. "So, we agree De Bracy did this?" he asked softly. It was the tone of voice of Robin's that Blaith knew people should mind.

"What other Normans would go that far into Cymric territory on such a targeted extermination mission?" Gil said.

"Even more so to the point, what other Norman lord with the resources to hire all those mercenaries knew for*certain*where Robin's people were camped?"

"It's damning," Blaith agreed. "When put together with the fact he's a madman who we know doesn't like being said no to."

"How do we know that about him?" Jack queried.

Blaith understood these days that he wasn't being argumentative; it was the older man's way of thinking to test all assertions and assumptions to make sure they held weight. He was coming to see that this habit made him an excellent second, though at first it had rubbed Blaith like a cat stroked backwards.

"Because it's why he killed my aunty," Robin replied, his voice shifting to a different kind of quiet that came on the back of a deep sigh.

"If that was a grave enough crime to die for it, then it seems in character that Gil and Augusta refusing him our heads, and his bounty, would easily be enough cause. Whether he knows Blaith and I are still alive or not, he obviously knew someone among us cared for those people back at the caravans, and he wanted to punish us."

"It fits with his character certainly. Well, it sounds more convincing than it being a random Norman attack. A farmstead with some tinkers staying on it is hardly a high value target in a civil war," Jack agreed.

"It is cowardly of him when he could have picked his fight with me who did the denying," Gil said.

"All bullies are cowards, my friend. That is also in his known character. It was my weird, touched, faerie child self he was bullying when Eliza caught his attention by yelling at him to stop hurting me. Who does such a man that beats up on a touched six-year-old choose to attack, the lord with a garrisoned

castle? Or the tinkers living in a field?"

Blaith had heard enough a long time ago. It was all words, words, words, until he was able to gaze down at De Bracy's face being covered over in dirt with the man's own severed cock crammed between his teeth. "We kill him." Blaith hadn't consciously used his Magister voice, it happened nonetheless. His tone suggested it was a decision made already. "You and I, Hob. We go in there at night and infiltrate his stronghold. We slaughter him like a pig in his own bedchamber."

Robin blinked twice, then nodded, quiet determination clear in the set of his chin. "There is no other way out now."

"Surely there is though!" Gil exclaimed. "You have me. I could demand to walk straight in the front door because of who I am."

"And for walking out again afterwards?" Robin queried. "After you've done it?"

Gil opened his mouth but didn't say anything. He clearly hadn't thought far enough ahead to his own extraction.

Robin just nodded, as if to say it was as he thought. "Bless your heart, Gil."

Blaith moved closer to him and took Gil's hand in his, lacing his fingers through his before bringing it up to his mouth to kiss. "I know you would throw down for us. I see it and love you for it." Blaith's words of love were known for being sparing, for this reason when he used them, they always landed with great impact.

Gil blinked away tears. "I'm just not ready to lose you."

Lux hugged the bucket to her in between retches. She hadn't been able to bring herself to use the castle privy. Even though the place was kept better than her family home anywhere where people continually shit down a hole in a castle wall has a smell. And she was particularly sensitive to smells ever since Eldri's story. Lux had found herself haunted by the scent of curing venison, mingled horribly with proud flesh and burnt caravan. The devastation of it

was sensory and saturating.

Robin had thrown up after Eldri's story too. Then they had all drunk an excess of alcohol on top of the grief and shock. Lux had needed to drink just to drown the sound of Eilish's wail of grief from her memory. But nobody else had vomited again the next day like she was doing. Just as she was trying to get control over her desire to dry retch over and over Augusta let herself into the room. They had all been living like this, treating the rooms more like camps than separate, private spaces. Most of the tinkers couldn't stand it all the time and would go and spend some time in their tent. This was one of those moments where Lux wished she had some privacy.

"You didn't make a merry begot baby at Roodmass with Hob and Blaith did you?" Augusta asked.

"No! I mean, why would you just come in saying something like that?" It felt to Lux almost as though the other girl were trying to ill wish her.

"Well, I ended up getting pretty drunk at Roodmass myself..." She rubbed both her hands against her face as though still a bit surprised by what she'd participated in. "It was extremely fun at the time because I knew I could get off Blaith if I wanted to... Now my blood is a couple of days late. Maybe three? So it was on my mind to ask it. It's probably nothing though. It isn't always on time anyway."

Lux didn't say so, but her blood was also late. Though for Lux the assertion that it was never terribly reliable was true, whereas for Augusta it was less so. Living as close together as they did she knew her friend's cycle very intimately. Nobody could really accurately track Lux's except Robin's nose, which could usually smell out when she was fertile. On such days, where he said she smelt most delicious, they would avoid sex of the cock in cunt variety. At Roodmass, he had come inside her multiple times.

"I think I'm fine, it's just the stress. You should talk to Eilish about getting some of that pennyroyal and rue tincture to get you bleeding, just in case. Blaith and yourself would make a beautiful lord or lady of darkness, but you are too young to risk childbirth."

"You are not wrong there." Augusta passed Lux a cup of water and a rag she'd brought up for her. "My uncle is busy comfort-sucking Blaith. So, I got the idea to come in here with you but then you were all covered in vomit…"

Lux laughed. "What a sweet thought, though!" She drank from the water and wiped her face with the dampened cloth.

Quite suddenly the fun, sexy moment was gone and Augusta sat down on the edge of the bed looking quite serious. "Lux? I think there's something I should have told Blaith. Or Gil. Or Blaith and Gil and Robin."

She frowned. Immediately her pulse went off like a runaway horse. Lux knew to listen when her fetch did things like this, it meant she was in danger. "What should you have told them?"

"I did something crazy."

"What kind of crazy?"

"I went to see De Bracy. To try to see if I could find out an answer for them about what happened to the rest of the family."

"You did what?"

"I just thought maybe he'd be the bragging type and that he might just tell me he killed them. At least it would have been an answer for Eilish. Not a good one, but an answer."

Lux was still staring at her with her mouth slightly open, her heart pounding harder and harder. "Did he say he did?"

Augusta shook her head. "Not in so many words. Gods he is a *bad* man though, Lux…" The way she said it carried deep significance. Lux knew what Augusta's eyes had seen when it came to bad men and that her emphasis on the word would not be used lightly.

"Well of course he is, Augusta! Do you not know the full extent of what was done to Robin's aunt? –Not that anyone but Robin does- He didn't just rape her in front of a child, and kill her, he tortured her, disemboweled her, in ways that Robin *still cannot fully talk about* to this day! Of course he is a bad man! What were you *thinking*, going there without Gil?"

She continued to look down and not meet Lux's eyes. Her shame was

palpable as she shrugged. "I suppose I wanted to be a hero."

The words seemed to cut through the air with how deeply they resonated for Lux. She couldn't help nodding to herself. Had she not felt the same thing, over and over again? A desire to be the one to be able to save her beloveds, to accomplish the rescue, to risk life and limb for Robin as he had so many times done for her?

"I can understand that, I really can actually. But this was too important for it to be about what you wanted, or what I alone wanted, because we are part of a team, and you could have provoked him by going there! We can pretty much infer his feelings towards our sex. Why would you think you'd have influence with a monster like that?"

"It's just that I'm sick of it, Lux! I'm so sick of them! Living with this 'don't provoke the beast' business! I was trying to use my privileges to help my friends, just like Gil does."

"Of course you were! But their society hasn't given you the same weight in its world that it's given Gil! How could you be blind to that? That's why I chose a different world! Now you need to go and tell our men immediately before I do!"

Jack felt funny around servants at the best of times. He had to admit that the people in service to Gil loved him with a very real loyalty. He was good to them. *As much one man can be when he owns the means to another man's basic ability to get food and shelter.* Most didn't think about it like that, or at all, so he could afford to trust them. They would be hard pressed to find a kinder master in the realm of masters, and the realm of no masters was unknown to them. Their loyalty was proven by the fact not one of them had spoken in the town about the presence of the tinkers in Gil's life, or the fact he slept with men.

"Enter," Gil cried out, in response to the knocking.

The young man looked shaken, which quickly had Jack on his feet. "My lord, there is a carriage and a company of two dozen soldiers at the gate. They wear De Bracy's colours. De Bracy claims he comes in peace merely to talk and

505

insists on bringing his guards inside the walls while he speaks to you. But will leave them outside when he enters as a gesture of good faith."

"By the balls of god," Gil muttered, followed by smacking his desk with his fist. "Alright. Well, we need to get all of the Twll Du people out the back way first. Get Robin to-"

"Uncle, I need to talk to you- what's going on," Augusta asked, brushing passed the servant who still hovered uncertain of his instructions.

"De Bracy is here," Jack answered, unable to spare the mental energy to elaborate.

The girl's face went visibly pale in moments.

"I'll tell Robin and get them all out of here," Jack said, on his way out of Gil's study. As he went, Augusta grabbed his arm. "Come back when you're done, your place is beside Gil in this. We are going to need as many De Biron men here as possible. The word of a noblewoman isn't worth much more to this man than that of an expensive nightstand."

"It will be done," he agreed, before getting off down the hall as fast as his uneven gait could take him. He had agreed so easily partly because he was still a little in shock. It was, after all, the first time one of the legitimate De Birons had ever applied his father's name to him. "Robin!" he cried out as he came down the stairs. "I need Robin and I need him fast. Everyone start gathering up what you'll need on the road! We need to make it look like you've not been here." By the time he reached the base of the stairs Twll Du people were running around everywhere, rapidly and efficiently beginning to decamp. "De Bracy is at the gate!"

Just as he had said this Robin appeared walking quickly towards him. From the look in his eyes Jack knew he had heard that last statement. Robin paused for a moment. While he did his whole body seemed a shuddering live-wire of unspent force, his hand hovered around his sword hilt. For a terrible moment Jack feared some crazed, berserker response. Jack raised his eyebrows and his hands,very slowly and significantly he shook his head. He walked towards Robin and put his hand on his shoulder, giving it a good squeeze to

remind him he was human and in a body. "Just get them out, Robin."

Then the moment had passed. He snapped back into hyper-efficiency mode and had them evacuated fast. Afterwards Jack was left with a sense of Robin as that eye of the storm among the moving people, holding a potential inside him that was dangerous to be close to. Jack didn't know exactly potential for what? Only that it was something that had a fallout zone.

Nobody questioned the fact that they didn't just exit via the back entrance and wait in hiding until Gil would say it was safe. When instead Robin led them at a gallop in a wide arc around the castle and through the woods before heading east, it seemed as if they were of one mind. The gallop itself was stress relieving. It reminded them they were still free. Of course, they were safest if they remained on Gil's land but safe and free are not always the same thing.

What was Gil's in title deed by other laws had been the outlaw territory of John of Hathersage. According to the rules outlaws self-governed by, when Robin had defeated him, it gave him first run of the place. John's territories had been vast but what Robin was doing was placing his people between De Bracy's lands and the road he would have to take to return to his castle. Robin also knew the land ahead like the back of his hand, because it was the land between De Rue's former property and De Bracy's.

He had not been anywhere near here since he first abducted Lux. But somehow Fate's threads had drawn him back here full circle, and he remembered all the paths as if he just walked them yesterday. De Bracy's property was surrounded by a rich game preserve Robin had poached solidly before without ever knowing he hunted on the lands of his aunt's murderer. To the east of that forest was a path that led to the sea. Robin was well familiar with it because he had used it to get Lux on a boat and outwit the clever noses of De Rue's hunting dogs. When they finally stopped to rest, just within the outer reaches of De Biron land, Blaith dismounted and came over to him. "We are decided then. We ambush him on the road? Kill him in the environment we are most at our advantage?"

507

"I can't see that we have a choice."

"You keep saying this. I don't like it. I want choices."

"I suppose if we're thinking just for ourselves, we have a choice to cower inside Gil's walls and keep hiding rather than fighting back. But what if in this time where I hesitated, knowing who he was, what if he did it again to someone else, Blaith? What if he did *something like what he did to Eliza* again, because I didn't act soon enough someone else-"

Blaith laid a calming hand on him, taking the side of his face. "Cariad, nothing he's done *has ever been,* or ever will be, your fault. Do you hear me?"

Robin nodded, though he wasn't sure he believed he was absolved. He had been taught so early that strong gifts required equally strong service, and he knew he could do things not everyone could do. *To each their need, from each their capacity.* Or put another way, take all you need, give all of yourself. Therefore, it seemed to follow that he *must* do the things others could not. "We can take out his armed guard with our archers right when they are almost home and tiring. Travelling with a carriage we will be way ahead of them and well rested."

Blaith nodded gravely. "If something goes wrong, we have more chance of escape in the forest than if we try to infiltrate the castle. Most of our evasion and tactics training was in the trees, not a huge stone tent. Our success would rely entirely on rapidity and surprise. We would need all of our people, the women included, to have two-dozen men dead before they begin to return fire. Think about it, how many men can you shoot before the first person recovers from surprise and returns fire, on average? If it's at close range?"

"Four or five on a good day, depending on the range and how seasoned they are."

"I can probably do about three, same for Rory and Zorien I'd say." He stopped to add the numbers on his fingers. Robin took in a deep breath and slowly released it. He frowned, looked outwards the horizon and rubbed at his stubble. He knew Blaith was right. Even a vaguely competent marksman would determine the position of someone firing on them quickly and return

fire, unless all of their targets died within those first crucial three to five seconds. Without the women they were only four archers, with the women they were seven. "I don't like putting them this close to seeing action, especially with Eilish..."

"I don't like it either, brother. I think she can do it at a pinch though, I think they all can. Our women are warriors, Hob. Like Gwenllian, Creirwy, and Aunt Eldri."

Gil had met plenty of evil men before. He had probably without knowing met others who had done terrible things and had no idea of it. These were the things he tried to tell himself. This Lord Malcom De Bracy would be just like a lot of other Norman nobles he'd heard laugh at how their fathers had slaughtered dozens of Saxon peasants. Theirs was a world that bred people like him, surely? That nurtured a place for these pitiless men... De Bracy wasn't special. He wasn't going to get one over on Gil mentally.

None of this interior monologue was helping though. He had heard one of Hob's nightmares once, the kind where he would talk in his sleep, when they were on the road together during the war, and it had chilled his blood to ice. De Bracy had Gil faintly spooked he had to own that. When his men admitted De Bracy and he strode into his hall, his step reminded Gil of the sound of his father's spurs coming toward his room. *Well, if nothing else that old bastard had taught him how to take a punch.* He had learned to take an emotional punch too, so whatever he felt on the inside he wouldn't be showing blood in the water.

Gil made a point of remaining sitting for a time after De Bracy entered, a conscious show of power. It was important to remind the other man that he was no longer in the presence of people who must get up when he entered a room. Most of his game he'd learned from Nanette, in truth. As the older sister she had mastered the arts of jostling and maneuvering among the upper class long before him. When he got up Gil was careful not to appear in any hurry. Just as he'd made De Bracy wait at the gate even longer than he'd

needed to for the exit of his friends. "Greetings, De Bracy. To what do I owe this unexpected visit?"

"My lord," De Bracy said, bowing to him. When he looked up, Gil caught his eyes for the first time and something happened inside him, his fetch seemed to jump up against his rib cage. It wasn't a fear response it was something even more primal still, it was a certain type of knowing he'd never had before. *I am going to kill you, or you me.* That was the simple understanding that came with the feeling. It was a clear fate. He had meant it when he'd shared blood with Robin on the battlefield, they were brothers, and this revenge was his weight to carry just as it was Blaith's and Robin's.

Jack only moved now, having sat very still off to one side the way a good hunter can. It was clear when he got to his feet that De Bracy had missed him when he entered the room, believing himself to be alone with Gil. For a moment he was thrown and it was strategically valuable. "This is my brother Jack De Biron," Gil introduced him.

"De Bracy," Jack said with a nod of his head, not managing a 'my lord' or anything beyond an acknowledgment that he knew the other man's name. Jack wasn't as good at tucking in his contempt as Gil was. De Bracy didn't respond to the contempt in kind. This told him that De Bracy knew less about his family that he knew about the other man's. Otherwise, he would have known Gil had no legitimate brothers and would have treated Jack accordingly. To the observant Jack was clearly older than Gil and this alone would have sparked doubt, considering it was he who held the titles. Though this man possessed a low cunning he clearly wasn't quite as sharp as he thought he was.

"Please forgive the intrusion." He smiled after this, and Gil rather wished he hadn't. His glassy, cold eyes were unpleasant enough on their own without him apeing human expressions. "I was hoping to talk to you on the matter of the outlaw problem in these parts."

Gil's facial expression didn't alter in the least but he was glad the other man wasn't standing too close lest he could smell his sweat. From his experience he knew that these types without pity seemed to be able to smell things

like fear from a greater distance than most. "Can't say I've noticed any increase in the problem. Game is still abundant in our preserve. Has there been a shortage in yours?"

De Bracy made a wheezing sound that he imagined was meant to have something of a laugh in it. "Ah, my lord, one hears some strange things about you and your family out in the world… Silly peasant rumours, I suppose."

"Ah, I see… I've always considered it one of the privileges of rank that I don't have to bother myself with silly peasant rumours. Otherwise, I might start believing the rumours I hear about other lords. Where would it all stop?"

There was steel in their smiles, and though he disliked it immensely Gil never dropped De Bracy's gaze. After a moment he could tell the other man had taken the measure of him and nodded to himself in silent acknowledgment that he had met a worthy opponent. "You need to watch that neice of yours, getting her to run all around the countryside like you do. She's a pretty little thing. Something could happen to her."

Gil concealed the faint twitch in his lip by biting it from the inside. He was thrown by the fact there was clearly some information here that he was missing. One could not let his enemy see them divided though. "Do you mean Lady Augusta De Biron, granddaughter of the Earl of Leicester and heir to one of the most lavish land and gold parcels to exist in the hands of a woman? I think she'll do alright."

He made a snorting dismissive sound. "Women need a strong tether, whatever their rank. Otherwise, they start running off and doing things you didn't ask them to do." The words found their mark. Or at least Gil now knew that De Bracy strongly suspected the truth -being that Augusta had clearly done something without consulting him first.

"Did you just come here to give me advice about how I run our family? Or is there more to cover on this outlaw business?" Gil tried to deliver it with the right level of haughtiness, one that properly conveyed that De Bracy had overstepped his place, without showing his hand on how disgusted he was by his treatment of women.

De Bracy tried to affect a mien of one to whom it was all the same either way. "I just came to let you know I've been hearing those rumours... Even people who say that Robin Goodfellow character has sprung up from the grave you put him in and is committing thefts still. He's targeted a few men of means. The people say he uses it to buy bread for refugees.

"They're making a hero of him. So I've taken some action rather than ignore it. I've assembled some of the best ex-mercenaries, assassins, and marksmen as foresters and household guards. I'm sick of refugees and bandits poaching my game preserve. I've got people in position on my land now in the hope that seeing my carriage move from there to here would flush Robin out. I mean, that's of course if he escaped before you could kill him? I'll keep you informed by sending you one of his hands so we can verify his identity. Or something else of his you might recognise? I've never seen the man personally."

"Yes, you have."

"Sorry, my lord?" he asked, pausing after having turned to go without Gil's leave.

"Well, you did not meet the man," Gil said, his gaze feeling like it was boring into the empty hole of the other man's, looking for the flinch. "But you met the boy."

There was a long moment where De Bracy just looked at him, did not speak. His eyes confirmed that he understood what Gil referred to and he smiled slightly, nodding his head. "I think it's really good of you, you know? The way you've kept Augusta's secret about murdering her brother? A lot of people would want her brought before the law to lose her head, especially considering how much she benefitted financially from it. I of course am not one to interfere. You De Birons really know how to stick together. Good day now, my lord."

"Can't sleep either?" Blaith asked, as Sariah sat down next to him outside the abandoned gamekeepers hut where their people had taken shelter for the night.

"It's this wind. It makes me nervous."

He nodded. Blaith didn't like it either. Being on watch could have better been named being on listen. Normally, if anyone wanted to get close to them, they would have had to take the risk of getting into position during the day. Tonight, though, you couldn't make out anything over the distress of the leaves and upper branches. "Me too," he admitted.

"Has anyone seen Eilion during any of this?" she asked.

"I just asked Hob that this evening. In short, the answer is no."

"What do you think that *means*, Blaith?"

"One of two things. Either he is too much wrapped up in Lux these days to appear. Or…" He sighed. "Robin once said to me that Eilion had never appeared to him on any day when what was about to happen to him was inevitable, only when there was action that could be taken, another thread to follow, to fight for…"

"You think it's the latter, don't you?"

She could always call him out on the hidden element of things that he wasn't planning to say explicitly.

"I'll admit it, I think we are in the grip of something inevitable. When I think about that it gives me courage. When you've got options, it feels good to have options. When you don't have options then you have nothing to worry about anymore. You just throw yourself as hard at what Fate has in store for you as you can. You try to leave a mark against the edge of life, even if it's just a Norman's blood splatter."

She smiled in a way that possessed a little of humour and much of poignancy, while reaching over to take his hand in hers. *Ah damn it all if her hand doesn't remind me how much I love life and still mean to fight for it, even if there isn't many ways left to turn.* "You are a beautiful, uncompromising creature, Blaith Dhu."

"And you? What do you sense?"

Sariah after all had been partially the bearer of two great prophecies and directives, without which many of them would now be as dead as Bran was.

"This wind isn't good for us."

"I've tried to talk it down and even to tie it down. It doesn't listen to me like the winds of Gwynedd."

She snuggled against him, seeking his closeness, and he opened his cloak to put his arm around her. "If it won't listen to you it won't listen to anyone, because unless that's a boy inside Eilish you are the last direct male descendent of the *nadredd* men."

"Well, if it is a boy, I'm going to have to die to see him safely into the world, aren't I? I often wonder about that… with my father. If there was some prophecy he never told me about? Some greater reason why he left us when I started to come into my own?"

"Garet was a mysterious man. I doubt your mother even knew all there was to tell of him or his motivations," Sariah observed. "Even more mysterious than you."

Blaith laughed quietly. "You know me better than most, Sariah ferch Gaelyn. In truth I am less comprised of mystery than I am of silence. They are not always the same thing. Garet talked more often than I, yet he did not say the things that matter most."

"Such as that he loved you, which I know he did. In his way"

"Ach. I don't care so much for the saying of it. I watch what people *do*." He kissed the top of her head and bundled her close. "And I watch how well those actions match the words. Everything else is piss and wind."

"A waste of the gift of speech, one might say. In all honesty then, are you afraid?"

Blaith shook his head. "I'm too angry to be afraid. Are you?"

Sariah laughed quietly. "The horses are unsettled, and I am almost peeing in my pants. But I'm here. I'm with you to the end, even if I pee."

For a moment he thought his tenderness and love for her would break him, somehow he wrapped around it. In size it was as great as his rage and made it all seem worth it. *Just that someone like her was able to exist in these diseased times will make it all worth it.*

514

The wind had died down a little now, yet still Robin was up and armed to the teeth and waiting. He had taken a seat on a makeshift chair that had been cut into a tree stump. Somewhat macabrely the back of it had a very long time ago been used for target practice, and the old arrows were partly decayed.

"Something's wrong, isn't it?" Lux murmured, crouching down beside him.

"Yes. The scouts should have been back by now." His voice was steady and tight-lipped but the alarm his words set moving through Lux's body was quite complete. In Robin's understated terms this meant he feared for the absolute worst. "We can't know when to move into position without a sighting of them."

"I'll go," Lux said immediately. Without meaning to she had shown her full heart in these two words. There were fierce tears springing to her eyes. She saw him look at her as if he was about to say no, as if he was about to say that if the scouts were missing, he wasn't about to send her to check the horizon of the road, then he'd seen her eyes. He took a moment to appraise her and she could tell it was despite himself. "I'm the junior maiden and I'm not pregnant." Lux crossed her fingers behind her back in case this was in fact a lie. "I am a fast runner, and I'm not afraid."

Robin did something with his mouth that she couldn't have put words to but it might have been him biting his lip from the inside. Then he shut his eyes and nodded his head. He knew as well as she did that with only the five of them there that this indeed matched protocol. He must stay to defend the Magister and First Maiden to the last and Eilish was pregnant.

"Alright. What I want you to do is go to the edge of the road, go carefully and stealthily. The boys went south along the road so I want you to head a bit further north. When you get to the road find a position where you can see the carriage coming from the greatest distance and when you see it come straight back. If something goes wrong-"

She smiled at him. "I know what to do. Call out 'Robin Goodfellow' three times."

515

His smile back held a great poignancy as though her referencing this aspect of their shared past cost him a sweet sort of pain.

It was true that she wasn't afraid when she was moving like this, running and ducking, doing what her animal knew best. The only time fear started to get the best of her and put a wobble up in her legs was when she was forced to sit and wait, like a rabbit holed into its burrow and about to be dug up. Lux hoped Robin understood that she wasn't taking this mission in a glib way. It was clear that Rory and Zorien could be in danger and at the very least something unplanned was happening. For a while she would run, duck, listen and there was nothing but forest sounds around her. But as she drew closer to the road, she became aware of another sound. It was some way off for the time being, yet it was drawing closer.

When she reached the roadside, she cautiously entered the bushes and peaked out in the westerly direction. What she saw caused Lux some cognitive dissonance. She was correct in having heard the approaching rattle of a carriage and the clip-clop of horses burdened with one. It was also possible to discern that it was De Bracy's carriage, as she had seen it yesterday from one of the arrow-slits in Gil's castle. The difference was that it was no longer travelling with two-dozen armed archers… Then she remembered her training, it wasn't for the scout to interpret the information, you just had to get it back to the group at all costs. She began to run.

"What does it mean, Hob?" Eilish asked. Her frightened eyes and her pale face seemed to fill up his entire visual field. It seemed there were more eyes turning to him than there really were. In truth it was only Sariah, Lux, and Eilish who were looking at him, Blaith was watching the tree line. But when the most precious people in the world were the ones looking in almost helplessness and he feared he was about to face a potentially unstoppable enemy, one who had been dogging his steps since he was six, the responsibility was the heaviest thing to exist in creation.

"We have to assume the worst."

"What's the worst?" Blaith asked, never taking his eyes off the trees.

"You know how people fan out in a line when flushing out pheasants so others can shoot them?"

The dread caused Eilish's bottom lip to tremble and tears came into her eyes as she took in the implications. "Our poor boys…" she whispered.

Robin nodded slowly. "We have to assume it's a trap. We need to mount up and ride hard east before attempting to outflank them by swinging south. If they are treating us like pheasants then they are driving us somewhere, they want us to go north, so north is bad for us. Let's ride. Stay close. Everyone keep Eilish to your left at all times."

He knew this instruction was against protocol. Normally he would be the first to say that protocols existed because they had saved their forebears lives and life-way more times than they hadn't. It was perhaps the man in him rather than the warden that instructed the others to all behave like human shields to the pregnant woman. Or perhaps it was just the human in him, for she above Sariah appeared to be the most afraid. If Robin knew anything from enduring a number of forms of suffering in life he knew the greatest and most crushing of all of them was fear.

"What if we can't outflank them?" Blaith asked.

"Ride like there is no backup plan."

He gave a little click-click to his horse and they were away. They galloped seamlessly together on the weaving path, ducking branches, falling back when they had to but trying to stay two-abreast at all times. Lux's body was shielding Eilish's, and Blaith's Sariah's, Robin rode at the front to show them how hard he wanted them to go. He wished he could be between Blaith and the source of danger, the place he'd been trained to be. But there was no way to lead them and be a human shield to them at the same time, so he just focused on speed.

Suddenly a cry from both horse and rider made him to pull his horse up fast, causing him to come back into a half rear and almost collect those behind him. Robin steadied his horse and swung him around. Immediately he dismounted when he saw Lux was thrown and ran to her. Her mare was

limping on a bleeding hoof but Lux seemed to have landed well. He was only able to offer her a squeeze on the shoulder that said something between: 'are you alright?', and – 'Good fall'.

Sariah examined the horse's foot while Robin doubled back to confirm what had lamed the horse. "It's a damn horse spike," he murmured.

"What is a horse spike?" Eilish asked.

"It means this is a trap," Robin muttered.

"She's not going to be able to continue," Sariah said, after gently placing the mare's foot down. "The poor girl served well."

He turned back to Lux. "You'll have to get up behind me."

"What are we going to do with her? Just leave her like this?" Lux murmured, looking over at her poor limping mount. They tried not to give them names exactly but she'd ridden with this mare for years. Without hesitation, Blaith rode past the mare, took out a metal spike, placed it against the right spot at the back of the neck and slammed it home with the butt of his hip dagger. Her legs dropped like she was a horse puppet. He got down from his own horse.

Grief lurch through Lux's face but there was no time for beloved horses. "Get down!" he said it quietly but it was easily audible to all of them and carried urgency without the requirement of volume. They all took cover, just as an arrow thudded into the tree nearest them. Eilish made a yelping sound and tripped inadvertently making her a target. Blaith instinctually grabbed her, rolling her out of the way and covering her with his body, covering her face also so she couldn't see as the second arrow thwacked into the place she'd just been.

Robin closed his eyes for just a second before swinging around to where the arrow had come at them from. There was the by now familiar thud and grunt sound Robin recognised as having successfully shot someone. He made the gesture of silence to them. They all stayed in position and waited to see if they would be fired on again. There was a lull in the wind that allowed them to catch a strange sound. It was like the half-distorted yelp of a hound being

518

hurt by something followed by the unmistakable whiz-thunk of arrow fire.

"Oh gods," Sariah whispered, her face was blanched with fear.

"It's happening," Blaith murmured.

Robin's senses clicked into place with the kind of hyper-clarity and slowness he experienced in an emergency. Unless the man he'd just shot was the furthest extent of the line any moment they were going to shoot the horses. If they didn't, it meant they were clear. Quickly Robin took stock of his people. Blaith's battle-readiness was evident, the consummation of a growing unquenchable rage, fed at its roots by equally unbearable grief he'd been forced to nurse the foreknowing of almost alone for years. He knew Blaith down to the bones. They trained together as boys, so he knew the terrifying force of nature Blaith could be when unleashed in his battle fury. He also knew the one thing he was never meant to do was put Blaith in a position where he needed to do this.

Eilish's lips were grey and her hands trembled on her bow. He doubted she could even shoot it. Sariah was pale too and her hand wasn't steady either, but he could tell from her eyes that she wasn't going to freeze. She would do what she had to, she would do it while afraid, but she'd do it. Lux's hand was steady, she had lost colour too, yet her eyes were as steely like the night she'd held that arrow on Nanette. This was all he needed to see. The decision was going to hurt whichever way he cut it, but there wasn't time. If this was the extent of the enemies fanning out it could be their last chance to get the Magister and Maidens to safety, and his horse carrying two would only slow them down.

He grabbed Blaith on the shoulder and looked into his eyes. He could tell that Blaith knew as he did that this was the last time. "My love, I need you to ride east like the devil's on your trail, and when it feels right try to swing south. Get Sariah and Eilish out, get them to safety no matter what."

Blaith nodded tersely. "Understood." Robin took his face in his hand and pressed their foreheads together in a firm hold that despite its brevity was full of intense emotion. "It's been an honour."

A last squeeze of the hand, one of so many thousands shared and then they

were away. It was a relief to Robin to see them go though because every second they got ahead equaled a greater chance something of them would go on, as Aunt Eldri had asked of them.

"Are you alright?" he asked before re-mounting.

"No. But I got up behind you under arrow fire on that first night, and I won't falter today."

"I'm going to move for my horse now, keep your bow ready, Lux. Because I might need you to cover me and return fire while I do."

She nodded and notched her bow. The plan could never be carried out though because a twig broke and then the serious arrow fire began, with arrow coming after arrow in quick succession. Instinctually he threw his arms around her and turned his back in its direction, covering her with his body just at the moment of impact. He felt the power of the blow before any pain. It hit him almost directly in the back on the left side. It wasn't a longbow; he knew that, not like the last thing he'd been shot by. It knocked his body into Lux like a solid punch but did not throw him to the ground. He saw blood splatter on her dress and sort of wondered where it came from.

"Onto the horse, Lux!" he cried out. Again, he closed his eyes and returned fire at the exact angle he'd been shot from. It must have hurt to draw the bow, yet it was distant by comparison to the urgency to fire. He opened his eyes again and sent subsequent shots into the places that corresponded with the arrows lodged in trees. Something seemed to yield fruit because the arrow fire slowed. Yet the arrow he'd feared came, straight into his horse's neck. Lux screamed for the first time, in the face of the horrific gurgling sound of the horse and the animal's strangled bellows of pain. Robin ran towards her.

Wounded as he was his hyper-alertness only increased. He could hear a lot of things at once. There was the possible sound of arrow fire to the east, and the clear fact that they must have had several clear shots at Lux they had chosen not to take. He wasn't sure if he was the target and they'd been asked to take her alive or if they were just prioritising killing him. "Get in here!" he said, pushing her into the interior of a hollowed out oak. "Shoot them if they

come near you. Do you have your exit strategy potion? Or do you need mine? I don't think I'm going to need it," he tried to joke but it didn't go over.

"I have mine. I won't let them take me alive. I promise you," she said, in a tiny little thin voice. "Is this it then, Robin?"

"I'm afraid I think so, cariad. I've loved you more than I love a May morning, but I have to go now and keep my promises."

She seemed to get control over her trembling chest with a proud sucking in of air. "Shoot straight, First Warden Robin son of Sifanwy. Save our Magister."

He nodded once to say he would and began to run towards the sound of arrow fire. Sometimes he wasn't even sure if he was going the right way, then he'd spot one of Blaith or Sariah's horse's tracks. Robin could feel his blood running down into his underwear from the front and back but his entire concentration was trained and tuned towards one thing. There wasn't any warning between the wind and the massive adrenal rush he was getting when he was shot in the back again, twice, a second and a third time. This time he pitched over in the leaves and got a face-full of dirt and forest loam.

It was no longer his brain assessing the damage and how much longer he could likely run for, or his chances even if he did make it, something else was making these decisions now. Something that seemed comprised of the entire will of every warrior in his blood, every man who stood his ground to give his family chance to escape, every one who ever had to make an enormous run to warn his people, every one who ever had to lift a terrible weight off another person trapped.

When he got back up it was his mother whose birthing travail had given him that stamina, who had said 'save my baby', who kept going against her own agony for an idea that was bigger than her own life. It was Eldri in him who walked her horse across a war-torn landscape, who got back up. It was the combined manhood of the Cymric people, honed for hundreds of years against relentless hardship, that got back up.

Through the trees he discerned flashes of a fight ahead. He was still a per-

son enough to pray it wasn't his people who were fighting -somehow. There was no time for sedentary prayer though. He had only what was left of the strength his mother's body had gifted his, and the little spark of the impossible he'd been gifted from his father, to place between his beloveds and danger. Something shifted in him as he struggled to his feet. It had something to do with the certain knowledge that he'd just received a mortal wound, or wounds that would prove fatal at their leisure.

What this meant was that everything left to him was comprised of two forces, Love and Will. When he began to run again, he was doing so at full extension allowing the white-hot intensity of the pain to fuel him with rage. The arrows sticking out of him, and another that hit him while he was running were a goad. Everything he was and ever had been became this one monumental effort to make it to Blaith.

To ride these feelings that were bigger than death itself, just above the cloud cover. Below lay the frenzy of pain and violence but he was higher enough he had the thermals under him. He was running to his people, his gifted people who held in their hearts and memories all the stories, songs and healing knowledge of the past. If he could save them then the caravans were not really burned, the thread was not really broken. His run was an act of physical prayer, for is defiance not the origin of all human prayer?

Blaith kept Eilish on the inside like Robin had told him to. When they were hit by arrow fire, he grabbed her bridle and rode for both of them. He could feel her whole body shaking hysterically with terrified sobs. All at once he knew they weren't going to make it to outflank the enemy. Just as he thought it he felt the impact of the arrow hit his horse's belly, just behind his heel, taking his wind out of him. Blaith's body was pitched from the saddle by his horse's fall, but he managed to roll free from being landed on or taken by the animal's flailing heels.

Eilish screamed and Sariah pulled up for him. He got up and ran towards her waving his arms. "Peel her off, make a distraction!" As he looked at her,

522

tears stood in her green eyes, so much like Robin's eyes, he knew with a terrible ache this was the last time he would look into them in this world. "I love you. Show me you're brave." With that he smacked her horse on the bottom so hard it galloped away from him for the last time. "I've got this," he whispered to himself.

Blaith crouched down beside his wounded horse. "It's alright, old friend, I've got you too," he said, before sending his mount to the Underworld with a savage tenderness.

With all the instincts of his training coming alive in him as if he were taught forest escape and guerrilla tactics only yesterday, Blaith went for the trees. He could hear some horses coming along the track. Something cruel allowed him the hope it was Robin and Lux, to believe for a moment that they had somehow got through and now for some reason had more horses.

But it was not, it was more of these mercenaries still fanning out. Blaith felt an unholy rage gurgle in his guts and peak like a black explosion into his mind. *Not one more step.* Only throats would be enough now. They were trying to go the way the girls had been riding, and he knew he wasn't able to let that happen, and protocol be damned. *When they burned the caravans they burned protocol. There is only the natural law that leads a man to defend his pregnant partner.*

Blaith undertook his work much as Meredith would have done, spying from above and then positioning himself on an above branch. He went out onto the branch and did the opposite to what a scout is meant to do. "I'm over here with one of those heads you're after, you cowardly Norman fucks!" He yelled at them in his very ordinary Saxon English, in the hope they would understand. Then as the arrow fire came in he'd already taken cover and they were firing at the wrong spot. While they tried to work out where he'd gone, he planned his moves for maximum number of enemy dead. There were five of them.

When they were about to ride by him, he held on with his legs and swung himself down from the overhanging branch. He drew out the two blades from

his sleeves and slit two of their throats with a smooth elegance. Flipping he landed on his feet in a crouched position while slashing another man's Achilles heel open. It felt in some ways like a dance he'd been training for all his life. Close range grappling violence like this was always where Blaith excelled most.

He used the corpse as a human shield while he delivered throwing knife killing blows into one man's neck, while the other moved in to try to grab him, Blaith surprised him by tossing the corpse at him, and then stabbing him over and over and over again with a kind of frenzy born of a life-time of denial and oppression.

He was brought down from his feet stabbing as many men fatally as he could. "I refuse your laws, and those of the coward you do a coward's work for!" He cursed those left who survived his blade in Cymric, though they understood not a word of it. There was, until the bursting point, only the hot upsurging of his total back-arching resistance, followed by the final freedom that sprung forth from him with black wings through his jugular.


"Go, Eilish, go!" Sariah cried, as she forced Eilish to peel off. "Ride for your baby!" She had tears streaming down her face and only one thought left. When they had begun this mission Robin had asked them all to gather with their weapon of choice. Sariah had lied when she came with her bow. Gaelyn had taught his daughter to shoot well, but in this moment her bow was still on her back. It never was, after-all, her real weapon of choice.

When it came to running distraction for Eilish all she could think of was the many times she'd used her body to distract while the men did their work. Her heart was hammering as she used her dagger to rip open the lacing down the front of her dress. Once it was pulled back her breasts came free. Somehow, she was less afraid then. In the action she had evoked what she stood for. She was no longer just Sariah riding alone into the forest, no idea if her beloveds were alive or dead, she was a proud Twll Du woman. She rode as her foremothers might have ridden into battle, her breasts and hair flying free in the breeze, hollering and whooping to cover the noise of Eilish's es-

cape. "Come on boys, why don't you come after me?" she cried out, her voice echoed in the forest drear.

It seemed the defiance of her act and the noise she was making did as she hoped and covered Eilish's escape. *Dear gods and foremothers please help her. Go fast, my girl. Go fast.* To think of her capture was impossible, too horrible to contemplate. *She is so afraid…* She probably wouldn't even be able to fire her bow upon them in her fear. There was a terrible feeling that the outcome still hung in the balance, and it was indeed all up to Sariah now. Fear and pride warred in her, still she managed to cry out one more time, egging them on to follow her. The horse was at a full gallop when the blow connected. Robin always seemed to hear shots coming before they landed, but at the speed she was going Sariah wasn't aware of getting a warning.

Something of enormous weight hit her in the throat, throwing her straight from the horse's back. So many times she had managed to stay on under all kinds of adverse circumstances, or to at least land well. These things were no longer an option as no horsemanship in the world could have prepared her for the speed it all happened. She lay there undulating in the leaves as she tried to breathe, gasping, trying to form a word or a cry, to scream out for help, or to warn others.

Nothing came and she couldn't get air. It felt like she was sucking blood. Down with her came a lineage of maidens stretching back into times even their caravan's stories didn't accurately record. Down with her came two hands that had brought relief to so many, and a body that had brought unbinding to her people. She felt her blood joining the loam and the smell of it near her face.

Sariah never fully had time to understand the arrow to the throat that put her down there. It took her into sleep it seemed. When she woke with a start, she knew she must have fallen asleep in the saddle, for she was back on her horse again. It wasn't the first time she'd been tired enough to fall asleep in the saddle, or her first terrible dream. There was a mist ahead of her out of which a man walked. At first she startled, then she recognised him, by his stance, and

dress, as one of their wardens.

She had to get closer still before she fully knew him. "Papa!" she murmured, taking in the implications of this reappearance of a dead man.

He took her reins in his hands and she experienced the sensation of being quite safe again. "I'm so proud of you, my brave strong girl," he said. Tears of pride appeared to shimmer in his eyes. "I'll take you from here."

Lux hadn't grown up expecting to get a lot of choices in life. How she was going to die certainly hadn't been one of them. Her sister had died because of male violence, and her mother had taken her life for the same reasons. From what she'd learned as a girl along with death in childbed those were your immediate options if you couldn't bear to live in slavery.

Calling out for Robin Goodfellow changed everything. It had caused reality and possibility to unfold before her like an opening fan. One could say he was like the element of chaos in all situations, the wild card. Or one could say instead there were a lot of very powerful men who saw chaos in anything where the people called women were suddenly given choices.

Lux felt that now she could choose to stay inside the tree where he had left her, waiting, hoping they would survive. If it turned out that all hope was lost she could drink the exit potion in her belt purse. Or right now she could choose to fight in any way she could for them. Robin had told her to stay inside the ancient tree, yet now she could hear active combat and the flight of so many arrow shots it sounded like then were trying to fight something that just wouldn't fall.

She had a horrible feeling she knew exactly what it was, as ideas are always particularly hard to kill. With this dawning awareness of the significance of the moment and what it meant to fight or not fight it became impossible to choose anything else. Perhaps, it is an illusion we all carry right up until options narrow starkly, toward our final road, to think there were many ways we could have turned, many paths to be chosen. Mostly who you are as a person makes the decision for you so that there is in fact only one way. Who Lux was

as a person decided in these moments.

She ran from cover to cover in the direction of the danger. Robin's blood trail became easier to follow. Thanks to Jack's instruction in tracking the ground told the story of all the places and times he'd fallen and got back up again to head towards the defense of his Magister. Sometimes she found the lower branch he'd gripped in his bloody hand to pull himself back up. It was like some kind of horror tale they tell the children at Hallowmass, where the storyteller holds off the thing that you fear most to see. All of this blood and still no body... Part of her didn't want it to happen because the story she was reading had him still on the move.

Lux had learned years ago in her first winter that whilst he was strong Robin was also a human, he felt cold and pain like everybody else. What if she could help him in some way? What if rather than a rescue he needed help to die? He is alone and gravely wounded, that much was clear. Lux was in awe and terror at how far he'd run. He wasn't a creature that knew how to die off his feet, or perhaps quite how to die at all... After a while she started to run too, careless of whether an arrow knocked her off her feet and sent her where he was headed. She wanted them to say of her that she died in action, not in hiding.

Was it that the will to protect Blaith had been bred into Robin since such an early age that it remained the final instinct? Or was it simply all the times it had been his brother's hands who had visited kindness upon him? That now brought him up out of the loam and dragged his body to his feet. There is a kind of pain where you know you are doing all the wrong things for your body, there is a kind of blood loss that reduces your faculties. Robin was in that place when he used some low birch branches to get to his feet.

For a few breaths he hung onto the branch, trying to get enough equilibrium. It wasn't like he knew what he was going to do when he got there, only that he must get there so they did not die apart. Instead of a forest full of signs of conflict and strife Robin saw before him when he managed to open his eyes

nothing but light for a few breaths. It was much like gazing directly into the sun, yet it was a different kind of light, a cooler sort which remained stronger than that of the moon.

He blinked to try to clear his eyes of blood. He heard more than saw the sound of the giant pale stag come forward on the forest floor. As he looked up he saw a male figure astride the animal, in the way one might ride a horse. His eyes were light grey and as cool as a snow-drift. As the enormous, long-extinct animal with its antlers each as long as an average man's height settled into stillness the faerie man held out his hand as if to offer help or succour. "Are you ready?" his father asked.

With great effort Robin shook his head. "I have to… I need to…"

"Ah…" Obreon murmured, as though in a philosophical vent. "The prime statements of human-livingness." He looked behind himself then. "Eilion? He needs you right now then."

Just as he'd always dreamed Eilion was as real as another human man as he took the weight Robin had been giving the branch. "It's alright," he said near Robin's ear. "I'll get you to him. We'll do it together."

Those were the last steps that Robin remembered walking, his arm slung over the faerie man's shoulders.

"I love you," he whispered, shortly before he began to drop the thread of consciousness.

"I have walked you here to your moment, Robin. The prime moment of artistry in your myth."


Finally, she came upon him where he lay stuck with about six arrows. Quickly she ducked behind some bushes when she heard male voices speaking Norman French. She had come just in time. Through the bushes she could see two men walking towards him with bows out and notched but not yet drawn. They were sure he was dead so they weren't on full guard, yet there was also the caution his reputation demanded.

"Are you sure he's really dead?" one said. "I was starting to think he'd never

die. I've heard he's already come back to life once."

"Well, we'll be sure when we've got his head." They both began to walk towards him. One of them nudged him with their boot and tried to half turn him over onto his back cracking some of the arrows in the motion. Lux felt it like it happened to her own body, embroiled in fierce tears of grief and rage. It didn't matter whether this was her lover's corpse or if he was still conscious. There was no way before the gods that live above, and those that live below, that they were touching him, let alone taking his head. Lux drew her bow-string back.

"Get the fuck away from him!" she screamed, sending the arrow square into the chest of the first man, before launching another at the second with wild cries of effort. It missed him. Still, he was forced to take cover and to step back from Robin. During this moment where his bowstring was no longer taut Robin suddenly moved, taking out his boot dagger and throwing it short-range into the man's throat. Lux stared at the man she had shot as she ran towards Robin. He died looking at her in confusion like he didn't understand how his death had happened. How was it his death looked like a girl?

"Oh gods, cariad," she sobbed, not sure where to touch him as he just seemed to be made entirely from broken arrow shards, unbroken ones, sucking chest wound, blood rushing out of his mouth, leaves stuck to blood...

"Lux..." he whispered. "Don't cry... Look! Blaith and Eilion are here with me."

At this Lux looked further beyond Robin to where several bodies lay in a great welter of fresh blood splatter. There was nothing to be smelt beyond the copper and the sweat of extreme stress. "Oh no," she said as she realised what he'd done. Blaith had peeled off to fight and save the maidens... He had died fighting before Robin could make it to him... She wanted to keen aloud. Among the other bodies Lux could make out Blaith's familiar form, stretched out in crucifixion pose with a dagger in each hand, with one of his legs bent awkwardly off to the side in a posture few would choose to be in if living.

"Did the... girls... make it?" Robin managed to get out between the

blood that was coursing freely out of his mouth.

"I haven't found them. They were last seen still riding." She reassured him though she had no way of knowing if it were true.

"Good," he whispered. "Blaith saved them then… He took the men I couldn't…" He smiled to himself with his eyes closed. "He always had a lot of… fight in him."

"What can I do to ease you?"

"Can you help me turn over? I want to look at the sky."

"Oh, Hob," she murmured. "That's going to make it hurt more…"

"Only for a second…" Immediately she went about breaking off the arrow shafts that prevented him rolling. It felt like brutal work but he did not complain of it. "I think I can see Mumma," he said, once over. "She looks like if Blaith… were a woman with my colouring. She's so beautiful…" He reached out his hand she grasped it firmly. "There is always so much light…"

A ripple of something that half lifted his body off the ground went through him from head to toe. He smiled faintly, his lips opened slightly like the breath in he'd take before orgasm, and his gaze disappeared somewhere into that distant sky he was looking for. Maybe they do things differently there. The feeling of him leaving to the place his gaze was set was like the rumble of distant thunder through the forest. She gently covered his face over with his cloak.

Sitting there with his blood still on her hands she sat there and turned her six-pence in her hands. It was the one Blaith had given her all those years ago at her initiation. He had told her to pull it out on the worst day of her life and throw it over her shoulder… It was blood-stained now, like everything else. Her hands shook as she reached deeper into her pouch for her exit-potion.

By the time Lux found herself running from people chasing her, she had been freed of the illusion that she had multiple options. These men were perhaps the last ones left alive and they seemed to want to catch her rather than shoot her. As far as Lux was concerned while De Bracy's last men were chasing her they were leaving her loved ones bodies alone, and the moment when Jack

and Gil would arrive was drawing closer. That the De Biron men wouldn't be far behind, well, in that she trusted.

It seemed in the stark clarity of her grief she ran without getting tired, like the spirit of the hare possessed her. The wild that had long ago got up inside her skin had turned her into a superior creature to these men. They ran fast at first, pushed her for a short burst of speed, her slight, highly-fit body rose to the occasion for the sprint as well as the long haul. For their endurance hadn't been forged in the hardship of eight wild winters and was far inferior to hers. How else did they think she'd survived out here? She would have lost all of them in time, was she not heading in the direction where the earth had its end.

Over fields, through woodlands… The paths were the same ones Robin had taken her down so long ago, and she knew them all like it was yesterday. In fact, she wasn't altogether sure the two escapes were two separate things. It was as if she were running in both at the same time, and all of them had always been running the whole time, running from a world that refused to include their difference. Hiding and then running as so many before them and after them would. Running to try to die under one's own conditions and to own themselves, even if it must be in death. *That was what they tried to take when they take a head, their last chance to own a person like a trophy.*

It didn't take long for her to understand the ritual she was in, or to know where it led. Because along this path she'd once arrived to see the sea for the first time… Below, on the sand and rocks, she'd cut away her long hair and her skirt at the knee for riding and performed the ill omen. Robin had picked up some of her girlhood hair and saved it from the sea, but some the current had claimed.

It was a long run because they had fled that first time on horseback. In those days she could barely ride it, let alone run it. She would make it today though, because she didn't need to keep any strength saved up for anything anymore. It was the only meaningful thing left, to run in the free state she'd promised Robin she would die in. As she ran, she tried to imagine running as Robin had, so that she was shot with him in stigmatic union. He hadn't saved

Blaith, he'd saved himself from captivity, and all of their souls would always now see the way out of the world's traps along with him.

When she saw the land disappear in front of her and heard the crash of the sea below the ocean breeze hit her as once the forest air had. Lux knew, just as she did that first night in the forest, that this too was the smell of freedom. As she reached the edge she slowly turned around and put it at her back. In her hand, her six-pence was lathed in sweat. She turned it over and over in her hand.

There it was the billowing emptiness at her heel… she had felt it so many times in life, as if she'd always been walking out her steps to this moment. She didn't know why she put her arms out at her sides except that perhaps it was the posture into which Blaith had fallen, their dark anti-christ.

"Come on, lass. Don't be silly. They'll go easy on you because you're a girl."

One of them said to her in Norman French. She laughed in his face, with what must have seemed to them the laughter of pure insanity. How could they understand how ridiculous their words were these people never forced to walk a mile in petticoats? Since when had anyone in their world started going easy on girls?

Her heels felt their way backward against the crumbling edge of reality, and beyond it the grasp of the sea. They looked spooked by her laughter, as if in refusing to be afraid she had robbed them of their power and they felt the cold breeze touch of that powerlessness rub up against them. She tossed the coin over her left shoulder over the edge. The sound of the wind and the billows of the ocean overcame the sound of the impact, as if it were stolen by the air.

That look on the men's faces was the last thing of the world she was ever going to see as she let herself fall backwards. Then there was only the ambush of the senses, of speed, and rushing air, a terminal velocity. With her eyes closed she was on Robin's stallion again, feeling the terror and elation of a form of motion more powerful than she had ever known before.

There wasn't long though before she was caught in the arms of her war-

dens. When she opened her eyes they were there again, all her dead boys, and her dead men… catching her in their hands, looking down at her to see if she was alright. Robin, Blaith, Meredith, Rory, Emrys, Zorien, even Bran and Ethan were there…

She smiled.

# 7

Gil was shaking visibly by the time De Bracy's carriage rattled away. To his credit he hadn't shown it before his enemy. The extent to which he'd repressed his feelings was reflected in how strongly they took hold of him now. "I am going to kill him! And when I've finished killing him, I'm going to dig him up and kill him again!"

"Not if I get to him first," Jack growled. He took Gil around the shoulders in firm hands to steady him, because the hatred, pure, physical, visceral, was dizzying. It had been all Gil could do not to kill De Bracy where he stood when he'd smugly unveiled his plan. He had taken a thorough measure of the man instead. Gil's playbook contained the considerable combined knowledge of Nanette, Blaith, and Robin, when it came to assessing an opponent.

De Bracy was an experienced fighter, tough, wary and well-seasoned. He wasn't getting any younger though and you could tell from his walk and stance that some joints were stiffer than they once were. These were all areas Gil's comparative youth and suppleness might be able to exploit. There would be no point trying to surprise him with dirty fighting. Because the low blow, the death from above blow, the side swipe, these were all part of De Bracy's natural assumptions about human nature. Assumptions he'd no doubt formed about the world informed largely by his own base nature.

"I'm going to track them. I'll go fast and bring them home again. And you-"

"I'm going after him. They won't be safe here until that creature is dead. God damn it!" Gil kicked out at a stool, upending it loudly on the stone floor.

"We need to go fast. You take my horse; he's the best in our stables. He's in peak condition and he's a good heart in him, he'll get you there as well as any horse alive. I am going to need a carriage and a sizeable bodyguard if I'm going to pull this off."

"He knows though, Gil! You heard him; he knows everything."

"He *suspects*, and there is some measure of difference between those two things. Especially when the person you suspect out-ranks you. If he were wrong it could be a costly mistake for him."

"He's not wrong though, is he? Even on a suspicion, why should he let you in through the gate?"

"Oh, he *shouldn't*. But I suspect he will. This man doesn't just enjoy killing, he likes to play with his food. He will want to continue the joust with me for as long as possible, draw out my pain more before showing his hand. I'm *certain* of it."

He could tell Jack was reluctant to believe him, yet was going to. "Even Nanette admitted you have good game play in you, so I'll trust your instincts. All I know is he's an evil bastard, and you are in love, so your judgment's compromised."

Gil shook his head. "I disagree. I am in love, so I'm at the top of my game. I will never again fight harder for anything than this. Come; let's get you on a horse. You're the best tracker in the country they say, and I will feel a whole lot better the moment you are on their trail."

Jack always said that you could either have a good tracking, or you could have a fast tracking. Luckily there wasn't much need to do good tracking when it came to finding and staying on the tail of seven galloping horses. As soon as the work began, he could see that they had indeed done what he feared they would do. Had it even been a fear or was it a knowing? Jack hadn't just sat with, ridden with and listened to Robin for all those years without paying attention to who he was as a man. When Jack really liked someone he studied them the way he studied changes in the earth's floor. He had felt his nascent

revenge in every line of Robin's body when he'd heard De Bracy's name. *There are some meetings on Fate's crooked path that even Robin Goodfellow can't outrun.*

Those words haunted him on the road, and when he had to rest to water the horse. In the heart of the forest he was alone with the churning in his gut and those words. Why had he let Augusta convince him to stay and support Gil when his real family was out here in danger? That thought came up occasionally. It had to be pushed away though, because too much thinking gets in the way of making the inferences that are the next step after the noticing.

This practice ran off a form of intuition that went beyond rationality. As he got further away from Gil's land the story told by the dirt became more complicated. He found a place they had rested and got off their horses. It was easy to infer from impressions in the damp loam them coming together to discuss tactics, make decisions. From here two of their company had departed, in slightly different directions, probably the scouts who were to check the road for De Bracy's return.

"They were planning an ambush," he murmured to himself. Here his tracking had begun to become more of a witchcraft than an explicable science. The tightness in his gut told him this was where they'd made it explicit, the intention to go for De Bracy and begun to put a plan into action. Jack had to admit that whilst it horrified him to think about the risk they were taking, he couldn't blame them either. The man had not only murdered their kinswoman, he had burned their caravans and killed their men, uncles, cousins, he was now arriving on Gil's property posing a threat directly at their very door. He had to be dealt with. Would Jack indeed have done any different had it been up to him?

Even with his extra decades of mellowing, his blood still burned as hot for the avenging of kin as it ever did. Nor was he someone to sit and wait to be hunted down like a dog while penned in. All this aside, when he found the body of Lux's horse and the bloodied horse spike, he felt sick and hollow with regret that felt both new and ancient at the same time. It was if part of him always knew this would happen, that it would be the price of deciding to fol-

low Robin Goodfellow.

It was now necessary to dismount and cautiously choose his horse's path in case of further sabotage or other booby traps. Gil's expensive stallion was high spirited and shyed from the scene of equine murder. *If only most humans sprang back from the sight of our own ruin as strongly as these beasts do we'd have had a better world, instead we have this one.*

He stared at the tree stump that had been cut into the shape of a seat with the broken and decayed arrows sticking out of it. It appeared to him like some horrific omen or symbol to do with the Witch Master's sacrifice. The story the forest loam was telling became complex here and was redolent of action.

The wind spoke in riddles of it. After a while he was able to puzzle out that three horses had ridden away. Nearby he found Robin's horse dead, this time with an arrow sticking out of its throat. *Lux's horse was sent lame by horse spike and then mercy killed.* It was only then Jack found an arrow sticking out of a tree and knew for sure they had fallen under some level of attack at this spot.

He dressed in his finest scarlet leather jerkin, over black pants and boots. It was partly because it was his most expensive-looking outfit and, if he were to be honest, also because it was something both Blaith and Robin always said he looked handsome in. Somehow if he dressed for seeing them again he superstitiously hoped it would increase the chances of it happening. Gil finished off his presentation with a wolf-fur capelet and sheathed his broadsword. That is that then, he thought as the sword found its home in the scabbard, he would next draw it in violence upon Malcolm De Bracy, and he was either coming home having defeated and killed him, or he was not coming home at all.

Right before he strode out the front doors to his waiting carriage Augusta waylaid him. "Uncle, a moment, if you will?"

He sighed. "Augusta, not now. Whatever it is you have to tell me, or to confess, it's not as important as getting to our-" As he said this he realised she was crying and rolled his eyes. He did so in part because of the urgency of the

situation, but also because he couldn't help but be affected by seeing her look so vulnerable with her hard exterior stripped away, and it annoyed him that he felt it so.

"I went to see him, Gil! I went to see De Bracy without your permission! I'm afraid it was me who made him angry and caused all of this to happen…"

As the impact of the words settled upon his soul like lead he nodded to himself and took a deep breath. This was what De Bracy had referred to then, about her running all about the countryside…

"I'm so sorry!"

Gil struggled to speak for a few moments holding up his hands as if begging quarter from her voice. His tender feelings hurtled away from him as if taken by a slingshot, and he began to turn away from her in the immensity of his disappointment. Too many times had he borne the results of Nanette's dishonesty and manipulation to do otherwise for her daughter. As he tried to go she grabbed his arm and tried to prevent him. "Don't you at least want to know why I did it?"

He shook his head. "If you had indeed been born a boy I would hit you right now, Augusta," he said coldly, pulling his arm away. "And frankly I don't care why you did it. Only that you did." Gil walked away from her down the front stairs and didn't look back, neither at her or his home, for he was heading to his home, it was where his brothers were. *Let me know no comfort, respite, or solace from this moment until my brothers' enemy lies dead at my feet.*

He had begun to enter the bargaining phase. With his heart pounding in his chest Jack came to understand that someone had died in the forest that day. Maybe it was the scouts? Jack allowed himself to imagine there would be one fatality, one of the most important people to him in the world would be laying dead here wreathed in the cast offs of autumn… If all had gone according to custom it would be Robin, who was perhaps the dearest of all these precious souls he loved more than life -if he'd had to say, though he'd have preferred not to. There were a lot of blood stories to read in the leaves, some

of them could have been told by wounded horses, he tried to calm himself with this thought.

Firstly, he followed the three horses that had separated because their tracks were easier to see. It was also another form of bargaining, for while they were still in the saddle, he had the greater chance of finding them alive. Then he found Blaith's horse dead. "Oh gods," he whispered. So the forest's tale had Robin, Lux, and Blaith all down and on foot and as yet no bodies. Blaith's worried him more than the other two because Lux would be with Robin, and if there was anyone who could defy the odds and the natural limits of things and somehow come out victorious when it was that weird faerie bastard.

The death of Blaith's horse without a warden with him was dire indeed. It was grave circumstances indeed that had put them in the position where Jack was reading them to be. The two sets of horse's hooves that went on beyond the black beast's body would be Eilish and Sariah's. Once again, he chose to prioritise following the horse tracks over finding and following Blaith's tracks.

This in itself did not fit with how he was meant to do things, as Robin's second he should have taken on the job to prioritise saving the Magister. This avoidance was guided by his ever-rising dread of the silence all around him. A terrible quiet that suggested there would be something to find. The two horse tracks went on together for a time before one peeled off, appearing to, in essence, gallop back in the direction of danger, whilst the other swung south-east.

By this time the hairs were standing up all over his body. The line between tracking and pure intuition had frayed to nothing now. It also made sense to assume that the final horse track swinging more to the south was Eilish's horse. "God damn it to hell," Jack said aloud, his hand going to his mouth and his eyes stinging with the threat of the kind of tears a man might weep once in a decade if he was lucky. Sariah... "You went and covered for her. Created a distraction... Of course you did..."

Hurrying back Jack covered the tracks of the peel-off horse that he both dreaded and knew was Sariah's mount. It didn't take long before he saw up

ahead what he feared to see, the bodies of two creatures, the human and the animal. The woman was on her side; the blonde braids her braided hair had been arranged into partly concealed the site at which the arrow had punctured her neck. He ran to her side as if there might be something left to be done and turned her over onto her back.

He did not need to check her pulse, for to his horror she was stark pale and her green eyes were empty of expression, pupils dilated as if she were gazing into the night. He didn't cry. Not yet. He felt so much rage to see her so callously broken like this, a being they saw no value in that the world would not soon again see the likes of. His hands shook with the too-muchness of knowing they had broken paradise, or at very least the door.

His eyes scanned the tree line. Not because he was worried about being attacked. To be shot along with her was suddenly his only wish in life. He knelt beside her and closed her eyes. Her flesh was cool but not cold and her blood was still fresh and barely coagulating. It was only now that he knew exactly how recently this had all happened. The old necromancer looked for the spirits of the dead with his other-eye, hoping to see her standing there in the trees, but there was only a stirring of the dead leaves by the wind and no other sign nor sound. Though so recently flown wherever she had gone, it was far from the world of man.

Gil's plan for getting inside De Bracy's stronghold was based on pure, brazen entitlement. He simply arrived assuming he would be admitted. It seemed to work. If you went in somewhere believing there was no possibility of being denied then people tended to comply. The first evident thing in arriving at the gate was that the place seemed under-garrisoned.

It hadn't been lost on Gil when he got out to look around while the guard was absent that the other man's carriage was still being cleaned in the yard after arrival, and there was no sign of the two dozen armed archers he'd previous been travelling was. This thought was deeply alarming to Gil because it spoke of this extra force being involved in whatever kind of trap he had set for

Robin. The only positive take on the situation was that the De Bracy residence appeared understaffed for fighting men.

Smoothly Gil got back into his carriage before anyone saw his casual recognisance. "Only yourself be begging pardon, my lord. He requests if you would be so good as to leave your bodyguard outside the gate?"

"I bet he does," Gil muttered to himself, and then more loudly. "Alright." That was what Hob would do after all. Just walk in. He drew heavily on advice Robin had given him in the past. *Walk in like you assume yourself to be a one man army and get your enemy to believe it too. That's half the battle won in the mind before a move to draw is even made.* Problem is though, Gil thought, is it's only *half* the battle, because if this fight could be won on pure bluff alone Gilbert De Biron would have put his money firmly on himself. As his carriage went through the gates of the De Bracy property, and they closed behind him Gil felt another fate rivet its way into place, solidifying his lack of exits.

He confirmed through the arrow slit a distinct scarcity of guards, just as he had noticed around the entrance. When the carriage pulled to a halt Gil took a moment to gather himself. Or did he in fact gather a face from elsewhere? He tried to draw on the magical signature of Robin's blood, shared with him on the field of the Battle of Crug Mawr.

Without thinking or planning he must let that blood-thread open up now into something that would be an act of magic as much as it was one of combat. For it was only right that he act as nothing but a hand to hold the blade that would allow Robin and Blaith to have their revenge through their blood brother. Gil had always been good at mimicry. Today his impression would have to be the best one of Robin anyone had ever done, it would have to more than that, it would have to be real.

As he walked towards the hall it was his spurs that rang out with rude volume on the stone. It was he (or was it he?) that dismissed the footman who opened the doors for him with a firm: "Leave us." They obeyed him and hurried out again, closing the doors behind them. Gil didn't bother to observe De Bracy's expression when he noted Gil ordering his servants around and it

working. He knew Robin well enough to know the contempt he would offer to someone he planned to kill. If Hob had decided on your extermination, then he had already buried you in his mind and your emotions were of no interest to him.

"Well, this is a surprise. It's like you can't keep away from me," De Bracy said, getting to his feet. Nobody had dared ask Gil for his weapons at the door. He hadn't bothered to plan for what if they did ask for his sword, because back-up plans were a sign of lack of belief in your ability to carry out plan a) – this was straight out of the 'what would Hob do?' manual. And it worked. De Bracy certainly caught the atmosphere of Gil's approach, and though he didn't draw his sword his hand was rested in a position that would facilitate him going for his weapon very quickly.

"I was hoping to have something for you by the next time we met. Turned out with all those men sent out so far they've failed to bring me the wolf's head. The job is done, though, I'm told."

Gil felt faint and giddy for a moment as if the ground had been whisked away beneath his feet. There was a very real threat and he perceived it quite suddenly, a cleft opening up in the situation where his emotions could let death step through and claim him. Instead, he sidestepped the feeling for the time being and doubled down on giving his body to Robin.

*If what he says is true then use me now, Robin. Though I think I can beat this man, I am not certain. My gut says it would go down to the wire. But I am certain that you could kill him. For if you are indeed laying slain, then all the fires of hell light up in me and will not be quenched but for this man's blood upon my sword.* Some white-hot centre of emotion that was also cold rippled through his core, it was something so fundamental it had a part to play in the emotions of both love and hate. Without even bothering on the element of surprise he methodically, almost meditatively, drew his sword. *"En guarde."*

Jack knelt and put his fingers in the blood before smelling and lightly tasting them. It was Robin's blood alright, and from the quantity of it he was

542

gravely wounded. Whoever had done this to his friend had paid a heavy price to get so close to him. Littered to the left and right along the path were dead snipers sporting an arrow from Robin's bow, dead men still aboard anxious horses, and spooked looking horses with no riders.

The forest was haunted by these wraiths of the disturbance it had witnessed. Even the trees seemed unnerved. What Jack counted so far as over two dozen people had died in a very short time here. One of the horses he believed was Rory's. It was in his instincts as a horseman to calm the horses and gather them up, there was no time for that though. He had to read the whole story, and walk the way Robin had walked, to even ape stumbling where he had stumbled.

From the tracks it appeared Robin had been running, whilst being relentlessly shot at and also shooting numerous attackers. There were misfired arrows in the ground around the blood-stained leaves. If he was running towards something then he was likely trying to save the life of his Magister, the job he'd been trained for since he was eight years old. Yet the story was further complicated by the smaller tracks, suggesting he was not the first person to track Robin's blood trail. Eventually he found a clear one that he recognised as Lux's boot-print, heading in the direction he had gone. Jack shook his head with consternation. The story was getting ever harder to endure though it was easy to read.

There were five or so marks where Robin had clearly fallen and slid, before getting back up again. Then, seeming to appear while he was looking down at the ground a body lay upon the path ahead. Again, Jack ran forward, leading his horse by the reins until he reached the spot. Even blood-bathed and through the welter of wounds and broken arrows as he was, Jack recognised Robin's form and clothing immediately. Jack fell to his knees beside Robin and pulled back his hood that had been used to cover his face.

Upon his face was the most beatic expression that seemed so far removed from the pain he must have suffered before death. His eyes seemed set on something very beautiful that he alone could perceive, and his pupils were

yet to even fully expand to fill most of the iris. Though his heart clearly no longer beat in his chest when Jack touched his face Robin's much renowned body heat was still not fully faded. "My poor, beautiful boy," he murmured, his voice disappearing into a burr of emotion as tears wracked his throat. He took the young man's much broken body in his arms and rocked him like he were his own dead child.

"You should take my head," a voice said, causing Jack to start back and go for his weapons, seconds before realising it was Robin's voice that had spoken. A strange unearthly light drew his eye away from the body to the stump of a forest giant, which had long ago crashed to earth to accommodate the grand table of some Norman lord's hall. Upon it he saw Robin seated, one leg drawn up and his arm resting on it. He was free of blood and marks of violence and his brow itself shone with inner fire. There was a circlet of some intricate design as fragile and skilled as the cobweb upon his forehead that he wore with the naturalness befitting the Crown Prince of Faerie. Jack was filled with such a disarming sense of reverence before him that what these ignorant humans had done to his human vessel seemed a profanation that would mark mankind ill for a hundred generations.

"It's worth a fortune. Would set you up for life. And what a jape it would be to think it was my dear friend and my sweet cousin Eilish who lived soft and fat forever on my bounty!" Robin swung his legs over so he looked almost as if he were about to spring or take flight on enormous, terrifying wings. His feral, faerie eyes met with Jack's gaze intensely. He smiled. "Go on. I'm not attached to it."

"Hob…" he hoped that using his nickname would allow access to the human dimension of his friend. For despite his rich experience as a necromancer Jack felt like all the people in the bible to whom the angel says 'be not afraid'- afraid. "Are you with Eilion now?"

"I am. He walked me to my very death steps. Blaith's body lies further up the path. You will find him by following my body's reaching hand to where he lies reaching out in death also. Place us so our hands find each other's again

544

and turn us back into fire. Lux has returned to her ocean lover; you will find what is left of her by the sea. Sariah… You already know…

"And Jack? It is a heavy thing to leave upon one of the best friends a man could have, to burn us, pick up our pieces, to protect the last maiden with the last Magister's child inside her, to be the bearer of witness, and of story… I would not curse-bless you with it if I had another way of showing my immense love, trust, and respect for you. But I do not, for this earthly burden of love is all that is left of mine to bestow now —that and my head if you want it. You'll have to excuse me; I have an appointment with an important fight. But if you ever need me, just say my name three times."

De Bracy's laugh sounded in response, that chill sound that had something a little off about it. "Oh, this is too much fun… You're going to be honourable about it and allow me to draw and get my guard up? Alright then, let me get my sword out for this. You do know I fought in the First Crusade and survived don't you?" he said, drawing his blade in a way that suggested he would be merely playing around with Gil.

"All I hear you saying is that you're old," Gil replied between gritted teeth that positively refused to move very far apart. It occurred to him that Robin probably wouldn't have done that. He was never one to waste his breath on trash talk and repartee with an opponent. Not when he'd come there to kill someone. He was usually deadly quiet and focused. As he had come in with the appearance of honour Gil was counting on De Bracy to not expect how he would fight.

Normally Gil had been the kind of fighter to test his opponent's strengths and moves a little before moving in for the kill. Today he came out fighting like he normally would only at the very climax of a conflict. It was the style of someone who was used to fighting for his life, a total commitment of will and a spiritual coalescence of presence. De Bracy was immediately thrown off and was very suddenly scrambling desperately to survive.

It wasn't rage but something that lay at the centre of it like a calm eye in

a storm. A strange mode of being where rage revealed itself to be as much an expression of god as love is, for were they not the same thing in this moment? Gil had been right when he told Jack he was at the top of his game because he was in love, for he would indeed never again fight the way he did that day. His sword was moving so fast, demanding defensive action from De Bracy over and over again and the fierceness of his attack did not relent, nor did the strength of his arm.

There was certainly to be no time for banter or De Bracy playing with him, or assuming Gil was food. His eyes now told a different story. It had been a long time since this man had seriously thought he was about to die, and for him Gil as a risk had come straight out of left field. He might have even cried out for help if he wasn't using all his breath. Gil felt it when De Bracy took a backwards step, and then three. Something Other surged up in him, a determination he had never known the likes of, even when he'd defended Robin from Nanette in Wales. What he had imagined as an idea took on magical reality. He *was* Robin and he took up this fight with the confidence and utterness Robin would have.

De Bracy was stiffening with age alright, his range of ability to swing the heavy broadsword was not as wide as Gil's and he was puffing from the exercise. There was no time to lose on breaking him down, who knows how long they would have before someone heard the sound of fighting? *Ghosts of the sons of Twll Du mothers guide my sword arm.* With that prayer in mind Gil moved in so boldly that De Bracy managed to cut through some of the fabric on his clothing. It had an air of desperation about it, as he tried not to step back again. Gil countered so firmly that their swords connected right near the hilt, flat on flat, so that the force of the blow knocked De Bracy's sword out of his hands.

It was Robin's eyes that fixed upon De Bracy as he put his boot over the weapon De Bracy was scrabbling for. Without hesitation, Gil lunged and stabbed him through the chest, before pulling out and allowing the other man to stumble and fall to the ground. He held his sword point pressing against

the man's bloodless lips. "This is for Eliza of caravan Ama who has waited too long for her vengeance," he said, thrusting the sword into De Bracy's mouth until his eyes went big.

Gil hadn't been expecting to do something this brutal, but he discovered it was important to Robin that De Bracy's death be both a penetrative and a silencing one. He struggled for a moment and as Gil's weapon cut through his soft palate, just before entering the brain there was fear as well as pain in his eyes. Only for a second or two though because the death, though brutal, was immediately mortal, as neither Robin nor Gil were the type of men who could have inflicted on De Bracy what he had upon others.

Gil waited until De Bracy's eyes had gone fixed and still. They were in truth not that much colder and emptier than they had been in life. It was only then that he started to shake, and finally to cry. Cold all over, Gil was suddenly bald and empty of Robin's fire. He turned on his heel and walked from the hall. When he reached the first other human he saw, he didn't try to conceal his tears. "I wouldn't go in there just yet if I were you. He's enraged and not safe to be around. You know how he gets when he's angry." He could tell from the man's eyes that he knew exactly how much to fear De Bracy's wrath and would certainly hesitate to check on his lord for some time. With that Gil walked out to his carriage without a scratch, someone opened a door for him, and he got inside. Without anyone preventing him he was let out through the front gates.

At first Eilish had ridden the way the others told her to. She took her pelvic weight off by holding herself higher in the stirrups and her legs were trembling with the extra effort. Ever since she'd first begun to gallop Eilish had been crying hysterically. As she rode for her baby like Sariah had told her she couldn't really see anymore for her tears. The intelligence and also the fear of her horse carried her rather than her steering her mount. In a way her sobs were a mercy as their intensity and the beating of her pulse in her ears blocked out the sound of arrow fire through the forest.

Never in her life had she been alone like this. Although her unborn child was in this with her this aloneness felt hermetically sealed. Born into tents, caves, and caravans as she was, clambering over and around other bodies since birth, there was not really an Eilish that didn't involve them until this stark moment. Her flight began to slow as this feeling creeped through her. She had to walk the horse now, as her legs were shaking with the effort of keeping her pelvic floor from fully resting on the saddle. She had already lost bladder control some distance back, now it simply felt as though her pelvis would split apart at the muscle if she didn't release it from the violence of a full gallop.

Even though she was moving slowly she kept moving. It was the last thing Blaith and Sariah had told her to do, so in this aloneness the instruction was the only part of them she had with her. If no one had come for her she might have walked the horse south until she herself or her mount collapsed with exhaustion. When she heard the other horse coming there was more of hope in her than of fear. It must be Hob coming, she thought. In her extremity he had always arrived before, pulled off the impossible, snatched them all from danger. Of course, he had overcome whatever tried to make a play for him. She dried her eyes hard to try and see clearly.

It wasn't Robin though it was Jack. And even from that distance and through her salt tears Eilish felt a terrible drop in her stomach when she saw his face. "Oh gods," she whispered in total dread. She began to sob convulsively again, this time something closer to hyperventilation. Within an improbably fast seeming moment Jack was suddenly at her horse's head, calming her mount, guiding her in.

"Easy there… I've got you."

"Just tell me!"

He drew his breath in but it was too much for him too and he began to sob, those painful, wretched type that crackle through a grown man's voicebox. For a while all he did was look at her and shake his head.

"But who? Robin? Lux?"

"All," he managed, between his own sobs. "Oh gods, I'm sorry, Eilish. All."

548

"All?" she repeated it back. "Even... even Blaith?"

Jack nodded, unable to look at her for his emotion.

"Then I am lost, if he is lost," she whispered, "-then we are all lost." She must have collapsed off her horse in a couple of motions because Jack had enough warning to help her down onto the leaves. Inwardly as she wailed with a grief that threatened to burrow a hole through her like the ocean does rock, she blessed Jack for not trying to say all wasn't lost, or trying to remind her think of her baby that was the future, that she must carry on for him because he was all that was left of Blaith, or other benign twaddle. He knew her too well to think she would want to hear platitudes and his own soul sat too close to the darkness and grit of things for it anyway.

She had to throw up then. The baby shifted nervously inside her with the squeezing of her heaves. She acknowledged that it was good he was still moving, but she couldn't really feel the goodness of it at this time. *Not Sariah, too...* Eilish was moving into bargaining and disbelief. "But Robin... he won't really be... he can't actually be... I've seen him *not actually die.* I mean, how did they?"

"With very great difficulty, my sweet girl." Jack dried his eyes with the back of his fist. "He fought with everything in him to save his Magister. Every last thing... I saw him though, you know, after he'd slipped his skin? Afterwards... he was..."

"Like an angel," she whispered to herself more than him, her mind tended backwards upon a memory of Robin as a little boy appearing to her to be standing in a ray of sunlight looking towards it. Then she had realised there was no sunlight, the child stood in a column of light larger than himself. He had turned to her and smiled, making the sign of hush across his lips. She felt a little delirious as if her shock and distress had made her high.

"Or a faerie prince... or a god," Jack murmured, the awe his vision had left him with evident in his voice like it had cracked right through him. "A heretical god of witches and outcasts, but a god nonetheless."

"It has been both our privilege and our price of admission that we have known great men and women. It is a miracle that unfolded around me, just like the heather blooming, and I was as an innocent babe, a naïve bystander who never saw it fully clearly till the Otherworld snatched it back again... I have lived in a time of gods and heroes and have known wonders from which I doubt I'll ever recover."

"Aye. We had to hear the faerie music, you and I."

# AFTERWORD

A story usually begins much like an explosion. Gifted- usually young- people throw themselves heroically against the walls of the world. It's often set during one of Blaith's violence holes where nothing much gets told of events, or lives lost, beyond that event horizon. Some facts die an immediate death from the human perspective, falling to the ground unwitnessed, or joining the heavy atmosphere in the wind at a massacre site.

Quickly both the glory and the damage scorches across the minds and hearts of those left in the comet tail, they begin to outsize some things and tactfully forget others. Little parts aren't told anymore, things that might have made it grittier and less romantic seeming. Until perhaps, many years later, the children of one of the people partly responsible for the glut of human sacrifice the story demanded, will play with the children of those who lost the most... Worn away by the passage of many long years where only so many remain who knew the heroes, and can tell the old stories, grudges wear away and fade from view, like an old plaid set to unravel on the thorn trees.

The story does some years on a front porch with an old man in a rickety chair who would tell you about the adventures of Robin Hood -whether you liked it or not. The left-behind woman who knew them better than anyone almost never speaks of it, and yet somehow in hushed whispers it gets told to the children nonetheless. The children who fidget and sometimes wish their parents would forget the past and come with them into the future, a place they seem to barely be able to look at. Yet years later when they find themselves in their first moment of life and death danger, it rises up within them, that strong-making story, and they scream 'Robin Goodfellow!' three times aloud to the sky.

"And did he come, Papa?" that man's children would ask years later. And their father would smile. He didn't know how to say it to them that he hadn't come, not in so many words at least, but something had, some pride, some determination seemed to come from the forest itself, and it had made him stronger. It had made him run faster, fight harder. But children don't understand that kind of adult equivocating, so:

"Of course he did, sweet child. That's why your papa lived to tell the tale."

In the quiet times though, parts get replaced, an axe handle here, an axe head there. Grandchildren assert it is their grandfather's axe still. The eyewitnesses fall softly silent. After a few generations people stop using their names. The wind fills in the details to those who'll listen. Sometimes someone raises the name and places it on the brow of a new baby. Other names hurt too much to say for a long time. Much is worn away in this manner, via human feeling for those same memories, like the re-used clothing of a dead man tends to do so quickly.

The story becomes frayed to gossamer, until it is more of a feeling than a tale, a haunted sensation when the wind blows a certain way and moves the leaves of the ancient oaks. They aren't as prone to forgetfulness as we are. There are other things also whose memories are even longer still and less prone to fraying than ours, things with diamond eyes unblinking against the distracting carnival of history. It is still debated whether such beings can learn to feel human love, and rumoured that although they can't, *if they could,* some stories might yet be told of forever.

Printed in the USA
CPSIA information can be obtained
at www.ICGtesting.com
CBHW031019311024
16683CB00043B/227